THE FOOTBALL FACTORY
HEADHUNTERS
ENGLAND AWAY

John King lives in London and is the author of four novels,
The Football Factory, *Headhunters*, *England Away* and
Human Punk. He is currently working on a fifth.

John King

THE FOOTBALL
FACTORY

HEADHUNTERS

ENGLAND AWAY

VINTAGE

Published by Vintage 2000

2 4 6 8 10 9 7 5 3 1

The Football Factory
Copyright © John King 1996
First published in Great Britain in 1996 by Jonathan Cape
Vintage edition 1997

Headhunters
Copyright © John King 1997
First published in Great Britain in 1997 by Jonathan Cape
Vintage edition 1998

England Away
Copyright © John King 1998
First published in Great Britain in 1998 by Jonathan Cape
Vintage edition 1999

Vintage
Random House, 20 Vauxhall Bridge Road, London SW1V 2SA

Random House Australia (Pty) Limited
20 Alfred Street, Milsons Point, Sydney
New South Wales 2061, Australia

Random House New Zealand Limited
18 Poland Road, Glenfield, Auckland 10, New Zealand

Random House (Pty) Limited
Endulini, 5A Jubilee Road, Parktown 2193, South Africa

The Random House Group Limited Reg. No. 954009
www.randomhouse.co.uk

A CIP catalogue record for this book
is available from the British Library

ISBN 0 09 928268 2

Printed and bound in Great Britain by
Cox & Wyman Limited, Reading, Berkshire

CONTENTS

THE FOOTBALL FACTORY

TO MUM AND DAD

Thanks to:
Anita Nowakowski for the kick-start,
Kevin Williamson and Irvine Welsh for encouragement,
and Robin Robertson for taking me on

COVENTRY AT HOME

COVENTRY ARE FUCK ALL. They've got a shit team and shit support. Hitler had the right idea when he flattened the place. The only good thing to come out of Coventry was the Specials and that was years ago. Now there's sweet FA and we've never had a decent row with Coventry. The best time was two years ago in Hammersmith with a bunch of Midland prototypes looking for a drink down the high street. About fifteen of them. Short cunts with noddy haircuts and tashes. Stumpy little legs and beer guts. Looked like they should be on Emmerdale Farm shafting goats for a living. They clocked us coming the other way and took off. You could smell shit over the petrol fumes, which is saying something in Hammersmith.

It was a stupid move. They should've piled in the nearest pub and sat tight. We weren't looking for them. We don't expect Coventry to perform. We were on our way to King's Cross to meet Tottenham coming back from Leeds. Saturday night battering yids. But the Diddy Men were running into the precinct and when you see something run you follow. Pure instinct. They were moving fast as their little legs would carry them. Red faces reflected in shop windows along with the hi-fi gear and baked beans special offers. We were right behind as the bloke at the front took them into the car park. Like those sheep who lead the flock to slaughter. You'd think they'd smell blood and hear the knives being sharpened. Not this lot. Straight into the car park with the last of the Saturday shoppers standing aside to let us through. We had them boxed in and gave them a hiding, working fast because someone would've called the old bill. We had the numbers and kicked them into next week.

Harris was there and opened up some cunt's face with his hunting knife. Said later he should've signed his name, so if the bloke ever managed to get his end away his kids would know the old man had been to London. That he wasn't just a goat fucker. But he was joking. That's just the Harris humour. He's not one of these sadists you read about who torture kids and give them chemicals to loosen their arses. Time was short and we were in and out of the precinct. Straight down Hammersmith tube before you could chant Harry Roberts. The Coventry boys would know next time. Don't walk around taking the piss. If you want a drink after the game, fuck off out of West London.

It's one o'clock and we're having a pre-match pint. It's been a hard week at the warehouse and the lager gives me a kick-start. Stacking boxes five days solid takes it out of you. Cardboard rubbing against your hands eight hours a day takes away the feeling. You go into remote control and the brain goes numb. Worst of all are the forty-footers full of pressure cookers. Four thousand of the bastards and you sweat your life away for three hours stacking pallets for Glasgow Steve the Rangers fan driving the forklift. A tall, thin bastard who spends his days shouting Fuck The Pope as he buries each pallet in the racks. He's one of those Ian Paisley Rangers fans who talk politics all day and wish they'd been at the Battle of the Boyne. Thinks he's King Billy. He's got a sense of humour and comes down Chelsea sometimes now he's exiled from Ibrox. Says Chelsea are a good Protestant team. Doesn't know any of the names but comes along anyway. Not with me though.

It's a closed shop round this table because since the old bill got serious with all those undercover operations you have to watch yourself. It's not like the old days. Not like when I was a kid sitting in front of the telly watching football riots with Jimmy Hill or some faceless cunt giving us a commentary and slow-motion replays. Today there's surveillance gear and you have to remember the cameras. But it's all a bit of a joke, because pitch invasions and riots for the cameras never compared to the trouble away from the ground. Your actual nutters do damage miles from the stadium in a tube station or down a back street, not behind the goal with a telephoto lens shoved up their noses. You don't stop that kind of thing. You can't change human nature. Men are always going to kick fuck out of each other then go off and shaft some bird. That's life. Mark's always going to get his end away.

– That bird last night was well dirty, he says, scratching his bollocks for emphasis. I got back to her flat in Wandsworth and she gave me a can of Heineken, then told me to go sit down in the living room. I'm sitting there with the telly on pissing about with the remote and she walks in tarted up in suspenders and crutchless pants. She's only shaved herself and walks straight over, kneels down and takes my knob out.

He looks at a couple of lads as they walk in the pub. Jim Barnes from Slough and someone I don't recognise. A tall bloke with a silver earring who looks knackered with a bruised right eye and cuts along his knuckles. Must've had a good Friday night.

– She starts sucking me off and there's this bald presenter on the box talking to a sex therapist. One of those stuck-up slags who've probably never had a decent shag in their lives. Talking about safe sex and how queers are taking the blame for Aids.

Barnes goes to the bar and orders. There's a few of his mates on the piss and he gets lumbered with a round. Takes it in his stride. Slough's well the drugs town but it's a Chelsea town as well. Shit hole basically, but a Chelsea shit hole. Croydon's another new town with Chelsea credentials. West Ham have Dagenham and Spurs have Stevenage. They're welcome to them.

– There's this bald TV head nodding up and down as he listens to the woman and this bird's head banging up and down giving me a blow job. A bald head and a bald cunt, and I'm sitting there with my Heineken resting on her shoulder. The TV personality is making a couple of thousand quid, but I'm getting the business off some dirty old slapper from South London.

Mark's a mouthy bastard and who'd want a bird sucking them off with a sex therapist on the screen watching? Those studio experts are ugly cunts and if Rod's description of Mark's woman last night is anything to go by then she was no oil painting either. Rod had to make do with a hand job and a large donner from the kebab van off the Hammersmith roundabout. Just down from the Palais where the freaks and niggers hang around. All those stroppy little cunts acting smooth in one of those fun pubs where a pint of lager's only worth the price if you're looking to get your end away fast or make do with smacking up a few kids. Rod wasn't impressed with Mark's bird. Reckons she was a bit dodgy. Off her head he says. He walked her mate back round the corner.

– She was only on, wasn't she? Rod's aggrieved. We go back and she lives with the old girl near the flyover. We're sitting there waiting for her mum to go to bed and when she finally leaves I think right, I'm in now, but the mouse was in his hole and she just tossed me off over the couch. She got angry when I shot my load over these cushions with pheasants on them. Indian she said. Bought them down Wembley market. I couldn't be bothered with all that bollocks and she stunk of blood. I just told her to leave it out and walked off. I mean, why hang about when you've dumped your load? I went down the van and nearly got in a ruck with these Shepherd's Bush raggamuffins. Chains and leather jackets and patterns shaved into their heads. They were young enough, but I thought next time you fucking black bastards. You've got to watch it on your own. Any of them could've been tooled-up and I'd be dead now and you lot would be listening to Mark, believing he pulled himself a stunner.

– Fucking did mate. Why waste time with pig meat like that bird of yours last night when you can get some woman dressing up for you and buying the rubbers. She had her bedroom kitted out with a mirror and all these different condoms to choose from. Not that I bother usually, but all the packs were open and she takes out this gel and the tube's half empty so she's been a busy girl. If we'd been playing someone tasty today I'd have left after the blow job and got a decent night's kip. It's only Coventry so I put myself through the grinder. She was a dirty cow. Swallowed it like a trouper. Not a moment's hesitation. The only downer was she kept biting me. Put big teeth marks into my arms and back. Bloody painful it was. Woman needs to go on a diet.

I go to the bar to get a round in. The service is always slow and you'd think they'd get more staff in when Chelsea are playing at home. It never changes. It's a captive audience so they make us wait. The lager tastes watered down and they serve it in plastic pints so no-one gets glassed. It makes sense I suppose, but the plastic means the lager smells like piss. It's another fun pub and it got done up after Chelsea and West Ham clashed a good few years ago now, during the peak of the original Headhunters.

Eleven o'clock in the morning and the ICF are turning up in Chelsea pubs. It was a golden age back then. West Ham hate Chelsea like we hate Tottenham. They reckon we're all mouth.

4

That East London is the real London. That Chelsea's mob is full of wide-boys and new town delinquents. They come in, get a warm welcome, and we're lumbered with an amusement arcade. They all think they're related to the Krays. Bill Gardner with your cornflakes and *Sun*. They'll be down here again in a couple of weeks. Tottenham one week, West Ham the next. You couldn't ask for better.

Dave Harris stands at the bar moaning about the six-month sentence handed out to a mate for fracturing a copper's cheek down in Camberwell. Says he didn't know the bloke was old bill because he was off duty outside a club. When he started acting cocky his mate nutted him. Thought he was a cockney Yosser Hughes. Broke the bloke's nose as well and the old bill made the effort to find him. Wouldn't normally have bothered. They take care of their own. Six months isn't a death sentence but it's long enough. Harris says the bloke's Millwall. That he's sound. There's grudging respect for Millwall and a few names have been known to grace Chelsea in the past, but when we play them it's war.

Funny how it works. It's like blacks. People say they hate niggers but if they know one then he's okay. Or if he gets stuck in then he's a Chelsea nigger. Or like when you watch England away all the English get on, although there is occasional trouble, between Chelsea and West Ham say, because some riffs run deep. Generally you're broken down into people rather than mobs so somehow the whole thing works. But no-one gets on with Tottenham because they're yids and the scousers are all thieving little cunts. Talk to a Man U fan and they'll tell you about scousers.

Harris turns to me as I wait to be served. He's a nutter, but friendly with it. His head's together which is something you can't say about one or two of the blokes who hang around this pub. He's got a brain and uses it to good effect. Runs a roofing company, or something like that. Must be in his mid-thirties and he's been around.

– It's half-eleven in King's Cross for Tottenham, he says. Flash yid cunts coming down here last year having a go at our pubs. It'll be worse than usual next Saturday. You don't come down here and take liberties like that. You lot will be there, won't you? I'm running a coach to Liverpool as well, so tell me if you want seats. We'll stop in Northampton on the way back. It's a good town to

5

go on the piss in and you can get back to London in an hour or so on the motorway. We've got a bog and video, and the driver's an original Shed skin from '69 so he'll hang around till Northampton closes down. Quality travel and we'll be getting tickets lined up. Let me know. Fifteen quid for the coach and the price of the ticket on top if you want one.

There's a lazy cunt behind the bar serving and some of the lads are getting pissed off waiting, telling him to get his finger out. Coventry never pull a big crowd and the pub's half full, but still they take their time. Try and make the punters wait. We're only football fans after all, but if we decided to turn the pub over they'd get it sorted quick enough. But you don't piss in your own lift. Or if you do, you've got to be a bit slow. Finally a bird with black hair in a pony-tail serves me. She looks at the glass she's filling or over at the wall the whole time, as though I don't exist, so I just stare at her tits so she knows I'm alive. She goes all red, the dozy cow. I take three pints of lager back to the table and Mark's into one about the Liverpool game.

He's got a cousin Steve who lives in Manchester and says we can stay with him after the match. Manchester sounds better than Northampton if you've got somewhere to doss and you don't have to worry about the trip back to London. We've been to Old Trafford and Maine Road enough times but not seen much of the city centre. That's the way with football. Unless you get it organised and get there early you just see the train station or coach park, the old bill waiting to escort you to the ground, and all the local slums. The natives do their best to have a go at you and, if you're smart, you get away from the escort and find them. Usually that's about it. You go up, see the game, have a punch-up if you're lucky, then get out.

Old Trafford's a smart ground and when they write about Man U being a great club you know deep down they're right. Going to places like Old Trafford and Anfield gives you an extra kick. Football's all about atmosphere and if the grounds were empty and there was no noise, there'd be no point turning up. Chelsea have had some good rucks in Manchester. Piling out of Maine Road when the old bill haven't got it together. Running fights along the side of the ground. Last year, walking back to the coaches, a mob of Moss Side niggers started lobbing bricks and we were straight

They couldn't act but the girl was alright. It made me
k though, seeing some bird getting treated like that.
was over Marshall said it was the real item. Paid a
id for the video. It was made in Aldershot. Authentic
ntic squaddies. The lads just laughed, but you knew
like that kind of scene. You have to be a fucking nonce
watching rape. Just sitting there with your camera
he barmy army waiting for them to do the business.
oing, pay your money and then send them down for
made my excuses and pissed off. After I left John
hreatened him with a knife from the kitchen. Kicked
ead and told him he was a cunt. Then he put a chair
screen. Only honest bloke there.
oy pumps out Liquidator, the Sixties Chelsea anthem
And The All Stars. It's a ska classic and belongs to the
. Next up is Blue Is The Colour with Peter Osgood
udson in the Top Of The Pops studios. The teams
he pitch and we stand to clap. The players wave and
ch kickabout begins. The crowd looks a bit more
Men coming in from the pubs. A zigger zagger chant
choing through the West Stand, video camera
image. Coppers sit at the controls. The pitch is a
h of green catching the sun. Harris laughs with Billy
k reads his programme moaning about the price,
kins up and adds a bit of blow. I sit back and wait for
o toss up and the game to start. Coventry get a bit of a
nd half the West Stand looks their way. We raise our
nd give them the wanker sign.

after them. They just ran further down the road, then started
chucking more bricks. We'd chase them again, but they'd just
move on. We had to give up in the end because we were out of
breath. There was only twenty of us by that time and they
could've been leading us into a trap. There's a lot of ways and
places to die but hacked up by Man City fans in Moss Side isn't a
chart topper. Niggers don't fuck about. They can't afford to and if
you see one in a white mob you know he'll do the business.

   - If we take the Harris coach up we can get a train to
Manchester from Liverpool, says Mark. Or if my cousin comes to
the game get a lift back, have a wash and some mushy peas and go
into town. Steve says it's more than just Coronation Street. Some
of those places are mental. You can get a cheap pint and northern
birds are friendly. Mind you, that bird last night was friendly
enough with her mirror shaking as I gave her one from behind.
Banging her head into the wall waking the neighbours. I had to
shut my eyes after a while and think of England, because the way
the street light was hitting the mirror it looked like I had my cock
wedged into the wall. One day that mirror will come unstuck and
there'll be two dead strangers found shredded in Wandsworth.

   Coventry at home is always a bit of a letdown compared to Man
United and Leeds. There's a lot of boring home games but you
turn up because what else are you going to do? We sit around a bit
hungover from last night, then at twenty to three drink up and
leave. There's a crowd building up along the Fulham Road
heading for the ground. We wait for the traffic to stop at the lights
and avoid the police lined up outside Fulham Broadway. There's
the smell of horse shit and hamburger meat, coppers on horseback
telling the crowd to go separate ways when they get to the gates.

   A van full of coppers moves slowly, eyeballing everyone under
the age of forty. Outside the church hall tables sell fanzines and
souvenirs. Kids with blue and white scarves hold the old man's
hand. More vans are positioned outside the entrance to the North
and West Stands, though fuck knows what they think's going to
happen. A pissed up old geezer stumbles off the pavement and
three coppers go over. They're young and mouthy and if there
was a decent sized crowd and there weren't those fucking cameras
up on top of the flats maybe they'd get the kicking they deserve.
But they've got uniforms and overtime and they nick a harmless

drunk. Bundle him into the back of the van well over the top with their attitude.

— I went round Andy Marshall's this morning, Mark says, handing his ticket to an old boy behind bars on the turnstile. Haven't seen Marshall for a good two years, but he lives near that bird in Wandsworth and I thought I'd find out if he's still alive. He's got a beard and long hair. Right hippy. Sits in front of the telly watching old Arnold Schwarzenegger videos. Thinks he's half man, half machine. He's just started lifting weights. Says it kills time as he waits for a job to come along. He wants to join a gun club and kill twenty chinks with one bullet.

— They should sign him on and send him off somewhere, Rod says, leading up the steps, weaving through railings. Marshall was a Special Constable. Wanted to become a copper but they wouldn't have him. Even the old bill have standards. He's the kind of bloke who sits in front of the box all day and then goes out and does a Hungerford. Imagine that cunt with a shooter down Wandsworth shopping centre. Just walk through the crowd and think he was Arnie on patrol in the jungle.

We're at the top of the steps leading into the West Stand. It's a clear day and I turn and look over the surrounding scene. It's a good view and I remember a clear evening with a gold sunset and West Ham turning up outside the North Stand. We were already inside the ground when it went off along the Fulham Road. I can hear the police megaphones. Visitors keep moving. North Stand to the right. Everyone stay on the pavement. There's more vans coming along the road and coppers giving it the big one.

Cameras are busy recording life. Videotape rolls and faces are saved for future reference. We go for a slash and wait for space. The bogs are full of piss and this is the kind of Saturday you have a few pints and don't worry about aggravation. We show our tickets to a wanky-looking steward and are in the West Stand. We look towards the visitors to see how many have turned up. There's a few hundred Coventry in small groups. There's empty spaces all around the ground, though there's still time before kick-off. But the price they charge nowdays what do they fucking expect?

We're in our seats and all the usual faces are here. Harris sits two rows in front flanked by a couple of evil cunts I know from sight, sipping a cup of tea. He isn't a big bloke but gets things organised

8

DOING A RUNNER

YOU'RE WELL FUCKING pissed on ten pints of lager, with a decent jukebox and a bit of fluff knocking about, mostly slappers in mini skirts, black cotton wedged up their arses, just what you want after a few sherbets, wide-boys and tarts with wide open thighs, spread easier than margarine, telling them to wait a while because you're drinking with your mates, downing the cheapest lager like nobody's business. Eight, then nine o'clock, evening's steaming past, end of the week job with two days off, and the lager tastes like heaven. Cold and sharp against the throat. Chemical bubbles brewed quickly for lager louts. All the lads on the piss talking bollocks, nothing you'll remember tomorrow, and the music's cranked up so you have to shout, but the electric beat is what counts, gives the place a bit of rhythm, drowns out the need to think about what you're saying and means you don't have to make any sense, just keep talking, moving the tongue, and the more pissed you get the more you find the words in the brain aren't what come out through your mouth. You could be saying anything. Fuck it. Drop your money in the slot, press a button, flick the pages and choose your songs. Dead simple. A fucking idiot could do it without thinking. But it's hard getting in at the bar if you're not half cut, fucking difficult, but it's easier now because you're pissed and don't give a toss about fine edges, just blunder your way through, push and stumble towards the barmaid with big tits bursting through her blouse, pouting painted lips and a bit of a stroppy method, knows she can afford to act like she's something special because there's enough pissed-up blokes looking her way, fucking loves it, time of her life, and you tell her you'll have two of those darling, you with the blouse at breaking point, tits knocking forward, showing your wares getting the hormones going, and if some cunt doesn't like you piling through

II

they shut up anyway because you're pissed, but mostly because you're with a tidy mob of blokes who'll put a man through a plate glass window for looking at you and your mates. No fucking strop steaming into ten o'clock, evening flashing by, all those faces under the lights, blending together, skin tone changing with each pint, waxwork reflections and suddenly it's last orders, always comes around too fast after ten, white faces melting through the smoke haze, the smell of perfume in the air, a sweet smell, but you want another drink, getting double rounds in, a couple of pints to knock back, and the cunt behind the bar wants you out of his pub sharpish now he's got your money and the till is loaded, he wants to fuck off upstairs and watch his new surround-sound TV, that till full of cash, your cash, you should rob the place, smash a few windows, that slag of a barmaid on all fours getting shagged by the landlord's dog. Lot of laughter from the lads imagining the picture. And the landlord's got a Rottweiler out back so drink up lads, drink up gentlemen PLEASE. Otherwise you'll get the dog set on you, that's what he really means, nice little warm up for the mutt before he slips the woman a canine length. And in the street it's cold and you're hungry, fucking starving because the drink gets you going and it's only poor cunts go down the burger van to stand in the drizzle, it's a long hike for a burger made from cat food and you're all agreed, it's straight down the curry house. Can taste it now. Red velvet wallpaper and Ravi Shankar sitting out back tuning up the sitar, and though you don't admit anything you know it's a fucking good sound, magic music when you're pissed and staring into the pilau rice doing an acid turn in front of you, buried deep in the plate, multi-coloured spin washable, the original bangra sound without the electrics, just the old rishi on a mountain top job stroking passing tigers. Like fuck. But you've got to get inside the curry house first so you have a few minutes making the effort, acting sober though the waiter giving you the table isn't convinced, you all know the real state of affairs, the cunt must be able to smell the hops or whatever shit they put in your drink nowdays, who knows, imagine that, not having a fucking clue what you're drinking, same goes for your food down the supermarket, it's dangerous thinking about that kind of thing, but so fucking what anyway. Money's money and the waiter knows your face. It's the easy option. Better than an argument and there's hard-earned cash into the bargain. The curry boys can't lose. You're wedged in ordering a stack of papadoms and six pints of lager, and you know it's going to be Carlsberg, that it's always Carlsberg in curry houses, that it tastes wrong if your Indian isn't accompanied by a bit of Danishhhhhhhh. Maybe it's down to bulk buying or something. Brewed by Danes for Indians. Fucking right. What else does Europe give you apart from a few dodgy lagers? Not like the Commonwealth, shunted out the back door, you'd rather have a curry any day of the week, none of that French muck the rich bastards eat, fucking wankers, if they want to be French fuck off to France. What have the frogs ever done for the English? The cunts come over in 1066, stick an arrow in someone's head and build a load of stone churches. Then they make the rich cunts speak their language while the rest of us are told our words are filth. Fuck off. And they fucking sided with the Germans when they rolled into France in the war. No bollocks those cunts. No fucking pride. Hang on to the curries and JA sound systems. But the place is packed and you're lucky to get in because there's blokes being turned away a few minutes later, mobs of geezers, not taking it well, stroppy cunts can see there's no tables left, too fucking bad pal, and there's four birds at the next table, right old slags by the look of them, fit bodies a couple of them but fucked-up faces, all shagged out, cunts like the Mersey Tunnel most likely, what was that Stranglers song, something about making love to the Mersey Tunnel, you can't remember, kiddie memories, fuck it. They're pissed-up looking over and you start giving it the classic chat while you're waiting for the papadoms and they're dopey cunts, know fuck all about curries, just looking for a length, then they get their kormas delivered, and what's the fucking point coming for a feed if you go and order a korma? Should be embarrassed with a full tandoori menu in front of them, but that's women for you, and they're going on about it being hot, how the fuck can it be when it's full of yoghurt or whatever the bastards put in it, probably spunk, have to laugh, telling them the korma's full of it, a line of waiters wanking in the sauce. The birds look disgusted but only halfway, and then the lager arrives and you're straight into the papadoms giving the main order, bhajees all round, digging into the chutneys, lime pickle and mango, chopped onions, fucking beautiful, the business, talking with your mouths full, then the various vindaloos and Madras dishes, Bombay potatoes and bhindi bhajee side orders, ladies fingers wrapped round your knob, but the girls next door are no ladies, no chance, and you order a stack of nans, half plain, half Peshwari, then the waiter fucks off and your mouth's like a dam. Peshwari nans, fucking beautiful, and you're telling the lads about your Irish mate who went overland down through Iran and Iraq, hard trip through the desert but good people, sound people, and he ended up in Peshwar during the war against the Russians, and the town was the base for the Mujaheddin, fucking hard cunts, a real wicked place on the North West Frontier, the Golden Crescent, and he spent a couple of weeks there out of his head. Some cunt says he should watch it because those Muslims would have him, specially the desert warriors, they have no qualms about shit-stabbing a bloke, and your mate said they were good people, no hassle. Still, you don't want to take chances. Not in Pakistan anyway. And the slappers next door are giving it the big one, always some mouthy cow leading the charge, some body-builder slag with a wet pair of knickers, always those birds have the biggest mouths to go with the biggest leg muscles, telling you they're putting it on a plate for you, eat your curry lads and come back with us for a drink, for a fucking shag you mean, but you're hungry, really fucking hungry, and you just want them to shut up so you can concentrate on the food. Either that or fuck off girls, go and pick up some other cunt. Doesn't matter who it is, but the food's important, watching the trolleys get rolled out, tandoori chicken sizzling for the mob a couple of tables along, look like off-duty squaddies, shaved heads and straight clothes, smart wearing blazers, none of the crisp Fred Perry gear, must be soldiers, can't read the words on the blazers but know it's some kind of crest, fuck them, you're not getting involved because the army's always on the lookout for a bit of aggravation, a couple of hours out of the garrison and the cunts need a ruck, it's essential to their training, Queen and country and kick some cunt's head in, basic training is what decides a soldier. Shut the old brain down and learn to obey orders because the Eton wankers in charge know best, just do as you're told, follow orders, and one of the lads says his great granddad was a soldier on the North West Frontier, up on the Khyber Pass, must have been fucking mental and you wonder what it was like being a soldier in the Empire, keeping the Commonwealth together, and the old boy saw a donkey one time loaded down with bricks or whatever, and the poor fucker was breathing fit for a heart attack, about ready to explode, and the soldier called the man over, the cunt who owned the donkey, and cut the rope holding the bricks and told him not to overload his donkey, because the English love their animals. No fucking cruelty mate. Or not much anyway, except for the scum who burn cats and drop dogs off high rise blocks. Cunts you read about in the paper but never see, because if you did you'd be straight in and break their fucking necks. Cunts. Just eat your curry when it comes and the lager's sliding down a treat, the onion bhajees arriving with a sweet mint sauce, salad arranged around the sides. There's a slice of tomato, bit of cucumber and lettuce. You get stuck into the bhajees, order more lager from the waiter, call him Abdul, he's Abdul and you're Mustafa Curry, bloke just laughs because he's heard it all before, every fucking time. You're starving and there's four prats to the other side, away from the birds, two couples with their food positioned in front of them, and you're looking all envious, then the big cunt with you, always the big bastard who's one hundred per cent beer monster, gut spilling over the front of his jeans, old lager drenching his hair, the kind of bloke who'll never get married or have kids, you know the one, he's fucking famous and you meet him all over the country, he's everywhere you go whether it's a city centre or village high street, wherever you go he's there after the pub's kick out, rain or shine, well, the big cunt leans over and sticks his hand in the middle of the nearest plate, pilau rice and dhansak, and you laugh and feel for the bloke who owns the curry, because he's not exactly Henry Cooper, splash it all over, or Frank Bruno, first of a new generation of black boxing heroes, and the prat can't do a thing about it, just hope his woman isn't the kind who demands honour gets defended, one of those cunts who think they're the fairer sex and should be fought over, fucking slags, and he takes it well when the big cunt leans over with a smile on his face, stopping with his hand in the bloke's food, saying YOU DON'T MIND DO YOU MATE? like he's worried, really worried he's gone too far, and maybe he is because the messages are getting delayed on the brain-to-tongue trip, but you know he could go a lot further, fucking headcase that bloke after a few sherbets over the top, but he's your mate and you forgive most things if it's your mate. Poor bloke just laughs a bit and shakes his head and the fat bastard lifts a hand full of Persia and stuffs it in his mouth. You're so fucking pissed you're cracking up, start pissing yourself but keep control of the old bladder, mind shifting round all the time, watching the squaddies getting in a bit of an argument with some long-haired cunts at another table, trendy wankers or something, you don't mind a bit of dub-smart drumming and synthetic magic but you don't fucking dress up for it, slags to one side moaning the fucking korma's too hot, stupid cows, forgetting about the happy foursome with the wrecked dhansak. The onions in the bhajees are harsh as fuck and you wash them down with more lager, feeling a glow inside, get up to go for a piss, stumbling along between the tables, the racket must be turned up but you don't register because you've drunk your fair share. The door slams and cuts off the Ravi Shankar tunes, fucking tunes mate, Toon Army, geordie bastards, and you unzip and rock forward against the wall, piss bouncing against the marble, solid marble like the Taj Mahal, that picture above your table sticks in the mind, real love story behind that, the waiter told you once, a few months ago when you weren't so pissed, and the marble's being destroyed by pollution and the Government wants to close down the factories in the area, save the Taj Mahal, fucking beautiful building, but more for the tourist money it brings in, and the factory owners say they'll bomb the cunt, jobs are jobs, fucking right they are, and you think of your head leaning against the wall and how some sick cunts wipe their snot there when they're pissing, you've just washed it as well, rock back too fast and nearly fall over. What a way to die. Back of the skull cracked by a sink. Sad. You zip up and wash your hands and wipe your head, squaddie coming through the door, doesn't fucking see you, walks like a prize bull, fucking animal, Stone Age man in slacks and blazer, hard cunt you wouldn't fuck about with unless there were some very good odds, ten onto one. You've grown up in the Slough-Windsor area and seen plenty of aggravation with the army, fucking wankers, and this bloke's not exactly a raw recruit, more like a career soldier, well into his thirties and you reckon he's killed his way round the globe, cutting throats in the Falklands and shooting his way through

Northern Ireland, all over the shop, and you get out of the bog because it smells like fucking death in there, you don't want to get on the wrong side of the bloke, by standing too close or sneezing, breathing too heavy, it just needs an excuse. You're back at your table and the waiter's come along and taken away the plates, put out the heaters, and you down a third of a pint chatting with the tarts next door who've finished their meals and ordered ice cream, congealed spunk this one lads, ha fucking ha, telling you to hurry up with your food, they're waiting, and you tell them they can wait as long as they want, they just laugh, playing hard to get are you lads, the mouthy slapper, real pig meat, though the bird next to her's nice enough, jet black hair and massive eyes, but when she opens her mouth the teeth are rotten, fucking horrible, you don't want that wrapped around the old anti-tank missile do you, and then the main meal arrives and they can fuck off home for all you care. It's the business this and you're getting stuck in, everyone sobering up fast, sharing fair and square, and the two couples next to you ask for the bill and are on their way, and you're lifting the first few forkfuls into your mouths, heaven, fucking beautiful, the meaning of life, Ravi Shankar going into one in the background, the strings vibrating like they're about to snap, listen to the fucking music you silly cunts, real music, none of your mechanised bollocks you long-haired cunts, did you say that, the squaddies laughing and the long hairs looking round, don't know where it came from, the birds are laughing too, one of them leaning over rubbing your leg. You tell her to leave it out, all good things come to the slag who waits, and they don't like that, what do you think we are, common or something, fucking right darling, flat out on the parade ground with a queue of squaddies in line like that video you heard about, that's not nice boys, but so what anyway, fuck them, and the couples have gone leaving their money on the plate with the bill and one of your mates leans over and pockets the lot. You see what's what and keep the momentum, cracking a joke with the slapper acting aggrieved, they haven't seen a thing and neither has the waiter who comes over, looks round, asks his brother, then one of them goes to the bar, they're confused, talking among themselves, arguing, Abdul going outside looking up and down the street. There must be some kind of mistake, decent citizens don't do runners, not respectable little men and women in their best clothes who go to the theatre and have nice jobs in finance. Not those cunts. And you're trying not to laugh because this is what it's all about, all that wealth distribution bollocks, this is what makes the country tick, petty thieving and sharing the cost, money safely tucked away, bunking the trains and being ready to pocket the difference. You order more Carlsberg and it's there in front of you, nice white head, the Danes know what they're doing, most of the time, like when they won the football and voted no on Europe, but then they fell apart on the pitch and were forced into another vote, and said yes, silly cunts. Just had enough of the old pressure politics and let the businessmen have their way. You're washing the food down, throat burning, magic this, and there's a bit of a commotion as the squaddies and a mixture of acid casualties and other lads start fighting. It's a right fucking grin because it's all slow motion and the bull soldier tries to smack someone in the face but he's too pissed and the other cunt jumps up on a chair and kicks him in the chest, more like a push with the bottom of his trainer, and the bastard falls back through a table letting the regiment down, then a couple more soldiers in casuals who aren't as pissed come over and the whole lot of them are into it, waiters running behind the bar taking cover, you wave to Abdul and he half smiles, not sure this time, what a way to make a living, and the phone will be going for the old bill. You're sitting there watching the show, everything moving out of time, punches missing their mark, talk about a drunken brawl, like something from a Carry On film, Carry On Steaming, you can't remember the name, but it was that Western, Carry On Cowboy, something like that, with Sid James, the great British hero, a fucking Aussie or South African one of the lads reckoned, part of the Commonwealth, a bunch of convicts shipped off for fuck all, raped on the ships, not a bad job if you're a sailor, it's not fucking funny though if you're one of the women or children. And your meal's nearly finished and you've only got half a pint left, lift the glass to the lips and there's a table emptying across the room, all the waiters out back now, the bar end of the restaurant a big fucking bundle, playground fight, hasn't got that nasty edge yet, not vicious or anything, just because they're all so fucking pissed, though it won't be long before someone gets hurt, and more people are joining in, a little cunt who must think he's a karate master or something, chopping some scruffy pissed cunt, his bird jumping on the bloke's back, ski pants and legs wrapped round his body, cunt wedged up against the base of his spine, like something from those karma sutra cartoons, smacking his head with her fists, fucking lovely, real laugh, and the old bill won't be long and maybe she'll get a cell all to herself. Fucking wicked. Rakes her nails down the man's cheeks. Long red slashes. You wipe your mouth and the whole table's up on its feet heading for the door, a right fucking laugh, and the cunt with the nicked money says next time lads, next time we pay nothing, though you're paying nothing now, but it's always good to have something to look forward to, something that's planned, you've got to take your chances in life, don't ignore the opportunities when they crop up as you don't get that many, every little helps, the small victories are important because that's your lot, and the half of the curry house not involved in the punch-up is doing a runner, eighty per cent anyway, a few dozy cunts too honest or thick, what's the difference anyway, they stay where they are, but you're outside in the street and the lot of you are doing a runner, saving your hard-earned cash for the future, out in the evening air shooting round the corner, out of sight. You're pissed and running and soon you're fucked, leaning against a wall, panting, breath gone, laughing and wheezing at the same time, and when you catch your breath you know you've been a bit silly, that you'll have to tread careful next time you go to that particular curry house, maybe leave it a few months, go back when you're pissed and think you won't be recognised, but fuck it anyway, and there's always one cunt who thinks with his knob and wants to fuck the girls at the next table. Did anyone see where they went, did they do a runner as well, who fucking knows, who fucking cares, and a couple of the lads piss off home with the sound of sirens in their ears as three cars flash past and you shout that they've got a major disturbance to worry about. They don't give a fuck about a bunch of wankers who've just done a runner, they're interested in the ruck demolishing the curry house. Problem is, the running got your head straightened out a bit and the curry's soaking up the drink, you've got your breath back and you decide to take a wander, should have got it lined up with those slags at the next table, so you start walking back in the general direction, get

19

near and see the wagons pulled up outside, blue lights pulsing like bedlam, setting off epileptic fits, fucking video games, playing police and thieves nicking a load of blokes, some short-haired figure, not a squaddie because he's not thick enough, he hits a copper and the bastards have him on the ground and start kicking the shit out of him. Battered to fuck outside the tandoori by the old bill. The waiters are looking through the window. The English are a race of barbarians and the Indians get their revenge, like the time down that curry house at the seaside, well pissed, and the bastards only laced the fucking meal, you thought it tasted a bit iffy at the time but put it down to the heavy water beer up north. You remember it well, have to laugh, you deserved it trying to throw a table full of food across the room, and you got the train back early the next morning shitting fluid the whole way. If you ever go back the lads are going to wreck the place, put a fire bomb through the window because your arses were burning all the way back to London, talk about the big smoke, then the tube home, but credit where credit's due, those northern waiters were smart. And you're no fool either saying enough's enough, turn and take another road, no point being spotted, making it easy for the old bill, more cars steaming past, looks like World War Three has broken out, Islamic fundamentalists on the rampage, more like Christian militiamen. You walk down by the station and there's two of the tarts from the curry house by the taxi rank trying to pull soldiers, three blokes from the tandoori, one the white buffalo soldier from the bogs, they must've done a runner as well, woke up half way through battering some cunt and realised they were in trouble and got out before the old bill turned up. And the mouthy slag is giving them some chat, but the blokes are too pissed, you can see it in their faces, jaws hanging down dribbling over their clothes, no chance, rough bastards who'd give the girls a hard time of it, but they're going to be suffering brewer's droop soon as they get back, and the only hard things left will be their fists when the girls start laughing, pissed, too much vodka, too much something, but they work it out and they see you coming and blow the squaddies out, leave them for the taxis and come over and it's getting late and a bit cold and they're inviting you back for a drink, a shag, whatever you want lads, bit of music, don't have anything but shitty sounds, nothing worth listening to, who cares, it's somewhere to go, something to do, better than nothing, just standing around idle. But the squaddies are up and moving and there's a bit of an argument about nothing in particular, the sound of a police car nearby, they say you can have the women boys, you're welcome to them, and the squaddies return to the rank, jump in a taxi, fuck off back to barracks or wherever they came from, and you're standing against the wall, listening to the siren cut off, knowing you've got off lucky. The two birds are telling you not to worry about it, those squaddies mate, those fucking squaddies are bred to kill, trained to inflict brain damage and other serious injury and the mouthy slag is looking a bit more human now, her perfume is strong and doesn't let her down, makes her warm and female, but she's a pig, you know that, a pig in knickers, though her mate's not bad, but those rotten teeth, rough as fuck both of them, be honest about it, you're well pissed, and your best mate has just walked off in disgust and left you to fend for yourself, you can't believe it, the smell of perfume and warm breath, wet pants and a beer gut, rotting teeth and a dose of the crabs, you've got to make a stand, show a bit of class, all you've got to do is say no, but you know you're going to hate yourself in the morning.

TOTTENHAM AWAY

HALF-ELEVEN ON the dot and we're in King's Cross, standing at the bar in our North London local. The city's wide awake and there's a good mob packed into the pub. I'm sipping a pint of lager. Taking my time. Making it last. Mark's making do with orange juice and Rod holds a bottle of light ale. Harris is by the door watching people come in. Seeing who's who. He's got his usual firm on hand and there's small crews from all over West and South London. We're exclusive. There's no room for part-timers. The landlord must think it's Christmas because he's in the right place at the right time.

We usually use this pub before a game in North London, or when we've come back to King's Cross from up north. It always works like that. You find somewhere in a handy location where you can get together without the owner calling the old bill. You keep using it till it gets sussed. When there's a police van sitting across the road you know it's time to move. We just want to be left alone. Dress sensibly and leave the army fatigues and funny haircuts for school kids and sillies. You have to be casual and blend into the background.

Tottenham away is a cracker. There's always been a healthy hatred for Spurs. They're yids and wear skullcaps. They wave the Star of David and wind us up. We're Chelsea boys from the Anglo-Saxon estates of West London. Your average Chelsea fan coming up to Tottenham from Hayes and Hounslow is used to Pakis and niggers, but go up Seven Sisters Road and it's all bagels and kebab houses. Greeks, Turks, yids, Arabs. The Spurs mob like to get us going and it works both ways. Tottenham have always had a reputation for being flash. Silver Town yids. They're the rich spivs to West Ham's poor dockers. At least that's how the story goes. You go through Stamford Hill and Tottenham and

22

you wouldn't think you're in the same city as Hammersmith and Acton. We've got our Paddies down in West London, but none of these yid ghettoes. I'm no Christian myself, but still Church Of Fucking England.

Tottenham sent us down to the Second Division in the mid-Seventies and most of the Chelsea mob got locked out of White Hart Lane before kick-off. It went off inside and there were battles all over the pitch. Spurs had the numbers and though Chelsea put up a show they gave us a kicking. Tottenham won 2–0. Chelsea went down. They've been paying for it ever since. Talk to other clubs' supporters, whether they're from up north or London, and everyone hates Tottenham. But we're Chelsea and proud of the fact. Harris has had the old brain ticking over since last Saturday and we're working to a plan. Know where to find Tottenham before the match. There'll be a good turn out for this one because Chelsea always show up in force for Tottenham away.

Black Paul is next to us at the bar. A Chelsea nigger from Battersea. He lives in a tenth floor flat looking over the river and sees the Stamford Bridge floodlights every morning when he gets out of bed. David Mellor shagging some bird in Chelsea gear's nothing, because Black Paul knocks them off with a view of the fucking ground. You can't get much better than that. He's no mug, Black Paul. Built like a concrete bunker and works on a building site. None of the lads wear colours because club shirts are the mark of a wanker, but Paul always has a kit top under his sweat shirt. Gets away with it because he's a mean cunt and nobody's going to say anything. He must be six-foot four in his bare feet and his hands are full of scars. Building walls for the white man.

He makes up for this by shagging the white man's women, winding us up something chronic with stories of the blonde birds flocking round his big black cock. It's always the same kind of birds. Blonde hair stacked up on their heads listening to digital drum beats. Your typical ecstasy girls from the inner city estates. Kids who won't touch a white bloke. They look us over like we can't compare with Black Paul and the niggers from Shepherd's Bush and Brixton. Like we're not up to scratch and it can cause bad feeling. Paul gives them a dose of jungle spunk but he's a

23

Chelsea nigger first and foremost. Do the business for Chelsea and that's all that counts.

I fancy a decent drink but take my time. Last night was quiet. A hard week at the warehouse. It's a boring place to work but you've got to do something. Didn't want to shag myself out with Tottenham next day so had a couple of cans and watched this film about some smooth cunt who makes a fortune buying and selling property. Knobs everything in sight, jacks up on heroin to help him cope with his millions, but gets a bit careless and shares his works and then finds he's got Aids. This makes him look up his old man who he's ignored for the last five years and they become the best of mates. The bloke dies and the old boy gets the cash. Rags to riches tale. Pile of shit basically, but there was nothing else on.

The lager tastes good but there's no point getting pissed and nicked for mouthing off along Tottenham High Road. You have to keep your wits about you when you're looking for a ruck. Get pissed and you're on for a kicking, not to mention a threatening behaviour charge. Assault if the old bill are around to see you in action. The cream of every club knows the score and leaves the pissheads to make lots of noise, jump up and down, and generally create a show for the TV cameras. It's a mug's game. Like the older chaps dressing for action. Like they're out on parade with their boots and fatigues.

We call them sillies because it's all about melting into the background. You can be twice as tasty without the show. Just do the business and piss off before you're spotted. It's all about calculation. Think before you pile in. Use your brain. Don't rant and rave and give yourself a heart attack. Look after yourself and stay healthy. Find the opposition and batter them into the concrete. You don't have to march in with a brass band playing. Do it on the quiet and you get the same result with none of the comeback. It's basic politics. It's great though, because the papers and television always miss the point. There's no reporters down Kensington High Street when we pull scousers off the train and kick them into next week. The cunts are in the East Stand rubbing shoulders with the money men, hoping a politician will look their way. The commentators don't sit in a block of flats with their camera crew zooming-in when we steam geordies at King's Cross

They're editing highlights and pocketing the wage packet. Suits us fine. Who needs the hassle?

One o'clock we start moving. It's a fair old walk along the Euston Road. We're out in the open then safe underground flooding the northbound platform of the Victoria Line, clockwork soldiers moving in time. Wind rushes down the tunnel and a Walthamstow train piles in. It's packed with Chelsea heading north. There's small mobs, kids and decent citizens. Older geezers with lion tattoos and granddads who remember Bobby Tambling and Jimmy Greaves like it was yesterday. There's nothing aboard to compare with us though and we get a few nervous looks. No colours. No sound. We wait for the next train a couple of minutes later, watched by London Underground lenses.

Video cameras see everything. You have to be sharp to achieve your ends because there's a market for Peeping Toms. Like this crime programme on the box hunting a serial killer wiping out sado-masochist queers. They took the cameras to a grubby flat in East London. Inside a bedroom with a body wrapped up on the bed. They were everywhere. Even went upstairs to talk with a granny who said she saw the victim and another bloke come home on the murder night. Said her eyesight wasn't too hot, but if the bloke's a nutter, which by rights he has to be, then he could well top the old girl as well.

They fucking loved it in the studio. Letting the country get off on the forensic team checking the flat. Pointing out old condom packets and an empty tube of KY. Then a camera at Waterloo picks up the killer with another bum bandit on their way to Putney and another murder. Cameras have a lot of power, but they won't stop anything. If you've got the urge to do something then it takes a special kind of strength to resist the desire. You don't have to get caught just because London's turning into a surveillance arcade. Not if you're clever.

The second train's half full and we spread out and take over. It's sauna conditions in the carriage with Mark and Rod pressed up against glass and Jim Barnes sweating last night's curry, moaning about some pig he shagged. Harris is in the next carriage down. I can see the back of his head through the door. Black Paul's against the wall, eyes to the ceiling. The train picks up speed. Curves through tunnels. There's a few women caught on the wrong train obviously worried, but we're Chelsea, not fucking Tottenham. We're not interested in bothering women. True, there are wankers about who'll get pissed up and give them a bad time, but they're nonces who wank their days away and spend their evenings telling everyone how hard they are.

We stop at Highbury & Islington and Finsbury Park. We check the platforms for Tottenham. If they're out looking for us and we get them underground that's their mistake. But the platforms are empty. Finsbury Park's Gooner territory, but Arsenal are away today, though there's a few memories of that particular area. The doors close and there's reflections in the windows. The next carriage starts singing Spurs Are On Their Way To Auschwitz and our lot joins in. A gang of kids in their late teens smell of too much drink. They start pulling at a seat. Flash a knife. One of them puts his hand on the emergency lever. Rod tells him to leave it out, we don't want the old bill fucking up our Saturday. Little hooligans showing off is okay when they do it away from us, but we don't need that kind of behaviour. You have to have standards. Would have done the same when I was their age, but I'm not. Now is now. There's no room for nostalgia. The kid does the sensible thing. Puts the knife away. Rod's not a bloke to annoy.

When we arrive at Seven Sisters the platform is all Chelsea. There's jokes about what will be first on the menu. A launderette or kebab shop. Harris is ahead now and the rest of us filter through the crowd trying not to draw attention. Tottenham offers a bonus because the tube's so far from the ground. It's a long way down Tottenham High Road and the old bill can't police all the different routes properly. Gives us the chance we're looking for. The crowd spills through barriers into the street. There's a kebab house opposite and a queue forms at the counter. Fair dodgers get pulled at the barriers while we move onto the main road. Keeps the old bill busy. Makes them feel needed.

There's traffic clogging the street and men run for buses to save their legs. Harris is on the other side of the road with Black Paul and some of the Battersea lads behind him. There's Hammerhead, a fat cunt from Isleworth who never runs because he's too fucking heavy. He got a bad kicking at Leeds last season and reckons he didn't suffer permanent damage because of his weight. Sixteen stone of blubber. He's more a mascot than anything and heads for the kebab house saying he needs a feed. He's a funny bloke. Lot of humour about him. Not the kind of bloke who deserves a kicking. Leeds are scum doing him. Ten onto one. It's not the odds, just Hammerhead doesn't want to know when it comes to a fight, which is fair enough.

Tottenham's a dump. There's holes in the pavements and more fumes than Hammersmith. Pensioners sit on benches looking into space and an old black woman pushes a supermarket trolley packed with flattened cardboard and empty cans. There's a heavy smell of kebab meat and even the niggers look different. The streets are wider. Derelict flats boarded up against squatters. These are the areas kids from up north head for when they come to London. Cheap accommodation. But there's plenty of builders looking to do them up and make a few quid. Plenty of nutters around who'll carry out the eviction. You've got to look after yourself. Nothing comes free and you've got to do the other bloke before he does you. That's what the pensioners on the bench don't realise. They might be owed something but there's nobody left to cough up. It's a different world now. The war spirit is dead and gone, packaged and sold off to the highest bidder.

We cross over and follow Harris, the crowd from the tube stretching along the High Road. We're dedicated in our mission. Getting in tight behind the leader. Black Paul telling us he's going to have a Tottenham nigger. Makes the lads laugh. His mate Black John with him. A smaller bloke with a shinehead and a way of making you nervous. His eyes are always darting around and you know his mind's working overtime. Only turns up for big games. Usually the aways. Paul told me on the quiet John makes a packet flogging crack in South London. Five hundred quid for a couple of night's work in Camberwell and Brixton. He's worth having along because you know he's always tooled-up. There's enough full-time, would-be yardies around who don't like him hanging out with the white man. He has to watch his step. Loves going up to Tottenham and Arsenal. Gets to deal with his North London rivals, or at least their brothers.

There's a few yids hanging around further down the road. Half white, half black which means they're Spurs. They're scouting and move away all stroppy like. Look back and we're together now, spilling off the pavement into the road. They turn a corner and the wanker at the back disappears sharpish, as though he's running. They're trying to play it cool, at least till they're out of sight, but we're looking for their mob and they're off to give the warning. Harris moves a bit faster now, telling some of the younger lads to hang back, take it calm, don't spoil the party. We come to the corner and the yids have disappeared, a pub further down the street on another corner the target. We turn right and spread across the road. You can feel the tension and I'm buzzing. Been looking forward to this all week. Washes away all the boredom and slaving over hot cardboard boxes.

Some of the lads start kicking at a broken wall, breaking away chunks of brick and masonry. Harris is trying to keep things together. Black Paul's handing out half bricks. A professional who knows his trade. Makes me laugh. Rod and Mark's eyes shine. A chunk of concrete with wire sticking through the middle rests in my hand, and then we're running down the street and there's that noise that comes from somewhere deep down inside when you steam in. No words, just a roar like we're back in the fucking jungle or something, and the bricks are flying through the pub windows and I can see shapes inside already heading for the door, vital seconds lost with indecision as the scouts got back and made their report. Tight cunts should try investing in a couple of mobile phones.

My hand's in the air and I see my lump of concrete among the bricks caving in windows, the sound of glass shattering a soft noise in the din of voices, and Tottenham are breaking through the doors but we're there to meet them and Harris is leading from the front with Black Paul and a load of other blokes, pulling the first yids into the street, weight of numbers piling out of the pub so we spill everywhere, Harris copying his mate from Camberwell, nutting a big cunt between the eyes, bridge of the nose job, no copper this one, and Black Paul kicks him in the bollocks, and as he stumbles forward a few of the blokes start kicking him in the head and gut, driving him under a parked car.

Rod's laying into some bloke with a Tottenham shirt on, silly cunt, and we're shoulder to shoulder, smacking a nigger in the mouth feeling the pain in my knuckles as I don't catch him right, try to kick him in the balls, but Mark's in first and we're in a position by the door of the pub, more yids inside trying to force their way out, but we've got the strategy and I do the geezer now, he falls back against the wall, Chelsea piling in and he sinks into the pavement, feet catching him in the head and for a split second I see his eyes glaze then he's fighting to survive, panicking in the crush, but they're piling into the street now because someone's lobbed tear gas into the pub, and we back off because it makes you choke and you feel like you're going to suffocate.

There's a split in the road and we're further back, those of us near the front rubbing our eyes, all the pub windows smashed, just long shards left, a pint glass flying through the air catching Mark on the side of the head sending blood down his shirt over his jeans, and the yids are getting it sorted out, a few of the cunts dazed on the pavement, others helping them away where they can half walk, half crawl, and we get ready to steam in again, the noise cranked up, car windows kicked in as the energy has to come out some way, held back by the gas, and there's a fucking giant Irish-looking geezer with red hair and pasty white skin coming through, and he's with a nigger with a machete and nobody's going to tangle with that cunt, the only weapons bricks which batter him and then Paul's saving face taking him out and the mob piles in kicking the bastard to fuck, paying him back for their fear, head on a stick, everyone reads the papers, and I'm in there feeling the sheer joy of kicking a deserving bastard in the bollocks, head, gut, anywhere we can get the cunt, in among the wrecked cars in this broken down North London slum.

The two mobs clash again and this time it's less frantic, trouble flaring across the street, mostly punches and kicks, a couple of blades coming out, flashing in the early afternoon sunlight, sparks of silver fear which make you pull back and everyone mob together and do the offender. Martin Howe's in there, only got let out two weeks ago, did four months for smacking a bloke who cut him up at a set of traffic lights, and he's bleeding from his leg, pig stuck by Spurs, and it's slower now, picking our spot, and I'm after a mouthy cunt shouting insults and he goes for my head and misses and I do my kung-fu impression because he's small enough and split his mouth open, Mark following through trying to do his knee like a kickboxer, Rod the man in the know using his karate to bruise his throat, sending the cunt spluttering into the crowd, choking on his words.

The battle moves along the street, the pub empty, scared faces watching from behind net curtains. A shitty street with broken walls and small rundown gardens. Piles of rotting rubbish left uncollected. Rusted bike frames on the pavement. Place smells of curry and decaying big ends. There's pale kids on doorsteps shitting themselves and you have to feel a bit bad for them, because when you're young you don't need this, not with your mum and dad at each other late into the night, but they'll get it from somewhere and we've all been through that shit ourselves anyway.

There's sirens screaming in the distance and one by one we take them in, know where they're heading. The sound sends us moving back towards the main road and there's a van flashing blue murder, just one of the cunts, and a brick sails through the windscreen, back door opening and the old bill are looking for aggro. They're tooled-up and Tottenham have scattered into the back streets. I turn round and Mark's holding his head together okay, Rod next to him, and I'm with Harris and his mob, looking further up the road. There's only the one van, and the old bill are sizing the situation up even as they pick on a young lad nearby and crack his head with their truncheons, one cunt with stripes smashing his head into the side of the van, another one kicking him, splitting his lip with the truncheon, screaming abuse, voice and siren together, fucking Chelsea scum. Somehow knows we're Chelsea.

The other coppers are lashing out and trying to nick some of the younger element, but they know they've fucked up and we're mobbing together and the cunts are on for a kicking. I want to laugh and shout because this is Tottenham. A fucking shit hole and the old bill don't put cameras down poor people's streets. They're only interested in protecting City wealth and the rich cunts in Hampstead and Kensington. Fuck the scum round here. There's no cameras this distance from the ground. No fucking chance. The old bill know they haven't got the numbers and there's no videotape deterrent. The road's jammed with traffic and we can see flashing lights further down the street blocked by buses. You couldn't ask for more.

There's a few seconds of quiet and everyone knows the score. We run towards the van and the coppers are shitting themselves.

Even the sergeant leaves the kid alone. The boy murmurs to himself on the pavement. They've all got their numbers covered so there's no chance of identification and you know that any complaint you make against police brutality comes to nothing. They love football fans because they can do what they want. We're lower than niggers because there's no politician going to stand up for the rights of mainly white hooligans like us. And we don't want their help. We stand on our own feet. There's no easy place to hide. No Labour council protecting us because we're an ethnic minority stitched up by the system. No Tory minister to support our free market right to kill or be killed. The old bill are the scum of the earth. They're the shit of creation. Lower than niggers, Pakis, yids, whatever, because at least they don't hide behind a uniform. You may take the piss out of the bastards occasionally but you have some hidden respect somewhere.

But the old bill? Leave it out. We have the cunts in our sights. We pile in and the bastards don't have a chance. The sergeant takes the worst of it because he's all stripes and mouth and we've seen him batter the kid. Somehow he's worse because he's got a uniform and authority and we've been trained to respect uniforms and believe in the idea of justice. He shouts out as he sinks to the road, pulled to his feet by Black Paul, and a few of the Battersea mob take turns kicking him. His eyes are shut and bruised. Blood spews out of his nose. His head snaps back and opens up on broken glass. He's getting his reward and we're so frenzied we couldn't care less if he died.

The sirens are louder and police vans mount the pavement. We move off. Another train has arrived at Seven Sisters spilling more people onto the pavement, the vast majority of football fans who hate violence. Content to sing songs and have a few pints. We're evil bastards in their eyes and it gives us a special position. We split up and leave the battered coppers and the old bill unload their vans and block the road, a few coppers going over to check their mates, the rest piling into the crowd fresh off the train. They tug the nearest blokes and start laying into them. We look back and they've got some kids under a bus stop, kicking them black and blue, and a black woman's screaming at them to stop, that they haven't done anything wrong. A copper turns and lays her out with a single punch. Calls her a fucking slag.

The old bill are going mad and there's a couple of thousand people along the road now, and they lose it and start fighting back, defending themselves, and that's how you get a riot going. It only takes a few of you to start things off and the old bill are so fucking thick they whip everyone up. There's a helicopter above and more coppers piling down the road. They've got their shields out and try to form a barricade as Chelsea move forward, covering the area, kids and older blokes joining in. It's paradise this. A great way to spend your Saturday afternoon. There's a few bottles bouncing off shields and snatch squads running out to pick off young lads who look the business but are just caught up in the spectacle. We're ahead of the main lot now, nearing the ground, trying to suss out yids among the onlookers, but doing it from habit more than anything.

There's people in the street watching the battle. It's turned into a stand off with the crowd singing and smashing the odd car window. They've missed the nasty part and it's turning into a show. Something to put the shit up Spurs. Mark and Rod catch up and we're on our own approaching the ground. I feel great inside. The rush is there and my body tingles. Sounds funny but it's true. It's better than shafting a bird. Better than speeding. Mark's head's a mess but the bleeding has stopped. My knuckles are bruised and Rod's eyes have gone a bit mental looking. We join the crush trying to get in the ground. The crowd's already buzzing inside and we can hear the constant chant of CHELSEA. This is what life's all about. Tottenham away. Love it.

WORKER'S DREAM

SID CHECKED HIS watch and wiped the sweat from his forehead, annoyed at his aching muscles. He smelt of salt, and the close atmosphere of the lorry he was unloading made him feel as though he was working with a surgical mask over his face. Tom was by the doors stacking boxes for Steve on the forklift. It was hard work, and boring, very boring, so Sid just daydreamed the morning away, imagining he was playing centre-forward for QPR in one of the finest football teams the world had ever seen.

He was having an excellent game. It was the Cup Final at Wembley and he was on a hat-trick. His first goal had come just before half-time as he finished off a long run, which had seen him cover the length of the pitch, by rounding the Man United keeper and slotting the ball into the back of an empty net. The second was scored midway through the second half, a diving header from a pinpoint cross from the left wing, Sid ducking his head in among the flying boots in a magnificent display of sporting bravery.

Now he was considering the options on how to complete the scoring. Leaning his back against the cold metal of the lorry's wall, he hitched faded jeans over a sweltering beer gut and decided on another pitch-length sprint with a pile-driver of a shot which burst the back of the net and sent the commentators into a frenzy of familiar football clichés. The voices of Brian Moore and John Motson echoed through the living rooms of a watching nation, the praise of Alan Hansen and Gary Lineker hailing the young West Londoner as the greatest living footballer since that Argentinian hand-of-God merchant Diego Maradona. Sid was a George Best for the modern game. A worthy QPR addition to the Rodney Marsh/Stan Bowles hall of fame. He closed his eyes to stop the flood of sweat from blinding his view, watching his own celebrating run towards the royal box, where Princess Di cheered

33

her favourite player with a look on her face which meant one thing and one thing only. Romance.

– You want a cup of coffee Sidney? Tom asked.

– No sugar or milk. I'm trying to watch my weight. I'm up to seventeen stone again.

– Right.

The Chelsea bastard pissed off to the hot drinks machine and Sid was left with the image of a beautiful princess spread out on his bed in a silk negligée, looking seductive. Her elegant fingers were covered in diamond and sapphire rings, and she wore a sparkling tiara. Sid had other things on his mind though. He was running around the room making sure there were no journalists hiding in the wardrobe, sticking their lenses through his dirty washing stacked up in a corner. Once the bedroom got the all-clear, he tried clicking back to the expectant royal awaiting his plebeian touch, but he wasn't much good with pure fantasy. There had to be a bit of reality to make the daydream work. He had too much respect for Lady Di. Anyway, he'd read somewhere that she'd had that illness girls got sometimes, where they stick their fingers down their throats and make themselves sick so that they can stay skinny. It was disgusting. All that skin and bones. They'd never catch him making himself sick just so he could lose a bit of weight.

Sid wondered if he was pushing it a bit by scoring a fourth goal in injury time, just so he could rub Man U's nose in shit. Why not? You only lived once and he'd got his second wind after completing the hat-trick. Steve was busy messing about with that last pallet they'd loaded, trying to work the forklift into the grooves, the sound of creaking wood and nails vibrating through the trailer. Sid switched back to the Cup Final, immediately setting off on an intricate dribble, a slimmed-down vision of his former self, ten years ago as a twenty-year-old, twisting and turning this way and that, nutmegging the centre-half and chipping the keeper. He ran to the QPR fans and sunk to his knees, enjoying their hysteria. Grown men spilled onto the pitch and hugged him. Sid was a hero.

– Here you go, Tom said. You look fucked. Out on a bender last night were you?

– Seven pints of London Pride and a couple of cans of Tennants when I got home. I was only planning a quick one, but it was Kevin the landlord's birthday and he had a bit of a lock-in to celebrate. You can't be rude.

– I thought you were going to lose some weight?

– I was. I am. Starting today. There's no time like the present.

Steve finally got the troublesome pallet up and moving, and soon had it stacked in the shelves. Tom dragged a new one into the trailer, as far as it would go up against the boxed pressure cookers rising above them, and they started the process again. Sid pulled boxes out and threw them to Tom, who formed precise rows. On the next pallet they would change over. It was a shit job, unloading these big efforts, but it did make the time pass if you could keep your mind busy, and Sid was having no trouble there.

He had won the pools and was signing on the dotted line. He was the biggest winner the competition had ever known, a cool forty million pounds topping up his savings account, which at the moment stood at a modest seventeen pounds and fifty-six pence. He had decided to buy up Queens Park Rangers Football Club, thereby fulfilling a childhood dream which showed no sign of fading. He would invest in new players and assume the managerial role. True, he had not played the professional game himself, though he'd had trials with Watford and Orient as a kid, but so what? He was an innovator ready to break the rules. He was rich. The rules didn't mean a thing if you were loaded.

– Slow down a bit will you Sid, Tom said, grinning. There's no rush. You're getting a bit excited up there. You're not imagining yourself in the cab with that French bird are you?

– I just won a fortune and bought Rangers, and was planning my first signing, he said, slowing down. He liked Tom.

– Hear that Steve, Tom shouted, turning towards the forklift driver. Sid's just bought your club and he's going to sign a team full of Catholics. He's signing Fenians behind your back.

– He fucking isn't.

– QPR, mate, QPR. I'm not interested in your Jock football. It's all haggis and kilts in the centre circle at Ibrox.

Sid had his say and didn't wait for a reply. He was back at Loftus Road with Rodney Marsh and Stan Bowles sitting on either side of him in the director's box. Chelsea were getting hammered 5–0 and he'd tipped the old bill off. He laughed as Tom and his nutter mates were led down the tunnel for a good spanking. He didn't approve of hardline policing, especially at football grounds, but neither did he like trouble-makers spoiling things for everyone else. He was a football fan. A programme collector. A third of the way to being a trainspotter. He was busy building a team the fans would love to watch and he had already halved admission prices. Soon he would redevelop the ground and crowds of fifty thousand would be common. The whole of White City and the surrounding area would flock to see his team of stars perform. Rodney, Stan and Sid would wave to the punters and share an after-match pint or three with Gerry Francis and Ray Wilkins.

– That new bird in the office is well nice, Tom said, watching Janet walk past on her way to the foreman's office.

She was. Very definitely. Sid couldn't disagree. But he was too busy in the director's bar to bother about fanny, sitting at a table with Rodney and Stan and Gerry and Ray. It was Gerry's round and he was on his way to the bar as Tom spoke. Rodney and Gerry had become best of mates and it was turning into a good evening. Gerry came back with five pints of the new Dave Sexton Best Bitter which Sid was having brewed on the premises. They were a bit pissed and talking about going for a sitdown curry when the bar closed. Terry Venables was coming along a bit later, when he'd got his England squad sorted out, as there'd been important matches played that evening and there was bound to be five or six players reporting themselves injured.

– Hurry up Gerry, you grey-haired tosser, Rodney shouted.

– Oh Rodney, Rodney ... Rodney, Rodney, Rodney, Rodney, Rodney Marsh, chanted Ray, obviously unable to handle the Dave Sexton Best.

– Shut up you bald sod, Stan mumbled. You'll get us kicked out and we'll have to fuck off down the Springbok.

– Baldness is a sign of virility, I'll have you know, Ray said. Remember that next time you're doing the business. Anyway, how many caps did you win for England?

– It's you wearing them every night in the bath that's turned you into a baldy bastard, Stan laughed, secretly cursing the former midfield maestro for highlighting his own lack of international recognition, simultaneously comforting himself with the know-

36

ledge that he had just been too talented for the limited thinking of the England set-up of his day.

Sid thought about telling the lads not to worry about getting kicked out because he owned the bar, the ground, everything, but he didn't want them to think he was a bighead. He kept quiet. Gerry was downing his pint in one and Stan was smirking to himself as he watched the former England skipper, at the same time trying to open a pack of salted peanuts he'd been saving since Sid bought the first round. Good old Stan. A great player. Unique talent. Sid was in heaven. A rich man surrounded by the greatest players he'd ever seen. All of them QPR men. He wished the night would last for ever, but knew time would pass quickly and they'd have to get down the curry house fast before the Indians locked the doors in the vain hope of keeping out the drunks who treated every tandoori house like an assault course. Sid was well used to eating his prawn vindaloos surrounded by rambling men, but tonight he preferred a quiet corner where he could talk the lads through the four goals he'd scored at Wembley, then tell them how he'd felt lifting the FA Cup, and how Lady Di had slipped him her number on a piece of paper torn from her autograph book.

– I heard about you and the princess, Stan whispered when they were outside the ground, waiting for their cab to arrive. She's a fine-looking woman, though I heard she sticks her fingers down her throat and makes herself puke.

– That was years ago, Sid said, keeping his voice down, because although he respected Ray and Gerry and Rodney, he was a discreet character. There were no kiss-and-tell betrayals falling from the lips of Sid Parkinson.

– Lovely princess, Stan whispered again, nodding his head thoughtfully. I remember the day of the Royal Wedding. A fine event. A day of celebration for the entire nation.

Sid thought of their first meeting. It was in McDonalds in Shepherd's Bush, just after midday, and they'd spent the afternoon window shopping before Diana had hopped on a bus back to her own manor. She'd had two hamburgers, small fries and a large strawberry milkshake. He timed her when she went to the Ladies, but she'd been quick, too fast to make herself ill. She really was cured. He had made the decision that their relationship would remain purely platonic. He was at the peak of his football career and in the finest physical condition. He couldn't afford rampant unbridled sex sessions with a member of the aristocracy. He knew Di wanted more, but he remained firm and knew that his moral stance was understood. She was a class act.

– I've got to be honest lads, said Rodney, once inside the taxi and racing towards the White City Balti, I don't fancy the old ethnic food much. Let's go to Tel's club and have a few sherbets there.

Sid felt a bit disappointed at first, but then reasoned that Rodney had been in the States so long that he had fallen behind in his understanding of British culture. Anyway, it would prolong the meeting of five great footballing brains, and Tel was bound to turn up sooner or later. Sid leant forward and told the driver the change of destination and, with the screech of tyres and a few choice words, the car was on its way to El Tel Palace in Camden Town. They raced along the Westway at seventy miles an hour, passed Baker Street tube and then cut past Euston to Camden. Once safely inside El Tel's, the Rangers contingent pushed their way through the hordes of blonde-haired Page 3 girls crowding around them to a private table boxed in with mahogany wood panelling. A bouncer stood nearby deterring the beautiful women pestering Sid and his mates, while El Tel's favourite hardcore beats blasted from an adjacent sound system. Sid thought he recognised Mixmaster Incie playing the England manager's CD collection, but knew he must be mistaken.

– It's five past eleven, Tom shouted, obviously narked.

El Tel's vanished in a sea of cardboard boxes and Sid was sweating in the back of a forty-foot lorry. He had lost five minutes of his precious tea break and wasn't too pleased. He left Rodney and Stan and Gerry and Ray without a word and went into the warehouse, swore as he had to return for his cup of coffee, then entered the tea-room. The rest of the warehouse crew were either playing cards, reading their papers or staring through the glass partition towards the loading ramp, waiting for something to happen.

– That driver's been in his cab with that French bird the whole time we've been unloading, Tom said.

Nobody answered. A couple of card players looked towards the lorry and then returned to their hands, a stack of small coins piled in the middle of the table waiting for a winner.

– There should be a law against us working our bollocks off while he's on the job emptying his, he added.

Still nobody answered. Why torture yourself with visions of female beauty and the joys of sex when hours of mindless warehouse tedium was the best you could hope for from the rest of the day?

Sid stood up and took his sandwiches out to the ramp; round the corner and out of sight of his fellow workers. He had to graft with these men five days a week and wasn't in the mood to share his tea break with them as well. Good luck to the driver if he was getting his end away. He watched cars and people arrive and leave the car park. He saw Janet getting into her company car. She waved and he smiled. Then she was off. Heading to El Tel's midday ambient room perhaps. He shook his head sadly. What would he really do when he won the pools? He liked to think he'd make QPR a power in the land, but would he when it came to the crunch?

First off he'd buy himself a flat and move out of the dump he rented at the moment. He'd tell the landlord what he really thought of him, the arrogant bastard. He'd spread a bit of wealth around to family and friends, maybe one or two blokes in the warehouse, though he wasn't sure about that one. He'd have a holiday and go somewhere interesting. He fancied Brazil. A trip down the Amazon and the street carnival in Rio. Maybe meet Ronnie Biggs and discuss the talent crowding the Brazilian beaches. He'd invest his millions, but then what? Money for players? Wages of fifteen or twenty grand a week? He didn't think he could justify the expense. Professional footballers were over-paid as it was. Would he really want to meet Rodney and Stan and the rest of them? He'd gone to the Rodney Marsh-George Best roadshow at the Beck Theatre in Hayes, and much as he loved Rodney and those childhood memories of genius with a ball, the bloke was a bit disappointing, with his comments about British passports and the Indians in Southall. Most of the crowd laughed, but Sid thought it was all a bit naff. He expected more. Footballers were just that, footballers.

When he had his millions invested, perhaps he'd look into

doing something with the homeless. Or start up an organisation to help people with psychiatric problems. Buy up some old houses and turn them into homes for the kids who ended up on the streets of London and were forced to sell their bodies to paedophiles. If he had all those millions of pounds in his account he'd help the doctors and nurses struggling against Government cut-backs, or aid protests against vivisection and the veal industry. He'd pour funds into a non-aligned progressive programme for the prisons which would re-educate people rather than drive them to suicide and a hardening attitude to the world. There was a lot Sid could do with the cash and when he heard the foreman shouting that it was time to get back to work, that there was work needed doing, he knew he had a good line of thought which would take him right through to dinner. Then there would be the short walk to the bookies, for a fiver on Sir Rodney, running at Cheltenham. Sid was feeling lucky.

ROCHDALE AT HOME

I'M LATE MEETING the others. Had to finish off the lorry from France we started in the morning. A late delivery arrived at two which needed seeing to and then it was back to the French job. Untold pressure cookers and the driver's a flash cunt with a tasty blonde bird he takes into his cab and gives a good shafting while we're breaking our backs in the trailer. Couldn't exactly hear him doing the business, but it wasn't hard to imagine. Specially when you're knackered and just want to get away, and Glasgow Steve's going slow on the forklift because he's angry with the foreman.

It's six o'clock and there's a crowd building up on the Wimbledon-bound platform at Earl's Court. There's a fifty-fifty mixture of Chelsea going to the Rochdale cup game and smartly dressed wankers from Fulham and Parsons Green. Always makes me laugh the rich cunts who live around Stamford Bridge. They must hate us lot coming along, messing up their Saturday afternoons. The blokes act like they're lord of the manor and the birds all think they're the Queen. They look down their noses at the world, but it's a doddle staring them out. Every single time they look away, shitting themselves.

A train shows on the board and the coppers standing by the stairs check their watches. The attendance will be low tonight which translates as easy money for the old bill. A grey evening and it's been raining on and off all day. A midweek League Cup game against Rochdale isn't going to stir up much passion and I need a drink to warm my spirits. I'm on edge. It pisses me off when the warehouse interferes with Chelsea. Beggars can't be choosers, but I do my duty and want to leave on time when there's a game on. Steve can rant and rave about Glasgow Rangers, but the Scottish cunt should learn to move a bit quicker when Chelsea are at home.

The train pulls in nearly empty and it's a quick ride through West Brompton to Fulham Broadway. I flash my ticket and dump the *Standard* I've been reading since Hammersmith in a bin. There's print on my hands and I'll get rid of it in the pub. Paper says Chelsea are in the market for a goalkeeper. I wait for the lights to change and cross over. The kebab house on the corner stinks. Reminds me of Tottenham. Mark and Rod are by the door with FA Henry, a funny-looking bloke with thick glasses and FA Cup handle ears. Only comes along to the midweek games because he works on Saturdays.

– Alright Tom, lager? Mark says as I walk in and he empties his glass. Perfect timing. Henry's getting married next week, aren't you Henry? Lucky bastard.

– Congratulations Henry. I mean it too. He deserves a bird in a white dress even though it's all a big con. He's a romantic bloke. Wouldn't hurt a fly. We've known him since we were kids.

– Who you marrying?

– Lisa Wellington. Henry's chest puffs up with what I imagine is pride. You remember her from when we were at school, don't you?

– Course I do. Thought she moved away. Ireland or Scotland. Something like that. Somewhere with their own language and drinking laws.

– She did. Married an Irish bloke, but it didn't work out. Gave it a couple of years then packed her bags and came back here. My old girl knows her old girl. That's how we met up. By accident really, or maybe it was fate. One of the two.

I remember Lisa when we were teenagers. She was a good-looking girl and I wonder what she's like now. Black hair and Slav features. Her old girl was from Bucharest and came over in the war. Hated communists if I remember right. There again, who doesn't? But the woman was always on about them whenever I saw her. Fucking hated yids as well. Them and the gypos. Well over the top on the subject. Lisa was all right, even if she was a bit laid-back and into hippy drugs when everyone else was speeding. Makes sense her marrying FA Henry. He's a sound bloke and has never done too well with the birds. As well as the FA Cup ears he's Fuck All Henry. Women like him well enough, but most of them are looking for a quick length, not Henry's thoughts on creation.

– Where you having the stag night then, Henry? Let us know and we'll come along. Give you a good send off before you disappear into the twilight world of sweat and tears and supermarket trolleys.

– I'm not having one, he says, looking a bit nervous. I'm not bothering with all that. I've never been into those sort of things. Rod's was enough for me.

Rod has the decency to blush, and he should as well, the dirty cunt. Speeding through space like the Starship Enterprise at the time, hitting warp factor 700. A hall off the Fulham Palace Road and there was this stripper on stage. Dirty-looking tart with a fit body and I don't know what the fuck she was stripping for because she could have done better for herself. Real cracker. She got Rod up there on stage with her and he was out of his tree. Let her strip him stark bollock naked, spread him out on a table and shag his brains out. Mark had a camcorder and Rod was shitting it long after the wedding came and went. It was surprising he managed to get it up he'd drunk so much, but he says it was the drugs.

– It was enough for Rod too, wasn't it mate, and I slap him on the back and he's looking a bit uneasy. Sometimes you do things under the influence you just don't want to admit.

– Don't remind me. I remember it well enough but it was like someone else on that table. Like I was in the operating theatre getting my balls stretched or something. That bird was leaning over telling me she'd had five Taffies on stage in Cardiff the week before. Five of the bastards for a hundred quid. Talk about bulk buying. Told me I had to compete with five Cardiff City leeks. That she was full of Welsh spunk and wanted to see what a cockney could do. It got me going at the time, but looking back I must've been mad to dip my winkie in that old slapper.

– I don't want that kind of thing happening to me. Henry's face is bright red, his ears a very dark purple. Looks like he's about to explode. Suspect device primed to go off with a two-minute warning.

– You're right Henry. That's what tradition does for you. But what about Lisa? Hen nights are worse than that. Birds get together and they go fucking mental.

– Lisa's not interested either. She's not that sort of girl.

Don't believe it mate, but you can't blame Henry, knowing how he runs his life. Rod let his standards slip and it wasn't a pleasant sight watching one of your mates on the job. I felt sorry for Mandy more than anything. Mind you, she was probably up to no good on her night as well, so there you go. It all evens itself out in the end. You can't trust anyone. Certainly not women. They're at it like fucking rabbits then act all coy when you swear in front of them or turn up with a black eye. It's a load of shit, but you'd be a miserable cunt if you didn't hold out hope for people like Henry. Let him have his dreams and believe in love and romance. Suppose we all do deep down if we thought about being honest.

– Here you go Tom. Get that down your throat and give us a smile you sad cunt.

Mark hands me a pint. I smell the familiar football mix of plastic and lager. The bubbles feel good down my throat even though it's cold outside. It's a depressing evening and the place is dead. Couldn't be more different than Tottenham. Days like that don't come along very often. Still, you have to make the effort. Just like the Rochdale fan walking into the pub. Must be well into his fifties and wears a scarf round his neck. A few of the lads look his way but he's an old geezer and harmless. Why fuck about with civilians? You just make yourself look a cunt if you start having a go at old men and kids. Leave that to the yids and scousers. They go back to their drinks and conversation. The Rochdale man buys a pint and stands nearby. I wonder if he's carrying a wooden rattle. Probably an engine driver or machine minder. Looks like something out of the Fifties. Thick hands and steel under the nails. Northerners are all the same. Dopey cunts the lot of them. I tell him he'll get a decent pint now he's in London.

– Not bloody likely son. He appreciates the humour.

Northerners are always moaning about the beer in London. They reckon it's piss. Expensive piss. The cunts up north don't believe it's a proper pint unless it's got an inch of froth on top. Can't handle that kind of head myself. They're right about the prices though. It's a scandal what they charge for drink down here. We're getting shafted left, right and centre, but there's nothing you can do. You just have to get on with it, otherwise you'll end up doing fuck all because you're looking at the price tag the whole time. It's not fair, any of it, but that's life. You work hard and the more you earn the more worthless cunts are after you for a slice of your wage packet. Mouthy wankers in suits acting big, but when it comes down to it they're bottle merchants to a man. Get rid of their suits and give them the options and they'd disappear up their own over-mortgaged arseholes.

– We've got a good team coming through, lads. We might beat you tonight. How do you fancy a trip to Rochdale if we get a draw? Chelsea won't like a replay.

– I'd rather we had an away game against you lot than play at home, says Rod. Gives us a chance to get out and about. It's more of a laugh. Small town like Rochdale would suit Chelsea fine.

– Same here. I like going away. I'd go watch England, but it's all young hooligans who go overseas and spoil things for the rest of us.

– You shouldn't believe what you read in the papers. Those blokes writing the stories know fuck all. They're too busy getting pissed to leave their hotel bars and discover the truth. Too scared. If you don't want to get involved, you don't have to.

– True enough, but you can't trust the Frogs or dagos, or whoever else you're playing. You pay for the sins of others.

My glass is empty. The others have hardly started. I go to the bar and get a refill, remember I need to wash my hands and go to the bogs. The water's freezing but I get rid of the shit. There's no towels but at least the print has been washed off. I've never seen a decent pub toilet. It's all shit, piss and graffiti. Not surprising really. The bowls have flooded so I stand in the cubicle and undo my buttons. My bladder burns as I piss and splash the plastic seat. Fuck it up for the next cunt. There's a bog brush with white bristles. It's got *Ken Bates* written in felt pen along the handle, a face drawn at the end. I button up and go back to the bar. The Rochdale fan's already pissed off to the ground. Should have stayed for another drink. I was even planning to buy the old sod one. There's not exactly going to be a crush getting in.

– Tom was on the pull Saturday night after Tottenham, weren't you mate? Rod's filling Henry in on the details. Aims to get his story in and whitewash the memory of his stag night. He can do what he wants. It was him on that stage performing for the lads, not me.

– We had a skinful in the Unity and went to this party in Hounslow. The three of us got a taxi down with this nigger playing jungle shit all the way. Tom was hanging out the window puking down the side of the car, but he couldn't say anything otherwise he'd have been on for a kicking.

– I don't remember Tom doing that, Mark says, trying to picture our journey down the Great West Road. Remember that fucking jungle nonsense though.

I can see bits as Rod tells the story. It's those few pints over the top, when you steam into the shorts like there's no tomorrow morning and next thing you're fucked for the duration. I was leaning out the window watching the road thinking we must be near Griffin Park and my guts were churning. Didn't need to hold back because my head was outside picking up the sweet smell of Brentford. Splattered the back wing. All the time there's some tape playing and it was making me think of Nelson Mandela with a spliff wedged in his mouth, for some strange reason, and of how the last thing I wanted now was my lungs full of poison and the brain mixed up. But once you clear your guts you're okay and ready to live again. The bloke driving wasn't too impressed but so what? It's all part of the service. What does he expect?

– We get to this party and there's this geezer on the door telling us we can't come in without bringing some drink, but we're not bothered with the small print and Tom's lining up to take the cunt out. He's too far gone to do the job properly and it's all getting a bit iffy. It's about to go off with the bloke on the door and a load of his mates when the bird having the party turns up and we're in without hassle.

There was fuck all drink around but I got hold of a couple of cans from somewhere and at least there was a bit of talent knocking about. Makes a change. Some places you end up it's full of pissed-up wide-boys, which is okay because you can wind someone up and give him a hiding, but it's not the same if you've been steaming yids all day. It works both ways. Either pull a tart and fuck the arse off her or fuck up some arrogant pisshead with a kick in the bollocks. The easier option is to get hold of an old slapper and give her a seeing to, specially after a good day out like Tottenham. Get in a ruck in a house when you're pissed and chances are you'll be on someone else's manor where the numbers are too heavy, or some bird'll phone the old bill. Try doing a runner at two in the morning when you're pissed. It's a big mistake. Like we tried it once at this house in Acton. Rod nutted some bloke who was getting lippy and the whole place went up. We got a bit of a hiding and next thing there was the old bill kicking the door in and everyone scattering out back. We did a runner over the fence and down an alley. Nicked a vintage Rover and I'm driving to Hammersmith whizzing trying to keep my thoughts together. Mark was chewing a lump of dope mixed up with gum. Laughing like a psycho in the back seat. It was bad news all round.

Nick a motor when you're fifteen or thereabouts and go joyriding, fair enough, no-one's going to think bad of you, but when you're working you need to show a bit of class. Nobody wants to get done for thieving a car for a two-mile trip down the road. If you're going to get nicked then get nicked for something major. Best off, don't get done at all. I mean, we've all got previous, but not for petty theft, at least not since we left school. You have to move up the rankings. It's all about respect.

– We're standing round listening to this fucking greatest hits shit, says Rod, going back to the party, and Mark's giving this tall cunt the eye looking to start a bit of trouble and we're telling him to leave it out because there's loads of skirt walking around waiting for three Chelsea boys to give them a good servicing.

– Fucking was as well, says Mark, waking up. All a bit young, but if they're old enough to bleed then they're old enough to shag.

– Tom pulls straight off, says Rod, and this bird's into him like nobody's business. Wasn't bad after a skinful and she's pissed or stoned or both, fuck knows, and she's giving him the come on so obvious even we could see it clear enough in the dark with this fucking android music breaking the eardrums.

– They're only talking a few minutes and they're off. Cunt doesn't even stop to say goodnight.

This bird comes up all confident and asks am I the romantic type? I nod my head and say nothing. Never commit yourself. Never give a statement. Deny everything unless it's going to serve the greater good. She looks alright and I can see the curve of her tits through a tight T-shirt she shouldn't be wearing if she wants to keep them to herself. Purple with patterns and snug enough to show off her nipples. She's made up like a fucking doll and her hair's dyed a mix of red and brown, but she'll do, can't complain. Her body's well put together and she's in jeans, baggy round the waist showing the shape of her arse. Probably bought them a couple of sizes too big to make her look thinner. Says I look like a romantic and her breath stinks of fags and gin. I agree, remembering the romance of turning Tottenham over and seeing those coppers get a kicking. That's pure romance, natural justice. Next thing we're outside walking down the road. She shares a place with four other birds and it's one of those big West London houses, rundown with bay windows to let in the light, overgrown front garden and peeling paint on the front door.

There's the sound of the telly in the front room and we have to walk quickly but quietly up the stairs. Her mate's watching a video and is expecting in a couple of months. The bloke's done a bunk. Gone to sea or prison. Can't remember the specifics. The sound the video's making it's one of those love stories women like watching. A girl with a fat belly and box of chocolates wishing life was like it is in the videos. Not abortions and stitch-ups. We get up to this bird's bedroom and she turns on a lamp by her bed. The place is a mess and the bed's unmade. Pisses me off a bit, but if that's how she wants to live it's up to her. Can't stand dirt and mess myself.

I go for a piss because if there's one thing worse than going home with your balls loaded it's trying to shaft a bird when you need a slash. The bathroom's a state with bras and pants hanging everywhere, a year's supply of tampons in with a couple of hundred toothbrushes and almost as many empty containers. I go back into the bedroom and this bird's only lying on the bed asleep. Didn't take her long to forget what she was supposed to be doing. Right dead loss. I think about waking her up, but I'm knackered myself so just pull a blanket off the floor and go to sleep in a chair. The bed's too small for two people unless one's on top of the other and Tottenham has made me tired. A good day all in all and next morning I take a look at the woman and she seems like the sort who'll want to talk and I'm not in the mood for idle chatter.

I call a taxi and let myself out. It's early, the streets are empty and

I'm freezing. I feel dirty and my neck's stiff like I've been strung up for murder. The cab arrives and I'm on my way home listening to some chirpy cunt on the radio telling me what a fucking great life it is and how we should appreciate the time we've got before God calls us back up to heaven. Cunt must be doing some serious drugs. What does he know?

– Tom disappears and we don't see him till Sunday night and he looks shagged, says Rod. Which he obviously has been. He only goes through her handbag and nicks twenty quid. Says she was so pissed she'd think she spent it, that he needed to get home and was skint. But he's just a fucking tea leaf on the quiet.

Rod and Mark like winding me up. Henry looks on a bit disgusted. Fucking idiot. This isn't Alice tripping through Wonderland. There's no magic bus back to Hammersmith at eight on a Sunday morning. It's a long hike from Hounslow and I'm not in the mood. The bird looks like she's got a bit of money so she won't miss twenty pounds. Spent enough on the fucking make-up. Henry wants to grow up sometimes. What's he going to do in a couple of years' time when he finds his wife's been shafting the plumber, dustman, local fire brigade? You have to be careful. Look after yourself. Fuck them before they fuck you.

Henry drinks up and he's off. I ask him what's the hurry. Have another drink. But he wants to get down the ground. Rod goes to the bar. I tell Mark he doesn't like being reminded of his stag night. Mark agrees. We should wind the cunt up a bit more. The image sticks in the head. Spread out on a slab and this old tart on top, tits hanging into Rod's mouth. She was tasty all right, but rough as fuck. Mark says he gave Rod the videotape in the end it was causing the bloke so much grief. Mandy would have done her nut if she'd found out. Of course, Mark would never have shown her, but Rod was worried and you can't really blame him.

I can just imagine the wedding reception. Mark's had photos made and they get passed round with everyone pissed and Rod's old man making his speech about his son turning out okay in the end. Has another drink and says he had some difficult times when his son was a teenager growing up, but that's understandable because he's a young lad getting to grips with the world, sowing his oats, no offence Mandy, moving into manhood, all the usual bollocks. The blushing bride who Rod met pissed one night and

49

when they went home together he couldn't get it up. Probably made them, that lack of a hard-on. Something special as the films say. Pulling a bird and not shafting her right off.

The old man's giving it the big one about the reformed young hooligan with a good job as an electrician, making a bit of cash, buying his own flat, still into his football. Rod the good son taking out yids and shooting his load over Indian wildlife. Rod the honest lover stripped off ridden half to death by a whore with a cunt full of Cardiff City fans, Chelsea tattoo coming out well in the video, face dazed and distorted in artificial light. Everyone wants to have something to look back on. That period of being a bit rebellious then growing out of it and turning into a nice boring citizen. Fuck that for a game of soldiers. Talk to people like that and they've done nothing. They just like to think they have. Blokes and birds. They're all the same. Wankers the lot of them.

– You know, Rod, I've probably got a copy of that tape knocking about somewhere. I'll have to give it to you. Mark starts winding him up.

– You gave me everything you had. Rod holds his pint still, stuck on its way to his mouth. That's what you said. I got rid of it straight off. Obscene propaganda. You're a fucking pervert taking those shots. You're not an iron by any chance? Keeping it quiet because you know you'd wind up on the end of a serious kicking rather than some queer's joystick.

– I didn't give you the copy, just forgot about it, but it's got to be somewhere. I'll dig it out and pass it on.

– You sure? Rod looks worried. Then starts laughing. You're winding me up. I know you are. Why would you make a copy? It wasn't exactly a pro job. The picture was out of focus half the time. It's not like you're going to make a packet selling it to Marshall.

– Just forgot about it, that's all. Mark's voice has an edge. If you don't want the tape I won't bother.

– I was pissed and did the business when I shouldn't have. So what? Rod tries the big bluff but he's looking bad. Poor cunt. Why crucify the bloke for making a prick of himself?

So he shagged a whore on stage in front of his mates. He was out of it and everyone makes mistakes. Better than going out and raping someone. Or watching squaddies doing it on video for you. We've all followed the urge and serviced things that didn't need servicing. Why have regrets? There's no place for sentiment, though Rod's only bothered because he's worried about Mandy somehow getting a glimpse. Who cares. None of us are into being a spectator. Leave that to the pundits on telly. All those noddy gameshows. The cameras looking for a bit of football violence, getting off on the lads steaming in. But it's a con. If you want something like that go out and get it yourself. Don't sit at home flicking channels expecting someone to live your life for you. We may be cunts but we're not hiding the fact. Unlike the docile majority. So silent you can hear their thoughts quivering with outrage. I tell Rod we're joking and he says he knew it all the time. We start laughing. There's twenty minutes till kick-off but bollocks, we'll have another quick pint. It's cold outside. We need the warmth.

Shame it's not someone like West Ham tonight. It would be good to have a bit of a punch-up. We don't have to justify ourselves to anyone. Like those wankers running the army or killing grannies because they won't give them enough money to pay their heating bills. Kicking fuck out of someone is excitement. It gives you a buzz. You can dress violence up anyway you like but it's still there. Why play games and try to justify your actions? All these plonkers with their politics and moral outrage are kidding themselves. The kick is seeing your first ruck, a mob of Cardiff chased down Fulham Broadway and battered by Chelsea when I was a kid. Pure and simple. No explanations. I ask Rod if he remembers Chelsea running Cardiff that time. He does. Says it was justice. Paid those five Taffs back years before the event. That he was looking ahead even in those days.

HOOLIGANS

POWERFUL WINDS BATTERED the multi-million pound structure, yet for the assorted players, officials, sponsors and media personnel cocooned inside the East Stand it could just as easily have been a warm summer's evening. The last spectators had left the stadium, driving rain forcing hunched shoulders deep inside coats, the visiting contingent facing a tiring trip north, clothes soaked and a heavy defeat for cold comfort. The glow of floodlights had vanished, brilliant illumination replaced by deep shadow. Stamford Bridge stood out against the rolling clouds, light from a near-full moon catching the angles of the towering main stand.

In a corner of the bar, Will Dobson was educating Jennifer Simpson, a rather attractive young hopeful, in the wicked ways of the press. Will was a good teacher who knew the football world inside out, all the gossip and a few of the facts, filling his belly with bottled bitter and a steady stream of double vodkas. It was humid and sweat stained his white shirt, every now and then his eyes straining for a peak at Jennifer's slender legs.

– It wasn't how I thought it was going to be, Jennifer said, learning the lesson and downing half a glass of white wine in a single gulp. There wasn't much of a crowd and those who came were pretty quiet. The game was very boring as well, don't you think? Where were the hooligans we read so much about?

– In here, Will laughed, tapping his temple. A figment of the imagination. An editor's wet dream. Sadly our hooligan friends are a thing of the past.

Jennifer let her eyes wander to the bar, allowing Will an escape route from any embarrassment he might feel at the sexual reference, watching casually-dressed young sportsmen rub shoulders with older, heavier men in suits. Will didn't seem bothered about such niceties though. He probably thought a new man was a type of service robot, and in a way he would have been right. Jennifer congratulated herself on the humour, and determined to use it some time in the near future.

The bar blended athleticism and new money, its own small world lost in the enormous concrete structure, an almost unique aura of big pay cheques and wholesome job satisfaction. Jennifer was aware of Dobson's occasional glances under the table but not averse to letting the old boy get a glimpse of her legs. She knew she was good looking and didn't believe in false modesty. He wasn't a bad sort and it did no harm. If she was going to make a career for herself in journalism she would need all the help she could get. Connections were vital in every walk of life, probably more so in this particular line, and even the likes of Dobson might prove useful in the future. She wondered what he had meant by a figment of the imagination.

– The hooligans faded away after Heysel, Dobson confided, lowering his voice because the subject was a taboo which turned off the sponsors. Before that they were a bloody nuisance, but they shifted papers and journalism's all about circulation figures. My theory is they either got into drugs like ecstasy which destroyed their violent tendencies and/or organised crime, or got married and settled down, and the kids today can't afford to go very often which means there's no new blood coming through to fill their shoes, Dr Martens if you like, so the hooligan drifted towards extinction, just like the dinosaur. The police became experts in the field of crowd control and introduced video cameras and the yobs decided enough was enough. A few tough sentences and they handed in their Stanley knives and started new lives. There's a pitch invasion now and then, but that's just a handful of idiots pissing in the wind, if you'll excuse my French. Football violence is dead and buried. Society is much better balanced these days. The Tories have eradicated the class system. The angry young men of yesteryear are either sitting in bed smoking cannabis or wandering around their local homestore trying to decide what shade of paint to buy for the baby's room.

– What about the trouble at that England game? Jennifer asked, remembering the televised pictures and endlessly reproduced face of a frightened child, the wide eyes sticking in her mind, the media's innocent-victim line of emphasis working a treat. There always seems to be a riot of some kind when the national side plays overseas.

– I'm not saying there aren't one or two bad boys around, but they know to behave themselves, more's the pity. I had my best bylines during the hooligan era. All you needed was a half-decent photo and it didn't matter what you wrote. There was a lot of glory to be had back then. You couldn't fail. But that's progress I suppose. Then there was the Taylor Report and the clubs aren't stupid you know, they've increased their prices and blocked out a lot of people, priced the hooligans out of the game. When they go to Europe the policing's not up to scratch so the thugs see their chance and go on the rampage.

– Well, if they do that, then they must come from somewhere, surely?

Will had given up looking at the girl's legs and was concentrating on the alcohol situation. That was the trouble with these bloody women, they never got their round in because they were always too busy asking pointless questions. Things changed and he was the first to welcome progress, sound investment and all that, and a lot of people were getting mega-rich from the beautiful game now it was adopting sensible business practices. His own match-day experience was vastly improved, but women should remember to move with the times as well and get the fucking drinks in. He liked Jennifer's legs but wasn't sure about the rest of her, the knowledge that she was studying at university a major turn-off. They thought they knew everything, these further-education people, and he wasn't conned by her mild manner. She was an arrogant bitch if ever he'd seen one. He had only brought her along as a favour to the editor, who was a lifelong mate of her father, a bigshot in the armaments industry with serious political clout. Then he remembered he was drinking at the paper's expense so didn't need to worry about enforcing equal rights, but he was too late.

– Would you like another drink, Jennifer asked, standing and walking through the crowd to the bar once the experienced pro had delivered his order.

Will was feeling tired, what with filing his report, walking to the bar and drinking his fill. Chelsea were on his patch and the old hooligan-heavy days really were a thing of the past. It *was* a shame as well, because apart from the opportunity to file some fine moral outrage and amuse the sub-editors, a punch-up was an exciting distraction from the dire games he'd been forced to watch through the years. As much as he loved football, and he honestly did, he wouldn't have paid to see more than five or six matches a season, and with so much football on television now he would probably just stay at home. The atmosphere wasn't like it used to be, whatever the vested interests said, and if the major clubs kept alienating ordinary fans and trying to attract a so-called upmarket clientele, they would eventually go bust. There was no loyalty in money. Even Will Dobson realised that much. But football was his livelihood and he had done very well for an ordinary lad from Swindon. He couldn't complain. He preferred to go with the flow.

– How many games do you watch during an average season, Jennifer asked, carefully placing Will's order on the table, not waiting for a reply. Did you go to the Tottenham match at the weekend? Everyone seems to be talking about it at the bar.

Will's eyes widened. The Spurs-Chelsea fixture of the previous Saturday had shown the sport at its very best, a great advertisement for the modern game. There had been plenty of goals and goal-mouth action and the crowd had roared its appreciation. In the old days that particular London derby meant trouble, but now the spectators were as well-behaved as a party of boisterous school children. True, there had been a few anti-semitic songs which the club was trying to stamp out, and the usual gestures, but nothing particularly violent.

– Mind if I join you, David Morgan asked, arriving on the scene and taking a chair between Jennifer and Will. Bloody terrible match wasn't it? They should refund our money.

– But we don't pay, Will laughed.

Morgan worked for a rival paper and was a full-time shit-stirrer. He had been widely accepted as having his finger firmly on the pulse in the mid-Eighties. While he'd never pushed himself more than his contemporaries, he always seemed to be in the know. Will suspected that this was because he was a little more liberal with the truth than the others, which in turn reflected the attitude of the title paying his wages. A readiness to shell out hard cash for dramatic pictures of supposed hooligans was legendary. He had his story and the subjects of the photos were generally well pleased with the extra cash and fleeting fame. The lads had welcomed the attention at first, treating the hacks as an amusing sideshow, pissed old geezers chasing ghosts, always a mile or two behind the action. Professional football journalism was a small circle and they were doing very nicely thank you. If people on the outside took some of their stories a little too seriously, then whose fault was that? Will raised his glass for a toast, eyes bleary from the blend of beer and spirit.

– Here's to the next round.

They drank up and Jennifer felt part of the gang. She had accepted the chance to get involved with the sports desk even though her eventual aim was to write celebrity features for a better-class newspaper. It was all worthwhile experience and would stand her in good stead when it came time to send off job applications. Looking around, she had to admit that they were a bit oikish, the lot of them, and the hooligans had rather let her down, but at least she would be able to tell her friends that she'd been to a football match. She could always lay it on a bit. She thought of her part-time boyfriend Anthony, assistant editor on a trendy style magazine which was forever pushing imagined left-wing credentials. Jennifer was always taking the mickey out of poor Anthony, asking him what expensive clothes, consumer pop and an obsessive interest in bisexuals had to do with socialist politics.

Jennifer smiled as she remembered Anthony's warning that same afternoon, delivered via his company mobile from a champagne-lunch CD launch party in Soho. He really cared for her and had insisted that the Chelsea crowd revelled in indiscriminate violence. He firmly believed Stamford Bridge was a breeding ground for white supremacists, where black players had been hounded off the pitch and black spectators went in fear of their lives. She should watch herself. Chelsea fans were brain dead and even capable of gang rape on terraces which no longer existed, rambling on about the notorious Shed and those metal kung-fu stars which would blind her for life, a backing soundtrack of synthesised music filtering its way down the phone line.

Anthony was drunk and had tried to talk her out of attending the match, but Jennifer had been determined. It was a shame he had been so mistaken, though she would lead him on all the same.

She had a vindictive streak and enjoyed his discomfort. He was rather childish sometimes, possessive and even hinting at love, yet was little more than a convenient London stopover. He came from money and was well-meaning, but lacked the calculation Jennifer found so attractive in a man. She was meeting him after the game, although her thoughts were with Jeremy Hetherington, who she had recently met at university. She was visiting his parents' manor house in Oxfordshire the following Saturday and was looking forward to following their initial drunken coupling with something a bit more satisfying. They would make the most of the countryside during the day, then attend the local hunt ball in the evening. It would be an experience.

– How did you find the game? Morgan asked. Will says it's your first time inside a football ground.

– It was interesting.

– You should have taken her last week against Spurs, Morgan said, turning to Will. Now that was football at its best. Passing and movement from two teams dedicated to the art. But you know, those bloody little North London sods only scratched the side of my Volvo. I managed to squeeze a line into the end of my report concerning the state of today's youth, but those moronic subs chopped it out. The politics of envy I'm afraid to say are alive and fermenting. It might not have been football fans of course, just the local population moaning about its lot, but it's going to cost a bit to get fixed. I'm taking the car to the garage tomorrow for an estimate. The paper will pay the bill but it makes me angry when the havenots take their petty frustrations out on me. It's a bloody nuisance more than anything else. I'm a busy man.

They had another round of drinks and Morgan took over in his usual way, bending Jennifer's ear with the story of a politician who had been discovered in Brompton cemetery with a thirteen-year-old rent boy, a young lad from Burnley whose homelessness was a direct consequence of Government cutbacks. Apparently they'd been caught at it in one of the crypts, a family vault with ripped coffins stacked on shelves along the walls. It was an excellent story, and Morgan had toyed with the idea of somehow introducing vampirism and Aids, but due to political considerations the papers were hushing up the affair, and even if there had been a decent left-wing paper it would have ignored the story, dealing as it did with homosexuality and the individual's right to privacy. If they could just get hold of something similar on a high-ranking Opposition figure they'd be away.

As Morgan talked, Will started drifting. He vaguely heard his colleague listing the buzz-words and phrases which made for a good hooligan article – 'scum', 'mindless yobs', 'thugs', 'ashamed to be English', 'not true fans', 'bring back the birch', 'give them a good thrashing' and 'now is the time for the courts to hand down tough custodial sentences'.

– Just shuffle that lot around and you're there, Morgan laughed, subtly checking the girl's legs under the table, marvelling at the texture of her skin and deciding the stockings she was wearing went right up the crack of her arse.

– First comes the titillation and gory details, then the condemnation which masks the pleasure the reader's had from the story. Call for the return of the cat o'nine tails and demand some good old fashioned square-bashing and everyone's happy. It makes the public feel secure.

He had little call for such specific vocabulary now, with the death of the hooligan and his own shift to more meaty subject matter – the general moral decay afflicting society, spongers living off the taxpayer and any kind of violent sex or sexual violence involving the rich, famous and/or politically unsound. Homosexuality within the clergy was another favourite. It was an interesting job and if Jennifer ever fancied discussing her future career she should give him a call and perhaps they could meet for lunch. He had seen everything during his time as a roving reporter and could share some interesting stories which had never made it into print. There was an excellent Italian restaurant he frequented in Knightsbridge. It would be his treat. He handed her his card.

– Perhaps I'll take you up on that, she replied, smiling, and adjusted her legs so David had a better view of her upper thighs, filing the old lech's face in her memory and his card in her purse. He would certainly be more useful than Dobson who was an old duffer in comparison.

When Morgan offered him a lift home, Will gladly accepted. Jennifer was meeting Anthony in a restaurant on the Kings Road and David was more than willing to drop her off on the way. They drank up and left the bar, surprised by the ferocity of the wind when they got outside. Jennifer sat in the back seat as the two journalists talked about mutual friends, a Frank Sinatra CD playing in the background. They pulled away from the stadium and Jennifer checked the streets for life. A couple of nearby pubs were doing good business with groups of men staying on till closing time, features distorted through the windows. The streets were windswept and empty. It was a pity. A gang of hooligans on the rampage and a quick exit in a fast car would have made up for a wasted ninety minutes watching the football.

– There it is, she said, spotting Bo-Bo's halfway down the Kings Road, purple neon lights above the door, flickering white candles inside. Just drop me off anywhere. Thanks for the ride and I'll see you tomorrow Will. Thanks for taking me. Nice to have met you David. It was fun.

– Phone me about lunch, won't you?

– I will. See you soon.

Jennifer waved at the Volvo as it drove away and looked for the scratch but saw nothing, then she pushed herself forward through the gale, opening the door to the restaurant. She was greeted by a burst of warm air, cigarette smoke and excessively loud laughter. She immediately felt at home, the clientele class-conscious and suitably confident. Looking around for Anthony, she flushed when she thought of those toads sneaking glances at her legs. Then she was angry at the boring game she had witnessed, the loss of a good evening, and not a thug in sight. At least she was on familiar ground in Bo-Bo's and could act normally again. The common people really were common as muck. You could give them money, but couldn't fake breeding.

WEST HAM AT HOME

THE PUB'S MAKING a racket and the old bill have pulled a van up outside. Everyone's trying to get a view through the window and there's a lot of movement in the street. Mark reckons they're bringing a train straight through from East London. Don't know how he knows this, but that's how football works. It's all rumour and speculation which fast becomes fact. The two blend together and in the end it doesn't really matter where they meet. It's logical enough though. We've already been down Victoria looking for them and come back with nothing. You never know with West Ham. They could turn up anywhere at any time and Victoria is a good place to meet up and sort things out. There again, they want to get into our streets and take the piss so why waste time messing about in the West End?

The tension's been building since early this morning. Mark banging on the door at nine telling me to get up. That I'm a lazy cunt. A cup of tea and some toast and I don't feel too bad after eight pints in the pub last night. He looks happy enough. Got his end away with some spaced-out blonde kid who couldn't have been much over the legal limit. Looked like she knew the score well enough and Mark confirms this as I get myself a second cup. Thin legs and small tits but was on all fours in the hall with her mum and dad asleep upstairs. Says she had a cunt so tight he thought he'd got the wrong hole. Had to take a look to make sure, though she wasn't complaining so doesn't know why he bothered.

We walk down the station and Rod's already there getting impatient. We catch a train to Victoria and there's a mob hanging around looking for West Ham, taking the tube to Tower Hill, then back along the District Line. Harris doesn't know where West Ham will turn up and we start getting worried in case they've gone straight down the ground. They could be turning the place over while we're stuck on the tube. We decide to go back to the ground and stop off in Earl's Court. There's fuck all going on there, so we head for Fulham Broadway where we've got a view of the tube and are guaranteed to find them in the end. We're on edge the whole time because West Ham's no joyride. Not like having a go at Arsenal or Tottenham.

Now we're out of circulation. There's dogs barking in the street and the hollow echo of horse's hooves on concrete. Traffic is diverted away from the run between Fulham Broadway and Stamford Bridge. There's a pub full of needle bottled up and confined by coppers ready to steam in at the slightest provocation. There's fuzzy police radio messages and a flashing light, Harris talking into his cellphone, scouts out and about, then we hear the West Ham anthem Bubbles coming up from the tube into the street and we're pushing towards the door, but the old bill know what they're about and they're laughing, pretending they're in control, and they are in a manner of speaking because they've got us locked up safe and sound.

I can see the scene through the window as West Ham pile out and the old bill have them contained well enough, but the Hammers breed lary cunts and the main faces are at the front, older blokes and nutters from Bethnal Green and Mile End, fucking headcases the lot of them, and they've no respect for coppers, taking the piss, trying to push past the British bobby looking towards the pub. There's psychos in leather jackets and a kid in dungarees and flat cap. The ICF and Under Fives mean more around Upton Park than Ron and Reggie Kray. History stays around for years. But who cares about names.

West Ham are forced towards the ground and they're letting everyone know they've arrived. The pub's singing as well but we feel like a bunch of wankers locked up out of contention. West Ham keep coming out of the station trying to turn right, forced left, and they've come down from the East End mob-handed, strolling along taking their time, but Stamford Bridge is one of the safest grounds in the country these days and the old bill have got everything tied up. Those cameras on rooftops record the scene but most of the faces are well known. These blokes are professionals. Not your average snotty-nosed hooligan. There's vans across the street, flashing lights through glass, horses helping the crowd along, shitting everywhere, the familiar mix of horse shit and hamburgers.

A few harder cases try to push their way back down the road towards the pub. The dogs go mental straining at their leads keeping things civilised, walking on two legs. Two legs good, four legs bad. Like they teach you in school. Lights flash and more horses come along the street. All those coppers think they're the business. They're keeping the lid on things and West Ham are moving reluctantly towards the ground.

Harris is near the door and we're getting wound up locked away, freedom of expression denied for the duration, but know it's the wrong location. Talk about civil liberties. West Ham are walking our streets, controlled it's true, but we're at home and it's up to us to do the business. If they can walk in here then it's half a result. Turn us over and we'll never hear the last of it. East against West and it goes back decades. Something you grow up with. It's all about territory and pride and having a laugh. They're fast disappearing down the street and the police will shepherd them into the away section, unless some of the cunts have tickets for the West Stand and are looking to have a go inside the ground. But it's unlikely. What's the point?

When West Ham are out of harm's way the old bill pile into the pub and empty the place. They're in a stroppy mood and line up outside the door. Think they're a firing squad except they've got no guns. One day that will change though and they'll walk more cocky than ever. A fat bastard punches me in the gut as I go past and I stare straight into his face asking him what the fuck he's doing, let's see your number, then he's telling his mate to put me in the van and nick me, but I get lost in the crush leaving the pub and they're thick cunts with the attention span of a goldfish and are already into someone else. Mark gets a knee in the bollocks from a copper which doesn't connect properly and I hate the bastards worse than West Ham and Tottenham combined.

Fucking scum the lot of them hiding behind uniforms, licking the paymaster's arse. A van escorts us towards the ground and when we get to the West Stand we're trying to bluff our way further down the street but only half heartedly because there's video cameras burning on overtime and West Ham are probably inside by now anyway. I'm well narked and have to remember Tottenham and the old bill getting a pasting just to calm things down and look on the bright side. I try and see it as a bit of justice but it doesn't work. We've all seen enough of them in action to realise the score. The old bill are just another mob but they're getting paid for their Saturday entertainment while we fork out for the privilege. They're hiding behind some kind of fucked morals where they're right because they've got a uniform and we're wrong because we haven't taken the oath. We're our own bosses and they're working for the courts. It's enough to turn you into a fucking Trotskyist, except they're a bunch of bent student wankers who spend all their time making placards and shafting your ordinary white bloke.

They're all the same those kind of people. Politics is a load of shit basically and you'll find little of it around here. True, there's a few blokes into the fascist bit, but the old men at the top would wipe us out if they got into power. Line your football hooligans up against the wall and blow their brains over the pavement. That's their idea of law and order. But it's a crack winding up scruffy rich kids selling Marxist papers and fuck knows what other dodgy reading matter. Give them a Nazi salute and watch the bastards boil up inside knowing they'll do fuck all back.

We're soon in the ground and West Ham are into another round of Bubbles. Chelsea are singing around the ground. The game kicks off but we're watching West Ham. They're a fair distance off and there's little chance of it going off, but they fucking hate Chelsea. Reckon we're mouthy bastards. They fire a rocket into the stand and it bounces off the roof. Lands a few seats back. Flares for a second and I wonder if it's about to set the place alight. I think of Bradford and all those people burnt alive. Then of Hillsborough and the scousers killed by fences.

Thing is, the people who wanted the fences put up never admitted it was the fences responsible. Just shifted the blame onto terracing. Give us seats and we'll all behave. Some chance. Your harder cases have been going in the seats for donkey's years. It's another mark of class. We're no grubby paupers. No lippy hooligans mouthing off doing fuck all to back up the words. We're the business. The people who run football are redundant. Clueless the lot of them. Hillsborough was one big scam from start to finish. They were all in it together. Politicians, papers and the old geezers running the show. But what can you do? Fuck all at the end of the day.

– Bunch of cunts aren't they? Harris turns to me. We'll have them outside if we can get hold of them. Kick them all the way back to their East End plague pits.

There's a lot of the bastards and they're no pushover, but you've got to have belief. West Ham and Millwall are always the bad ones. Must be something in the water. Some strain of infection which affects the brain cells. Rabies is alive and well and flourishing in the East End. Probably came into the docks before the area fell apart, then stayed in the bloodstream. Some people don't fancy having a go at West Ham but if you're in a mob you can't afford to bottle against anyone. West Ham are hard, true, but they don't bother me. If you can get everyone to stand firm and the odds are even you've got to have a good chance.

It's all about presentation. If you've got a reputation then half the job's done before you start. It's everyday propaganda. Make yourself believe something and it's easy to persuade everyone else. There again, you end up getting every cunt in the country wanting to have a go and prove themselves when the odds are stacked. If you get picked off and cornered and you're on the receiving end then there's no mercy. It's survival of the fittest and the law applies everywhere. The weak don't last long in this country. There's no help for those who can't look after themselves. It's primitive man talking. Real Stone Age society where the biggest lump of rock wins. That's why you have to stick together.

– East London cunts. Rod's giving them the wanker sign. I fucking hate those bastards. Reckon they're so fucking hard with their cockney coons and Brick Lane Nazis. Fucking cunts the lot of them. Muggers and Paki-bashers. Same fucking gene working overtime.

– Scum, that's what they are, and Mark's got a soft spot for West Ham, bad memories from when he was a kid seeing his old man having the piss ripped out of him outside Upton Park. A split lip for the old man and a kid's blue and white scarf in the gutter.

The game kicks off and Chelsea cut their way through the West

Ham defence at will. We're knocking the ball around with style and it's great watching the Blues when they play like this. A reward for all the bad performances. The rain's hammering down and the players have trouble keeping their feet. We score twice before half-time then add a third near the end. It's a dull day with heavy clouds and a vicious wind but we don't care. We're stuffing West Ham on the pitch and it's good to see the bastards getting their noses rubbed in it. The rubbish they write about West Ham being a football academy is all in the past. More television nostalgia. They're more Billy Bonds than Trevor Brooking. We know the truth. They're cunts and they'll be twice as wound up by the time the ref blows the final whistle.

We're making the most of the score winding the Happy Hammers up and they're not taking it well. Even from this distance I can see the expressions on their faces. Sullen and narked as fuck, the Irons are simmering under the surface. They're like a pan of boiling water waiting to spill over and melt some cunt's face. They're all in there. Just like Rod says. The lads from Bethnal Green and all the other bomb sites stretching to Upton Park and on to Dagenham. But we're stuffing them on the pitch and enjoying the chance to take the piss.

The final whistle blows and most of Stamford Bridge is celebrating a good game, cheering victory over London rivals. For the majority of people the football is everything and they don't want to know about what's going to kick off soon as we get the chance. I can feel the pit of my stomach getting tight. I follow Mark, Rod and the rest of the lads up the steps and West Ham are moving towards their own exit.

Behind the West Stand there's a bit of a crush and the light covering the pitch is shut out. Floodlights burn high above but they're pointing the other way. That's the stage the media focuses on and once we're out the back of the West Stand it's just another Saturday night. There's a few small lights burning but more shadows and the smell of piss and dirty rain water. We get to the steps and there's a bit of singing and we can hear West Ham coming down the road already. We're moving down the steps with Harris getting everyone together. We've got to keep tight and act together once it goes off.

We're out in the street with police vans everywhere and we're looking into where we think West Ham will be, but it's all decent citizens and the old bill are moving Chelsea along, serving the community keeping the scum in line. There's a tense silence and everyone's giving everyone else the eye and we're getting down towards the tube. It just needs a spark. There's a few lads hanging around the flats and we start moving over as well but a couple of horses come up the steps and the old bill are moving everyone on again.

We're getting pushed down by the tube but we don't want to go home yet. We follow the happy supporters down into Fulham Broadway station. It's all Chelsea in here now and the tube pulls in and we take it up to Earl's Court, check the platform which is full of old bill, and continue to Victoria. We get off and hang around the platform, doing our best to blend in with the Saturday evening crowd. It's all backpackers and shoppers. We've clocked the cameras and Harris tells a couple of kids to smash them when West Ham pull in. We're taking a chance but acting camera shy. Just put a cross on the coupon and take your chance. No publicity and no video evidence. We're waiting along the eastbound District Line platform knowing West Ham will come through sooner or later.

Trains pull in and we scan the carriages, taking the piss out of a few civilians with West Ham colours, but their firm is nowhere to be seen. It's getting on for six when the tube we've been waiting for finally arrives. We know right away it's West Ham and the cameras are put through with bottles and before the doors open we're kicking the windows in. The mob on board are booting the doors trying to get out and there's the vague sound of crying from women and kids. The doors open and the bastards are on the platform, and it's real toe-to-toe stuff and we've picked a good mob here, a lot of older blokes but not too many of them, more or less equal odds and Harris kicks a squat bastard first off the tube in the bollocks, and Black John kicks another cunt in the gut. Rod kicks him in the face and the front of the train empties, a running battle now along the platform because out of nowhere the old bill have appeared.

Transport police on the platform and it's chaos and I can't believe they've got here so fast. Both sides are trying to get out of the station. Get above ground and the old bill have got no chance. There's coppers piling in forcing us through tunnels and up the escalator. It's all gone wrong somehow and then we're in the flush of Victoria jumping over the barriers, mingling with the crowds. We're out and about and move into the bus station waiting for West Ham to find their way. We move back as police vans arrive, doors flung open and coppers heading underground, sprinting to get stuck in. Then we see West Ham across the station and we're running into them but the bastards just stand there laughing like fuck and it goes off again in a big way, people running everywhere and it's a bitter punch-up this one and Black John's getting the shit kicked out of him when he goes down on the floor. We try to get over to the bloke but a mob of West Ham are around him and he's down for the count.

Some West Ham cunt lumbers into me, fist connecting, and I feel a numb throb through my jaw as I kick out at him, missing any decent kind of contact, then he's back in the crowd and my head's spinning. I focus myself and get my mind in gear, but I don't see anything now, just hear the racket of shouting men and alarms, then mad barking as the old bill get into the battle again, dogs on the rampage, always one step behind, and we're moving across the bus station, lobbing bottles and whatever else we can find at West Ham who are busy having a go at the old bill. I look over and Black John's on his own on the ground and a couple of coppers are looking down at him, and we've got to keep moving because there's vans and cars coming in from every angle and the last thing we want is a ride in a meat waggon. There's a few running fights with West Ham but everyone's getting split up and the old bill are nicking everyone they can get their hands on. I jump on a bus with Mark and Harris and a few other blokes. Rod's got lost in the commotion. Victoria's a no-go zone now if you're looking for trouble and we're on a bus heading for the West End. We're well pissed off at the old bill turning up so quick and just sit back and go with the motion.

– Black John was getting a hiding last I saw of him. Harris is leaning back over the seat in front. I tried to get to him but there were too many West Ham.

– The old bill were helping him up. Dusting him off making sure he was still alive. Mark scratches his bollocks. Hope that bird I shagged last night was clean. Last thing I need is a dose. Specially off some juvenile delinquent.

I reckon Black John's going to be visiting a doctor before Mark. He got a heavy duty kicking and I hope he wasn't tooled-up like normal. Coppers don't like knife-carrying black boys and any sympathy they might feel calling an ambulance would disappear once they got him for carrying an offensive weapon. But there's no finding out now. Not tonight. We've just got to fade away and old Rod's going to be a bit pissed off losing us in the chaos. But John's a cunt and a wicked bastard. Wouldn't want to cross the man but you can't feel too sorry for him because he's done enough bad things in his time. Couldn't cut a bloke myself, but I wouldn't knock him on that score. Just as long as we're on the same side.

– John'll be alright. Harris is laughing. It'll take more than West Ham to put him out of action for long. It'll just make him meaner next time around.

– Like a short sharp shock to the system, Mark backing him up. Give someone a dose like that and they're twice as bad in the future.

I lean against the window and watch the plush rows of houses pass. There's money in these streets, home to gun-runners and oil merchants. Millionaire flats full of Stock Exchange cunts with acne-free upper-crust birds choking on the property developer's plum shoved half way down their throats. But we're just passing through. We're content getting away from our battleground in Victoria. Fighting among ourselves. East against West. But West Ham's over for us now and when we get up to Oxford Street we decide to go for a few sherbets.

The centre's lit up for tourists and everywhere you look there's Arabs selling plastic police helmets and models of Parliament. It's all bright lights and fast food hamburger meat. An amusement arcade full of dagos. It's a black hole in the middle of London. We walk along the street and turn into Soho. Another fucking abortion with its fake reputation for sleaze, but it always pulls in northerners down for the football because they haven't got a clue where they're going. They see this area and no wonder they think London's full of queers and posers, rich slumming bastards and fashion queens. It's a magnet for scum. We go to a couple of pubs but they're dead so we move down towards Covent Garden, find a pub. There's eight of us in all and Harris says Derby played in

London today, away to Millwall. Maybe we'll pick up on a few of the bastards.

– Where did you get that tan from darling? Mark's into a small bird with dyed hair and a skin colour which means she's been abroad flat on her back shagging dagos or spics for a two-week break from the routine of shagging white men in London.

– What's it got to do with you?

She's a stroppy bird that's for sure and we're all laughing because Mark's gone red in the face. Obviously embarrassed and not pissed enough to take it in his stride. He's made a bad move here, that's for sure, and I can only see it getting worse.

– Who do you think you're calling darling anyway? Her mate's telling her to be nice, that Mark's only being friendly, but Mark snaps back.

– Fucking dyke.

– Macho wanker.

– Don't call me a wanker.

– Then don't call me a fucking dyke.

– I was only being friendly. Like your mate said.

– Well go be friendly with someone else.

– What's the matter with you anyway?

– I don't like being called darling for a start. And I'm talking with my friend and don't need you butting in.

We're cracking up laughing and tell Mark to leave it out. Fair play if the girl's not interested and, anyway, we're on the lookout for a few Derby fans, or even West Ham strays if we get lucky. There's a long way to go till closing time. What's he going to do in the meantime? Spend the whole night chatting up a couple of dodgy birds. Mind you, the dyke's mate seems game enough. Same suntan so must have been on the same holiday. But Mark should sort himself out. There's a time for shagging and a time for fighting. He should think twice about mixing the two. He'll just end up getting himself confused.

NEVER NEVER LAND

DAD IS HOLDING Mum's hand and I run ahead of them along the beach and Sarah is trying to keep up, yelling in my ear, and I'm a year older and a bit stronger and I don't want her to start crying so I slow down and let her catch me, but don't let her know what I'm doing because that would spoil the race for her. We get to the water together and stand there out of breath and we're holding hands like Mum and Dad. I look back to where they are and they're laughing about something and Mum's waving to us and Dad's kicking sand up which blows back because of the wind and then Mum's turning away so it doesn't get in her eyes, and then she's got her hand through his arm and they're getting nearer.

– Put your foot in the water, Sarah says.

– I don't want to, I'll get my trainers wet, I answer.

– You're just scared.

– I'm not scared of anything.

– Yes you are. You're scared Dad'll tell you off and Mum'll smack you.

– Dad wouldn't tell me off. He doesn't care if my trainers get wet because we're at the seaside and it doesn't matter at the seaside, nothing matters at the seaside.

– Mum would smack you though.

– Maybe.

I run on a bit further and Sarah follows and then we stop and look over the mud to where a big black dog is running out towards these wooden boats that are sitting on the mud. He runs very fast towards a load of seagulls floating on top of the water and when he gets near they all fly away and they're skimming across the water and this dog is doing his best to catch them and then they're up in the air like magic and I wish I could fly as well. I'm a bit worried in case the dog gets the birds and tries to eat them but they aren't stupid and just let him get near enough before they take off. I watch them go up in the air and the dog does a big circle with the water over his paws and then he's coming back to the sand and at first I think he's coming for me and Sarah and I'm moving in front of my sister because boys have to walk on the outside of girls to protect them from traffic so they don't get knocked down and hurt by cars and lorries and I'm stronger than my sister and other little girls and must never hit them because it's a bad thing to do, but then I see a man in a black jacket with a metal dog lead calling him and the dog changes direction and speeds up a bit and when I look back to where the seagulls were they've come back again and now they're sitting in the same place.

— You both won the race together, says Dad, and he lifts me up in the air above his head because my dad's big and strong and the strongest man in the world apart from boxers and people like that, though maybe he's even as strong as them, I don't know.

— You're both winners, he says, putting me down and lifting Sarah up in the air and she's laughing but looks a bit scared at the same time, not sure what she's supposed to do next.

— Mind you don't drop her, Mum says, and she looks worried as well.

But Dad's like Superman with his muscles though Superman doesn't have a West Ham tattoo on his arm and Dad doesn't wear a suit and cape. He says he can fly like Superman high in the sky and visits planets in outer space when we're asleep but I don't believe him, I think he's joking, and if I could fly like a bird I could fly with Dad as well but birds can't go to the moon and planets and I wouldn't want to go too far away because there's no air in space and I would choke and maybe we'd meet aliens and spacemen who would use us for experiments, like people do with rabbits and dogs and other kinds of animals. Anyway, if he could fly then he would have carried us all down to Southend on his back instead of in the car and we would have got here much quicker and Sarah probably wouldn't have been sick all over the back seat, but she might have fallen off or something and then Dad would have had to move fast and catch her again before she hit the ground and broke into small pieces.

— Is anyone hungry? Mum asks, and Sarah says she's starving but

I'm thinking of her puking in the back of the car and shake my head no.

– Not even for chips? Mum asks, and I nod my head up and down because chips are my favourite food.

– Come on then, Dad says, and we walk over the sand to the pavement and climb up and go along the front to where there's a cafe. We sit by the window and we can watch the boats coming in and Dad says they're heading into London along the Thames and that they used to go all the way to the docks in the East End, but that was a long time ago now before his time and times change and people move on and there was a big war or something and later on there was unions which the rich people didn't like and then the rich people built big luxury buildings and the poor people got nothing.

– What would you like? asks a girl who Dad tells me is a waitress, and I have fish fingers and chips and peas and a glass of Coke.

Sarah has the same. So do Mum and Dad, and Dad asks for some bread and butter as well, and then all of us ask for some bread and butter, and it's warmer in the cafe than outside and Dad says we timed it right because there's more people coming in now and we wouldn't have been able to sit by the window if we hadn't hurried here and then we wouldn't have had such a good view of the water. I like watching the ships move slowly along and wonder how big the bottoms of them are because the smaller boats on the mud have big bottoms to them, to make them stand up in the water Dad says, and the small boats are painted in lots of different bright colours but the bigger boats carrying stuff for shops and factories are grey and black.

Sarah kicks my legs under the table and I kick her back and she makes a noise like it hurt and Dad tells us both to behave. He winks at us and when the food arrives he says he's starving hungry and asks the waitress if we can have some more ketchup because the bottle's almost empty and she nods and goes back to the counter and then she comes back and puts a new bottle on the table. Dad says he'll put the ketchup on our food but I want to do it myself because I'm a big boy now, seven years old, and he lets me but it comes out too fast and there's a load of ketchup on my chips but I don't mind because I love ketchup and Mum and Dad raise their eyes into their heads in the way which makes me look away because it looks like their eyes are going to disappear into the back somewhere and then they'd have to go to hospital for some help. Sarah has to have a go with the ketchup as well but Dad helps her a bit because she's smaller than me.

– There's a train we can go on later, Dad says. It runs right out into the water, to the end of the pier.

I start asking questions because I love trains and sometimes Dad takes me to Liverpool Street and we go and look at the trains coming in, but best of all I like Thomas The Tank Engine, though not as much as I used to because I'm getting too old for Thomas, he's for smaller children really, and I think Sarah likes trains as well now, and I'm looking forward to going on the train over the water, but I like the fish fingers and chips and will think about trains in a minute.

– I'll be a train driver one day, I say. If not I'm going to be a policeman or a doctor.

Dad coughs and says a doctor would be best, but being a policeman is tough work, and he laughs and says a train driver would be best of all, but not a policeman, anything but a copper, and laughs some more, but Mum frowns at him and says that the police are good, that they protect us from bad people, and if there were no police we would soon miss them. I scrape ketchup off my chips and cut bits of fish finger and put it in my mouth and chew with my mouth shut when Mum tells me, and when I've swallowed a mouthful I have a drink of Coke and it has ice in it which makes it hard to drink, and I have to wipe my nose on a piece of toilet paper Mum gives me. I keep looking out over the water at the boats coming in and wonder what it would be like being a sailor living on a boat and I think I would be scared because if the boat sank I'd get eaten by sharks or at least have one of my legs bitten off and I can't swim properly yet though Dad has started taking me on Sunday morning.

– Don't play with your food, Mum tells Sarah, and she's full up and has only eaten half her dinner, and I'm almost done and so are Mum and Dad.

We walk along the front and I'm thinking that I'd like to be a policeman and help people, I suppose Superman's a sort of policeman, then suddenly I see a pirate ship next to the pier and I try to run towards it but Dad's got my hand because of the cars along the road and he holds me back and I've forgotten that, and I want to go see the pirates and he says okay, but first we're going on the train because it might start raining soon and it could get more windy, so best to get the train ride done first because it goes out over the water and we don't want the kids getting a cold or sore throats.

I'm sitting on the train which doesn't look much like Thomas because Dad says it's a big children's train and I wonder what the driver calls it, and Sarah keeps looking back at the pirate ship, but once the train starts moving it's more exciting and I'm looking down at the water and I don't like it much because what if something breaks and we fall in and Mum and Dad and Sarah and me get eaten by sharks or crocodiles or submarines or something even worse. I don't say anything because I shouldn't be scared and have to be a brave man and boys don't cry either, though I did at school last week when that kid hit me with a lump of wood because of some black man who got beat up by white men but that wasn't my fault and I told him that but he just laughed and ran off and the teacher asked what happened but I shut up and didn't tell because telling is the worst thing you can do.

There's a man driving the train and he has a whistle and blows it every now and then and I like that and I feel safe because the driver's in charge and knows what he's doing, that's what Dad tells me when he puts his arm around my shoulder, and I like the ride now, so does Sarah, and then we're at the end and have a look around and see the ships coming in a bit closer and Mum says that one's from Russia and another one's from Africa. There's wolves in Russia she says, and bears, and there's all kinds of animals in Africa like lions and elephants and giraffes and other things I don't know about, but some people are bad and kill elephants for their tusks and Sarah starts crying and Dad says it's okay it doesn't happen much now and he buys us both crisps from an old man with a box of different stuff.

We get the train back and I can see the pirate ship ahead and wonder when the pirate ships come down the river into London, though Dad says there aren't pirates any more, only in the sea around Vietnam and places like that and they've got new boats

now and it's not like the old days. We get off the train and hurry to
the pirate ship because it's starting to rain a bit more and Dad
pays the woman some money and then we're walking onto the
ship that's made of wood and has a mast and bits of rope and
loads of other stuff and some big guns on wheels which Dad says
aren't real, but then he says they are but not dangerous so don't
worry, and I'm glad they're not toys and they don't look like toys
either.

There's writing when we get inside and Dad tells us that the
pirates wore baggy trousers and they were covered with tar to
protect them against the cold and their buttons were sometimes
made from the backbone of a shark or pieces of cheese that had
gone hard. He says that the pirates often ate their food in the dark
because the food was horrible and they drunk lots of rum and
suffered from a lot of illnesses like things called scurvy, typhus,
typhoid, dysentery, malaria, yellow fever and another kind of
disease to do with men and women. Pirates liked gold and silver
and even though they'd been around for a long time before, it's
for what they did in the seventeenth and eighteenth centuries that
they are best known. They were mostly Dutch and English and
French and at first they robbed Spanish galleons coming back
from America which was called the New World at that time and
took their treasure.

Dad says the pirates lived mostly in a place called Tortuga near
Haiti and in the Bahamas and in 1663 there were about fifteen
ships and a thousand men who lived around Tortuga and Jamaica
and though they started off working for the kings and queens of
their countries after a while they just attacked anyone and became
their own bosses and then the kings and queens didn't like them
any more because it was alright when they were robbing and
killing for their countries but they weren't liked much when they
did it for themselves. Francis Drake was a pirate and that's why the
Spanish sent their boats in the Armada to stop his attacks on their
boats and he was sent by the first Queen Elizabeth.

Pirates were called buccaneers and corsairs and filibusters and
freebooters and gentlemen of fortune and privateers and sea
wolves and Henry Morgan was one of the best and everyone was
scared of him. Dad says that all the sailors on a Spanish ship killed
themselves rather than get caught by Henry Morgan. He was

captured and went on trial in England but Charles I made him a knight instead of killing him and then he was made Governor of Jamaica. Woodes Rogers was another pirate and he later became Governor of the Bahamas and there was Edward Teach who was also called Blackbeard and he was a giant who swore a lot and had a long beard that had ribbons twisted in it and this looked like dreadlocks and Dad says he liked to put gunpowder in his rum. Calico Jack had two women in his crew, Anne Bonny who was from County Cork in Ireland and was his girlfriend, and Mary Read who had been a soldier. Dad says one of the fiercest pirates was a Welsh man called Bartholomew Roberts who often killed people and he had a dandy look and wore a red feather in his hat.

We walk through the boat looking at guns and pictures of big ships with sails and drawings of pirates drinking and fighting. Sarah says she doesn't like it much and it's boring but I wouldn't mind dressing up like a pirate and having sword fights but I don't think I would want to kill anyone or make them walk the plank and get eaten by sharks because I wouldn't want that to happen to me. Dad says there was Captain Kidd who was Scottish and there was a flag called the Jolly Roger which he points to on the wall and it's a skull and crossbones and not very nice and when the pirates put it at the top of their mast it gave the ship they were after the chance to surrender but if the ship didn't give up then a crimson flag was put up instead and it meant everyone would be killed with no quarter given.

The captains made their own versions of the flag and we walk up some steps onto the deck of the ship again and look over the side at the water and there's big ropes everywhere and Dad says a pirate's life must have been tough with storms and hard conditions but it must have been exciting because they got to live in the West Indies where the weather is nice and different to England where it rains all the time and they were their own people and didn't have to worry about electricity bills and gas bills and taxes and paying for the phone and local council charges and they didn't have all the insurance people and rule-makers after them all the time making their lives a misery. Dad says maybe he'd have been a pirate and smiles at Mum, with all that drink and beautiful women with big earrings and necklaces and stacks of gold and sword fighting, and she could have been a pirate as well like Anne Bonny and Mary

Read who they didn't hang because they found she was going to have a baby. There would be no more laws to tie them down and steal their wages for stupid reasons and someone is always after Dad's money, trying to take it away from him, making him pay lots of money for the rent and they just have to make a law and he has to pay what they say otherwise he goes to prison.

I can imagine Dad being a pirate with pistols and a sword and baggy trousers and he's got a big black eye where he got punched by a Chelsea fan when he went to see West Ham play there and I bet he would make the men who punched him at Victoria station walk the plank. Sarah wants to go to Never Never Land across the road so we walk back through the exhibition and I have a final look at the pirates and the guns and then we're waiting to cross the road.

– That's the sixth Rolls I've seen since we've been here, says Dad. I wonder how many millionaires live in Southend.

I look and there's a black Rolls-Royce along the road and this is where the people who get rich in East London come to live and there's a cartoon picture of a man in a coat with a funny look on his face and I ask Dad what that is and he says it's a police warning about flashers and he says that flashers are men who show their willies to people who don't want to look at them, and Mum says that's one of the reasons we need policemen and Dad nods and agrees. I laugh because it seems a bit stupid showing your willy like that and it must be freezing with the wind blowing and we cross the road and Dad gives the old man some money and we go into Never Never Land.

Mum leads us through the big cartoon pictures and says it's all about Peter Pan who was a boy who never grew up and I say that's strange because I'd like to grow up and be like Dad, but he says not to rush because he'd rather be a child again, that's the best time in life because you don't have to worry about anything and you can just play and go to school and be yourself. He says if he could have his childhood again he would learn stuff at school and he's always saying this to me, that it matters when you grow up, and Mum tells us about Wendy and Tinker Bell and Captain Hook and a crocodile. Sarah wants to be Wendy and I'll be Captain Hook because there seem to be pirates all over Southend and I could carry a sword and I'll tell them at school and maybe we can play it in the playground. Sarah likes Never Never Land and wants to see Tinker Bell and Mum says it's just folklore, there aren't fairies and little people any more but Dad says yes there are, and they laugh, maybe Mum says, but not around where we live, we'd have to go right out into the country somewhere, or across the sea to Ireland, and even then we might miss them because we're not used to seeing this kind of thing. There's a shop with books and toys, and Mum and Dad buy Sarah the Peter Pan book and I get a sword.

When we get outside again it's not so cold as before and we walk along the seafront. There's more people around now and we get some donuts from a little shop and watch the lady making them and they're brilliant when I bite into them. Mum says she'll read us Peter Pan tonight when we get home and I keep thinking of pirates and would like to see a real pirate ship sailing towards us and I'd wear a patch over my eye and have sword fights if I had the chance. Dad says we'll walk to the end of the wall and turn back. Then we'll go back to the car and drive home so we miss the traffic and we'll see Bobby who'll be waiting for her dinner, and Mum says she just hopes that bloody dog hasn't been in the bin again.

LIVERPOOL AWAY

LIVERPOOL ALWAYS BEAT us at Anfield. We don't expect anything result wise, but the team generally puts up a good performance. It's a funny ground. Gets a lot of good press but I've never liked the place. There's a cold atmosphere. I don't go for that chirpy scouse wit bollocks. Unity in poverty. All that shit. The real Liverpool is gangs of scrawny scousers with blades trying to pick off lone cockneys on their way back to Lime Street. Shitty streets and piles of rubbish. Under-age scallies throwing darts and dropping concrete slabs on the trains back to London. Indiscriminate scum.

They can put Brookside on the box and try and bring the place upmarket like they try and do everything else, but Liverpool's just forgotten housing estates, Toxteth riots and the scousers moaning when they lose a game. Cilla Black and all those professional scousers make money out of the myth. But you never believe that kind of stuff. You believe what you see and Liverpool can be a nasty bunch of knife merchants and there's never been press about what it's like to get bushwhacked on the streets of Merseyside. Trophies count and nobody wants to know.

The ground's emptying and we've lost again. Mark's cousin, Steve, is with us. Met him outside the ground. He's parked up by Stanley Park and we're driving back to Manchester. It feels like half a day out this one, because there's Harris and the regulars trying to work out a way to find the opposition, but they know the old bill have the situation tied up. They picked us up coming into Liverpool and we didn't get a look in.

We shuffle our way to the exit and now we're out in the grim Liverpool night, dark streets and a flood of coppers. Same scene as London. The bastards on horseback carry long sticks and serious attitudes. The old bill are scousers themselves and hate Chelsea

79

like everyone else in the country. They don't take any lip in this part of the world and if you step out of line they'll have you. It doesn't impress the harder element but makes them wary. Harris tries to con his mob away from the coaches but the old bill aren't daft. He's got fifty or so blokes hanging back. No chance. Vans block their way. They smell of trouble and they're caught in the trap.

We follow Steve and persuade a copper we're going to the car. It takes some doing but we're walking along the side of Anfield, large areas of concrete and men and kids hanging around talking. We feel obvious. There's paranoia because all we need is a mob of scousers to come round the corner and we'd be cut up in seconds. They'd fucking love it finding four Chelsea boys on their own. We're keeping our voices down because there's no point being careless and getting overheard. My fists are clenched and the first scouser who mouths off is going to get his nose broken into tiny bits of shrapnel. Drive the bone into the brain and maybe it'll sort out that whining scouse accent. Steve better know where the car is because it'll be a sprint job.

There's no hassle though and any interested scousers must be waiting towards Lime Street, mobbing up down one of their concrete tunnels. The thieves I've seen watching England are human rats. Pale white skin and that fucking accent which nobody understands. They brag about being good robbers and they did the business following Liverpool around Europe nicking expensive gear from Switzerland and Germany, starting a designer trend with stolen property which dozy followers of fashion, missing the point, went out and paid through the nose for years later. But when it comes to doing a few Dutch equal odds in Rotterdam the scousers would rather turn over a jeweller's. Thieving little cunts the lot of them. We're in the car and I've got a thirst and a hard-on. Some Manc bird's going to have a good time tonight.

– Turn on the radio, will you? Mark's in the front seat with his cousin. Let's hear the other scores.

It starts to rain outside and our glimpse of Liverpool is huddled figures and street lights, bricks and mortar shining under artificial lights. Tottenham have lost and we cheer. Steve's windscreen wipers sweep side to side clearing a path through dirty streets, chip shops packed with scouse kids and old men. Mushy peas and chips with curry sauce. It's a fucking sad place and as much as I hate the bastards I have to feel a bit sorry for the young kids in thin rain-soaked shirts. This is bottom of the shit heap this city. They can keep their Boys From The Blackstuff and Derek Hatton. I'd die in a place like this after growing up in London. I mean, London's shit, but it's home and nothing like Liverpool. This city has to be the arsehole of England. I don't blame Yosser Hughes nutting everything in sight. I'd do the same.

– Fucking zoo this place, says Rod, following my train of thought like he's a mind reader. No wonder the bastards come down to London just to sleep on the streets. At least in London they get to suck a rich man's cock and earn a few quid. What are they going to do round here?

– Fuck all, says Steve, keeping his eyes on the road. Liverpool's a dying town. It's gone. There's too much Irish blood and Toxteth's full of kids left over from the slave ships. Liverpool was the original slave town. They bought the bastards here from Africa before shipping them to America. The past has caught up with this city.

– I don't know about all that, but the place should be bulldozed and the scousers sold off to the highest bidder. Rod stops to think. Not that anyone would want the bastards even as slaves. Wouldn't get much work out of them. He starts whistling the tune from the Hovis advert.

– Manchester's class in comparison, says Steve. Mancs and scousers hate each other's guts. You've never seen anything like it. It's worse than what you get in London. You go see Man U play Liverpool and it's evil. Real hundred per cent hatred. Only thing worse is Rangers against Celtic. Total civil war that one. It's religion tips the scales. Protestants and Catholics living like they did a hundred years ago. There's even a bit of that kind of feeling left over between Liverpool and Everton, Man U and City.

We start picking up speed and soon we're on the motorway to Manchester. The results come through the radio and we swear and cheer as our prejudice takes us. We're feeling good now leaving Liverpool behind, even though Chelsea got beat. We're in a relaxed mood. You get out of the situation, away from the mob, free from alcohol, and you're not bothered. We've done our bit for the Blues and I just fancy some food, a few pints and maybe a decent woman. Steve's putting his foot down and the rain's coming heavy now. We're steaming along surrounded by lorries and cars, dim outlines which could be anywhere in England but somehow we know we're up north. There's a definite smell and feel to the place, even on a stretch of motorway. Go into a service station and it's all fry-ups and strong tobacco. Like going back in time. You get spoilt living in London. It's a different world up here. A primitive world full of primitive people. Different tribes for different parts of the country.

When we get to Manchester, Steve parks up outside his flat. It's a dead area but only a short ride into the city centre. We haven't brought any gear with us, so pile in the nearest pub. It's early yet and there's a few locals staring into their pints, all laid back and reflective, which makes us feel noisy till we've downed three pints and calmed the nerves, and it's going to be a good night. I can feel it somehow. You go through the routine all week, keep your wits about you down the football, maybe do the business, maybe not, but now we're relaxed and out to destroy a few brain cells.

We end up having six pints in an hour and a half and Steve is pissed. Can't make my mind up about the bloke. Whether he's alright or a bit of a cunt. There's something not quite right about him. He's not a full shilling. Not thick, but not all there. Not sure what, but there's something. He goes off and calls a taxi. The pub's filling up now. Mostly middle-aged couples. A good laugh most of them, dressed up smart like Northerners tend to do. They're sound people, and I suppose if we were sitting in a boozer full of scousers they'd be alright as well. We make the last pint stretch and the taxi arrives to take us into town.

– There's a fair bit of crumpet knocking about, says Rod as he pays for the drinks in a done up pub with glass mirrors and leather bar stools. One of them's going to get a strong dose of Chelsea tonight. A dose of London infection.

I have to agree with the bloke and the pub we're in is packed solid. They all seem a bit sweet somehow, students or something probably, and I'd rather get hold of a real chunky northern girl than one of these inflatables. A hundred per cent Manc. The music's okay though and the lager's cheap so we stay a while and try sussing out some Man U or City fans but this lot are more into their clothes than rucking. Poor little babies wouldn't want to get their costumes messed up. Fucking idiots all think they're Peanut Pete and it's daft really because wankers like these deserve a kicking just to bring them into the world with a bang. Slap their bottoms and force them to breathe in the fumes of an English city, but when there's no resistance you don't bother. You want a bit of conflict, not one of these docile wankers who hate violence yet use it in their language and manners.

I pinpoint a mouthy cunt near the bar with some of his mates. Dressed up like a clown obviously thinking he's some kind of Saturday night special who's going to show his bottle down some flash club impressing birds who reckon being hard's a haircut and expensive gear. Cunt. I'm going to take the bastard out no problem, but my head's still together enough to know it's early in the evening and I'd get tugged within ten minutes. I've got to keep things sharp and pick the right moment. No point making a prat of myself. This one's personal and not something to share with an audience. I know the time and place well enough. Piece of piss and the bastard's going to have a split head the next time his bladder starts hurting him.

– I only go down the clinic and the bloke there tells me to drop my trousers. He has a bit of a look and then starts scratching round my knob. Mark's pissed going into one about his visit to the STD clinic.

– I'm thinking whether to nut the bloke, whether he's a fucking iron or something, and he must have the problem all the time because he starts talking about his wife and kids. How well his young ones are doing at school and all that family stuff. How he hopes his kids will go into the medical profession like their old man.

– You're better off dying of the clap than having some doctor playing with your balls, less it's a bird of course, and Rod's laughing into his drink spilling lager down his front, over the floor, everywhere. Scratch your own bollocks. Least you don't have to give up drink.

– It's professional, isn't it? It's different than some queer trying to get to grips with you and I was clean enough first time round, though I've got more tests coming back next week. Said I should watch where I dip my todger, not in those words exactly, but I started thinking about that skinny bird I had and what a tight fit she was. That's a real blood job. That's where you get your Aids from.

The mouthy cunt I've been watching puts his bottled lager on the bar and fucks off to the bogs. I follow him across the pub. Music's loud in my ears, some old Happy Mondays wank, I don't know, but I can hear the bloke's voice and see the cockiness in his face. Cunt. Reckons he's something special. I go in the bog and he's having a piss, leaning over the bowl admiring himself. There's another geezer zipping up ready to leave and I pretend to wash my hands. When he's gone I walk over to the wanker at the bowl, grab a handful of his golden locks, pull his head back and slam his skull into the wall hard as I can. There's a heavy thud of bone and concrete. I pull his head back and slam his face into the tiles. I feel the shudder through my arm. His knees go and he's sliding into the piss down below, blood splattered across the wall. Fucking lovely pattern. Poor little darling's fucked and his clothes are fucked as well. Blood and piss, the great British cocktail. A national institution. I walk out and tell the others we're leaving, that I've just done some Manc cunt. We get out of the pub sharpish.

Manchester's buzzing and there's a real flavour to the place. I feel better. Brought things to a natural level. Cunt deserved a bruising. Hope his fucking head's split in half. Hope the stitches dig in deep. That the doctor fucks them up first time around. But it's no time to linger so we get walking and ten minutes later we're in another pub better than the last one and there's a couple of tasty girls at the bar. They're well moulded. Built for one thing. Remind me of Letter To Brezhnev, but then I remember that those girls were scousers, that there's a difference, that Mancs hate scousers, and scousers reckon they're the business when it comes to thieving. Have to watch my money with these two.

I'm leaning across one of the girls ordering four pints of lager. She smells strong of perfume and she's laughing with her mate making no attempt to move away. I lean into her a bit more a little unsteady on my feet from the drink, using it as an excuse to test her and she doesn't shift an inch and I know I'm in. I can feel her tits through the thin material of her top and know she's wearing a low cut bra. It gives me a boost just getting the scent and texture.

– Get any nearer and you'll be sucking my nipples, she says with a smile which spreads lipstick across her face, and her mate's laughing, choking on her drink.

They hear our accents and know we're from London, but it doesn't phase them. They've been down a few times themselves but reckon it's a shit town full of posers. It's expensive and the clubs are full of silly little kids. The girl with the strong perfume and willing nipples will be no problem and Steve's straight in with her mate. Doesn't waste any time, I'll give him that much. He's giving her some nonsense about how much he loves Manchester. How London's a dump and even though I should be concentrating on the bird next to me who's flashing her eyes in that way pissed girls tend to do, he's winding me up without knowing it, all in the cause of getting his end away.

I can take a bit of a pisstake from the girls because at the end of the night I'll be doing the business and it's all in good fun. But Steve's got nothing to offer. I mean, if it was a mob of blokes in a pub I didn't know and they were taking the piss out of London, or worse than that, Chelsea, then we'd just steam in without a second's thought. But with the girls I can take the joke, basically I suppose because they're women and there's some kind of inbred respect deep down inside, buried under all the insults and jokes. Steve's a relative of a mate so I have to play the game, but he can go too far with the slagging. He's a bit of a smarmy cunt, but he's Mark's cousin so I keep my mouth shut.

– I was glad to get out of London and move up here. The people are more genuine and you don't get so many madmen walking the streets. Up here people talk to each other and everything costs less so you can afford to go out more. The people are real. They're not so bothered with their image and how much they earn.

I notice Rod giving Steve the eye, picking up on his line of chat. He looks my way and I know we're thinking the same thing. I mean, he might have a point about some of the things he's going on about, but at the end of the day you don't slag your own kind. The truth's often hard to swallow but you don't abandon your culture whatever anyone tells you. Steve might have lived in Manchester for the last six years, but he was born and raised in London and he's always going to have a bond with the place.

It's like the Indians in Southall. You might take the piss

occasionally but they're not just going to come over and ditch everything because they're in England. They're not going to give up their curries and start eating beans on toast every night. They can mix respect with their own ways. You're always going to push your way of life, but deep down you understand what's what and Steve's just making a cunt of himself in my eyes. He's like those wankers who are always slagging off the Union Jack. Say it's a symbol of fuck knows what. They all have the same accents. All follow the same kind of politics. Posh accents, posh politics. Intellectuals they like to call themselves, but they're just outsiders who don't belong in their own culture.

Maybe Steve's one of those misfits, but he hasn't got the accent and I doubt he's got any politics other than the politics of dumping his load. But that's just as fucked as the tossers who deliver lectures on something they've never experienced. Steve's following the politics of promising anything and slagging everything off just to shaft some pissed bird who'll knob anything she can get hold of because it's Saturday night. Steve's just fulfilling a social obligation. Saturday night. Bloke shags bird. Girl shags bloke. Says anything to achieve that goal. Basically, the man's got no pride. No self-respect. No nothing. He's one of those people you meet who needs to impress and has no solid foundation. He'll say anything, do anything. Another cunt in a world jam-packed with them.

I finish my pint and Mark's at the bar ordering. I think his cousin's a wanker and I'm wondering whether to let him in on the secret, but we're not pissed enough yet. Steve's like a fair weather football fan. He'll go along with the atmosphere when the team's doing well but you won't see him for ten years when they're losing. He'll come along to Anfield because it's a short drive down the motorway, and he'll rant and rave because everyone else is doing it, but that's as far as it goes.

– The worst thing about London is places like Brixton. You go down there and you might as well be in New York. It's a dangerous place not safe for a woman to walk around once it gets dark.

I'm looking at the back of his head as he rambles on and he's giving her a long line of shit because he's been slagging off Moss Side and Hume for the same reasons when we were at Anfield. I don't know, maybe I shouldn't get so wound up about things. Maybe it's just me. He's pissed and talking shit. I should let it go. Not worry about what Steve has to say to shag a tart. But then I think of football and how you go everywhere through thick and thin and it represents something, like being faithful maybe, but he just doesn't understand the notion. I go for a piss.

I'm standing with my head against the wall pissing away the lager. I think of that smarmy wanker in the last pub. Must be down the hospital at this very moment. I could have killed the bastard and I start thinking what it must be like to go down for twenty years. To find yourself banged up slopping out every morning. Shifted around the country from prison to prison, trying to keep your nose clean so you can get time off your sentence, but the whole time bottling everything up just wanting to kick fuck out of someone and release the tension. I do my buttons up and wash my face in the sink. I'm wound up worse than normal and I don't know why. I'm on for a shag, seen Chelsea, even though we got beat, and I've had the bonus of smacking some wanker already tonight. Even so, I want to nut Steve, but know it's not on because he's Mark's cousin and Mark's a good mate. A diamond. We go back years. Same with Rod. Another diamond. Both do anything for you. We stick together and help each other out. I let the cold water wake me up and I feel in control again. Go back in the bar and take the drink Mark's just bought.

– Are you coming back then? The girl I've been chatting with leans into me, rubbing against me. She's already sorted things with her mate. We could go on somewhere if you want, but I'm pissed.

– You can come back to my place, Steve says, interrupting. It's not far. We can get a cab. I'll pay if you're short.

– No, I don't fancy odds of four onto two. I look at the woman wondering if she thinks we're sick or something. Rapists or gang-bangers.

– Nothing personal. She looks me square in the eyes, a serious expression on a nice face. A girl's got to be careful these days. There's a lot of weird men around. Make the wrong choice and you could end up hacked to pieces with bits of your body scattered around Greater Manchester.

Steve shakes his head and turns away.

– You coming or what, and the woman's on her feet leading me to the door. I tell the lads I'll meet them tomorrow at twelve at the train station. Follow her outside.

She bundles into me and we start walking. It's a cold night and I forget about the rest of the lads and she's not bothered about her mate either. Too pissed to think. Too pissed to argue with another drunk. We walk for what seems like ages, but it's only ten minutes and I'm climbing up two flights of stairs in the dark. The light doesn't work, but when the front door opens we're in a warm flat with nice wallpaper and purple carpet. I don't have much time to enjoy the surroundings, though, because the woman's leading me into the bedroom without bothering to offer me a drink or go through the normal routine of coffee and dull background music. We strip off and before I stop spinning from the excess lager flooding my brain we're banging away with the bed threatening to cave the floor in.

She's a good ride, no doubt about it, which is unusual when you're pissed and maybe the lager has an effect because it's a fair old while before I finish and collapse in a sweating lump of rubble. We're both fucked by drink and sex and next thing I know it's morning and she's handing me a cup of coffee. Tells me I've got to drink up and get out in fifteen minutes. Nothing personal, her mum and niece will be round soon. I'm not feeling bad and, to be honest, wouldn't have minded another pop at the girl with a clear head, but you can't have everything in life and it was a good bit of sex last night so that's a bonus over the usual drunken effort.

I'm sitting on a bench, reading the football in the papers for half an hour before Rod and Mark turn up. They look rough and eye me with suspicion. Must have got rid of something more than the standard with that bird last night. I feel good. Set up for the trip back to London. Rod goes to get a cup of tea and Mark sits on the bench next to me. He's shaking his head. Doesn't look too happy with life.

— I'm fucking dead when we get home. He stretches his legs out and kicks at an empty fag packet. Misses and stubs his toe. He swears.

— My cousin, Steve. Fucking did the bloke last night. He only persuades that bird, the one whose mate you went off with, to come home with him. Me and Rod kip down in the living room and then he comes in about three in the morning with a towel

round him, wakes us up and tells us to come in his bedroom and
fuck her.

– I tell him to piss off. I'm not some fucking pervert. Anyway, I
think he's joking but then I hear this crying, like a kid, and I get up
to have a look and he's only battered her. She's shivering in bed
with bruised eyes and blood on the sheet. He's shouting that she's
a fallen angel and deserves everything she gets.

– I just went mental. Kicked the shit out of him. I hate that kind
of thing. I mean, the girl was suffering. He was a wreck the time I
got through with him and we just sent the bird home in a taxi. Left
Steve this morning and told him to get himself an ambulance. I'm
not helping the cunt. If he comes round my place again I'll kill
him. Talk about bad blood in the family.

Rod comes over and sits down. Sips at his tea blowing the
steam away. Looks my way to see if I've heard the story. I raise my
eyes. I knew there was something dodgy about the bloke. Makes
you wonder what else he gets up to if he goes that far when he's
got witnesses around. The first time I've met the bloke and
hopefully the last.

– You missed a bad night, Rod says.

– I'm history when I get back to London. He won't tell the old
bill but I wouldn't put it past him telling his mum. Maybe he
won't, I don't know. It's sick though. I've known him since we
were kids, though we didn't exactly see a lot of each other. I never
had a clue. I hope he keeps quiet about me having a go at him. My
aunt Doreen's a strange woman. She'll set God on me if she finds
out I touched her Stevie.

SWEET JESUS

SHE KEPT HER mouth shut most of the time and just spoke when she was spoken to, which was quite often really, considering, what with people wanting to leave their washing and needing change for the machines, maybe poking their heads around the door to ask what time the launderette closed. And this suited Doreen fine because it meant she didn't have to talk about the weather and how bad the Government was unless she wanted, though working in the launderette meant being discreet and knowing when to speak and what to say to a particular person at a particular time, judging their moods, but generally life panned out fine, only now and again one of the old girls, older than her, would come in and spend her time getting in the way, talking to herself or some invisible friend, more mumbling really than talking, they'd gone a bit dotty and, because they'd been through it all, the war and everything, they thought they didn't need any answers, so Doreen had to bite her lip when she wanted to warn them of the Devil's influence, of the salamanders in the heat spitting fire, salvation a short walk away at the altar of the Protestant church she attended twice a week.

It was too much time on their own that did it. Usually their husbands were dead, a lot of them killed by the Germans in France, or else run off with a younger woman though, to be honest, the state of most of the men around the neighbourhood you wouldn't think they'd be able to attract anyone decent, but life was full of surprises, none of them that surprising. Like Walter, wandering around the streets on his own all day, then he'd visit the launderette on Friday afternoons with his plastic bag, the same plastic bag which gradually fell apart until by the end of the month Doreen had to give him a new one from the supermarket, one that they used to make you pay for, stronger than the rubbish given

90

away free, but they wanted to switch back again, or so she had heard, nothing was free in a man-made world, only the air and sunlight, and they belonged to God. She would tell Walter that the bag was sitting around forgotten, doing her Good Samaritan act, not letting on that he was in her thoughts and he should think about a conversion for the good of his soul.

Walter did his own wash and whistled old Dubliners tunes, and occasionally he would shout out loud about the tears of Ireland and how the Catholics had been downtrodden for centuries, mourning those who had died fighting the English. Then Doreen would have a quiet word because nobody wanted politics in the launderette, it scared the mothers in with their kids, or at least she imagined it did, and there might be a man in reading his paper who would have his own views and then there would be a fight, and blood, and damnation. Politics worried Doreen. It was a bad word and life was hard enough anyway thank you very much. God was watching his flock and the men in new suits kept getting in His way. But once she'd had her say, smiling all the time and talking in a soothing voice, Walter was quiet and she would hear nothing more from him. He just kept his head down looking a bit embarrassed and sometimes Doreen would feel uncomfortable, that she should have let him get the ideas out, that he was from a different people who didn't have the ability to bite their lip and take everything on the chin. When she felt this kind of guilt she was stern with herself and knew she had to enforce some kind of standard.

Walter couldn't come in ruining things for everyone else, making the launderette an unpleasant place to visit. Business would fall off and Mr Donaldson might be forced to close down or cut back and that would be Doreen on the dole with her begging bowl pleading for charity. She paid her taxes and gave generously when the collection came round at church. Calm was restored and it was always the same youngsters who came in with the family wash, because their mums and dads were saving pennies and didn't put it in for a service, and boys sulked and girls talked too loud, really irritating it was, swearing sometimes because they wanted to be noticed, but they were seeing things through their own eyes only and hadn't learnt about other people's feelings, not yet anyway, and when it got too bad Doreen had to put on a stern voice and tell them to watch their tongues or they would be banned.

Most of them were fine though, like young Ronald who came in every Saturday morning, only eight or nine years old, and he shouldn't have been doing the washing, but he always had a smile on his face, like a lot of darkies, though not the youths with anger in their faces and shiny cars with that music all tinny through open windows, but real darkies, the ones that came over when she was young, guest workers from the Caribbean, and Ronald's smile was the same, real ray of sunshine whatever time of year it was, summer or winter, and Ronald came from a good Christian family who went to church regular as day followed night. He wasn't aggressive like some other children she could mention and Doreen would tell him to leave the wash for her, to go and play on the swings but watch out for the older boys selling drugs, remember to avoid temptation, and he would go off and she would do the wash for him, it was a pleasure, no charge, a labour of Christian love, just did it along with the rest. And when he returned he was always nice and polite and said thank you Mrs Roberts, it's very kind of you Mrs Roberts. Off he would go to his mum and dad, and children should play more, like she had done when we was a little girl.

Things were different now and some of the things she had heard about, the stories she read in the newspaper, all these men who molested children and mutilated their bodies. That monster who killed a child and buried the body in Epping Forest, then went back and dug the poor little thing up, took photographs, it was so hard to understand that kind of thinking. It proved what the vicar said, that there really was a Devil lurking in the shadows, in the dark recesses of the human mind, a monster preying on the defenceless, the old and the young, small boys and old ladies, the raving lunatics turned onto the streets for some care in the community. It was really shocking, as though the world was going mad, people turning in on themselves and falling prey to wicked thoughts. Doreen hadn't slept properly for months. She just didn't understand the frantic scramble that surrounded her.

Children had forgotten how to enjoy themselves and they shouldn't need lots of computerised toys to be happy, video games and cartoon superheroes, and their parents were to blame dressing the girls up like painted dollies and the boys were turned into miniature soldiers. But there again their mums and dads were copying what they saw on television, in the adverts and shop windows. Some of the things Doreen saw in the windows of toy shops made her wonder where it was all going to end, how far God would let His children go before He lost His temper. All that money spent on plastic guns when so many of the people who used the launderette were dressed like scarecrows. Doreen never got near their clothes because they did their own washes, but it was obvious, the colours gave it away. Drab and worn out colours faded because they'd been washed too many times. But it was their own business and during the winter it was a good job in the launderette, with the door closed and the radio going and the machines and dryers working flat out.

It was so warm, it was a job, and Doreen felt sorry for the down and outs living on the street at this time of year, the boy who slept in the Post Office phone boxes at the end of the high street. The first time that she saw him she'd thought he was a bundle of rags, a pile of lost washing, but then the legs moved and he couldn't be more than twenty or so, poor little lad, and she'd seen him the day before sitting there in the twilight with a pair of sunglasses covering his eyes, staring at the wall. In winter the launderette was a haven and every time the door opened and a gust of cold wind came in she remembered how lucky she was to be inside out of harm's way, the Lord watching over her. The window dripped with condensation and the heat from the dryers made her perspire, those tumble dryers spinning round and round, with the clank of motors and steam from the washing machines and the strong smell of powder. In the summer, though, when it was really hot outside the windows sweated as well and Doreen wished that her customers would take their wash home and hang it out to dry instead of wasting good money on the dryers. It became so hot in the launderette at this time of year and it would be better for the ozone layer and the polar ice caps wouldn't melt, bringing on another Flood. It would save energy as well, but they still got the dryers rolling and Doreen had to go to the door and stand on the pavement for some fresh air, but when there was a lot of traffic the carbon monoxide fumes were over-powering and her skin itched, though it could have been the powder she was using, but most likely it was the poison in the atmosphere.

Doreen's back ached more in the summer and she felt lazy, but her job was important, she couldn't complain because she was fit and healthy and working, and at least she didn't perspire as bad as some people. It could be horrible at times, the state of some of the clothes she had to wash. It just showed how different people's sweat glands operated, or the food they ate perhaps, herbs and garlic and spices, and then there would be bags of washing where the clothes seemed clean already, she just didn't understand why they bothered, maybe they thought they were the Queen and wore something different ten times a day. Not the English Queen, of course, because the older generation knew all about recycling and making things last, they wore their skirts and trousers and shirts longer than the younger people, they weren't so regimented, they made things last, made do with what they could get.

Now and then Doreen would wonder whether she had developed her own smell after twelve years working in the launderette, because people did, and their odour came to match their occupations and lifestyles. She could tell the bankers and solicitors who came in because their blouses and shirts smelt sharp, as though all that frustration and paperwork created a build-up of acidic sweat, a really disgusting smell, and the people who did manual work, whether stacking shelves or digging the roads, they had a heavy kind of smell which wasn't so unpleasant somehow. Then there was the girl who worked in the pub across the road, and she smelt of drink, quite a nice smell really, Doreen had to admit that much, and the Rastafarian who came in, his clothes were so sweet, lovely colours as well, and his hair was all knotted and clean and sometimes she just wanted to run her hands through it and let her cracked fingers get snagged on the knots. He had bought her a yellow china teapot at Christmas, a present he said, for being so nice to his nephew Ronald, and she made a cup of darjeeling on Christmas Day morning, such a lovely man, about the same age as her Stevie. She used to run her hands through her son's hair when he was a child, such lovely hair, and sometimes she wished she could move up to Manchester and see him every day.

Everything Stevie told her was honest and true, he was the best son a mother could have, so when he had that trouble with the drugs she knew it couldn't be wrong if Stevie said it was okay, what did she think helped Jesus with his visions and miracle cures, and she loved Jesus and her son Stevie, he was almost holy in his sweet innocence, such a good boy, and it was a good job James was away visiting his sister when the police came to the house about that horrible girl who said Stevie tried to touch her in the park, a wicked vicious lie, because her husband never loved Stevie like she did, no mother could love a son like she loved that boy. James had always been hard on poor Stevie, said the lad wasn't all there, and it was the only thing they had ever argued about.

Certain drugs were better than beer and didn't do so much damage to the body, it wasn't like drink which led to violence and caused death, it all made sense that time when Stevie was younger and sat her down and explained things in his special way, and she ran her fingers through his hair which needed a wash, but he was so innocent he didn't realise that appearances were important. But if she was honest with herself, Doreen could see the other side as well because if someone took drugs every day there was no way they'd get into work on time and it would be a quick walk to the social. It was the same for everyone. Punctuality was important. Even Mr Donaldson was a businessman first and foremost, and though his favourite worker got on with him she knew he would send her on her way without a second thought if he felt she wasn't doing her job properly. Life was like that, making choices and putting things in perspective, and some of the people who came into the launderette were all nerves and misery, crushed by society, right across the scale, from the poor to the not so poor, they all had their problems, doesn't everyone, though Doreen understood that she had less than most, but it was the rich ones who had moved into the area, the estate agents and insurance brokers, all those men and women under thirty who were power dressers or whatever they called it, they just gave her their underwear and talked like they owned the world, which they did really when it came to property and bank accounts.

Doreen had never known that only twelve and a half per cent of money actually physically existed, that the rest was just numbers in computers, until Stevie told her, when she caught him going through her purse that time, a difficult period of his life, it wasn't his fault, the power of the Devil trying to work its way into God's finest creation, and it was handy to know, something they should put in Christmas crackers, because she looked at the arrogant little so-and-so's with their expensive clothes and upturned noses and wondered if they realised what that meant. Did they? They moved into the neighbourhood for a couple of years and then sold the property for a profit, and the locals couldn't afford to buy a home in the area in which they'd grown up, that was greed for you, Jesus just turned their table over and threw them out of the synagogue. If Stevie had been born two thousand years earlier he would have done the same, died on the cross for suffering humanity, and the Son of God might return one day, the vicar didn't know everything, good man though he was, and she could see Stevie in the desert through the mist coming off a pile of shirts, and hear his voice above the roar of the dryers telling a crowd of people to love thy neighbour.

Sometimes she felt guilty for her good fortune, but James always told her to enjoy life while she could because they would be dead one day, it all ended in the grave, and that's why it was good to have a religion, it didn't really matter which one she supposed, though she couldn't imagine being anything but a Protestant, and she would have liked Walter to convert for the good of his soul, but it was just what you were raised with, and it was best to get on with it because if she looked at what the vicar said too closely maybe she would find some of the ideas a little bit suspicious, and then where would she be? Doreen hoped she wasn't being blasphemous because she knew God was listening to her thoughts, but surely he would understand, because she was a good woman really and she knew that God loved her.

James was away again visiting his sister, poor Kate was ill, the air in Wiltshire didn't seem to be doing her much good. She was lucky to have such a dedicated brother, they'd always been close, both their families were close and the children were always around on Sunday for their dinner, though not Stevie who was doing well in Manchester, they didn't see him very often, never anything but smiles, truth be told there were never many problems, a few when the children were teenagers and they were having trouble making ends meet.

Doreen snapped back to the launderette and she was watching

Mrs Atkins load a machine, the poor woman had lost her husband the year before and had apparently turned to drink though she never smelt of the stuff and was always well turned out, though they said she stuck to gin because it leaves no trace. Doreen hoped she would be okay and she was coming towards her suddenly, swaying a little, asking for a twenty pence piece, and Doreen went into her little room and took the two tens she handed over, gave Mrs Atkins the coin, exchanging pleasantries about their respective children, what good people they had turned out to be, free from the drugs which destroyed so many youngsters today, nothing wrong with a little cannabis now and again Doreen told herself, hearing Stevie's voice, and the dryers were spinning behind her, the door opening and closing, the hatch a nice addition, thank you Mr Donaldson.

Then Mrs Atkins turned back towards the washing machine and Doreen was wondering what she would eat that night, perhaps she'd treat herself and have a couple of samosas and a big bag of chips, maybe a pickled onion, that would be nice. She started thinking about the man who ran the kebab house, she could never pronounce his name properly, but how the place smelt of grease and meat, and when she met him in the supermarket and said hello he smelt just like the kebab house, all that fat and frying oil, a mix of kebab meat and battered fish, it was awful, made her stomach turn, it was as though he had no personality, like it was swamped in bubbling oil, doused in vinegar and chilli sauce. It was disgusting, the poor man, with a wife and children and maybe that's why his sons were always in trouble, fights and drugs, his eldest son was in prison for beating up a policeman, because kids could be cruel and violent when they got into their late teens, just look at her nephew Mark, though he'd straightened himself out now and was good as gold.

Doreen wondered if the other children had made fun of their father, because he really was foul-smelling and she felt terrible because he was such a nice man when he was in the kebab house, so friendly, and he gave her big portions when she went in, a Greek or a Turk, she was never sure which and didn't want to ask because she knew the two countries didn't get on, but she never saw him in the launderette and she was quietly and guiltily pleased because she would hate to have to handle his clothes, poor man, what a terrible thing to carry around with you, and it started her thinking, making her a bit nervous, that parable about casting the first stone. He had been behind the counter for such a long time that he had picked up the smell of the place, and Doreen wondered if the same thing had happened to her.

She thought of the clothes that she washed day-in day-out, and how each bag had its own unique smell which told everything worth knowing about the owner. But what did other people think of the woman from the launderette when she passed them in the street? Did they smell dirty clothes? Perhaps all the rotten fumes she dealt with through the years had worked their way into her pores and mutated her glands. Maybe she turned heads when she passed, her odour one of dirty socks and smelly underpants, curry-stained T-shirts and bloody jeans. She had been in the place so long now that she was used to the stench of dirty laundry when opening bags left for a service wash, pushing their contents quickly into the machines, washing away the sins of the world, turning her head away, turning the other cheek, giving her customers the chance of a clean start in life though she knew well enough they would never learn from the past but make the same mistakes all over again and then come back to her looking for one more chance. Like Stevie. She was just another cog in the machine, her purpose in life the cleaning of soiled shirts and dirty hankies.

The poor man in the kebab house probably smelt her coming and thought poor Mrs Roberts, she reeks of other people's dirty washing, she has no identity of her own, a faceless woman in other people's clothes, washing and drying and folding shirts and towels in neat little piles, and if that was what he thought then Doreen told herself that it was only right, a just desert for thinking the same about him, poor man. She looked up and Ronald was trying to cross the road with his washing, the bag heavy over his shoulder, weighing him down, a police car stopping to let the boy across, and he pushed the door of the launderette open and looked at Doreen uncertainly. She knew what he wanted but was too polite to ask, such a lovely little boy, perfect manners, no trouble to anyone, and she smiled at Ronald and told him he should be off playing, that he was a child and children should play games, that they should sit on swings and climb slides. He grinned and handed

98

Doreen the bag, said thank you Mrs Roberts, and Ronald was an honest boy, a good boy, all children were honest up to a certain age when it all got too much and they became confused, poor Stevie, God's suffering children, but this boy was different, she knew he was a good boy, and he would tell nice Mrs Roberts, the woman who went to the same church, the truth, he would tell her the truth so she asked him what she smelt like, and he didn't flinch at such a strange question, and it was best to be direct with children, no point hanging back keeping her mouth shut with this little boy, the salamanders in the heat digging their forks into the launderette lady, some kind of punishment, heaven and hell on Earth. Ronald said she smelt clean. Like nice new clothes. Then he turned and left the launderette and Doreen smiled as she watched him walk along the street towards the children's playground.

NORWICH AT HOME

NORWICH ALWAYS BRING a lump to the throat. It's like some old fossil in power has decided to bring back hanging. That's what happens when you look back. You stitch yourself up. Get all emotional. Pensioners live off memories because they get nothing from the Government. Enough for light bulbs, but forget about the electricity to make them work. But I've got my own memories. None of those wartime stories of the Blitz. Chirpy cockney bollocks about sticking together in times of trouble. It doesn't work like that. Not these days. Not outside a few good mates. Not in Norwich.

We were kids at the time. Seventeen or eighteen and a bit slow. It was me and Rod after a game and we took the wrong turn outside Carrow Road. We were talking about nothing and not looking where we were going, like you do when you're a kid, and suddenly there's twenty Norwich fans in front of us. Just our dress sense must've told them we were Chelsea. They asked more for effect and I told them straight out because I knew we were going to get a kicking, but didn't realise how much it was going to hurt.

They didn't hang about. I dodged the kicks at first as they went for my balls, then looked to Rod, but he was on his knees in the street with his arms held out like he was being crucified and there were three or four farmers taking turns kicking him in the head. I went back and smacked one across the side of the face, then some cunt bundled me forward and my head hit a concrete post. I was on the ground and just remember being dazed. They were soon busy kicking seven shades of shit out of me and I must've been down for a good while.

Don't know how, but we managed to get up and stumble along an alley. It was a real panic job. My legs were fucked and Rod was swaying from side to side. Couldn't see much as we went. There were no pretty sights, just wood and bricks, though I remember the smell of rain on concrete. A strong, stale smell. We were on a slope which helped us along and we jumped over a fence and sat on the ground surrounded by stinging nettles, breathing heavy like we were old men choking to death.

The Norwich lads didn't follow us and we looked over the fence after a while and they'd fucked off. Melted away like they never existed. We just sat there. Didn't even get stung too bad which would have been the final insult. Rod was lying back against the fence saying fuck fuck fuck to himself like the needle was stuck. His eyes looked a bit mental. I thought his brain had gone, but was more bothered about myself. Must've sat there for half an hour and my body was beginning to ache and my head cracking in two. We were shitting ourselves because it was a fair walk to the station and we didn't fancy a second helping.

Eventually we got the bottle together and climbed over the fence. Walked up to the street and turned back along the side of the ground. There were people buying tickets for the next game. Young boys with Norwich souvenirs. Men, women and kids. The great farmer support playing happy families. I wondered if they'd seen us get a kicking. They weren't giving anything away. Just living their lives. Maybe they watched the show, maybe not, I don't know. But nobody came to help us when Norwich were trying to inflict a bit of yokel tradition.

Can't blame them, of course. Scared people living shit lives aren't going to help a couple of teenage Chelsea boys. But they could've come down the alley and seen if we were still alive. They did fuck all. Left us to rot. Makes you think about all that decent citizen stuff. The public wants law and order and all the other stuff that goes with it, hanging and castration and short sharp shocks, but most of them are just small minded cunts who don't want to get their hands dirty. They'll have their say as long as it doesn't go against what everyone else says, but they'll do fuck all when it comes to the crunch. They flow with the tide. A great tidal wave flowing through the sewers. Shit and used rubbers. Maybe they were just embarrassed, or reckoned we deserved it being young and away from home, but after Norwich we realised the score and grew up. A bit of an initiation really.

I had a headache for a week after and, being a kid and thinking too much about mights and maybes, started getting worried I could be brain damaged. Imagined this blood clot spinning around my head waiting to kill me. None of it seemed worth the agony but once my head cleared I was fine and sense returned. Sometimes you need a bit of reason kicked into you and the whole thing raised the stakes. We realised there's more to life than being a cocky hooligan with a big mouth. If you're going to run the risk of getting a kicking it's better to get in first. Travel with a crew where you get maximum satisfaction and hopefully not too bad a hiding if things go wrong.

It's all about belonging and working together. Like in a war everything changes. Everyone pulls in the same direction and all the peacetime nonsense is knocked on the head. It's doing what's got to be done to survive the bad times, and when you're up against the wall you find all kinds of hidden strength. When he was still alive, my granddad called it war socialism. Said all the rich bastards bit their lips and reverted to a system they normally slagged off. It was different times and my granddad grew up with different notions, but the idea's the same, more or less. Makes sense that if you're going away looking for trouble you need a good mob that's going to get stuck in together. There's no point ten of you going somewhere like Leeds looking for a row because you'd last five minutes.

Flies around shit, those Norwich farmers saw us standing out and gave us a kicking like they were tenderising some of their pigs. We were mugs and it hasn't happened that way since. It's all a bit of a laugh, because if you've got a good firm together you can turn a place over and generally walk away without too much damage. Of course, things can go wrong, specially against big clubs, or when it's an important game. The locals make an effort and you turn a corner and find yourself up against a thousand psyched up Northerners determined to send you straight to Emergency. You shit yourself inside but the rush is so good you love it more than anything. You push yourself through the fear and you've done something that'll last you the rest of your life. They say it's adrenalin and that may be true, but all I know is that nothing compares. Not drugs, sex, money, nothing.

One day I'll be an old geezer pissed on a couple of pints and fuck knows what kind of world I'll be living in. I'll have some crippling disease and get mugged every time I walk out the door. There'll be no more pensions and I'll just be sitting around watching an endless stream of soap operas waiting to die. But at least I'll have lived a bit while I had the strength. And I won't be paying for my own funeral either. Dignity in death? Fuck off. I'll have stories to tell anyone bothered to listen and the kids will be surprised there was life in the good old days. They'll look at me a bit different.

I've done it myself. Listened to old geezers ramble on about their youth. But if you stop and listen it's not that at all. People are impatient and call a slow delivery rambling. The old people hanging around bus stops and libraries, the pub if they've got a bit of money spare, looking for something to do with their time, those are the ones who teach you about history. They can tell you about football riots. Or sex. Or drugs. Or anything you're into. Nothing's new. They just laugh and tell me we're nothing these days. That London's gone soft.

Nothing's changed. We're just more global and the village idiot gets a documentary made about him by all those people who want to be John Pilger. Everyone's in front of the screen watching everyone else. Listen to a pensioner and there was plenty of football violence in the old days. Look at Millwall. They were closed down enough times and nobody's seriously telling me that those boys didn't get stuck in on a Saturday afternoon. I've heard a few stories and I believe them. There's never been a golden age of love and peace. That's just down to the papers and television. Public exposure. Entertainment for the masses. One big fucking peepshow.

Despite the kicking we got at Norwich, I still enjoy watching them play football. A team's tradition gets handed down through the years and every club has its own approach to the game. It's the same as inheriting your dad's violent tendencies. Not that my old man got up to that much, or at least not as far as I can make out. Seems to have played it safe most of his life. Kept his head down and done his duty. But we're talking football teams and Norwich like to knock the ball about and entertain. Every football fan respects that. Whether it's your nutters concentrating on the movements of the opposition, or programme collectors guessing a player's vital statistics. I look over to the Norwich fans and wonder if those blokes who did us are there. I wouldn't recognise them and expect a few have fallen by the wayside through the years. Got married and stitched up with kids, mortgages, visits to the in-laws, whatever. But odds are there'll be at least one or two of the blokes here today.

Funny, really, I don't feel any hatred for Norwich. Not even those pig fuckers who gave us a kicking outside Carrow Road. They're just shapes without faces. I know it's nothing personal. It's all a dream now, like it happened to someone else, as though I'm watching it on a video with all the slow-motion replays and still-frames you could want. It's so long ago, but just yesterday when you think of the memories the Chelsea Pensioners must have sitting in the East Stand.

They line up in the middle tier, up the back, and you can just see this row of red jackets across the ground. White blobs where their faces should be. Same as the Norwich crew. It's a bit frightening thinking those blokes go back so far, the First World War probably. Don't know if there's any of that lot left now. Must've been kids at the time. But who's the mug? A handful of poor old sods get to sit behind the directors and politicians, but when half-time comes and everyone else is off for their drinks in the bar, the old boys are still there in their seats. Makes you laugh. A nation fit for heroes and they're the lucky ones because at least they've got a home and the chance to watch Chelsea play.

Then you think of their mates who didn't make it and ended up getting their heads blown off. Or fucked up with mustard gas. Bitten and infected by rats. Drowned in mud. Slaughtered by machine guns. It's a nightmare and my granddad told me stories about that one. I mean, I don't reckon I'm a coward or anything, but there's no way I'd have gone over in the First World War because some stuck-up cunts ruling the country thought it was a good idea. King and country and all that shit. If I want a punch-up I don't have to go and sit in a trench for a year up to my knees in diarrhoea. Making do with French whorehouses where every other British army cunt's been dumping his load. Beats me how they could let themselves get conned.

It's different times I suppose. The pressure must come when a war gets going and you had those women sending out white feathers to try and shame the sensible blokes who wanted to stay at home into wrecking their lives. A lot of them must've thought it was a bit of an adventure, but more probably they just didn't want to stay at home and have their lives made a misery. Everyone looking at them thinking they're bottle merchants. Better to die in the trenches than at home eaten away and tormented by vermin. Can understand that, but on my own terms. Sit in front of the TV watching war films and drama series, or get out and find your own excitement. Let everyday work and play grind you down to a dribbling video game boy, or open the front door and put yourself on the line.

With football you make a choice. It's no easy option. You don't want to bottle out in front of your mates, and the more your reputation develops the more pressure there is to perform. Still, it's freedom of choice because I'm doing it for myself, not because the wankers in power tell me. That's what they don't like. When it really goes off the show's so far beyond their control it's unreal. The fat bastards who think they're in control realise how much power we have. Mob-handed we can do whatever we want. That's why they make a big noise about it all. Spend millions on cameras and police bills.

Look at a war and they kill millions, but how many deaths have you ever had through football? Not from fences or wooden stands, but from the fighting that goes on between rival mobs. Everyone says look at Heysel, but if you get the story from scousers, blokes who were actually there, then according to them it's a lot different to what you're told back in England. Nobody wants to see people die at football matches, nobody, but at the end of the day they reckon Heysel was an accident. There was trouble inside the ground, it can't be denied, and anyway, so what, but the way it's painted is a con. The Italians have their own nutters and anyone who knows anything about football knows they're a bunch of knife merchants. Just like niggers, they're always tooled-up, and when you talk to scousers, like I do occasionally at England games, you hear that Liverpool fans were getting slashed before the game.

Add that to the match in Rome a year before when Italian mobs went mental attacking anyone English – men, women, children – anybody that supported Liverpool, something that the papers and Government conveniently forgot, and what do they fucking expect? Of course the scousers steamed in, but the dagos who were having a go when the numbers favoured them should take a bit of the blame. From the telly it even looked like there was a fence between the two sides. But who gets killed at the end of the day? It's all the people there to see a game of football who aren't interested in causing trouble. It's like everything, it's always the bystanders who get slaughtered. The old bill went mad trying to identify the scousers involved. They had the video evidence so why not check out the Italians as well? Because it's all down to public opinion, which is dictated. The whole thing's political, but people are too thick to understand. Talk to a Liverpool fan who was there and they'll go on about it all night.

Funny thing is, people look at football fans and think they're scum. But your regular football supporter, right across the board, from young kid to old man, nutter to trainspotter, has seen the propaganda machine in action through the years. First hand knowledge. You can go to a game and see a bit of trouble and then when you get home and read the papers, or turn on the TV, you think it's happened somewhere else. The amount of time and effort they put into minor outbursts, the way they exaggerate, makes you think seriously about what's true and what's a lie. The great thing is, though, that it's us lot, the scum, especially the major firms, who understand it better than most. We know the truth because we've been there.

When I was younger I was at games where there was supposedly major aggravation. While we enjoyed it, and it did get out of hand at times, it was generally more show than anything, happening as it did inside grounds. But the way it was painted you'd have thought it was an alien invasion. The truth gets twisted. There's always someone messing things up. Worse that that, your average person likes to believe the lies. Saves them making the effort. People don't think for themselves. That's why politics is such a load of wank. It's all about mindless prats standing in line obeying their masters.

There's this bloke Big Bob West, goes down the Unity regular as clockwork every Friday night, and every Friday night, regular as clockwork, he gets pissed. I'm not talking pissed as in drunk, I'm talking pissed as in out of his fucking tree. Gets as much beer down his throat as he can without puking then hits the double whiskies.

Doesn't get wound up or sad, or anything dramatic like that. Just sits in silence by ten o'clock and you don't know what the fuck he's thinking. Everyone else is generally pissed by that time as well, so to notice him acting unusual means something.

Big Bob served in the war against Iraq and reckons he saw enough sights to make any one of us sick. Says us lot back home know nothing about what went on. That tens of thousands of Iraqi kids got wiped out by the weapons we've been told to respect. It was high-tech warfare and the Iraqi army was useless. Conscript village boys and a few full-time soldiers trying to keep them in line. Says the Allies bulldozed thousands of bodies after the Iraqis abandoned Kuwait. That they slaughtered them as they withdrew. Shot the cunts in the back. Says the yanks called it a turkey shoot. Formed big queues in the sky lining their planes up. Everyone wanted to get in on the kill. Says we'll never know the truth.

First time he started going into one some of the lads in the pub were getting a bit narked. They knew he'd done the business and wasn't one of these pacifists, but still didn't want to hear news like that. I was the same. I mean, Hussein was a cunt doing what he did, even if he got started with British backing, but deep down you want to believe in all that bollocks about strategic weapons and smart bombs and fuck knows what else. It means you can have a couple of cans of lager, sit in front of the box and enjoy the special reports and newsflashes they put on TV. It makes it more like a film than anything else, and even though you're not there and it's got fuck all to do with your own life, you get a bit of a thing going because they convince you it's you and yours involved.

But Bob never bottles out. I look at his eyes when he gets going and they don't shift around like he's trying to impress people. He isn't one of these cunts you see who wants everyone to think they're different, or care about their fellow man, or something special like that bloke I did in Manchester. He talks to himself more than us. Isn't gutted or spaced out. Nothing emotional. He's just realised a few truths. Some of the blokes in the Unity were pushing it a bit first time, and I wondered if Bob was going to go all the way to Kuwait and come back with his health intact, and then end up getting glassed in West London. They were getting the idea he was a traitor or something, but I understood a bit of what he was saying when I got over my first kneejerk reaction. Maybe it was my granddad telling me about being a soldier, but more than that it was going down the football.

I know how the media distorts everything. I've been around when the law's making things heavy. But now it's supposed to have changed, as though you change anything in this world, and that's the ultimate revenge. They've taken away the shine but now we're so far underground they haven't got a chance. They say the harder cases from the Eighties grew up and built new lives selling drugs and running other petty scams. But there's always new talent coming through and a lot of the older chaps are still around anyway. When there's a big match familiar faces come out of the woodwork. Standing in the shadows using their experience, beating the cameras. A big black cross marks the spot. You do your time and who knows, in another five years I might have burnt out and be content to sit back and let the younger blokes have their say. But I'll still be down Stamford Bridge. That won't change.

Norwich hit a beautiful long pass that cuts through the Chelsea defence and the farmers bury the ball in the back of the net. We swear and tell the bastards to fuck off back to their cabbage patch as if they can hear us. Harris sits with Black Paul and Martin Howe shaking his head. Rod shouts abuse, talking about Wellington boots and the art of pig fucking. A copper's looking his way but leaving it alone. We all admire the goal, the forty-yard precision pass and the forward's instant control, then the first-time shot into the roof of the net, but you don't stand up and clap the other side. There's no room for that kind of behaviour. No chinks in the armour. You have to stand firm and dedicated, always loyal. Present the world with a united front.

Sometimes it can mean hiding your feelings, but not that often, and never to any serious degree. True, it's a good goal. Worth seeing. But none of us have any desire to be fair. We get no pleasure from the goal even though we recognise the skill involved. We're Chelsea and that's that. There's no place for indecision or dissent. It's something that doesn't come into the equation and as the Norwich players celebrate we're telling them to get on with the fucking game, illiterate pig-fucking farmers' sons. They can't read and they can't write, but at least they can drive a tractor. We all laugh.

Half-time comes and I go for a piss. There's a queue of blokes pushing their way in, lager held back. Nobody wants to go for a piss during the game and risk missing any of the action. Happens to everyone, of course, that moment when you think it's a safe time with nothing happening on the pitch. Then you get there, whip it out and feel that orgasm of exploding piss, and suddenly there's a roar that sends your bollocks shooting up into your body like some Millwall bastard's foot has just made the fatal connection. Chelsea have scored and you're a cunt missing it, and the pleasure you get from having a postponed piss is ruined and you hurry back with your jeans wet from a serious lack of concentration. When you get back your mates are calming down and having a laugh at your expense because you've missed out. It happens to everyone sooner or later and then you spend the next year holding on for half-time before you dare take another risk. Then it happens again. It's sod's law.

I get a cup of tea and go back to my seat. Mark and Rod are talking to Harris. He's telling them about Liverpool. How they had the coach windows put through by some scouse juveniles. Coach was making its way out of Liverpool and five or six kids came running out of nowhere and lobbed an axe through the window. The glass broke its flight but it still ended up in the side of Billy Bright. We laugh because he's just lost his job and things usually come in threes. What's next? The bloke had better keep his head down for a while.

He lost his right hand in woodwork class as a kid, but tells the lads he had his fist wedged up some black bird and she started contracting on him telling him what a fucking stud he was. Says he started pulling out because she was coming off and he had to remember his fascist principles. Didn't want to give pleasure to the inferior black race. But he pulled out too quick and was a hand short. The story always gets a laugh. Billy never says it when Black Paul or John are around.

Mark decides to have a bit of fun and rub salt in old wounds. He asks me if I remember that time at Norwich. When me and Rod got a pasting. I nod my head and he tells Harris the story. How Norwich sorted us out. Rod's a bit red in the face feeling embarrassed and I hope the blood's not showing itself with me. Mark knows he's winding us up. Harris is laughing out loud and so is Martin Howe behind him. They're laughing because Norwich are nothing. What a place to get a kicking. Insulting more than anything. Done by a bunch of farmers. It's a story that will spread quickly. I feel a bit humiliated. Tell Mark he's a cunt and try to laugh it off. Tell him that at least I was fucking there.

HAPPY EVER AFTER

ALBERT WAS GOING to be late for his appointment. He was due at the social in ten minutes. He had to get to the bus stop, wait for his transport to arrive and make the journey. If things went well he would only be fifteen minutes after the appointed time. He put on his coat and combed his hair in front of the mirror, then scrubbed his teeth and washed his hands. He dried them on a towel. He was ready to leave and checked his watch. Went into the kitchen to make sure everything was turned off. He looked at the taps. Counted them. ONE, TWO. Checked the knobs on the cooker. ONE, TWO. THREE, FOUR. All turned to OFF. He examined the knob for the oven. OFF. The control read HIGH. But that only mattered when the oven was ON. He couldn't smell gas. That was the confirmation for which he was looking.

Albert left the kitchen and put on his jacket. It had been expensive when new and he always made an effort when dealing with authority. It was part of his upbringing, something inherent in his generation. It made him feel clean and gave him added confidence. A person could never have too much confidence. He did up a button and walked into the bathroom. He looked at the taps on the sink. ONE, TWO. Both OFF. He wanted to tighten them but the plumber had already changed the washers because Albert tended to turn them too tight. He looked at the bath, squinting his eyes. ONE, TWO. He waited for the hot tap to leak. A lazy drop of water built up and fell. There was a vague sound.

Albert moved into the room and sat on the edge of the bath. He waited for the next drop of water. It took time to form. He moved closer so he could see the water gather. It swelled, then burst its skin and fell against the white bath tub. He looked at the plug and knew it was out of harm's way. The last thing he wanted was the bath to overflow and flood the flat below. The man who lived there was a nasty bit of work. Albert was too old to fight angry young men. His heart wasn't what it was and the doctor had told him to take things easy. His nerves weren't as strong as they used to be, and his thoughts had started turning inward. Confusion built up and he was a bit worried about the future. He had his faith, though, which pulled him through.

Albert wasn't a rich man and had to get to his appointment, but was worried about the tap. He argued with weakness and felt disgust at his lack of decisiveness. He had to get a grip and take control of his life. If not, he would lose his self respect, and once that went he was doomed. He reasoned with fear and knew that the bath wouldn't flood. The drop of water was too small and the plug far from the hole. He stood up defiant. Buttoned his jacket which had come undone. He held a hand under each of the taps. The taps in the sink left his hand dry. He did the same with the bath. The cold tap was tight and secure. He felt a drip hit his palm under the hot tap. It would be okay. He shouldn't worry. He checked the taps in the kitchen and made sure the cooker was safe. He went down the stairs and closed his front door.

It was a beautiful day. The sky was clear and though it was cold Albert didn't mind. He promised himself he would get out more often. He hadn't left his flat for four days and was missing a burst of crisp, clear weather. The winters were getting harder the older he became. He couldn't afford the heating bills and the doctor had told him to eat a high-protein diet. But protein cost money. He had three hundred pounds in his bank account and it would go towards his funeral. The winter months dragged and Albert was sure the temperature was falling each year. Perhaps another Ice Age was due. He wished he was a young man. He wished he could sit with his brother in the pub and drink and laugh like they did when they were young men. But his brother was dead. Everyone was dead. Albert was alive. He was living and should be making the most of his time. Things could have been worse. And he had that three hundred pounds set aside. They couldn't take it away from him. He would pay for his own funeral.

Albert Moss was no sponger and he didn't expect charity. He had his self respect. He made it to the corner and then stopped by the estate agent's. He felt water drying on his hand. Had the tap been secure when he left? Was the front door shut tight? Would the gas escape and destroy his home? He was late for his interview and needed the extra fiver he was trying to claim for heating, but he had to go back and check. He would hurry. He would walk briskly back to his flat and have one final run through the routine. If he was quick everything would be fine and everyone happy. That was all he wanted.

Michelle Watson was keen and sincere and working for the state. Albert Moss hadn't kept yesterday's appointment and she knew enough about the pensioner that it would be his condition more than anything keeping him away. It had happened before. As a dedicated socialist Michelle was appalled at the way working-class pensioners had been conditioned to regard their financial entitlements as charity. The idea was changing, but it should never have existed in the first place. She would write to him because he didn't have a telephone and line up another date.

At times Michelle despaired of the working-class people with whom she dealt each day, especially the younger elements of the community. They had no idea of directing their anger and aggression in the cause of class solidarity, preferring to drink themselves near to a state of coma and then fight each other over trivialities. There was no logic to this self-destructiveness when the people who crippled their lives with unjust laws and oppressive propaganda were so near in the Houses of Parliament. The young men kicked and stabbed each other at closing time, or in clubs, or when they were cut up at traffic lights, yet they allowed weak, chinless men in suits to rob them blind and tell them who they should hate.

If the joyriders and ecstasy users woke up and looked around they would find better ways of using their energy. Michelle could find no logic in drugging yourself up to the eyeballs and ignoring the realities of life. Everything that happened in society was political. Those football hooligans she'd read about were avoiding the issues, kicking lumps out of each over a sport. It was unbelievable. Sport was the ultimate indignity of a capitalist society, resting as it did on the importance of competition, the wastage of resources, concentrating people's energies away from the class struggle towards silly games. So many of these young men were reactionary right-wing thugs and she could well believe that a good ninety-five per cent were bordering on membership of extremist organisations. She had never been to a football match herself, though she had listened to gutter conversations in her local, but felt qualified enough to comment.

Michelle's great hope, as a radical socialist raised in deepest Hampshire but now living and thriving in London, was the black population. Downtrodden through the centuries they were the ultimate in crushed humanity. With the help of left-wing, educated whites such as herself the blacks would gradually fight their way up the scale, and in the black youth out on the streets there was potential for a political cadre of fit young men ready to overthrow the barriers of white capitalist racist oppression. She listened to gangster rap by the likes of early pioneers such as NWA and Public Enemy, though the violent and sexist lyrics were not exactly conducive to informed political struggle. Even so, they were talking about life on the streets of Los Angeles and New York as it appeared in the flesh and therefore a little slack could be allowed.

She shuffled the papers on her desk and opened the next file. Billy Bright. A deformed neo-Nazi by the look of the man when he responded to the raffle ticket he was holding in his one good hand. He had the short hair and black combat jacket she had seen on TV reports covering fascist activity in Brick Lane, and appearances while generally deceiving could easily be assumed correct in such right-wing instances. She studied his file, making the man wait. This was the kind of thing socialism was up against. He had been made redundant and expected the state to help him out.

Mr Farrell had become a gardener after the war. He loved plants and flowers and had been lucky enough to get in with his local park's commission. The seasons came and went and because he was outside Mr Farrell was able to appreciate the changes. The work kept him healthy and now that he was retired he benefited from a life of moderately superior health. He walked most places to keep the flow of energy circulating through his body and also because he appreciated the ability to move freely in a democratic society. He knocked on the peeling door and waited.

– Hello Albert, Mr Farrell said, when his friend opened up.

Albert Moss stood back and Mr Farrell entered. The flat was spotless and Mr Farrell marvelled at the order and control of Albert's life. He scrubbed the place weekly and kept the fittings and furniture in pristine condition. He walked down the hall to the living room and saw that Albert had everything ready for his arrival. There was a nice pot of tea on the table and the two easy armchairs had been moved from their normal positions so that they were now at an angle to each other.

– Would you like a cup? Albert asked, looking to Mr Farrell for the biscuits he always brought along.

– I'd love one. It's a nice day out, but turning a bit nippy.

The two men sat in the armchairs and blew on the tea to help cool it down. They said little and worked their way through the pack of biscuits. Mr Farrell enjoyed the calm atmosphere and liked Albert's flat.

His friend had gone to the trouble of framing old photographs and positioning them strategically around the room. Most were black and white, which worked well against the white walls, although Mr Farrell wondered what the golden pagoda in Rangoon would have looked like in colour. Albert had taken it during the war while he was serving in Burma and said that the original image was there in his memory and would never be dislodged. There was a colour drawing that stood out, a present from someone at the Spiritualist church he attended. It represented his aura. Mr Farrell didn't understand exactly what it meant, but found it interesting in its way, like a piece of abstract art.

– Are you ready then? Shall we get started?

The curtains were drawn and the two men sat in silence, their eyes closed. Soon Albert would begin talking and Mr Farrell would have some kind of contact with those he loved but who had passed over to the other side. Albert tried to relax his thoughts and let the spirits come to him. Leaking taps were the last thing on his mind.

Number 46 studied the woman interviewer in front of him as she examined his papers. She was a fair looker but he wasn't wanting female company at the moment. He was skint. Made redundant by the captains of industry who spent their time bleating on about national identity and then invested British resources overseas. He felt the hatred deep inside, shoved forcibly down his throat and left to rot and fester in the pit of his stomach. The woman looked like a right Trotskyist with her specs and clear skin, scruffy long hair and roll-up stained fingers; the kind of know-nothing outsider who came onto his manor and practised so-called positive discrimination for every minority that could ever possibly exist. These people talked about the working-class but didn't have a clue what the working-class was all about. Maybe he was wrong, but he doubted it. They all looked the same. Dykes and Marxist theorists with mortgages and framed university degrees next to the futon.

He wasn't saying anything though, because he didn't have a grievance with the woman and he wanted some cash to keep him going till he got a job. The cunts in charge of his firm had shifted their resources around to save a few bob and thirty people had ended up on the dole. Top management within the firm had awarded themselves big increases on the savings made. Fascism was an attractive proposition. Listening to speakers at local, clandestine meetings and their calls for the hanging of child molesters, rapists and the scum in the Tory party made a lot of sense. Blokes with the same attitude went along and the social workers and students with placards shouting Nazi at them from behind police lines just made him more determined. He wasn't into the Combat 18 bit but was gearing up for the push. He was white, Anglo-Saxon, heterosexual and fed up of being told he was shit.

The queers and Jews in the Tory party were shafting more than each other. They were stitching up the white population for the liberal wankers in the BBC and got all the plum jobs in the media. It was a cliché but true that Zionists controlled the media, and there was no need to look further than Washington's manipulation of the British establishment to understand the reasons why. The Klan had been making itself understood in the States and it was time nationalist groups in Britain became better known. It was like any ethnic or religious minority who wanted could walk straight in, get their benefits, shoot to the top of the housing list and the whites were expected to sit back and listen to the left-wing set up shop and slag off the native way of life.

Billy Bright hated the Tories even more than the scum on the Left. The Tories had taken charge of the patriotic stance, waving the Union Jack around while milking the common man as though he was a factory farm animal. He would gladly have seen the cabinet strung up in the street. They were con artists with their plum accents and even though they made subtle noises about race he didn't trust them. Jews in high places were talking double standards. Hitler understood what was what and while he didn't exactly go along with the mass extermination of a race he had to admit that he would probably have stood back just like the majority of Germans had done and said he didn't know what was going on. It was easier to let the subhumans in the East do the dirty work than get their own hands dirty. Sometimes, though, he got so fucking wound up by the whole thing that he could see himself out on the streets shipping the bastards off. He knew the official line, but would have preferred the bankers in the City and all the other public-school wankers to be on the first trains out of Paddington. He would have to change a lot himself, though, if the thing became official, because there would be no more drugs, drink or random violence. He would have to become a new man and hoped his deformity wouldn't count against him when it came to the crunch.

Everyone was as happy as could be expected given the circumstances. Albert Moss died peacefully in his sleep and his body was found four days later when Mr Farrell became concerned by an unanswered knock on the door. Mr Farrell was sad, but knew death came to everyone and that Albert would find things easier in the afterlife he so strongly believed existed. At least he had gone peacefully in his sleep and hadn't been forced to endure years of treatment for a crippling disease. He hadn't died of cancer or spent his last years paralysed after a stroke. He had gone with as much dignity as death allowed and had paid towards his own funeral. Prices had rocketed since Albert last looked into the matter and Mr Farrell was glad the tight-fisted bastards in the council were being forced to contribute.

Albert's neighbour downstairs was happy in his own way

because though he felt a bit sorry for the old boy, who had fought in the war in Burma and along the Malay Peninsular, he wouldn't have to listen to him moving around upstairs any more. It drove him mad at times, furniture being shifted at three in the morning, and whenever he said hello Mr Moss wasn't exactly friendly. He'd heard the old man was into Spiritualism and though he wasn't superstitious and didn't believe in all that ghost stuff, Mr Moss's neighbour didn't fancy his flat ending up haunted by a spirit which came for a chat and fancied staying.

Michelle Watson was happiest because Mr Farrell had discovered the body after four days. She could have found herself in trouble if the corpse had remained undiscovered for months on end and a local journalist had got hold of the story. There had been other well-publicised incidents in the national media and that kind of thing just did not look good whichever way it was explained. While the locals would get much of the blame, the social services would have come under scrutiny and it would have done her career prospects no good at all to be involved in something so messy. She was ambitious and knew she had what it took to make the grade.

NEWCASTLE AWAY

I'M PISSED AND hungry and telling the bird behind the counter to get her finger out. The coach will be leaving soon and we haven't got time to fuck about. The chinky's packed with closing-time pissheads but we're taking priority because it's Friday night and we're on our way to Newcastle. It's a daft time to leave but that's the way it's got to be when Chelsea play away and you're lining up a major beano. Mark's chatting up a couple of birds and he's obviously in with one of them, and her mate's going spare, but we'll just have to do without. A shag's a shag and no bird can compare with a trip to Newcastle. Would we rather take them back and give them a good servicing? Full lubrication job and a tank full of petrol? Wake up with a slab of freshly greased tart on the pillow tomorrow morning? Or open our eyes in Newcastle with the lads looking for geordies?

It's a cold night and these two sleep in beds kept hot with the flow of one-nighters. It's so fucking easy you want to laugh. No need for electric blankets with these two slappers. It's a long trip to Newcastle, uphill all the way. The inevitable hangover and a broken night's sleep. That or a takeaway girl. Number sixty-nine on the menu. No contest. The chink bird hands over a white plastic bag and the smell hits me full frontal. Mushroom noodles and sweet and sour. An away day special. I tell Mark to leave the slags for some other cunt and he smiles when they tell me to fuck off. Turns on his heel.

Rod's outside sitting in a doorway. Been mixing shorts with lager and it knocks him out. He should know better. We've got five minutes to get down Hammersmith roundabout and meet the coach. We start running and I'm huffing and puffing like a fat bastard, the night's lager rumbling inside, but I'm more concerned with spilling the sweet and sour because that's the fucker that always goes over. I get to the roundabout first and the coach is nowhere to be seen. Gary Jones and Neil Kitson sit on railings by the subway. We're in time.

– I'm going to have a fucking heart attack in a minute. Rod's the last one to arrive. I'm fucked.

– It's because you're Chelsea. Mark's quick with the oldest line around. Not used to running. Yids would have set a new world record. Don't know what I'm doing this for when I could be at home tucked up with that bird.

– It's because you're Chelsea. Anyway, it saves you getting a dose. They were well rough those two. Wouldn't have touched them with yours.

– Fucking unbelievable, Mark says. I can hear my heart beating.

– Least you're still alive. I was wondering for a while tonight. Mister fucking interesting sniffing round birds every chance you get.

– Leave it out. We're not at the football yet. It's just something to fill in the time. Let me think straight and get my breath back.

– You want to get on the weights. Do some running.

– Like you? I've really seen you down the gym pumping iron.

– I'm married mate. Nothing's expected once you put that ring on a woman's finger. Get married and it doesn't matter what happens to your body. Mandy loves me for my brain.

– What fucking brain? Only brain you've got is wedged between your legs.

– That's where I get my exercise. Fifteen times a night. Regular as clockwork. I'm a sex machine. Fuelled up on lager and ready to shag her rigid. Fifteen times a night, every fucking night without fail.

– Once a month more like. Once a month with Mandy anyway. You're a pig fucker on the quiet.

– Piss off. Only regular sex you get is off your right hand. And I hear that's getting fussy these days as well.

Ten minutes of Rod versus Mark banter and the coach pulls up. Ron Hawkins the retired skin is at the wheel with Harris sitting at the front, ship's captain, in charge of a select crew. We climb aboard and there's one pick-up left, at Hanger Lane, then we're off to the miserable north. We go to the back. It's a class coach with a toilet and video. Blade Runner's on the screen. I've seen it before but don't mind because it's a smart film. All robots and changing times. Specially the language and new breed of people. Bit like London really. Mutants in the underground. Harris says he's got a pirate Clockwork Orange for later if anyone stays awake past Birmingham.

I sit by the window and share out the food. It tastes good. The Chinese know how to cook. Them and the Indians. Best food you can get. I open a can of lager and watch London pass by. We roll through closed pubs, packed takeaways and pissed couples to the Western Avenue. Then down to Hanger Lane. There's ten or so blokes waiting across from the station outside a parade of shops and Harris has a full coach. Good news for the man's finances, though he always has a decent turnout for the aways because there's enough people around who respect his ability to sniff out trouble. We pile round the North Circular and pick up the M1 heading north. The engine pulls at the gradient. The coach is heated and slick, motor humming with confidence. Ron puts his foot down and Blade Runner replicants stick the boot in. It's man against machine and I want the replicants to batter Harrison Ford to a bloody pulp. Want the cunt to spit out bits of broken teeth. I know the finish but you always hope for something a bit different. Break the routine with a happy ending. Bit of magic.

Rod's head has snapped back and he's deep asleep. Dreaming of Mandy. I nudge Mark and get down on the floor. Tie his laces together. Silly cunt's out of it which serves him right for mixing shorts and lager. Mark hands me a lighter and I set a lace on fire. The flame takes off and in twenty seconds there's smoke spiralling up from his trainers. Still the cunt sleeps. Must be a good dream. Mandy getting her fifteenth portion of the night. Rod'll be so knackered when he finishes he won't be able to play fireman. He's the dummy on the bonfire laughing at death.

– Rod is burning, Rod is burning. Mark to the tune of London's Burning. Call the engine, call the engine.

– FIRE, FIRE. FIRE, FIRE. The back of the coach joins in.

Facelift, a headcase from Hayes or some other West London building site, leans over. Taps Rod on the shoulder. Tells him he's doing a Guy Fawkes. At first Rod doesn't understand. Looks around confused caught with his trousers down, Mandy asking what the fuck he's stopping for halfway. Finally he picks up on the smoke, looks down. Panics. Kicks his feet against the seat in front and he's going to set the whole coach alight if he's not careful. But everyone's laughing, even Facelift, though with him laughter could mean anything.

– You cunts. You trying to kill us all or what? Leave my darling wife a widow with five hungry mouths to feed?

– You haven't got any kids. Mark looks like his head's about to launch into space he's laughing so hard. Fifteen times a night and you can't even get your woman up the duff.

– Least I'm not some bent cunt servicing my hand.

– Could just be a cover. Marry a bird and it throws the rest of us off the scent. Closet bum bandit mate, that's what you are. Fucking iron on board a Chelsea coach. Doesn't look good, does it? That's a hanging offence.

– Piss off to the bog and give the five-fingered widow a portion.

– Fuck off.

Rod's swearing and banging his feet trying to get rid of the flames. They jump a healthy six inches in the air. Red and white whiplash effects. Stronger by the second. But he kills them with a bit of effort and starts having a go at me for some reason. How he knows it was me I don't know.

– Don't just sit there with that stupid grin on your face. Has that cunt sitting next to you been having a go at your arse? Is that what the smile's about?

Eventually Rod sees the funny side and the whole coach is cracking up. Even Harris and Ron the driver who have a stake in making sure we don't end up a burnt-out wreck on the hard shoulder. Just our luck. Coach wrecked before we get to Watford. But Rod's pissed and tired enough not to want revenge which is fine by me because I'm not in the mood myself. He plays the white man, takes stick, and goes back to sleep. I'm knackered and though I'm in the mood to hand it out, I don't fancy taking it as well. There's cans going round and Facelift's into a bottle of quality vodka. Tattoos cover his arms and his gut spills over his jeans. One of the few football stereotypes on board. The rest are nutters, but smartly dressed nutters. Facelift's pissed and moaning about Black Paul and John. Talks under his breath. But they're sound blokes and do the business. He'll learn soon enough when the geordies pile in. Geordies always get stuck in against Chelsea. They're no bottle merchants.

Have to admit I don't like Facelift but wouldn't want to cross the man. He did nine months for glassing his brother-in-law after a row in some snooker club over in Hayes so wouldn't hesitate with a casual acquaintance. Says he just lost it and cut the bloke up. Ran home and the victim's mates were round the house trying to kick the door down when the old bill arrived and nicked him. Said it was the only time he was glad to see the bastards, though he reckons his brother had a shooter stashed upstairs and he'd have used the fucker no problem. You've got to be a bit mental to take life so seriously and Facelift's the kind of bloke who'd do it all again. Prison just makes people like him worse. Makes everyone who goes down bitter and more fucked up than ever. It's not a pretty sight seeing someone's face sliced open, even if they're a cunt and deserve the grief, but you can half understand someone doing it in a blind panic to a stranger. But not your sister's husband. You've got to have standards or you're nothing.

Motorways are all the same by night and you don't get to see the rolling fields of England's green and pleasant land because the dark shuts out the housing estates and dead factories. Cities of the living dead; Derby and Wolverhampton and then up to Leeds and Huddersfield. England's full of shit towns. Places like Barnsley and Sheffield. They can't compare with London. We're out on our own and don't belong with the rest of England. Northerners hate us and we return the compliment. We're just a bunch of flash cockney bastards as far as they're concerned. They think we're all Mike Baldwin wide boys because we treat them like country bumpkins, even though they come from some fucking rough cities. It's two countries in one. Different ways of thinking. Though when you get to a football ground we're all the same really.

Mind you, go see England away and Northerners turn human. A bit like Blade Runner in a way. Android lads from Yorkshire take on new identities when you're in Poland or some other East European slave state. When you're facing a couple of thousand mad Poles aiming to kick you into the next world the sight of a mob of fat geordie bastards steaming in washes away all the problems. It's an odd experience and you have to push yourself at times not to lose the edge. You know you're fighting blokes with the same attitudes but it doesn't stop anything. If you sat down and analysed it you'd end up doing fuck all. You can't apply logic. Just blank the situation and enjoy yourself. Watching England's different and you have to remember your priorities. If you clock a familiar face back in England you're obviously not going to pile in. You'd avoid it somehow, though the situation's unlikely to come about. But no matter what, I'd have a word and save the bloke concerned. If I couldn't I might as well give up. That would be me ground down standing to attention. Sitting on this coach speeding north it doesn't pay to think like this too much. It serves no purpose. You want your fun and that's the end of the matter.

– Arsenal had their moment for a while. Facelift's holding court behind us with Martin Howe and some bloke who used to be in the Marines. Dave Cross I think he's called.

– They were never going to touch Millwall or West Ham, Dave says. Too many fucking niggers.

– They've had black faces in their time.

– Not like fucking Arsenal. It's all the kids from Finsbury Park and Seven Sisters. Paddies don't get much of a look in these days.

Black Paul's down the front of the coach. I can tell he's listening. Him and Facelift don't see eye to eye on a lot of things and it'll come out one day. At least Billy keeps his mouth shut. There's few niggers in this mob but the couple we have are here on merit, plus something extra. It's down to geography more than anything. Black Paul gets up and walks down the coach. Facelift sends him a look that gives nothing away. Their eyes lock on. Nothing's said. Black Paul goes for a piss. Facelift has a swig of vodka and says he's looking forward to doing a few geordie cunts.

I last through Blade Runner but fall asleep before Clockwork Orange gets going. Next thing I know the sun's making me blink. I never remember my dreams which suits me fine, but it makes the night go quick. Seems I've only been asleep a few minutes, but once I straighten my neck I'm feeling good. Rub my eyes and look out the window. Don't know what the time is and fuck knows where we are, but the coach has stopped and there's a green field and blue sky outside. Facelift stands in the middle of the field with his empty vodka bottle at his side, pissing away the dregs. Steam rises from the grass. A fucking slob that man. If he wasn't so hard he'd be an embarrassment.

– Piss stop lads. Harris looks fresh as a daisy, but all the daisies are getting pissed on by Facelift. Time for some fresh air. Last stop before Sunderland.

I get up and go outside. It's a crisp morning and it's a good piss. Maximum relief. Full bladder orgasm. Better than the chemical job on the coach which isn't working properly. I look over the fields and there's birds singing and mist rolling across lush grass. There's hedges and old oaks. There's a couple of houses in the distance surrounded by green trees. There's cows grazing on the side of a hill and when I look up at the sky there's just a dome of brilliant blue with all these weird little clouds floating around. And there's a tattooed Hayes cunt turning back towards the coach. He throws his empty bottle into a bush. There's the smash of glass and a couple of distant cows turn their heads and they're probably thinking the bloke's a right wanker doing that in such a beautiful bit of countryside.

– Could do with a good fry-up lads. Facelift wipes his face with the back of the hand. Set me up for steaming geordies.

Some of the lads standing around pissing in the grass laugh because he's like something out of a newspaper cartoon. Of course he plays along to the crowd at times because we all understand the difference between this bit of England and our own lives. It doesn't have to be spelt out. We stop, have a piss and get back on the coach. We leave our empties behind without a thought. There's no time to muck about with nature and romance. Start thinking like that and you'll be old before your time. Maybe we think we're shit and don't deserve something this good. The coach moves off.

The idea of the early start is to get to a pub in Sunderland where Harris has organised a get-together. The plan is to meet up with various Chelsea firms, have a few sherbets, then catch a train into Newcastle. That way the geordie bastards won't know where we're coming from and the old bill won't be there hanging around playing big brother. The Newcastle boys will be standing about with their noddy kit tops and Newcastle Brown beer guts when suddenly there's a flash of smoke and Chelsea steam in. That's the idea anyway. By the time the old bill get their truncheons out of each others' arses there'll be fuck all left except a few fat geordies to scrape off the pavement. Harris has got the day organised and if he pulls it off there's going to be some bruised heads by three o'clock. The cunts deserve it for all the fucking mouth they carry around with them. If the master plan works it'll be a tasty row.

I'm feeling great and there's not a hangover in sight. The chinky must have soaked up the lager and a few cans of piss water to wash it down beat off dehydration. Rod is awake and moaning about his footwear which doesn't look too damaged from where I'm sitting. Mark's just staring out the window watching the world pass. I feel fresh but wouldn't mind a bath. Don't like to do without. Can't understand those dirty hippy crusty bastards.

– Old bill ahead, lads. Harris calls back. Keep your heads down. Pretend you're asleep or something.

It's a turn-up for the books this one. Eight o'clock Saturday morning and there's a police car with a flashing light ahead and a copper waving us over. Could be chance, but this seems unlikely when a van pulls round the corner. A copper gets on and talks with Ron. He looks back and grins. We sit expressionless, good as gold on our way to church. Maybe we should practise a few carols. Ron switches off the engine and goes to talk with the old bill. Harris sits at the front boiling. I can feel the heat from here.

– That's all we fucking need. Mark's shaking his head. What are we going to do from now till three o'clock? I should have knobbed that bird last night. These bastards will probably send us back to London.

– We've got tickets, says Rod. It might just be a check. How would they know we'd be coming into Sunderland this time of day when Chelsea are playing in Newcastle at three?

It makes you wonder. The old bill must have had advance warning. Makes you think of undercover coppers and ten-year sentences. Things are tight these days and the serious firms have to watch faces and suss people out. You tend to know people over a period of time so anyone turning up on the scene is always treated with suspicion. You have to be careful. If you're not in the club you can fuck off. Ron is arguing with the old bill, raises his arms in the air, then comes back to the coach. He says something to Harris who tells us the bastards aren't letting us into Sunderland. They're taking us to a service station where we can have breakfast, then a pub outside Newcastle where they're holding all the Chelsea coaches till an hour before the game. Word's got out somehow and they're making sure Chelsea don't get loose in Newcastle.

There's nothing we can do and we're just sitting back playing it calm. We don't know if the old bill have got specific information about the meeting, or just know something's been planned. It's a bit worrying. Like you're being watched and your conversations taped. Seems you can't do anything these days without spies recording the event. If it's not a video camera watching you it's some undercover cunt keeping his head down passing on information. It's like being in a South American dictatorship or something.

The police car turns and we follow with the van behind. It's a fucking joke this. Their lights are flashing like we're some kind of virus that can't be allowed too near the locals. We're lepers. They think we're vermin and they can treat us how they want. We pass through green countryside and dead houses, and finally we're entering the services. Haven't got a fucking clue where we are. The day has gone seriously wrong.

– I should have shagged that bird last night, says Mark, who's talking bollocks going on about it because there's no way he'd miss a trip to Newcastle. Instead of some woman giving me a blow job I'm stuck with you lot and a motorway fry-up.

We take over the services and I'm sitting at a table getting stuck into a full English breakfast. It's expensive for what it is but we're no grubby paupers and aren't complaining. We're all making money and it has to go somewhere. There's a few families looking at us a bit nervous but fuck knows what they think we're going to do. True, we've had a couple of good punch-ups at services through the years, but service stations are easy for the old bill to police so you have to be careful. You can end up trapped. Even so, when another team's coach pulls in you have to do the business if they're interested, otherwise you look like a bunch of cunts. The old bill keep a lid on things. They know what they're doing.

We see a coach arrive with a police escort and look to see where it's from. Obviously Chelsea, but we're checking the name to see if it's a load of trainspotters or another firm. Turns out to be a Slough coach. A mixture of older blokes and younger lads. The men are well into their thirties and we know the faces and some of the names. They've been around years those blokes and don't take any lip.

– How's it going lads? Don Wright stands over the table. Must be forty if he's a day. Old bill picked us up like they knew everyone was mobbing up in Sunderland.

– Makes you think who's been tipping them off. Mark flicks beans across the table at Rod. It's going to be a long wait till three o'clock.

– All gone a bit wrong somehow. Don goes off to get his breakfast, eyes glazed.

– That bloke's a fucking schizo, says Rod. Used to work in a morgue, or so they say. You look at his eyes. Looks like he's pissed or stoned, but he's not all there. You've got to be off your head to work in a morgue with all those dead bodies.

– I heard he was a brickie. Mark leaves the beans alone. Even Don Wright wouldn't work in a morgue. You've got to be sick to get into that kind of life.

– I saw him jumping on some Leeds cunt's head one year. The bloke's out cold and he's using the man's bonce as a trampoline. Real brain-damage job. I don't mind giving someone a pasting, but trying to crack their head in two like a coconut is out of order.

I try to think what it would be like working in a morgue. They drain the bodies of blood and you'd see all kinds of mutilation from road accidents and that. You'd start dreaming of corpses and it would do your head in. Suppose you wouldn't think anything about jumping up and down on someone's head if you saw bodies being sliced up every time you went into work. Only thing I can think of worse than that would be working in a slaughter house. Least you're not killing them in a morgue. I watch Don Wright at the counter inspecting the menu and wonder.

Two hours later and we're bored to tears hanging around. Another couple of coaches have pulled in and the old bill are ready to take us to the pub they've been talking about. We get back on the coach and there's a delay as an argument gets going between the old bill and the driver of the Slough coach. Apparently a load of them have phoned for cabs and pissed off. The old bill are well narked. They want to know where everyone's meeting up but nobody says a word. They're pissing in the wind. Not sure of the facts.

We're up and running and kicking ourselves for not having the idea ourselves. Mind you, it would look a bit obvious the whole fucking services emptying and a convoy of cabs shooting off to Sunderland. We sit back and have to admire the nerve of the blokes. Fuck knows what they're going to get up to this afternoon. We arrive at a big pub set back from the road and within a couple of hours the place is packed with Chelsea. Everyone's getting pissed and the walls are vibrating. We have a few sherbets and watch the old bill outside in the car park with their vans and dogs. It's getting like an open nick in this country. Whatever happened to freedom of movement and choice? It's always been like this I suppose, but it pisses you off at times. About two o'clock they clear the pub and we're in a line of coaches with flashing lights around us heading into Newcastle.

Mobs of locals hang around giving us the wanker sign as we enter the city and approach St James Park. The coaches park up and we're on Newcastle's manor. There's a bit of geordie singing down the street, but no attempt to have a go at us. We're into the ground without aggravation and the Newcastle support is into Away The Lads. Don Wright and the others are already inside and the man's got a black eye and skinned knuckles. He's laughing and telling us we missed a treat. He's well pleased. Says they made it to the pub and a two-hundred strong firm got into Newcastle without an escort and turned over a pub in the city centre. The geordies were surprised, but got themselves together and put up a show. Says it was well worth the cab fair. That a bit of travel's good for the soul.

RUNNING THE BULLS

THE SUNSET DAZZLED as it creaked through trees and rock, a stunning orange Vince Matthews had never seen in London, though it could have been that he had never really looked. Whatever the truth, the sun was burning a path through the Basque country, and the hot sweaty trip up from Madrid was nearly over. Another half hour and they would be in San Sebastian and could enjoy a few days in the quiet of a friendly town away from the fumes and aggravation of Madrid, the capital's police and right-wing thugs out to batter the famous English hooligans attending the 1982 World Cup finals.

There were six of them in the compartment. Four Southampton lads and Vince's mate John. They were exhausted. The cheap beer they'd brought aboard was long gone and dehydration was taking hold. Only Vince was making the effort, watching the sleepy hills and scattered peasant homes drift away, the steady motion of the train a perfect complement for the country smells and waving children. It was a great trip and he was taking it all in because he would be back home soon enough. Back in London with its tower blocks and dead ends. True, London was better than Madrid, a nightmare city, but the Basque country was in a different league.

Madrid had been an experience, Vince had to admit that much, but it was too heavy by the end. Especially after the Spain match when they'd come out of the Bernabeu and the locals were lining up for the kill, pulling knives from glossy satin shirts. The English piled in and the Spanish scattered. Then the police arrived with their truncheons raised and set about cracking every English head in sight. There were hundreds of them tooled-up like they were extras in a sci-fi film, each man pushing for a starring role. They battered the English for the Falklands, showing the papers that the hooligan legend would crumble under the majesty of Spanish civilisation. Vince and a couple of others, isolated, worked their way around the ground, separated from the English mob which stuck together for protection as much as anything. There were kicks and punches from the Spanish, but they survived without a knife in the ribs.

Vince had a lot of sympathy for the Basque cause. They didn't want anything to do with the Government in Madrid. They were fighting for independence and Vince had learnt from his stay in Bilbao during the World Cup's first round that this was a different set of people, like the Scots, Welsh and Irish in Britain. The Basques treated the English as though they were people and not tabloid thugs, during the first round games, before England moved to the capital. Getting drunk and playing football on the beach was a great way to spend ten days. Vince had blacked out before leaving for Madrid. A local paid the fare and put Vince's wallet back in his pocket after taking the necessary amount. He woke up in Madrid, his only problem a hangover and some lost mates. Now they were heading north again, escaping the dust and hate of the capital.

While in Madrid, they stayed in a pension in the red light district, which was run by six identical women in their sixties. They were darlings really, with their grey hair tied back tight and always dressed in black. It was just how Vince imagined Spanish women. Either that or the younger Mexican bandit whore in a Tijuana-type border town, with her tits on the counter and hair soaked in cooking oil. Films and newspapers always had the same angle on foreigners. They didn't stretch the images, which was no surprise. The way the media represented the people who followed football was a mirror of their wider approach.

Vince was on a roll. He'd looked forward to the World Cup and saved for two years. It had been an eye-opener and he'd met some great characters. A lot of blokes travelled on their own, and everyone had a few drinks and stuck together. Some of the lads reckoned it was like the war, the spirit of the Blitz and all that, but Vince thought it was better. It was England away and the lads from Scarborough, Exeter, Carlisle, anywhere you wanted to mention, all had something to offer now they were outside the local scene. Club rivalries were for the most part forgotten. He wasn't saying the English were perfect all the time, and there had been a few people out to hurt as many Spanish youths as possible, but there was always a small number of headcases wherever you went. It was better than a war. There was no killing for a start.

He watched the villages pass and tried to imagine himself living in the mountains. There was so much scent in the air and the sun was warm and kept the forests full of light. It was a glimpse of a totally different kind of life and he had the bug. He'd get home, save for a few years, really make the effort and cut back on unnecessary expenses, and then he was off. Everywhere he thought about sounded good.

When he had the money he was going to India. In a few years' time. That was the place Vince wanted to see most of all. First he would go walking in Nepal. It was full of travellers, or so they said, but the Himalayas were the biggest mountains in the world, and even if Kathmandu was a bit commercial, what could they do to the likes of Mount Everest? He would acclimatise and get a bus to India, then he was going to Australia to work. It would be a culture shock, of course it would. Vince was no fool, but Spain was his first time out of England and it was excellent. He felt no pressure. Like the peasant's yoke you saw in school books had been chopped up and thrown away. The trains through France and into Spain, Bilbao, Madrid with all its aggravation, and now this journey to San Sebastian.

He was going to have a different kind of life. Friends and family would still be there when he got back. A year away, maybe two, three, four, five. His mates would be in the same pubs, pulling the same women, talking about the same things, and this gave Vince added courage because he didn't want to go away for ever. He wanted to see the world and come back to England and find everything the same. He didn't want great changes. Things could be better, they could always be better, but he wasn't one of those people who held a grudge.

The train was struggling to make it up a hill. The mechanism groaned and Vince listened for voices, the grumbling of an old man embedded in the system, a story from when he was a kid. He heard nothing. The other lads were sleeping and he was glad he hadn't gone full throttle with the drink. He left the compartment and stood in the corridor, window down, hanging his face through the gap. The air was warm but fresh. He breathed deeply and saw himself on one of those travel programmes, rambling on about paradise. Then the train was approaching San Sebastian, countryside giving way to the town, and Vince was back in the compartment telling the others they were a bunch of lazy bastards and it was time to get their gear together.

It took time to find a pension, a nice effort near the sea with blooming flowers in the garden and clean rooms, the only problem was that they were a bed short till the next day. The woman was middle-aged and efficient, wore a white cotton dress and didn't flinch when she saw the six English boys enter. That was nice. They looked rough in gentle San Sebastian, a mixture of beer guts, tattoos and dirty ripped jeans. One of the Southampton boys, Gary, carried a suitcase tied together with a length of rope. They were a mess, barbarians from the industrial slums of the freezing north. Vince laughed at the description. But that was what three weeks on the piss, staying in cheap pensions with cold showers and limited washing facilities and a long, slow train trip did for a bloke. The woman didn't care. Vince wondered if maybe she didn't even notice, but then she told them to give her their washing and she would have it cleaned. That they should have a hot shower.

When it came to a decision, Vince opted to find somewhere else to stay that night. He left and arranged to meet the rest of the lads in a nearby bar. He couldn't be bothered finding a pension and, anyway, he needed to save money. He was near enough skint and a night on the beach would do him no harm. The fresh air was still a novelty after the clinging, polluted atmosphere of Madrid. It was a warm evening and he went down to the sea. He crossed the sand and took his shoes and socks off, then followed the golden curve. There were a lot of people walking, mostly families and couples holding hands, stretching their legs before an evening meal. Vince was hungry. He didn't care if he was out of place and had none of the expensive gear worn by the Spanish. Fair enough. No complaints. England was all about poverty, and he was very definitely English.

He chose a place to sit at the far end of the sand and watched the sea gently sway back and forward. Most of those on the beach obviously had money, and he tried to distinguish the holiday-makers from the locals. This wasn't difficult, but he didn't feel the same anger he had for the rich bastards at home. He couldn't understand the language for a start, so couldn't make out the different accents. Most of all, he wasn't that bothered. He was on his own and had shed the responsibilities stacked on his back in London, where the class system was becoming so confused and distorted it took a full-time academic to break it into accurate categories. It was something Vince had never taken time over. He had an Englishman's distrust of politics and intellectualism, yet his life and behaviour was ground in a hatred of wealth and privilege. Outside England, he was able to relax. The normal rules and regulations no longer applied. He wished he didn't have to return home yet, but money was the big decider. Still, at least he had a plan. He had an escape route worked out. Like in the Second World War films. Except the POWs were heading in the opposite direction.

Vince sat on the beach for a long time before giving up his daydreams and heading for the bar. On the way he saw a place to sleep, under the promenade, tucked out of sight. Lovers sat on the wood, while a group of people had started a fire on the sand and were cooking fish. The darkness covered his wrecked appearance and it wasn't till he was back on the road, with the lights shining, that he felt like an outsider again. It was nowhere near as bad as Madrid, but that had been something new, going into an angry city where the looks told him he was inferior. It was the first time he had been on the receiving end of racism, and the old men in the square where the English went to drink had been one hundred per cent fascists, supporters of Franco who saluted Hitler at the England versus Germany game when the national anthem was played. It was odd, conjuring up old grainy film of Nuremberg, and made the mocking, cartoon salutes of the English pointless.

He would have to get used to the feeling, because he was going to see the world one day, and if things went really well who knows, maybe he would never go back to England. The thought made him jolt, though it was all in the future. He was hungry but had to save money, have a couple of drinks and get a decent night's sleep. It would be good in its own way, sleeping on the beach alone in a foreign land. Now he fancied an ice-cold drink. He entered the bar.

– Alright Vince? We thought you'd forgotten about us. John was propped against the bar looking scrubbed and polished, even if the clothes he was wearing were creased and unwashed. Tomorrow he would look the part. Or so he hoped.

– Did you find a place to stay? Gary was in a round with the other Southampton boys, and he ordered a bottle of piss water for Vince, who gave him the money. They were sticking in small rounds because none of them had much cash. Buying your own drinks was unheard of at home, but these were difficult times. Vince told them he was sleeping out.

– I didn't think of the beach, John said. It's a good idea. You'll save a bit. But the shower was fucking heaven and there was hot water. Haven't felt that for three weeks. You wait till tomorrow.

– Decent bogs as well, you can have a nice sit down without some bender peeping through holes drilled in the walls.

– You remember when Sean was sitting there reading that dirty mag he got off that old boy in the square? He's sitting there having a wank and then he looks up and someone is watching him perform.

Sean looked embarrassed by John's story. He sat on a stool with the other Southampton lads Gavin, Tony and Gary. He was always calling John a chirpy cockney, and the Londoner was doing his best to live up to the pisstake. They'd known each other since their arrival in Madrid on the same train. The others just laughed.

– He comes running out with his jeans round his ankles with a hard-on and the watching eye has legged it, but one of the old dears is passing and she stops and just stands there staring at him. He turns and runs back in the bog with his arse hanging out.

– Those old girls were alright, said Vince. Nice ladies. What a place to live, though. Smack in the middle of the red light. They weren't bothered by it much, were they, and they were off to church every evening as well. The Spanish are a bit funny like that. They have Franco in charge all those years, and their coppers are nutters who must've been trained up by the Gestapo, and the Government's worse than Parliament, and then they all march off to church together.

– It's like the Mafia films, said Gary. You look at a film like The Godfather and they're cutting bits off each other and shooting people for fun, and then they're there in front of the old cross giving it a load of chat, asking God for forgiveness.

Vince drank from the bottle of lager. It was freezing cold. He was used to the taste of Spanish beer now, but couldn't say it was that good. He tried not to moan too much, because all the other lads were always going on about drinking piss water, but he told them he'd never drunk piss before so didn't know what it was like. It got a laugh.

– It makes you think about the old Catholics, doesn't it, he said. You look at it, and what countries were fascist before and during the last war? Italy had Mussolini and Spain had Franco. Germany ran the show with Adolf and he got a lot of his support from the Catholics in the south, in Bavaria and thereabouts, while the Croats and Ukranians both joined up. The French split in half and shipped their Jews off to Germany, while the Poles didn't exactly love them and if they got out of the Warsaw ghetto they had the Polish partisans to face. Then you've got Latin America and all the dictatorships. They're all at it, aren't they?

– How do you know so much? asked Sean.

– I read the occasional book. Watch documentaries on the telly and things like that.

– What about the Irish then? They weren't a fascist country, were they? My mum and dad are from Ireland. They would've told me if Hitler had been in the running over there.

– The Irish are different.

– How's that then?

– They're Gaelic. They only became Catholic because the Scots that the English brought into Ulster were Protestant. They just went for the opposite. That's what it was like then. And anyway, the Irish aren't exactly the most open-minded people in the world, and they didn't back up England in the Second World War either.

– Why the fuck should they back them up? What did the English ever do for the Irish?

– We gave them Oliver Cromwell, said John, laughing, trying to calm things down.

– Yeah, right. Oliver Cromwell. Murdering bastard.

– I'm not having a go at the Irish, said Vince. I was just saying it's a bit odd how the Catholics seem to go towards right-wing leaders. I'm not saying whether it's good or bad or whatever, I'm just saying it's a bit of a coincidence.

– It's because the Jews killed Christ, said Gavin. Yiddo bastards killed the Saviour. That's why they all hate the Jews. You look at the Catholics and they're fanatics, aren't they? You saw how they were in Madrid. It's buried in their heads. They don't know why it is, but they have to obey the leader. They obey God or Franco or Hitler or Mussolini or who fucking knows who. It doesn't matter. It's built in. Comes with the religion.

– The Irish aren't like that, said Sean.

– They're different. An island race. A different tribe. Gaelic like Vince said.

– Why does everyone hate Spurs then? asked John. They're the yids and every club hates those bastards.

– That's because they're flash, Vince answered, laughing now. It's there, but not the same. There's no religious mania in England, just a few vicars man-handling their flocks. A few old spinsters in the shires wishing they could get a length off the farm hand, but knowing they can't and pointing to the Bible and saying if they can't get a good poke then why should anyone else?

They were all laughing now. It was an interesting point, though. Vince had never thought it all the way through before. He would have to give it some more consideration in a quiet moment. He finished his drink and got a round for John and himself. A couple more bottles and he would piss off for the night. He was looking forward to a hot shower tomorrow, but had to make the best of tonight first. There were some nice birds in the bar, though he could tell they were well off and the English boys were a bit cut off from the rest of the people there. It was mostly men and women in their early twenties. The majority were dressed in white and had scooters parked outside. He paid the barman and took the bottles.

– That bar was great in Madrid, wasn't it? he said, when he turned back to the others. Poor old Lurch didn't know what was going on half the time. Poor bastard just stood there trying to keep tabs on what we were eating and he had no chance.

– It was a lot cheaper than here, Gary said, looking at his beer. And there was all that food up for grabs.

The Madrid bar had been near the pension where they stayed.

It was the first one they went to in the evening and the last after they'd been for a wander. They generally polished off the evenings with a couple of hours drinking the dirt cheap wine and beer Lurch served. The counters were covered with big trays of food, everything from battered fish and chicken wings to paella and bread. It was greasy, working man's food, and the idea was that customers helped themselves and paid their bill at the end of the evening. The English, as was the custom when following England away, just jumped in and helped themselves, then denied any knowledge when it was time to pay. They figured that the Spanish treated them like dirt, as though they were the scum of the earth, so they went for the herd approach and reasoned that if they weren't seen as individuals then the locals wouldn't be able to tell them apart.

Lurch ran the bar until one in the morning and then he was off, an older, fatter man, who owned the place, arriving to take over. Lurch was alright, and got his name from the typical horror film butler, tall and leaning forward, never showing much emotion. Occasionally he would smile as the England boys went about their business, and though there were no big conversations between the two sides, they always paid for their drinks and he rarely lost his temper. Maybe he decided that it wasn't his bar, Vince never worked it out. It was a strange situation because they were back there night after night, thirty or forty pissed-up English lads in shorts and T-shirts, singing songs about the Falklands and chatting with the prostitutes out on the pavement.

– Remember when we were coming back from that shitty disco and those street cleaners came along and hosed us down? We were pissed up on cooking wine and they soaked us and then just drove off.

When they left the bar, Vince turned towards the beach while the others made a big fuss about the crisp white sheets waiting at the pension. Vince could handle the pisstake though and walked through the near empty streets to the spot he had lined up for the night. A breeze had picked up and he took his jacket from the bag he'd brought to Spain. It wouldn't give much protection if the wind really got going, but he would survive. He got on all fours and crawled under the promenade, smoothed the sand and put the bag under his head. He raised his legs up into the foetal position.

The drink would help him get to sleep. It had been a good idea. Mind you, he was hungry, fucking starving if he was honest, but there was no chance of any food now. He wished Lurch was running a bar in San Sebastian.

Vince was soon drifting away, shifting his position in the sand, which wasn't as comfortable as he had imagined. It was a different texture to the actual beach. This was a mixture, with heavier earth and stone from the promenade's foundations. The sea was faint at first and he enjoyed the idea of water moving up and down the shore, the steady rhythm which would rock him to sleep. This was what living was all about. He was seeing a bit of the world. The sea would eventually become faint and then disappear, but it wasn't working out that way, and after half an hour the noise was deafening, a dose of Chinese water torture which wouldn't let him sleep. The wind was getting stronger and he was cold. His mind raced. Thinking of Madrid.

There had been a bad atmosphere in the city. That night they were in the square drinking at three in the morning, going from bar to bar, thirty or so English singing songs about the Falklands, using the term Malvinas so the Spaniards would understand. Three English lads had been beaten up pretty badly by a gang of fascist blue shirts armed with iron bars while asleep in the park. Then a Derby fan was surrounded by a big mob of the bastards and stabbed through the heart outside the Bernabeu. They were scum. Knife merchants the lot of them. He hated people who used knives. Some of the English started arming themselves for their own defence. Then a mob of Spanish came to the square where they were drinking and piled in. The English ran them all over the shop. A bunch of shitters. That's why the Spanish used knives and needed numbers of twenty or thirty to one. The Derby lad was lucky to survive.

That night they got back to the square at two in the morning and for once weren't going to end up in Lurch's bar. They were sitting at tables when the waiters started pulling out guns. They all had pistols and suddenly the square was full of police carrying machine guns. The English were lined up against a wall and the old bill went along searching everyone. Two men stood behind the person they were searching. Vince felt a muzzle in the base of his back. Hands worked up and down his body looking for something. He wondered if it was drugs. If they were going to plant something nasty on a select few and bang them away for ten years. Then they were surrounding the three German skinheads knocking about with the English. The police were screaming at the Germans and one of the bastards was cracking Jurgen, the leader, in the jaw with the butt of his gun.

Vince remembered the Germans had a pistol and gas cartridges. They were going to let them off in the subway after the Spain-Germany game. He figured it out. Someone had reported seeing a gun and the police had gone into action. They must have been watching all the time and had lined it up. The Germans were getting a battering while the rest of the police kept the English faces to the wall. It was a flies round shit job. Then the skinheads were bundled into a van which skidded off with lights flashing and sirens cranked up doing their best to wake the locals. Coppers loved making a drama out of nothing. It was the same all over the world.

It was only a flare gun or something similar, and the gas would have got a few people coughing but wasn't going to cause mass death. The Germans were daft flashing it around. They had all the skinhead gear, bought in The Last Resort shop in Petticoat Lane, and the first time the three had come into the square Jurgen stopped, pointed to his DMs, and called them nigger kickers. They had the clothes while the English were more of a scruffy casual crew, and this was a time of skinhead revival in London and English club sides in charge of European competitions. He wondered if the Germans would get a sentence or be on the first plane back to Düsseldorf.

The sea was driving Vince round the bend. He wondered what the time was but didn't have a watch. He'd sold it in Madrid for a giveaway price, needing the cash. Some of the lads went to the embassy and pleaded poverty for a ticket home, but Vince was making his time last and wanted a few days away from the football. Scousers were best at getting a long way on zero resources. The Liverpool fans especially, who had been following their club around Europe for a number of years, had it down to a very fine art. They paid for near enough nothing, with stories of blokes travelling under the carriages of trains, and they robbed any shop going. It was established that when Liverpool played in Europe the scousers would hit the clothes shops first and then the jewellers. The Swiss and all those rich, decent-minded countries didn't understand this mentality. They had polished streets and intense discipline while the young men arriving from the English estates were robbers and villains on an early Eighties free for all.

The scousers were leading the trends in football when it came to gear, and they nicked all the expensive sports stuff, wearing some and flogging the rest. They made a decent amount from their raids on jewellers' shops. Get a riot going and the scousers would loot the jewellers and stash the stuff in railway station lockers. They'd return to England for a few weeks and then go back to the Continent and bring the valuables home, where they'd make enough to keep themselves going for a couple of months. The Manchester lads were next in line, and had started boasting that they were better robbers than the scousers.

Vince wasn't a good robber. He could nick a bit of gear, but wasn't dedicated. It was more when he was a kid and it was something to do because it impressed. But he wasn't bothered about England games now, he'd had enough and just wanted to sleep. It wouldn't come. The hours passed and he was floating when the smash of glass woke him with a bang, and he was under the promenade as a group of drunks threw bottles against a wall. He had the image of himself in a hole, like a mole or frightened rabbit, but it was just annoying. They banged their feet on the wood and eventually were gone, shouting into the darkness at nothing in particular. He tried to sleep but couldn't. The dark began fading and the sun was just below the horizon. He knew it was going to be a beautiful sunrise, but didn't care.

A tramp crawled under the promenade early in the morning with the sun starting to rise. He was drunk and surprised to find anyone, let alone a famous English hooligan, asleep in a pot hole under the promenade, there in San Sebastian. He blinked and thought he was hallucinating. Too long sleeping rough. Too much cheap drink. Then he accepted Vince was real and tried to teach him the essentials of the Spanish language. A half hour of this and Vince had to leave. He didn't want to move but his head was banging. He was hungry. And tired.

He walked along the beach and laid out on the sand. This was better. It was much more comfortable and soon fitted the shape of his body. The sun was warming things up quickly and then he was dozing. Later he took off his top and replaced jeans with shorts. He fell asleep. A deep sleep. And when he woke it was with a shock, his head buzzing. People were talking. He opened his eyes and looked around. The beach was full. He looked to his right and two topless teenage girls were eating ice creams. He looked to his left and a body-building Spaniard passed by with some kind of G-string half covering his vitals. Everyone was tanned and saw themselves as beautiful. Vince moved and felt the pain. He looked at his chest and legs. He was red. It hurt. He had fallen asleep and not felt the sunburn. He pulled his shirt on and walked up to the road. It hurt more when he moved. He asked a woman the time and it was eleven. It was painful but it could have been a lot worse. He could have slept till three.

The rest of the lads were sitting outside a café sipping coffee. They looked refreshed. They were wearing familiar, shabby clothes, but it was great what a bit of soap and effort could do. He went straight to the pension and the woman started making a fuss when she saw his burns. She took him to the room he would be sharing with John and gave him some cream. He eased back on the bed and looked towards the open window. Everything smelt so good. There was the same scent in the air he noticed coming up on the train. He wondered what plant or flower it was. He closed his eyes and went to sleep.

– You alright Vince? John was sitting at the end of his bed.

– What time is it?

– Nearly two o'clock. The others are down on the beach.

– I just lay down for a minute and I was out.

– You should see some of the crumpet down there. All a bit young, but they don't mind stripping off. Very nice. The others have got their Union Jack out and put it on the sand. They've dug a trench around themselves and built a castle. The kids love it. They're heroes.

– More like freaks.

– We're a bit different. It's the sense of humour. There's no aggro in this town. Even the body-builders in their plaster-on suntans are laughing.

– England on tour.

– You coming down? The woman who runs the place says we

can have a special rate if we stay three days longer. What do you think? It's a rest after Madrid. I'm in no hurry to get back to England. My job's gone anyway so I might as well get the most out of it now.

– I haven't got much money left. I'm skint.

– Me neither. But I thought we could bunk the train back to England. Enough people seem to be doing it.

– Could do I suppose. We could use the money now and worry about the ride home when the time comes.

– Have a think. I'll be down the beach. Turn left out of here and we're straight ahead. You can't miss us. We're the white-skinned bastards with club crests on our arms sitting on a Union Jack.

When John had left, Vince went for a wash. The sunburn didn't seem as bad as he'd feared. There was a bath and he filled it up with warm water. He sat in it for half an hour. There was nothing like it in the world. He thought of the tramp and wondered when he'd last enjoyed something so good. Poor old sod. He dried off and put on some cream. His clothes were still dirty, but it was hot so a T-shirt and shorts would do. He washed his gear in the sink and hung it out on the balcony. Then he went to find the others on the beach. It wasn't difficult. Just as John had said.

– Alright Vince?

– You fancy a drink? I'm not sitting in the sun right now. I don't want to die on the first day.

Gary and Sean followed Vince to a bar along the seafront. They ordered beer. Piss water. But it was cold piss water. They sat in the shade and Vince watched the waiter and thought of the undercover police in Madrid. It must have been a bit mental for the blokes working there full-time when the old bill arrived and told them they were taking over. They even had striped shirts on, or so he thought. He was pissed at the time but was sure they were dressed like the bicycle-riding, onions-round-the-neck caricatures that screamed out from every tabloid whenever there was a cross-Channel disagreement. There were probably enough police on the lookout around San Sebastian. The Basque separatists didn't sit about waiting for the Government in Madrid to get generous. They planted bombs just like the IRA. Except Vince understood the Basques much easier than the IRA, even though he didn't know anything about the history of the conflict. The IRA were too close to home.

– Dear oh dear, look at the tits on that, said Gary.

– Not bad. You should watch what you say, though. Walls have ears and so do women in shorts.

Gary laughed and looked away. They'd been sitting in the square in Madrid in the afternoon watching the time pass, waiting for the England-Germany game the next day. A nice looking woman in tight black shorts passed their table. The shorts ran up the crack of her arse. She was dark skinned with blonde hair over the collar of a short-sleeved shirt. She was a cracker and Gary, sipping his lager, casually asked if she took it up the bum. The other lads at the table laughed. The woman turned round and came up to them.

– What did you say, you filthy bastard?

The accent was educated and English. A school teacher working for the British Council maybe. Gary squirmed in his seat. His face went red. Like Vince's sunburn.

– Who do you think you are, talking to a woman like that? You bloody animal.

The woman lifted a jug of sangria from the table and tipped the contents over Gary's shirt. Then she stormed off. Total humiliation. The three of them laughed remembering her lesson in good manners.

– That was a nightmare. Why did it have to happen to me? I didn't know she was going to be English and understand. None of the people in Madrid speak a word of English and you can say whatever you want and they just scowl at you. Trust me to choose her. Nice arse though. Has to be said.

They passed the afternoon in the café and Vince filled up on a couple of long bread rolls stuffed with cheese and salad. He was going to stay the extra days and bunk the train back. It was a good idea. The fare saved meant he could enjoy himself. When he returned to the hotel John was just getting back. A couple of blokes he recognised from Madrid were standing outside the pension. John had had a run in with them the week before.

– What are you two doing here?

– We're looking at the accommodation. You staying here? What's it like? Looks like a free bed to me.

– It's an alright place. Nice woman runs it.

– Likes her sex does she?

– If you fancy fifty-year-old women she's okay. Old enough to be your granny I expect.

– I don't mind. I'll fuck anything.

John moved towards the kid doing the talking and leaned into his face. They were a few years younger. Skinny runts. The silent youth moved forward looking to have a go and then saw Vince approaching.

– Listen to me you cunt. You can fuck off somewhere else. You're not staying here. You try it and you're in the fucking hospital. We've got a nice little place. No problems. No aggravation. The woman's alright. She's not some rip-off merchant. You fuck it up for us, you'll have your mate's trainers sticking out of your arse with your mate still inside them.

They moved away. They weren't going to risk a kicking. They'd been round Europe on the blag and would probably be going home with a profit out of nothing. Vince had even seen them ponce a couple of drinks from a Scrooge of a barman in a bar outside the Bernabeu. Wankers were nowhere to be seen when the trouble started though. Spics with English passports those two.

– See you later boys.

Vince had a sleep till nine, then the Southampton lads were knocking on the door and he was washing his face, lining up a few beers and some food. He wasn't out to get pissed like back home. It was a different approach in Europe. Better licensing laws for a start and there wasn't that need to get down the pub in the evening and shove as much beer down his throat as possible before the barman did his town crier impersonation and started ringing last orders. True, you could go on somewhere, but most clubs were interested in fashion victims and silly little disco girls. A bunch of lads on the piss meant trouble and they were generally left out in the cold to fight and break a few windows. In Europe you could take your time.

They were soon in another bar on the seafront, the best place they'd been so far, with a mixture of locals and pretty young Spanish holiday-makers. They got the usual looks and the clothes horses kept their distance. Vince didn't care. He wasn't looking to get his end away. Certainly not here with one of these pin-ups.

What was the point trying? They were like the clones who entered Miss World competitions. Perfect tans, capped teeth and no personalities. Still, at least these kids were one up on the Miss World girls. The lager was good in the bar. It was on tap and hit the spot. They were soon getting pissed. A Man United fan they'd met in Madrid saw them through the window and came in. He was a big, friendly bloke. Hands twice the size of Vince's and a gentle way of talking. But he was well into a bit of aggro after a few drinks. If the situation was right. He hated scousers. Vince was starting to feel a bit sorry for the old scousers. It seemed like the whole world was against them.

– Me and my mate were coming back from Liverpool last year, and the scousers had been singing about Munich during the game, and the two sides just fucking hate each other. You know what scousers are like. Anyway, we're coming onto the motorway and there's this bloke hitching. We thought he was a Manc so we stopped to give him a lift and he gets in the back and he's only a fucking scouser.

– He doesn't realise and starts going on about how he was with this other lot who gave these Man United boys a kicking. Really going on about it, laughing and boasting, but he's wedged in the back and I haven't said a word yet so he hasn't heard my accent, and he's saying they really hurt them badly, no ordinary kicking. I let him go on and I looked at him and told him I was Man United. His face froze. I battered fuck out of the cunt and we pulled up on the hard shoulder and I threw him out. We started driving away and his leg was stuck in the door, caught up in the seat belt, and he was bouncing along the hard shoulder for twenty yards or so. The wanker got what he deserved. He shouldn't go around beating up Man United fans, should he?

– You know what it is tomorrow? Sean looked round, waiting for an answer. Nobody spoke.

– I heard it from this Spanish bloke selling ice creams and souvenirs in a jockstrap. It's the running of the bulls in Pamplona. He said it's not that far away. You can easily do it on the train. We should go down and have a go.

Vince felt the strength of the drink inside him. The others were well on their way already, the effects of the sun and lazing around. They started making plans. It would be something different. They all felt confident. People got killed running the bulls and bull fighting was a crime the English couldn't handle, but they were convincing themselves Pamplona was okay. It wasn't like the bull in the ring, where the creature was castrated and mutilated and had spears stuck in his shoulders, just so some flash poof in a cape could ponce himself up and torment the poor animal.

They decided they'd leave early next morning. Talking about bull fighting had raised a few doubts, but it would be okay. It was a bit of a laugh. A couple more beers and they'd be fine. A mob of bulls didn't hold much threat with a belly full of lager. They were more like friendly English dairy cows than rampaging killers. It was the chance for the bulls to get their own back. It was survival time. They would have to be able to shift though. True, none of the English lads were particularly fit, and they would be going into the thing blind, but who cared anyway? None of them after a few drinks.

– It goes a bit against the grain, though, doesn't it? Vince said when they were about to go back to the pension. They were drunk and had to get up early next morning to find a train for Pamplona.

– I mean, it's not like the English to run, is it?

The others laughed. It was a good line, used by everyone at some time or other. They went back to the pension and told Man U they'd meet him and his mates the next day. Back in his room, Vince dipped his face in the sink and when he got in bed the idea of running the bulls had turned bad. He smelt the blood of the animals as they were slashed, and then he smelt the clean sheets and fragrance coming in through the open window. There was no way he was going to get up early in the morning and torment an innocent animal, and maybe get his back broken. What was the point? Ten minutes later he asked John what he thought. Vince reckoned it was the drink talking. It was a waste of time and effort. And anyway, the English were supposed to love animals. He asked John if he was definitely going in the morning.

– No chance. Everyone will accidently oversleep. I bet you a curry when we get home.

WIMBLEDON AT HOME

I WATCH THE game but don't see the football. It's a fucking sad effort in the rain and the flu's cutting through me like nobody's business. I should be at home in bed with a bowl of soup and someone to look after me, but when you live on your own and you get sick you take care of yourself. Like when you get past fifty and develop cancer or something. Get a fatal disease and you're fucked. Left to die because you're weak and can't defend yourself.

The secret is don't get ill. You have to stay healthy best you can and be your own person. Shut up shop and don't let anything in. If you've got the will power and resist the dangers lurking round the corner you'll come out a winner. But sometimes you can't fight off all the little germs and microbes waiting to stitch you up. Like the cunts going through my head eating brain cells. The doctor just sits there looking at me doing a Prince Charles imitation, then starts making jokes that aren't funny. All this after I've been waiting for an hour reading dodgy two-year-old magazines full of nonsense about junkie aristocrats and the sex lives of pop stars. Fashion models with capped teeth straight from Bugs Bunny's worst nightmare. Truth revealed in yellow newspapers packed with football rumours that never happened.

I don't really dream, but the flu makes up for all that deep sleep. It's like I'm tripping. Not that I'm into crust mode, but my thinking's muddled. It's a bad world when you're sick watching life pass by and Wimbledon bypass the midfield with their long ball game. They're backs to the wall that lot and you have to admire them on the quiet, doing so well with zero resources.

The wind's blowing a gale and even though my hands are buried in my pockets they're frozen. I try and move my toes to keep them from snapping off but feel nothing. Mark comes back with a cup of tea and I hold it with dead stumps. Like I'm an out-of-work bomb disposal expert signing on for my weekly reward. It's a shit crowd and shit atmosphere. All those cunts in warm television studios insisting football hooligans aren't real fans don't know what they're on about. No clue. They're licking the arse that feeds them. Saying what they're told to say by the money men behind the camera. It's true there's blokes who only turn up for big games when there's the chance of a ruck, but they're a minority. Of course there's hangers on. There's hangers on in every walk of life. But not that many at football. Just like the nutters. There's a few of them, and a lot of fans who if there's trouble outside run around and swap a few punches, but most people just don't want to know.

– You look bad, Tom. Mark's watching me shiver. Look like you've got malaria. You should have stayed at home in bed.

I've been off work four days and it drives me round the bend sitting at home doing nothing. The warehouse can be a boring place, but there's people to have a laugh with and Glasgow Steve to wind up. The flat's nice enough and I've got the heating cranked up full blast, but it's just me and a box full of rubbish. Sometimes there's a good film on during the day. An old war effort maybe. Real propaganda jobs raving about freedom and the right to do whatever you want. But then there's the endless love stories and soap operas doing your head in. Makes you understand why women go off their trolley stuck at home all day with a couple of snotty-nosed, screaming brats. Why they end up in bed with blokes they pick up down the supermarket. Why they batter the kids against the walls.

– I hope it's not catching. Rod leans over. I don't want you giving me any tropical diseases.

– Only tropical disease you'll get is Aids, Mark replies. Six inches up the arse and a dose of blue monkey infection.

– You look fucking terrible. Seriously ill. No wonder you didn't come down the pub last night.

I know they're trying to cheer me up but I'm not in the mood. Get sick and you want to curl up and jump back in your old girl's belly. All your confidence disappears. Your bollocks shoot up into your gut. You don't feel cocky any more. Most days you're giving it the big one because you're in the prime of life, doing well, nothing can touch you, then suddenly it's gone. It's like you're a kid again and don't need the hassle. No fighting or shagging. The whole thing's fucked sitting here with a head full of feedback. As though everything catches up with you in the end.

Guilt doesn't come into it. That's a mug's game just down to education. They train you to obey the rules and regulations. Try to control the way you behave. They do a good job because it's buried deep inside and the cunts running the show get a tidy bonus. You reject what they say but when you get weak all that programming returns. They work their way under your skin but we've got them sussed because we're out on limb beyond their ideas of what's right and wrong. They don't understand and we prefer it that way. I can see the teachers when we were kids. Me, Mark and Rod. Getting the cane and a lecture off the head. All those cunts with their speeches telling us what's right and wrong. They do their best to gear your thinking, but they don't come from where you come from. They get up your nose something chronic. Make you go off and do the opposite to what they tell you.

The three of us have always stuck together. Your mates are what's important. You don't get to choose your family and if you end up with a bird, like Rod has, then it all comes back to men against women eventually. You can con yourself there's something more with women, but it's wishful thinking. Nothing's like the films. People should grow up. Your mates are what count but don't expect too much sympathy when you're ill. There's no shoulder to cry on.

– I'm glad that's over, says Rod when the ref blows the final whistle. Come on. Have something to eat and we'll buy you a pint. It'll help clear your head. Have a couple and go home.

We leave the ground and walk towards Fulham Broadway. It's raining and the street's full of dark figures bundled up against the weather. Few people speak and nobody sings or chants. It's a fucking ghost town. The stench of meat cooking makes me feel sick. I think I'm going to puke in the middle of the street. That would give the lads something to laugh about. We go in a cafe and I order eggs on toast. That and a pile of chips. It's well cooked food and I reach across Rod for the ketchup. We drink coffee and it warms me up. People queue at the counter for chips and pickled onions. Some go for the works with fish or pies. The windows are steamed up and sweating like a monster getting her third portion of the evening. Mascara smeared across her face like an inflatable doll. The bird in question was a right goer. Can't remember her name. It was years ago now. Appreciated the attention because beauty's only skin deep.

When we leave half an hour later the streets are clear. Nobody hangs around for Wimbledon. They don't have many fans let alone a firm. It's all greyhounds and sex killers on the common. There's only a few clubs worth bothering about when it comes to the crunch. Most are useless. We walk past the tube towards North End Road and into some fun pub, with tables for burgers and salads. There's a few birds sitting around and Mark's eyeballing them with all the subtlety of Chelsea bushwhacking Spurs. Rod gets straight in at the bar. We sit at a table and I down half my pint of lager. I shouldn't be drinking with the medicine I'm on but fuck it. It's Saturday night and there's fuck all else to do. I'll have a couple of pints and get a taxi home. Leave the other two to get on with it.

– My old girl's started seeing this fucking Arsenal fan, says Mark. He's ten years younger than her. He's the brother of some woman she works with. I met him when I went round last week. Big cunt with tattoos all over his arms like he's a fucking Hell's Angel, except he's got no hair and talks like a mincer.

– It was bound to happen sooner or later. Rod looks at a mob of girls talking too loud, trying to get noticed. Your old man died three years ago. Not many women would last that long.

– I know all that, and I'm not having a go at her or anything, but it's still strange going in and seeing her sitting on the couch with a stranger watching the telly. Just like she used to do with the old man.

– Your dad would have wanted her to get someone else. She's a good woman. She shouldn't be on her own the rest of her life. Not at her age. She's still young enough.

Everyone likes Mark's old girl. She was good to us when we were kids. Always made us a sandwich when we went round. That and a glass of milk. It nearly killed her when the old man died. He was alright. Never a day's illness and looked younger than his years. Then one day he complains about pains in his head. That night he goes for a piss and falls down dead. Just like that.

Doctors said it was a blood clot on his brain. One day he's there laughing with the family, the next he's down the undertaker's having his blood drained. Whatever you do in life there's always something waiting round the corner. That's why those dozy cunts moaning about football firms rucking each other are out of order. We're only interested in the other team's mob and don't care about anyone else. They let the fucking queers and sadists batter each other, but when it comes to something like a bit of football violence they get on their platforms and start preaching.

What do they think they're going to get for their talk? Do they think they'll go to heaven and live happily ever after? Or live right here for ever like some of those religious nutters who come round banging you up at eight o'clock Sunday morning believe? They're mad the lot of them. When your time comes you'll be sitting in your own shit and piss gagging for breath and everything you've done in life will mean nothing. Those cunts you see Sunday evening polished up for the television cameras in gold-plated churches will choke on their own sick like the rest of us, wishing to fuck they'd had a bit of fun while they had the chance. Imagine being seventy years old watching all the birds passing without a second look for a hunched-up old man who can't get a hard-on any more. End up like that and you've wasted your life. Mark's old girl understands, now her husband's dead and she's left alone. Mind you, she wouldn't say it in those exact words.

– She shouldn't have chosen a Gooner. Mark laughs. That's the main problem. Mind you, he could be a Tottenham yid with the curls and hat. Real Stamford Hill effort.

– Or a nigger. Original Gooner from Finsbury Park.

– Not my old girl. She'd never go with a nigger.

– Might be some old West Indian geezer with a bit of dignity and a sense of humour.

– No. She wouldn't go with a nigger. Not her generation.

The birds next to us are talking louder the more they drink. They're well groomed with long hair. Typical prick teasers. Not bad looking though. Like all prick teasers.

The pub's filling up quickly. I'm forcing the lager down but I'm dead. I was hoping it would get me going. There's something happening but it's no miracle cure. All I can think of is Mark's old girl flat on her back with Tony Adams in full Arsenal kit slipping her a length. A horrible thought. It's amazing what the brain can do. Must be what happens to your serial killers. One day they're good as gold going about their business, the next they're sitting by the radio tuning in to Jack the Ripper. Disease gets into the brain and all the messages get scrambled.

– The old girl's got to have her life but I don't like seeing her with another bloke. Someone other than the old man. It's wrong somehow.

Mark's getting a bit emotional on us and it makes me feel uncomfortable. We're mates and help each other out and everything, but we handle our problems alone. The things that go on inside your head. There's nothing anyone else can do for you. It's down to personal responsibility. You can't show weakness in this world otherwise the virus gets into your blood and you waste away. There's no mercy and my temperature's racing. I'm burning up. It's no ordinary infection. Doctor says it's come all the way from Asia. I think of Mark's old man. About when we were kids. About Rod's family and Mandy at home with a different idea of what the bloke's like when he's out with his mates.

I know he's into Mandy in a big way, but if truth be told he shouldn't be shafting birds behind her back. It's not on really, but I don't say anything because you can't. I'd just make myself look a cunt and what's he going to say anyway? He'd just tell me to fuck off and mind my own business. Mark would pile in as well because he doesn't like Mandy much and reckons all birds stitch you up soon as they get the chance. We've all been through it. You're trained up to believe the films and all that love bollocks but you soon work things out. There's no place for sentiment unless you want to end up a snivelling wreck.

I always wondered the reason Rod got married and one day when we were on a bender I asked. Just said he got lonely. That she was the salt of the earth and he had to grab her while he could. He'd never get something better. Real diamond. Said he knew he was a cunt fucking her about, but one day everything would be fine and they'd live happily ever after. Just like the films. I laughed when he said it, but he wasn't joking. It's all a bit sad really.

– I thought about having a word with the old girl. Mark looks

153

miserable as fuck. Tell her to get herself something better, or do without. Respect the old man's memory.

– I know what you're on about, but the point is she's got to get on with her life. She can't mourn for ever. Nobody can. I wouldn't like the idea of some other geezer shafting my mum but it's a different situation now to when your dad was alive. You say something like that to her and you'll just make a cunt of yourself.

I remember my old man arguing with my mum when I was a kid. Telling her she was a slag. That she could fuck off back to her family in Isleworth if she ever did whatever it was she'd done again. My mum was crying and I asked her what was the matter. She laughed like she was going mental or something and said she'd been peeling onions. My old man pissed off down the pub with a red face. I knew she wasn't peeling onions. We'd already had our tea and we didn't eat onions much. I never found out the truth, but it's not hard to guess. Things like that you have to ignore. Push it down and keep it there on a back burner. Bury the bad times under concrete. What's the point of thinking too much about things? It just fucks you up. Like the dossers you see begging round tube stations and sleeping in doorways.

Usually I'm fine with memories. Just remember the good times. All the Chelsea games we've been to through the years. The laugh we've had. Good times as a kid. Of course things go wrong now and then but it happens to everyone. You can't dwell on it or you'll end up a basket case. I see my mum and dad once or twice a week. There's no bad blood between us. It's funny I should think of that time now. It's the flu that does it. Makes you lose your grip. Everyone has black spots in their lives. Things that go wrong. It can't be denied some people get it worse than others, but most of us just roll along with the occasional hiccup. We've chosen our way and the three of us at this table haven't done too bad. We're working, with money in our pockets. We've got good mates and tight families and we don't go without birds when we want them. We have a laugh.

I suppose we're like niggers in a way. White niggers. White trash. White shit. We're a minority because we're tight. Small in number. We're loyal and dedicated. Football gives us something. Hate ar ' fear makes us special. We have a base in the majority which means the cunts in charge can't work us out. We have most of the same ideas but we've worked them round to fit ourselves. We're a bit of everything. There's no label. We're something the rich cunts hate and slumming socialists can't accept. We're happy with life and there's no need for social workers. None of us are sitting in the freezing cold, lonely and depressed, fucked up on drugs or drink or sex or whatever else is out there waiting to do your brain in. Our heads are together. We're three normal blokes and we go along with the football bit because it's part of our lives. Some people join the army, others the old bill. Some go in for killing people with politics and others finance.

Everyone's in a gang. Everyone has some kind of badge. There's uniforms everywhere you look and they all mean something. Something and nothing. So when the old bill and the politicians and the mindless Joe Public cunt down the high street get together and moan about the scum rioting in their back streets, shaming the good name of England, we laugh in their faces. Laugh in their faces and piss in their eyes. It's not what you say or do, it's why you say and do it. That's what counts. Two people could go out and each of them kill someone and both could have different reasons. One would be right, the other wrong, depending on your viewpoint. It's a hard thing to be honest about. The same if you go out and fuck the arse off some tart. The same with everything. We all think we're right and the other bloke's wrong, that's natural, but listen to the cunts delivering lectures and despite their educations they haven't even worked out the basics.

I'm going back to Hammersmith after the second pint. I leave Mark and Rod getting wound up by the screaming birds and get a black cab home, glad to find a driver who doesn't want to talk. There's a time and place. Sometimes you want to be left alone. We cut through the side streets and along the Fulham Palace Road. I watch people going into pubs and restaurants. An outsider. The cab drops me at the bottom of my street and I go across to the Indian. I drink a pint of Carlsberg as I make my choice, then sit back watching the happy couples in action. Psychedelic music floats in the background while men and women stare into each others' eyes. Waiters push trolleys glad they're serving lovers and not the closing-time drunks they used to rely on before half the curry houses went upmarket, but who will probably turn up later all the same. When the order's ready I finish my lager and go home.

It's cold in the flat so I turn the heat on, put my dinner on a plate and sit on the couch. I flick through the channels looking for something worth watching on the telly. There's the usual blockbuster, murder and mystery in a foreign city. I don't follow the story but it's good having the noise. My nose runs more than usual as the Madras makes its mark. Maybe I'll burn the flu away. It's fucking hot enough. When I've finished I start dipping in and out of sleep. Saturday night and I'm stuck at home like an old man. Mark and Rod will be laughing their heads off, slagging off those birds maybe, or moving to a better pub. They'll be talking football and sex, steaming on lager. It makes you appreciate life when you get sick. All the simple things. That you have a bit of excitement with the football and relaxation with your mates down the pub. It's a shame there's all those poor bastards alone the whole time, with nothing to do but work, wank and worry about the future.

I think of the Tottenham game and it cheers me up. People join the army and sign away three years of their lives just to find a bit of danger. Films can't do it like the real thing. It's the difference between wanking and shagging a bird. We need more than videos. Watching films about psychos isn't enough. Or the cunts going on about sex the whole time like they're dangerous. That's almost as sad. If that's the biggest thrill they get they've got no chance. Not that I'm ready to go without the business of course, but the way some people go on about it you'd think they were going into a war zone. I mean, we're not queers or anything, but you get your sex and it's good while it lasts, then you go away with Chelsea for a high-profile match, when there's the chance of trouble, and the excitement lasts all day.

It's a hard thing to explain. It's not that it's like sex, just that there's a bit of risk involved. People watch horror videos and whatever to feel a bit of danger. The urge is still there even if they live boring, everyday lives. Mind you, service a bird nowadays and you're taking a risk with Aids and everything, but even that's not new. We've never thought about getting a dose more than having to queue up down the STD, but there was enough people died of syphilis in the old days.

When the football finally comes on my head clears and I forget all the bollocks floating around my brain. I still enjoy football on the box. Not like when I was a kid learning about the teams and players, knowing all the line-ups and names of grounds, but it's a Saturday night tradition you don't get when you're in your prime because you're out and about. Maybe when I get older it'll go back to the beginning again. Maybe I'll lose my desires, for violence as well as sex, and make do with the things I enjoyed as a kid. It's all that second childhood stuff. They've got the usual selection of studio experts, some talking sense, others shit. There's a Manchester derby between United and City. They go on about big city rivalry till I get bored, but they're even showing highlights of Chelsea-Wimbledon. I'm like a child watching United and City rip each other apart with their different styles of play. It's a good game, but you don't feel the same watching clubs you don't support.

There's under ten minutes' worth of the Wimbledon game. It's dire football but you have to admire the characters Wimbledon bring up from South London. A few minutes of decent action is what the armchair fans get. It's all they want. All they deserve. The day's been a waste of time but it would have been a total write-off staying away. What's the point sitting at home all your life in a chair with football on the screen when you could be there in person? They show every goal from the division. I've been to all the grounds and see the stadiums as more than the view on the screen. To me they're towns. There's streets, pubs, shops, people. Everywhere has its own character. There's Everton getting stuffed at home and behind the stand full of scousers I know the streets are terraced throwbacks to another era. When Villa go on the rampage through the Coventry defence I imagine the park next to the Holte End and the brickwork of Villa Park's main entrance. And when Norwich put three goals past West Ham I have to smile even though I'm picturing the street behind the stand where me and Rod got a hiding.

All your average bloke sitting on his arse fiddling with the remote control gets is the pitch and three stands. He wastes his life flicking channels, pulled back to the football by the sound of the crowd and the passion that makes the game special. None of the TV companies seem to care about supporters, but without the noise and movement of the fans football would be nothing. It's about passion. They'll never change that. Without passion football's dead. Just twenty-two grown men running round a patch of grass kicking a ball about. Fucking daft really. It's the people that make it an occasion. When they get going it takes off. If you get any kind of passion it spills over. That's what can happen with football. That's what makes it for me. It's all connected. All part of the same thing. They can't separate football from what goes on elsewhere. They can make you stand to attention when you're being watched, but when you get away from the cameras fantasy ends and real life takes over.

POPPY DAY

MR FARRELL WALKS to the newsagent's for his morning paper. He pays his money and takes his choice. He argues over the local election result with Mr Patel. The Tory candidate has been defeated by his Labour opponent, yet neither has much to offer. The BNP has been attracting those white working-class voters alienated by the established parties. Mr Farrell and Mr Patel agree that a right-wing local councillor would mean more racist attacks, and that the bangra kids in the next street should turn their music down after midnight. But there's no telling the youngsters of today. They shake their heads sadly and Mr Farrell leaves.

— A white boy got knifed last night outside the youth club. They say he was stabbed through the heart. If he dies it'll be halal murder. He's on a life-support machine and they don't think he's going to survive. The police are trying to hush the whole thing up so they don't have a race war on their hands, but people should know the truth. People have a right to know what's true and what's a lie.

A woman with curled hair and glasses held together with sticky tape has stopped the old man. It takes Mr Farrell a few seconds to recognise the face. Mary from the White Horse. She's getting on in years now and the joke doing the rounds among the younger men is that she was shagged silly in her youth. Mr Farrell remembers Mary when she was a young woman. He sees her partially naked on the common more than half a century ago. They were teenagers at the time. There was cold grass and the smell of her excitement through the beer fumes. Mary had firm breasts in those days. Rock-hard nipples. A sharp brain that lost the thread during the war. People say it's the effects of untreated syphilis, but Mr Farrell puts it down to the Luftwaffe. Nobody wants to hear about the realities of mass bombing. They just want a soft memory with Churchill walking through the wreckage and the royal family taking enemy flak.

– It's those Pakis again. Hooligans the lot of them. They should send the smelly little bastards back where they come from. Hang the ones who stabbed the white boy and kick the rest out. Put them on a slow boat to Calcutta or wherever it is they come from.

Mr Farrell wonders if Mary remembers their night on the common, but doubts it very much. She has changed. Not so much her body, which is bone white and wasting away, because this is inevitable, but more the eyes which have emptied and sunk into the skull. Gossip says she's a drug addict. A slave to heroin and the men who keep her supplied. He sees little truth in the rumour. Mary is too old for this form of recreation and, more importantly, she doesn't have the money. Unless the other rumours are true. But who would pay to have sex with such a woman?

– Their time's going to come. You mark my words. How much longer do us whites have to get pissed on before someone does something? They give them the best flats and what do we get? Nothing. We get nothing but promises and excuses from the council. This new one will be worse than the last.

Mr Farrell continues. It is Sunday morning but the streets are busier than usual. It is Remembrance Day. A time to conjure up the Mighty Fallen. Friends and relatives rotting in the Channel and mud of France. But the old man won't remember quite yet. Not till he's had his breakfast and read the paper. Then he will let the memories come back. Relive the good old days.

– I've made you a nice cup of tea, dear. Milk and two sugars. I saw you talking with Mary Peacock. I watched you from the kitchen window. What was she saying? She looked upset, but she always looks upset these days. She's not well that woman.

Mr Farrell goes into the kitchen. His legs ache from the four flights of stairs. The kettle is cold. He turns it on and puts a tea bag in his favourite red mug, then gets the milk and sugar ready. He looks at the mug and sees a small crack he's never noticed before. Bangra vibrates through the brickwork. The smell of curry. He likes Indian food. When the kettle has boiled he makes his cuppa. He looks at the old photo, a picture of his wife who has been dead for the last three years.

– There you are. That will warm you up nice and quick. It's

hard this time of year, but we always get through the cold weather in one piece, don't we? There's Christmas to look forward to, and then the new year. A brand new start.

Mrs Farrell had high blood pressure but the doctors operated anyway. They made a mistake. An honest mistake. Mr Farrell has seen death many times and understands, but he loves his wife. He is careful and keeps his wits about him. People can be narrow minded. It makes him happy that his wife is still there, that he hears her voice and sees her face even though her body is in the cemetery. If he didn't have her he would be sad. Lonely even. But he will never be defeated. He has the blood of the bulldog breed flowing through his veins. He will stand tall and see the thing through.

– I hope you're still going to Whitehall. You haven't changed your mind, have you? You always say you'll go, but you never do. You always leave and return before you're halfway there. I've got your medals ready. Let me see you wear them. Go on, put them on your chest. They should have you laying wreaths. Poppies for your friends. How many of those bastards lost people on D–Day? Politicians start wars, they don't fight them. They cause the trouble and sign the forms and hide when the bombers come. How many of them suffered like I did? Answer me that.

When Mr Farrell has finished his tea he takes the medals from his wife. He doesn't like it when she swears and never uses bad language in front of her. She saw and heard enough before he found her. They made her suffer and then he played the hero. The medals gleam and he is embarrassed, but somehow proud at the same time. His wife's eyes light up when she sees the ribbons pinned to his chest. Most of his mates sold their medals to collectors to help pay the bills, while some threw them away in disgust, but Mr Farrell kept his for a rainy day. Mrs Farrell admires her soldier. Her knight in shining armour. The Englishman who looked for her two months after the concentration camp was liberated, to find if she had survived.

– I hate that woman. Mary Peacock is a fascist. An English Nazi. Whenever I speak with her she is criticising the blacks and Indians. And me with my accent and history, though she'll never know everything that happened.

Mr Farrell stands behind his wife. He runs his hands through her hair. The same now as it was a year after they were married. After it had grown. She was beautiful with long hair. So much different from the shaven skull. He remembers the texture of her head when he helped lift her into the truck. The stench of death is overpowering. Mortal flesh and broken limbs. He sees a coffin disappearing beneath the soil, but the Nazis didn't waste money on wooden boxes. He wonders how many times she was raped by the Ukrainian guards. He tells her that Mary Peacock is a sad and bitter woman. That life has been cruel to her in its own way. That she needs something at which to direct her hatred. It is not right, but it is the truth.

After reading the paper and eating a breakfast of egg and toast, Mr Farrell smartens himself up in front of the mirror. He spends time on his hair making sure it is combed properly. His wife is sitting at a window staring towards the common. She will stay at home while he attends the ceremony. She prefers to stay indoors these days. Three years since she last left the flat. He kisses her on the cheek and she pulls him towards her. There are tears on his cheeks. He smells the salt and disentangles himself. He must go. He doesn't want to miss the train.

Fifteen minutes later Mr Farrell is standing on the platform at Hounslow East. A train arrives and he chooses a seat. The carriage is almost empty. Two youths in leather jackets sit opposite a man with two young children. They are the only others aboard. The youths consider themselves patriots and verbally abuse the man and his children. They are smelly Paki bastards. They should be exterminated. Wiped off the face of the earth. The only good wog is a dead wog. Adolf Hitler had the right idea. There ain't no black in the Union Jack. The holocaust is a myth. A blatant lie put about by the Jews who control the media. Part of a Jewish Bolshevik Asiatic Zionist world conspiracy. Look at what the Zionists have done to the Palestinian people, though they're just a bunch of smelly Arab shit-stabbers. Nothing's as bad as a Paki though.

The Indian leads his children to the doors at the next station. The taller of the boys stands, follows, punches the man in the face, splitting his lip. He laughs because the blood is red. The doors open and he kicks the kids onto the platform then turns back to his friend, the father torn between his children and the kind of violence which goes against his nature, opting for the crying kids.

The youths share a joke and feel good together. The doors close and the train gathers speed. Mr Farrell is alone in the carriage with the two boys. He feels no fear. He is a white Anglo-Saxon Protestant male. He served in the war. An old soldier with the mark of the bulldog on his forearms, cut into the skin and filled with blue ink. He has killed for England and the English way of life. He is proud of his identity. He wears his poppy with honour.

Mr Farrell is saddened by the changes destroying his country. Things aren't what they used to be. Foreign influences have eaten away at the fabric of the society he once knew. Hospitals, schools, social welfare, unions, industry, everything has been obliterated by transatlantic dogma. England has changed and changed for the worse. Nobody takes a stand against the invasion. A revolution has occurred which Mr Farrell doesn't understand. He has been left behind by the acceleration of change. But he has his pride. He looks at the boys in leather jackets. More people should stand up for what they believe in, but nobody does because they feel there is nothing worth believing in any more. The majority have little genuine pride in their national identity.

He sits back comfortable in his seat and thinks of the war. Only those who were alive at the time care. Everybody else has forgotten. Politicians make noises which mean nothing. They use the annual occasion of Remembrance Day for their own ends. Individuals don't matter because the greater good is what is important, but the greater good has been redefined by arrogant men in expensive suits. Pride has been reinvented as cash flow charts and excessive profit margins. Mr Farrell pictures a young German recruit in a nameless village. Younger even than his killer. The mad rush of war. How many men did he kill? He isn't certain. Six or seven for sure, probably a few more. There are no regrets, he did his job. It was their lives or his. But the boy was different. In an ideal world he would have reasoned it out. The lad was badly wounded but still had a gun in his hand. There was a possibility he would have shot Mr Farrell, though in hindsight it was unlikely. There was no time to think. He blew the boy's head apart. He remembers clearly.

He tells himself that people are the same all over the world. There is good and bad everywhere. He tends to believe human beings are essentially well-meaning, that evil is conditioned by fear. Men raped Mrs Farrell while children were incinerated in nearby ovens. Maybe even they had their reasons. But the next station has arrived and he has no time for such emotion. He ignores the smell of dead flesh and burning hair. Walks towards the door, catching the two boys off guard. He breaks the first one's nose with a straight punch. He is a strong man who boxed in the army and worked outside till retirement. He is reminded of the young German soldier with half a head, face down in the dirt, brain mixed with mud. The second youth is surprised by the assault and Mr Farrell has time to deliver another punch, sending him onto the floor, blood coming from his mouth. Mr Farrell stares at them for a moment and sees the cowardice, nothing more than stupid kids repeating slogans and picking on an easy target. He wishes he had a gun in his hand. Then the anger is gone.

The station is busy and the youths don't follow. It is the Lord's day of rest and Mr Farrell is a dark shape walking with his head down. Nobody really notices the elderly. They are considered an outdated irrelevance. Even hospitals shun them for fear of wasting money as they strive to hit financial targets. The world has moved forward. He will leave Remembrance Day until next year. Mrs Farrell will be disappointed but the good old days can wait a while longer. She will make him a nice cup of tea when he gets home. With milk and sugar. Nobody makes tea quite like Mrs Farrell.

MAN CITY AT HOME

THE CUNT GETS me round the neck and jams my arm behind my back. Pulls me over to the van where one of his mates pokes me in the balls with his truncheon. The pain shoots up through my gut, a short sharp shock to the system. I say nothing because I'm not giving them the satisfaction. The old bill hate it when they can't get a reaction. This is bad news, but I'm not getting into a discussion on the subject. They can make up any story they want. My lips are sealed.

– In the van you fucking animal. They pull and push me into the transit. I make it as difficult as I can, without actually resisting arrest.

The one with the truncheon pokes me again. This time harder. More a stabbing movement. My bollocks jump into my body and my eyes are watering. I don't want them thinking I'm crying like some ten-year-old wanker. Your balls are sensitive and getting wacked with a truncheon hurts. It's a chemical reaction. There's nothing worse. It's fucking agony. They bundle me into the van and I can smell the copper's breath he's so fucking close. He's put his truncheon away, sweating, and I reckon his face is going to melt if he doesn't calm down. A waxwork with an erection. He loves the image. A hard man. Someone to be avoided. Keep your head down when you pass him in the street. Keep on the right side of this cunt.

– You're scum. He leans into my face. Breathing all over me. The smelly bastard should brush his teeth if he wants an answer. I look out the window.

– You lot should be lined up against the wall and shot, then hung up from lampposts between here and the ground and left to rot. They shouldn't cut you down till you're a pile of bones.

I watch Mark and Rod further down the street. Moving away

from the old bill. They're acting casual, melting into the crowd. Getting lost in the mass of people heading towards Stamford Bridge. Two more innocent faces among thousands. Half of me is glad they're getting away, the other half a nasty bit of work wishing they'd got nicked as well. It's no fun getting done, but it's worse when you're on your own.

The old bill are excited. I keep my eyes trained out the window and don't answer when they speak, knowing the more I do it the more it's going to wind them up. It's not a good idea, to be honest, but there again neither is getting yourself nicked in the first place. It's turning into a bad day. I should bow down and act humble, show how fucking sorry I am, admit what hard bastards they are, but they can fuck off. Coppers love showing off their power. They want me to act gutted, come over all repentant like, but I'm not. I'll survive. I should get some kind of connection going because they've still got to write their reports, and even though they're thick as shit and twice as smelly they have a way with words. Know how to tell a good story. Over-active imaginations and a mean streak that runs through the system, right to the bone. The courts believe what they say without a second thought. I should play the game. Play the white man. But I'm not interested. I'm narked with myself more than anything, but I still hate them.

– Wait till we get you down the station. You won't be so fucking cocky once you're in a cell. Scum like you are destroying this country. You give the rest of us a bad name.

I wait for him to go into one about that golden age of law and order when everyone did as they were told. Never questioned anything that happened to them. When people were happy with their lot and front doors never got locked. Back in Toytown the Englishman never stepped out of line. There were no pissheads, nutters, perverts, junkies, killers. There was no sex and everyone was a virgin. Walking around with swollen balls hanging down to their ankles. It's a miracle the race didn't explode in a puff of smoke it was so fucking pure.

– They had the right idea in the old days. They should bring back flogging. That would make you think twice about breaking the law. The Arabs have the right idea. An eye for an eye and a hand for a crime.

There's nine of us in the van. Six Man City and three Chelsea as

166

far as I can make out. The City lads are mostly sloppy geezers who've been doing some serious drinking by the smell of them, though there's a black boy who looks a bit out of place. They're fat cunts with red faces and bloodshot eyes. The biggest one's got love and hate across his knuckles. Real wank job that one. Should have a bit of respect for himself. Born in Strangeways the way he's decked out. But now we're nicked there's no trouble because we're separated and the old bill are in the middle keeping the peace. The moment's gone and I'm feeling a right cunt letting myself get pulled into a punch-up round the corner from the tube. That kind of behaviour gets you nowhere and belongs in the days of fifty-thousand crowds when the old bill had better things to do and the Government was more interested in keeping the country running than fights at football.

We're walking down from the Maltster and there's ten or so Manchester lads pissed up and mouthing off. Walking around our streets like they own the place. They're not a firm or anything like that, but they're not exactly peace and love merchants either. A few Chelsea beer monsters start having a go at them, and before I know what's happening I'm joining in. Nothing serious, but well fucking stupid. We weren't looking for City and had been down the Maltster to see a mate of Rod's. We hung about too long and got stuck drinking. But the sight of a ruck just sucks you into the centre. Specially after a few sherbets. That's what too much lager before a match does. It's rubbish and nobody has to tell me. I've messed up and let my standards slip. I've been pulled into the gutter with the chancers and pissheads. Bad news all round and now I'm sitting in the van like a prat.

– We'll book you down the station, but the cells are getting full so we'll be taking you over to Wandsworth nick.

I want to laugh in the man's face. He thinks he's getting us worried. I want to look him in the eye and tell him he's wasting his time. That he's a cunt and I hope his family dies before he gets home. There's no way the cells are going to be busy against City and I've heard the line before. Why does he bother?

The bloke doing the talking has a thin face and bulging eyes. Bullfrog breed. There's a dedicated look about him. Believes in what he's doing. Wants to make the streets safe for pensioners and kids on their way home from school. Probably collects stamps in his spare time, but the fat cunt he works with is more into hardcore porn and fifteen pints of lager. They should fuck off and hassle some real criminals. The rapists, muggers, nonces. Instead they're wasting their time at football. They're missing the point. But they're also taking home a healthy wage packet for having some fun at the taxpayer's expense. I reckon some of them love it more than us lot.

– You won't get much joy in Wandsworth lads. The fat cunt joins in. Better make sure your arses are ready because they don't like football hooligans in the nick. You'll be walking with a wiggle by the time you get released tonight. Shitting yourself something rotten because your arses have been split.

The man's a hundred per cent wanker. Who does he think he's conning? Just because a bloke goes down doesn't mean he turns into a fucking iron. The copper knows he's talking bollocks, but he has to try it on. It's part of his thinking. All that wanking in Hendon as a boy recruit. He's repeating the same nonsense trendy lefties like to put about. All that bollocks about everyone being a bum bandit on the quiet. They fucking love it those cunts, with their scabby clothes and wishful thinking. Their world revolves around the male arsehole. They lecture the rest of the country about equal rights for queers and how shafting other blokes is natural, then rant on about prison bum bandits to try and prove the point. If it's no big thing like they say, on all those late night programmes on the telly, where the cunts sit around slapping each other on the back trying to be all unemotional, then why go on about it like it's some kind of exclusive?

Basically those cunts know fuck all about reality. They get their piece of paper and think that's it. They get a plush job and retire to the TV studio to continue their lectures. Cradle to grave. That's why nobody in London wants to know about today's Labour Party. They should roll up their sleeves and get their hands dirty. Build up a sweat. A day's hard graft would kill them. They're the cunts who wash their hands after they've had a piss, never before.

– Right, Bob, let's get this rubbish down the station. The fat copper shuts the back doors as he calls to the driver. I need a cup of tea and a cheese roll. Put your foot down will you, I'm starving.

The van starts up and we're crawling through traffic for the short ride to Fulham Police Station. I've been there before. I think of the time against West Ham. Got nicked when West Ham piled in the pub we were drinking in and it went off right there in the door. I'm standing around minding my own business and the doors burst open and a mob steams in bopping up and down like jumping jacks. I turn round and I've just got this whistled Bubbles going through my head before one of the cunts smacks me in the mouth. It was a split second thing with no time to react. The pub was packed with Chelsea and West Ham were there for five seconds before bottles, glasses and some chairs and tables sent them back into the street. West Ham piled out fast as they'd arrived and the old bill took their place. They steamed in with truncheons and I was one of the unlucky ones. The copper who nicked me just grabbed the nearest body. Just like this one now.

That was a wicked day with West Ham causing havoc all over the shop. The cells really were full, and the old bill were giving it the big one then about putting us in Wandsworth, but nothing happened. They got us down the station and moved us to a truck with cells. We sat there for two hours. Real premature burial effort. Half of us needed a piss and kept asking the coppers, but they were laughing like the cunts they are, telling us we'd get a kicking if we pissed ourselves. There were three of them sitting at the front telling stories. One with a bigger mouth than most going on about a queer he'd nicked down some bogs who wouldn't go in the cell. Said he was scared of being in a small space. The bloke promised he wouldn't close the door. Soon as the queer goes in, bang goes the door. Said the queer was screaming and going mental when he turned the key. Frothing at the mouth like he'd picked up a dose of rabies and the copper just laughed and walked off. There was a bit of laughter from the lads in the cells. The old bill liked that. A show of unity.

– What are you looking at, you black bastard? The fat copper gives the City nigger a bit of verbal. You don't come down here causing trouble in the white man's streets. You should've stayed in Moss Side where you belong with your drugs and whores.

It's a slow ride. The traffic's diverted away from Stamford Bridge causing a jam. All the people on foot move in one direction. Off to football like they do every Saturday. It's like those fish that go back to where they were born. They have to return. Something inside forces them back. It's in the blood.

Upstream all the way, but you just have to get there. It's going on all over the country and Chelsea's one of the bigger clubs. I think of all those shit teams who will never do anything, only get a couple of thousand through the turnstile, and know that if Chelsea were the same I'd still be there.

– You lot don't care about football. You just come along because you want a fight. You should piss off and let the other idiots get on with it. If they're stupid enough to come along every week they should be able to watch the game in peace and quiet.

He doesn't have a clue. He's talking to himself repeating the rubbish he hears on the telly and reads in the paper. Five minutes later the van arrives at the station. Things have quietened down because the old bill get bored when no-one answers back. The day's grinding to a halt. For me it ended getting nicked. The City fans have come a long way and they'll be into their hangovers soon. A wasted trip. Manchester to London for a few hours in a cell and a date in court. Now it's just down to procedure and the petty digs. The endless wind-ups and irritation.

– Right, out you get. The coppers are outside standing by the doors. Hurry up. We haven't got all day. Sooner you get in and we check you out, the sooner you can go home.

I expect a kick or punch but they're standing back bored out of their skulls. The excitement has quickly died down and they've realised it was a small scuffle and not the start of a major riot. It's not like the system's going to be overthrown or anything. You'd think after all these years policing football they'd understand what goes on, but they still haven't got a clue. It makes you wonder where they dig them up from. And who's in charge of the operation? Probably some old geriatric with a cabinet full of recommendations he never did anything for and a brain rotting with the clap.

We're led inside to be charged. The bullfrog copper holds my arm like I'm going to do a runner or something. Public enemy number one. Don't make me laugh. I take my turn and give my details. Tom Johnson. No previous. Just say what's necessary and the copper behind the desk writes it down as though he's on a go slow. He's got glasses which keep slipping down his nose and a bald patch at the back of his head like a monk. Doesn't look at me the whole time. Just stares at the forms. I'm not important enough.

Another statistic. He takes his time and the bullfrog next to me shuffles his feet getting impatient. That makes two of us. They take me to be photographed and fingerprinted. It's a load of shit and I've told them I've never been nicked before because, who knows, maybe nothing will show up on record. It happens sometimes, or at least that's what I've heard, so it's always worth a go. I haven't been in trouble with the old bill for a few years so it won't count when the case comes to court. That's the theory anyway. But a simple lie keeps them off your back.

The copper leading me round tries to make a bit of small talk now the commotion's over and the paperwork's got to be done. I'm just looking at him thinking I'd like to nut him. Break the bridge of his nose and see those eyes pop out of his skull. Or stick a banger in his mouth, watch the fuse burn and his head explode. Wanker. Why don't they turn a blind eye now and again? It's not like it's anything serious. A few punches and a bit of shouting. Nothing more. A scuffle which generally looks worse than the reality. Major efforts like Tottenham only come around a couple of times a season.

I'm led to a cell and put in with some other Chelsea lads. City get their own accommodation and that's the last we'll see of them. I nod to the others and sit down. Time to go through the boredom of waiting till the game finishes, the old bill check my details and decide to let me out. Then I'm going to be down Horseferry Magistrates listening to three old squires who should be six feet under telling me what a fucking evil bastard I am. I'll have to stand there listening to the usual bollocks and, worst of all, I'll have to pay the cunts a fine for the privilege.

– I'm just standing there trying to keep out of the way and I get arrested. A skinny kid looks to the rest of us for a reaction. There's these blokes having a go at each other and I'm trying to find a way past and suddenly someone thumps me from behind. Right across the back of the shoulders and I feel him against me and I use my elbow to get him off. I thought it was a City fan and when I turned to get away it's a policeman.

– That's bad luck, says an older bloke trying not to laugh. You're a football hooligan now.

– It's not fair, though. I'm not like that. I've never been in trouble before and I'm going to plead not guilty. I'll say it was an accident. Do you think they'll believe me?

– You've got no chance, but have a go if it makes you feel better. There's no such thing as accidents when it comes to the old bill. You can do fifteen years for nothing, because the bastards decide to stitch someone up, but they never apologise do they? Look at all the cases that get shown up years after the event. It's no honest mistake. They need a conviction and they grab someone off the street. They just want to look good. They're not interested in minor details like innocence and guilt.

– I spat in the gutter outside the ground and a copper on a horse tells me I'm nicked. Another bloke joins in the discussion.

– I just laughed because I thought he was taking the piss and he calls his mate over and here I am. They'll nick you for anything. They're probably on a bonus scheme and get so much for each arrest.

I listen to their stories. The skinny kid getting charged with assault when it was me and the others to blame. The young lad spitting in the gutter. The other blokes swapping punches with Manchester drunks. A man in an anorak like the trainers wear, pissed and bleary-eyed. A bunch of losers. Me included. It's all minor league stuff and just goes to show how the old bill waste time on trivia. What are they bothering with all this for when they could be putting themselves about where it counts. This is the easy option. Get hold of some bystander and spend the rest of the afternoon writing it up. I pay my taxes and this is what I get in return. Mind you, I reckon a few of them agree, just following the political line wasting resources. Rod reckons there's more people employed monitoring football hooligans than there are tracking down child-molesters. Don't know if it's true, but if it is then it's got to be down to politics.

– My brother's mate was in Belize, says the pisshead. He says he was on a bounty for the guerrillas he shot. Bounty-hunting in the army. Says he bagged five of the bastards. He was stationed in Belize City. When he wasn't training he spent his time with the whores, getting drunk or in the jungle killing guerrillas. Says it pissed all over patrolling Belfast.

The drunk must be lying. Either him or the soldier. Can't imagine the army paying bounties. There again, when you stop and think about it, that's what the blokes who sign up are doing anyway. Then they slag off mercenaries. Everyone has a go at us lot as well, but what's the difference? Only ones I can see is your average bloke who gets in a fight in his own time doesn't get paid and isn't killing anyone, but maybe I'm missing something.

— City got a kicking before the old bill got there, says one of the two blokes with a strictly casual appearance. More of a nutter than the others, though I don't know his face. They were sounding off and you don't have to take that from anyone. Serves them right.

I start thinking about that bird Steve battered in Manchester. Now that's the kind of bloke who should be sitting in here. Not us lot. Steve should be in Wandsworth or Brixton or some other hole getting a hiding from the other prisoners. Nobody likes a nonce. They reckon there's honour among thieves. Maybe there is, maybe not. Depends who you're talking about. But one thing's for sure, sex offenders and queers are the scum of the earth. More so inside because there's got to be some kind of standards when you're being treated like shit. If the cunts aren't sectioned it doesn't take long before they get carved up.

Mark did three months for assault after he hospitalised some bloke outside a club in Shepherd's Bush. He was out with his older brother Mickey and some of his mates. Must've been twenty at the time and he was the only one got done. Said it wasn't as bad as he thought because there were some interesting men inside. Old-time crooks and apprentice hoods. As long as you didn't show any weakness you were okay. Mind you, it's no way to live, and he swore he'd never go back. Not that Mark's changed his ways, he's just a bit smarter than the rest and keeps his wits about him.

Mark kicked the fuck out of this nonce one time. Says the screws stood back and watched. Laughed as he sorted the bloke out. Didn't give a fuck. Says the bloke raped a kid or something and deserved what he got. Says the blood was thick like he'd hit an artery and he got a bit worried because you can't hide a murder inside. The screws told the bloke to get up and shut his mouth. Took him off to see the doctor and sectioned the bastard. It made Mark feel better because he was boiling up and had to take it out on someone. I suppose there's a pecking order everywhere you go. People follow the same rules whether they live in a fifty-room mansion in Kensington or five hundred to a cell in Brixton. Everyone's trying to better themselves. We all want to get another rung up the ladder and make ourselves feel important. There's always got to be some cunt worse off because if you reach rock bottom you're fucked. Mark says he has no regrets.

– Chelsea are getting stuffed, lads. A copper looks in through the hatch and laughs. City scored three times in the first twenty minutes and your new goalkeeper's busted his leg.

It's hard to know if he's telling the truth. They get a thrill out of winding you up. It's all cat-and-mouse once they've got you under lock and key. It keeps them on their toes. It's all mind games and though you blank the comments and insults it starts to get on your nerves after a while. One time I got put in the cells overnight for being pissed on a Friday night in Hammersmith. I woke up with a hangover and a copper said I'd raped some bird. He said I followed her after she'd got out of a taxi and fucked her round the back of the optician's. I was so pissed I went for some chips and they caught me. I couldn't remember anything and was shitting it. I'd lost two hours of my life and only just remembered getting nicked. Everything else was blank.

The copper went off and I was sitting there for half an hour. I saw myself sent down for ten years ending up like the nonce Mark battered. I wanted to tell someone it wasn't me responsible. That I must've been on remote control. That I didn't remember anything, so how could it be me? If you don't have a memory of what you've done then how can they blame you for the crime? I was sitting there feeling like shit. Knew that's what nonces say. That they hear voices, or can't help themselves, whatever. I could see it all coming my way. Up in court and the shame, everyone turning against me and then the years inside. I'd rather have topped myself. Then another copper comes along to give me a cup of tea and I ask him what happened. He said I kicked some dustbins over and was singing football songs in the middle of the street dodging traffic. I was drunk and disorderly but they weren't going to charge me. Just give me a warning and send me home. I was so happy I could have hugged him. My hangover disappeared as I drank the tea. He was alright that one.

I sat there waiting for them to let me go home and the bloke in the next cell had killed his wife the previous night. I could hear him crying. They had an argument and he knifed her. Just went mental according to the policeman. Said the bloke didn't know what happened. One minute his wife was there shouting at him, the next she was going stiff. I felt bad for him. Life is shit sometimes and there's always going to be someone round the corner waiting to take advantage. Slip up and every cunt's on to you before you've hit the pavement.

– What's the score at the game? The drunk asks a copper passing the cell.

– One nil to Chelsea.

Silence.

– Has the Chelsea keeper broken his leg?

– Not as far I know. He just saved a penalty. Radio said it was one of the best saves seen at Chelsea for years.

BOMBAY MIX

THEY PROBABLY THINK Vince Matthews went a bit mental when he left England, that he came back a shadow of his old self, but it doesn't bother me because I view everything from a different angle now, seeing things in perspective, skinheads running over the bridge heading for Hayes with a big mob behind them, locals outnumbering the shaven-headed aliens ten to one, and they're big blokes with machetes and those kung-fu sticks Indians use when they're looking for trouble, and then there's this nuclear explosion as the pub blows up, or petrol bombs inside more like, popping glass, and everyone sort of hangs in the air for a second like the film's been stopped and someone in a recording studio's chopping up the negatives, but then their brains click into what the noise is, because, after all, they were there a few minutes before watching the Business 4 Skins Last Resort play, or in the case of the locals armed and called out for duty, probably angry because of the NF march when Blair Peach got a pasting, and that sort of thing sticks in the memory, so when a mob of skinheads comes on your manor you're not going to muck about asking questions, because tabloid pin-ups go a long way, read your papers and every skinhead is a white fascist who hates brown and black faces, never mind the JA music and clothes, the old rude boy style, and anyway, there's stories going round about these East London hooligans thieving from shops and slagging off Indian women and girls, someone's mothers and daughters, and if you do that you're asking for trouble because, the thing is, white blokes from outside the area think Indians and Pakis can't look after themselves, which is a load of shit, and everyone goes along with the easy image that blacks and what have you, even the Greeks and Turks up in North London, are so fucking hard that the Indians just follow in the wake of their mums and dads and inherit all the cornershops and cash-and-carries, but if you knew some of the blokes in Southall, like George, who got embarrassed when his old man stopped to give him a lift home after school when he was with his mates, when it was summer and he had the windows open in his Ford Estate, playing devotional sitar music you usually hear down the temple, yelling at his son to be careful crossing the road, and George knew a load of blokes in the local National Front, or at least blokes who said they were NF but understood none of the politics and wouldn't believe Martin Webster was bent, just thought the NF badge made them hard and got the Socialist Workers Party and Anti-Nazi League going, the same kind of thinking that makes the Union Jack an anarchist symbol, and George said he saw their point of view, in a funny sort of way, and he was like an honorary white boy though he was no Uncle Tom doing tricks in the white man's circus, a hooligan who worked as a hod carrier for a while in Hanwell then built himself up with weights and did some kind of training so he was hard, one of the martial arts, maybe it was kung-fu, and nobody would push him because he'd been inside, did borstal and was never that bothered, but fuck knows where he was when the skins got steamed in Southall, he'd been around a few years before when the NF tried to march through and the whole area got mobbed up and there was a right royal riot and Blair Peach, a red teacher militant or something according to the papers, got killed, battered to death, and a lot of people say it was the SPG, they've changed their name now, big deal, and the studios of the Ruts and Misty In Roots got trashed, black and white united, the West London punk and reggae bands, and George and his crew were down there that day, rioting along the Uxbridge Road, he kicked a copper in the bollocks and his extended family were straight in, all that lot, real Indians without the cropped head and natty clothes George wore, but when there was trouble they'd turn up with ceremonial swords in the boots of their rusty imports and do the business, I got a kicking a couple of times off Indian gangs, after dark at closing time, it was just part of the landscape, but Southall was rioting in broad daylight and the police steamed into everyone in sight and George and the family nicked a bus, gave the driver a kicking, bit out of order that but bad things happen in times of war, people go too far and commit atrocities, it's always the innocent who get lumbered, and George himself was up behind the wheel, putting his foot down racing through the streets, a double decker 207 I think it was, but who cares about numbers, they never paid the fare on that trip, Southall looks after itself and you go down there it's another world with people all over the place and the shops full of food spilling onto the pavement, there's always something happening, a different kind of culture which younger whites find it hard to get into because the blacks have their own thing and the music lets whites get in on their life a bit, but the Indians, they're another story, just do it and live it and there's a single attitude and that's why West London is a different place to South London, or even North London, because it's got that history, that punk flavour, whether it's the Ruts or that Oi riot, two strands of the same thing, and I think about all this sitting in the cafe I use, the most authentic Indian cafe in the whole of Southall, a bit unusual for this part of the world because it's mostly South Indian food, massala dosas and thalis, even idlis in the morning which I have on the way to work if I've got the time, but this place is the business, because when I say authentic I mean the real thing, the best way to spend Saturday evening is sitting in here, I haven't been in a Southall pub for years because they're all shit, basically, and who needs drink when I can come here and have my food then wash it down with a bang lassi, the original item, the bang lassi is a lassi with a bang, and the bloke who runs the place remembers me from when we were kids, I knew his cousin, George, the hooligan who went back to India and runs a guest house in Bombay, some people reckon he's a fool because Bombay's full of junkies, others say he's into the old export business, maybe he is, maybe he isn't, could be he just wants to live there, I don't know the truth about the situation, don't ask me, I haven't seen the bloke for a good ten years, maybe longer, he's like two different people, and the bang lassis take my head off and the prices are authentic as well, or near enough, a special rate because I'm a familiar face, one of the old herberts, thanks for the cocktail of drugs mixed in with the lassi, and it's Saturday night and I'm watching the people pass outside, like I'm back in India, the other side of the globe, and I don't have to move from this place to see the world, just let the lassi take effect and look through the window, and it's a good mix tonight, the chaps have done me proud, a jug of water on the table with dents in the metal, and my hearing must be going because I can hear the voices change in the background, the sound of punk, a good memory, from the Ruts to the 4 Skins, but at least it seems to have quietened down these days, though you go across London to Bethnal Green and Whitechapel and it's another story, another story altogether, and you'd think it would have sorted itself out by now, especially after the Trafalgar Square riot, that was the last punk riot, and there were a few political groups there but there was a lot of everyday people as well, everyone up for a go at the police, and that was the dirty side of punk after it went underground, animal rights and squats, white dreadlocks, but a lot of ordinary people, because how I remember it that was what punk was all about, ordinary people with nothing to say about fashion, except that it was shit and a con and a giant rip-off, morons, and Trafalgar Square was surreal, whatever the word means, South Africa House on fire and bongos vibrating through Nelson's ears, smoke everywhere, horses and riot police, bricks and truncheons, and the police lost control that day and it was the big restaurants in the West End that got wrecked, must be a good feeling putting bricks through the windows of McDonalds and steak houses, and none of the Indian restaurants got touched, just the big corporations and banks, serves them right, all that bad investment and manipulation, and I'm moving now, my head working in a lot of different directions, the peaceful bustle outside has the same kind of electricity as those riots, somehow, shouting voices and political violence without the organisations, youth rivalries, the race question which those at the top keep using, and I wonder where these people come from, they should try living round here for a while and they'll know what's what, because they always go for what they think is the easy option, and that's why the Indians get attacked so often, because of that belief that they're somehow incapable of defending themselves, that they're weak, that they're all peace and purity, a punch bag for the rest of the country to have a go at when they need to unload a bit of frustration, but it's not like that, I know that from growing up in the area, it's bound to happen, different groups maybe but you're living in the real world, not some whitewashed Tory idea of a constipated paradise or socialist ideal of good-natured underdog, just people, that's what it is, just

people, and this bang lassi is doing my brain in, and I see Rajiv
coming in now and he's sitting down opposite with the small
wooden chess set, Punjabi-made he tells me, and he's knocking
back his bang lassi talking quietly, too quietly, and I know what
he's saying but can't get to grips with the words, funny that, and
he's setting the chess pieces up and there's no place for violence
and riots any more because it was a long time ago and we've all
grown up and, anyway, chess is a gentleman's game, a bit of
logical thinking and calm, fucking right it is, and we're starting
with a bang, big bang theories, the Saturday night ritual for the last
six months now, and my mind's set on the king and queen,
washing away the aggravation, something inbred and part of the
culture, my life story, something that gets dismissed and ignored
and it's easy to see how history is just the winners telling everyone
how bad the losers are, Johnny Rotten said that, should call the
boy Lydon I suppose, classic line which sums the whole thing up,
and even he's got another life now, maybe that was what started
me thinking about all that punk stuff, how everything's gone back
to square one again, and then those stories on the telly, about the
BNP in the East End, and the NF have changed their name as
well, just like the SPG, and I would have thought that was all in
the past now, that we'd gone through a bit of a breaking point
with those two Southall riots, and I grew up with Indians and
Pakistanis and know the difference, two separate countries, they
killed hundreds of thousands just to get that border, and don't
forget Bangladesh, and that was the starting point, knowing the
difference, and maybe there was a bit of aggro now and again, but
that was just different gangs of kids, even Paki-bashers used to be
black and white, that was bad enough, sad bastards, but not like
this new stuff, young kids getting stabbed to death, what's going
on, and even that Oi riot, who's to say those skinheads were
racists, I don't know, it's all up in the air and there's accepted
stories about history, invented by those in power who weren't
even there in the first place, and I can't get my head round it, can't
get my head round this game of chess, three moves in now and I'm
looking down through the board, down through the white
squares and they're tunnels drilled through the table, except
there's no bottom and the sides are red, marble instead of wood, a
translucent red haze, very odd, some significance I suppose,

symbolic maybe, or just confusion, I don't care, I've got to make the next move, another step forward in the evolution of man, this man, move a piece forward and put the opposition under pressure, shift the emphasis to Raj so he has to work out a plan, and it's all about clear thinking and seeing beyond the initial action, making the right decision when there are so many different versions of the truth, getting beyond the generalisations and having respect for the opponent, and chess is more than competition, of course it is, that's why me and Raj play the game, every Saturday without fail, George's cousin brings a massala dosa over and Raj is getting stuck in and, I can't remember, I just can't remember, trying to think whose go it is and I don't want to ask, there must be a bit of something special in this lassi because I'm having trouble keeping my thoughts together, pulling the different strands tight adjusting the contradictions, like the information has got tangled together and my brain is being squeezed by the rush of images, and I'm thinking back again into the past, trying to remember if Raj made the last move, or was it me, I just don't know, I can't ask, can't ask the question, I can't fucking speak, just can't get the words together clearly, no such word as can't, that's what they say, a full steam ahead attitude, and Raj is sitting dead still with a chunk of dosa in his hand and sambhar sauce dripping onto his plate, just silence now, then the sound of the Ruts in the background, I can hear ghosts, Malcolm Owen singing H-Eyes, poor bloke, and it's all there in the song, no need to say anything else, imagine writing a song about your own death, how did his mum feel, poor woman, and his dad, it makes me miserable, such a waste of a good life, and then his voice is fading and the 4 Skins are singing Wonderful World, going on about the suss laws, and it's a strange moment because the Ruts had a song called Suss, imagine that, never thought of it before, not till this second, but you'd be hard pressed to find anyone who wouldn't consider the two groups on opposite ends of the political spectrum, but maybe they just don't understand, I don't know, it's just a thought, and what has he put in the bang lassi, I've got that paranoid feeling, like everything I think I'm saying out loud, that there's no secrets, and I've got to ask Raj whose move it is, the words are there now, full frontal delivery, he's lifting his head looking up from the board telling me that he doesn't know, he can't remember, and there's a bit of a gap in the conversation as we both try acting with a spark of dignity, the clatter of plates as the cafe closes up for the night and the plate cleaning gets under way, they always let us keep playing till we're finished, but we have to know whose turn it is to make a move so me and Raj start playing backwards, trying to retrace our steps and see how we ended up in the present situation, making slow moves on the board so we don't forget, looking back on choices, turning time upside down and shaking it so the answers fall out, I must remember my original position, but after a couple of backward moves I've forgotten, I hope the same goes for Raj, that he's not carrying the image in his mind, I don't want to look stupid but somehow I know he's in the same state, those bang lassis, talk about value for money, that's what we're getting, no doubt about that, because this is the authentic India right here in this cafe, and we could be in Rajasthan right now, sitting in a desert town confused by the Golden Crescent's finest export, brought across the desert by bandits, the Thar Desert here in Southall except there's no Pakistani border to cross, and it's magic because I don't have to leave London for a taste of the East, all that travel overseas, the clatter of plates in the kitchen, water running, and we're sitting here staring at the chess board, lovely colours too, pulsating and swaying, wooden fractals going with the grain, and there's not much to say, it's all quiet, just my heart thumping, nothing to think about but the next move.

THREATENING BEHAVIOUR

I SIT IN a cafe watching people pass in the street outside. Monday morning and they're hurrying to their offices. The men are identical with black suits and noddy haircuts. The women don't vary their style much either, but there's some nice birds around. Dirty office girls. Just like the one serving me coffee and a Danish. She walks around with her nose in the air like she's renting a room at Buckingham Palace. Can't be more than twenty-two but thinks she's a cut above the rest. Birds like this are easy to work out. They come from money and are bred to be arrogant. They look down on ordinary girls. Slag them off as common. But get one of these stuck-up birds between the sheets and they're away. It's all down to upbringing. They're arrogant like nobody's business, but arrogant makes for a good shag. They don't care about anybody but themselves.

I smile at the girl as she gives me my order. She lifts her head and turns away. She'll get a fucking nose bleed if she's not careful. Her nostrils are up there in space denting satellites. Real Himalayas job. But I let her think I'm hooked. That I reckon she's a cracker. That somehow the fact she's good looking and well groomed makes her more than another snotty nosed slag. She stalks off rolling a shapely arse and I keep my eyes on her. She can't resist looking back. When she catches me staring she marches into the back of the cafe. I want to laugh. It's a classic.

I've got half an hour before I'm due in court and I'm killing time round the corner from Horseferry Magistrates. I've been in these courts before I got wise. I know the place well enough, but it's a good job time has passed since my last visit, otherwise the magistrates might even be looking at something more than a fine. I bite into the Danish and wish it was a proper cafe with decent food. Not a greasy spoon, just somewhere that doesn't have its head so far up its arse it could get some decent food together. Danish pastries, croissants and all the other European shit leaves me cold. That's the kind of rubbish you have to put up with when you go abroad. What the fuck is it doing here? It's taking over in the rich areas because every cunt thinks the Frogs and Eyeties are better than us. It's because they don't belong in the culture around them that they have to look over the Channel.

When it's time I give the waitress a big friendly smile and ask for the bill. She's toned down a bit now and when I've paid I leave a fiver in the dish. I make sure she sees it then flash my teeth at her like a prize wanker. Real devil worship stuff. Done up in my best gear for the magistrates she might even reckon I'm worth a few bob. She's sweet now because a whore's a whore wherever you go and whatever the accent. Only difference, birds on street corners are up front about what they're doing. The girl returns the smile.

I walk round the corner and up the steps leading to the court. The foyer's full of nervous first-timers and cocky pros who think the whole thing's a joke. Sick humour. The other Chelsea boys are up as well and to make things interesting there's four Millwall lads down the corridor. I know they're Millwall from the crest and slogan sweat shirt one of them's wearing. They're scruffy bastards. Haven't made any kind of effort. No respect for authority. We'll be down there in the League Cup in a couple of weeks and it'll be mental. They're ragged and even if they didn't have the cunt with the shirt it would still be easy to tell them apart by the rest of the gear. It's easy working out where football fans come from. It's not even the style. That spreads fast enough. There's something more. Scousers look like scousers. Geordies are geordies. Forget the clothes and look at the haircuts and tashes for Northerners. Their heads are a different shape. The faces look like they belong to another race. Must go back to tribal times.

Take London. Go to any derby game and you can tell different firms apart. It's not just the niggers at Arsenal and yids at Tottenham, it's something more. You know from experience where they come from. West Ham and Millwall are tatty even when they're looking smart. There's common blood with West Ham and Millwall, and the difference from living on opposite sides of the river. Same with Arsenal and Tottenham. Then there's

Chelsea and nothing clubs like Rangers and Brentford. The Millwall boys are giving us the eye and there's no love lost. Chelsea generally have a bit more cash because West London's a classier place than the likes of Peckham and Deptford. Acton and Hammersmith piss all over the Old Kent Road. I feel a bit of a cunt in my Sunday best but that's why they're on a hanger in my cupboard. Weddings, funerals and court appearances. All the sad occasions. If you can save a hundred quid dressing up for a couple of hours then why not? The waitress was obviously impressed.

I look at the sheet pinned to the wall. It's a mix of drunk driving, theft, assault, the standard football charge of threatening behaviour, and a rape. Bad news that last one. People mill around talking. A cross section of everyday blokes, though the men doing the defending all come from the same classrooms. They're easy to tell. No need to look. They're the cunts with the clipped accents. Stroppy the lot of them. Relations of the bird in the cafe. It's all men as well, not a woman in sight. Suppose it's true what they say. It's a man's world when it comes to crime.

The kid on the assault charge talks with his brief. Shitting himself. He doesn't belong here and it's out of order they put that kind of bloke through the grinder. Shows what cunts the old bill are when it comes down to it. They stitch themselves up in the end because they turn everyone against them. I think of Tottenham. Anything they give me today will be okay because I'll be watching the coppers, magistrates and all those other snides sitting around wanking themselves off. I've been in there with the lads doing some of their own and they haven't got a clue.

I haven't bothered with a brief. No point. Just plead guilty and get it over with. Nobody saw me do anything, but bollocks, why bother? The first time I got nicked I'd done fuck all. I was just a young lad into football, a drink and a quick punch-up if one came my way. The old bill turned up after a bit of trouble and I was straight in the van even though I was just passing by. I was down Fulham nick in ten minutes and when I got to court I pleaded not guilty, which was a big mistake. Whatever they say about the British legal system being the best in the world, it's shit. They say you're innocent till proven guilty, but the first thing the magistrates did was order me to sign on every Saturday when football was on till my case came up. I waited two months and learnt a lesson from a bloke up on the same charge. He was another teenage bystander who'd done nothing, but he was smart. Pleaded guilty. Paid his fine and took his chance. Said he couldn't be bothered and didn't want to miss Chelsea.

It was funny that one. He's telling the magistrate what happened and the old cunt is looking into him like he's a nuclear scientist gone mental. Says that if what the kid's saying is true then he should be pleading not guilty. The bloke knows that if he does that he'll have to sign on like me. He wants to watch Chelsea. They've got some good games coming up. He tells the magistrate he just wants to plead guilty. Everyone knows the score. It's a lottery. The kid's almost begging the bloke to accept he's guilty even though his statement says he's not. The magistrate convicts and fines him.

For two months I signed my name at three o'clock while everyone was down Chelsea. I could have shot down the ground for half-time but what was the point? It was a miserable time. I was shitting it as well. It was like being a virgin or something, not knowing what to expect. I got myself a brief and he was a plonker if ever there was one. I'm standing outside waiting to go in and it's the first time I've seen him face to face. He says a few words and makes a crack about not liking Saturdays because all the riff raff comes in for the football. He lives in Fulham. One of the cunts who pushed house prices up and gave the area a dodgy reputation. Wanker with a plum in his mouth.

Having said that, I went in court and the copper who nicked me must've been brain damaged at birth, though that's being unkind to flids. The bloke representing me did a good job. I got Mark and Rod to give evidence and the arresting officer mucked up his story. The magistrates didn't like it, but they couldn't really get away with a conviction. The old bill were gutted. It was a good moment. My brief asked for costs and the cunt in charge snaps at him and says no. Says I shouldn't have been where I was when I got nicked. I can't dwell on the past, though, because what's done is done. But it shapes you for the future. When my turn comes I plead guilty and tell the three waxworks staring at me that I regret my actions and was only defending myself. I wait for the speech. There's a lot of cases lined up, so the man in the middle, a prat with greasy black hair who looks like he hangs

186

around schools at closing time, gets to the point and says I should be ashamed of myself. He asks me what my parents and friends think about me being in court?

I have to tuck my head into my chest so I don't burst out laughing. He probably thinks I'm ashamed. I should tell him to shut up and stop molesting kids, but what's the point stitching myself up? I've got to keep quiet, take my punishment and come out smelling of roses. I look up quickly and see the fat woman next to him nodding her head. Real dyke prison warden effort in desperate need of a length. The third magistrate wishes he was inspecting his stamp collection. He wants to go home and seems a bit embarrassed by it all. Like the rest of us.

I walk out with a two hundred pound hole in my pocket. It's a con but I've seen it before. I don't hang about. There's no point trying to say anything because it's meaningless and I've got nothing worth saying. These people are scum. Everything's sorted before the accused arrives. Sometimes you get lucky but even then you still have to put up with the hassle. There's never an apology. Look at all those Paddies who got stitched up by the old bill, not to mention all the other bastards through the years. There must be loads of poor sods rotting away inside framed by bent coppers. I've got the old bill's number. Just keep away from them and live your life on the quiet. It's only wankers who get done. Wankers like me.

I walk away from the court and remember the waitress. I look at my watch and it's half-twelve. It's worth a try. I head back to the cafe and go in. Sit at the same table. The bird sees me come in and though she tries to hide it I see she recognises me. When she comes over I tell her I've had a hard morning. Been busy signing a big contract. Made five grand in my pocket but it took a bit of doing. She raises her eyebrows. I tell her life is hard on the streets. She nods and says she knows what I mean. I want to crack up but keep a straight face. The slag walks to the back of the cafe to get my order. I sit back and watch the people outside. The streets are getting busy with office workers running around looking for food. The fine doesn't phase me. It's a risk you take. I don't like the law or any of those involved, but there's no point getting wound up. Two hundred quid's a drop in the ocean. The amount of gear I sell on the side from the warehouse keeps me going. That

187

and a modest wage. It's always the fringe benefits that see you through. Leave it to management and you'll lag behind all your life.

I drink more coffee and eat a sandwich. Life's okay if you know how to handle yourself. Horseferry Magistrates is a minor inconvenience, not the end of the world. Just keep your chin up and they can't touch you. I'm thinking how to spend the rest of the day but have a good idea the way it's going to go. I'm on a near enough cert. There's no point going into the warehouse this afternoon. I told them I was going to a funeral. They won't miss me at work. Everyone respects death. I don't fancy a day off my holidays for the old bill. Far better to invent a family tragedy.

When I start getting bored I catch the waitress's eye and she comes over. She's a good looker and has that rich bitch sleaze about her. This is the fucking class war. Not a bunch of cunts dressed up thinking they're hard when they're more into their clothes than getting stuck in. If they want to go on about class they should have a bit of this bird working out my bill. Or just give up the notion and get stuck in at the football where you avoid the limelight and do the business without justifying yourself. Aggravation without the excuses. I ask her if there's a decent pub nearby. She gives me directions. A five-minute walk. I ask her what time she knocks off. Half-two. Ask her along for a drink and she says yes. Not a second's hesitation. I think about giving her another hefty tip but decide against the idea. A bit obvious that one and I'm into her for a fiver already. We give each other the eye and I watch her arse move all the way back to the kitchen.

I find the pub easy enough and sit down with a pint of lager and the paper. It's one of those Central London pubs done up nice enough but without much character and hardly any locals. The dinner hour mob are clearing out when the bird from the cafe turns up. She looks fit without her uniform. A nice body with good legs and a healthy pair of lungs. She's got a short haircut which suits her bone structure. I know she's going to be a dirty cow. Everything about her spells it out in giant letters. She's got a strong line in confidence and gets the drinks in, then sits down at the table. Her legs brush against me straight off breaking down space.

Her name's Chrissie and she lives in a flat in Westminster.

Belongs to her parents. They live in the Far East and she gets the place for nothing. They're into drugs, the legal variety. It works out well for her because she doesn't have to worry about rip-off rents. She tells me London's full of high prices for studios in dodgy areas. We have the one drink and then she's taking me back to her flat. There's an entry phone downstairs and a video camera bolted to the ceiling. We get in the lift and Chrissie's sticking her tongue down my throat while I'm still swearing at myself getting caught on film. What happens if I want to come back another time and turn the place over? I'm on a mission, doing my bit for the workers. Muscle relaxation after the tension of a court appearance and maybe the chance to make good my losses.

We go into a luxury flat on the eighth floor. There's a view of the surrounding buildings running down to the river. I look out and it's a nest in the clouds. You don't imagine this kind of world exists. I mean, I've seen the sights from tower blocks, but there's an atmosphere to this place. It even smells different. This part of Westminster means money. Big money. There's no rundown cornershops or takeaways. Nothing but luxury flats and Government buildings. The flat's in the middle of London but it doesn't belong here. It's another dimension. A world without people. The place is massive. Three bedrooms, Chrissie tells me. Decked out with paintings that look like they're worth a bomb. There's pictures from all over the world and the carpet must be a good inch thick. There's even a leopard skin on the floor with glass eyes. What a way to end up.

I feel like James Bond or some other upper-crust playboy as Chrissie starts kissing me again. She has me out within seconds and she's got a grip like a pro. I can see us in a big wood trimmed mirror and imagine a camera on the other side with MI5 agents recording the details. Like I'm important or something. Not just a football hooligan fighting my own kind. But Chrissie's groaning like mad and I haven't even got inside her top yet. She's got me stripped in a couple of minutes and she's down to her bra and pants. She won't let me take them off which is getting me wound up. She gets down on her knees and starts in and I have to make do watching her in the mirror. Then she's on her feet going to a bedroom. I'm told to wait a minute before following. I feel like a right cunt standing in the middle of the room with a hard-on, stark bollock naked.

I'm summoned by her highness and Chrissie's on a giant bed with a vibrator wedged up her. She's still got her bra on but I can't see her pants. She's saying she wishes one of my mates was along so we could do her in tandem. I'm smiling but she's bad news. I'm not that kind of bloke. The very idea makes me feel like throwing up and turns me right off. What's the point? It's supposed to be some kind of turn on this line of chat. Breaking down barriers she says. But all I'm interested in is a bit of one on one. I pull the vibrator out and we're going at it, but when it comes to the business Chrissie starts prick teasing. You can usually tell when a bird gets mouthy they're not going to deliver. Same with blokes. The ones bragging about how many birds they've had are the same ones wanking their lives away.

I get her worked up and she lets loose. Makes a liar of me. She's pulling a condom over my knob which I hate but this bird prefers burning rubber to riding bareback and the woman always knows best. I'm banging away for a while but the delay's blocked me up which isn't a bad thing I suppose. Means I last a bit longer though I'm not that bothered either way. She starts telling me she wants it from behind so I have to pull out with this fucking robber's mask over my knob while she gets on all fours. Chrissie assumes the position and raises her arse in the air. She leans over and picks the vibrator up from the floor. She starts sucking on it, groaning like she's auditioning for a film. I start laughing but she doesn't hear. I'm glad I've got the rubber on now because if this bird wants a threesome then fuck knows what she's been up to over the last few years. She's getting well horny and it's no problem keeping her going. Then I'm giving her the business with just the back of her head for company realising that this isn't any kind of revenge, just a good one off.

I shoot my load eventually and roll off. We lean against the pillows with nothing to say. It's that moment of truth after you've done the business with a stranger when you wish there was a button nearby. Hit the switch and the bird disappears. I'm James Bond again. Activate the ejector seat and you're alone to carry on down the road without the model. In the films the woman always gets killed off so Bond never has to bother about small talk after he's done the business. I hate the after-shag chat. I want the bird to disappear so I can be on my own. I nod off for a while and Chrissie's dozing as well. It's an easy option because you wake up later all refreshed and you've got the urge again. There's no need for idle words.

I'm drifting, half asleep, feeling I've let myself down. It's alright when you're going for goal because you've got a bit of steel in you and this kind of shag's about invasion. Instead of sticking the boot in you're using your knob. An invasion of privacy. But once you've delivered you look at what you've done with a bit more vision and see it's shit. You've opened yourself up just to exploit someone else. Violence and sex. Sometimes there's little difference. Not like cutting someone up or torturing them, but it's all about boosting the ego. At least when you get in a punch-up it's power pure and simple. You keep your identity. It's more honest somehow. Not like this set-up where you're conning each other the whole time. Talking shit just to get your end away.

I get up and go for a piss. Chrissie's asleep. It's a palace of a flat and I help myself to a drink from the fridge. A bottled import. All the nobs drink this kind of lager. I sit on the couch and put my feet up. My flat's not bad but it doesn't get near this place. I must have dozed off again because next thing I know it's dark and Chrissie's dressed up in red stockings. The TV's on and there's a bird on the screen getting serviced by a nigger. It's a bleary recording but I recognise the body. Chrissie's smiling for the camera as Dildo Boy does his duty. It's a rich man's paradise and she's telling me nobody does it better than a black man. She's looking in my face for a reaction probably thinking she's radical or something. Probably is for her line of thinking. Chrissie can't compare two different cultures.

It's all a bit of a comedy. The faces are so serious that I see the angle. I feel like a vicar because I'm supposed to be impressed and turned on more than usual. Chrissie looks at me again for a reaction. She starts lecturing me on racial equality and sexual freedom in her pinched upper-class voice. I hate the accent. I realise that now. Maybe that's what does me in, even though she starts sucking my knob again telling me she loves the taste of rubber. Half of me is laughing, the other narked. Suppose I thought I was going to get one back on those miserable cunts in court. Thought I was going to stitch up one of their own. Get the business and turn over a stuck-up slag's flat next time she's selling over-priced coffee. It's no victory. I'm getting a lecture on niggers by a slag in an ivory tower using a black man for her own ends. Arrogant brat's setting herself up as some kind of expert. Actually thinks she's dangerous.

Mind you, I can't get too upset because she gives a good blow job and I'm happy enough shooting off in her mouth. She chokes a bit and I cheer up because she's pissed off. Tells me the one thing she doesn't like is a bloke spunking up in her mouth. At last I've got a blow in against the magistrates. She'll take anything shoved her way but doesn't like a mouthful. Too fucking bad darling. What's she's doing down there in the first place? Chrissie storms off to the bathroom to rinse her mouth out with disinfectant and I go to the fridge for another bottle of lager. I'm sitting on the couch dressed when she comes back, wondering what the fuck I'm doing here. It's raining outside and it's a long way home. The day hasn't really worked out. That's what happens when you get involved with the law. They come at you from every direction. They pull all the strings and have their way every time. The cunts are everywhere.

I watch Chrissie walk in with her cockiness and set ideas. She goes on about niggers but how many mates has she got who are black? Shafting a black man doesn't prove anything. She uses her sex like a hammer and it's me that's being used here. At least I got a shot off in her mouth, though, so something good's come of the day. That and six inches of Chelsea aggro. Expensive though. Two hundred and five quid for something I should be getting for free.

BOMBER COMMAND

THE PICTURE FLICKERED for a fraction of a second, causing Matt Jennings to lift his head from the newspaper he was reading, a plastic mug of steaming tomato soup frozen halfway to his lips. He concentrated on the screen that had attracted his attention, eyes trying to make out a vague object in the darkness. It was nearly two in the morning and the conditions outside were fair for the time of year. It hadn't rained for three days and the wind had calmed after its earlier rage. There was something in the shadows on the far side of the car park, though he couldn't see more than a faint quiver on the rolling film. Jennings put his mug down and was tempted to pour the soup back into his flask, but kept his gaze on the dark corner, automatically switching the angle of camera 6.

He punched the correct buttons and achieved the desired view. A jolt of recognition identified a human form. Jennings zoomed in, wondering what he would find in the recesses of the car park, up against the wall, fearing the worst as a reel of psychopath blockbusters hovered. Day followed day, weeks turned into months and years, and now he was cruising down a tunnel into God knows what. Cushioned by warm air and surrounded by high-tech surveillance gear, he didn't really want to know what went on in the depths of night, the endless repetition of empty car parks and sidewalks, metal gates and driveways suddenly appealing in the face of murder and mutilation. Despite himself, he felt the anticipation of puberty, a twinge of excitement penetrating thirty-five-year-old bones, adrenalin flowing as a ghost began to form. He felt exposed as the camera hit its target and a face looked straight back.

A drunk glanced over his shoulder, the stream of hot liquid running back between his legs across the patterned concrete, harmless dregs, a million miles from the torrent of thick jugular blood Jennings had feared. Disappointment gave way to joy, embarrassment replaced by a sense of the absurd as the drunk walked back towards a small side gate dedicated to those who had fallen in the Falklands, out of the company car park, off along a side road towards the train station. The figure swayed gently from side to side and Jennings imagined him singing a song, a happy song of dancing and love, on his way to the all-night kebab house for a large donner with chilli peppers and chilli sauce. That would sober him up quick enough.

Jennings clicked into the various cameras and enlarged images flashed across the bank of screens surrounding his desk. He was safe and sound, a politician in his nuclear bunker immune to the outside world, removed and cut-off with a one-way view of life that strayed across his line of fire. But he could do nothing other than pick up the phone and call the police station. He was a peaceful man. Violence scared him and, despite the repetitive nature of the buildings he had watched over for the last three years, he was content with the safety of his hideaway, the consistency of the work, the chance to read newspapers and travel magazines, and dunk the sandwiches Pat made him each evening into a mug of soup while planning for the future. Tomato was his favourite flavour and he had this on Tuesdays, Thursdays and Saturdays, while chicken filled in the gaps on Wednesdays and Fridays.

Jennings was thorough in everything he did and had great pride in the knowledge that nothing would ever get past his command post. But there were no bitter winds blowing across his face and no searchlight with which to examine the surrounding jungle. He tried to picture himself with his finger on the trigger of a machine gun, smiled, glad that he wasn't hoisted up as a sitting target for Iraqi commando raids or South American peasant rebellion. He was happy with the warehouses and concrete walkways, the passing cars and drunks emptying their bladders when they thought they were safely hidden from prying eyes, the prowling cats and stray dogs.

Once his shift was finished, Jennings exchanged brief pleasantries with Noel Bailey and was straight out of the door. His replacement would go through the formality of checking the cameras and have an excellent view of his colleague crossing the car park. It was six in the morning and still dark, but Jennings was conscious of the lenses. He didn't like being watched. He got into his car and was soon home, the journey taking ten minutes, the roads practically empty of traffic. He walked through the small front garden and was safely behind the front door, bolt in place and chain hooked. His sigh of relief was audible in the silence of the hall. He was king of the castle once more, back in total control.

He went into the kitchen, took a carton of grapefruit juice from the fridge and filled a tumbler. He drank slowly balancing calories with vitamin content, rinsing the glass when he had finished, leaving it to dry in the empty rack, changing his mind and wiping it with a cloth before putting it back in the cupboard; then tiptoeing upstairs to the bedroom he shared with his wife. He could see the outline of Pat's body under the duvet, the friendly smell of sleep and perfume, earrings and bracelets on the bedside table. The door clicked when it was closed and he listened for the sounds that would show he had woken her, but there was nothing. He went directly to the boxroom at the end of the landing which had been converted into a small office. This was his workshop and the nerve centre of their future success. Jennings plugged in his Macintosh and switched on, a crack of light burning through the screen, the mouse tight in his right hand, finger on the button.

The man from the surveillance unit was soon surfing the Internet, information setting wires alight, ridding him of the need for conversation and puerile social skills, the warehouses and empty car parks blasted into the void, technology maximised. It was so easy on the superhighway, the world at his fingertips waiting to be explored, and all for the price of a local call. The only light came from the screen and he was all-powerful, sitting back in the dark, a white knight in the London metropolis, the figure lurking in the shadows serving humanity. His fingers pounded the keyboard, eyes flitting up and down, left and right.

The downloaded image of a red-headed woman filled Jennings with great expectation, the transparent negligée and welcoming smile a subtle turn-on, the red painted nails long and exotic, text running ragged around partially concealed breasts. He felt guilty and turned to look towards the door, fearful Pat would wake and find him examining other women. It wasn't right, but he was curious all the same and there could be no real harm in looking. He knew there were harder services available, that he was a child in the world of international pornography, a naive boy scout in a web of middle-aged perverts.

With a burst of decision Jennings cancelled his last command and dragged the image to the dustbin, then confirmed the option. He switched off and sat in the dark, thinking and plotting the future. He was ambitious. A winner. He was a clean-living man with morals and a beautiful wife, a woman he loved dearly, someone to cherish and respect. He didn't urinate on private property and hated the thought of having his soul caught inside a surveillance camera. He let his mind race, living the future, then started dozing, dreams setting foundations, jumping awake and going to the bathroom, ripping the woman's memory into tiny pieces and flushing her away. He looked at his watch, mouth watering as he realised it was almost time for breakfast.

Jennings waited for the bacon to crackle and the tomatoes to melt, the smell of fresh Colombian coffee filling the kitchen. He had always wanted to visit South America. Brazil, Colombia, Peru, Bolivia. The names were magical, but a fear of disease, filth, macho violence meant he would make do with glossy magazines and the Sunday papers. Pat was still asleep and he would eat his breakfast and watch twenty minutes of morning TV, wash the dishes and take his wife a cup of coffee in bed. She wasn't working today, but rarely slept in. She was at her best in the morning whereas he was the kind that enjoyed the evenings. The night-shift suited him and it gave them both the space they needed, which in turn helped to keep their marriage fresh. He was a lucky man.

Jennings had plans. Big plans. He was working for the future, clicking into the modern age, his computer a lifeline, a connection with the rest of humanity. Technology was making world travel redundant. Everyone wanted to watch satellite TV these days. The planet's population was tuning into the same news broadcasts, while personal computers would soon be as essential as electricity. Virtual reality was the new reality and Jennings was smart enough to adjust his thinking and move with the times. He was progressive.

– Are you awake, dear?

He saw Pat's bare back in the half-light of the curtained room. He slipped into bed next to her and she turned around, healthy breasts pressing against his sweater. A wedding photograph on the wall showed family and friends, a country church, flowers and confetti, smiling faces.

– I didn't hear you come in, Pat said.

– I've had my breakfast already. It's only half-seven though.

Pat sat up and took the mug of coffee, shifted over a little so that her husband would be more comfortable. The coffee quickly had its effect and Jennings felt his wife's hand moving across the inside of his thigh tugging down his zip. He took the mug of coffee, careful not to spill it on the bedspread as Pat moved nearer, placing it on the bedside table, mildly irritated he had forgotten to bring one of the Windsor Castle coasters to protect the pine. Jennings watched the motion of the bed clothes and noticed the freckles on Pat's face and shoulders. He loved his wife. She was everything a man could wish for in a woman.

– Come here and kiss me, he said gently.

Husband and wife kissed with the solid romance of companionship and ten minutes later he was moving softly, timing his run, high above the clouds riding on pure oxygen, bringing her to climax with his precision performance. When he had finished he timed the withdrawal perfectly, simultaneously positioning his discarded briefs below his wife's buttocks, thereby avoiding stains on the sheet. They lay in each other's arms and rested. Soon Pat was quietly snoring and Jennings began drifting, musing over the wonders of his invention, Smart Bomb Parade, and the deal he was about to sign with a major video games manufacturer. Youngsters would love Smart Bomb Parade. It would satisfy their natural instincts and make him a rich man. He would move out of London and enjoy some clean Gloucestershire air. Perhaps they would try for a child once they were financially secure. He knew Pat was proud of his inventiveness and technological know-how. They were going to be rich one day.

He imagined amusement arcades full of Smart Bomb fanatics splashing out on merchandising. Living rooms echoing specialist sound effects. Personal computers pulsating to the red and yellow flashes of incendiaries. He saw that kid Dave from next door hooked and benefiting from a healthy outlet for misdirected energy. The game would wean him off ecstasy and channel his thoughts. It was good, clean fun and the boy would look good with a short RAF haircut and Smart Bomb T-shirt.

Jennings moved towards sleep, Smart Bomb Parade playing in his mind. There was a hum deep inside the machine and a blaze of ticker-tape street scenes. Blonde virgin girls waved white hand-kerchiefs and a stern middle-aged man wiped a tear from his eye. The graphics were excellent. A brass band played a familiar tune and this filled the combatant with hope and glory. The sound effects were perfect. Jennings was a fighter bomber pilot for the New Economic Order; power of decency pitted against the evil General Mahmet. He was ready for take-off. Red digits flashed across the screen counting down seconds. The computerised faces disappeared as he prepared for the dangerous task ahead.

An electrified crucifix melted through fading street scenes as the military took charge of the operation. To progress through the ranks he needed a high score. It was a question of discipline and the will to win. Individual thoughts had to be controlled and his life donated to the greater good. If he lived he would be a hero with all the benefits such selflessness brought. If he perished, he would be a martyr, and his memory live forever. His family would quote Shakespeare, the message flashing briefly across the screen in a font he had designed himself, that a coward dies many times but a hero dies just the once. He was proud of the artistic touch. He was a man of culture.

Jennings took his place in the massed ranks of fundamentalist crusaders. Modern weaponry was quiet and efficient and only punished the guilty. There was a rigorous points system that recognised decisiveness in battle and the ability to smart bomb a nation's infrastructure back to the Stone Age. He felt the thrill of conflict. He was on the march, part of an organisation based on chivalry and the highest moral principles. He was justified in whatever actions he was forced to take to save his way of life, community, nation. His finger tingled on the mouse deciding life and death. Although strategic missiles and smart cluster bombs were readily available, there was a bonus for decisive strikes. Waste not want not was the NEO motto.

The score was scaled according to a target's military import-ance. A secret bonus scheme operated, details unknown. Schools and hospitals recorded points, though this was officially denied for reasons of political politeness, while other more complicated factors were also taken into account. Kill ratios were broken down and categorised. The player would never question the machine. Deep in NEO circuits the publicity network protecting Jennings from mass opinion called for extra memory. Nothing was left to chance. Lights flickered and the eyes of the General burned communist red. A blood red craving for infidel babies and homosexual deviance. The General was flanked by sadistic mullahs, Korans held to the sky, thunderbolts cracking the minarets of the East. There was no need to consider the strange mixture of Islamic and communist ideas. As far as the game was concerned they belonged together.

Rockets spat flame and Jennings was soaring through the skies on the crest of an adrenalin rush, thoughts sucked towards the hard disk. He crossed parched desert landscapes and spotted a Bedouin camel train, insignificant and unarmed. He considered a strike but would be wasting time and ammunition for a low points return. He switched to control frequency, briefed by a computer programmer tapping into detailed information banks, digitised kill potential passed to a gunslinging pilot. Righteousness flooded his brain. He was a prophet in steel casing, a clean-killing European superman. He launched his craft in a calculated arc, technology confirming creative genius. Missiles burnt beneath an Arab sun. A row of slum housing exploded in dust storms. Colour was added to a drab world of hunger and disease. The gleaming dome of a mosque stretched outwards and then melted back into itself. He hit the water works, score rising as black ants ran beneath falling debris. Chemical weapons were the reward for experience. Death better than continual poverty.

The Smart Bomb pilot turned in semi-consciousness, bumping his wife, turning for home with joy in his heart, knowing he was safe from ground attack. He had one rocket left and turned a victory roll, spotting a bazaar on the outskirts of town, a tangle of bright stalls and frantic insects. He clicked the mouse then shouted into his radio as a school exploded. The score increased, machine buzzing with complicated equations. It was an easy ride back to base, but he had to keep his wits about him. He was ecstatic with success. Mundane existence was transformed.

The score was high and Jennings translated the success of the software into hard cash. There would be steak on the menu and congratulations from his comrades. He would drink cold American beer and listen to relaxing mood music, take a shower and enjoy the praise. He was a credit to his country. He timed his approach and felt the bounce of touchdown. Pat was awake and getting out of bed, on her way to the bathroom to clean up the mess. He hoped she hadn't leaked on the sheet.

VILLA AWAY

WE'RE STUCK IN traffic on the motorway looking over Birmingham. It's a fucking horrible place. Ties with Liverpool as the worst place I've been in the last few years. That's saying something because the North is stacked with dead industry and ghost towns where the kids are deprived and the parents depraved. The traffic's died a death and we're pissed off because it's getting late. Half-one and we're still on the flyover. There's cars and coaches and lorries backed up. The cars carry happy families and decent football fans. There's Villa, Chelsea, Arsenal scarves hanging from windows. A couple of other clubs I don't recognise. All the colours of the rainbow. Rod says Arsenal are playing Everton away. Wankers wearing colours.

Birmingham stretches as far as you can see. All the way to the horizon. There's no colour, just grey warehouses and derelict buildings dwarfing identical houses full of Jasper Carrot Brummies. There's mist floating around but it's no natural beauty, more like poison from the traffic clogging the motorway. Traffic speeds in the opposite direction while we sit tight like a bunch of cunts. Coachloads of grannies and Paki pilgrims head south to London. Can't blame them wanting to enjoy a bit of civilisation. Anything for a break from a lifetime stuck in a slum clearance like Birmingham.

We're not going as far as Spaghetti Junction, turning off for Villa Park before we're sucked into that particular abortion. But we've been through enough times going to away games to know about the jams and fumes. Space Age gone wrong. When we go away it's either coach or train travel and both have their advantages. At the moment we're using coaches a lot because you avoid the aggravation and expense of travelling on British Rail. There's no coppers standing at the barrier watching you from the moment you pull out of Euston or King's Cross till touchdown in Manchester or Leeds. There again, when you go by coach you end up tied to the fucker. That's if you want to get back to London without forking out for train fares. Nothing's perfect in this world.

The old bill have Saturdays sewn up and are always on the lookout for coaches, so you have to work things out in advance. The more they install cameras and set up cordons around grounds like it's some kind of war zone, the further away they push the problem, stretching the Harris imagination. That's all anyone really cares about, keeping their patch tidy. No major disturbance translates as a clean bill of health according to those in charge. But nothing gets solved ignoring the problem. It just sets up shop somewhere else. It's human nature and that's why banging someone up never does much good, because even though it's no picnic inside, the causes are still there bubbling away.

– Mandy thinks she's up the duff. Rod's been a miserable cunt since this morning and now it's easy to understand why. He sits there looking at us like a stray dog feeling sorry for itself.

– What do you mean? Mark looks puzzled.

– What do you think I mean?

– What do you mean she's up the duff?

– Well, mate, it's like this. Blokes have this lump of meat between their legs that fills with blood when it sniffs a bit of gash. The bird gets greased up when she sees the bloke. The man shoves this stiff object into the hole between the woman's legs, moves back and forwards for a while, in your case a couple of seconds, and shoots off this white washing-up liquid. Nine months later, if the timing's right, a screaming brat pops out and the cunt responsible gets to pay for it for the next sixteen years.

– Are you serious?

– That's how it works Mark. I wouldn't lie to you. Not about something that important. It's in all the medical books and most of the programmes on telly, though they don't show all the details. It's the birds and bees. Watch them next summer if any of the cunts get lost and fly down your street and you still won't have a clue what I'm on about. I'm surprised your old girl didn't tell you when your balls dropped. They taught us at school when we were kids, but you were always skiving so you were probably down the arcade or something fucking about with the Space Invaders.

– Very funny. Are you sure about Mandy?

– She's two days late. Didn't seem bothered when she told me this morning, but it felt like she'd kicked me in the bollocks. I'm getting dressed ready for a day out and she comes back from having a piss and breaks the good news.

I tell Rod that two days isn't a long time. Birds can be a lot later than that. Some are so fucking dozy they can't count past ten so they never know what time of the day it is let alone the month. I can see he's gutted. It's there in his face carved in deep like he's been glassed by some headbanger. Even Mark sees it and he usually misses the subtle things in life. Like his time in the nick. He's always been like that, even as a kid. He's thick-skinned like a pissed water buffalo. Just says what comes into his head and doesn't give a fuck if it winds people up or not.

He's leaving well alone at the moment. It's a good idea, because though Mark can be a nasty bit of work sometimes, with a mean streak that makes you think he's a closet psycho or something, Rod can be a bit naughty himself. If Rod gets pushed far enough he snaps. Goes mental and then he's worth two of Mark. I remember him at school in the playground when some kid picked a fight, said his old girl was a prossie, and Rod went off his rocker like someone had pulled the plug. Had the bloke on the ground with his shoulders pinned down, smashing his head on the concrete, again and again. I had to pull him off in the end before he killed the cunt. It's not part of his basic character, but it's there all the same. Everyone has a breaking point. I can't imagine Rod being a dad.

– What are you going to do if it's true? What if Mandy is in the club? Mark looks worried. Kids are bad news all round.

– Don't know what I'd do. Mandy wouldn't get rid of it and it's not like she's some slag I've serviced in a doorway after one pint over the top. She's my fucking wife. I suppose I'd end up being a dad. Either that or kick her down the stairs.

– That's a fucking stupid thing to say.

– I wouldn't do it. Don't know why I said it. I'm a cunt, alright?

– You could buy it a Chelsea shirt and bring it to games. You wouldn't be out with us lot much, would you? You couldn't go out steaming Tottenham with a kid sitting on your shoulders.

I start laughing and Rod gives me a nasty look. He asks what's so funny. I tell him I'm imagining him kicking some Spurs cunt in the head with a kid on his shoulders directing operations. He could be the firm's mascot. He doesn't see it himself and shakes his head. The idea starts growing on me but I'm not telling Rod. He'll end up like one of those blokes you see on a Saturday with messy grey hair walking down from Fulham Broadway, who goes in the ground and has to sit in the family section surrounded by brats while the lads are having a good time. If Rod ends up like one of those cunts I'll get a shooter and put him out of his misery. Play the vet doing the decent thing for a poor dumb animal. Otherwise he'll end up another one of the walking dead. The people milking the game say football should be family entertainment and all that nonsense. They say more birds should go to football. There's enough of them there already and who wants a stand full of screaming kids like at England home games?

We cheer up as the coach pulls off the motorway heading towards Villa Park. We've got a different driver with Ron Hawkins off with the flu and he doesn't take long to get lost in the traffic, missing the signs, and the old bill are dozing and don't see us go past. We end up on the other side of the park backing onto the Holte End. He's a fucking wanker this driver. Doesn't want the ticket Harris always gets Ron for the game. We get the bloke to drop us off. Tell him we'll walk and he can meet us at the same place after Chelsea have stuffed Villa.

– You'll be alright, Mark says, trying to cheer Rod up. I wouldn't worry about it too much. Not yet anyway. Every bird is late now and again. That's how it goes. She could've had a shock or something, or not been feeling well. Maybe she was frightened when that thing you were talking about filled up with blood and hit six inches. Fright of her life after getting used to six centimetres.

– Mandy looks after herself. Rod laughs despite himself. She knows what's going on inside her gut. Mind you, she said she didn't think she was in the club. Reckoned she'd be able to tell though fuck knows how.

– Forget it. Maybe we'll find some Villa fans. That'll cheer you up. Batter a few Brummies and you'll be smiling.

– Some chance. Remember how they scattered that time on

the pitch? Last game of the season and they get steamed by fifty Chelsea and do a vanishing act.

– Bunch of cunts.

– Thought I'd been slipped a nasty chemical. One minute they're standing there like they want to know, the next there's nothing but thin air and a pile of steaming shit.

We walk down a terraced row of houses. There's two beat up cars and a load of kids playing on the sidewalk. Small scrawny bastards shivering in the cold. There's a Paki shop on the corner with bare metal shelves and a few tins in the window. Curried beans and chopped mushrooms. A rack of newspapers with a bird on the front in suspenders and a headline accusing a leading politician of adultery. A gang of black kids stands around the corner watching us. Must be eight or nine with oversized coats and trainers. They've got flash bikes and bobble hats as well, so they must be doing something right.

They're waiting for cars coming to football, trying to make a bit on the side, offering protection from other kids they say are going round slashing tyres. You have to admire their understanding of the free market. It's basic economics, because you take something like a major war and it's a money spinner. Bomb the place till there's nothing left standing and then a few years later put in bids for work rebuilding the place. There's big money in sewage systems and fresh water. It's sound business sense. Build and destroy. Or when you can't go out and smash it straight off, put a timing device inside so after a few years the fucker breaks down.

We head off across the park. A coachload out for a stroll and it must be an odd sight. It's a mild day in the park with green grass and trees, and a loving couple walking their dog take one look at us and head in the opposite direction. It's funny, but I feel uncomfortable. We're out of our surroundings and must look a right bunch of cunts. It's like when we stopped for a piss on the way to Sunderland for the Newcastle game and Facelift was doing his best to pollute the English countryside with an Agent Orange piss attack. We didn't belong and now we're taking it a stage further. The fat cunt's not with us today, but Harris is up ahead getting muddy, looking left and right like one of those bouncing toy dogs Pakis carry round in the back of their Datsuns.

There's a smart red brick building to our right and we're coming over a ridge walking through dead leaves. Like a tribe of Apaches on the skyline. There's locals heading in the same direction, little knots of teenagers who you know straight away have never been in trouble in their lives. We come to the street along the side of the ground and turn right into the buzz of Saturday afternoon. The main entrance to Villa Park is impressive. It's old brickwork from another era, a nice bit of history. Classy but ancient. It's two o'clock and the place is packed with people walking up and down, a lot of them wearing Villa tops. We go towards the Holte End, a wedge through the middle of the street looking for reaction but not expecting much. The crowd melts away. They know we're Chelsea and know we're a firm. No colours or shouting, but it's obvious. Any cunt could tell us apart. Harris slags off a few blokes walking the other way but it's a waste of time, they don't want to know.

– What's the matter with these cunts. Mark is laughing because it's a bit of a joke.

– They're not interested. They just want their football.

I look at the blokes walking along holding the hands of small children, making sure their kids don't get lost in the crowd and trampled underfoot. They look at us sharpish with a bit of dread mixed with disgust. They're older and not exactly trainspotters, but they're on their own with the kid and we're just another problem along with the bills and dole queue. They want to watch the football while they can still afford to get in the place.

We're outside the Holte End and nothing's happening. There's no Villa mob in sight and even the groups of three or four young lads hanging around look like the last thing on their minds is a row. We walk back the way we came with Villa fans hurrying the other way. They're real Brummies this lot with their dodgy gear and accents. It's obvious we're ready for a bit of conflict, but for something to happen you've got to have opposition. We're up here for the day, all the way from London, ready and willing, but there's no-one worth steaming. We're walking up and down the street outside their ground and it's up to them to do the business. They should be having a go at us. We need a Villa firm to make things work. These cunts around us with their programmes and rip-off club shirts don't count.

– Don't know what's the matter with them. Harris is laughing because if you make an appearance there's nothing more you can do. You've done your bit and it's the other side that looks bad.

– There's a few pubs round the back of the away end, says Billy Bright. Let's take a stroll down there. See if we can flush the wankers out.

– They'll be shut up, says Mark. Worth a try though.

We turn through a set of gates leading to the away end. There's a mesh fence with a crowd of people peering through waiting to see the players. I hate that kind of thing. Real hero worship. I mean, I support the team and everything, but I don't want to talk to the players. At least not through a fence with my tongue hanging out like a demented polar bear in the zoo, like the players are something better than me. You get enough of that during the week. It's bollocks and we keep going through a small car park and down to the away entrance. Suddenly it's all Chelsea and it's good how you just walk round a ground and the people all have a different accent and way of dressing.

– Down here. There's a couple of pubs at the bottom of the street. Billy Bright plays the Pied Piper and leads the way.

There's a transit with a riot shield across the window full of old bill. They watch us pass in silence. Make no move to interfere. We're going against the flow of Chelsea coming the other way. It's sunny out, but cold as well, and the area around the ground is dead. No character till we come to a stone pub on the corner which is closed and then a junction that's more Midlands depression, crumbling in front of our eyes. There's a pub across the street with a couple of police horses and a transit van parked outside. There's the sign HOME FANS ONLY in the window. Now and then some cunt in an anorak knocks on the door and goes inside. It's not exactly going to be a major Villa firm inside so we take a wander. There's nothing. All the pubs are closed and there's no Villa in sight. We've done our best and turn back to the ground for the kick-off. Have to admit I didn't expect much. We have to queue for ten minutes and there's some kid copper explaining that having too much to drink before the game means you're pissed and not allowed to watch the football.

I get a cup of tea inside and we sit in small plastic seats waiting for the match to start. Villa are singing in the Holte End but

Chelsea always give it some good vocals when we play away. It's all end to end stuff which warms us up and takes Rod's mind off Mandy's missing period. I start thinking about this bird I went out with when I was a kid. Two years it was before I found out she was knocking off some bloke from Kilburn. Claire thought she was in the club one time and I made the mistake of telling Mark, who passed the news on. Soon I was getting the piss ripped out of me left, right and centre. She was black and they were giving me stick asking what the kid was going to look like, whether it was going to come out half man, half baboon.

I was shitting it because I didn't want to be a father at fifteen and they were trying to ease the agony with a bit of humour. It turned out alright in the end because she came on and we went out and got pissed on snakebite. We were out of it and I shagged her in the back of some car we broke into and the next morning I was red as a beetroot. She was alright Claire, really into the old music and that, and became a dancer when she grew up. She moved out of the area years ago and went up to North London. Moved in with some kebab merchant. She was one of those birds who if you met her twenty years later you'd probably end up staying with. I remind Rod about Claire to get him looking on the bright side.

– She was a cracker, he says. Well tasty.

– I'd have fucked that if I'd had the chance, Mark joins in.

– Fit body on her. She made a bomb as a dancer, didn't she?

Chelsea break clear of the Villa defence and we're on our feet. The ball hits the net and we're jumping up and down going mental and Claire and Mandy are forgotten. It's a good game of football and when the ref blows the whistle at the end we leave happy. The dark's starting to come now and we're going back across the park with a good chunk of the crowd. Billy Bright stands against a tree having a slash and a woman coming the other way looks at him like he's committing a major league crime. He flashes at her and she runs off.

The coach is waiting and we're ready for the trip back to London, planning a stop in Northampton. The kids guarding cars are still there, but don't look like they're doing much business. Times are hard and those at the bottom of the pile are always first to feel the pinch. Harris has slipped the driver twenty quid to stop in Northampton so everything's sweet. We move slowly through football traffic. Once we get to the motorway we're off with everything moving nicely. Should be in a Northampton pub within an hour or so. Now the game's over Rod sits frozen looking out the window watching the world pass in the opposite direction.

– Phone Mandy when we get to Northampton. Mark is sitting next to Black Paul, leaning over the seat. She'll have come on by now. She's got you worried so she'll start bleeding.

– I'll phone her but I'm not holding my breath.

We're soon pulling off the motorway and stopping at a pub we've used several times before. We're straight inside lining up the drinks. Rod fucks off to the phone. I watch him and he looks like he's talking but comes back and says there's no answer. He's been chatting with himself. Mandy must be round her mum's, but there again she could be doing a Claire. You can never trust a bird because they give it the big one about honesty and everything, then soon as you turn your back their pants hit the floor and they've got their ankles digging in some other bloke's arse.

– I fucking need this, says Rod, lifting the glass to his lips. Beautiful.

– That'll sort you out. Black Paul is next to him drinking orange juice. It's thirsty work waiting for women to get their act together.

– Why don't you drink then?

– Don't have problems with women. Treat them like shit and they love you. Give them a bit of leeway and they'll take liberties. It's a fucking war.

– Mandy's alright. She's straight. Solid.

– She might be, but what about you? Mark joins in. A few beers in your belly and you're sniffing round anything that moves.

– It's different. It doesn't count.

– How's that then?

– Don't know, it's just different somehow. I know I don't mean it I suppose. It's just the alcohol taking charge.

– You drink it in the first place, says Paul coming on like a fucking agony aunt. You want the effect otherwise you wouldn't get pissed. You go to football and you lay off it because you know

209

you'll get out of hand. Go out in the evening when you're socialising and you don't give a fuck.

– I don't know. You can't think about these things too much.

– It's war. Just remember that. But it's a psychological war. Lift a hand to a woman and she'll never forget it. You can treat them like shit, but show respect when you're doing it. Lose your temper and it means they've got under your skin.

– Paul's right in a way, says Mark. Getting pissed is no excuse. Everyone says it is, but it's a bottle job. But who needs an excuse in the first place?

Rod gets the drinks in and we're knocking them back fast. After five pints Rod goes over to the phone and tries again. I watch the bloke and know he's not talking to himself any more. There's a big grin on his face. Ear to ear job. Real Joker effort. He puts the receiver down and comes back. He's got a result and Mandy's got a Tampax earning its keep. He clenches his fist like he's just scored a goal.

– One-nil. Came on this afternoon.

– Told you it would be okay. You shouldn't worry.

– I know. But you do, don't you? You just see your life going down the bog with the used rubbers. You know you'll never fuck off out of London or do anything different with your life, just keep on going till the day you die, but you like to have the option. Kids stop all that.

– Depends how you look at it, says Harris. I've got two kids myself. It doesn't change anything. It's all in the mind, like everything else. I see them twice a week and everything's okay. I wouldn't swap them for anything, even though me and their mum don't live together these days. We get on alright and the kids are the most important thing in your life once you have them.

I look at Harris a bit different. I'd never have guessed it, but that's not unusual. You see some blokes at football and you'll only ever know some of them one way. Then they melt into everyday life. They don't walk around with a sign round their neck telling everyone they're the hooligan element or anything. They've got their jobs and their loves, though that's not to say they're saints. Football is just a focus, a way of channelling things. If there was no football we'd find something else. Probably be a lot more indiscriminate as well. The aggression's got to get out some way and the authorities know the score and want you signed up, standing to attention killing Arabs or Paddies or whoever's flavour of the month on their behalf.

– I'm a free man, says Rod. I feel like I've been let out of the nick. Ready to pass go and collect my cheque.

– No you don't. Mark speaks up. That's something you've got to go through to understand. It's a different thing being inside, like nothing else. Take my word for it.

– You know what I mean.

The night passes quickly and we're hammered by ten. The coach driver says he's leaving at eleven. We're trying to persuade the cunt to stay on, to come along to this club we know, but he's not interested. Says he's got a wife and kids at home waiting for him. We're undecided, not fancying the hassle of trying to get back to London at three in the morning. Rod makes the decision. Says he fancies a bit of bloodsport when he gets home. It's the man's night so we let him have the final word. He tells us to drink up. We've still got another hour till we head back to London.

ASHES TO ASHES

A CHEERFUL YOUNG man said a few words, the mourners sang a song of remembrance without musical accompaniment, and the deceased's remains were sent below to melt into nothingness. Mr Farrell caught his line of thought, stopped it dead. It wasn't emptiness but a new beginning; if that's what Albert Moss really believed, then why not? He had no deep-rooted faith of his own and doubted whether his Spiritualist friend would have trusted in a greater, all-loving creator if he'd been inside a concentration camp, but that was the democratic way.

With Albert's corpse went visions of Mrs Farrell. Her husband was finally at rest; one day he would visit the headstone, read the inscription he had chosen after much careful thought and days of indecision, then trim and arrange her favourite red and white carnations. He saw flesh slowly rotting, skin sucked into itself and wrinkles exaggerated, below ground with the sewage pipes and broken bones. A shudder passed through his body, starting at the shoulders and racing down to his feet, forcing him to lean forward in his pew. Nobody paid attention. They just saw an old man expressing his grief.

When the congregation filed out of the chapel, Mr Farrell stayed behind, sitting with his head in his hands. Tears trickled beneath strong fingers but didn't reach his lips. He hadn't cried properly since he was a child, though he couldn't remember even that, and he wasn't exactly sobbing now. He was sad but at the same time relieved. He remained solid for a long while, flashbacks coming in bursts then slowly melting away, the stacked corpses and rotting bodies of his army experience swamped by happy memories; family and friends and a pride in his role in the war.

While others his age fumed at antagonists who had only ever known peace, Mr Farrell just didn't care. Perhaps Bomber Harris had been wrong about Dresden. There was no glory in fireballs and burning human beings, how could there be, yet he couldn't see what could be gained attacking pensioners who had done what they thought best. They had been kids at the time. Teenagers in uniforms. But he marvelled at the spiral of history, rewritten and revised and turned inside-out. He was living history, for as long as his memory held, and he would be dead in a few years, perhaps sooner. Then it would be left to books to tell the story secondhand.

Eventually Mr Farrell stood up and pushed through the weakness, because that was all tears could ever be. His sex and class meant he was denied the right to act soft, to shed tears and openly mourn. That was for the privileged, with time on their hands and a need for excessive psychology. He wasn't complaining, because you needed an inner strength to get through life, the ability to face everything and come out on top. The weak sank into depression, names unknown and reason lost. Perhaps he'd been on the brink himself, suffering hallucinations and seeing his wife where she couldn't possibly exist, hearing her voice in his head, allowing himself to drift towards Albert's way of thinking. But he was finished with all that now. She was dead.

He didn't care for religious ceremony or images, the only reality body fat melting in intense heat, bubbling up and dripping from the oven, turning to stone. Deep down he envied Albert his Spiritualism, yet could never become immersed himself. Belief was ingrained. If a person created their own afterlife then who was to say it wouldn't come true; like wishing on a star. Time was the crux and while the past was reinvented daily it was too hard an exercise for him to follow at his age, all the bickering back and forward, the future an easier and more positive option.

– How was it? Vince asked, his grandfather opening the passenger door and getting into the car.

– A funeral's a funeral, though this one was better than most because there was no organ player going through the motions and hitting all the wrong notes, and they kept the speech short. At least there wasn't the fuss of your gran's burial. I remember everything like it was yesterday. The organ blasting away out of tune and echoing through my head driving me mad. Then the vicar rabbiting on about someone he'd never met, not even knowing she was born a Jew in Budapest and died an atheist in London, that she was a million miles beyond his forgiveness and taking a plot in his graveyard. I swear if he'd gone on much longer I'd have swung for him.

Vince Matthews nodded his head, not knowing what to say. He turned on the ignition and pulled to the edge of the road, looking for a way into the traffic. The old boy'd had a rough time of things since his wife died, but seemed to be pulling through now. He found a gap and put his foot down, leaving the crematorium behind as quick as possible. The lights were rolling in his favour and before long they were cutting along beneath the Chiswick Flyover gunning towards Kew.

– You should come out to Australia when I get set up over there, Vince said. Give me a few months to get things going then come and stay for as long as you want. I'll get work no problem, I know enough people, and we can drive into the outback and see the sights. It's relaxed and you don't have to worry about politics and getting mugged, or how much the council's going to tax you next month.

– I could have gone years ago you know. A mate of mine emigrated after the war and wanted me to try my hand, but I didn't fancy it somehow. Mind you, maybe I'll take you up on the offer, though it'll cost a bit to get over there. I didn't know what was going to happen after the war. It was an exciting time in its own way, coming out of something like that with all your limbs and half your mind left, then after a while the relief just turned to sadness. There was no help in those days. Nobody you could go and talk to about what you'd seen and done, and your gran was such a mess after everything that happened to her. You got through it though. You had no choice. It was either that or the madhouse. Maybe we were stronger then, I don't know. Not like you nancies today with your counselling and social workers.

They both laughed. Vince wondered if he'd killed anyone during the war, but would never ask. Even as a kid he had known enough not to put the question. That would be hard to handle, even though it was war and a fight for survival. He thought about the punch-ups he'd been involved in when he was younger. He couldn't link the two characters even though he was the same person. If he got himself in the situation he would fight for survival, but he preferred overseas travel to a trip up to Liverpool or Manchester. Losing his head over a bang lassi was better than a two o'clock kicking outside some dodgy club with your eyes bleary from the drink and your brain about to get another pounding from some nutter out to do you serious damage.

– I'll pay your flight over, don't worry about that. You've done enough for me in the past, when I was a kid and all that. You just get yourself down Heathrow and enjoy the ride. Don't let me down either. Mum and Dad said they'd be over but you come on your own and we'll have a good laugh. You drive out in the desert over there and there's nothing to see but sand and the horizon, burning mountain ranges the Aborigines say are sleeping animals that created the world. It does something to your head. There's no crowd mentality in the desert, just kangaroos and maybe some Aborigines out in the heat living the dreamtime.

– It'll be my second youth, let alone childhood, my first time abroad since 1945. I've never been on a plane you know. They say it's an experience, a bit better than jumping out of a landing craft with German machine-gunners trying to cut you in half if you get to the beach and a bastard of a sergeant at your back with a machine-gun threatening to chop you down if you don't get out quick enough. It was like that, you know, because if you didn't shift you risked the other blokes as well as yourself.

– You get treated with respect when you travel to Australia because you've paid a fair bit for the seat. It's not like some two-hour tube trip to Spain or Greece. You go long-haul and they look after you. Free drinks, meals-on-wheels and films. You get some crackers working as stewardesses as well.

– Maybe I'll find myself a dolly bird and get her to look after me, you never know. I'm not past it. Even when you're old you still get the urge now and again.

Vince was embarrassed. He didn't want to think of his granddad on the job, shagging some British Airways bimbo on Bondi Beach, giving her a nice line of chat, pulling the rubber on and spreading the woman's legs, dipping his winkie in a piece of BA hardcore, bony arse moving up and down in time to a brass band, voices in the distance, the blonde with blue eyes captivated by the pensioner's charm, the medals he rarely wears because he thinks they're rubbish, digging ten-inch purple fingernails into sand-paper skin, coming in a groaning tribute to age and experience, the skeleton shag-machine from West London on tour down under, bikini blondes flocking around the pre-war model sex instructor tucking into his early morning breakfast. Vince shook his head. That lassi must be lingering. It was disgusting. Child-molesting in reverse. He took the techno tape his brother had made up and slipped it into the cassette-player, Spiral Tribe, turned the volume down so it was just about audible.

– You get high above the clouds and next thing you're flying over all these places you hear about on the news, Kuwait City, New Delhi, Singapore, the works, right there in space looking down on everything, the shapes of the clouds, and when the sun comes up you look through the window and you can almost see a curve in space. It's like you're halfway to being an astronaut riding with the gods. You feel special. Nothing can get near enough to harm you.

– It sounds good. We'll see about it later. You might not go back.

– I will. Give it another six months or so. I love England and everything, but it's shit really. It's all the stuff you have to carry on your back. I mean, I know it's the same anywhere you go, but I'd rather just be on the outside looking in, keeping my head down, rather than in the middle of things getting battered all the time.

Vince crossed Kew Bridge, indicated right and stopped, waiting for a gap in the South Circular. He pulled off towards the front of Kew Gardens and easily found a place to park. At this time of year there was always free space around the common. The houses were more like mansions and he wondered what it would be like living there. Not bad probably. It wasn't London really, at least not the London he knew. During the summer there was a cricket pitch and the old church opposite served tea and cakes. It was more like a country village. They got out and walked to the main gates, Vince's treat as it was expensive to get in Kew Gardens these days.

It had been five years since Mr Farrell's last visit, a summer's day walkabout with his wife, his former occupation adding to the attraction of the botanical gardens. Vince had been as a child with both his parents and grandparents. He especially remembered the time his brother got lost in the trees off towards the river. Their dad gave him a hiding when they found him. They went straight then turned left towards the lake, the Palm House to their right. As a kid Vince was convinced it was a spaceship, the shape and glass panelling elegantly contoured and maintained, as big now as it had appeared then. They stopped by the water. There was an elderly couple on the opposite side and three Japanese tourists, but this time of year saw only a fraction of the summer rush. The earth was black and rich, clouds blocking the sun, a relative solitude and promise of life under the soil waiting to rise up and take over.

They went to the Palm House, heavy doors sounding behind them. It was warm and humid, the glass sections above just visible through lush foliage, a regular hiss of sprayed water. They were transported to the Amazon, the rainforests of Asia, around the globe in minutes. Everywhere there was exotic life and lush vegetation. They climbed circular stairs to the walkway above, stopping to look down on enormous leaves and intricate bark formations, lost in a Victorian jungle.

– They did some good things in the old days, didn't they, Vince said, finally breaking the silence, footsteps on metal. It wasn't all blood and theft. You know, I read that they used to castrate Aborigines and bet on how long it took them to die, but you come here and see what other people built and it's another story. You look at this place, the parks in London and all the museums, and you don't see anyone doing that nowadays. It's all cutting back and closing down, and if they could get their hands on Kew the developers would chop down the trees and flog the land as prime real estate.

– Things get better in some ways and worse in others, Mr Farrell replied, the load just gets shifted around. Look at my day. World war and millions murdered, raped, tortured. That was Europe and now we build the guns for others to do the killing, but there's nothing on that scale. It depends which way you look at things.

Mr Farrell was glad when they left the Palm House. The humidity was affecting his breathing. Vince enjoyed the fresh air as well. It made him happy seeing the old boy in a positive state of mind. He was always talking about his wife in the present, like she was still around, sitting at the table in the flat maybe, or resting in the bedroom, watching through the window for her husband's return. It was a bit sick somehow and Vince was thinking of his gran, the way she laughed deep in her throat, but now his granddad was talking about her in the past tense. It made him feel a lot easier.

They went towards the river, past the second lake with ducks on the water and duck shit on the bank, circling around so they eventually arrived at the Evolution House. Vince read about asexual and sexual reproduction, the roles of bats, bees and butterflies in pollination, the extra strength to be gained through sexual production, the addition of new genes which made for a better chance of survival. It was all there in the bang lassis, the great British mega-mix.

– I'm glad we came, Mr Farrell said, sitting in the nearby restaurant half an hour later, a squirrel sauntering up for a piece of cheese sandwich. It gives you a lift, somewhere like this. This is the real world, what it's all about, trees and plants and flowers and scientists looking at the medicine we can get from nature. It's all this that you never hear about. You just get the negative angle the whole time.

Vince nodded. He was right. Kew just meant happy memories as far as he was concerned, but there was something even more positive about the place now. It was more sophisticated, like they were trying to get people involved in the work, attempting to educate as well as everything else. Maybe he'd just not been looking before. But how were you supposed to know the truth about the past when on the one hand you had stories about Aborigines getting castrated for a wager, yet at the same time there were naturalists and horticulturists travelling the globe fascinated by trees and plants and the benefits they offered humanity, trying to preserve nature.

– What do you want to go to Australia for when you've got this? Mr Farrell laughed. It might be nice over there but it's never going to be home, is it? That's probably why I never went and tried my hand over there, I remember now. It would have been admitting failure, that a part of me was no good, that the country that made me was nothing. The future's got to be worth seeing, just finding out what's going to happen next, even ten or twenty years down the road. That's what keeps you going. You sit in the past and you never move forward. It's half and half. Keep the good things and add to them, but throwing it all away and starting again is as bad as never changing anything at all.

– You sound like a politician, Vince said.

– I've never heard a politician worth listening to, and I've heard a few.

Vince was in Australia, north of Sydney along the Great Barrier Reef, sheer beauty beneath a clear blue ocean, diving down into another universe of fish and coral, shoals of minnows darting back and forward, thousands of tiny lives, bigger multicoloured fish looking at him with enormous eyes, a harmless shark in the distance. Below the surface life was vibrant and alive, finding its own way to survive, all the colours mixed in together, and he was thinking about asexual and sexual reproduction, vindicated in his role, thick sand and the Italian girl he met diving, that evening sitting on the beach looking into the darkness, the outline of her long black hair against a cloudless sky covered in stars and trailing meteors, waves crashing on the shore taking him back all those years to San Sebastian, trying to sleep under the boardwalk with drunks smashing bottles up above, and he'd done what he planned, got out of the rut, out of his environment, so now he could see what was under the surface, deep down, all the colour and movement, people like himself too far into their world to see there was something outside, something bigger, and the great thing was that it didn't really matter one way or the other, just that Italian woman was important, total beauty, a soppy way to describe a human being but that's what it was, pure magic, the realisation that he, Vince Matthews, had made it to the other side of the planet and had seen more than seven wonders on the way, almost laughing out loud thinking of the lads in San Sebastian, the bulls they were going to run and the sunburn, where were the poor bastards at that precise moment, the bulls dead, what about John and Gary and all the others, then they were gone again, as Vince focused on the red burns of space rock millions of miles above his head.

– There's one or two politicians who made the effort, but they got shouted down, so now none of them bother any more and make do looking after their own little bit of power. They blend in with popular opinion and settle for an easy life. Suppose we all do. Not you and me though. We've been outside and seen the options. I had no choice and didn't like what I found, but you had the nerve to do it on your own and you'll probably be going back for some more. What are you smiling at Vince?

– Just the thought of those explorers and how they must've travelled. There were no round-the-world airline tickets or backpacker hostels in those days.

When they'd finished their coffee and Mr Farrell had attracted another couple of squirrels with hand-outs, they started walking again. The clouds had gone and it was a fine day. They passed through a ruined brick arch and were about to pass the Marianne North Gallery when Mr Farrell caught Vince's arm. Neither remembered the building and they walked inside, reading the details of a Victorian artist without formal training who had travelled the world painting plants and scenery.

Hundreds of brightly coloured pictures covered the walls, each with a black wooden frame holding it in place. There was no space between individual paintings, the walls literally covered. There were details of plants, their intricate forms painstakingly recreated, and wider more general views. There were few people, just plant life and incredible scenery. The woman who painted them looked dour in a long dress, round glasses and hair held in a scarf, but that was just her appearance. She had been everywhere; Borneo, Java, Japan, Jamaica, Brazil, India, Chile, California, New Zealand, more places than either of them could absorb. There were plants and flowers and trees, seascapes and volcanoes, snow-capped mountains, kangaroos in the outback, walking from picture to picture, a monkey eating fruit, the mass of colours a kaleidoscope of impressions.

Vince had never been inside an art gallery before. Art was something for the people who lived in Kensington and Hampstead. Mind you, there'd been that time with the school when they'd gone to the Tate Gallery, but they'd had a fight with some kids from Lewisham, even at that age West London fighting South London, and Vince had hit one of them. A teacher saw him and he'd got the cane, then been banned from the next trip, a visit to the seaside which he'd have liked seeing as he didn't go on holiday very often. But he'd done well when he grew up and had been to more places than most people managed and wasn't finished yet, a bit like the woman in the photo at the front of the museum or art gallery or whatever they called the place. He bet she didn't care about Victorian bullshit when she was off travelling, fighting back against her set role in society, refusing to be ground down, showing more bottle than he ever could, and he had total respect for Marianne North, though he knew nothing more about her than what he saw on the walls. She showed what was possible.

– She saw a lot didn't she Granddad?

– Just saw the beauty. That's the way to do it.

Mr Farrell went briskly from one picture to the next, matching images with the text below. They were nice enough though a bit close together. She was an example, someone who had a passion for a subject and really lived. That was all you could do. Then he was finished and outside waiting for his grandson, ready to go home and sort out his wife's clothes and give them to the jumble, clear out and start again, wash the floors and scrub away any lingering scent, the wind cool on his face, refreshing and invigorating, like he was waking up after a long sleep, his grandson inside still, looking at volcanoes in Java and then a picture of a plant whose name he couldn't pronounce, thinking of that Italian girl on the beach, an old Spanish tramp trying to teach the Englishman his language, glad they'd left the bulls alone, something worthwhile that, knowing some people were more up-front and took protest further, something beyond class, like Marianne North, daughter of an MP, just people in the end, looking inside the plant past the shape and seeing all that detail, Vince wondering whether its genetic survival depended on a bat, bee or butterfly.

MILLWALL AWAY

WE'RE HARD AS nails going into the Lions' den, warming up on a couple of slow pints, enough to get the courage flowing in this nothing pub, something to dull the blows if things turn bad. The kids are bragging and singing while the older blokes play it calm knowing mouth and action rarely go together. It all comes from experience. Apprenticeships have been served and lessons learnt. There's no room for chancers tonight. Everyone here has got to stand up and be counted. There's a lot of pride at stake and self-respect is all important. If anyone bottles they better not show themselves again.

I look at familiar faces. Mark and Rod standing next to me. Harris with Martin Howe and Billy Bright. Black Paul putting coins in the fruit machine acting casual and pulling it off. Black John lucky to be back in Victoria after West Ham. Facelift and Don Wright. Everyone is primed ready to get stuck in. Doing their duty when it matters most. Behind the scenes maintaining reputations and promoting the good name of the club, our select club. We'll put on a show tonight and if we're the only ones who see it then so fucking what. It's not one of those things you do for someone else. You do it for you and yours and we're peering through the pub window seeing what's what in the station.

There's not a lot of drinking going on because two pints is the limit if we want all the benefit and none of the weakness. A lot of the lads make do with soft drinks. Alcohol dims the brain and kills discipline. If you want a punch-up and not just the chatter you've got to watch what you drink. You can't afford to get careless away to Millwall. Make a mistake down there and you're dead. There's no second chance against that lot. We have to keep alert and see what's going on. Act straight till the second it goes off and when we get stuck in take no prisoners.

Harris stands at the corner of the bar with his squad taking the nod from new arrivals, clocking faces knowing who's who, wary of outsiders more than ever since Newcastle. We're a tight mob tonight and it's only the full-timers who make the trip to Millwall because it's major aggravation down in South East London. True, there's one or two kids knocking around, youths pushing into their twenties, but they know the score and are older than their years, keen to prove themselves and move up the pecking order. It's games like this when a kid can arrive, getting stuck in with the best of them, building the base of a reputation that will see him alright if he stays solid. If a bloke does the business when it counts then it doesn't matter what else he's about.

We're building up for Millwall away and it's going to be nasty, yet we respect Millwall somehow, deep down, though we'd never say as much, knowing New Cross and Peckham are the arseholes of London. The Bushwhackers have been making people take notice for years. As far back as our memories go Millwall have always been mad. Something special, mental, off their heads. They've got the reputation and they deserve it, raised on docker history spanning the century. A hundred years of kicking fuck out of anyone who strays too far down the Old Kent Road.

Their old men were doing the business chasing visitors around Cold Blow Lane when we were kids into toy soldiers, before they moved up the road to Senegal Fields, and before that their granddads were handing out sewing lessons when West Ham strayed too far through the Isle of Dogs, bringing in bad habits from Poplar and Stepney. Knives, bottles and running battles before, during and after the game. All that before my old man was even born. Back in the good old days when Britannia ruled the waves while parts of London were no-go areas for the old bill on Bank Holidays, when the locals went on the piss in a big way.

Human nature translates as human nature, and if the old bill nick you and worst comes to worst and you go down for a couple of years, banged up for affray, then your mates will come along to wherever you end up for a visit, and when you get out you'll be made. That's how legends happen. Names from history that mean more than all your Nelsons and Wellingtons put together.

Millwall, West Ham, Chelsea. F-Troop, the ICF, Headhunters. Waterloo is just the name of a train terminus and the best the blokes who died for their country got was a station named after the place where they fell. Going to Millwall is what it's all about today and it makes more sense than fucking off to France to get your head blown off.

We're killing time in the pub, stronger by the minute as fresh faces arrive, keeping things tight, being discreet. There's no need to attract attention, tonight more than any other time, the old bill primed for trouble with their riot gear and half-starved Alsatians tucked away down dark side streets on standby. There's expectation and it's a balancing act keeping the momentum flowing in the right direction, looking for a result. Harris tells the kids to lay off the noise and they respond straight away, toning down the songs, tight lipped, understanding that Millwall away is the big one and no time to lose control, the majority of the firm older with a few well known faces who only turn up for major aggravation.

We leave it till half-six, then Harris starts moving and we're following him out of the pub, through buses packed with silent citizens into Victoria. We're remembering West Ham briefly but it's in the past now filed away and we're into the moment looking at the departure times, Harris knowing where we're going, the plan to get a train to Peckham Rye. We want to avoid New Cross and South Bermondsey, where most of our support will arrive. If everything goes to plan we'll be walking around Millwall without an escort while the old bill are focusing their attention elsewhere. They'll be lined up doing their duty while we're wandering around out of sight looking for a good night's entertainment.

The mob's filled out by now and there's a good three hundred of us. There's a lot of muscle around, the older element, some nasty cases straining to hold back the violence. Every firm needs numbers for major games like this. You're no good with twenty or thirty headcases, however tasty, and we're having a laugh thinking of Pete Watts, how he got thrown through a pub window at Millwall fifteen years ago, another slice of Chelsea myth, knifed in the leg before the police pulled up and nicked him. Cost him fifty quid that one.

We're on the train filling the carriages knowing other

passengers fear us, but we're not interested, keeping our affections for Millwall, not wanting trouble, none of that juvenile hooliganism throwing light bulbs on the platform and touching up office girls. Millwall's a corner of London where time stands still even if they do have a plush new ground. The streets and people remain the same and Cold Blow Lane was a wicked place full of nutters, and the New Den may look flash but it's full of the same old faces standing in the background waiting patiently.

Those days of everyday Millwall theatre riots are part of the past, our fun out in the streets, as it's always been anyway, year in year out, away from reporters and photographers. What do they expect the old bill to do? Put cameras on every roof of every house in every street in every city hoping to get a recording of the latest assault? They're not interested. It costs too much and they're only moved to act when it gets in the public eye, a dead fly irritant washed out with a good caning and some outraged words from the tabloids.

The doors close and we're moving away from Victoria and the plastic Disneyland of the West End. We're moving through London with its granite blocks full of official secrets and money managers, arms dealers and legalised drug barons. There's glass offices reflecting light and buildings, empty of life, full of advertising strategies, the river a great sight this time of night, a harsh city London where the lights are the only thing that stop the place exploding. We gradually pick up speed, train rocking gently side to side with flashes of electricity on the tracks and the whole thing could grind to a halt at any second. The windows are full of reflected faces and soon we're rolling through Brixton and Denmark Hill, travelling in silence. Turn the lights off in London and the whole place would go up. They've got to keep the fires burning no matter how much it costs. Pull out the plug for more than a few minutes and there'd be nothing left.

Harris starts talking in his precise way, giving instructions and warnings, his reputation sound despite Newcastle, that wasn't his fault, beyond his control, but he still has to deliver because the rush is there and we're ready for it to go off in a big way. There's been too much frustration over the last few weeks, the old bill sticking their noses in all the time, doing their job, messing things up. Tonight has to happen. It's vital for confidence. Suppose we're like junkies in a way. Clean-cut junkies looking for the kick of a punch-up. Except we don't take the easy option sitting in our own shit jacking up, out of sight trying to impress the neighbours. We get out there and put ourselves in the firing line. It's a natural high. Adrenalin junkies.

The train pulls into Peckham and we pile onto the platform. Queen's Road is nearer the ground but it means hanging around waiting for a connection and it only takes one phone call and we'd be lumbered with an escort. It's looking good though and we don't see any coppers. Looks like we're in the clear until some wanker nicks the ticket collector's small change. The man's a Paki or something and he's shaking a bit, obviously shitting himself. Don't blame him really. But Harris shouts at the bloke to give the money back and the British Rail man seems happy enough, not wanting trouble, doing his best, earning a crust, Harris coming on like some kind of Robin Hood, and we're laughing inside knowing he doesn't give a fuck.

We're just keeping our noses clean for the moment. Petty theft and vandalism are the mark of a cunt, and Harris doesn't want the ticket collector on the phone. That's the last thing we want. We pile out of the station and are on our own, spilling into the road, geared up because we're steaming, moving away from the station, over the street not waiting for the traffic lights to change, energy flooding our brains and we're on their manor now strutting along and we know the bastards will be around somewhere with their scouts out, mobile phones in small fists for a quick call to the Bushwhackers switchboard.

We look at stray males with suspicion and head towards the ground, buzzing inside the whole time. It's going to go off in a matter of minutes rather than hours. It's a fucking unreal feeling getting into a place like this knowing there's another mob nearby looking to do the same thing, and the fact they're Millwall makes the whole thing major league. This is top of the table. Millwall and West Ham. But we're united, all together in this, and we're telling ourselves that Millwall are mental, but we're mental as well, like we were against West Ham at Victoria, and it's all about pride and self respect. Traffic piles up as we cover the street, taking over, total control, a shot of power. We're on Millwall's manor and it's up to them to stop us taking the piss otherwise they won't be able to hold their heads up till the next time the two clubs meet and they get the chance to try and turn us over.

We're taking liberties but they're smart cunts, it can't be denied, like the time they mobbed together and cut a tree down blocking the Leeds coaches heading back to Yorkshire, or the two thousand a side they had against West Ham. That takes organisation. The tension rises. We're nervous and cocky at the same time. Somehow we've got to control the nerves and make it work for us. It makes us more violent. More determined. When it goes off we'll have to be brutal if we're going to survive. We're putting ourselves on the edge and when you're in South East London it's a fucking long way to the bottom if you get thrown off. It's like we're on the edge of the world sailing along with Christopher Columbus against the tide and you have to keep your momentum otherwise you're fucked.

There's not a copper to be seen, only Peckham locals and flashing amusement arcades. Every pub holds potential as we pass, Millwall holding up somewhere trying to find us, playing the same tracking game, cat and mouse, hide and seek, through streets they know like the back of their hands. This gives them the advantage because you could get lost for days in the blocks, houses, empty yards. There's no colour in the buildings, bricks identical and wasteland overgrown, rows of broken walls and barbed wire, smashed glass and rusted metal, dull new houses that remind me of Bethnal Green. It's a fucking joke thinking about Millwall's flash stadium set in among this shit. Makes you think about priorities in a dump like this. We turn right at a set of traffic lights moving with more of a swagger because we're pumped up to breaking point, Harris shouting at a few lads to tone it down. Keep calm and hang back. We've got to behave ourselves for a bit longer.

We can hear the crowd singing in the ground streets and estates away through the darkness, the station way behind us now, mist coming off the river drifting across the rubble, a white chill infecting dead homes. It's fucking eerie this place. Full of decaying dockers in flat caps bombed and left to rot under a collapsed London. People talk about concrete jungles and that's what this place is, a perfect description, a fucking nightmare world without any kind of life, but we know once we find Millwall that's all going to change, that they'll come out of the brickwork and then disappear into the tunnels when the job is done like they were never there in the first place. Fog drifts through blocks of flats in and out of stairs and balconies, a mugger's paradise, the chance to earn a few bob carving up a skint granny, scum of the earth niggers. The air is cold and evil and it's only our energy that keeps us warm. London's a ragged place now, full of mute pensioners and sullen rappers, past and present melted down and spat into the gutter.

We turn a corner and there they are. Millwall up ahead. There must be a good five hundred of the cunts and they've got the numbers and we could be on for a kicking. But there's quite a few kids with them, though there's a few niggers as well and they're always carrying. They're mobbed up in a patch of wasteland the council calls a communal garden, in among a tunnel of concrete blocks, and they start moving our way slowly, coming down from the New Den maybe, or just standing around out of sight, waiting for the right moment. Time gets lost as the clocks don't matter any more and we're shouting Chelsea as the bricks come raining in, bottles lobbed by kids on the balcony of some overlooking flats.

Millwall are moving faster now, getting things going and we can feel the hate coming our way like they're gasping for air or something they're so fucking wound up, and you can understand the thinking of these blokes nailed into a slum like this, but we're strong united, and we're Chelsea, and this is what we've been looking for, out to settle a few scores, showing our bottle, making a point that we're here at all, and we don't feel Millwall's hate any more because we've got enough of our own.

We return the bricks and steam in. There's a roar that sets heads racing and we feel the rush, the buzz of fighting shoulder to shoulder, for status and our mates, the first punches and kicks landing, both sides piling straight into each other. We've got the front in this slum they call Peckham, New Cross, Deptford, wherever the fuck we are, who knows where we've wandered, trading more kicks and punches in a madhouse, the usual gaps appearing in the street as the two sides clash, the crack of glass and a couple of men going down on the concrete, immediately set upon kicked black and blue from head to toe, and some poor bastard's going to have a serious headache in the morning.

There's no time for fear as we kick out and six or seven older geezers into their forties come through the crowd at us, real old-time street fighters these ones in their donkey jackets, with scarred faces and poxed skin, uneven haircuts and dead eyes even in dim street lights, but they get bricked and hammered. One bloke's on his own with everyone scrambling to kick him and use up some of that energy, threatening to break him in half, send him back to his family and friends in a wooden box. But Millwall act fast and he's dragged back along the concrete unconscious by some of his mates, Millwall winding themselves up, an uncoiling spring with a sharp edge, Millwall going mental, Chelsea going mental.

We're holding our own, but there's just too many of the bastards to run them right off, fights breaking out back and forwards through a kiddies' playground, bottles smashing against the climbing frame. One day we'll think back and see it as a bit of a laugh, if we can think straight, because there's swings bouncing around and some kid trying to get up the slide, pulled back with his head slammed into the metalwork by a couple of older blokes taking turns, Chelsea boys battering the Millwall kid's head trying to dent the fucking thing. It's mental rucking in a playground, seriously funny when we think about it later, reminiscing over our Millwall trip. Childhood fucked up by grown men who should know better.

More Millwall start appearing through the concrete like soldier ants, flooding through the precise angles and stacked piles of rubbish. Battles are kicking off towards the ground, houses and flats around us coming alive with old men hanging out of high-rise windows cheering Millwall on. Their bitter voices echo through the concrete, locked in cells with only the telly for company, taking their hatred out on West London. The roundabout in the playground is spinning with an unconscious youth bent double like something from a war photo. He could be Millwall or Chelsea. Nobody knows what side he's on, or what he's called. What's the fucking difference anyway? And it's all there, the generation gap closed, with the swings and slides and men in their prime cheered on by men ready for the grave.

The fighting's confused now, Chelsea and Millwall getting mixed up. The sound attracts more people coming over from the direction of the ground, but there's still no coppers in sight. It's a kind of heaven this, even though it looks more like hell with the low wattage lighting and dirty mist turning everything inside out. We can feel the anger and hate coming out all around us, flushing out the locals, dragging them from their caves, their kingdom under attack, moving through the age groups, women's voices screaming from the balconies up above now as well as the old boys, the sound of fighting cats late at night, shrieking like babies, a seriously sick sound, turning the air blue with the best Queen's English.

Things are getting worse and we look down the street and there's a few of the lads getting the shit kicked out of them. They're too far gone and we're unable to do anything to help. There's no mercy on sale and we're yelling at each other to stick together, loving every second of what's going on, and Harris starts going mental with his hunting knife, a six inch blade and a dark wood handle, it sticks in my mind, time stopping for a second then speeding up again, didn't know he was tooled-up, his arm moving forward slashing some Millwall cunt across the face, the bloke in shock, expression frozen, a thick groove across his cheek, jaw to the edge of his eye, those Millwall around him holding back as he staggers.

There's Millwall everywhere now. Must have been waiting mob-handed further down the street. It's out of control and they're coming for us desperate for blood, kicking to kill, more bricks and bottles landing on our heads though fuck knows from where unless the pensioners on the landings are dismantling their flats. We don't know what's going on up above because our attention is on the aggro two feet in front, ears burning with the din, the movement and dull blows, the thud of fists and kicks, an iron bar or something catching me across the side of the head.

Suddenly I'm on my own. Isolated. Face down in the street eating dog shit. Forehead in a puddle. Grit cutting my hands. Up against a wall. The smell of crumbling brick and wet concrete. Weight of numbers forcing the main battle further along the street. Off to the football. To the Millwall-Chelsea match. A game of football. It's only sport. Should be an attractive match between two sides who love to go forward. But I don't reckon I'm going to make it because the kicks are coming in, a mob of blokes surrounding me, kicking to cause maximum injury, numbing my body, digging in, breaking blood vessels. I feel the kicks bouncing off my head and shoulders, along my spine, the crush to get stuck in my only protection as Millwall get in each other's way, kicks aimed at my bollocks and I'm tight in a ball trying to protect myself best I can.

There's a ringing sound all around me as most people move off down the street taking that deep roar with them, individual words coming through now, just nonsense, and hatred, fucking Chelsea cunt, fucking cunt, fucking Chelsea cunt, fucking cunt, fucking cunt, fucking cunt, the kicks slowing down but better placed, evil bastards picking their spot, the numbers thinning, leaving the sicker ones to work me over, probably scrawny kids with no bollocks. Seconds turn to minutes and I have no idea to get up and run away, because I'd never make it and only open myself up, expose my balls and face, escape impossible not even considered, must take my punishment like a man, like I'm taught in school, by my mum and dad, hit them harder than they hit me, don't cry, don't tell tales, stand up for yourself, be a man, have a bit of pride, some self-respect, violence without a happy ending.

There's no way out of this and I want to shout but nothing comes out. My throat is bruised and the chords rigid. I'm scared like never before as I realise it's me against the whole of South East London, less than ten of the cunts left now I suppose, and they're hammering me into the concrete. Trying to force me through the gutter into the sewer. The kicking doesn't stop. I feel sick. Like I'm going to die. I'm shitting myself and it's turning to panic. Sheer blind panic which grips me inside as the kicks bounce off my head, spine, even my bollocks as I roll over opening up. I taste sick in my mouth as I try to keep the ball shape. Protecting my bollocks. Hiding my head. But the blows crack against the back of my skull and along my back. I imagine myself in a wheelchair, in a coffin rolling down the chute, burning in the furnace paying for my sins, corpse melting like a waxwork puppet, strings cut one last time.

Where the fuck are the others? Where's the rest of the lads? Why don't the cunts help me? I shouldn't be left alone like this. It's not supposed to be this bad. Football should be about running punch-ups and a few bruises. Nothing too serious. A quick ruck and some mouth. I've been left to fend for myself. I'm losing my grip, going into some kind of junky dream world, thoughts cracking up and drifting along, floating, and I can feel the blows but none of the pain, just numb now, like I'm pissed or something. But through it all I've still got my dignity, a dull voice in my head telling me that we did the business. We've done ourselves proud showing we've got the bottle to take on Millwall and we've held our own against superior odds. I can hold my head up high if I get out of this, but my legs have gone dead and my skull's aching. I've had enough. Thank God for the sirens.

LIQUIDATOR

THE EDITORIAL TEAM was in place and ready to get down to the evening's business. There was a lot of planning to do for the next issue and once the content had been decided on there wasn't going to be much time left to write, edit, design and get the pages down to the printer. If they missed their allocated slot it would mean a two-week wait, and a lot could happen in that time. It was the difference between a well-run operation with its finger on the pulse and a cowboy outfit that trailed in the wake of its contemporaries.

The editor came into the room with a wooden tray, carrying mugs of steaming hot coffee. Maxwell was a big man with badly cut hair and a chubby face. He had bushy eyebrows and a square mouth. He placed the tray on the table and the rest of the editorial team took their drinks. Maxwell lowered his bulk into the editor's chair and picked up his clipboard, paper and pen which had been cast aside in the rush to make coffee. Maxwell was one of the troops and didn't want his colleagues to think he was taking the piss. There was a chocolate cake and plate of crackers for those who fancied something to eat. Maxwell had already cut himself a slice of cake and took a big bite, then leant over and added three spoonfuls of sugar to his coffee. He stirred the mixture and marvelled at the whirlpool effect.

– Issue two sold well, said Vince, who was new to the team. Two thousand copies is a lot of magazines to shift in two months. You must have been so busy flogging them I'm surprised you had time to see any football.

He had been introduced to the others by his younger brother Chris, and they found him an interesting character, having spent two years in Asia before travelling to Australia where he'd worked on the railways. He was a bit older than the rest of the squad and had a good knowledge of Chelsea history. He was planning a return to Australia at some point so his contribution wasn't going to be long term, but the more people they could get interested the better. The editor had been going through the mail before the rest of the lads arrived.

– We're picking up momentum, said Maxwell, who had been nicknamed after the slightly more famous Robert. We doubled our print run for the second issue and sold out. We'll be challenging the other Chelsea fanzines soon if we keep going at this rate. We've got twice as many letters as for the first issue and there's still a couple of days left till the deadline. We've also had three articles sent in that aren't bad; one on the Rangers-Chelsea connection, another moaning about the lack of skill in your modern professional and the last one going on about the club in general.

No Exceptions had started up in the wake of the more established Chelsea fanzines *The Chelsea Independent* and *Red Card*. There was no serious sense of competition despite the editor's remarks, but more an attitude of if-they-can-do-it-then-why-not-us? Maxwell was the first to acknowledge the *Independent*'s determination at getting the punters a say in how their club was run. Indeed, he had every issue lined up next to his programmes. Like many others, he strongly believed that the club belonged to the supporters, because the players, chairman and backroom staff came and went through the years, but the hardcore fans were there from child to pensioner. The name of the fanzine had been Maxwell's idea and he was proud to have come up with such a clever title. It had been lifted from the club's own terminology when telling people about ticket arrangements. To buy tickets for big games there were often long lists of conditions and qualifications with NO EXCEPTIONS tagged on the end to prevent further discussion. The lads felt it summed up Chelsea's attitude perfectly.

As well as the Matthews brothers, Tony Williamson and Jeff Miller were also making the most of the coffee, cake and crackers, both of them long-time mates of Maxwell. The core three had inevitably been strongly influenced by *When Saturday Comes*, and their broad socialist/anarchist approach to life meant they appreciated the worth of fanzines such as the *Independent* in reflecting the natural grassroots acceptance of black players within the English game. All three had been at the Crystal Palace-Chelsea match in the early Eighties when Paul Canoville had been booed by a big chunk of the Chelsea support when coming on as a substitute. The arrival of a black face in the Chelsea first-team had upset a lot of people and many had walked out, the three of them talking about it in the pub later that evening.

Maxwell had argued that it was a beginning, though, and Canoville soon won over the majority of Chelsea fans, his performances on the pitch and some vital goals putting an end to the abuse. Since then numerous black players had become big crowd favourites. The editorial team believed that football more than any other area of society, with the possible exception of popular music, had accepted the shifting make-up of England's working-class population. It had done this without the help of any of the latter-day interest groups which, now that they felt safe to get involved in football following a middle-class media-inspired acceptance of the game as something other than the domain of Neanderthals, had jumped on the gravy train ten years after the event. Maxwell, Tony and Jeff agreed that those who had founded fanzines such as the *Chelsea Independent* should be getting the credit, not people within the media establishment who had spotted a good career opportunity.

– How about a cartoon strip? Vince asked, shifting the conversation. I'd be up for doing it. It would be this character Liquidator, after the song. He'd be this bloke with a mean streak mixed with a Robin Hood sense of justice, and he'd go about righting wrongs at Chelsea and within football in general.

– We need a few images, said Chris. It's all text and a few lifted newspaper photos at the moment, which never show up all that well. It's either arguments about team selection or club politics. We need to lighten up a bit and keep expanding without losing the edge. After all, two thousand happy customers can't all be wrong.

Maxwell nodded and heaved himself up from his chair, then walked to the bathroom for a piss. He left the door open a bit so that he could hear what the other lads thought of the idea. If Vince was good with a pen then why not? He made sure he hit the side of the bowl and avoided the water. The rest of the editorial team seemed enthusiastic, discussing various ideas and laughing as they pictured Liquidator in action. Maybe they could do something about Dean Saunders. Liquidator could take Paul Elliott along with him on the mission. Maxwell shook himself dry and washed his hands. He examined his face in the mirror. He was an ugly bastard and hadn't been near a woman in five months.

This made him feel like a professional publisher, or maybe a journalist working on one of the tabloids or a shitty football magazine. They were the scum of the earth, some of them at any rate, and he was happy enough as he was, driving a delivery van and taking the *No Exceptions* pages down to the cheap printer they'd found in Crystal Palace. They used paper plates which meant costs were kept low and the manager even looked a bit like Dave Webb, which was a bonus. It was fine as a hobby but he wouldn't want it as a job. Maxwell was honest if nothing else. He turned away from the mirror in disgust.

Vince, meanwhile, was busy giving life to his creation. Liquidator would be a bit of a boy, he wasn't going to make him into one of these TV celebrities who went on about football but when questioned a bit more closely knew few of the specifics and skirted the issues. Liquidator would have a semi-aggressive appearance and would go to the heart of things. Perhaps he would be half-man, half-machine. There would be no trial by jury and his justice would be instant and final. Vince tried to think up a story-line, veering from the hypocrisy of politicians and those running football to the money-madness the game had developed. All the time he was looking at the wider angle, football a microcosm of society.

— I reckon something about football's pricing policies would be well appreciated, said Tony. Everyone I speak to thinks they're being stitched up, no matter what club they support. It's going to hit breaking point and then they'll just give up.

Jeff was weakest on this angle, trying to convince the others that while he didn't agree with the price hikes, if English teams were going to compete with the big boys in Europe, the Italians and Spanish clubs which were backed by corporations and seemed to have their own mints built into stadiums that easily held a hundred thousand people at a go, then money was needed. There would only be a drain of talent to Milan or Barcelona and where would that leave the English game? Top players were going to go where the money was and, if they were honest, wouldn't any one of them jump at the chance to live in Italy and earn twenty grand a week? The others nodded, quickly pointing out that from Chelsea's point of view the argument about a player drain didn't hold. The Italians and Spanish wouldn't want any of their lot.

Maxwell said it was sickening the amount footballers were paid. How could anyone justify ten thousand pounds a week and up? Vince agreed, though they weren't exactly going to turn it down. But it was a subject that needed addressing and Liquidator would deal with a couple of well-paid Tottenham stars and their agent, but first he was going to settle old scores and pay Thatcher and Moynihan a visit. Vince let the story develop, the pictures he would draw already forming, revenge the driving force as he thought about identity cards and expensive seats in all-seater grounds.

Liquidator was on a train south to Dulwich, bunking the fare and covering the walls with marker-pen graffiti. He'd heard Maggie was at home after her latest world tour and would probably be suffering from jet lag. He knew the address, found the house and climbed over the back garden fence. He broke a window and was soon inside. Denis was crashed out on the couch with an empty bottle of champagne discarded on the floor. Liquidator kept moving. Thatcher herself was upstairs in a deep sleep. The house was expensively decorated and ornaments from all round the globe were positioned in strategic places. Vince was impressed by the Iron Lady's choice in artefacts, but Liquidator told him not to be such a prat, that they were on a mission. He told a humble Vince that they were probably fakes and the originals stashed in a bank vault. Maggie would be saving her treasures for a rainy day.

Liquidator was looking good. Vince had the curves of the face and the assassin's expressions perfectly formed in his mind. He thought about doing something with the eyes, making them oversized or filling them with reflected images, but decided it would just make the CFC superhero look a plonker and anyway, it would be too difficult. He didn't know how good his drawing was going to be yet. Liquidator was casually dressed in jeans, trainers and black jacket. His hair was short but not shaven. All he had to do was transfer this mental prototype to paper and he would be away. That was the hard part.

Liquidator led the way upstairs and stood over the former Prime Minister, the woman Vince whispered would have been Queen if the Queen had allowed such a constitutional oddity. She was bald and a wig rested on the bedside table. The Iron Lady was getting old. Now that Liquidator was in a position of power Vince didn't know what to do. Murder and torture could well upset those readers who had an inbuilt respect for the fairer sex, not to mention age, so instead he chose a tattoo. Using chloroform to anaesthetise her, Liquidator added the original club crest to the Iron Lady's right forearm. The next time she shook hands with a foreign dignitary it would catch the cameras, the Chelsea lion wrapped in a Union Jack. Thinking about it, the flag probably wasn't such a good idea, only adding to the nationalistic mystique. On the way out of the house Liquidator ransacked Denis's drinks cabinet.

Vince knew the plot wasn't strong enough. His audience would demand a more decisive thrust if the Chelsea hero was going to live up to his name. That was the modern way. Things had to be clear-cut, with good and bad aspects separated and no common ground in between. Moynihan was next. Perhaps he could do better there. Moynihan was working as a newspaper boy in Surbiton and Vince decided on a puppet characterisation. Once Liquidator had recovered from his Thatcher-fuelled hangover, he tracked Moynihan down and, using the chloroform, bundled him into a suitcase. He would keep the former Parliamentarian in cold storage until the Millwall-Chelsea game which had just taken place. Then he'd take him down to South East London and at the exact moment when the two mobs were about to steam into each other he would produce Moynihan and, in a frenzy of working-class recognition of a common enemy, they would join forces and rip him apart.

Maxwell came back into the room and took his place. He felt like a major publisher right enough and wasn't there something about the big boys being able to do whatever they liked? Imagine having that kind of power, influencing and deciding democratic elections, forming opinion in millions of people around the globe. What would Rupert Murdoch do next? He only had the job for a year and then it was going to switch to Tony or Jeff. They'd adopted a democratic approach to *No Exceptions*. Maxwell cleared his throat and prepared to speak. He was gearing up for something profound, about to stun his comrades with insight and publishing acumen, but bollocks to all that, it was only a bloody football fanzine, it wasn't like they were trying to bring down the Government or something. He was thirsty despite the coffee.

– Does anyone fancy going down the pub for a bit of inspiration? We can continue the editorial meeting down there. The Harp does a decent pint and they've even got Liquidator on the jukebox. Anyone thirsty?

The team collected their coats and Maxwell switched off the lights. Everything was going well. He could murder a nice pint of Guinness.

SOMETHING SPECIAL

THE NURSE ADJUSTING my pillows smells of roses. Something like that. Some flower melted down and turned to liquid, stuck in a bottle and flogged for a small fortune. She's a nice looker. The uniform does her no harm either. Not that I'm into birds in uniforms in the sense of shafting them just because they've got the official stamp, but this one makes her different. Something a bit special. Nurses serve time helping the likes of me and that makes her more a woman than the mouthy regulation slags you pick up, shag, then never see again.

Mind you, there was this time in Chesterfield, coming back from a game up north. Can't remember where, though it might have been Oldham. We ended up at this club full of off-duty coppers. I was pissed, drinking shorts, past the point of no return, and I'm sitting at a table talking to this woman in a black pencil skirt with fishnet stockings wedged up her arse and Gary Glitter heels on her feet. She wasn't bad and I was getting in there. Then she leans over and tells me she's a copper. Tells me she loves being in the force because she can sit back watching the world go by, knowing she can nick anyone, anytime, anywhere.

I was gutted. She was filth and I was lining up a good bit of sex and I find she's got the plague. But I got myself back in the swing and started thinking what a laugh it would be shagging a copper. It would be a crack telling the lads I'd knobbed a WPC. I tried to imagine her in uniform, but it didn't work. She looked like any other Saturday night bike ride. Then she starts going into one about how she's got the cuffs tucked away in her handbag and if anyone starts anything she'll be over in a flash, kick him in the balls, then nick the bastard. She says she's not scared of anyone tonight. She's got plenty of work colleagues around to back her up.

240

My head was spinning and I went into one saying how much I hated the old bill. That I'd love to fuck one up. Luckily the music drowned me out and she just smiled and rolled her eyes like any other bird looking for a bit of stiff. She was pissed as well, so nothing was making much sense. I realised what I was saying and toned it down, still thinking I was in, but ended up getting blown out. It would have made a good story, but soon as she pissed off I had a word with Mark and Rod and we got out sharpish. That's all you need, socialising with the old bill on a Saturday night. I'll have a drink with almost anyone, but there's a limit. You have to have standards.

The nurse asks how I'm feeling. Not too good, I'm afraid. Still, that's what happens when Millwall get hold of you. I tell her I must look a right state with two black eyes and cuts and grazes all over. My body aches from head to toe. She says I look worse than I am. I've got three cracked ribs, a fractured cheek bone and bruising over a good chunk of my body, but I'm lucky it isn't worse. She says there are some sick people in the world. That she can't understand why a gang of men would attack someone just because he supports another football team. I shrug my shoulders. The slightest move hurts. I say I don't know either. It doesn't make much sense. She tells me I probably owe my life to the policemen who got there in the nick of time.

– There's so many people come in here suffering, really suffering, that when drunks arrive with sick down their clothes and their heads split open from fighting each other, I feel more angry than anything. They've got their health and money in their pockets, and yet they go out and get into fights for nothing.

Her name's Heather. Comes from the West Country. I think of Bristol City and Rovers. Always football. Heather is a Lady With The Lamp throwback. Suppose all the nurses are really. A romantic view because there's no glory emptying bed pans and scrubbing the incontinent, but maybe there should be, because the cunts who get the headlines and congratulations deserve sweet FA, earning more in a week than nurses do in a year. It's all about public service.

– You get kids come in here with cigarette burns all over their bodies, where the parents have stubbed them out, tormented all their lives. Little bodies covered with cuts and bruises and hair pulled out in lumps. Then you get the men at closing time full of beer and filthy language. You hate them because they just see themselves and nothing else. They're angry but they don't know why. They don't try to work anything out. They spend a fortune on drink and drugs and where does it get them? Their Saturday entertainment is damaging people.

Heather has a chirpy voice despite what she's saying. It's positive. She's tidying my bed, clearing away a plate and cup. Keeps moving, doing things the whole time, twisting her body, almost breathless the way she darts around. No pause for rest. Nurses don't have time to hang about talking rubbish. Every second counts. They have to keep cheerful otherwise they'd crack up seeing all that misery and shit every time they come into work. There's no way I could handle it.

– Try and get some rest. The doctor will be along to see you later. You'll be fine after a couple of weeks doing nothing. You've got to give yourself time to heal. You'll be right as rain and we won't have to see you again.

Heather walks down the ward. She's got a nice body. I think what it would be like if we were tucked up in bed together. She stops at a middle-aged man with a sad dog look on his face. Don't know what he's in for, but it's not going to be anything good. I can't hear what she's saying and he just nods his head up and down. I'm not interested in what the man's about, keeping my eyes on Heather. She doesn't look back the whole time she's with him, then she's moving further down the ward out of sight. She's a nice lady, Heather, real class act, but I know I'm never going to get near her.

We're moving in opposite directions and if I'm honest I have to admit she's got it sussed. But it takes all sorts, and I'm not going to sit around thinking I'm shit because thinking too much can seriously damage your health. Like the official Government warning. I've enough to get on with at the moment. My right arm is bandaged along with my ribs. I'm a mess. Heather says I've got enough bruises to open a market stall. She's got a sense of humour. They've done X-rays and given me a brain scan. I'll be okay. Got to stay patient. I'm better off than some of the poor cunts in here. I try to keep still. Feel like a geriatric confined to bed for the next twenty years. What a way to spend your life. I feel bad as fuck for all those poor sods stuck at home from the day they're born to the day they die. Worse than the physical side, it must seriously mess up your thinking. It's the boredom that would do me in. Even now I want to get up and move about, but at least I know that if I keep my head down for a couple of weeks or thereabouts I'll be on my feet and out the door. Good as new in fourteen days.

– She's lovely that nurse. She can come and give me a blanket bath any time she wants. I won't disappoint her. I may be getting on but I still know what it's for.

I say nothing and pretend to sleep. The ward goes about its routine and I'm not interested talking with the bloke in the bed next door. He's one of those cunts who's into every little detail. Talks all the time but says nothing. Reads all the papers and knows a million facts and figures. Reckons he's the dog's bollocks when it comes to politics, with the brainy papers stacked next to the comics. I don't give a toss about committees and arguments between party leaders. They're a bunch of wankers and their publicity stunts do nothing for me. He's welcome to them. I keep my eyes closed. Start drifting off.

– Wake up you ugly cunt. Rod's voice makes me start. Pain racing up my spine. Foot on the accelerator. His words a kick in the balls.

– You can try hard as you like but you're never going to fool anyone you're Sleeping Beauty. No nurse is going to creep up and give you a kiss, hoping you'll wake up and save her from all this. Not looking like that she won't.

Mark and Rod stand over the bed looking down on me with a plastic bag of biscuits and Lucozade. They look fit and healthy, prime of life, though Mark's got a bit of a shiner where his right eye used to be. Apart from that, not a scratch. Shows it can be done. You can go to Millwall and come out in one piece. Even do well out of the experience. Learn a few things without paying for the lesson. It's the luck of the draw. They're a couple of pretty boys looking the part. Making the effort because this is a hospital. Real end of the line job.

– Come on, Tom. Mark is eating biscuits from one of the packs they've brought along. Speaks with his mouth full. Fucking slob.

– Pull yourself together. It's visiting time. The nurse said we've got an hour if we want it. Said you're going to live and that you're

243

lucky to have come out of it with your head still on your shoulders. Silly cow. What does she know? She needs a good six inches up the arse. That would sort her out quick enough.

They pull up chairs and sit down either side of the bed. I prop myself up feeling a bit useless and reckon they should give the nurse a break. I feel like I'm a pregnant housewife or something waiting for the kid to drop. Or some invalid with disease eating my insides away, working itself up to the brain so I end up a haggard old dosser talking to chocolate machines down the tube. It's the same feeling you get with the flu but a hundred times worse. It's being out of circulation with your defences down. At the mercy of something beyond my control. Something I made for myself.

– We just lost you. Rod shakes his head and forgets to hand over the bag he's been carrying. Just puts it at the foot of the bed. Two unopened packets of biscuits spill out. They don't notice. Rod continues.

– It was mental, Tom, fucking chaos, and you're just thinking about what's going on in front of you and you don't see anything else. You know who you're with and everything, but it all gets mixed up and confused because you can't be looking over your shoulder every other second.

– We didn't know you were getting a hiding till we saw Millwall kicking the shit out of this ball of clothes on the ground, and even then we weren't sure it was you. Mark looks at the ground. Focuses on the tip of his right foot.

– There was no way we could get to you. Rod looks guilty and I know they think they've let me down.

– There's a hundred or more people in the way and it would've been like going into a tidal wave. It was just the numbers. Millwall were everywhere, but we did the business alright.

– One minute you're there, the next you've gone. Mark looks up. It all happens so fast you don't have time to think.

They're acting like a couple of grannies because I know the score. They'd have done whatever they could. There's no need for explanations. Most of the blokes there would have as well, but in that kind of situation there's no organisation and little chance going against the flow. The whole thing's a lottery and if you're unlucky enough to go down you're fucked. I tell them to leave it out. It wasn't their fault. Nothing they could do. Diamond blokes. Bit of emotion. Embarrassing really. We avoid each others' eyes. Get into that kind of position somewhere like Millwall and you have to take what you're given. Take it on the chin.

The cunts in charge say there's freedom of choice, but the options are lined up before you start. You don't get to pick and choose. A bit of luck and you're king for the day. Fuck up and you're straight down Emergency. Mark and Rod look relieved. Like it's been on their minds. I can understand it easy enough because the big thing isn't really winning or losing, it's having the bottle to have a go in the first place. It's about sticking together. About getting onto Millwall's manor and making your mark. It's pushing yourself a bit further showing what you've got inside. But there's been no overall winners or losers anyway, just a good row, though considering the odds I reckon Chelsea came out looking pretty good.

– After we lost you it went on for ages, says Mark, cheering up, turning the Millwall game into a bit of history, something that'll develop and grow through the years.

– Millwall are fucking evil, but we didn't put up too bad a show considering. Facelift got four stitches in his head where some cunt lobbed a brick. Blood down the front of him like the fat bastard had puked up. Except it was red. Thought the cunt would have blue blood or something. He was well narked about the mess. Said he'd send the bill to Millwall.

– It was a bit tense inside but apart from a couple of scraps down the side of the ground not much going on, says Rod. But afterwards Millwall went mental and had a go at the old bill.

– We come out of the ground and we're held back by vans and dogs, says Mark. They've been at the stores and the shields are out and the truncheons oiled. Half of Battersea Dogs Home was on overtime working for their extra tin of Chum. Alsatians everywhere and vans packed with psyched-up coppers. They looked nervous as fuck. Millwall were off down the end of the street and they were going mental trying to get at Chelsea.

– All you could hear was smashing glass and riot police legging down the road to get stuck in. We were penned in and the old bill shunted us down to South Bermondsey and sent us back to London Bridge. They were on the trains, everywhere. Up at

London Bridge in case Millwall followed us and tried to have a go there or we tried to double back. We hung around for ages but nothing happened. A lot of Chelsea got the tube from New Cross and it went off at Whitechapel.

There's a sudden silence and they're thinking they shouldn't be going on about Millwall, especially the buzz they got out of it, because in the end it was me who got a hiding, me sitting in hospital suffering, me who Heather reckons owes his life to the Metropolitan Police. I'm not bothered. It gives it a bit of meaning and when I'm fit it'll be another story. But last night, when I'd got my head together, I was in bed looking at the ceiling with the breathing of all these sick, sad men around me, wheezing and coughing and half drowned with disinfectant, and I started thinking about Millwall. Like it was a nightmare but real.

I was fucking scared when I went down, though I feel a bit of a wanker now and wouldn't tell anyone. Never known anything like it. Norwich was a playground punch-up in comparison. At first I was thinking I must be a bottle merchant, but it wasn't that, not really. You just realise you could get yourself killed, crippled, blinded, brain damaged, something that would stay with you your whole life. Suddenly you don't want to be there any more. You want to turn the telly off and tell everyone that it was only a joke. One big grin. No hard feelings. Why take life so seriously? Because, after all, we've heard the soundtrack and football's only a game.

– How long before they let you out? Rod moves the conversation on. You look a mess. That yokel nurse told us she thought you'd get better quick. She said you're young and strong so you've got a head start on the old men. Nice bit of skirt. Reckon she fancies you the way she was going on. You should get her out for a drink. When you get yourself fit. They reckon nurses are dirty as fuck. They see so many bodies and that, they're not scared of getting stuck in.

I think about what Heather was saying. Men kicking lumps out of each other and she has to put the pieces together. I know what she says is right. I understand the argument. But it can't change anything. She'll never know what it's about because her thinking is different. Suppose the whole country works along a million different wavelengths. Getting battered at Millwall was bad news, but I know why it happened and it's not a surprise. Other people would feel disgust. I just feel the pain through my body. Head to toes kicking. Right now I care because I'm hurt. In a couple of weeks, who knows.

– I spoke to that Scottish bloke at the warehouse, Mark cuts in. Told him what happened and he said he'd pass the message on. The foreman phoned up and said anything he can do I've only got to let him know. He said some of the lads would try and get down to see you. Seemed like a decent enough bloke.

– Your old girl phoned up as well. Wanted to know what happened. Then your old man got on the phone. They came down yesterday but you were out of it. Said they'd come again tonight. They were worried.

I wonder how they found out. It's not the kind of news you want the old girl hearing secondhand. When I was a kid and the old bill came round my dad used to give me a whack, but Mum just cried and drank half a bottle of whatever was handy. Went on about how she'd failed her kids. That was the only time I felt guilty. Like if I got done as a juvenile for nicking a car or something she was gutted like it was her fault. It's a dumb way to think and it makes you feel a cunt. I never forgot that, but you get older and you don't want your parents involved.

Mark and Rod stay until their time's up. The hour goes by fast. When they're about to leave they remember the biscuits and Lucozade. Hand it over a bit embarrassed because they say they should have brought some porno mags and lager to ease the pain. I tell them the biscuits and Lucozade will do fine. They laugh. I watch them walk down the ward. They look back and give me the wanker sign. Laugh again as they turn the corner.

I'm soon dozing. Down in South East London again. It's six o'clock Sunday morning and the streets are empty. The sun's shining so hard it must be summer. There's this gold plaque on a wall that's just been rebuilt. The only clean bricks in the area. The plaque reflects sunlight. I have to cover my eyes to read the words. I'm an old man. My hair is grey and I walk with a limp. I'm suffering from arthritis. I've got a walking stick with the Chelsea crest painted on the handle. The name on the plaque is mine. Says I died for my country and have been buried where I fell. I look around but there's just concrete and a cross in the street.

I jolt awake. Remember the dream. A load of old bollocks. I drift off again and I'm with Heather in the nurse's hostel. She's got a room on the tenth floor overlooking London. I watch trains cutting through houses like mechanical snakes. There's no sound. It's late at night and the lights make the trains stand out. I can see miles of vague terraces. No detail. The Post Office Tower in the distance with a flashing light on top. I'm in the spotlight but nobody can see me. I like Heather. She's different. I turn around and she's naked, her back to me, opening a cupboard full of whips and vibrators. She reminds me of that posh bird after Horseferry Magistrates. She lies on the bed and tells me I'll be fine in a couple of weeks. Mark and Rod are laughing on a television screen. They tell me she's just another money grabber. In it for the dosh. That there's good money in bed pans and shovelling shit. Cold hard currency.

– Tom. You alright son? I jolt again. It hurts. My old man's standing next to the bed. I look past him and it's dark out. Must have been asleep for ages.

I've got a depressed kind of hard-on under the covers because Heather's turned out different to what I wanted, but I'm expected to perform. It disappears in seconds. Heather is forgotten as I get accustomed to the light. The old man's got a pile of newspapers under his arm. Something to read, he says. A good draw in the next round. Home to Derby. He smiles a bit uncertain and sits down. Stands up again to take his coat off. Lays it across the bottom of the bed. He starts talking to me a bit nervous like, but his eyes are checking the bandages and bruises. After a while he gets used to the scenery and I don't feel so awkward.

– Your mum was going to come down with me, but we didn't know how well you'd be, and she's got some overtime tonight, but she'll come along in a couple of days. We were here yesterday but you were sleeping, then we phoned up this morning and they said you'd be alright.

The old man looks healthy. His eyes are burning like he's been on the piss. Silly old sod probably thought I was going to snuff it or something. Suppose you worry a bit when it's your kids. Least he knows not to go into any lectures or anything. Unable to move much you've got no chance getting away.

– I spoke to a couple of the nurses and they said you'll be good as new in two weeks. We heard from Gary Robson's old man. Gary heard it off Rod. We got a bit worried at first. We thought you might die or something. It was a shock. Still, you don't seem too bad. I mean, I know you're not in perfect health and all that, but at least you're not maimed or anything.

For some reason I think he should be more upset. Don't know why. A bit daft really. I mean, I don't want a fuss or anything, and I'd prefer it if he didn't come along at all, but now he's here the least he could do is see that though I'm still alive I've been through the grinder and it's going to take a while for the pain to go away. Mad I know, but these ideas spring up from fuck knows where and before you realise what's happening you're thinking gibberish. Must be the drugs. Dad stretches his legs out. He's going to tell a story. Give me a few pearls of wisdom. Real father and son job.

– There was this time when we were kids. Me and your Uncle Barry. We went down Acton to this Irish pub with a load of lads from the area. A couple of them had been in a bit of bother down there and these Paddies knocked one bloke's teeth out with a hammer. We took the train down and had a drink in a pub round the corner. We knew what we were doing. We were in the pub for three hours and when we came out we were raring for a punch-up.

– We got to the Mick's pub about closing time. They were coming out blind drunk. Real hard bastards they were. Navvies the lot of them. They beat the shit out of us. I got stabbed in the stomach and lost two pints of blood. I could have died but I survived. Someone got an ambulance and the hospital stitched me up. I remember the doctor. Indian he was. He said he was from West Bengal. There weren't that many of them around then and he stood out. Looked a bit like Gandhi. It's funny the things you remember. They're good people.

I look at the bloke a bit cockeyed. I'm surprised. Couldn't imagine him doing the business like that. It's not that I'm amazed those kind of things went on, and you always know your parents weren't lily-white like they try to make out when you're a kid growing up, but even so. I wonder what he's telling me for now. Probably his way of saying that he understands. I don't care if he does or doesn't, but he keeps going. It's all good stuff, and I'm interested now, but he doesn't need to say anything. Some things don't have to be said. Families and mates don't need big speeches.

– Then I was in the army. We were doing our basic training. It was down near Salisbury and it was hard work, but it toughened us up. There was this bloke from North London, Edmonton I think it was. He thought he was the king. He was a bit of a spiv but liked having a go at the boys who were easy targets. He tried it on with me once. He just went on all day, taking the piss. He said I had no guts. I was frightened of him. I don't mind saying it, but by evening I'd had enough. Something in my head clicked. It was like I'd got a big dose of strength from somewhere. It's like the stories you read in the papers about crack.

– He went out of the barracks and was shining his boots round the back. I walked straight up behind him and put my knife across his throat. I had him in this lock they'd taught us in training. I nicked his throat with the knife and the blade was over his jugular. It was just like they taught us. I wanted to kill him but held back. If I could've got away with it I would have done it and been pleased, but I controlled myself. He started crying. I told him if he hassled me again he was a dead man. He was sobbing and said he didn't want to die. He said he was sorry. I walked off and he never spoke to me again.

I'm trying to work out why he's telling me this. If it has some kind of hidden meaning or whether he's just trying to show me he was a lad in his own youth, in his own way. He smiles when Heather walks past and says hello, doesn't make any comment though I can see he's watching the way she moves. He asks me if I fancy a drink. He's bought a small bottle of gin with him. I shake my head and laugh but tell him to go ahead. He makes a big deal of keeping the gin secret, so that if anyone was bothered they'd work him out straight away.

He says he feels better. A bit of gin and old stories to tell. Says he never liked Millwall. They were always a bunch of hooligans. He'd thought trouble at football was a thing of the past. You don't see it much on the telly these days. He seems happy. He's actually smiling which is unusual for the old man. It's a bit of a funny situation. You'd think he'd be gutted, but for some reason he's really enjoying the visit.

DERBY AT HOME

I FEEL LIKE a kid. Full of life and raring to go. Nothing can touch me. Millwall's another story to tell in the future, again and again, over and over, small boy sitting on my knee watching the old geezer with drink on his breath, dentures chattering, gasping for air; but for now I make do with thirty of us wandering the streets between Earl's Court and Fulham Broadway. A Derby firm has been spotted and we've had a call on the mobile. If we find them it's a chance to make up for lost time. I'm in the mood. Feel good. Derby may be fuck all when it comes to football, but they've got a few faces prepared to do the business. These midweek Cup games in winter are ideal. There's added needle because of the competition and darkness for cover. As long as it doesn't get too cold and freeze your bollocks off it's a good night out.

We're walking down from the Jolly Maltster. A couple of the lads go inside the first pub to check for Derby. They're straight back shaking heads. The pub's full, but it's all Chelsea. We keep moving. Going against the flow of decent citizens coming out of dead back streets, heading for Stamford Bridge. Eyes full ahead, inspecting concrete as they pass. But there's no pavements of gold, just fag ends and old paper. Even Dick Whittington gave up when he got to London. Made do with shafting his cat. They're looking to get in early and beat the crowd arriving just before kick-off, lapping up the atmosphere like we all did when we were kids with big eyes believing we'd be out on the pitch playing some day. No chance. We check another pub round the corner. It's my turn, and I go inside with Mark. Nothing happening. Just a crowd of men with papers and programmes talking football. We go back out.

— Let's have a drink and wait here for a while. Harris takes command once we're back outside. I fancy a pint. It'll warm us up and get the blood flowing. If Derby walk down from Earl's Court they'll have to come this way. Either that or North End Road, and that's the long way round. Chances are they'll come to us whether they know it or not. If we sit tight we'll be okay. Everything comes to the man who waits.

Half of us go in through one entrance. The other half the side door. A couple of the younger blokes go off to have a look around. There's no point standing on street corners looking like a bunch of orphans, making cunts of ourselves. We go in the pub and though there's no direct look the volume dips a bit as the men inside keep talking but have a quick glance, working us out. Robot mouths moving in time. All the usual chat. It's obvious we're Chelsea and the noise goes back to normal, a group of men arguing the toss about the England side and what's wrong with football in general. Same old words and opinions, year after year. Daft cunts should let it be. You've got no comeback against the men in charge. Goes for everything in this country. England's feeling the strain.

– What do you reckon on Derby then? Mark rubs his hands together. Like an excited schoolboy who's just nicked a dirty mag from his local paper shop and can't wait to see the beavers tucked in his jacket, burning a hole.

Mark's in a good mood tonight. Haven't seen him this happy for years. He's being made redundant in the next couple of months and is due a healthy pay off. He's done his time and is looking forward to the cheque. Thinks he's got it made, Mr Big, but he hasn't stopped to think about the future. He hasn't planned on what happens when the money's spent. Says he's not bothered. Hasn't given it much thought. Says something will turn up. No trouble. Does he look like a tosser or something? Thinking short term as usual.

– They'll have a few boys down tonight.

Rod pours his bottle of Light Ale into a glass as he speaks. Acting flash like he's a genius on remand. Fucks up the image making me laugh. Swears because he's given the Light Ale too much head and the cunt's threatening to spill over. He puts it on a beer mat and lets the advert take the strain.

– We steamed this vanload of Derby up by Earl's Court, about five years ago, says Harris, coming over with his tonic water. We were on our way back to the tube. Been hanging around for an hour after the game, but nothing was happening so we fucked off to the nearest station. Well pissed off we were, slagging the cunts off, then this van stops at a red light. Right rust bucket. Must've been running on a bent MOT, but it had Derby inside so we tried rocking it over and suddenly the back doors swing open and this tribe of Midland headcases piles out. Fuck knows how they all got in the van. Couldn't believe it. Must've been auditioning for the circus, though they weren't exactly a bunch of clowns or beauty queens practising for the high wire.

– I remember that one, Martin Howe joins in. Don't know where you lot were. They were mental. Big bastards in donkey jackets. Never heard the war was over. Still hanging about in the jungle eating roots for twenty years in gear that went out in the Stone Age.

– About twenty of the cunts steamed us, says Harris, taking over the storyteller role. Must've been hiding under the seats or wired into the electrics. Lary as fuck. Tooled-up with iron bars and baseball bats. Cunts pushed us halfway down the street we were so fucking surprised. It was the shock that did us, nothing else. Didn't run us, more like we moved back to clock the situation. Looked like they lived on shit burgers and twenty pints of stout a night. It gave us time to get ourselves sorted. Lobbed a few bricks and tooled up, then chased those Derby bastards back to their van.

– Billy puts a bottle through the windscreen and the driver's panicking and tries to run the cunt over. Up on the curb thinking he's on the dodgems. There's a bit of a barney and everyone backs off and Derby are back in the van safe and sound and just piss off. Cunts were laughing as they disappeared. Flashing their arses as they went. Fucking irons. Went up in a puff of smoke.

– Must've been a cold ride home without a windscreen, says Rod. Thick bastards probably didn't notice till they got halfway up the M1 and started dropping dead with frost bite.

I knew this Derby nutter a few years back. Met him in Poland watching England. Mad as they come, but a good bloke all the same. Was in the army as a kid but got kicked out after one punch-up too many while he was stationed in Germany. A smart bloke. Read a lot of books and could tell you the prime ministers and wars from a hundred years ago. Knew his history and geography. Any capital in the world. Didn't drink and spoke so quiet you had to stop and listen to what he was saying. Kept himself in good nick and got stuck in at the football. Haven't heard from him for three years now. Last I knew he was inside. Could've been a year. Don't remember exactly though the extra months would've meant a lot to him. A mixture of football, thieving and general mischief. The big one he got sent down for was assault.

He was alright. Sort of bloke you knew was going to do something with his life. He wrote me once when he was inside. Said things were getting wound up tight as a queer's arse at a fascist rally because it was summer and rumours were going round the whole time. Said everyone was on edge waiting for the place to go up. Wrote his letter dead straight. Very factual. Clinical way of thinking and I could see him working his way up through the system, building a name for himself, football a hobby, bit of an apprenticeship even, though probably one of the last ones going because they don't have apprenticeships these days. No cunt running a company's interested in anything but quick profits. Still reckon Derby's done well, whether legit or otherwise.

– You recovered now, Tom? Facelift stares me in the eye. I look at the scar where Millwall damaged his looks. He's ugly and the stitch marks aren't exactly going to turn a mob of screaming birds off him. They're cunts Millwall, but we were there, and nobody's going to take that away from us.

Can't be denied. We were on Millwall's manor giving it the big one, taking the piss, mob-handed walking around, but who was it left behind? Me and a few others. Real brain damage material. Don't remember seeing this cunt much when it went off but it's a bad way of thinking because Facelift's no bottle merchant. He's a nutter. A cunt. A mad bastard. A slob. But he's no shitter. That's all that matters at the end of the day.

– Next time we play Millwall we'll make sure we give some of their boys a hiding on your behalf, Facelift says, smiling, mouthy as ever. We'll do it even if we have to go down there five hours before the game with a shooter. Next time. There's always the next time. Take a shotgun along and blow some Bushwhacker cunt's head off. But it was a mental night whatever way you want to look at it. One to remember.

I think about arguing the toss but what's the point? Now I'm on my feet again, Millwall's something to talk about and look back on. I don't think too deep about it, specially being on the ground with half of South East London doing their best to kick me to my reward, but there again the whole night was mental. It rarely happens that bad. You get a handful of decent rucks a season, but Millwall was something else, and though I got a kicking it gives me a bit of respect from the other lads.

If I'd been hiding, holding back even, then I'd probably never have got done. I suffered, but it gives me something in return. Respect. Bit of a name. That's important. You have to earn respect in this world, unless you're one of those bent public schoolboy politicians. There again, that's just their own idea of respect because every normal person thinks they're scum. There's no way you can con your way through life. Comes a time when you've got to stand up and be counted. You can hide, but if you hide you don't live. Definitely not at football. You get sussed soon enough and if you're a wanker you can fuck off.

– I hope they bomb fuck out of those Arab cunts, Billy Bright's watching the telly propped at the end of the bar. Fucking animals. They should use a warhead on them. That would sort the ragheads out. It's all desert anyway, land's not worth a fuck, so why not drop something special and get rid of the bastards. Just make sure the wind's blowing away from England and you're laughing.

The woman on the box is going on about possible air attacks on a Middle East dictator. The volume is down low but I pick up some of the words. Same old phrases and excuses. Usual bollocks. Like a fucking advert. We're sick of hearing about it. Nothing but the threat of bombing for the last week and it's obvious the Government's softening everyone up so there's no protest when they steam in. Public relations. Stand together. Another showing of Coronation Street or Eastenders. Formula curries. Bulldog breed. We won't see the cunts burn and so we don't care. We've got our own lives to worry about. There's no tin soldier gear or guns for us lot.

– What happened with that nurse at the hospital? Mark waits for a story but there's nothing to tell. Did she spit or swallow?

I asked Heather if she'd come out for a drink. Couple of pints and a meal. Said I wanted to show my thanks for getting me put back together again. My treat. She laughed all embarrassed like and said she had some late shifts coming up, but leave my number and she'd give me a bell. It was a nice way of getting blown out and it made me feel stupid asking her in the first place. Knew inside there was no chance getting in there, but if you don't try then you don't know. Said she'd call this week sometime, but I know she won't because Heather had me worked out by the end of my visit. She was half keen, but knew I was a cunt. And that's the way it goes. You get the kind of birds you deserve. Just another piece of skirt looking to turn you into a Saturday afternoon wanker down the high street shops. Life's a bitch, then you marry one, then you die. Saw a sticker saying that on a Jag once. But only if you're a cunt to start with. Nobody makes you into something you're not.

– There's Derby coming down from a pub off North End Road. Harris has the phone to his ear and is relaying the message. Don't look like anything major but there's forty or thereabouts. Look like they could be up for it with a bit of encouragement. A lot of pissheads but a few boys in there as well. A mixed bag of treats. They'll be here in a few minutes. They're not exactly in a hurry. Taking their time seeing the sights. Terraced streets, cockney dustbins and the like. Should charge them for the tour.

– Give it a couple of minutes and we'll give them a running commentary on the wonders of West London, says Rod.

We're outside and suddenly it's a perfect evening. Sharp but clear, and not that cold. Makes your mind concentrated. It feels good to breathe in and out, without the death fumes and disinfectant of hospital. Rain has washed away the poison. We walk along keeping to the pavement, heads down like decent citizens, near enough silent. We turn a corner and Derby are up ahead. Silly bastards are laughing and joking like they're on holiday with a plate of Spanish baked beans in their guts. We stand back in a junction and wait. They're a bit slow and don't clock us right off. Then they see Chelsea waiting and stop. It's a bit of a comedy really. Like stray dogs with ruffled fur, scratching their heads wondering what the next move is. We're two different dimensions. Chelsea are smart and without colours. Derby old-time drunks with kit tops. Obviously not a serious mob. Just a load of geezers out for the football. They're not the ones we were expecting to find, but still, sometimes you just have to make do with what you're given.

– Come on then, you Derby cunts. Harris gives the visitors a warm welcome. Steps towards them. Best foot forward.

– Fuck off cockney, shouts a big bloke in club top, flanked by the half smart element, backed up by the pissheads with beer guts and bad reflexes.

We laugh and move. It's hardly big time this but it'll do for now because major London derbies like Millwall, West Ham, Tottenham are all about inter-breeding and bad blood. Northerners are aliens and you don't expect large-scale aggravation, at least not for a midweek effort this near the ground. Not with modern technology and everything. Amusement arcade battlegrounds and video cameras on rooftops. It's slow motion again and Harris puts his leadership up front and the Derby cunt with the mouth tries to headbutt him, misses, hits cold air, off balance like the mug he is, gets a bruised jaw for his trouble. There's a brief punch-up, a lot of front and kicks, and Derby do a runner as though it's synchronised. All turn and run at the same time. Should be on a fucking ice rink. We follow at a jog, knowing their hearts aren't really in this, follow the trail of shit for a bit, then give up. We walk back the way we came, Harris shaking his head. We're half sad, half narked we've only found a bunch of drunks and not some decent opposition.

– Shitters. Facelift laughs like a Rampton special. What the fuck are they doing down here if they're going to run soon as it goes off? Makes you wonder, cunts like that. Can understand the old men and kids, but not blokes on the piss on someone else's manor. Waste of effort that lot. Should have stayed in Derby with their whippets and pigeons.

We melt into the side streets away from the busy glow of North End Road. Leave the shop windows for people with nothing to hide. Heads down hurrying to watch a ball kicked up and down a patch of grass, maybe even between a set of posts. Fucking dumb when you stop and think about it, but there's something more for me, Mark, Rod, all the boys here, the whole thing that goes with football, the way of life you can't see changing but know it will eventually, when you get tired and old and a younger firm comes up and makes a name for itself, carrying on the tradition with a new set of rules, shifting the emphasis to avoid detection, always a few years ahead of the old bill and five or so in front of the media and public opinion. It'll either be that or I'll end up like one of those trainspotters who never change because nobody notices them, so they just get on with it day in, day out, undisturbed.

I see kids with their old men down North End Road. Lit up 3-D by street lights, cartoon cut-outs, electricity in the air. There's cold and rain and burning bulbs everywhere, the only bit of warmth during winter, and when they pass the Maltster and get down to Fulham Broadway they'll be nearly home and dry. Then they'll see the floodlights glowing like some kind of spaceship. Get all religious, and it was Bill Shankly said football was more important than religion. A famous quote that one. They'll hear the crowd and it's unreal when you're a kid. Like when I first went down Chelsea and saw the Shed singing its head off moving back and forward, on its feet, and there was that passion all round Stamford Bridge which could spill over into a punch-up or pitch invasion at any time.

It was supposed to be dangerous but somehow you felt safe at the same time, because apart from a few headcases that you get everywhere, there were rules. Even major aggro looked worse than it was. You soon got to understand what is and isn't important, because the people running the show were outraged when shop windows got smashed and a few hundred lads ran onto a piece of grass. But out of sight of the cameras and reporters it was a different story. It's like those monkeys. See no evil, hear no evil. It's all cosmetics which isn't a bad thing really because as long as we keep out of sight we can have our fun and games. Just don't shit on the grass.

I feel like the kid I was, thinking about it all these years later. Must be more than twenty years since I first went down Chelsea. All that time and I've grown into what I am now, and after that first game at home to Arsenal I latched on to the Blues. It's just how it happens. It's part of you and what you are makes you what you are at football. If you're a programme collector you're the same outside. If you're mad you don't turn into a

Samaritan once you walk out of the gates. Makes me laugh the cunts calling it football violence when it's nothing to do with football. Nothing at all. Anyone can work that out if they take the time. But they don't because they don't really care. Just drop everyone in a filing cabinet and give them a label.

Suppose you get cynical and ground down the older you get. England's changed since I was a kid. Sound like a real old geezer ready to collect my pension, so fuck knows what it's like for people who can remember back sixty or seventy years. Change comes gradual and worms its way under your skin, irritates the fuck out of you in your sleep so you start scratching like you've got a dose and wake up with the inside of your legs ripped and bleeding. But it's different now, because when I was a kid there were a few punch-ups and whatever, and it went off inside grounds fairly regular, but today, with everything crushed, and more and more people plugged into their TVs and video games, everything's about having money and doing the right thing. Looking like you're behaving yourself. Least that's what they'd have you believe.

— When I get my redundancy I'm lining up a coach for the first away game comes up. Mark wants to share his fortune. No-one pays a penny. It's coming out of my pay-off. Bit of wealth distribution.

— Look at those cunts getting out of the car, Facelift's butting in, bringing us back to the here and now.

— Who you looking at?

— Four blokes across the street. Just parked up. They're Derby alright. Bit smart like they've got money in their pockets.

I look over and see the four men Facelift's pointing out. Blokes in expensive gear. Dressed to blend into the background with a bit of style. Keeping quiet but not through being scared.

— Oi, you, Derby. Facelift shouts across the street.

One of the men turns. I recognise his face. A bloke who did his time in the services. In Poland when the Poles were going mental having a go at the famous English hooligans, lobbing bricks, bottles, anything you can name. Getting stuck in for England. All grudges forgotten for a while. Another flag to fly. Petty local rivalries suspended.

— Fuck off, you cockney bastard.

No fear in Derby's face. Looks older than I remember. Same close-cut ginger hair. Expensive coat and the look of someone who's made a few bob. And I'm just a cunt working in a warehouse who doesn't do too bad selling gear on the side. But he's got more than me, making me the nigger locked out of the shop again, looking in through the window, denied access.

Facelift walks across the street and Derby stands facing him, his mates on both sides, broad faces, cut faces. I hang back watching, wanting to say something but thinking there's nothing I can do. The odds are stacked and when all's said and done it's one of those situations you swear you don't go in for but with Facelift and Billy Bright around, Black John as well, it'll happen because the rules are drawn a bit further down the line for those cunts. The rest of the firm don't care because these are bad odds, thirty or so onto four if everyone goes for it, though I reckon one or two will stand back. Makes me feel sick inside. The odds and the man.

Derby's a good bloke. I want to say something but don't. Just bottle out. He knows the score. He's no fool. So I just stay where I am and don't bother. I'm not going to cover my eyes like a kid, because you see enough blood and guts on the telly so what's a bit more, except in real life it's always raw and dull. No romance. Not now with Derby about to get a kicking and me keeping quiet. Knowing I should speak up, but telling myself this is no innocent sneering at Facelift.

Suppose when it comes down to it I don't want to look bad now Derby's had his say and no way is Facelift going to back off. Don't want the lads thinking I'm a wanker. I have to belong somewhere and when you belong you don't stitch yourself up. You eat shit and follow the rules, even though you keep telling yourself you don't. But I'm trying to persuade myself that Derby's got it coming in a way. Rough justice. He's been in enough trouble in his life to know what's what. But I'm not in the swing of it so it's going to be worse somehow. Like the cunts who watch life through their videos and TVs and clips of porn. The old bill with their surveillance gear and Marshall with his soldier gang rape show. Rod on stage getting the business off some old slapper. The whole fucking game recorded and examined.

Facelift gets close enough and Derby's arm shoots up from his waist, knife buried in Facelift's gut. I want to hear a popping sound. Like the balloon's been deflated or something. But I just hear someone yelling down the road a bit and a load of men coming our way. I look back towards Facelift and he slumps over a car bonnet. Derby slashes his arse with the knife and I want to laugh because he's going to have a lot of grief when he sits down over the next couple of months. I pity the poor bastard who gets the job of sewing him together again.

I look back and there's the old bill escorting some Derby fans and Harris reckons we should get moving. That it's not the time or place. We melt away and a couple of the lads are bent over Facelift who's bleeding into a puddle. Blood and water mixing patterns. A copper comes over from the firm we must've been looking for originally. We keep moving away because the streets are narrow and we don't want to get boxed in by the old bill. We leave Facelift to himself and I've got away without seeing Derby battered. It makes me feel better. I'd have felt a cunt letting him get done like that. He's moved on himself and I've been saved any feelings of guilt.

HEADHUNTERS

TO ANITA

'What was even funnier was what happened when I
went to sleep that night, O my brothers. I had a nightmare, and, as you might expect, it was one of those
bits of film I'd viddied in the afternoon. A dream or
nightmare is really only like a film inside your gulliver,
except that it is as though you could walk into it and
be part of it.'
A Clockwork Orange, Anthony Burgess

PART ONE

BEAUTIFUL GAME

CARTER WAS FIRST off the mark, and it wasn't much of a surprise. He walked into The Unity with a smile that didn't need explaining. The dirty cunt had been dabbling again. The others likened him to the Ooh Ah Cantona Man United side – he had flair *and* the ability to grind out a result when the occasion demanded. The lads did this on the quiet as they didn't want to give him the satisfaction. He got enough of that elsewhere.

The other four members of the Sex Division nursed half-full glasses, watering hangovers, prepared to wait for confirmation of the Carter score-line. If the result wasn't in much doubt, then there was still the small but important matter of totting up the points. But the shag man was going to take his time and passed the rest of the boys on his way to the bar. He ordered a pint of 4X and chatted with Eileen behind the counter, enjoying the warm smile, talking about electric shavers that break down a week after they've been given as Christmas presents and the odds on it snowing before the end of the week, both agreeing it would be nice to see everything painted white, though in London snow usually translated as slush. Carter finally went over to the Sex Division HQ in their usual place by the window. Will had left for the fruit machine while Carter was ordering, feigning disinterest but listening to the conversation with Eileen.

'Well?' Harry asked, forcing a note of indifference into his voice, not wanting to break rank with the rest of the service crew, but keen to get the facts sorted and filed so he could get on with life, always needing to have things straight in his head.

'Well what?' Carter settling into his seat, dipping his hand between his legs to pull the chair under the table, lifting the glass to his lips and savouring the taste, taking his time and doing his best to wind the others up.

'How many points did you get last night, you flash cunt?'

Carter smiled his Well Lads I'll Tell You When I'm Good And Fucking Ready smile and continued with the lager, exaggerating movement of arm and hand. He wondered if 4X was brewed in Australia by Australians. Crocodile Dundee's cousin giving it the big one down the brewers in between knocking off sheep in the middle of a radioactive desert, oversized wellies for the back legs just like the sheep-worriers he'd heard about on the Scottish islands; shearing the bastards then slipping them a length. Mad Max holding the poor little fucker still, rusty Harley parked up with an overheated engine. Probably not. The Aussies were all in Earl's Court and Dundee was working for the yankee dollar. Him and the yardies. He looked at Harry and Balti, the Fat Bastards, then Mango, all of who'd stopped drinking and were waiting for an answer. The season was under way with a vengeance and they had to know exactly where they stood. Perhaps it was early doors yet, as Ron Atkinson would say, but what did the northern gold merchant know anyway?

'Well lads, it was a free-flowing game as I'm sure you've already guessed, taking into consideration the quality of the opposition round here. I was up against a feeble defence trying to con its way through with a clean sheet, and I'm glad to say the old skills didn't take long to have the desired effect. I was pissed and can't remember the build up, but as you'll imagine it was quality footwork, playing it through the midfield, out to the wing, a bit of skill, dribbling and all that, end of the knob job, a bit of muscle getting past the hatchet tackle, a quick one-two, chipping the keeper. You know how it is when you're one-hundred-per-cent quality.'

'I don't,' Balti smiling despite the headache he was carrying and narked he was behind less than a day into the season, already following a leader he'd never catch. If only a self-made millionaire would turn up on the doorstep and offer to bankroll a successful championship push. But that kind of thing only happened up north.

Will came back to the table and remained standing. Carter got on his wick sometimes, but he said nothing, waiting for the mouthy bastard to get his bragging over and done with. He didn't like the idea of competitive football, turning the beautiful game into a business. He wasn't a tart like the rest of them. His sex was his own business. Even as a kid he'd never been into all the mouth, getting a couple of fingers in and running off to tell everyone. But he was signed up now and had to go along with it otherwise he'd look a prat. That's what a moment of pissed weakness did. The resolution had been made the previous night and if he bottled it he'd be branded.

He would keep his ideals, though, and wouldn't be changed by blatant commercialism. Play his natural game and bollocks to the rest of them, do an Ossie Ardiles even though Will was a Brentford man, do a Brazilian orange-juggling-on-Rio-Beach effort. It meant a place at the bottom of the table because he was no Pele and Ardiles was Argentinian, worse than that Tottenham, and they were charging over the top for oranges at the moment, vitamin C a luxury, but at least there was no chance of relegation. He could handle the tag and would live off the respect due a man with convictions, though when he left Rio and started filtering back into the pub, sucked under a dirty London sky, he knew it wasn't worth holding his breath.

'Get on with it will you,' he said, more to his Guinness than Carter. 'My pint'll be solid by the time you get your report filed.'

'It was a four-pointer.'

'Four points?'

'Four points. That's what I said. That's the way it goes. I got lucky. I was expecting three and ended up with a bonus for good behaviour.'

'You gave that bird one up the jacksie?'

'That's right. One point for a knuckle shuffle, two for a shag, three for a blow job and four for six inches up the arse.'

Will shook his head, more in sarcastic mock awe than real disbelief. Balti smiled and yawned, rolling a stiff neck. Harry sipped his drink, frowning, looking at the floor, following the faded pattern, an intricate network of faded red and black lines, a bit of yellow tucked away, holding the information for a while before storing it in his memory. Only Mango wasn't letting the unstoppable sex machine claim instant glory and further develop his cult status. If he wanted to go round shafting birds up the arse, then that was his problem. Must be a fucking iron on the quiet. He couldn't imagine a bird taking it voluntarily first time between the sheets. Not unless you paid them.

'You're a fucking bum bandit mate.'

'That's right.' Carter fixed on Mango's eyes without much humour in his voice. 'Four points in the bag and the bird's got a dose of vindaloo fall-out for the next couple of days. Serves her right as well. Do you think I'd have shit-stabbed her if there was no points in it? It's total football. I'm like the fucking Dutch. Johan Cruyff and Neeskens. A touch of Rudi Krol and Johnny Rep. Keep the tradition going. It's like that with the clogs. Bit of blow and black tarts sitting in the window waiting for their share of the Englishman's wage packet. Pride of Ajax. Cross their palms with guilders and sample the dark African continent, or at least the Dutch colonies. Have a Jakarta special with the gado gado at half-time. Total fucking football. You should try Amsterdam. The Dutch have got it sussed.'

'Were Cruyff and Neeskens bum bandits as well?' Harry asked, confused by the carpet, formation spinning and sending his head into orbit, red and black doing something to his brain, wondering what the fuck gado gado was. 'Cruyff's got a son. Seems a shame somehow, brilliant footballer like that, European Footballer of the Year and everything. I didn't know he was a shirt-lifter.'

'He's not, you cunt, it's the football I'm talking about.'

'That wasn't what total football was about,' said Balti snapping awake, big belly grin on his face. 'Total football was the whole team attacking and the goalie the only one at the back playing sweeper. It was scoring more goals than the other side. They just went out on the pitch and played the game and didn't give a toss how many they let in. Didn't follow systems and did whatever they felt like. No rules. Natural, free-flowing football. If the other side scored five then as long as the Dutch got six they won and went home happy. It was a sound attitude. Like that Brazil team with Pele, Tostao, Jairzinho. Remember the keeper Felix. Dear oh dear.'

'Didn't they have Rivelino as well?' Mango asked. 'I remember him. Big bushy tash and always bending the free-kicks round the defensive wall.'

'We're talking total football, Dutch style. I'm a fucking Orange man stuck in Black Town, adding colour to London's black-and-white approach to the beautiful game. What do you know about football apart from how much Man U are worth on the stock exchange.'

Will sat down and deliberately placed his glass on a beer mat, Germanic lettering and a red coat of arms covered by the Irish stout. He was half cut. He still hadn't got over last night, New Year's Eve, and his right eye was murder. He'd left the party about four or so and was waiting for a cab with Mango. Fuck knows where the rest of the lads went. Pissed, stoned, useless. Except Carter on remote control looking to get his end away. Then Mango wanders off for a piss and the taxi pulls up. Three blokes appear from nowhere and try to nick it, a bunch of chancers, and when the barney started he got smacked in the head but was too pissed for aggravation and ended up in the gutter with decaying leaves for company and a kick in the head for good luck, that split second when he focused on the foot driving into his eye, like a slow-motion replay waiting for some expert analysis from Alan Hansen.

The cab left without Will, the driver only bothered about getting a fare, ignoring the body in the street. Mango returned too late, as usual, and found Will sitting on the curb, shaking his head, pissed off that they'd have to call another car, knuckles wedged into his eye socket replaying the kick. He didn't even know what they looked like. Didn't know them from Adam. Dark shapes with dark hair. White faces without eyes, noses, mouths. Moving, living, stroppy waxworks. Any one of them could be sitting in the pub and he wouldn't have known. Will hated violence.

'I'll tell you, Carter,' he said. 'You're more like Liverpool.

271

The old Liverpool. Grinding out a result. Going home with a 1–0. Or Arsenal. Boring, boring Arsenal. Up the arse with the Arsenal; 1–0 to the bum bandits. Tony Adams pushing up all the time playing offside then moving upfield for a ninety-eighth minute corner heading in the winner. Bad news that, getting a length off the Gooners.'

The Sex Division stopped talking and watched Denise, who'd just come in the pub. She nodded their way as she went towards the bar, dressed almost to the point of looking like a King's Cross tart; one of the girls Mango admitted shafting just before Christmas. A youngster. A nice treat for Santa. Not more than sixteen, he'd said, though he secretly reckoned she was fourteen tops. Plastic mini-skirt and six-inch heels, and the cut so short there was an inch of childlike flesh exposed, goosepimples and something extra in her Christmas stocking, just the strap of the suspender belt against innocent white skin. He'd paid his money and rolled the rubber on, knobbed her up by Regent's Park near the mosque, then dropped her off again in King's Cross. He had class, he told them. He wasn't shagging some Halifax teenybopper in the back of his car round the station, not with junkies and dossers everywhere, bloodless faces pressed up against the window screaming heaven and hell, Aids and smack and rich punters in the blood, a dose of new-economics care in the community. He got his money's worth and said the bird offered him the night for free. She'd liked him. Will knew it was bollocks, about the girl offering Mango a freebie, but the others believed him, reckoning he was bang out of order shagging a kid that young forced on the game, sixteen still the right side of a kicking. A year or two younger and Mango would've been in trouble. He knew as much. Will reckoned they were mugs. The lot of them. Especially Harry, who pissed his wages up the wall worse than the rest of the lads, a big man with his square, shaved head and dreams. Mango was a cunt. Someone's daughter, sister, lover.

'I'd love to knob that,' Balti said, watching Denise disappear into the back of the pub. 'She's beautiful. I'd settle down and work all hours to bring her the good life. I'd give up the drink and curries and eat bean sprouts and grated carrot on crackers, lose four stone in a week, leave the coffee alone and drink grapefruit juice. I'd go and buy myself some decent gear and get my hair cut in an Italian unisex effort rather than a Greek butcher's. We'd have babies. Snotty-nosed brats puking up all over the place, shitting themselves twenty times a day for fun, dribbling like they're a minute from the grave. Anything Denise wants. I'd even change them as well. I'd take electrocution lessons and have my teeth capped, get those broken fuckers at the front mended so I look good when I get to meet her mum and dad, roses in one hand, bottle of sherry in the other. I'd do anything for that woman. Build a family and live happy ever after in the Green Belt away from you lot. And if you called up and wanted to go out for a pint I'd just have to tell you to fuck off and put the phone down, get back to the dishes.'

The others were laughing, Will pointing out that if he took electrocution lessons Denise would get a shock first time he tried it on. Denise was a cracker in anyone's book. She was also going out with Slaughter, who happened to be a Grade 1 nutter, a bloke whose jealousy wasn't worth stirring up for something as minor as sex or love. They all knew the score. Denise could prick-tease as much as she liked when Slaughter wasn't around. Winding the blokes up. Flashing her teeth and the top of her tits. Bending forward to collect the glasses and leaving it that extra couple of seconds that made all the difference, showing off her figure. She enjoyed it because they were a bunch of hooligans in The Unity. Dead lager on their breaths next day and black eyes, like that Terry watching her bum move tight inside her jeans when she arrived. She liked getting them going, knowing they'd bottle it if she offered them the business. None of them would chance it with Slaughter around. But she liked Terry, specially when she heard the others call him Carter. An unstoppable sex machine they said. Denise liked blokes who preferred women to drink and football. Mango gave her the creeps though, and Terry wasn't exactly a teetotal or football-free zone. She wondered if he had the guts. Maybe, with a bit of encouragement.

'If you settled down you'd end up bottom of the league,' Carter said. 'Imagine that, Balti. Four points maximum all season. You'd be shacked up living the life of a cunt and your mates would be on the rampage enjoying themselves, running up points while you're shovelling gerbil shit for the kids.'

'I'd never give Denise one up the arse. She's too nice for that. What kind of woman do you think she is, a slag? Denise is a solid lady. We'd make a good couple. I can see us with the trolley now, working our way through the freezers, loading up on steak and burgers, frozen peas, a nice bottle of wine to wash the meat down and some of that expensive Italian ice-cream.'

'You would mate. Believe me. A bird like that needs a good six inches up the dirt box to sort her out. Dirty old cow. No wonder Slaughter's a headcase. She must shag him rigid. Mind you, any woman hangs around with that cunt isn't letting herself in for French cuisine and vintage champagne. Must be a fucking battlefield when they get going. Can't imagine old Slaughter's into hours of foreplay and romantic meals for two. More like a quick knee-trembler and a samosa with his chips.'

'Me neither, but it's bad news sticking it up a bird like that. Mango's right. That kind of stuff's for queers, even if it is worth four points. You'd never catch me going that way.'

Eileen came round picking up glasses. She was an average looker, but friendly enough. Denise had sex and Eileen warmth. Will reckoned that meant more. He'd fancied her since she first started working in the pub four months before, though she'd never paid him much attention. It always worked like that. The women you took a shine to were either with someone else or not interested. The ones that pushed themselves were generally a bit iffy, with glazed eyes and desperation in their moves, thinking they were getting left out, craving love and affection so they'd shag anything and hope to hang on after the event. Like a lot of blokes. Will didn't think there was that much difference. Women could have babies and men couldn't. Straightforward really. He hoped Carter didn't get to grips with Eileen.

She took the glasses to the bar. It was only half-seven, but the pub was busy. Will was surprised. First day of the year and the world should've been staying home watching the game shows. Mind you, he was filling up fast enough, and would have a few more before he went home. It was like all that enthusiasm had been watered down the night before, and though everyone was going through the motions, not admitting they'd been fooled by the Christmas tinsel and extended drinking, persuading themselves it really was a brand new start, that this was the year when they'd finally get somewhere, be happy and satisfied with their lot, they knew deep down it was just going to be more of the same old bollocks.

'Where did you get to with that bird then?' Harry asked. 'Last I saw, you were chatting up Mick Gardner's sister. She's a right old slapper, even Balti's serviced it. Fanny like the Channel Tunnel. Half French by the look of the hair under her arms, but then she's gone and Mick said you'd pissed off with some decent-looking blonde which seems a bit suspect because everyone knows you're a pig-fucker.'

'Don't remember Gardner's sister. I gave her one last year. Well rough. No. I said I'd walk this other bird home so she wouldn't get mugged. It might've been New Year's but businessmen never sleep. Time's money if you're a sick cunt waiting in the shadows looking for an easy target. She wasn't bad. Lives down Ramsey Road and has her own place. Looks over the train track, but you wouldn't know it at night, just in the morning when the wagons roll through. Fuck knows who travels that early. Probably shipping nuclear waste through or pigs for slaughter. That lot don't rest. They're the real pig-fuckers. But this bird was very polite when we got back, very proper, went and turned the lamps on and chose a CD, shitty music, Mango sounds, and then when I'd had a drink, a couple of glasses of quality Scotch to warm the throat and thaw the vitals, I delivered some of the usual patter and she was away before you could say "Mango's a wanker".'

Will went to the bar and ordered a cheese roll. He hadn't eaten all day and was starving, but still had enough nous to concentrate on Eileen walking along the counter towards him, plate out in front. He self-consciously watched her breasts move gently under the wrap-around top she was wearing, long silver earrings brushing against the fabric covering her shoulders. She had a small nose-ring all the way from Rajasthan via Camden. He was feeling embarrassed just thinking about her breasts so close to the material, nipples rubbing erect. He liked the smell she brought with her, character embedded in the face. Perfume always worked with Will. Made her stand out exotic in an everyday London boozer. He wished he'd asked for some salt-and-vinegar crisps or peanuts as well, but didn't want to send her down the bar again and make a fool of himself. Nothing turned a woman off more than indecisiveness. If a bloke stammered or didn't know what he wanted they'd look straight through you like you were scum. A man with appeal was a man who never glanced sideways. That was the way he'd been told to look at the problem. You had to have the dosh to back yourself as well, otherwise you were nothing. The rappers had it worked out well enough.

'What happened to your eye?' Eileen asked, a hard edge to her voice that he couldn't identify. 'Been getting in trouble, have you?'

'Three blokes had a go at me last night.'

'What did they do that for then?'

'Don't know really. I was standing there waiting for a cab, minding my own business, thinking about the new year and everything, wondering if today was going to be any different from yesterday, brand new life and all that, and when these blokes turned up and tried to nick it I told them it was mine, that I needed to get home because I was knackered and had been waiting around for ages. Tired and emotional like, with the end of the year and Christmas over. They just piled in. There was nothing I could do and after they'd given me a bit of a kicking they nicked the cab.'

'You should get it looked at.' She was more sympathetic now he'd shown himself the victim rather than one more pisshead causing trouble. 'They might've damaged your eyeball. You could've ended up getting blinded. The eye's very sensitive you know. It's come up quickly. You won't be impressing the women looking like that.'

She smiled and put the cheese roll on the bar and Will tried not to look at her tits, wondering whether it was a real diamond plugged in her nose. Whether she took it out at night so the butterfly didn't come out and slip into her head, working its way into the back of her skull, wishing he knew why she'd mentioned women.

Will hoped he wasn't going red, blushing like a kid as he paid his money and went back to the others without delivering the killer punch that would show he was a smooth cunt with a good line of humour. He should've followed up with a sharp one-liner, but words didn't come easy. Least not with the opposite sex. He was too much of a gentleman, that's what he told himself when confronting the truth that he was probably just shit at chat-up lines, though he'd never say it out loud. He just went along with things, they all did, expecting nothing, except for Carter always aiming to get his leg over. It was unnatural somehow, looking to get stuck in all the time, no chance for a decent chat with his mates, a couple of pints and he was off for the night sniffing round anything that moved. But she was alright, Eileen behind the bar, and maybe it was better he wasn't one of those blokes who could talk about anything and say nothing, because someone like Eileen, with a Rajput ring in her nose and classy perfume, would see through the shit and tick him off as one more brain-dead wanker thinking with his knob. One day though.

'Getting in with Eileen are you?' Carter asked, looking over his shoulder at the barmaid, talking now with Denise who'd dumped her handbag out back and was ready for the evening's work, having a smoke because the landlord was out and not due back till after closing. 'Didn't know you fancied her.'

'I was only talking to her. Why does everyone have to be looking to get into a bird's knickers just because they have a bit of a chat? She asked me about the eye, that's all. Wanted to know what happened last night. She's not going to stand there ignoring something like that bulging out of the socket at her, is she?'

'Alright Mildred, I was only asking. No need to cry about it. Here, I'll wipe your eyes. She's alright. A bit skinny in the legs but at least she's not a heifer you'd have to string up and open with a chainsaw, blood all over the shop as you hook up a rope and pull out the Tampax. I wouldn't say no if she was offering me a quick one in the cellar. Wouldn't turn her down so I could piss off upstairs and service old Balti breath over there.'

'What's wrong with my breath, you cocky cunt? Didn't even have a curry last night, though I wouldn't mind a bit of a feed right now, but I'm off them. That's my New Year's resolution, to shift a couple of stone and give those Kashmiri boys down Balti Heaven a break.'

'You're a slob,' said Mango, laughing as he rocked back in his chair.

'And you're a toerag who hangs about with nonces in pinstripe suits, sucking cock, so you can piss off back to your stocks and shares or whatever the fuck it is you do for a living.'

'I made forty-grand last year touching my cap for my betters, milking the smug bastards, getting them all worked up so they hand over their liquid assets. But at least I'm moving, not stuck in the shit like you or one of those kids in King's Cross or Streatham. At least I'm dealing in prime genetics, not the mongoloid swill kids from Halifax get shoved down their throats for a few quid. Wake up lads. It's a material world. Even Madonna knew that much. Maggie understood what it was all about. Best prime minister we ever had that woman. Gave me the break I needed.'

Balti felt himself losing it a bit, looking to smack Mango if he went on. His head was heavy and he wasn't in the mood for propaganda. He fucking hated Mango sometimes and everything he was into; the expensive gear and three-bedroom flat in Fulham, that Jag he'd bought and the holidays in Spain three or four times a year, the Jag with its five-grand stereo and automatic sun roof, Spanish resorts full of English slappers who left their knickers at Customs and collected them again on the way home; and the Jag shifted when Mango put his foot down, blowing the rest of them away. It made him sick just thinking about it all, and there was Balti, sweating his bollocks off lugging bricks around, coriander and garlic in his water, slave to a lippy Belfast cunt of a foreman, and the tosser opposite was sitting in a luxury office near Liverpool Street punching buttons on a keyboard, juggling figures and probably working out his own pay packet. It wasn't fair, and Balti was left behind in the wrecker's yard with his big end fucked while Mango cranked up the volume and disappeared down the Western Avenue in a cloud of lead-free exhaust fumes. It wasn't like Mango was smart, except when it came to maths and making money, dedicated more like, but he'd always been that way. Always had to have what he reckoned was the best of everything. Into the image rather than content. Listening to disco shit at school when the rest of them were into punk and 2-Tone, going for the soul patrol gear when he should've been wearing DMs.

The Sex Division members knew each other from childhood, sharing the same streets and school and most of the same lessons, once or twice the same girls. Like that time Balti had stopped seeing Helen Peters and Mango was straight round, filling the void. Now Carter was getting involved, telling Mango he was a wanker, that he thought he was better than his mates, that if he really thought odds and ends were all that mattered then he could fuck off to some other pub, back to Fulham and a poxy wine bar, or better still fuck off to where the cunts he worked with lived and drink cocktails and talk about the rugby, then bend over and touch his toes while he got some public schoolboy's fist rammed up his arse. You don't even like football, you tart. But Balti was giving up on the argument. It was the same old stuff that Mango dismissed as the politics of envy, turning off and drifting back to those turn-of-the-year days when he was a kid. Balti's dad would have a hangover so he'd keep his head down knowing he'd get hit if he made too much noise, maybe go see Chelsea play if there was a game on in London. Like that time they'd gone up the Arsenal, Boxing Day maybe, he couldn't remember exactly, when Micky Droy was playing and they'd gone in the North Bank, kept their mouths shut, shitting it, then there was a roar and the Chelsea North Stand steamed in and kicked the shit out of Arsenal who pegged out the other side. They were all there, everyone except Mango, even Will who supported Brentford, Mango busy with Zoe, that Iranian bird who got him into the soul music, knocking around with her Hawaiian shirt mates. He was a wanker even then, listening to love songs when any sussed kid was into decent lyrics.

They were good times. Eddie McCreadie's Blue And White Army and the Clash releasing White Man In Hammersmith Palais. That was the best song, fucking magic. Balti felt guilty suddenly, remembering Mango's older brother Pete who'd had all the records and lent them out left, right and centre, turning them in the right direction. Will, meanwhile, had always been a few years ahead when it came to music. Then one day Pete went missing. He'd walked down the tube saying he was off to Greenford and hadn't been seen since. No postcard, no letter, no nothing. The old bill had tried to trace him but without any luck. Everyone had a theory. Maybe he'd just had enough, signing on, not seeing anything on the horizon, just Maggie raving about law and order.

Balti looked into his glass and watched the bubbles popping, thinking of Mango sitting on the swings across from the station, waiting for his big brother to come home. It was seventeen or eighteen years ago now and Mango must've given up. Just before Christmas he'd seen Mango's Jag and the bloke was down the same playground, swinging back and forward. Every year he went back and didn't give a toss if the mothers down there thought he was a nonce after their kids. Maybe he cried when he thought about it all, the sadness and that, and Balti couldn't blame him. He wondered what Pete was doing now, if he was still alive, if he'd ended up on the game. Mango had told Balti that was the worst thing that could've happened, one time when he was pissed. Or a smackhead, clean now but a wreck, living in a graveyard in Stoke Newington or Hackney, sleeping rough. Mango was pissed Christmas Eve, mumbling on about Pete being a crack addict or a wino, weighing up the options. Balti had told him to look on the bright side. If his brother was alive he'd come back one day. But they were only words. Mango had never been the same since his brother went missing.

'Get a round in then, you tight cunt.' Harry was sick of the squabbling, like a load of kids the lot of them, back in the playground. 'You're the money man round here Mango, so shift yourself and go to the bar.'

'Alright. Forget I said anything. It's the change of weather, the time of year, just gets me going and everything and I've got to hit targets and keep people sweet. You don't know what it's like working for a bunch of stuck-up wankers who've got money behind them and sit there waiting for you to fall down and mess up. Forget what I said Balti. It's the pressure does it.'

'Leave it out. It doesn't matter.'

'Go on, give him a fucking kiss,' Carter said, puckering his lips. 'Couple of fucking irons you two.'

Mango stood up and went to the bar, Denise coming over to serve him, swapping pleasantries, the entrepreneur acting casual. Denise thought he was a wanker. She wouldn't trust him to water her plants. He was a right turn-off with the expensive clothes and big-man attitude, eyes shifting here and there, never following the line of conversation. His wallet was stuffed with tens, twenties, fifties, propped on the counter, credit cards jutting out. He thought he was special and she had half a mind to set Slaughter on him, take off the muzzle and let the pit bull loose. Except Mango hadn't done anything wrong really, it was just the way he stood and talked and everything about him. But that Terry, he was gorgeous when she concentrated on the back of his head and she knew he was interested. Those kind always were. She could see them getting together and though Slaughter would hospitalise them if he ever found out, probably worse, he would never hear it from her lips. Anyway, she could control him if a rumour started. She had him wrapped round her engagement finger. A sincere expression and good sex would convince lover-boy that the person spreading rumours was spreading lies and he'd be round to see them with that machete he kept under the bed looking to mend their thinking.

Slaughter was a nutter, mental about Denise and life in general, but it was amazing what a healthy bit of sex did for a man like that. It was the strippers on stage and bikini girls on advertising boards that caused problems. Agency models in sight but out of range; winding them up, taking their wages, then stabbing them in the balls for having tattoos and tatty gear, chasing wealthy fashion clones with funny haircuts. Slaughter would drink out of the dog's bowl if she told him. He trusted her, believed her sexual appetite meant he was major, more than sex and protection, that he was the man of her dreams or some other romantic rubbish. That Terry was smart. He was dead ahead. No complications. She'd ask him why he was called Carter when she got the chance, straight out, confirm her suspicions and learn the details. She'd blow his mind.

The man she was serving was going on about something or other, a film he wanted to see, and she was smiling and doing her job, nodding her head, raising eyebrows, but all the time she had her eye on Terry leaning forward over the table telling a story to the three others, Will and the two men who shared a flat down the road. She wished she was a fly on the wall listening, a wasp with a sting, getting hot and bothered thinking about Terry having it off with one of his girls. She guessed it was that kind of story. She felt annoyed for some reason, Slaughter getting in a punch-up with a bloke in the West End the night before, putting the silly so and so's head through a car window because he'd paid her a compliment, a bloody compliment, nice arse. Anti-theft device screeching in her ear. Slaughter ran off leaving her to follow as best she could. It wasn't the kind of life Denise wanted.

When they'd got back to her place he'd stripped off and she could see him standing there now. Covered in ink with a dead penis full of lager, body swaying side to side, head back looking at the ceiling. She'd been ready for a Slaughter special, rough sex which was okay if she was in the mood but not when he was paralytic and biting into her neck like Dracula on a bad trip. She thought of that time when she'd pissed over his face, both of them burning up. She'd covered the bastard and he choked when it gushed into his mouth, eyes wide hoping it was okay, looking to her with a kind of appeal, a dumb kid. But last night Slaughter had looked at the ceiling like he was trying to find skin in the plaster, first-year monsters in the woodwork. He fell back against the wall and sank down to the floor. Denise had to turn off the gas fire otherwise he'd have burnt alive. He didn't move till morning. Terry though, where was he last night? She watched the men laughing together, wishing she could get him on his own for a minute and arrange something.

'Here you go,' Mango was back at the table. 'Anyone want crisps? I reckon Denise fancies me.'

'Leave it out,' Carter said looking towards the bar. 'Take her on and you'll be into Slaughter as well. He'd fucking kill you. Chop you into tiny pieces and feed you to the penguins in London Zoo. Then he'd take your head and put it on a stake outside the Tower of London for the ravens and beefeaters, balls stuffed in your mouth.'

'Suppose so. Don't stare at her otherwise she'll think I'm talking about her.'

'You are.'

'What's your resolution, Mango?' Harry asked, bored with Denise, a right old slag by his reasoning. Those kind were trouble. They came in your dreams and gave you grief all night long.

'Going to get myself a Merc by the end of the year.'

'I thought you were shagging the Jag. Changed your mind a bit sharpish didn't you? Fed up creeping down at three in the morning in your boiler suit to get stuck into the exhaust?'

'I'll keep the Jag and get the Merc as well. I have to earn the money first. It's a target to aim for. You've got to plan ahead. It keeps you going.'

'Can I use the Jag when you get the Merc then?' Carter asked.

'Fuck off. You'd ruin the upholstery with all the birds you get through. It's a class motor. I don't want stains all over the leather.'

Mango regretted the comment right away because it recognised Carter's reputation. He liked to present himself on an equal footing, but never did as well as the sex machine and would have to lie his way up the table. That was okay, because Mango was good with the truth. The others wouldn't have the ability or desire to cheat, but a high position was important for Mango. He was a competitor and despite his relative wealth women didn't exactly come calling like they did for Carter. He did alright, anyone could do okay with a bit of effort, but he was nowhere near the Carter class. Sometimes it bothered him, but Carter had serviced some right old grinders in his time and Mango had long since convinced himself he was more into quality than quantity. Something stirred, the memory of that kid up in King's Cross, the girl from Halifax. Young and tender and fucked rigid by how many men he did not know.

'What about whores?' he asked.

'What about them?' Balti was feeling the strain, looking forward to a good sleep but too tired to get up and go home. He was fucked and not looking forward to getting up for work.

'Do prossies count?'

'Course they fucking don't,' Carter said.

He turned to look over his shoulder again and three Sex Division members considered the possibilities. Will wished they'd talk about something else, but was more concerned with the pain shooting through his eye than starting something off. Balti looked at Mango, then Carter, Harry catching his eye and winking as he lifted his glass and took a big swig of liquid gold.

'Why not?' Harry asked. 'After all, you're still doing the business. It's the same things you're doing so there should be the same points available. You've got to perform even when you're splashing out for the privilege. It's not that easy.'

'Don't be a cunt. What's the point having a league if you're going to pay some tart for points. It would be taking a bung.'

'No it wouldn't,' Harry was into the game. 'You look at the big clubs and football's all about how much money you can spend on players. It's like everything nowadays. Ask Mango what counts and he'll tell you money, and he should know better than the rest of us stuck down here while he's rubbing bollocks with the men who matter. Nothing else comes into the equation. You still have to buy quality players to succeed. It's not like you pay the money and everything's over with. You might not be able to get it up or something.'

'Fuck off will you. You're trying to wind me up. There's no sense having a league if you go out and pay for it. Where's the fun in that? It would be like you said, success geared by how much you spend.'

'Like professional football then.'

'We're better than that. We're in it for the love of the game, or at least I am. You lot might find it a bit of a struggle, not being into birds and all that, rather sit at home wanking over the cartoons, but some of us enjoy shafting beautiful women. Sex makes the world turn.'

'Well what about a points system for the state of the bird concerned if we can't get them for whores?' Balti asked. 'Give them a rating on looks and how much effort it takes. I mean some birds we could all have, but others are a better standard. You'll fuck anything with a dress on. Vicars, Scots, whatever. The rest of us are a bit more select. We don't scatter our DNA everywhere.'

'Is that the excuse then?' Carter was shaking his head. 'You're all going to say you're only interested in beauty queens. Next you'll be wanting points for blokes.'

'Do us a favour,' Balti said, choking on his drink, outraged. 'Any cunt does that and he's out of the fucking squad. Immediate relegation and a lifelong ban.'

The lads nodded their heads wisely and sat in silence.

'What about rape then?' Mango asked. 'What about twenty points for rape?'

'Yeah, twenty points for a rape. You fucking lemon.'

They were all laughing now, because the options were endless, and Mango was getting silly. Anyone who raped a woman deserved to be hung. They all agreed on that. It had to be the worst crime going. That and child sex. There were some fucking sick bastards in the world. Hanging was too good for rapists and child molesters.

'What about animals?' Mango asked.

'He's had a few animals in his time,' Balti said. 'Carter's not fussy where he dumps his load.'

'We all have, be honest. Get pissed and you don't know what's going on. A bit of meat would do when you're on the scent. It's programming. I mean, that's why God invented the orgasm. Nobody's going to plan kids are they, because it makes your life a misery and everything, so there's this implant wedged in the brain that makes you fancy the opposite sex, and when you're pissed you lose your reason and shag anything. A pig can still produce young, can't she?'

'I meant hamsters and stuff like that,' Mango was cracking up.

He didn't normally laugh much, but was feeling spaced out. 'Some people shag animals, don't they?'

'Anyone does an animal, a four-legged animal that is, and I'll chop their bollocks off,' Will said, piping up at last. He liked animals, saw them as defenceless victims. Even mentioning rape in the same sentence as sex was bad news. That kind of stuff was all about power and control. He was a romantic and couldn't really separate sex and love.

They shut up when Eileen came round again. Carter asked her if she'd had a good New Year's Eve and she nodded, saying she'd gone to her sister's house. A few people round for dinner, and it made a nice change from the usual drunk effort, an Italian meal which her brother-in-law had made. He was from Naples and a good cook. The Italians knew how to enjoy themselves without getting pissed, though she couldn't say much seeing as how she worked in a pub. She asked how Will's eye was and he stammered a bit and knew he was going red and said fine, thanks, then changed his mind and was honest and said it hurt, real painful like, and she told him he should go and see a doctor. Harry looked at Will and prescribed another pint.

'You're in there,' Carter whispered, when Eileen had gone. Will shook his head and felt awkward.

'How about shitting on a bird then?' Mango asked.

'Why is it always you that comes up with the sick stuff?' Harry asked. 'You've got no soul. You've sold it down the City. I bet it's sitting there in a bank vault wondering where you've gone. Why would you want to shit on a bird? You're sad even thinking like that.'

'How about shitting in their handbags then?' Balti flicked a dead match from the ashtray at Harry, which bounced off his number 2 crop before falling to the floor.

The Sex Division membership thought about this new development. It had a certain kind of appeal. There had to be something acceptable beyond a four-pointer, something nobody was going to achieve. Rape, animals, anything like that was obviously bang out of order, the mark of a pervert destined for a severe kicking. But shitting in a bird's handbag was funny.

'Five points. What do you think?' Harry liked the idea.

'What about ten points?' Carter was laughing, they were all laughing.

'Ten points for shitting in a bird's handbag then. We all agreed on that?'

Everyone nodded, even Will. It was the impossible dream, a Sex Division special that went beyond the everyday, a recognition that there was only one winner when it came to sex, unless Mango made a determined effort and Carter lost the urge. Will was negative about the league anyway and Harry and Balti would never be that bothered, maybe pulling once or twice if they were lucky, but more concerned with drink, football, food; preferring a laugh and a good wank to feeding someone a line. The handbag bonus scheme eased things and made the league more light-hearted. That's all it was supposed to be really. A bit of a laugh.

COGS

HARRY WAS LATE. Well late. And that lazy cunt Balti hadn't woken him. He sat up in bed and breathed out, watching the mist form and hover, then slowly disappear, pulling the pillows high behind his back, chasing the dream running out of reach, deep into his brain where it could hide in the undergrowth. The radio was talking about a fire on the tube, Clapham North evacuated and the London Fire Brigade in attendance, a train on the District Line stuck underground packed with commuters, passenger under the carriages at Whitechapel, leaves on the line outside Waterloo threatening derailment, a pile-up on the M25 with police cutting a woman and child from the wreckage; all the normal fun and games of a rundown infrastructure. He had fifteen minutes till he was due at work and wasn't going to make it, but bollocks, there was nothing he could do now. Then Balti was sticking his head round the door saying he'd just got up, the fucking alarm hadn't gone off, that they'd better shift. He started half an hour later than Harry so was alright, handing over a cup of tea and a plate with two pieces of toast floating in a puddle of melted margarine, then shut the door and returned to the kitchen.

Harry sipped milky tea with two sugars, still tracking the dream, his head clear despite the drink of the previous evening. They'd left the pub at closing-time, though Will had pissed off about ten, wanker, and the rest of them had got soaked on the way home. Typical Will picking the right moment and avoiding the storm. He looked round the room, curtains half drawn and his clothes in a tangled pile by the chest of drawers. He needed to go to the launderette. Then he was concentrating, like he could make something click towards the back of the skull, a switch setting electricity loose, current popping and the scene sticking, colour melting inside felt-tip outlines.

He was with Balti, a tropical paradise by the look of things, both of them in bright yellow shorts. He pushed harder retracing their steps, a long winding trail through pure white sand, a bit younger, four or five years, and they must've been in the Philippines or Indonesia, somewhere in South-East Asia, because there were skinny brown kids playing in the sand looking for crabs, changing to skinny white kids building castles, then brown kids again wading into a clear blue ocean with small nets held high above their heads, up to their waists in a gently lapping sea, white kids dodging sewage and used condoms, brown kids watching for fish, wary of sharks. He saw a fin approaching, the pit of his stomach drawing back as he pictured the monster lurking, teeth razor sharp for amputation, victims drowned and mutilated, pure blue water turned to congealed artery red, a dolphin leaping then belly-flopping with a smile splitting its cartoon tab-of-acid face.

He bit into the toast and pulled the bed clothes higher. Harry liked dolphins. Everyone liked dolphins. Except the American military who'd trained the poor cunts to carry explosives on kamikaze missions. Tuna fishermen didn't give a fuck about dolphins either. Then there were the amusement parks that kept the bastards confined and taught them to perform for their supper. Life was shit if you were a dolphin in the wrong place at the wrong time. There'd been two in the Thames a while back, but there was so much shit in the water they'd got sick and their skin peeled with the pollution. He couldn't remember whether they'd escaped, the faint voice of the radio missing the end of the story. Take a wrong turn like that and you ended up boiling alive in industrial waste. But it was freezing on the mainland painting a house in Wandsworth. They had to let the gas people in first so wouldn't be starting till a bit later than normal, which gave him an excuse. Fuck's sake. He'd almost spilt the tea.

Pushing his head again, Harry was back with that line of footprints across a near-deserted beach, an exotic hideaway, sitting with his best mate, like brothers, both of them tanned and fit, bare-chested, served a nice plate of rice and a yellow pineapple dish with grated coconut, thick banana shakes in tall glasses, sliced papaya and watermelon on a separate plate. There was a brilliant green snake winding its way down a palm tree and the two men watched it as they ate, trying to decide whether it was poisonous. The old lady serving said no, that it was just a tree snake, teeth long gone and the gums bruised dark black red. There were tiny transparent geckos on the ceiling watching the dream unfold and when he looked across the sand the kids were coming back to shore with their catch, lifeless silver strips of protein. He felt happy. Real contentment. The fishermen were children, but at the same time adults. They were old when they were young, yet would hold on to a brand of innocence till the moment they died. He couldn't remember much more. The rest of the dream was fading, just out of reach, a mystery washed away by last night's drink. He was late but didn't care now. Harry's dreams usually decided his mood for the day. He dreamt a lot. He was in a good mood and knew nothing could touch him for the rest of the day.

He heaved himself out of bed and stood naked in the middle of the room eating toast, nicely done with burnt edges. Balti would make someone a perfect wife. He imagined the fat cunt in a bride's dress with a veil over his head, some old slapper from Blues carrying the train, walking up to the preacher and taking the cunt's crucifix then driving it into his head, blood on the insignia, army uniform under the holy man's skirt. Harry laughed and wondered if it was part of the dream coming up. He walked over to the window and looked round the curtain, careful not to show himself off to the outside world. He didn't want to get done flashing before he'd even got out of the house. It would be just his luck getting dragged out in handcuffs. Straight down the nick for some instant justice.

The street was damp but it wasn't raining, a gentle wind rattling the frame which was rotten and needed replacing. He put his dressing gown on and went to brush his teeth, have a wash, making a note to get the dressing gown cleaned. It didn't smell too healthy. There was no time for a shave and Balti was in the kitchen telling him to get a move on, fuck off you cunt, you should've woke me up earlier, then he was back in his bedroom considering a wank before the first day's work of the new year, a quick meeting with the five-fingered widow. He reached under his bed for a magazine and pulled out a plum. *Red Hot Asian Babes On Heat.* He flicked through and selected Tash and Tina, who were busy servicing The Sultan Of Singh. The lager was still in Harry's system and slowed him down at first, but with a bit of concentration he was soon erect and beating out a familiar rhythm. Practice had made perfect and in under a minute he was unloading the white man's burden. He mopped up and found a clean pair of pants and a T-shirt that wasn't too bad, added his torn sweat shirt and jeans, and sat down to put on thick socks and boots. Balti was shouting he was off on his own if Harry didn't get a move on, get your finger out you fat bastard, stop banging the bishop. Just like a nagging wife.

Will worked his way through the albums, stopping at Yes. The sleeves were bent and worn, and the corners looked as though they had been gnawed by rats. He'd never listened to Yes, though he'd always been quick enough to slag them off. Long-haired hippy music. It was funny how it worked. He'd never been into Deep Purple or Status Quo as a kid, but had listened to Led Zeppelin's Physical Graffiti enough times. His first single had been by Elvis Presley, according to his old man, and later he'd found out Elvis was one of punk's many enemies. The same went for the Beatles and Stones. It was mental the way you had to act according to the rules, even as a kid. It was still there and he wanted to buy one of the Yes albums to prove a point, but if he did it to prove a point then he was still being told what to do in a roundabout sort of way. He could afford the record because it was secondhand, dusty vinyl, and he could buy it because he was older with money in his pocket. He'd pay a couple of quid, have a listen, confirm his opinion, then chuck the album out so it wouldn't pollute the rest of his LPs. But then he would have to do the same with every other battered piece of vinyl in the racks. He left well alone.

'Will? Is that you?'

Will turned and faced a woman with spiked jet-black hair

and a thick red cardigan, a well-worn, multi-coloured shirt peeping through. His surprise must have registered. He tried to pin a name on the face.

'I thought it was you. Happy New Year. You don't recognise me do you? I was in your sister's class at school. I came round your place a few times. Karen. Karen Eliot.'

'I remember. You look different. It's a long time since I last saw you, that's all. You were a kid then.'

'How's Ruth these days? Haven't seen her for ages.'

'She's alright. Living back round the old man's at the moment. She broke up with her husband a year back. Took it hard, but you get over these things with a bit of time I suppose.'

'I didn't even know she was married.'

'Bad news he was. Used to knock her about but nobody found out till she left him and now he's done a runner. Ruth didn't tell anyone because she knew he'd get his head kicked in. Left her with all the bills on the flat to pay when he legged it. She's getting straight again. Must make you feel like nothing when you've been battered and then you're forced to cough up for the honour. There's a lot of rubbish around.'

As they talked, Will discreetly checked the albums Karen was holding. U-Roy's With Words Of Wisdom on top, and under that what looked like Prince Far I's Free From Sin, judging from the thick red lines over a smaller black-and-white crisscross pattern on the edge of the cover. Not bad. A woman with taste. Nice body and a face with character. Classy album covers as well and they didn't go cheap, classic reggae vinyl. He hadn't found anything he wanted and was tempted to ask Karen if she fancied a coffee somewhere, a cup of coffee and a slice of cake. It was too early for the pub. But he bottled out, and instead she was saying she worked in The George three nights a week and if he came in later she'd make sure he drank for free. There was a late-night Moroccan cafe round the corner, so maybe they could have a coffee after. Then she looked all embarrassed and said she'd like to hear more about Ruth, stared at the floor, smiled a crooked smile, and was off to the counter to pay for the records. She turned back to say she hoped she'd see him later. When she went outside Will's eyes followed her down the street.

Carter cut up a Rover at the lights, pulling the furniture delivery van tight into the inside lane, his young assistant Ian, Boy Ian as Carter called him, raising his right hand to the mirror in a peace gesture, beating the wanker sign his work-mate was about to deliver. Ian was easy-going which meant he generally got lumbered with the heavy lifting when they were on a job together. Carter enjoyed directing operations, the hard graft never much more than a double bed that the customer had to assemble, though lugging the various parts up four or five flights of stairs wasn't much fun.

Ian was a heavy-built Irishman from Donegal, though he'd lived twenty-one of his twenty-two years in London. He was London Irish, a QPR boy with a Celtic top and cross round his neck, but went against the Paddy stereotype preferring dope to Murphy's, jungle to diddly-daddly, ecstasy to whisky. He worked the cassette player as they went which suited Carter, slipping in some On U-Sound or old techno compilations. Carter specially liked Gary Clail's Emotional Hooligan, heavy bass taking him back to when they were kids into reggae, dub, punk − following Will's early interests and Pete Wilson's readiness to lend out his albums. He liked the dog barking in the background, or whatever the sound was, probably a special effect. Bim Sherman was next. Funny how music reappeared. Everything went in circles.

He kept meaning to knock together a tape of his own but never got round to it, deciding he'd get Will on the job, as the bloke had all the same records plus a thousand or so on top. Will was the man in the know. He thought about the emotion bit. Tricky that one, though if you were in Mango's shoes then maybe there was a reason. It was sad how something like a missing brother stayed with you your whole life. Fucked things up badly. Mango had never been the same, though it could've been growing up responsible for the change. He hit the brake hard for a hunchback granny walking on to the zebra crossing not looking where she was going, glancing into the mirror at the Rover he'd cut-up, a big cunt behind the wheel staring back. He put his hand down the side of the seat and felt the sawn-off snooker cue tucked out of sight, ready for the bloke to try his luck. There was a dented skull waiting to happen.

Then they were moving and he watched the Rover turn off, a nice motor worth a few bob, near enough vintage, pointing out a couple of women with kids in push chairs coming out of the bookies. He didn't think kids were allowed in betting shops. Maybe they were getting kicked out or had been in to see the old man, begging for spare change. Kids shouldn't be hanging around the bookies. Ian followed his gesture and Carter was saying the taller one was nice and well worth five minutes of his precious time, shame about the sprog, that the other bird was a bit iffy but so what. He'd fuck the arse off both of them given the chance. Ian just smiled and put in another tape, fast-forwarding to a mixture of didgeridoos and cranking metal, like the van was about to explode. Then the whole thing was taken over by some brand of psychedelic Eastern trance, Kurdish according to Ian, religious and full of nailed down sex. It was alright and made up for missing out on Bim Sherman. Ian started skinning up.

While Harry sat on a front garden wall in Wandsworth with Dave and Bob from West London Decoration, banging his heels against bricks, waiting for the men inside to sort out the gas, Balti was down in Tooting breaking his back. He wasn't in the mood for the verbal he was getting off Roy McDonald, a mouthy Belfast cunt who was going to get a brick rammed down his throat before the day was out. Balti decided on a break and set his load down, going round the back of the parked-up tippers where he could sit for a few minutes. He was shagged out. Like he was sick. Every muscle ached and his head was weighed down. There was this thud of drills from deep inside the building and he was dizzy. Then he was trying to keep his balance. He'd been on one long beano through Christmas and into the New Year, on the piss with Harry and any of the other lads who happened to be around. Harry was the top boy though. He loved his drink more than the rest of them. He could never keep up with the cunt. He tried, but failed. Harry said the lager washed away all your problems. Add a few beans courtesy of Mango and he was fucked.

'What the fucking hell are you doing?' McDonald was standing opposite, fag hanging out of his mouth, shit all over his donkey jacket, dried clay covering his boots. He spat his words and Balti looked for red flames.

Balti wondered if McDonald was a devout Protestant. There'd been a lot about Ireland on the news, history and everything, stuff he didn't understand because he never paid much attention to the details and couldn't work out the logic involved. He didn't care one way or the other, staring back at McDonald unable to speak. He had nothing worth saying. He ran his eyes towards the opening behind McDonald, the area of the site that was visible and empty of workers.

'We're behind enough as it is without you taking a fucking nap. You lazy cunts get paid on time and you want to sit around doing nothing. We've got schedules to keep. I've been watching you and you're taking the piss. Get back to work or you're out. This isn't a fucking holiday camp.'

Balti stood up slowly, moved forward with a humble expression and headbutted McDonald between the eyes. The two men were roughly the same size and the foreman liked to think of himself as a hard man; hard but fair, respected by the lads who worked for him. But Balti wasn't watching the same video. McDonald rocked back against one of the lorries and a steel toecapped boot connected with his groin, pain racing through his stomach into his mouth, down the front of his coat. Balti pulled him forward and damaged the cunt's nose with his knee. He hoped it was broken. Heard a crack.

He stood and looked at the bloke half-conscious on the ground, breathing heavily. It was the surprise that made it so easy and there were no witnesses. For a second he thought about using a slab to smash McDonald's skull in, picking up a shovel and killing the cunt for his lack of respect. But he wasn't worth the aggro murder would bring. No way. You had to know when to stop. He was out of a job but McDonald wouldn't get the old bill involved. Maybe he'd come looking, but Balti could handle that. What did he care? He didn't need his nose rubbed in shit first thing in the new year. Like everyone else he just wanted a bit of respect. That was all. Respect was essential. Without it you were nothing. You might as well give up and top yourself if you didn't have respect.

'Any time you fancy your chances, you know where I am, you Irish cunt.'

Balti kicked McDonald in the gut and went to collect his sandwich box and flask, walked to the car, and was soon driving past Tooting Bec tube towards Wandsworth Common. He smelt the fumes and felt sick, moving slow then fast, lumbered behind a bus, changing down a gear and accelerating on his way, pavements full of people, then empty, breathing slowly returning to normal. When he reached the common he parked and walked over to a bench, rich green grass stretching out in front of him, a black labrador in the distant hunched up and straining. Time to rest and calm down a bit, watching the traffic lights click red, yellow, green; double-deckers rolling slowly along, top decks full of pinprick faces; people going in and out of a parade of shops; a couple of wankers over by the pond hanging on to their fishing rods looking to catch a minnow.

Carter was directing operations, carrying screws and a couple of planks, Ian bringing up the bigger parts of the bed. They'd already brought the mattress upstairs and a well-bred woman was flicking through the instruction manual. Carter was casting a critical eye over a fit figure showing off a pair of expensive slacks. He reckoned she was over forty. There were gold rings on her fingers and a couple of silver specks in nicely-groomed but fairly natural hair. She looked up and caught his eye, turning away quickly, something wicked on her mind. He reckoned there was a good chance of picking up a couple of points if he played the game in the right way. He would have to get rid of Ian for a while, but he was stoned and open to suggestion. It shouldn't be too hard. When the woman went out of the room he had a quiet word.

'Hurry up, my husband will be back soon,' the woman gasped. 'Come on you horny bastard. Faster.'

Carter kept pumping away, the plastic cover they'd half pulled off the mattress rubbing against his knees. She was a right goer this one, but he didn't fancy her old man opening the bedroom door and catching them on the job. He wasn't getting anywhere though, so turned her round on to all-fours, trying a different angle. As he did his duty he looked around the room, a gold-framed photo of the woman in question standing next to a man in a black suit, an accountant or solicitor by the looks of him, two blond-haired, blue-eyed boys in front of their parents, smiling. Their mother was moaning and the delivery man servicing her ladyship was totting up the points. Two plus four made six and they were only a day and a half into the season. Four points would make it eight and he slipped his hand between the woman's cheeks testing the ground. He didn't really fancy the shift, but there were points on offer and Carter wanted to get a healthy lead established as soon as possible. Then he could relax.

'Don't do that,' she ordered, sucking in her breath, a hand coming back to remove his finger.

Carter was getting a bit bored, wishing he could finish and get down the cafe with Ian. His work-mate was a good boy, understanding the situation. Carter was hungry and it was time the delivery man delivered his load. He fancied a good fry-up and a nice mug of strong coffee. Meat for the gut and caffeine for the brain. Bacon and sausage smells hit home, imagination working hard, picturing the look on the faces of the rest of the lads when he broke the news. Total football. Johan Cruyff was the master, like that time out on the wing he'd taken the defender one way, back-heeled the ball through his own legs and off he went. The tradition moved on. There was no real beginning and end. There was the Gullit-Rijkaard-Van Basten mob. Now there was Bergkamp-Overmars-Kluivert. It was in the blood and the rest of the boys would be gutted. There was a tank in a corner of the bedroom, tropical fish unaware of their origins. At least they were free of predators and fed regularly. That's the way Carter looked at the situation. Next to the tank was another photograph, in an antique frame that must've been worth a bit, two girls in sixties fashion. It was probably dog woman and a sister. They were wide-eyed, female versions of the two young boys. One of them held a hoop, both with ribbons in their hair, though the picture was black and white so he didn't know what colour. There was the same expression on their faces.

'Come on, don't slow down,' the woman was panting and Carter made the effort, concentrating on the job in hand, feeling the woman shudder, trying to forget about the bacon, his mates waiting down the pub, Ian in the cafe shovelling down egg on toast, Harry and Balti, Mango and Will the record collector sitting in The Unity, drinks lined up, having a crack, a good laugh, enjoying the show. A flash of inspiration hit the league leader, the kind of thinking that sorts the winners from the losers, championship material, the mark of genius, excitement hitting home, total fucking football. Total fucking football.

As the woman finished Carter felt the tension reach boiling in his groin, quickly withdrew, flipped her over and moved fast so he shot over her left breast then finished off in her mouth. His thoughts were with the manoeuvre, the distance between the first muscle spasm, the quick withdrawal and attempts to hold back, losing it a bit halfway, then hitting the jackpot. Calculations were all important and his tactics worked. He rolled over next to a satisfied mother and wife, the smell of pine from the bed all around them. They were strangers again in a clearing deep inside a Scandinavian forest with the trolls and lumberjacks and herds of reindeer. It had been a near thing, breaking the flow and diverting his attention, numbing the physical satisfaction. But he'd done well. Fucking brilliant. It was a three-pointer and the rest of the lads would be well impressed. The woman next to him laid her head on his chest. He couldn't wait to see the faces of his mates when he broke the news.

'You nutted him?' Harry asked, shaking his head. 'Nice one Balti, can't slag you off for the reasoning behind the action, but a job's a job you know.'

'He had it coming. I know it's not too rosy workwise at the moment, I mean it never fucking is, but he should've kept his trap shut. He doesn't pay enough to talk to me like that. He wouldn't do it off the site. No cunt talks to me like that. I should've bricked him as well. Should've killed the cunt. Who the fuck does he think he is?'

'Never mind all that. Drink up and I'll buy you another.'

'I can still get a round in. I'm not a beggar. Not yet anyway.'

Harry watched Balti go to the bar and order two pints of Fosters. Strange that the dream he'd woken up with was so positive, and now this. He tried to make sense of the beach scene, the kids fishing and everything. He must be getting his ideas mixed up. Usually he could work out his dreams by the end of the morning, often much quicker. It was either sorting out the past or, now and then, seeing something in the future. Maybe it was wishful thinking. Balti sipped his lager as he waited for the second pint. This morning Balti had been good as gold, up with the sun and everything, then a few hours later he's giving his boss a hiding. Maybe it was down to McDonald, fucks knows, though it must've been a bit of Balti as well. But it didn't matter, because they were mates and Balti's version was all that counted. If the bloke came down looking for trouble they'd give him another helping. Harry went back to the beach. Considered the tree snake.

'I think I'll shoot off after this one,' Balti said when he'd returned with the drinks. 'Go home and polish off a bottle of gin then start the new year again tomorrow. What a way to kick off.'

'Stay here and we'll have a drink. The others'll look out for me. It's a bit slow anyway. They're still fucking about with the gas.'

They stayed in the pub most of the afternoon, drinking at a relaxed pace. Harry was pushing a visit to Balti Heaven back home, but the Balti king was standing firm, leaving well alone. It was a question of will-power, something he had to prove to himself. He also needed to shift some weight if he was going to get anywhere in the league. Harry didn't care about such niceties, half a stone lighter than his mate. A midday session was just what Balti needed to forget about mass unemployment, McDonald just a stack of clothes with a pool of shit inside. So what if Balti didn't have the pleasure of killing himself hauling bricks. There were other things he could do. He was sick of labouring. He'd done it on and off since leaving school. Picking up the wage packet and out on the piss, down the football, feeding his face, keeping the curry houses going. It was a clean break. Better than a New Year celebration. The lager was doing its job and Harry talked him through with some expert advice. Life was good with a gallon of drink tucked in your gut. Harry was no mug. He could see the present as well as the future.

Carter and Boy Ian were making the most of the delay, sitting in the van behind Baker Street tube. The next delivery was due in half an hour and they were ahead of schedule. The man buying the large double bed wasn't due home till four. They'd tried him on the mobile but got an answerphone. Despite the fry-up, Carter was hungry, deciding it must've been that woman building up his appetite. She was a raver and suddenly keen for another portion, but he'd had to leg it. He couldn't leave Ian hanging round like a cunt all day and her husband was due back. She was mad. One minute she wanted him out, the next she wanted him to stay. It didn't matter to him, but she had a lot to lose. He couldn't work women out sometimes. Carter had a job to do, and it wasn't like he was going to add to his points total. She'd asked him to ring her and he was considering the request. He could put himself through the grinder – she'd offered to pay for a hotel room in the West End and obviously had the wedge – but the most he could hope for was an extra point, unless he saw to her handbag, and that wasn't being realistic. He would have to believe in the possibility of chalking up a bonus point before he called.

'Get us some chips if you go for a kebab,' Ian said, eyes bleary and his thoughts drifting. 'A can of Coke would be nice as well. A cold one.'

Carter made the decision and went over to the kebab house. It was different to the normal effort, a real Middle East job with Muslim girls in head gear behind the counter. Not the purdah stuff but scarves. They were in their early twenties and good-looking. Cheerful and friendly. Lebanese or Syrian maybe. He ordered a kebab and chips, two cans of freezing Coke, then sat down while the food was prepared, flicking through a magazine. Rain hit the window, Arabic script decorated the glass. It was a smart little place, big pictures of mullahs and minarets adding flavour. An old man shuffled in, smoker's cough in his throat. Too much hashish. Carter watched him, then the girls. Even the meat looked different. It wasn't the usual Greek-Turk effort he got round his way, a bit up-market seeing as this was Baker Street. He considered the girls behind the counter and whether there was any way he could top up his seven-point total. A couple of blow jobs out back, or at least a shag.

The man pissed off with his sweet cakes and Carter tried to work out whether the smiles and looks coming his way were an invitation or plain friendliness. It was difficult sometimes working things out, knowing what was true and what was fiction. The food was placed on the counter and he made the right decision, dipping his hand in his pocket to pay, leaving it alone knowing that success was going to his head, that sniffing around in kebab houses was a bit sad somehow.

'Cheers Terry,' Ian said when the chips arrived. 'I'm looking forward to these.'

Carter rolled the window down to let some of the smoke out. The wind cleared things nicely and he got stuck into the kebab, wondering what kind of meat was in the mix, the chilli sauce packing a powerful kick. They ate in silence, Ian more concerned with his chips than changing the tape. When they'd finished, he took the paper and empty cans to a bin while Carter called Mr Malik. A man's voice answered and they were in business, one more job out of the way. If they finished ahead of schedule they got off early. Carter would have a look in the pub, see if any of the boys were about. It would be a good evening if he could find some of the lads. He was on a roll.

The Lager Twins were well oiled and ready to eat, a full-scale Chinese takeaway and a couple of cheap bottles of cider to polish off the evening. Balti took two plates, knives and forks, serving spoons and the mushroom soya sauce into the living room. Harry meanwhile had the containers on a tray, leaving the lids in place so none of the heat could escape. Balti remembered the glasses and went back to the kitchen for two pints nicked from the pub. He shoved one of the cider bottles into the freezer and took the other. The telly was on in the corner, volume turned down low, a documentary on the chemicals in food packaging that were believed to be affecting male sperm counts in the civilised world. Balti said they should tell Carter.

'Look at those.' Harry had emptied the spring rolls on to a plate and was prising the lid off the sweet and sour, Balti opening the other containers. 'You get value for money down the Die Nasty. Like Carter. Value for money shag machine, always a cheap deal on offer. They're fucking huge these spring rolls.'

The doorbell sounded. Balti swore and Harry told him not to answer it. Balti looked out the window and saw the sex machine below. It was magic. Black, evil, twisted magic. Mention the cunt's name and he turns up on the doorstep just when you're about to get stuck in. Balti was starving and letting Carter in meant sharing the food, or at least offering, but the lights were on and he'd just keep ringing till they cracked. Mind you, they'd ordered enough. Gone a bit over the top in fact. He made Carter wait a minute and helped himself to a king prawn in batter, digging his teeth into the tender flesh, then poured a glass of cider and took a few gulps. It was warm and tasted like shit but at least it was wet. He banged into the wall a couple of times on the way down, almost falling arse over tit. He could think of better ways to die. What would they write on the grave stone – 'Here lies a pisshead who fell down the stairs and broke his fucking neck, the silly cunt'?

'Go get a plate if you want something to eat. We've got a chinky on the go in the front room.'

Once in the flat Carter made himself at home, filling his plate when the others had done, then another glass with cider. The drink was fucking horrible and he went to the fridge, into the freezer for some ice-cubes. He put them in a bowl and took them to the others. Then he was taking things easy, sitting back on the couch next to Balti, watching Harry in the chair opposite spilling food down his shirt. He was a bit stoned thanks to Ian, and had five pints inside him from The Unity, popping in to see if any of the lads were drinking there, having a chat with Eileen, asking after Denise who was off for the night. It was a shame seeing how he was moving, an honorary Dutchman in London, a fucking Orange man from Ajax of Amsterdam, part of the brotherhood. Then he was pissed off realising no-one was going to turn up, deciding to take the news on tour. But he wasn't getting the chance to tell them about the three points because they were pissed and into their own thing, fucking up his moment of glory. He took a ready-rolled spliff Ian had supplied earlier and lit up, passing it round.

'There's opportunities for people like me,' Balti was saying. 'Fit and healthy men in the prime of life, too good for the knacker's yard. I'm not thick you know. Just haven't had the breaks so far. I could do a lot in life, anything I fucking want. You understand that, don't you Tel? Travel the globe and create a bit of history.'

Carter wondered what the fuck Balti was on about. He nodded, his brain misfiring all over the shop, tiredness and the drink, a heavy dinner and kebab that made him feel sick when he thought about it now. There was food everywhere, everyone ripping at everyone else, cannibalism wedged in the mind, consumer society, sex consumption, bit of blow during the day, that posh old witch he'd shafted watched by the kids. It was a nasty business. The things he did for his mates, keeping the flag flying. Top of the league. Wishing he had the woman's arms wrapped round his back now. He noticed the screen for the first time with some boffin-type cunt and then these burning tadpoles that looked like fluorescent spunk under a microscope, tails banging away, sex on the brain. He had to clean his act up, it was taking over. There were other things in life. But nothing like sex. He loved it. Loved women. He wished there was someone at home when he got back, not an empty flat with cold walls till the heating got going, some tasty Swedish bird with legs right up the crack of her arse. Carter tried to work out what Balti was saying, clocking on that he'd given his boss a spanking and was out of a job. Silly fucker.

'It's alright,' Balti was saying. 'It's alright Tel. I'm fine. Don't worry about it. Something'll come up. I'm not bothered. I'm better off than most blokes, those poor bastards with kids to support. Think of the pressure. If I want I can piss off. No ties mate, no fucking ties. You should've seen McDonald go down. Didn't know what hit him.'

'That's living,' Harry agreed. 'No problems. Just keep on, full steam ahead. No surrender.'

Carter had worked it out. They were right. Fat boys in a two-bedroom flat. Looking after each other. Husband and wife. He laughed. Husband and wife without the sex to get in the way. They argued but it never lasted long. They were good mates who watched each other's backs. But Carter knew he'd always be the winner. He had his mates and kept his distance. He was his own man. He stood alone and preferred things that way. Dabbling like there was no tomorrow. He waited for the boys to finish their food and relax, waited till their heads were simmering, a late-night therapy programme coming on and the TV turned off sharpish. Then he picked his moment and broke the good news. He told the lads that their old mate Carter had pulled again and was on seven points. He watched their faces. Balti sunk his face into his hands and Harry shook his head slowly. Carter savoured the moment.

Will had to admit it wasn't a bad little place. He'd pushed himself to go down The George and Karen was right there behind the bar, like she'd said. It was a quiet evening and she fiddled free drinks for the hour till closing. When they'd cleared up she took him round the corner for a late drink that turned out to be coffee. Like she said. She called the waiter over and they paid the bill, Will waiting for the change while Karen went to the Ladies. He was chilling out nicely now, though he'd been nervous going down the pub like that, not knowing what to expect.

Karen was beautiful and he couldn't believe she was interested in someone like him. She was clever as well. He remembered her vaguely as a kid with long hair that had since been cut, and of course she'd filled out and become a woman. A real woman. He couldn't explain it properly, but it was the feeling that counted. He was conscious of mucking things up but she was easy to be with. But why him? A shabby herbert who collected punk and reggae records and made a living running a junk shop. There had to be a catch. Maybe it was a wind-up organised by the rest of the Sex Division. He sipped the coffee dregs and tried to work out the motivation. Perhaps Karen was leading him into a trap. But what kind? It could be personal. Like he could've been rude to her when she was a kid and she'd never forgiven him, showing her up in front of his kid sister. He wasn't like that though. Will was easy-going. Had she seen a chance for revenge? She could be lifting herself through the bog window at that very moment and doing a runner down the back alley, straight into the arms of the Sex Division champion who would take her back to his flat and chalk up a four-pointer. It wasn't a nice thought. He shook his head. Maybe she wasn't interested at all, at least not that way, wanting to talk about his sister who she'd hardly mentioned.

'I can't believe I've met you after all these years,' Karen said as he walked her home. 'You know I used to fancy you like anything when I was a kid. Ruth's big brother. You always seemed so mature. Funny we live so near each other, yet all these years have passed. I don't know where it goes. I shouldn't be saying this should I?'

Will wasn't sure. He couldn't work out the angle. They crossed the street and nearly got soaked by a double decker, Karen pulling him away from the kerb. They continued and she brushed against him very faintly, but enough for Will to take notice. He saw a group of youths sitting on a wall opposite, tensing as he tried to identify whether the faces were friendly, but they were talking and not interested so he concentrated on Karen. She led the way, turning down a side street, off to the left past cars parked outside a row of lock-ups, under an old railway bridge that was dark and smelt of rotten cardboard and forgotten engine oil, the kind of twilight corner where dossers slept and rapists lurked. The type of place where Batman dropped from the rafters, opened his cape and flashed his Batknob.

'It's a short cut home, but I never come down here at night,' she said. 'It's too dangerous. It gives me the creeps, but it's much faster than going the long way round. I don't mind with you. I don't even come through here in the day. You never know what's waiting for you.'

Will was a bit narked with himself, feeling a tingle, like he was the hunter-gatherer protecting the women folk, the knight in heavy armour telling the rest of the Crusaders to leave him out of the rape and pillage. He loved women. He thought about them a lot but in a different way to the rest of the lads, or at least how he imagined the others thought. He was attracted to warmth and imagination.

'This is it,' Karen said, looking at a three-storey house, the flat she lived in on the top floor. 'Home sweet home. Do you want to come in for a coffee?'

Will was going to say no, that he'd just had one and it had been a bit strong, that he'd be up all night unable to sleep and he had to get up in the morning for work. He realised he was being soppy and smiled again. He reasoned that coffee had to be responsible for a lot of people getting together through the years. Clichés everywhere. You couldn't turn around without one smacking you in the mouth. He told himself to shut up moaning all the time, trying to dissect everything. What should she say? 'Would you like to come upstairs you dirty bastard and fuck the arse off me and if you like I'll give you a blow job so you can impress that Carter mate of yours and go back down the pub with him and the others and make yourself out to be some kind of Alfie stud.' No thanks. He told Karen coffee would be nice. Perhaps they could listen to that Prince Far I album she'd bought earlier. He had the record himself.

PIGS IN KNICKERS

MANGO WAS THE only one still in the office, but was surprised to glance at the onscreen clock and find that it had already gone ten. His eyes were aching from prolonged use of the computer. He hadn't been taking the recommended screen breaks and leant his head back, swivelling in his seat. He turned away from the machine and focused on the far end of the open plan office that covered the ninth floor of the block in which he worked. Although designed to soothe the mind and create an illusion of free space, thereby maximising potential in the work force, the inevitable kingdoms had been built with the assistance of grey dividing boards and large potted plants. Cartoons had been carefully cut from *The Times* and *Economist* and pinned up for general appreciation. During the day there was the tangible thrill of expectancy. It was the expectation of either instant dismissal or a very large commission.

Although he appreciated the unique nature of corporate vitality, Mango, or James Wilson as he was known to his work colleagues, preferred the evenings when the majority of his fellow workers had left the office. It gave him the chance to fully relax and plough through data, pinpointing potential targets. Most of the people with whom he worked took a bit of stomaching, but he bit his lip readily enough. Compensation came in the form of hefty financial rewards. This in turn allowed him to leave the poverty of his childhood behind. Mango was good at what he did, very good in fact, which couldn't be said for many of his expensively-educated colleagues who were nonchalantly trying their hands in the world of fast-turnover commodities, little resting on their success. But results counted at WorldView, a model of multinational free-enterprise, and public-school education or otherwise, failure was not tolerated. Maggie would have approved. Mango owed the great lady a great debt. He was fortunate enough to work for a cut-throat company where weakness was erased with the punch of the delete button, and he firmly believed that the WorldView set-up was at the cutting edge of contemporary economics. He had made himself competitive and was reaping the benefits. James Wilson had ambition. He was forging ahead, making money, bettering himself.

Mango pinpointed a yucca plant. He concentrated on the exotic outline, trying to readjust his eyesight to the relaxed mood of the tropics. It was the biggest yucca he had ever seen and must have cost a hundred pounds minimum. The leaves were sharp and well defined, the bark grizzled and sturdy. Each leaf had been individually waxed by a junior employee so that it would shine brightly under the office's artificial lighting. His eyes gradually adapted. It was a lot to pay for a plant, but he was quick to put things into perspective. WorldView had enjoyed record profits during the previous financial year. Talk about wealth distribution. There was no such thing in Britain. He had learnt that growing up and it was this realisation that had made Mango determined to live in a flat where there was no damp and no chance of vandalism. He didn't want to bend his head with the continual scrimping and worry that had haunted his parents. Nobody was going to give him a helping hand. Maggie had understood this essential fact and was a true friend of those people prepared to get off their arses and graft. She was a patriot ground in the realities of multinational commerce. He had taken his chance and embraced the classless society.

Mango thought about his brother. Pete must've decided on something better as well, going off like that, though in his darker moments Mango always imagined the same thing, cruising through a red light area picturing Pete selling his mouth for a couple of quid to make ends meet. Rent boy on the game tiding himself over till he made it big, letting the politicians and financiers carry their policies through to the logical conclusion. Where was he then? Mango was waiting for his big brother to come marching through the door, part of a takeover consortium, nothing less than the top boy. Pete had been trying to get ahead. Maybe that was the true story, Mango didn't know, and although it was the only way he wanted to think, he had strong doubts. Who was he to judge his brother? Sometimes he went a bit spastic and imagined himself grabbing hold of Pete and telling him what a cunt he was, not leaving a body to drain and bury and mourn, just pissing off, before Christmas as well, hitting the bloke then sticking the boot in when he hit the ground, kicking his head till the face caved in, taking a blowtorch and burning the features, melting wax.

Every year Mango's mum bought Pete a present and put it under the Christmas tree. She bought it sober, wrapped it with a celebratory glass of whisky, put it with the other presents, then got pissed. It was always the same. Every year. Christmas morning came and the family was together. The old man with the stuffing ripped out. Mango's two sisters, neither married but wishing they were, right sad cases if he was honest. They all went through the usual routine, passing presents back and forward, delaying the moment, putting it off, scouting round for something else to open till there was nothing left, just a pile of paper with red-nosed Rudolph and shepherds tending their flocks ready for the slaughterhouse, and there it was, left at the end surrounded by shredded wrapping, as per fucking usual, Pete's Christmas present from his mum. Mrs Wilson said nothing as she took the gift and hid it away in the back of the cupboard in her bedroom with all the other presents, tears running down her cheeks into her mouth, the salt of a mother's misery, one more woman ground down and battered into the concrete. It was sad, so fucking sad that sometimes Mango wanted to cry like a baby.

He always wondered what she'd bought. He asked but she said it was Christmas and a surprise, that he was still a big kid at heart wanting to know what his brother was getting ahead of time. It would spoil the surprise if she told him. Jimmy would have to wait and see like everyone else. Did she still buy for a teenager? Did she think her eldest son was the same as the last time she'd seen him, still wearing the same clothes, the army surplus trousers and Harrington, pale face and spiked black hair, suspended in time? Mango did. Off to Greenford to see about a job and there was Mango sitting on the swing waiting for his brother to come back, stood up and let down, twisting the chain round and round, spinning back to earth feeling like he was nothing. He tried not to visualise the scene. He always saw himself in that playground like the spirit he didn't believe in was high above in a spaceship, looking down on the wickedness of human error. It was his own kind of death experience. He'd read about death trips. Sometimes he wished the old bill would come round, say they'd found a teenager's skeleton and DNA fingerprinted Pete, that it was his brother and no doubts remained. Murdered by a pervert and buried in a shallow grave. Found by an unemployed man out walking his dog. At least they'd know for sure. It was the suppressed hope that did them all in. It never seemed to get any easier, however many years passed.

After the regulation break Mango returned to the screen, eyes out of focus now confronted by regimented lines of white figures, digits marching in time and suddenly melting into a tangle of jagged edges. He tried to click into gear but couldn't get going. He was due in at eight the following morning, so surrendered to the inevitable and switched off his computer. He went for his coat and stopped at the drinks machine. He was groggy and tired. His thoughts were losing their clarity, the concentration essential for his success at work fading as his brother made himself part of the present. The ghost was back, ready to cause havoc. Mango chose coffee for a kick-start. It was bitter and tasted of chemicals, but would have the desired effect. He took the lift down to the ground floor and waved to the security guard, a big bastard with a starched collar and glass eye, the result of a pub fight in Bermondsey in his youth. One of the old Millwall boys. Mango passed through the heavy glass doors and into deserted City streets. The buildings towering above James Wilson were sand clean and well-maintained, architecture a fine balance of the old and new. He felt it worked well. A winning fusion of tradition and the modern element to take London deep into the new age. There was no point looking back, although the past was inescapable and had to be accommodated, so a compromise had been reached. The best elements were promoted, while those that had been ignored or pushed outside the area remained to blur the wider vision.

Mango loved the streets of the City when they were empty. He imagined the rest of the human race sucked into a vacuum, abducted by aliens, zapped by an intergalactic ethnic cleansing team. He would sit with the controllers and oversee the extermination campaign. Logic would prevail and he would be president for eternity. All around him there were buildings honed from quality masonry and shining glass, not the cheap stuff they used to house the masses. It was down to quality. If the buildings and environment were solid, then it followed that standards would be maintained. Put someone in a slum and they adapted in order to survive. He hated poverty and insecurity. It made him angry. He wanted the best on offer and fully accepted the survival-of-the-fittest dogma that had revolutionised British life. It was common sense.

The pubs were shut and most of the offices deserted. He walked down perfectly cut streets, very little rubbish to be seen, surveillance cameras on every corner protecting his interests. Mango felt safe. He went to the underground car park, paid his toll and slipped into the Jag. The smell of its interior filled him with a magnificent sense of satisfaction. He leant his head against the rest and inhaled deeply. His eyes ached and he had a pain above his nose, but the Jag was the ultimate relaxant. He closed his eyes and thought of the yucca tree. Perhaps he should buy one for the flat.

Mango drove an XJ6 3.2 Sport. It was a beautiful piece of technology. The machine oozed class and represented British car design at its finest. It had set him back a little over thirty grand, but was well worth the money. It wasn't a long trip from WorldView to King's Cross and he was travelling in style. Cleanliness and sharp design would soon be replaced by uncollected litter and inner-city confusion. Mango cut through Smithfield, past the church where Queen Elizabeth I had watched the execution of Catholics, past the market's meat racks and freezer lorries with their rows of dead pigs, ancient fields now a concrete landing pad for refrigerated truckers waiting to unload their cargoes. Mango's curiosity showed hundreds of pigs on steel hooks, deep black channels carved down the front of their bodies, from throats to missing genitals, straight through to the bone so that the insides could be hacked away, wall-to-wall, clogged together satisfying a pork-hungry public. Computers had given way to headless bodies, hard white digits to drained black blood. He put his foot down disgusted and the Jag soared through Farringdon and Clerkenwell to King's Cross. He became absorbed in the engine. The atmosphere was warm and comforting. Cold butcher's steel a mindless fantasy.

King's Cross was near to deadlock, traffic moving slowly in front of the station, paper flapping and neons flashing, cheeseburger takeaways and sex shop invitation. It was cold and dirty, the inside of the Jag the height of automotive luxury. He preferred the sound of the engine to the radio, working himself further inside the machine, feeling the power and rational precision of the XJ6 surge through the accelerator and into his body. He was part of the mechanism, naught to sixty in 7.9 seconds, cool and calculated, a top-of-the-range model beyond the tug of failure. Mango sat in traffic watching the crowds; half-drunk office workers and inter-city travellers weaving in and out of the festering scum. He stereotyped drunks, junkies, whores, drug dealers, spivs, pickpockets, pimps, muggers, rapists, hypermanics, schizophrenics, wankers. Every kind of mental disease was there in King's Cross drowning in drink and powder and lingering bouts of psychosis, too much for the clean-up campaign. He looked at thin girls and body-built men with gold watches and expensive designer gear. He thought about the girls on the game; addicts, abused kids, poor mothers. He considered the scum milking them, minor-league entrepreneurs dealing crack and selling women as a fast-shifting commodity, chopping their heads off and hanging them on skewers for roving punters. Mouths frozen and sucking devices installed. Blonde heads with bullet holes, American imports, back of the skull efforts where a man could insert his penis and fuck the pig's brains out.

Once away from the main flow Mango knew his way. He

saw pros along the side street, tarted up for a cheap porno mag centrespread, caricatures leaning into cars matching the advertising billboards lining London; black and white, old and young, fat and thin, ugly and one or two beauties. Some carried handbags for their accessories, others just had the clothes they wore, making do with spit where others splashed out on lubricant. A woman got out of a car and slammed the door, kicking the wing as it pulled away fast leaving behind a heavy smell of burnt rubber, screaming words Mango couldn't hear. He looked for the kid from Halifax he'd had up by the mosque in Regent's Park, more out of curiosity than any desire for a repeat performance. There were some sorry people about, so desperate they'd do anything for a pittance, spaced out on crack, smack, fuck knows what, amyl nitrate to help them with the big payers demanding a tight fit. His eyes glazed imagining the workings of the human body. He saw blood pumped through veins powering the heart, speeding corpuscles and heaving muscles, valves straining stress, popper acceleration, his own engine expensively tuned and ready to explode down the motorway at a top speed of 138 miles per hour. But these women were the wrecks, covered in rust, scabs, burnt oil. He saw the stockings and suspenders, black white red, the thin fabric and low-cut bras, high heels and thigh-length Nazi jackboots.

A black woman approached, thick red lipstick and hot pants wedged into the crease of her cunt. He looked at the crutch and imagined her shaved clean like the pigs in the refrigerated lorries, heads cut off for Queen Elizabeth I, chainsaw mutilation in the centre of town, Jack The Ripper in the East End slaughtering immigrant workers, Irish whores, operating and hanging their insides over the walls of Whitechapel. The woman was tapping on the glass moving her hand in front of her mouth, offering to suck him off, mouthing the words cheap-very-cheap as she faced up to economic reality, fluttering false eyelashes, star of a pop music video that would conveniently avoid the cold of a leaking one-bedroom flat in Hoxton. The skin was tight against bone but the thighs were too powerful, make-up overdone and smudged, rough as fuck.

Mango pulled forward leaving her behind, past three younger blondes; arms, legs, heads nailed together, mouths jabbering, powerpacks inserted. Plastic dolls on a street corner. Inflatable sex. Full of sickness battered by economy and gender. Aids blended with herpes, syphilis, hepatitis, depression, suicide, a couple of coughing under-five black bastards waiting in Hoxton. He felt confused and thought about doing a U-turn, but kept going.

Mango moved further along the street, cars slowing down so drivers could choose from the menu. He looked in his rearview mirror and saw Hot Pants get into a dented Granada. Then he spotted the one he wanted, a young girl up ahead, just what he was looking for, purity itself. She was in a doorway wearing a mini skirt, talking to a couple of bent-looking boys. He thought of Pete. Rent boy on the game. It was wrong, all wrong, that kids like Pete had to leave home and end up down at the bottom of the pile, pissed on by the world, a dumping ground for queers and sadists, the kind of people who deserved the death penalty. The Jag came to a halt and the girl approached. Mango pressed a button and the window noiselessly lowered, cool night air entering the cocoon. She was perfect. The hair was cropped short and dyed black, and she had a nice pair of lungs for a kid, not particularly big but jutting forward with sharp nipples he could see through the green cotton top she wore beneath an open PVC jacket. Mango imagined a red button in his mouth, digging his teeth in deep and tugging hard, pulling the nipple off and cracking it open with his incisors. The legs were thin but the skirt showed them off just right. The girl leant in and touched his ear sending a shiver of excitement through his body. Her perfume was strong, the smell of roses, resembling a sophisticated brand of artificial beauty. Mango knew that it was cheap shit. He smiled a paternalistic smile as he handed over his money and the girl walked round to the passenger's side. He pushed the relevant button to unlock the door.

Sitting next to him the girl was small and innocent, legs crooked and half open, a kid who was probably about thirteen. He glanced at the texture of her skin. The legs were pale white and covered in goosepimples. He increased the heat a little, attempting to thaw her out. She'd catch a cold standing around on street corners like that. He remembered his mum telling his sisters to dress warm when they went out. She'd said the same to him and his brother, but more often to the girls. When you were young you dressed to impress rather than look after your health. It was only when a kid got older they saw beyond all that. But the girl sitting next to him, flicking through his CDs, she was beyond that now. He wanted to give her advice. If he was sensible he'd give her the benefit of his years. He should tell her to sort herself out. Go back to school. Get some kind of an education. There were other ways of earning a living. Stacking shelves, cleaning offices, and factory work could pay alright if she got in to the right firm. Maybe she could do something with her life, like he had, get ahead, make decent money. She could become an estate agent. You didn't need a brain for that. Just flog houses to idiots who couldn't afford the repayments, take the commission, then turn your back when it came time for the eviction. Maybe Pete went that way, but no, he'd have done better, Mango was sure of that. There was more to his brother than shuffling deeds. Pete was international. Diamonds, technology, something major. Good old Pete. He should tell the girl about the success of his brother, the short black hair and everything, pale white skin, causes and effect, but he was a man of action and would rather drive up to Regent's Park.

The smell the girl brought into the car was irritating, breaking the Jag's magical aura, yet her presence was exciting, like Halifax, bringing fresh life and the promise of pubescent sex. He drove slowly along the corridor, watching for Halifax, saw comings and goings and the exchange of currency, market forces hard at work. Once on the Euston Road he returned to the girl next to him, buckled down behind the seat belt looking out the window saying little. He found this annoying. The silence put him on edge. Fucking slag. Treating him like one more sleazy punter looking to abuse underage girls. He should teach her a lesson. Put his foot down and steam out of London, 138 miles per hour, naught to sixty in 7.9 seconds, multi-point fuel injection, power-assisted steering, over thirty grand's worth of automobile. Somewhere they didn't interrupt a man going about his legitimate business. He was solid. Doing well. He drove a Jaguar XJ6 3.2 Sport and owned a two-bedroom flat in Fulham. He snorted coke on his own late at night watching videos of German au pairs flat on their backs as queues of Italian queers ejaculated over their grateful faces, while his mates made do with more lager, blow, kebabs. The gym in which he trained was exclusive. The mirrors were floor-to-ceiling and the clientele Eton-educated or London-done-good. Mango was going places. Foot down naught-to-sixty in 7.9 seconds, six in-line cylinders, piling through North London past Hampstead, Barnet, out into Hertfordshire or cutting along the M25 to Essex.

They'd find a nice little beauty spot surrounded by black fields under a locked sky. An abandoned lover's lane. Mango was erect. Space Shuttle job. Grabbing the slut round the neck he'd drag her forward, taking the cut-throat razor from his pocket and holding her down, the blade he kept honed tight on the jugular, maybe a nick or two to see the disease in her blood. He would demand an apology for her treating him like shit, like he didn't matter, like the Jag was just another car. She'd left him spinning in circles, dizzy and confused, just a kid, sitting on those swings like a right idiot for everyone to laugh at, trapped, surrounded by losers, going nowhere, round and round and round till his mouth filled with sick and he started to cry.

He'd remember the Jag's seats and take her out into the darkness. Do them both a bit of good, breathing fresh country air, the hum of the nearby dual carriageway keeping him sane. Subhuman vermin. Drag her to a ditch scaring away the rats and foxes lurking in hedgerows. Night prowlers. The sound of survival flapping in mud. He'd pull her beneath an old oak tree and wait for the moon to burst through a crack in the clouds. He'd see the face for what it really was. He'd force her to look him in the eye. The cropped hair and black dye. The look he knew so well. Selling herself like that, beyond sex now, a boy and a girl, bisexual psychology shifting from a kid growing up playing football to a youth roaming London alone, unloved, killed by a monster and buried in the same spot, under the old oak tree, the only possible reason for a teenager's disappearance. Somewhere there was a bit of English countryside that would remain forever English. One day they'd find the bones. Thousands of years into the future, fully-developed genetic technology readily available, a society so far advanced in its scientific understanding of the creation myth that nurses would be able to apply synthetic skin to the basic bone structure and rebuild the innocent victim. Mango saw Pete in a coming world of peace and love, where people stuck together and there was no need for competition. Right now it remained a masochist's fantasy and belonged to the dole queue. Mango did the sensible thing, fitted into his world and survived. More than that, he prospered. Learnt lessons. He had the strength and the power. He had power over the kid next to him, turning her head now from the Euston Road to the punter behind the wheel.

'Where we going?' she asked.

'Regent's Park,' shaking away the thoughts racing though his brain, imagination running wild, all that death and destruction bad news, something for the TV. 'It's quiet up there. We can be alone for a bit. No risk of the old bill or some headcase watching through the window.'

The girl laughed and her hand moved to his groin. Mango felt tense and turned right. They stopped at a set of traffic lights on the edge of Somers Town. He felt awkward with her next to him when the Jag wasn't moving. The girl leant over and undid his flies. The lights changed and they continued. He cut through back streets to the edge of the park, a quiet spot under a thick covering of trees. He remembered going to the nearby zoo with his family as a kid. Everyone but the old man. Mango must've been eight or nine at the time. It sounded grand when he was small, just the name London Zoo, like the animals there represented the city. They paid to enter another dimension. Watched animals move they'd only ever seen stationary. It was mental. Lions, tigers, bears, elephants, giraffes, crocodiles, snakes. There was a gorilla as well. He didn't remember the name. The poor thing sat there in his own shit surrounded by cold steel, banged up for the duration, sectioned like a nonce, though nobody on the other side of the bars seemed to realise what it all meant.

Pete smacked some kid making faces at the gorilla trying to wind him up, and the wanker had run off crying. The face of the gorilla was in front of him now. The dimmed eyes and broken frown, controlled and paraded for the crowds, unable to appreciate the innocent love of the children outside. The size and power of his body made it worse somehow. There was an unhappiness Mango understood but hadn't been able to identify till years later, thrilled by the strength of the beast, the gentleness and pride. It was all a mess, the lot of it, and now he was all grown up sitting in a flash motor in among the wealth and prestige of Regent's Park with a teenage tart from King's Cross threatening to splash his seed all over the upholstery.

Mango was a success. He had money in his pocket. Money in his various accounts. Savings schemes and investment plans. Now it was time for a bit of active socialism. He was spreading his wealth. The girl sunk her head down and started moving. He looked straight ahead, willing himself to remain interested as he felt the emptiness of paid-for sex, his vision quickly accustomed to the darkness. Apartments glowed red through the trees and occasionally a car hummed past on fresh tarmac. The girl was doing her work like the pro she was and he felt the tension quickly build, forgetting the romantic setting and confused motives. Mango's hands moved down to the back of the girl's head and he pushed the dismembered head further down, doing his best to ram his penis down her throat. She began to gag and pull back, but he pushed harder and told her to get on with it, not to muck him about, laughing that he was paying the wages and the employer always demanded more work for lower pay, it was just the way of the world, part of the boss-worker contract. Then he was coming and the girl was coughing, Mango pushing the button so she could open the door and clear her throat in the street, realising that the punter meant it when he said he'd send her home in an ambulance if she dirtied the interior. When she'd recovered they sat in silence as he did the decent thing and drove her back. Mango made a couple of attempts at small talk that weren't returned, one-word answers unwilling to forgive. When he glanced at the kid he saw her brushing a tear from her cheek and he felt like the exploiter he was, wanting to ask her name and history but knowing it was too late.

Mango felt the Jag vibrate as the girl slammed the door and ran off, a flash of anger replaced by a desire to get home. He needed to forget instantly and press on as he had to be up early and needed to be at his best. There was a big deal in the pipeline and he would have to be shit hot to get the best for both himself and WorldView. He retraced his route along the Marylebone Road, then on to the West Way, down to Shepherd's Bush Corner and through Earl's Court to Fulham. He tried not to think too much, all that stuff about cutting up kids and everything, what the fuck was going on in his head, that whore as well, the second bird under sixteen he'd been with for a wage. King's Cross was a cesspool as far as Mango was concerned and the sooner the police finished cleaning up the place the better for everyone. It was disgusting. It was his last time. Something had to be done. The country was going to the dogs.

He wondered what the lads were doing. He wouldn't mind a pint and some normal company, but it was late. He knew they thought he was a bit of a wanker sometimes, with the car and flat and money in the bank, but he preferred to dismiss it as jealousy. His mates were losers but they were also his history. It was where he belonged, though he hated the blind acceptance and broken pavements, the intensity of everyone knowing everyone else's business. He wanted privacy. He believed in breaking things down and separating interests. If he wanted to bring some tart home and cut off her head, maybe leave it sitting on the living room table for a week then he could. No other cunt could do that. Not that he was going that way, not James Wilson, no chance, but it was nice to have the option. It showed he was in control. It was all about freedom of choice.

When he entered his flat the first things Mango did was bolt the door, switch off the alarm, turn on the bath and get a shepherd's pie out of the freezer ready for the microwave. It was good to be home, the flat warm and welcoming thanks to the automatic timer he'd had installed. The thick carpet was a luxurious cushion as he stripped off and went to the main bedroom. The bed was large and custom-made from the finest imported hardwood and had set him back two grand. There was a big gold-trimmed mirror at the bottom of the bed where he liked to take women from behind, able to view his actions in widescreen format. He really should've bought that girl back and shagged her properly. He was wary of disease, but imagined himself sodomising her, ripping her apart, shoving his fist up her arse and pulling out the guts. He laughed. Sick cunt he was sometimes. He'd never do it though. He knew he was alright. It was just the stuff around him hitting home. Poor little thing stuck in a place like King's Cross. Probably milked by some dago, nigger or white trash pimp. Hooked on junk. Shafted by the male population. She'd been lucky to meet a bloke like James Wilson, Jimmy Boy, good old Mango, someone respectable from the City, a mother's son, a bit-of-a-chap soft at heart, a decent citizen who wanted to help. Least he wasn't a bum bandit like Carter or some death-tripper insisting on unprotected sex. He hadn't even tried. Shown a bit of respect. He wasn't tooled-up, a knife or pliers in his coat pocket, lengths of twisted wire to dig in her skin and find some kind of silver lining under the surface. Fuck that for a game of soldiers. He'd leave that to the wankers he worked with, going on about S&M all the time. It wasn't surprising some of it rubbed off after a while.

He'd even given the bird an extra twenty quid after the event and though she took it quick enough the ungrateful slag hadn't even bothered with a thank you. He got a bit carried away, that was all, trying to get deep down her throat like a man was told to in school, just to understand what was going on inside the system. And Mango stood in front of the mirror with subdued lamplight behind him, the edge of his skin dusted with orange-tinted angel dust, an aura of invincibility protecting him from harm. He worked his penis erect, walking over to the bedside table for the KY, returning to his original position, rubbing the lubricant in and aiming for the mirror. He thought of the girl in all kinds of positions, working through the options. When he was about to come he thought of the mirror's price tag and hurried to the bathroom, entering the steamy atmosphere heavy with bath salts, hanging plants placed strategically either side of a frosted-glass window, a rainforest atmosphere for a lithe animal. Mango was in good time and ejaculated over the toilet seat and into the bowl. He watched tinsel hang, glue stretching with the weight of his heritage. He felt patriotism and pride in the DNA he manufactured, a caste away from the mutant genes dominant in red light zones and other centres of genetic inferiority. There was some kind of regret for the sperm doomed to float in dead scented water, the goal never achieved, the only possible end a torrent of green bleached water from the cistern and a one-way ticket round the U-bend. Then there was the trip through the sewers, struggling manfully to impregnate rats, creating a unique monster race that would one day rise from the underground and proclaim a new social order. Mango laughed and noticed his face in the mirror. He was looking a bit strange. Fresh from a test tube. It was the coffee. He wiped himself with a length of toilet paper, then flushed it away, swearing at the bits that stuck. Typical. He turned the bath off and was about to get in when the phone rang.

'Mango you wanker,' it was Balti. 'Where've you been? I rang twice before.'

Mango checked the answerphone and saw that two messages had been left. Balti was half-cut, but he wasn't lying. He never did, the idiot. That's why he lugged bricks around for people. He needed to get himself sorted out. Move on.

'I was working late,' he said, sitting down in the reclining armchair next to the phone, naked except for the toilet paper.

'Till nearly midnight?' Balti asked. 'You want to have a word there. I mean, it's a bit strong.'

'I worked till ten, then went round this bird at work's place. She hung about and I knew she was asking for it because she's always giving me the eye and that, and then she was still there at ten, so when she invited me round to her flat in the Barbican I thought why not? She's tasty as well. One of those professional birds in dress suits that hug their bodies. Real quality, Balti. Not some donkey from Acton or Shepherd's Bush. She comes from class. Healthy food her whole life so she looks like an upper-class model. Privately educated, went to Oxford, you know the sort.'

'Not really,' the voice laughed. 'Sounds horrible to me, but I suppose as long as you don't have to talk to her and hear all about the country estate and that, how they kill foxes and torture the servants, and if she's a looker, then why not.'

'She's beautiful,' Mango said, smiling. 'Long blonde hair and the perfect figure. You wouldn't believe it if you saw her. I reckon I should get a few bonus points for class. Carter knobbing some brain-dead whale isn't the same as what I've just been dipping my winkie in. I think I'm in love.'

'How many points did you get then?'

'Two for a shag, then I followed it up with a three-pointer. Swallowed it like a trouper. Straight down, though I thought she was going to gargle at first. She fucking loved it.'

'Dirty cow. Mind you, you didn't hang about did you? I mean, you leave work at ten, get round the Barbican, maybe say a few words or something, then you knob her, give it a while to recover and next thing you're bollock deep in dentures. Then you have to stay awake and get back to SW6. Didn't she mind you pissing off like that?'

'She doesn't care. Just wants a good bit of sex without the hassles. Pure animal attraction. She's got one thing on her mind. You know what these office birds with a decent income are like. No morals. That's how their families get rich in the first place. It goes back centuries. They rape, rob, stitch up the serfs, then set up laws so everyone believes what they're doing is right because it's been written down. It's in their history. You watch them sometime. They've got no manners. Can't say thank you or please and take what they want. It's the ordinary people who've got morals. It's them that help others and know their right and wrong.'

'You sound like Arthur Scargill. Anyway, you're part of all that now.'

'You've got to get in there. There's no other way. No point wasting your life trying to fight the system. Didn't get Scargill anywhere, did it?'

'Three points puts you second. You know Carter's been up to his old tricks again. He shafted some bird when he was delivering beds. Three-pointer as well. Puts him on seven.'

'Sounds a bit iffy to me,' Mango said, narked that the shag man had maintained the gap at the top of the table. 'You sure about that?'

'He's not going to lie, is he?' Balti sounded a bit surprised. They were mates. If you couldn't trust your mates, then who could you trust?

'I know. He doesn't hang about, that's all. What about you and that dreamer you live with? What about Will?'

'Had my first wank the other day, and I've followed it up with a couple more since then,' Balti admitted. 'As far as birds go, sweet FA. Mind you, we're going down Blues tomorrow, that's one of the things I'm calling about, so I reckon we'll be getting stuck in there. Don't know about Will. Haven't seen him. You know what he's like. Sitting at home listening to music getting stoned.'

'I'll see what time I get finished tomorrow. I'll try and get down. Where you going first?'

'The Unity, then The Hide, then Blues. Should be alright. Don't suppose you know yet, I did the foreman the other day so I'm out of a job. If you hear about anything going let us know. Keep an ear out for us will you?'

'What did you go and do that for?'

'He was slagging me off. I hated it there anyway. It's time I did something different. It's like a new start. I need something to tide me over so if you hear of anything let us know.'

When he put the phone down, Mango thought about Balti for a few minutes. Maybe he'd get himself into gear now. He could offer him a few pointers. Apply some of Maggie's infinite wisdom. Balti would be better buying and selling. What he didn't know. Anyway, it wasn't his problem, though the news that Carter had been scoring points pissed him off. But at least he was second and the office bird story had potential. She probably had some dirty mates who wanted Mango to give them a good seeing to as well. He laughed as the word spread through the bistros of London. He could be their bit of rough, riding in a limousine down to Henley or Virginia Water, rows of upper-class birds lined up waiting for a good old-fashioned dose of pleb love-making. He'd make them pay through the nose, and he wouldn't be touching any grinders either. He'd keep his dignity. Loaded by other means but willing to service the aristocracy, for a fee, considering that he was in effect lowering himself in providing such a facility. It got him thinking. Instead of hanging around King's Cross he should try one of those agencies. The birds were probably a bit more up-market, with posher accents and cleaner gear, more into it than the worn-out street girls. It meant getting them round the flat, which he didn't fancy. Bollocks though. It was his place. He could do what he wanted. He lived in a democracy, not some communist slave state. He'd ask a couple of the chaps at WorldView. They'd know all the angles.

Sitting in the bath, Mango took the opportunity to relax. The bath salts eased the strain and he closed his eyes. Steam filled the room. The Arabs understood these kind of things. The old Turkish baths and that. The Scandinavians had their saunas. The American Indians their sweat lodges, though they went for the natural touch as well, turning it into a hallucinogenic experience. But Mango was happy with his bathroom, a boiling cave where he could unwind after a hard day earning a crust. He looked at his knob floating limp in the water, the paper melted away. It was funny how something like sex became so important. One minute he was acting like scum in some park, next he was content, ready to support any proposed government action to clean up the streets. He was alone. It was great. His eyes were closed and the strain of working on computers all day was beginning to slide away. It was tough sometimes, but rewarding. He had everything material he'd ever wanted. Rain bounced off the window, reinforcing his feelings of satisfaction. One day, long before he was the same age as his old man, he would be set up and retired. No financial worries. That was the crux. You were always going to worry about money if you didn't have any, but if you got a decent bit of wedge banked you could enjoy the finer things. It was security. Learning from the losers. Maggie knew.

He felt tired but wanted to make his time at home last. When the water began to cool, he topped up again with hot. The tap handles were period brass. They shone under the light which he had dimmed. The weather outside was getting worse. He heard thunder far away in North London. He thought of the underclass in doorways, shafted left, right and centre, then forced to sell their sex. His view was realistic. Mango knew he was right. Nobody chose to prostitute themselves. The thought struck that he was a tart himself, out of his environment, but he wouldn't think about all that. He was living proof of the longed for classless society. Or at least he was a representative of an early beginning. Mango didn't want to think. It was too much. Rows of figures beating drums, pigs on skewers, women on street corners, schoolgirls in his car, Balti on the phone, Carter on the job. His old mates. Good blokes they were whatever they thought of him. At least when things got too much, the pressures of achievement and all that, then he could go back to his own manor and fall into the old ways for a night. He didn't have to pretend. But neither did he want the pressure. He didn't care. There was no point caring too much because you'd end up in a psychiatric unit with the doctors pushing ECT, or on the piss like his old girl, or jabbing needles into your arm in Finsbury Park.

Sitting in his Rest-Easy armchair, Mango's right hand adjusted the relevant handle, lowering the back rest so that he could lie out full-length. It had been expertly designed to fit the human body and was well worth the thousand-pound debit. He flicked through television channels using the remote, crisp images beaming from the screen of the Nokia 7296, surround sound supplied by the Rock Solid speakers that had been professionally placed around the room. Mango enjoyed the full home-cinema treatment, flicking back and forward through terrestrial and satellite channels without finding anything substantial to hold his interest. Trendy cult-show presenters discussed myriad forms of sexual persuasion in minute detail, a blockbuster Hollywood movie revelled in the blood and gore of a faceless serial killer without bothering with the deeper

psychology behind the Razor Man's gruesome dismember-
ments, while the soft-porn channel to which Mango subscribed
grunted and groaned its way through a by now dull routine of
missionary/rear-entry/woman-on-top positions that only ever
revealed bare breasts and wobbling buttocks. For a laugh he
cranked the volume up full throttle to annoy the couple who
lived below, a right pair of arrogant yuppies. The room was
filled with the moaning passion of a full-blown orgy, female
ecstasy vibrating through the bookcases he'd had specially built
the previous year, shaking the books he'd never read. He did
this for a couple of minutes then turned the sound down. He
turned off the TV and went over to the separates system Will
had recommended.

Mango was making a brave attempt with the classics. His Best
Of collection included Beethoven, Mozart, Bach; all the
European masters he'd heard about somewhere along the line. It
was supposed to be uplifting music, the kind of thing that
imaginary blonde nymphomaniac from WorldView would be
listening to as she lined the coke up along some multinational
director's knob, stirring the soul. Mango skipped from one track
to the next. He found it pompous and dull, failing to do
anything but bore, the knowledge that it represented European
history and the ruling elite's cultural values not enough to make
it listenable. He had some of the best audio gear money could
buy but it was no use. Maybe it was a question of being in the
right mood at the right time. He should try listening with a bit
of blow, or Wagner after ten bottles of select German lager. He
wished he could get something out of Beethoven and the rest of
the boys, but it wasn't happening. He was uneducated. He
would keep trying and crack it one day. Some other day. He
chose another option.

The radio was repeating news items with a breathless,
speculative presentation that owed more to the need to fill the
airwaves with constant interest than qualitative news values. He
moved through layers of ragga, jungle, drum-n-bass pirate
stations, French- and German-language channels, Anglo-Indian
bangra where the sitars filtered through tablas seemingly boxed
into the speakers. The clock on the mantelpiece showed one

o'clock. He had to sleep. Had to stop his brain racing. Morning would come round soon enough. He closed everything down, went to the window and looked outside. He had forgotten about the shepherd's pie. He wasn't hungry. The rain slowed a little, then redoubled its pounding. Mango pulled the curtains tight and went to the fridge for one of the sleeping tablets the doctor had prescribed.

KICKING OFF

HARRY AND BALTI were the first ones in the pub, landlord Len pouring two pints of Guinness to bolster their guts and line them up for the long day ahead. It was the third round of the FA Cup and Chelsea were at home to Portsmouth. The previous night had been lively, a few lagers at the end of the week, Balti knowing he'd have to start watching the pennies now he was unemployed. He'd been down the social and had his interview the following week, ready for the grief coming his way. Bollocks anyway. Pompey would bring a mob up to London, they always did, and Tommy Johnson and his mates had been in the night before, psyched up looking to bushwhack them down Charing Cross, maybe the Elephant.

Portsmouth had always been a bit tasty and would want to put on a show, the 657 Crew in their designer gear back in the eighties, they remembered that well enough. Balti laughed, thinking of the bloke in the pink tracksuit who'd gone right over the top with his clothes getting the piss ripped out of him throughout a game at the Bridge. They'd had a few punch-ups in their youth but nowdays they were older and wiser and happy to let Johnson and nutters like that do the business. It was different now, deeper underground, not such a mass thing any more, though when it did go off in a major way there were plenty of older faces ready to steam in. But it was the past. Times changed. Balti took a long drink from his glass, letting the iron content work its way into his blood, a lethal pint first thing Saturday morning. Even Harry had a pint of Guinness now and then. He was no fascist.

'There was some Paddies in here looking for you last night,' Len said, once he'd rung up and taken Balti's tenner. 'Five of them. Big bastards. They asked for you by name. I said I hadn't seen you for a couple of weeks. They ordered, hung about for half an hour, then left. The one asking the questions looked like he'd been on the receiving end. Nose blown up like nobody's business. Even complimented me on the bitter. Said they'd be back for some more. They were looking for trouble. I could tell they weren't waiting around just to buy you a pint.'

'What else did they say?' Balti asked, knowing McDonald wasn't the sort of bloke to take a kick in the bollocks, then grin and bear it and put it down to experience. He'd hoped things would pan out. McDonald wouldn't grass him up, but if he was honest then the comeback was inevitable. He'd started something that was only ever going to end in tears.

'Nothing,' Len said. 'Nothing to me anyway. They seemed more interested in the door. Who was coming in and out, clocking faces. They didn't look too healthy.'

'They're not. Thanks. What did the others look like?'

'In their forties. Hard men. They all had coats on but I don't reckon they were tooled-up. One had some kind of Ulster tattoo. I noticed that much. Another smoked roll-ups. Right stink of tobacco but I wasn't going to argue the toss. You only missed them by fifteen minutes. Looks like it was a good job. You in a bit of bother?'

'Nothing to worry about,' Balti said. 'It's a shame we missed them though. We went down The Hide, then ended up in Blues. You should've seen the skirt down there. Carter only went and pulled again, didn't he? Don't know how he can be bothered all the time. Some slack black bird. Well nice if I remember right, but I was hammered so it could've been a pig with a suntan.'

They went to their regular table by the big window at the front of the pub where they could watch the world outside. Hungover parents led hyperactive kids in and out of shops, middle-aged women lined up at the grocer's and juveniles played arcade machines, the roar of rockets and buzz of lasers filtering into humming traffic. Two alkies sitting on a wall by the bus stop shouted gibberish, sipping Tennants, ignored by everyone who passed, a regular sight. The off-licence opposite had a jagged hole in the window that had been bandaged until it could be replaced, the owner sweeping glass towards the wall. It had been ramraided a couple of weeks before for the contents of the shelves. Business wasn't going well and the owner was seriously thinking of selling up and moving out of London. Balti looked at the familiar scene and wished he was somewhere else. Carter would be along soon and Will had said he'd be in later before he met his Brentford mates and got a lift down to Swindon. The third round of the FA Cup was a big day in the football calendar. Mango might even put in an appearance seeing as how he hadn't shown up the night before.

'So what's this McDonald about then?' Harry asked, looking towards the bar, out of earshot from the landlord who was interested enough but busy serving three noisy pensioners who'd just entered, taking advantage of the pound-a-pint special offer on bitter.

'Don't know him much outside of work really. Imagine he can handle himself. I'm not bothered about the bloke. If he's looking to have a go that's up to him. We'll just have to sort things out again.'

Carter came in with a smile on his face, stubble on his chin, same clothes he'd been wearing last night. He saw the lads were on the Guinness, went to the bar and ordered, sipping his lager while Len let the stout settle, looking around for Denise who wasn't in yet, knowing she often worked Saturday mornings. Len even put shamrocks on the cream, though it wasn't that professional a job and they might've been daisies for all he could tell from the vague outlines. Carter didn't know if the governor was Irish or what, and couldn't be bothered to ask. He didn't look or sound it, but you couldn't tell things like that sometimes. He carried the glasses over.

'Straight in another bird's bush and two more points in the bag,' he said, sitting down. 'That's me on nine and no-one else off the mark yet, unless you two got the scent.'

'I forgot to tell you last night,' Balti said. 'Mango shagged some bird from his work, then he got a bonus point on top. What was she like then?'

'Indian bird. Nice body, small tits, decent shag. E'd out of her box and if she'd been strong enough she'd have carried me through the front door she was so keen.'

'I thought she was black. Into the old jungle wasn't she, jumping around and that.'

'No, Indian. Dark though. You should've told me about Mango and I'd have put in a bit more effort. That's what it's like when your game's based on flair. You do enough to get by. It's only when you're up against it that you turn on the charm. Chelsea have always been like that. Look at the teams we've had through the years. Get beat by shit one week, then go and stuff Liverpool or Man U the next. Gullit's different though. Ruud's got everything. Dutch flair and discipline. Double Dutch. That's the mark of genius. Cruyff had the same ability. Forget the Premiership though for a minute and let's concentrate on the amateur game. What happened to you two? Pull anything last night after I left, or just your plonkers?'

'Leave it out,' said Balti. 'It was down the kebab van and straight off home. I was even too pissed for a knuckle shuffle.'

'Not even one point off that Greek serving chips in the back of the van? Big flabby arse and piss flaps down to her ankles. You service that and I'll slip you a back-hander. Anyone gets between the sheets with her deserves a couple of extra points.'

'You'd have to give me more than a back-hander to touch that,' Balti laughed, spilling his drink.

Harry was watching the street outside. He was pissed off that Carter had bought him another pint of Guinness. He'd wanted lager. The Guinness was lining. He wasn't going to make a fuss. The winos were up and moving towards the swimming pool. He was thinking of flabby arses and desert islands, crystal blue oceans where the only movement was the occasional fish jumping. Except last night it hadn't been a desert island. It was somewhere on the mainland. The east coast of Mexico fronting the Caribbean, golden beaches that backed on to thick jungle and ancient Mayan temples buried so deep that the syphilis-heavy white man had never set eyes on them. On the horizon lay Cuba and Haiti. He could smell Castro's cigars and hear voodoo drums. They'd been sitting in a bar with a couple of Aztecs. Balti was on the Corona while Harry was joining the warriors in the local moonshine. There was a worm in the bottle which the older of the Aztecs said turned ordinary men into gods. Bite into the worm and they would have visions that would change their lives. But Harry and Balti didn't want to change. They were staying in a nice little place with a front porch and two hammocks where they swung back and forward watching the village kids fish in the ocean. It was similar to Harry's last dream, with a few essential differences. They were more laid back now, like they'd been there for a while, although the same dangers lurked. As he enjoyed the hemp supplied by a retired policeman, he kept his eyes on the frail little Mexicans searching for fish, knowing from his experiences in the East that sharks were present everywhere. It was a worldwide problem.

Harry woke up and went for a piss. It was cold in the bathroom and he kept his eyes half closed in the bright light. He made sure he stayed with the fuzz in his head, got back into bed and returned to the dream, preferring the heat of the Gulf of Mexico to London in the winter. At first the dream was forced and not worth the effort, but then he began sinking down and when he woke the next morning he was easily able to concentrate and everything rushed back full throttle.

It was night and they were still in the bar. An all-day session. Fireflies danced in two-dimensional blackness and there was the bark of a monkey, the screech of thousands of tiny throats that hit a crescendo before stopping in perfect unison. The Aztecs were backpacking, Spanish passports tucked into fabric money belts, visiting the land of their Mayan brothers. Harry was laughing, telling them he knew more about the Aztecs than they did about the cockney tribe, that he watched a lot of telly when he wasn't on the piss. They were chopping up the maggot. Four equal pieces. One, two, three and the four men ate the maggot. They were in the middle of the jungle. The bar and sky had disappeared and there was a heavy smell of rotting vegetation. The Aztec warriors were leading them by the hand. Harry felt the sweat on his guide's palm. He felt awkward holding another man's hand but knew it was in the interests of survival. On his own he would be wandering blind and it wouldn't take long for wild cats to smell his fear and rip him apart. The guides were old and wise and with the help of mescalin possessed infrared night sight. With this sophisticated vision they were able to cut a path through the woven tangle of the jungle, ever-present fireflies hovering just above their heads the only movement, Harry feeling the gentle pricks of settling insects on bare skin, the rough texture of a heavy snake passing over his feet. He felt no fear with the Aztecs. These Indians knew the laws of the jungle. It was only European diseases such as the common cold that could destroy the natives. Harry wore the same bright yellow shorts from Asia, but with the dead maggot his dream had switched to black-and-white.

Eventually they reached a clearing and the colour returned with a flash. He was surprised to find Frank Bruno barring the way checking tickets. Big Frank was wearing a black flight jacket more common to Combat 18 than a great British heavyweight champion of the world. His hair had been dyed white. Harry was embarrassed to see that Balti was still holding his guide's hand, even though a computer-generated fire was lighting up the clearing. A temple towered above them. Harry admired the structure, the same Mayan temple he'd seen on the TV. There were hundreds of steps leading up through slanting stone, enormous carved figures positioned at regular intervals. It was a magical moment. There was a brief silence while he absorbed this wonder of the ancient world and then he heard the music, the blips and beeps and subsonic drumming of his own culture.

Dayglo graffiti had been painted on the trees surrounding the temple and he thought it was a shame. He read the nearest message, *Congratulations, you have just met Millwall*, a few words for anyone unfortunate enough to get a hiding off the pride of South-East London. He couldn't be bothered with all that violence. It just wasn't important. He felt good and was glad to see Balti had adjusted to his surroundings and was no longer holding the Aztec's hand. He asked Frank why he'd changed his hair. The British bulldog pointed out that despite being born and bred in London, he had been a big fan of Gazza since his Newcastle days, and had always wanted to be a professional footballer. Anything that was good enough for the Geordie maestro was good enough for Frank. Wor Gazza, meanwhile, had been in training and was looking to have a go at Mike Tyson. Frank pointed out that this was what being conscious was all about. Swapping things around and blending in together. Like the music.

The maggot was fast reaching the peak of its effectiveness and Harry found himself surrounded by a jungle that was becoming more and more distinct, a moving network of geometric patterns, complicated fractals that nevertheless made sense both scientifically and naturally, the kind of new age shit he normally slagged off. He sat on one of the steps with a girl he'd known at school. She'd been a good laugh but had been knocked down by a bus and this had left deep scars digging into her forehead and left cheek, so he'd never been able to think of her as female. She was alright though and they sat together, Harry's head held high, breathing deep and feeling content. He felt her hand in his, but there was nothing sexual going on. It seemed okay. He saw his best mate dancing around like a wanker but it wasn't important, the trimmed down beer gut still big enough to bounce. Nothing seemed to matter in a clearing deep inside the jungle. The girl whispered that the Aztecs were really Mayans. Because the Aztecs made human sacrifices they were easily understood back in London, while the Mayans had apparently invented the concept of zero and had been forgotten. The two guides just wanted a bit of respect. Then Balti was pulling his shorts down, fat arse on display, mooning for the crowd. A siren sounded and Harry wanted to tell his mate to pull his shorts back up because the Spanish riot police were on their way and they didn't appreciate traditional British humour. The feedback was too heavy so he maintained a dignified silence. He looked for Big Frank, but the heavyweight champion of the universe had taken the night bus home and Harry's alarm was sounding, a blitzkrieg warning that a wave of fighter-bombers were coming, loaded with napalm, intent on burning the ancient rainforest to a cinder.

It was daylight. Time to get up. Saturday morning. Chelsea-Portsmouth. Nine o'clock. Balti's arse was the last impression the dream left as it ran back into the jungle. Harry felt uneasy. He tried to move away from the thought but couldn't let himself bottle out and pushed back inside his head to find out what had gone before. Five minutes later he was on his way to the bathroom, satisfied the dream had been a straightforward replay of events, the night out at Blues with a repetition of the desert island theme, some little gems thrown in for decoration, that bird on the Es last night. The image of Balti's arse was obviously symbolic of his attitude, showing what he thought about losing his job, but when Harry went into the kitchen and his mate was sitting there with the paper, in his dressing gown, bollocks hanging out, he actually felt embarrassed.

'You're a bit quiet,' Carter said, emptying his pint, then holding it up for careful examination, as if by staring at the glass for long enough it would somehow fill up again.

'I'm feeling a bit rough, that's all,' Harry said.

'I needed that,' Carter was prompting now with the understanding that miracles had stopped in the years BC. 'It's the best thing when you've been on the piss. Dehydration causes all the grief, and half of it's in the head, mental like, so if you start filling up again you get rid of both the reasons.'

Harry collected the glasses and went to the bar. At least he'd get a pint of 4X now. Denise came in then and served him before she'd had a chance to dump her handbag out back, Len busy at the other end of the counter. He ordered a ham roll and bit into it as lager filled glasses. Denise smelt good. Better than Carter who was carrying a mixture of last night's drink and smoke fumes and a night's broken sleep. A couple more pints and nobody would notice. He was just about to return to the table when Will walked in. Harry ordered another pint, Directors this time, and Will came over to help.

'Alright?' Will asked.

'Can't complain. Got a bit of a hangover from last night, but nothing serious. Should be a good game today if the players are up for it. You never know though. Pompey could just pull off a result.'

'It's easier than a trip to Swindon. I wonder if you'd have bought Gullit if Dave Webb had stayed at Chelsea. He only signed because of Hoddle. At least we've got Webby. The man's a god.'

'He should've been Chelsea manager,' Harry agreed, thinking of the magic maggots that turned men into immortal beings and wondering if Webby had been hassling the insect world. 'Webb was the one who brought the Cup back against Leeds. He'd have done alright and he saved us from relegation in the three months he was there. Hoddle was a great player. He'd have got into any half-decent Dutch team lining up next to Carter in midfield, so it's no wonder The Dutchman decided to come to Chelsea. Gullit's on another planet. The bloke's got so much time when he's in possession. Never loses his cool. Bit like me really.'

Will swapped pleasantries with the rest of the lads and took over Harry's daydreamer role at the window as the other three talked football generalities and Chelsea specifics. He sipped his Directors and enjoyed the ten minutes of heat a hesitant sun fired his way. He was on a high. It was funny what a woman's interest could do for you. He mustn't let himself get carried away and start behaving like a lovesick kid though. Spending time with Karen had done him good. She had an interesting flat that reflected her character, full of posters and tropical plants. She'd invited him in for fresh coffee but he'd chosen tea bags instead. A plate of chocolate biscuits and a good look through her records and CDs. They had similar tastes. They'd sat there talking about music and everything for hours, and it wasn't long before the pressure Will felt to make a move disappeared and they were having a laugh like they were mates.

Before he knew what was happening it was four o'clock and she was nodding off and he stood up and said he'd better be off. He didn't even try to kiss her and she gave him her number on the torn edge of an old envelope and asked him to call. He'd been tempted to phone right away but had held out until that same morning. A simple call to say thanks for the free drink and company. She'd sounded pleased to hear from him and he was seeing her Tuesday night. There was a band she liked playing in Brixton and he was going round her place at six. He was excited. Daft really. It was nice though. Spending time with a woman like that. Better than eight pints and a drunken effort that no matter what anyone told him was useless. You never got to know what a woman was really like and the sex itself was rubbish. Waiting a bit was another brand of foreplay, building up to something, making sex a bit special. He wondered what Karen thought about it all.

'Carter's on nine points,' Balti told him. 'It's about time we got going. You're joint bottom with me and Harry. Mango shafted some Tory princess from his work, the arse-licker.'

'Nine? You were on four last time I saw you. How did you manage five more? I thought the maximum score was four. What did you do to the poor girl to get five points?'

'I serviced this sort when I was delivering beds. It was one of those instant on-the-job demonstrations. All part of the service and no guarantee required. Three points there, and the bird at Blues last night was another two. You'd have liked her Will, but I know you'd rather get into Eileen. That Denise keeps looking over and I reckon I'll be shagging that soon. She's a right goer. A four-pointer, but I'll settle for three. Depends on the table when I get to grips with it. Total football's fine, but you've got to get points as well or you're fuck all.'

Will was going to ask Terry how the sex had been. Forget the points for a minute and consider the act itself. Still, that was Carter. He didn't give a toss about anything, just living moment to moment without a care in the world, and if that's what he wanted out of life then who was Will to say anything? He was happy and not hurting anyone. Will wasn't made that way. He wished he was because it would make everything easier, but on the quiet he was looking for something a bit more permanent. At least he was being honest with himself. It would be nice to spend time with a decent woman for a change, with ideas and views about things, even a bit of politics thrown into the equation. Carter had probably pulled some good people along the way but he never got to see more than the paintwork. Then in the morning with the goal achieved he'd be out the door. Not that it was just blokes who were like that. Of course it wasn't. Will had met enough women whose social lives and prestige among their mates revolved around how many men they'd had. It worked both ways. Anyone who thought otherwise was squatting on the moon thousands of miles into space. It was just down to people once all the decoration was removed.

He returned to the scene outside, playing the Pogues' Dirty Old Town version through his head. If you could find love in among the fumes and debris you were doing alright. He looked around at his mates and felt sorry for them. They were a bunch of kids despite the language and manners, playing their role in the greater scheme. At least they were a bit more settled these days, getting through the problem years and all that banging heads against brick walls. He hated all that. Will was a pacifist of sorts. He'd defend himself but avoided confrontation as far as possible. It was hard sometimes. Like in the First World War they'd shot those men who refused to fight or were suffering from shell shock. Condemned the poor bastards for not killing their own kind for the scum that sat miles away from the trenches in their polished havens. Stood them in a line and had other men shoot holes in their bodies.

Life was short and on special offer if you didn't work things out. He just wanted to relax, put his feet up and listen to some boss sounds. That's what he liked about Karen. She had it sussed. There he was thinking about her again. To touch her seemed wrong. He smiled. Thinking of sin as though he'd been raised with religion. It was the princess thing they'd been talking about, Mango dabbling in the City. But a princess didn't need money to make her royal. That was down to the adverts. All that consumer propaganda.

'You should've come along last night,' Carter said, pulling Will back in with the rest of the lads. 'Where were you anyway?'

'I stayed in. Had a pizza and listened to some music.'

'You'll never get off the mark sitting at home.'

'I'm not bothered.'

'What do you mean you're not bothered? You'll end up in the relegation zone.'

Will didn't want to get into a discussion on the subject. The idea of a sex league was shit. He didn't know why he'd signed up in the first place. He'd have been better off giving up alcohol instead and it was the drink in his blood that had made him go along with the idea. That's what is was. Drink was a bad drug. He'd been talking about it with Karen. It didn't mean he was going to stop, because he enjoyed a quality pint, but it only ever led to problems. They made dope illegal and advertised alcohol because a good smoke kept you mellow while drink set everyone off fighting each other. Will was gearing up for something but didn't know what. Maybe he wanted to settle down. Live with a woman again.

He thought of Bev and the three years they'd had together, though it had never really worked once they'd settled into the routine of work, food, sleep. It was two-way and they'd parted on good enough terms. They'd kept in touch for a while, meeting up every two or three months, then every six months till she found someone else, and then there was nothing. He didn't feel bad about it, but at times he missed the companionship. She'd given him something he couldn't get from his mates. They'd been able to talk about things that he would never talk about with the lads, but they'd been too young for it to last. They were nineteen when they met. Twenty when they moved into the flat in South Acton. Towards the end it was obvious they were shifting in different directions, but they spent a year trying to con themselves. In the end it was a relief. He'd felt free again. She was a good person. He still loved her in a way. Nothing physical because that went years back, but she was a bit of the past and Will liked thinking back.

The only other Sex Division member who'd lived with a woman was Carter. Will reckoned it was a bit funny that, because they were so different. He'd been married to Cheryl for a couple of years, before the divorce. It hadn't worked out. He'd always boasted that with Cheryl nothing mattered and he was busy most of the time dabbling on the side. Will didn't know the truth about that, and when Cheryl slept with some bloke Carter had gone off the deep end. He'd been well gutted when she left but had recovered quick enough. Will couldn't live like that. He would've felt guilty lying and planning something. It wasn't in his nature, though he knew everyone was ripe when they were under the influence. Carter didn't care. He was a free man. It was his life and it was only sex and glands and nature, and he had told Will a couple of times that he should enjoy himself because that was why God had made women. Will couldn't think like that. They were miles apart, with Harry and Balti and even Mango in the middle, yet in some ways they were similar. It was like Karen had been saying the other night about party politics, that if you went far enough one way you eventually went full circle and ended up on the other side.

Carter and Will were the only two who'd gone all the way and moved in with someone. And Carter had gone right in and got himself married. Big wedding and everything. They'd all gone. He looked at Balti and Harry and wondered where they'd end up. Living together when they were forty? What did they think about it all? Probably didn't know themselves, so how could Will? Living day to day. Then there was Mango. He had enough ambition for the rest of them but somehow Will felt most sorry for him. Even though he had a bit of wealth it was a dead-end world, without soul or morality. Carter had few traditional morals but was honest and no harm was done, while Will was so moral he had to admit he sometimes verged on the self-righteous. He hated himself for that. Harry and Balti were decent blokes, but Mango lacked something, like a slit had been made and that part of the brain converting the relevant codes had been rewired. Will wondered if he was getting religious or whether that bit of blow he'd had last night had set off a forgotten circuit, turning him into a raving fundamentalist. He was smoking a lot these days.

Will saw Mango coming out of the bookies, walking with his head up for a bit, then bent forward focused on the pavement. Like he was proud, then ashamed, then proud again. Will thought of them playing that game as a kid, it didn't have a name, avoiding the cracks and lines, the slabs land and the cracks rapids that would drag them away. One day he'd ask Mango if he remembered. A car stopped at the zebra crossing and Mango was on his way to the pub. He often came down on Saturday to see his mum and dad, then have a pint with the lads if they were about. It was one of those loose rituals. He saw Mango stop and talk with a group of women, friends of his mum. When he stopped his face had been creased like he was thinking too hard, but now it had smoothed out, back in the community. When he left them and continued Will saw him stop by the drunks standing outside the swimming pool, begging, and hand something over.

'Alright?' Mango said, going straight to the bar to get a round in. When he'd brought the drinks to the table he sat next to Harry who shifted up a bit. Mango looked happy enough.

'What happened to you last night?' Balti asked.

'I had to work late.'

'On a Friday night? You must be joking. You were round that bird's place sipping champagne with your caviar.'

'Wish I had been. I was working my bollocks off till three. We had a big job going through.'

'She didn't want another portion then?' Carter asked. 'Once was enough, was it?'

'I'm going round tomorrow night. She's a real cracker. Seems like I'm in second place. How was it down Blues?'

'Not bad. I'm on nine points now so you'd better get out of first gear, but don't worry about these three. Will stays in these days listening to his records and these two are always so fucking pissed they can't get it up.'

The talk drifted back to the football while Mango started bending Harry's ear about dreams. Mango never remembered his dreams and wanted to learn the secret. He'd tried eating cheese because he'd heard from his old man that a good bit of Cheddar worked wonders, but nothing had happened. He couldn't get to sleep without his prescription, and then when he managed it the next thing he knew the alarm was sounding and he was getting up with nothing but a blank filling the gap. Without chemicals he would lay there for hours with his mind racing, the same thoughts that came in the day when he wasn't busy, but which his work helped him avoid. Mango was sensible enough to know that it was only his imagination speeding, but he didn't want to think when he was alone because the later it got, the darker the pictures became. He didn't mention his tablets or thoughts to anyone.

Harry thought of the siren and the bombing raid on a Mayan temple. Remembering your dreams proved you were alive, that you weren't just a machine put on charge overnight. They'd talked about it before and Mango agreed, but he wanted a bit for himself. He liked the idea of symbolism and another part of his head working free-style. Harry told him about his dream, about the bar and Frank Bruno, the Mayan temple and the music, how the whole thing had started in colour, shifted to black-and-white while he was in the jungle, then returned to colour. The others were talking football and he kept his voice down so nobody took the piss. He was selective in his account. Mango nodded. It sounded good. He wouldn't mind some harmless home cinema for himself rather than the late night horror shows he never spoke about. Hallucinating in the tropics would be better than running around North London with some kid next to him thinking of ways to chop her up.

'Harry, you remember that Cup game against Tottenham in the sixth round?' Carter was already getting pissed, topping up. 'The yids were coming down from Sloane Square and the old bill pulled up. We were down by The Black Bull, remember, and then they started running horses into Chelsea.'

'Course I do. I went under one but it was going so fast it didn't land on my head. Went right over me without doing any serious damage.'

'The rider didn't even look back. Just kept going.'

'I could've been brain-damaged. Sitting here now with a nappy on that you'd have to change for me.'

'Fuck that,' Balti said. 'When was it? Early eighties, something like that. The pubs were packed by twelve weren't they and everyone was looking to have a go. The Shed was full an hour and a half before the fucking kick-off.'

'Only because the old bill cleared the pubs and pushed everyone inside, closed the gates so they could get Spurs past.'

Will had to admit it had been a lively day out. Hoddle had scored for Spurs but he wasn't going to remind them. The North Stand had been empty and when Tottenham piled on to the terrace they got a warm reception. It had gone off in a big way outside afterwards and they'd nearly got battered by the old bill as the two sides clashed. It was a long time ago. He'd gone to a few games with the others when Brentford weren't at home, or playing a shit team. Chelsea had always been a bit of a cult side. Things were better now. Peace was better than war. Sex instead of violence. Bollocks, he was thinking along Sex Division lines.

'What are you lot doing tonight?' he asked. The drink was having an effect and he fancied a few more. It was fine meeting a decent woman like Karen, but he wouldn't mind a decent drink as well. He was thirsty after a quiet Friday sitting at home listening to records.

'Have a pint somewhere,' Carter said, considering the options. 'Pick up a Miss World and give her a good servicing. What I normally do. What else?'

'We'll probably come back here,' Balti said. 'Have a beer round Chelsea after the game and get back by eight at the latest. At least it's a short walk home.'

'What about you?' Will turned to Mango.

'Don't know yet. Might come down here if you lot are around. I'm shooting back to Fulham first.'

'You giving us a lift then?' Carter asked.

'Long as you don't piss all over the upholstery like you were threatening to do last time I let you in the car.'

Will left at twelve and the rest of them stayed till nearly one. Mango had a couple of pints and then stopped while the others started working their way into a session. He wanted to get back and go through some paperwork. He was toying with the idea of phoning one of those home-delivery services, a call girl in leather with stilettoes and high cheek bones. Like that bird in the Barbican. The others were pissing about pleading for another pint before they left. Mango stood up, took out his keys and the rest of the lads fell into line. It was still early enough to get down to the Hammersmith roundabout without too much hassle and then slowly roll along the Fulham Palace Road. He felt good behind the wheel. The Jag purred, though he doubted the others appreciated just how good the engine really was. They appreciated the luxury and interior, but with a bit of drink inside them the finer edges were blurred.

'You shagged anything in this yet?' Carter asked, sitting in the front passenger seat, Harry and Balti in the back.

Mango almost answered more or less, that the bird from the Barbican had been down on him the other night, sitting in the same seat as Carter, then remembered the story, confusing the down-and-outs with those who helped put them there.

'No.'

'You've got a stain here,' the unstoppable sex machine pointed out. 'Thought it might be spunk, that's all.'

Mango took his eyes off the road to look and almost went up the back of the car in front. He looked at the spot Carter was pointing to, a small blob ground into the seat. The fucking slag. He'd warned her. Fucking whore. It was typical. You couldn't trust anyone these days. That was the problem with England, the sorry state of the industrial base. He had forked out hard cash and received a shoddy service in return. That sponging cow should've taken a bit of pride in her work rather than falling down on the job. He was disgusted with himself for allowing such a thing to happen. Next time he wouldn't be so generous. He would make the woman perform in a doorway or under a tree. That's what happened when you tried to help the less fortunate. They were rabid and quick to bite the hand that fed them. The thought struck that the girl might have infected his knob, that soon he would start frothing at the mouth and go on the rampage, biting and breaking skin until he was shot down in the street by a police marksman, shot down like a mad dog.

When they were kids Kev Bennett had gone mental and held his girlfriend hostage with a shotgun nobody knew he had. Mango remembered it well. It was a major occasion. The neighbours had reported screams coming from his flat and after the old bill pulled up there'd been a stand-off. The area was sealed off. It had been quite exciting being a kid and that, with everyone talking about what was going to happen next, about the negotiators they would bring in to try some psychology.

344

Bennett was nothing out of the ordinary, just went off his rocker one day. He'd been in there for ages and everyone expected a happy ending when he got his head straight. They said he was pissed up. Then there was a bang from inside the flat and the old bill shot him. It was unreal, the pop of gunshots. Nobody ever knew the reason why Bennett did it and his girlfriend moved away. He wondered what she was doing now. Whether she thought about the boy who'd threatened to kill her all those years before. It was funny how things worked out. But he wasn't thinking of guns.

'Did you use a rubber with all those three birds?' Mango asked Carter.

'Course I did. Well, I did with the first one, but I was a bit pissed last night and let it go. I'm not bothered though. Wouldn't want to do it too often but she seemed clean enough, not some smelly hippy or scrubbed trendy who specialises in queers. Mind you, I didn't bother with that woman I was delivering to, but she was married so she must be safe enough.'

'What about when a bird gives you a blow job?' Mango asked, worried. 'Do you use one then as well?'

'Leave it out. What are you going to catch that way?'

Mango felt relieved.

'You should do,' Balti said, leaning forward. 'I read that if a woman's got a cut in her mouth then Aids can spread through the end of your cock. That's the weak spot.'

'They're not going to get stuck into a lump of stinking rubber, are they?' Carter laughed. 'It's all to do with blood and that. I mean, it might be possible to get it from a cut like you said, but the chances are small.'

'It would be a fucking horrible way to die,' Balti muttered from the back, his eyes closed and head leant back. 'Getting HIV or Aids, whichever one it is that comes first. Withering away like a skeleton. I feel sorry for people forced to die like that. Poor bastards. No-one deserves that.'

'You could die of anything though, couldn't you,' Carter said. 'As long as you're careful you're alright. I mean, you can't stop having sex just because it might kill you. How would the human race continue? It would be a bit boring as well.'

'It's a time bomb waiting to go off,' Balti said. 'It's blokes like us who are next on the list.'

He sounded like something from a documentary. Mango checked the mirror, Carter turned round and Harry moved back in the seat and looked sideways. Balti just sat there with his eyes shut.

'You miserable cunt,' Carter accused, not appreciating the tone. He didn't like thinking about Aids too much because he'd been through a fair number of birds over the years, and if the propaganda was true, that it wasn't just queers and junkies condemned to a miserable death, then by rights he should be shitting it. But it wasn't in his nature to think like that. You had to live right now. Forget the past and not worry about the future.

'You could die under a bus tomorrow, or that lorry over there could skid and wipe us all out. How many people die of cancer, heart attacks, blood clots? It's only because it's sex that they go on about it. Fucking hell, lads, live and enjoy it while you can. At least if you die on the job then you've gone out with a bit of style. I mean look at that bird over there. You're not telling me you wouldn't risk death for a poke at that.'

The other three looked at a tall, thin blonde, moving at the same speed as the traffic. Carter rolled down the window and hung his head out, trying to attract her attention. She smiled his way and went into a shop.

'I was thinking,' Harry said, once they'd got past the lights and were moving again. 'Maybe we should get Balti to write a report, like Taylor did for football. He could look at the safety aspects of the game and make certain recommendations.'

He saw Mango's eyes move in the mirror and a smile on the side of Carter's face.

'It would be for the good of everyone involved in the game. Look at Carter. He picks up some bird in Blues, goes home with her and gives her a good seeing to, but the main problem is that he's a bit casual about the whole thing and doesn't take any precautions. He's putting himself at risk, not to mention the woman concerned. Not that he's carrying any tropical diseases or anything like that, but he's taking a bit of a chance. Now say the Balti Report insisted that points couldn't be registered unless the person concerned had used a rubber. Carter would be about to get stuck in when suddenly he'd realise he was going to lose out in the league and make the effort, tell the woman to hang on a second, walk to the other side of the room, go through his clothes till he finds the custom-made, pigmy-size condoms, coated of course, chinky spare-ribbed efforts, then slips one on his knob and returns to the business in hand. That way he would be looking after himself and doing his bit for the human race at the same time.'

'Makes sense,' Balti said, 'but I don't see why I should have to write the report. Let Will do it. He's the sensible one. He'd enjoy doing it as well. I'm shit at writing.'

'You could limit the kind of birds as well,' Mango said. 'No junkies or those ones who go with dodgy blokes. No slags either.'

'Hold on, you were the one who wanted points for shafting prossies the other day,' Carter said. 'That's interfering with freedom of choice. I mean, I can see the point of rubbers and all that, maybe even avoiding junkies, that's common sense, and I mean, anyway, they're not going to be walking around with a sign round their necks, but just because a girl puts it about shouldn't be enough to cancel the points.'

'You're only worried because it would put you bottom of the league,' Mango said, turning off the Fulham Palace Road.

'Fuck off. You're slagging off some dirty old tart for shafting anything that moves just because she's a woman. That's sexist. I fucking hate sexism.'

The others laughed.

'Dear oh dear,' he said. 'Look at the tits on that.'

Mango parked and waited for the others to get out. He had a quick look at the passenger seat. He was thinking about the stain and whether to clean it himself or get it done professionally. All that talk about death and disease had put him off the idea of an escort girl, though to be honest he didn't have the nerve to get someone round the flat. He was tired. It was all catching up with him and he wouldn't need his prescription. The thought of curling up in bed like a kid, getting into the foetal position again with the doors locked and everything shut out, that's what he fancied more than anything.

'Come down The White Hart after the game,' Carter said, 'and you can give us a lift back. You can doss round my place tonight if you're coming down The Unity. We'll be in there till seven or thereabouts.'

Mango went indoors and Carter kicked a puddle of water at Harry who told him he was a fucking donut and tried to grab him, but the sex machine was too fast and ran ten yards down the street, then kept his distance till he reckoned Harry had forgotten about the wet jeans he was wearing. They turned towards the ground and a pre-match pint, building up for the kick-off.

BLACK VINYL

THERE WAS A break between bands and the DJ was busy mixing sound effects. Will had ordered two pints of snakebite and was weaving his way through the crowd towards Karen. There was a thin film of sweat covering her face and arms, red cardigan wrapped around her waist, black mascara very slightly smudged. The snakebite had been her idea. Will hadn't had the potent mix for years. A lot of pubs had stopped serving it, though Club Verbal didn't seem too bothered by the bitter-cider potential for aggravation. But it was a peaceful, largely anarchist gathering. He handed Karen a plastic pint and sat down next to her on the stairs, returning to their conversation as she folded the copy of *Two Sevens* she had been reading.

'My mum died three years ago today,' Karen said, Will noticing the mist in her eyes. 'She had a hard life, you know. All women her generation had hard lives. They say it's different now, and I suppose it is in some ways, but it's still a world built by men for men. My mum had to graft almost till the moment she died. She had a faith, though, that never left her. She was raised a Catholic. Believed in God and heaven and a better life in the ever-after, bearing everything as though it was her fate. Like an all-loving God would invent something as wicked as cancer.'

Will nodded. He couldn't disagree, though he didn't go along with the line that every male in the country had an easy ride. He thought class was more important, sexism one more element in a strategy of divide and rule. But he didn't want to argue. Will loved women. Maybe he even loved Karen.

'You take a man and if he has sex with lots of different women he's admired, but you catch a woman doing the same thing and she's a slag. Where's the sense in that? Why shouldn't a woman be able to go off and have sex with whoever she wants, when she wants?'

Will agreed. It was nonsense, but try as he did there was still something there in his head. He'd heard that it was to do with the male's in-built biological function, the need to keep his genes flowing through the generations. It was like a computer chip. A basic battle for survival. Genetic programming buried so deep in the circuits that any amount of reasoning and self-disgust would never be able to remove it entirely. Maybe there was truth in the theory. Will didn't know. But it was something worth considering. A woman could always be sure the kid in her belly was her own, but what guarantee did a man have? He vaguely remembered publicity surrounding the marriage of the century between Prince Charles and Lady Di, rumours of royal checks on the future princess's virginity. In the bad old days that kind of thing had been up front. Kings had their wives-to-be examined because they didn't want any doubts about parentage when it came to succession to the throne, no tainting of the divine DNA. He couldn't really believe that kind of stuff still went on though.

There had to be some kind of logic behind jealousy. Either that or men really were chauvinistic slavers. He was glad Karen didn't hear the way his mates spoke about women, birds, slappers, whores, tarts, grinders, slags, whatever. He tried to imagine her sitting in on a session with Carter and the rest of the Sex Division crew. At least they'd tone it down a bit if she was around. It was all about respect. She would have to put a bug somewhere, in the bottom of Carter's pint maybe, and record everything without moral constraints. Karen was right. She was beautiful as well.

'Don't get me wrong,' Karen smiled, the odd crack splitting her face, something Will was already used to and which seemed to fit her personality, a lop-sided grin that cut through her right cheek. 'I'm not into sex with strangers like some people. I mean, what's the point of having sex with someone you don't know when you're drunk or stoned or whatever drug's flavour of the moment, because it's not going to be much good, is it? I mean, this friend of mine, Leoni, she goes through two or three blokes a week, but she never gets anything out of it except a hangover and when she's careless too often a visit to the STD clinic.

'I went down the hospital with her once and the unit was just a mobile home on the edge of the hospital grounds, like something off a rundown caravan site. It put it all into place. It was raining and we got soaked, and the nurse was a right old hag, and I was just thinking all the time what a waste of something that should be full of feeling. Even so, there shouldn't be any judgement, should there? We should all have the freedom of choice. There shouldn't be all these religious relics weighing people down, covering up the truth. We'll all be dead one day, whether it's from cervical cancer or old age.'

Will nodded and said nothing. He had never had a venereal infection, at least not as far as he knew, but Carter had been down the STD a few times. He was a regular customer in fact. He should get himself a season ticket. Then there was that time Balti shagged some bird at a party, his first bit of sex in seven or so months, and it was just his luck that he picked up a dose. It was the lack of alcohol that almost killed him. Leoni sounded like a bit of a raver. Carter's long-lost cousin following the family trait, spreading peace and love and one-on-one mastur-bation techniques through the community. If Will was feeling generous he'd fix them up and let them bang each other into the next century, but he wanted to keep Karen separate from his mates. The drink was obviously going to her head a bit, because she kept talking without waiting for a response, as though he wasn't really there.

'I'd rather make love with a man. One day I suppose I'll find someone who's the other side of the same coin and we'll live happy ever after in our own little flat, and when we're together there'll be nothing like it in the world. It's the difference between making love and having sex. I suppose it sounds old-fashioned to you, but that's the way I look at things. You get more out of something if you build up to it and have some emotion. I mean, we're not machines are we, and we're not animals just interested in reproduction.'

It was strange, but all this talk about love and romance and emotions wasn't turning Will off. It didn't even sound that dated. If anything it was drawing him in. It was turning into a bit of a lecture but he stayed with her as she got scientific. He wondered what exactly progestogen and oestrogen did to a woman. Thrombosis was something to do with blood clots, but he didn't see how that connected with babies. She was ahead of him. He watched Karen's mouth move and thought how feminine she was, yet she had a punk look about her and was no damsel in distress, no frail caricature in a frilly dress picking wildflowers on her way to church. She must've thought things through a bit further than the usual kneejerk reaction. He felt his eyes drift down to her T-shirt and focus on her breasts, then down to her crutch. He tried to imagine what she would look like naked, and whether he would ever see her in that state. Maybe tonight would be the time, but he doubted it somehow. He didn't mind. It was nice to keep the thing going.

'What's old-fashioned anyway?' she asked, leaning her head back. 'Things are never how they appear. What's conservative and what's liberal? You look at the people here, and you could say that a good number of them are liberal in their outlook, whatever liberal is supposed to mean, but when it comes to an argument their views might be just as entrenched as those stuck-up bastards passing laws for themselves in Parliament. How many of the so-called alternative preach free sex and everything and dismiss love and faithfulness as conservative values? They wouldn't be able to even talk about the subject without sinking into worn-out rhetoric. Their own locked-in approach makes them the real conservatives. It's just another version of materialism. Communist or fascist, what's the difference. Where's the soul?'

Will nodded his head. He thought he understood what she meant. He was beginning to feel like a puppet having his strings pulled in time to Karen's words. He wondered where it was leading. It was a line of argument he didn't mind hearing because it added to her attraction, gave her strength of personality and independence, but he could guess the reaction of the rest of the lads. Carter would shake his head listening to such blasphemy and piss off, not bothering to waste precious seconds on a dead end, back on the trail of a quick knee-trembler. Balti and Harry would go along with a bit of the chat, liking the virginal princess angle, which would probably be the way they'd misinterpret Karen, a bit of a novelty, before getting bored with it all, just wanting the quick presentation and an instant succumbing to the fine love-making skills of the beer-bellied elite, or preferably a visit to Balti Heaven. Will didn't have a clue what Mango would think. He'd either walk away in disgust or set the woman up as a piece of prized property worth pursuing purely for the pleasure he'd get from charming his way past her resistance. Maybe he'd even fall in love with the imagery.

'This stuff makes my head go funny,' Karen said, leaning into Will. 'I haven't had snakebite for a while. Last time I drank five pints and threw up in the sink at home. That was soon after my mum died and I haven't had it since.'

The lights went down and the band came on, and a mixture of punk and rap kept them going for the next hour. They didn't wait around for the encore, hurrying to Brixton tube to catch a train to Victoria. The buildings were rundown and dark, the pubs kicking out, police vans patrolling the back streets. The wind screamed as it blew over dustbins and scattered flyers. Further along and a young raggamuffin had been stopped by a patrol car. Will was glad he wasn't black. The poor bastards didn't have a chance. Then they were in the sharp light of Brixton station past the Nation of Islam boys preaching fundamentalism and the avoidance of chemical distraction. The escalators dazzled under their feet, churning up warm snakebite, running for a train about to depart, the carriage almost full with people from the Academy. The blend of sweat, drink and happy faces made it a quick roll to Victoria where they had to wait ten minutes. There was more room and a different mix of office workers on the train, pissed and loud. Once in Hammersmith they took a bus to Karen's flat. Will followed her up the stairs. She fumbled with the key and then they were inside.

'What do you do for a job?' Karen asked, once she'd made

two cups of tea and was sitting on the sagging couch next to Will.

He wanted to pull her forward, but had to be careful, all that talk about making love instead of having sex. It made sense right enough, but it also made him hesitant. That's probably what it had been like in the old days in high society. The gentleman had to go through the routine and get things just right for the lady. They must've spent a lot of time making themselves blind; morning, noon and night. At least that's how period dramas presented life. Will couldn't stop his eyes straying and felt guilty because he was sure Karen could read his mind. She was peering into the place where his soul should be, deciding whether his intentions were honourable, reading the cartoon bubble above his head, words etched in scratch black ink. He looked away and her words connected.

'I run a shop, halfway between junk and antiques. I make a living and do my own hours. You soon know what to buy and what to ignore. Before that I worked for a cab firm. I saved up enough to buy some secondhand gear, rent premises, and I haven't really looked back. I'm my own boss, though it hurts when the tax bill comes round. I do the odd market. It's a good life. I've been lucky. What about you?'

'I work in the housing department at the council dealing with benefits. I get to help people at least.'

Will stood up and went over to the singles stacked next to the two long rows of albums he'd examined on his first visit. Karen had a good five hundred or so seven-inches. He sat down and pulled a few out at random. First was Gary Gilmore's Eyes by The Adverts. Next Penetration's Don't Dictate. He remembered seeing both bands when he was a kid. Gaye Advert speeding through Bored Teenagers. Pauline Murray fronting Penetration at the Roundhouse. Female vocals fitted punk to perfection. That had been a night out that one. He'd gone along with Mango's brother Pete, lying about his age to get in, taller than his mates then. Black Slate and Fusion had opened the bill and the place had been stacked with skinheads all going on about the forthcoming Slade reunion gig, the original skinhead band. Sham's barmy army was definitely mental. It had taken

Pete twenty minutes to work his way through the shaven heads five deep at the bar.

Wooden terracing led down to the dancefloor and Will had been bundled aside during Penetration's set as a big crew of skins piled through the crowd. Black Slate and Fusion had been okay, but Pauline Murray stood out. Will had wished he was a bit older and that the Penetration vocalist had taken a shine to him, spotting the boy in the crowd. Pete was at the back of the terrace during the break between Black Slate and Fusion, snogging with some punk girl with peroxide hair, torn fishnets and a PVC mini-skirt with a silver zip up the back. Pete was pissed and leant over the back of the terrace to puke on those down below, then went back to the punkette who didn't seem bothered by the new flavour. Will kept his eyes ahead most of the time, young enough to mix embarrassment with curiosity. A stream of Clash tracks blasted through the speakers. Pete had been wearing his Snow White and the Seven Dwarves shirt at the time. Poor old Snow White was getting a regular servicing from the sick midgets, stumpy erections jammed into every available orifice. Happy, Grumpy and Doc were doing their best to give the girl a night she would never forget. Disney's caring image had been given a gangbanging punk rock reinterpretation, a tribute to consumerism which the righteous majority condemned. Will looked at Karen sitting on the couch sipping her tea and smiled as he linked Pauline Murray and a similar look.

He pulled out the Sex Pistols' Anarchy In The UK. It was the EMI pressing and worth a bit. Will went into one, the snakebite hitting, telling Karen that nobody had ever matched the Pistols, the best working-class London band ever, despite the latter-day revisionism of middle-class journalists who insisted that punk was nothing more than an example of Malcolm McLaren and Vivienne Westwood's manipulative powers. Will told Karen that it was the natural progression of boot boy culture. That the new-wave term really got up his nose. It was always like that. History was written by a certain element in society and that was the only version left behind. Johnny Rotten was the top man, hearing that voice when he was a kid in school striking the right chord. The Pistols were an obvious development. Simple really. One hundred per cent boot boy music with a chunk of non-party politics thrown in which he had been able to appreciate because it came from his own experience. Paul Cook and Steve Jones were sound as well, West London boys. He liked picking up the records, looking at the sleeve designs and then pulling the vinyl out. Funny really, but he'd never been into the coloured stuff, the yellows and pinks and reds. He preferred black vinyl. Beautiful stuff.

He wanted to put the record on, preferring the B-side to Anarchy In The UK, but it was midnight and it wasn't the right time for good old-fashioned lyric-heavy listening. He was sitting with a classy woman and needed something a bit more mellow. He switched to the albums and asked Karen what she wanted. She didn't mind, so he took out a King Tubby collection and was back on the couch with the volume low and Karen leaning into him again. He stroked the back of her hair, looking at the perfectly formed ears, three earrings in the left, two in the right. She wore a silver necklace and the pendant had worked its way to the side, some kind of pagan latticework with a hidden meaning. He could feel her breasts against his stomach. The heater was working and the room was warm. Karen sat up and twisted her body, taking off the cardigan. Her breasts pushed forward against the top and Will could feel movement between his legs, noticing the line of a low-cut bra. He tried to think of something else, playing the gentleman. He was getting into the swing of the thing, deciding he would play hard to get. He went back to the records, back to the music, back to the Lyceum.

He'd been to quite a few gigs with Pete. The Lyceum had been a good Sunday night out. Like that time when the UK Subs had been due to support Generation X. The Subs had a hardcore following and for some reason Charlie Harper's band hadn't played, so the Subs element of the crowd was well wound up by the time Generation X were due on stage. Billy Idol was the cowboy of punk, with his pretty looks and plastic leer, and the Subs fans hadn't exactly welcomed him. But it was afterwards Will remembered most. Coming out and finding a hundred or so skinheads lined up across the road, a lot of them with bottles, waiting for the UK Subs mob to appear. He was with Pete on the Strand when the skins steamed in and then the old bill had arrived and broken things up. They'd walked towards Trafalgar Square and the skins were given a police escort along the Strand behind them towards Lord Nelson waiting with his press gang and the short sharp shock of naval service. A couple of stray German tourists heard the skinhead chant and shot off into Covent Garden. Pete had been good like that, taking a kid along with him to gigs. He'd been a nice bloke. Nothing was too much trouble. He didn't have to bother with his younger brother's mate who happened to be into good music at an early age. Most people wouldn't have made the effort.

Karen got up and went out of the room. A blast of cold air hit when she opened the door. Those gigs had been brilliant, the DJs either playing solid reggae between punk bands, or maybe throwing in one of two punk singles, playing them a speed too slow to take the piss. It was all the same tradition really. Ska and skinhead bands. Punk and reggae. Soul and mod. Then there was the techno and scratch, rap, jungle, drum n bass, all the colours of the rainbow. But he knew where the roots were. You couldn't beat music. Anyone who didn't like music wasn't alive as far as Will was concerned. It was something to be proud of, the way cultures had blended so successfully in music. That was the way racism broke down. Living and growing up with black kids, Asians, whatever. That's how they'd been raised. The whole skinhead thing owed its roots to the ska bands and all that old Jamaican dancehall style. Classic sounds. Boss sounds. And it was best heard on vinyl, with all the rough edges. CDs didn't compare, and they lacked the sleeve artwork and overall feel. CDs were convenient and polished and part of the technological age, and more sophisticated reproduction methods were on the way. New formats would be marketed and software pushed, then the hardware, raking in the cash. Will had a CD player, but whenever possible bought vinyl. Like Karen had said, soul was more important than mechanics.

He stretched out on the couch. The room was so warm with the gas fire burning. King Tubby soothed him. He was relaxed but far from tired. He heard water running and Karen stuck her head round the door to tell him she was going to have a bath. She felt dirty and smelly with the sweat frozen to her skin. She wouldn't be long, and Will was bending his head back just seeing the head detached, wondering what was behind the door. When she was gone he closed his eyes, concentrating on the music. He was okay for a while, then started thinking of Karen. He heard the water shut off.

He had finished his tea and fancied a biscuit. He went into the hall. It was icy. A lamp shone in what he imagined was the bedroom. There was a strange pattern on the whitewashed ceiling. The door was half-ajar. He heard Karen splashing in the bath, King Tubby in the living room. He poked his head round the door, peering into the woman's private world. He felt a bit guilty. It was a plant creating the shadow. A teddy bear drew his attention, sitting on the bed's pillows. There was a purple duvet and Islamic-patterned pillowcases, a pine chest of drawers and a small stack of clean clothes on a chair. The carpet was red and the curtains black, pulled together. Light from a streetlamp highlighted the material's texture. An electric fire had been plugged in and was beginning to have an effect.

Will went into the kitchen, remembered his manners and returned to knock on the bathroom door. He asked if he could have a biscuit. Said he was feeling hungry. Karen's voice was slightly muffled, and he knew the answer, but wanted her to know where he was. He went to the biscuit tin and took four custard creams, then sat at the small vinyl table. He heard the plug pulled and water rushing away. The bathroom door opened and Karen went to her bedroom. It was an odd situation and Will didn't know what he should be doing. Usually, you went back with someone and that was that, but here he was the second time round her place sitting in the kitchen eating custard creams while she was having a bath and, for all he knew, wandering around naked. He finished the biscuits and wondered whether he should go home. He was nervous. Something wasn't right, yet a little while ago everything had seemed perfect. His old paranoia started to return. What could she see in him anyway? What if it was a stitch-up by some of the lads? It would've been easier staying at home listening to music, then going straight to sleep. But here he was sitting in a strange kitchen.

Eventually he turned the light off and went towards the living room. King Tubby had fallen silent and the light had been switched off. He heard Karen call him from the bedroom. He stopped outside the near-shut door and felt his confidence go. It was the build-up that was doing it to him, the time to think and imagine. Then he was through the door and the light was right down low, the atmosphere friendly and warm, this stunner naked in front of him. Will hardly had time to look at Karen before she was up against him showing that it was no pisstake.

An hour later and Will was looking at the effect the street light had on the curtain and far wall. He'd played the same game as a kid at night when he couldn't get off to sleep, trying to create scenes in fabric or on wallpaper. Karen was asleep and breathing deeply. Her right arm was over his chest and her breasts against his side. He felt like something major. There was no way to describe it really, just the best shag he'd ever had, and yet it wasn't a shag at all. He needed another way to describe it. Making love, that's what it was. Like Karen said earlier. It was probably the first time since Bev really, but much better. He had to be honest that he'd never really satisfied Bev. He'd wanted to talk about it but had never been able to find a way into the subject. He'd just felt useless, but reckoned things couldn't be that bad because she seemed to enjoy it sometimes. She never complained or anything. Never said a word against him.

With Karen, though, they'd just merged in together. He'd felt her spasms and heard the groans and reckoned it had been alright. He hoped so, but somehow knew that the love-making had worked right away. Maybe that's what love was all about. Not the sex so much, more the feeling. Will didn't know about love, didn't want to think that far ahead. He was getting soppy. Acting soft. He had to keep himself in line and not give too much away, just go with the flow and hopefully things would turn out okay. Karen shifted a bit, murmuring in her sleep. She pulled in closer. He felt great. Really happy.

The clock on the radio said it was three and Will wasn't

getting anywhere. He wanted to sleep but couldn't. The curtain was made from fairly thick material and the light created different levels. He saw lines of men marching across an empty desert, off to war, travelling thousands of miles just to get their bollocks blown off. He thought about the teddy bear. Karen could have had it since she was a couple of years old. His own teddy bear was long gone. It was a shame really, and he wished he could remember the moment when it was forgotten. All those years and it gets dumped in the dustbin or given to the jumble. It was sad somehow, that kids had to grow up and have those kinds of things taken away. Peter Pan had the right idea. Peter Wilson forever young.

Half an hour later and Will gently removed Karen's arm from his chest. The movement disturbed her and she turned round, curling into a ball. He looked at her back for a while in the vague light, following the gentle ridge of her backbone from below the neck, between small shoulder blades to the base of her back. He pulled the duvet down, looking at the curve of her buttocks and the shapely legs, while she slept soundly, suspended in time, somewhere far away. He thought of Harry briefly, the dream master, that ability he had to remember so much the next morning. Will pulled the duvet back up and positioned it around her neck. He got up. The electric heater was still on so the room was nice and warm. He pulled on his shirt and jeans and went into the hall, then into the living room. It was cold. He put on the gas fire third go and rolled himself a healthy spliff. He laid back on the couch with his bare feet up, feeling the burn of the flames. He was doing well. Inhaling deeply and watching smoke spiral towards the ceiling. He looked at his surroundings with no music to distract his attention, moving from the records to a row of books, past a couple of prints on the wall towards a small, crooked pile of videos.

He went over and knelt down, looking at the titles written in pencil. Most were films from the TV or comedy series, mostly *Black Adder* and *Dad's Army*, one marked *Family* in black felt pen. He inserted the last cassette in the VCR and returned to the couch, remote control in his hand. He did the business and inhaled as the picture flickered and faces began to appear. It was old cine footage converted to videotape. Will was surprised by the instant close-up of a man's face, the camera zooming-out to show what he identified as Karen's old man. He looked like a decent enough bloke. He wore an oversized collar and sideburns and had the same crooked smile Will had seen on the face of his daughter. Karen's dad turned and walked across a small lawn to a woman sitting in a deck chair. Karen's mum. Had to be. The likeness was obvious. She seemed happy, waving at the camera and laughing, then turning her head away. He rewound and pushed the freeze-frame button. The face stuck in time. He leant forward and inhaled, the blow hitting home. He suddenly felt bad, like he was trespassing in a private zone, seeing the dead woman's face and looking for clues to the future. There were lines across her forehead, but that was nothing unusual. She was dignified-looking, her hair dyed blonde with an absence of make-up on her face. Natural beauty in a rough sort of way.

It was mental freezing a bit of personal history like that. Will couldn't imagine being able to watch a film of his own parents once they were dead and cremated. It was too much. It made death look irrelevant when in reality it was the ultimate degradation. Was she a bundle of bones in a rotting coffin or the woman he saw on the screen with a smile splitting her face? Will reached for the remote and pushed Play. It was bad news that frozen image. The frames flashed past and there was Karen running around with the brother she had spoken about. He tried to match the six-year-old on the video with the sleeping beauty next door. She was all grown up with the reproductive urge added to the equation, cleverly disguised as recreation. It was odd to think of making love so many years into the future with that small kid busy shouting and jumping up and down, without any kind of care or worry. He felt uncomfortable. But it was making love, not sex. Was that all sex meant, adding another division to male and female when you reached puberty? Was it possible to carry that innocence on when you grew up, or did it have to be destroyed with the toys that became childish?

What would Carter think, in his unbothered way, taking

some bird back and finding Teddy sitting there on the pillow waiting for his mistress to come home from a hard night's entertainment? Probably try and mount it into the bargain. He'd think it was soft. But it wasn't. Will didn't see why there had to be such a big divide. Why couldn't sex just be loving and everything, like Karen was saying at Club Verbal, a bit of romance without the materialist hard-sell? He watched the kids run and play and Mum and Dad kiss for the camera, holding hands, and he drew on the blow hoping to get to sleep. He stopped the video and rewound, pushed Eject. He replaced the cassette in its case.

For the first time he noticed a vase of flowers by the window. Every year Karen bought carnations on the anniversary of her mother's death. They'd been her favourite. The flowers were red and white and pink, and though he didn't like flowers much, at least not out of the ground and indoors, the ceremony made them worth something. At least the memory was preserved, a bit like his punk records, though he knew he was a bit of a tosser comparing vinyl and death. He'd bought Pete's records off Mango five years after Pete went missing. It bothered him a bit at first, but it was Mango who'd made the offer. Will had been into the idea of owning lots of records and paid the asking price, Mango using the money to go out with a millionaire's daughter from St John's Wood he'd been trying to impress. If he remembered right, Mango had taken her for a meal, got her pissed and then been blown out. He'd been well fucked off about it, but wasn't bothered about the records. It was a bit bad somehow. The whole transaction lacked dignity, even though the records were only objects.

Will finished his smoke, coughed, and went for a wee. He was halfway through when the fire alarm in the hall started sounding, a high-pitched scream that cut through the dull throb in his head. He splashed his jeans but was straight in pushing the right button. He sweated a bit listening for Karen. Silence returned. It was the smoke that had set off the alarm. Talk about touchy. He went back to the bathroom and tried to wash the piss out of his jeans, then returned to Karen's bed and crept in. It frightened him that she hadn't heard the smoke alarm. She hadn't even shifted her position since he left twenty minutes before. She turned in her sleep and cuddled up to him again.

Will lay on his back listening to his heart, her heart, both hearts together. The bass was deep and contented. His eyes were open and he became used to the faint light once more, thinking of the video and what a shame it was there was no film of Pete. It was probably for the best. It was better just to erase that kind of thing. He felt sorry for himself and Karen, whatever happened, even if he never saw her again. His heart beat had always worried him as a kid. It seemed so easy to die. A valve could go just like that, or a fatal disease appear and you'd be on the dissection table with your guts in a plastic bag and an attendant eating his ham sandwiches. That worry was in the past now. He was positive. He thought of his time with Bev. They'd been close at first, like this, but gradually the bed had been separated down the middle, especially in the summer when it was hot and sticky and touching another person made you feel clammy and dirty. In the winter it was different, closing up for body heat. But it was okay, because this was what life was all about, getting attached for a while and enjoying intimacy before moving on. A lot of people missed out. Couldn't make the connection because they were scared of the pain later on. Loads of blokes he knew didn't get the chance, whether the fault was theirs or a bit further down the road. You couldn't get the same fulfilment wanking your life away, even if it was in the shape of one-off sex.

Then the sun was forcing his eyes open and Karen was in her dressing gown next to the bed, a purple effort that rode above her knees, saying she had to get to work. She kissed him on the mouth. A long, warm kiss. She said she could always phone in sick if he wanted. She'd never done that before. It wasn't the right thing really, because she had responsibilities, but maybe staying home one day wasn't that bad a thing to do if there was a good enough reason. Will didn't need much persuading and was awake now, sliding her dressing gown apart. Karen pushed herself into the bed and for the next couple of hours everything centred on the bedroom.

Will sat up sipping his coffee, the smell of the soup Karen was making in the kitchen working its way under the door. It was raining out. The wind was blowing and the sun had been hidden by thick cloud. He was starving. It was yesterday dinner-time when he'd last eaten, apart from the biscuits, and the drink had made him even more hungry than normal. It was a good day to be shut indoors. It was the right weather for chips with brown sauce, crumpets with melted butter and jam, a nice tin of soup with the toast. He was tired after just four and a half hours of sleep, but beyond it now. His balls ached. After months of sexual inactivity, Karen's enthusiasm was a shock. He started wondering how long it was since she'd last had a shag, he meant made love, then dismissed the thought. There was no need to ruin things thinking like that. Maybe after the soup he'd be able to rest up a bit. The shop would just have to stay closed, but there wasn't exactly going to be a flood of eager punters braving the weather to spend their fortunes on his collection of tatty furniture and chipped ornaments.

The teddy bear, who Karen said was called Ted, sat next to him. Will was sure the expression had changed. There wasn't the same non-committal grin he'd noticed before, more a knowing leer with a bit of resentment thrown in as a bonus. Will stroked the bear's muzzle without response. It was just a toy. The blow was sticking around longer and longer. He turned quickly to see if it was watching him, but Ted hadn't moved. Poor little fucker, forced to listen while his childhood sweetheart made love with a strange man. Next time he would have to go and sit in the living room. Will laughed at himself and lobbed the bear in the air, catching him by the right ear. He held Ted out in front at arm's length. The expression hadn't changed. He was giving nothing away.

'Talking to Ted, are you?' Karen asked as she came into the room. 'What was he saying to you, Teddy dear?'

She gave Will the tray she was carrying and lifted the bear to her head. She looked at Will, then back at the bear. She frowned.

'Ted says you threw him in the air and made him feel sick, and that you caught him by the ear. He says that his ear is hurting. He thinks you don't like him, and if you're not careful he'll get you when you're asleep. You should treat him nice or he'll make you sorry.'

Will looked at the bear, then down at his soup. It was homemade and vegetable and a bit too healthy-looking for his tastes. Thick brown bread was buttered on a plate. He preferred his bread white and ready sliced, but said nothing. And you couldn't beat soup from a tin. Just get the old can-opener working, dump it in the saucepan, give it a few minutes over the flame while you buttered the toast, and there was a four-star meal ready and waiting. His mouth watered at the thought. He looked back at Ted, then Karen.

'Don't look so worried,' she laughed. 'Ted and me don't have any secrets from each other. We tell each other everything.'

Karen went to the kitchen for her soup. Will looked at the bear. It must've been a lucky guess. But he was beginning to dislike the toy, with its cocky grin and glass eyes. She came back and got into bed.

'How did you know I threw him in the air and caught him by the ear?' Will asked. 'I wasn't talking to him though.'

'I saw you through the crack in the door. You looked scared when I told you what he said. Toys can't talk. They're just toys, nothing more. Something for when you're a kid. Ted's a memory more than anything else.'

Will nodded. He was tired and his brain was misfiring. It was nice putting emotions into things which could never have that quality. That was what religious icons came down to really. Karen's mum shifting her feelings somewhere they couldn't do any harm, avoiding debate, hearing the sort of answers that made everything alright. If it helped her accept her own death then maybe it was okay, even if it was a con.

'They were fine when I phoned up and said I wouldn't be in,' Karen said, blowing on her soup and waiting for it to cool down. 'I was a bit nervous lying like that, but they told me to go to bed and rest. I said I had the flu. I said okay, that I'd go back and spend the day sleeping, but they didn't know I had a man waiting for me.'

She rubbed the inside of Will's leg and he was glad they both had trays on their laps. He didn't fancy sex again right now. He was a bit worn out. Karen had enough energy for them both.

'You didn't sleep well last night, did you?' Karen asked.

'I'm usually alright,' he answered. 'Just one of those nights.'

'Thanks for staying. Sorry I was going on a bit. I was depressed yesterday thinking of my mum. It was a nice night out. And it was even better when we got back, wasn't it?'

Will guessed he was going red and sipped from a spoonful of soup. It didn't taste bad for something homemade. He stirred it and noticed chopped carrots, mushrooms, onions, and a couple of bits of what must've been potato. He didn't fancy the bread much. He made the effort seeing as how Karen had fixed it for him, treating him like a king. It had to be the first time in his life since he was ill as a kid that someone had made him food in bed. The bread was alright. A bit chewy and that, but nothing he couldn't handle.

'It was a great night,' he admitted, feeling the enthusiasm in his voice but reasoning that it was okay to be open.

'What do you think of the soup? I made it with miso.'

'It's great.'

Will wanted to ask what miso was, but felt a bit of a prat. He'd ask one of the lads, and if they didn't know he'd go down the library and look it up in a dictionary. He was getting into the soup now, not pushing himself any more.

'I made the bread yesterday. Do you like it? You've only had a couple of bites. I don't like all that processed rubbish. You don't know what shit they've put in it and I never touch anything that's been in a tin. It's unnatural. I'm sure cancer comes from tinned food and preservatives. It seems a bit of a coincidence it's such a big killer in the West. My mum should've had a go at the food corporations rather than putting everything down to fate and trusting in God's mysterious ways. It was just easier for her to believe all the propaganda she was fed as a kid.'

'The bread's good. I've never met anyone who makes their own bread before. Never met anyone who makes their own soup.'

'It's easy enough, nothing special. Just a bit of DIY.'

Will wanted to tell Karen that he knew a couple of blokes like that. His old mates the Lager Twins. They were DIY merchants, preferring a J Arthur Rank to sex with a woman. You'd never catch VD that way. It was on hand any time of day, literally. Karen might have laughed but it wasn't the kind of humour he was going to introduce at such an early stage. He wanted things to be perfect. Romance, love, all that kind of stuff. Karen understood better than him. Maybe the Sex Division should split in two. Balti and Harry could form the Skin Flute League, where each wank scored a single point. It would be a local derby really, because they lived in the same flat and would have to constantly outdo each other in the quantity stakes. Quality wouldn't even come into the daily Skin Flute derbies. It would be non-league football, but would be better than constant battles against relegation where the beautiful game would be corrupted and reduced to a coarse scramble for points.

Will chewed the homemade bread as Karen went through the details of how she had made it, thinking of the Sex Division. If she ever found out he was in something like that she'd probably send him packing. Will felt righteousness take over. Karen would look at him in another way. Gone forever would be the caring, gentle Will she was obviously attracted to, and in his place a pisshead would rear up, or worse than that, a Carter cut-out. As for the Sex Division, he would never be able to claim the points of last night. It would ruin everything. But bollocks to all that. He would keep Karen away from the others for as long as he could, but eventually they would probably meet. Not that anyone would say anything, but he wouldn't feel good about it all the same.

Will had to get out of the Sex Division. Had to go into liquidation. A loss of assets. Sell his ground. Whatever it took. He didn't want to belong. He'd never liked the idea in the first place. Imagine meeting Johan Carter in The Unity when he was a bit pissed, maybe going into one, Karen telling Will what a wanker he was and that he could fuck off. It had to be done. He was getting paranoid. He'd been smoking too much blow. But it was only exaggerating things he already felt.

When they'd finished eating Karen took the plates away and washed them. She came back soon after, smiling, asking Will if he had anything left for desert. She took her dressing gown off and he admired her body. Despite himself he was aroused and the woman he thought he was probably going to fall in love with pulled the duvet back and got in next to him. He noticed that one of her earrings had fallen out. He was on for a three-pointer that would never be entered into the statistics. Will was with Karen for pleasure, not points. They were together for the purest of reasons.

PART TWO

DREAMSCAPE

THE HIDE WAS heaving and the boys were steaming, Carter well into a blonde number, her two mates waiting for Harry and Balti to show a bit of interest. Harry leant back against the wall and considered the options while Balti remained tucked into the side of the jukebox. One Step Beyond by Madness was playing and usually they'd go into a bit of sax imitation, maybe do a Suggs or something, but knew the girls would think they were a couple of muppets. Harry was thinking of saying something but couldn't really be bothered, and he'd had a good wank that morning before the football, sitting back in the bath with the water scorching hot burning the week's paint and turps from his pores, lager dregs melting away, his first chance to bang the bishop since Monday. Balti was weighing their chances up, thinking they looked okay but were a bit too fucking trendy for his liking, too fucking cocky for their own good. They were obviously out of it or they wouldn't be eyeing up a couple of herberts. He'd had a skinful and the last Saturday of the football season was always a sad time.

'Where'd you get the earrings then?' he asked, leaning forward and almost falling into the woman's chest, the support of the jukebox removed forcing him to stand on his own two feet, instantly regretting a shit chat-up line. When he looked more closely at the face in front of him, he realised she was the same age or older, that she had probably heard of Madness after all.

'A mate of mine brought them back from Goa. He DJs over there. They're silver and the stone in the middle's a ruby. They cost a tenth of the price you'd pay in London.'

'I used to wear an earring, when I was younger like, but

every time I got in a row someone pulled it out trying to rip my ear off. Nothing special mind. Just a silver hoop.'

'I was thinking of having my nose pierced but everyone does that now,' she said, eyes widening, circled with slightly smudged eyeliner. 'I've had my right nipple done, and my friend's got a stud through her lip.'

Balti looked sideways and saw the ring-free mouth, then thought about it for a moment. He wondered what it was like shagging a bird with a butterfly tucked in between her legs. A bit rough probably. You'd have to be careful. The one doing the talking was looking round like Mango did, checking for a reaction, a bit of recognition. She was nice though, despite the pose. The gear was a bit expensive and fashionable in that naff way that left him cold, all designer dago bollocks. But that was her trademark and if she'd been a heifer, or not paid him attention, just ignored the shit line and made him look a cunt, then he'd have been forced to dismiss her as one more dyke who didn't know what she was missing. One more dyke in a brave lager culture suffering from mass outbreaks of lesbianism.

Harry was moving now, uneven on his feet, feeling the effects, Madness replaced by some industrial effort neither of them could identify. For a second Balti wished he was back home where he could decide what music he listened to, like Will, who was sitting in with Karen again, the miserable git, but bollocks, he was having a laugh and if he'd been in Will's shoes, with a cracker like that on the go, a bit of class, then he'd be doing the same. At least he'd remembered to set the video for *Match Of The Day*. The Dutchman had played another blinder for the Blues. He wanted to see it again. All the flicks and feints, the surging runs ghosting past the opposition with an ease that made his team-mates look like Sunday league players. Even Carter had ditched Johan and was going on about Ruud's genius. Next thing he'd be growing his hair and wearing dreadlocks.

The idea of Carter in Gullit-style dreadlocks set him off. With the football season at an end, and that riot in Birmingham having run its course, the papers were looking round for a new public enemy. As ever, summer meant hippies, ravers and travellers were about to take the strain. Balti had always dismissed white blokes with dreadlocks as wankers. He didn't hold an opinion about Stonehenge and pagan rights of worship, though the media usually went into one when the summer solstice came round, denouncing the anarchist threat to democracy and the Christian way of life. The tabloids were comics anyway so he didn't take them seriously. He was starting to see the logic. Karen had set him straight, following the line of descent back to punk, the way the anarchist movement had rearranged and developed itself. She was alright Karen. And it showed what could be done. He didn't believe in all that nonsense, witchcraft and everything, knowing that it was too much drugs that did their heads in, but getting away made sense. He'd been signing on for five months now, going for jobs he never got, just sitting around. That was no life. He wasn't talking about Glastonbury either. That was just more wank. Paying through your nose to stand in a field. Playing at being something you weren't. They should bomb the part-timers. Like the football. All those cunts who came to five or six games a season and sat in the most expensive seats. Going walkabout for a couple of months would be a laugh. It was supposed to be alien, like it couldn't be part of your life because of the pictures you saw and the interviews you heard, but when Karen cut through the prejudice then it made sense. Like it didn't have to belong to someone else.

She was great Karen. He wouldn't mind meeting someone like that. None of the lads had seen her for the first couple of months and then Will brought her down the pub and everything was sweet. She got her round in. Everyone liked her. She had her view and could make you think things through. It was another angle. She wasn't some sloppy cow giggling the whole time, or some flash case rabbiting on trying to boost her ego. Karen was solid. Hundred per cent. She came down quite often now and none of the lads complained like they usually did when a bird tagged along. She wasn't a mother figure, nothing like that, more a sister. But even that wasn't right. Just a mate really. She had a different slant. Made them think. Most of all she was honest. She fitted in perfect with

Will. Balti didn't like posers. Mango pissed him off. Something chronic. This bird was pissing him off as well. But she was a good-looker. He didn't know how important that was, the sex appeal and everything, whether he should play the game and bite his lip, hoping to get his leg over. Act all impressed because she had a ring through her tit.

'I started stretching my bollocks last year,' Balti lied. 'Had the weights nailed on and my sack soon began sagging. Once I'd gained a couple of inches on the old scrotum I added more weights and my balls are down round my knees now. It took a while, but they got there in the end. It's something you just have to stick with and force yourself through the pain. I'm suffering for my body art. All you need is the time and a bit of patience. I've got time at the moment, being self-employed and that, though you get a bit impatient because you're so keen to see the end result.'

He patted his left leg. She looked a bit wary. Like she thought it was a wind-up but wasn't sure, trying to picture a stretched sack and a couple of chestnuts floating in the void. She powered into his face looking for an answer, but Balti kept his dignity and refused to crack a smile. She seemed a bit pissed off now. She sipped her drink and looked past them, then meaningfully at her mate, then her shoes which Balti reckoned must've left a serious dent in her wages. A waste of money you saw more clearly when you were living on pennies.

'I keep them tucked down my left peg because I'm right-footed and don't want to strain the veins. I can swing them side to side. My mate's the same. We're the Bollock Brothers. Surprised you haven't heard about us. We're famous round here. Balls down to our knees and now we're working on the guts, filling up nicely.'

'Nice one, Scrote,' Harry shouted, grabbing his mate by the knee, pretending to squeeze his bollocks. 'Just like knicker elastic. With all that weight attached it means the skin stretches and when you let it go again it snaps back to the body. It's like playing ping-pong.'

'Doesn't it affect you when you're with a woman?' The second of the two asked, moving closer and taking him at face value, maybe taking the piss, while her friend adjusted her stance. 'Doesn't it make things a bit difficult with all that skin getting in the way?'

'It takes a bit of imagination, that's all,' Harry laughed.

He was taken back to last night with the two women on top of the hill. He hadn't slept well, the weather hot and humid, summer arriving early with the effects of global warming and city pollution. The confusion of the seasons was mucking up his sleep. Everything was shifting around. In the winter he dreamt of the tropics and psychedelic jungles, where his surroundings were bursting with life and sound, the natural world mixed with futuristic technology, Mayan Indians disguised as Aztecs and Frank Bruno on the door. Now it was almost summer and he was stuck on a moor, without shelter, with seven thousand shades of black and white for company. He was part of a line drawing and there was a coldness about everything, the cracks in the sky cracks in broken bone china. There'd been a woman in a white gown laying on a horizontal stone, a woman in a black dress in the background next to a fossilised tree. It was a dead oak and the only tree to be seen. The woman on the slab was alive and tripping on special-offer button mushrooms. In a semi-conscious state with her brain frying from all the things she'd seen. Somehow it was up to Harry and Balti to show her that it was worth going on with life, that just because she'd seen a crow flap its wings and been able to follow the vibrations through the air, it didn't mean that boring everyday life wasn't worth living.

They were old men. With long beards and slight hunches. Merlin wizards without the magic. The end was near and they were dressed in rags. A couple of tramps on top of a moor surrounded by ancient stones not knowing what to do next. They'd lost their way. Balti leant forward and the woman's eyes opened. Harry remembered the black circles, the emptiness; eyes without pupils. A thin white arm pulled Balti forward. The woman turned sideways and Balti slid onto the stone. Harry turned his head away but heard their moans. She was a witch and was draining Balti's resistance. Harry tried to say something but no sound came from his mouth. He left the moor, the footsteps of the second woman right behind as he hurried towards the orange glow of London. He turned once and saw that the second woman was dressed in worn-out rubber and had the head of a giant insect. London was on fire. He ran from the moor, covered in a thick sweat that soaked his mattress.

The two women made their excuses and went off to the Ladies, and Balti and Harry had a laugh, not expecting them to return. Fuck it anyway. They were enjoying themselves, Carter well away with the blonde. Not a bad-looking bit of skirt if they were honest, but the music was loud and they were pissed and nothing could touch them, no fucking way. It was May and they'd been to a goalless draw in front of a full house. The Sex Division had gone a bit quiet as well, with Carter so far out in front now, Mango in second place with those posh numbers from his work, while Harry and Balti were in serious relegation trouble without even a sniff of a point. Will, meantime, had gone underground since he'd got all serious with Karen. They didn't even know how many points he was on, and Carter had stopped winding him up about it because Will wasn't shifting. But Carter liked Karen as well and didn't really want to know, just felt he had to ask. It was expected of him. Will said he wasn't in the Sex Division any more, which was fair enough really, when you had class like that, but they still included him. Who needed dodgy old boilers when a decent bird paid you attention?

'You in there or what?' Carter asked when the blonde had followed her friends to the toilet.

'If they like their bollocks hanging free,' Harry said, filling him in on the details.

'I don't understand you two.' Carter was unamused. 'There's two fit-looking birds obviously up for it, gagging for a good servicing more like, with studs in their tits and fannies, and you two start feeding them a line about having Plasticine balls. I mean, what's the game? Don't you like women or something?'

'Not Plasticine balls,' Balti said. 'Elastic sacks.'

The Bollock Brothers were cracking up. Balti looked like he was going to have a heart attack. He was doubled in half and there were tears in his eyes.

'What's the fucking difference?' Carter was getting excited now. 'Don't you want to get in there? I'm not surprised your balls are down to your ankles. It's the middle of May and you're not even off the mark yet. It's spring-time lads. Make an effort.'

'There's a lot of difference,' Balti insisted. 'We're not choirboys with our balls bit off by the vicar. You couldn't produce much with Plasticine balls, could you? But just because you've stretched your sack doesn't mean you can't bring pleasure to a beautiful woman. That's the problem today, nobody appreciates differences. We're unique. We're the Nut Crackers.'

Harry was laughing and didn't want an argument. It was good to see Balti enjoying himself. After five months signing on he was coiled tight. It was a long time living on a pittance. He thought about the desolate moorland and the rags they'd been wearing. Maybe it was a warning. He should watch out for his own job. That's what happened to you in the end. On a slab of concrete with blind birds the only ones willing to spend time with you. There was no helping hand when you went down. Mango had that much worked out. He'd said he'd be along later, they were meeting him in The Unity. Harry had forgotten about that, but Mango had been blowing them out a lot recently. It was his WorldView commitments and those posh birds he was into at the Barbican. It was another world. Harry knew it wound Balti up when Mango went into one, the fact that they came from the same backgrounds making unemployment something personal. The propaganda fired through the TV and radio, covering the front of the papers, that didn't do anyone any good either. Just made the likes of Balti feel more useless than ever.

Balti saw the three women come out of the bogs. He pointed them out. They stood for a minute talking, then left the pub together.

'Couple of fucking lesbians,' Balti said. 'Don't know what they're missing.'

'Dykes, mate,' Harry agreed. 'Fucking dykes.'

'Probably off to some queer club,' Balti said, knocking back his drink. 'Some place that costs twenty quid to get in just so they can pay three quid for a bottle of foreign lager surrounded by a bunch of fucking shirt-lifters.'

'More like fat birds with short hair and beards.'

'They didn't like the old stretched bollocks routine much,' Balti noted. 'Couple of posers. Seems like it's alright sticking a ring through your clit, but stretch your sack and you're an outcast. Where's the fucking equality in that?'

'Didn't fancy yours much anyway,' Harry said.

'Didn't fancy yours either,' Balti agreed.

'Lesbians.'

'Dykes.'

'Fucking horrible.'

'A narrow escape.'

'Fuck knows what's been up those two.'

'Right old slappers.'

'Another pint?'

'Don't see why not. No need to be uncivilised, is there?'

'What about you, shag man.'

'They just pissed off,' Carter said, stunned. He wasn't used to getting blown out. 'They went without a word. I was well in there. It's you two going on about your bollocks the whole time. You fucked it up. I was on for a minimum three-pointer.'

'Do you want a drink or what?' Balti was getting narked now, took the glasses and muscled his way to the bar.

'You ballsed that up badly,' Carter told Harry. 'You should play the game. Talk shit with them for an hour or two because that's all you've got to do and then you're in. Show them you've got a bit of a brain and think they're the cream and before you know it you're away. Birds are easy to work out. Flatter them. That's all it takes.'

'Can't be bothered,' Harry laughed. 'We're pissed. Who cares? We're having a laugh. If she starts off talking about piercing her tits then what does she expect? You've got to have a laugh. It doesn't matter, does it?'

'What about relegation?'

'Fuck that. I'd rather have a laugh and go down than say things I don't want to say just to get a few points. I'd rather have a wank than waste my time talking gibberish with some poser.'

Carter stood in silence looking around the packed Hide until Balti returned. Time was standing still with the music blaring and Harry couldn't get his thinking straight, that miserable dream of last night confusing things. He liked everything in order. Neatly filed and understood. The dream was all mixed up with what was going on around him. He was losing the thread and when Carter suggested going down The Unity he remembered Mango. They drank up.

They walked slowly and Balti stopped to get some chips. The door was open but it was still a pressure cooker inside, with the oil bubbling and fat frying and some skinhead on his way out with a half-eaten roti. There was a woman in front with a couple of small kids buying the Saturday night special. They waited while the chips were wrapped and Harry watched the woman disappear. Kaleidoscope patterns of passing traffic pulsed inside the window, light caught in blasted sand. He was feeling the effects of the drink and last night's dream still wouldn't go away. It bothered him. He was trying to think back but the winter setting kept getting in the way. He was sweating heavily. The weather forecasters said it was going to be a hot summer. Long and hot. Balti took his chips and they continued down the street. It was half-nine.

The woman's white gown had been almost transparent, but there was no warning that she would pull Balti towards her, that she was interested in anything other than what was happening inside her head. She belonged to a different tribe, with her long hair and weathered features. She wasn't ugly, but not exactly state-of-the-art Modern English. She wasn't what she seemed and Harry couldn't pinpoint what she represented. Those eyes must mean something. The scenery was sparse and brutal. It was going back to a primitive environment. Somewhere on the coast of Scotland or Ireland perhaps, though there was nothing to show they were outside England other than the barren landscape. He thought instead of the woman in rubber, the insect head that made him nervous. It wasn't much fun when you started dreaming of bondage insects, giant fuckers who would suck your blood and kick your carcass into the gorse. Past and present. Maybe that's what it was. It didn't sound right somehow. The stones were obvious, magic and druids, but what about rubber woman?

'These are fucking shit,' Balti moaned halfway down the street. 'I should take them back.'

Harry tried one. They weren't cooked right. He threw the chip in to the gutter. Even the chippies were going down hill these days. Balti ate a few more and put the rest in a bin. The Unity was up ahead. It was an odd feeling, the end of the football season and the start of summer. There would be a hole for the next few months. At least with the football there was something solid at the end of the week. They were all season ticket holders and averaged thirty or so games a season. They'd been going since they were kids. Older and wiser, they avoided aggravation, back into a second childhood of team selection and tactics discussions. The eighties had been a bit mental with Chelsea on the rampage week in, week out, but they'd got older and couldn't be bothered. Things had changed. All of them had the odd flashback to childhood, carefree days growing up.

'Alright Slaughter?' Carter asked as they entered the pub.

'Not bad mate,' the nutter replied, and Carter had a subtle look towards the bar where Denise was serving.

Unknown to the rest of the lads, Carter had been shagging Denise for the last month and a half. Dirty Denise. He'd been right about her, she was a right goer. The best bit of sex he'd had for years. She seemed to get off on the knowledge that Slaughter would kill them if he found out she was doing the dirty on him. Carter didn't like that part of the arrangement, but he kept going back for more all the same. He'd had his eye on Denise for ages and knew she was interested, but it had been an accident how she'd ended up round his flat. Carter and Ian had finished delivering early and he'd bumped into Denise in the street. She'd invited herself round for a drink and he'd been nervous in case they were spotted and word filtered back to Slaughter. They'd got pissed on vodka and Denise ended up staying. She was mental. There was passion there alright, but it boiled near to violence, which Carter wasn't keen on, but he didn't want to put her off, just keep it in line a bit. There was no way some bird was going to tie him up. No fucking way. He'd heard a story like that from some bloke down Chelsea, about some other cunt nobody seemed to know personally who'd picked up this bird down a club in Brixton, gone back with her and let her tie him to the bed. Next thing he knows a six-foot nigger turns up, shafts him up the arse so hard he needs thirty stitches, and then the poor cunt gets robbed into the bargain. Not that Carter reckoned Slaughter was an iron, but you never knew what else Denise might have planned. Trust might've been the basis of all good relationships, but he wasn't looking for any of that from Denise.

It was iffy, though, with Slaughter being a headcase and Carter slipping his missus a length, Denise a bit suspect. He didn't feel guilt or anything like that, it was just that he enjoyed life and wanted to die in his sleep or from old age, not under the fine edge of a machete. From the first time she'd come round, Carter had thought about knocking it on the head, but he still kept going. The longer it went on the harder it was going to be walking away. He would keep his head down, but knew he was asking for a kicking. She was a good ride though. He switched back to their last session as he worked his way to the bar, Denise with her vibrator and clitoral stimulator spilling out of her handbag. The dirty cow.

'Three pints of lager please Denise,' he said, avoiding the barmaid's eyes, then watching her move along the bar. She had a lovely arse. Eileen was back there with the landlord and his brother-in-law, who helped out sometimes.

'There you go Terry,' Denise smiled, eye-to-eye contact for a split second as he handed over his money.

'I thought you were coming down at nine,' Mango moaned, appearing from the mass of people crowded into the pub.

'Thought you'd be blowing us out again,' Balti said.

'I've got the night off,' Mango smiled. 'It's a bit quiet at the moment. That Saudi deal kept us up late for ages and now it's over we're left playing with ourselves.'

'What about that Penny you're always going on about?' Balti asked.

'She's alright. I saw her last night.'

Mango was moving forward in the world. He'd given up on the degraded scum haunting King's Cross and moved up-market. The old bill were cleaning up the area, moving the problem on with the help of the council which was looking for a bit of inner-city rejuvenation, and Mango was pleased. It was an eyesore and not exactly conducive to economic growth. A couple of the chaps at WorldView had opened his eyes to that one. Being men of commerce and in the peak of physical condition, training at a Mayfair gym which Mango was considering joining, they had little time for women and found chance meetings a waste of resources. Time was of the essence. Ridley and Hetherington would have been appalled at the thought of picking commoners off the street. They had outlined the best approach over a working lunch, and Mango had accepted the card Hetherington put on the table.

James Wilson was better than King's Cross. The agency supplied quality acts, and while he paid heavily for the privilege of shafting women with nice accents and expensive gear, he considered it money well spent. There was a selection of nationalities available. Models from Zurich, Paris, Copen-hagen. They would do anything for a price. Mind you, a pro was a pro, but they weren't so desperate somehow. Kids from Halifax were definite victims while at least Mango could feel the cold steel of a financial transaction with the call girls. They weren't even called whores. It was so much more sophisticated. Corporate sex. It felt international, with none of that Anglo-Saxon bawdiness he had grown up with. It was Eurosex. Multinational business transactions. There was a lot of religion at WorldView and the likes of Ridley and Hetherington had been educated in public schools rigidly controlled by the Church Of England. Perhaps it was being a Christian, making money and respecting wealth. It was the next stage in Mango's development. He reminded himself that he was a Christian. Fucking right he was.

'Penny's into it alright,' Mango explained, lowering his voice. 'She's got all the gear and I'm not talking your everyday stockings and suspenders either. Wanted to know if I wore hoods. Whether seeing as how I was a Tory voter, did I follow my masters and need a good caning and a night behind bars?'

Harry smiled and felt a bit better. Carter shook his head and marvelled at the workings of the female mind. Balti felt like he was going to throw up. A nightmare situation. It was bad enough the ruling class beat you into submission day after day, year after year, grinding you down and then screaming that you were a sponger for accepting benefits you'd paid for a hundred times over during the previous decade and a half. They humiliated you every day of your fucking life and then their women wanted to put a hood on your head so you didn't even have a fucking face, whipping you like they did in the Middle Ages. Fucking slag, and there was Mango, accepting the dogma and pissing on his own kind. Balti remembered those two kids he'd told them about. The bird from Halifax. He was on the verge of headbutting the cunt but held back. A year or two years younger and he'd have done him no problem. Mate or no mate. You had to have morals or you were fuck all in this world, but it was choosing the right morals and sticking to them that was hardest. There were plenty of wankers around who wanted to define the rights and wrongs for you. Karen had been right about that one. They'd had a long talk about it and Balti saw it more clearly. She was telling him that he was the victim and not the criminal. It was hard to see yourself as a victim, it made you look like a wanker and everything, like you were another castrated cunt on the box going on about the suppression of women and the white man's guilt. You had to work according to your own standards. Funny really, but Will had told him more or less the same thing, soon after he'd lost his job. But it had been presented in a different way. Not so direct. Karen got to the point. He respected her but he was no victim. No fucking way. He downed his pint and went to the bar for a refill, the others way behind, spending money he didn't have.

Nothing could compare with Saturday night. Except Friday maybe. And they usually had a few beers on a Thursday, warming up for Friday. Saturdays were good though. There was more of a mixture in The Unity whereas The Hide was a younger pub, pre-Blues drinking, people from all over West

London, The Unity more local. Carter seemed less rampant than usual, enjoying a drink with the lads. He pissed them off sometimes, sniffing around anything that moved. Slaughter passed them with a grin and went to the bar and kissed Denise on the cheek, leaving with a couple of his mates. Carter smiled to himself.

'Will, what the fuck are you doing down here, you cunt?' Balti shouted, wrapping his arm round the new arrival's shoulder. 'I thought your liver had given up now you've gone all romantic on us.'

'Fancied a pint,' he answered, a bit sheepish.

'Hello,' Karen said.

'Alright darling?' Balti said, more quietly. 'I didn't see you there. What do you want to drink.'

'I'll get them,' Will insisted. 'We're only having a couple.'

He went to the bar. The rest of the lads shifted a bit so Karen had some room. Balti was hammered but felt embarrassed all the same. It was bad manners mouthing off in front of a class bird.

'Didn't expect to see you tonight,' Carter said.

'I fancied a drink. I had to give Will a bit of a kick to get him moving. We got a video out but it was rubbish. We're going back for the football. I heard Chelsea was nil-nil. Brentford won though. Beat Cardiff 3–1.'

'It was a good enough game,' Harry said. 'Typical end of season match when you've got nothing to play for, but at least The Dutchman was making the effort. Earns enough mind, but I'd rather he had it than some wanker in Westminster. We were thinking of going over to Amsterdam for the weekend next month. Terry's spiritual home, isn't it mate.'

'Sort of.'

'Why's that then, Terry?' Karen asked.

'Just love Dutch football, that's all. As soon as I got into football I remember watching Holland playing when Cruyff and Neeskens were around. I love the idea of total football. Look at the team they've got today. Overmars, Kluivert, Davids. Brilliant players.'

'Have you heard of St Pauli?' she asked.

'What's that then?'

'It's a football team in Germany, in Hamburg. It's in the squatter's area and the police are banned from the ground. Most of the fans are anarchists and instead of the national flag they fly the black flag. When there were riots against the police in Hamburg some of the players were even supposed to have taken part. I read about it. It sounds good. It's not that far from Amsterdam, though I suppose the season would be over by the time you go.'

'I wouldn't mind seeing Ajax play,' Terry admitted. 'What are they called, the German team?'

'St Pauli. They're in Hamburg.'

'That sounds alright as well. Depends on the anarchists of course. If they're like some of the ones you get over here it wouldn't be much. Students playing politics for a couple of weeks till they get a decent job.'

'It's probably better than that,' Karen said. 'It's just something I read about, that's all.'

Will came back with two pints, Guinness for Karen, Directors for himself.

'We were thinking of going to Amsterdam for a weekend during the summer,' Balti told Will. 'You don't mind him coming do you?' He turned to Karen.

'Course I don't. Why should I?'

'Don't know. Some women don't like their boyfriends or whatever going off on their own.'

'You're a traditionalist at heart, aren't you?' Karen said, laughing.

'You coming then, Will?' Mango asked.

'Don't know. I'll think about it.'

'Plenty of dope over there.'

'Plenty over here. It depends on the money.'

'Mango's going to try and put the train tickets through his work,' Terry said. 'It'll be worth it just to get his company to pay for something like that. Mind you, can't see being able to put the drugs through, and the red light's a no-no as well. Not that I'd be into it anyway.'

'You lot aren't like that, are you?' Karen asked.

The Sex Division shook their heads. Mango most of all,

385

though he was the only one who'd ever paid for sex. He was looking forward to seeing Amsterdam's famous red light district, though from Carter's and Terry's descriptions it sounded like shit. Then there was the Reeperbahn in Hamburg. But he was up-market now. Call girls. He moved the conversation on, feeling uncomfortable. It was something you wanted to keep quiet, a failure really, and he wished he hadn't mentioned anything to the others in the first place.

'Will was saying you might be going down to Cornwall for a week in the summer,' he ventured.

'I've always wanted to go to Tintagel,' she said. 'Ever since I was a kid. It's beautiful in Cornwall. There's less people and the landscape's the nearest you get to Ireland in England.'

Harry was happy. He had the gift. Maybe he was psychic. Seeing things in the future. Of course, it was only now and then, but it gave him a buzz when it happened. Like he was above fate and in control. If he could get it a bit more accurate, control the gift, then he'd be away. Imagine being able to predict the future. You'd make a packet with the horses and win the Lottery every weekend. They wouldn't be able to stop him and he'd keep on taking their money. The world would be his.

'I dreamt about a moor with stones last night,' he told Karen, who seemed impressed. 'I've done it a few times now, seen things that happen later. It's never really clear at first, but when it happens I know right away.'

'Are you a lucid dreamer?' Karen asked.

'That's when you're in a dream and know you're there, isn't it, so you're able to control it and make it go the way you want. That wouldn't be a real dream.'

'Of course it is,' Balti said, aggrieved. 'It's like daydreaming. You can have dreams when you're awake. They don't always have to be buried.'

'That's alright if you can be honest with yourself, but the thing is, you're always going to be turning them your own way. It's better to be straight and let it sort itself out. Then you've got the problem of working out what it means and making sense of what you've dreamt. That's the part that does me in. But when you finally understand, you're made up.'

'Who says you can trust what happens when you're asleep? Anyway, everything's natural.'

'I'll tell you what's natural,' Terry said, getting a bit fed up with the dream shit, daydreams or night dreams, it was all images and airy-fairy hippy bollocks. 'What's natural is getting a decent pint down your throat.'

They all laughed. Karen liked Will's mates. Mango interested her. To see someone like that change their stripes, when inside he understood how things worked. He was aware, but had given up. Will insisted that deep down Mango was still the same person as when he was a kid, that it was to do with Pete.

'I'm going home to watch the football,' Balti announced twenty minutes before closing-time. 'I've had enough.'

'You're recording it,' Harry said. He had his second wind and fancied a few more. Carter knew he was in with Denise.

'Hold on and we'll walk back with you,' Will said.

They drank up and moved through the pub. Will was always surprised when he went into a drunk pub sober. It was mental, watching the deterioration, the conversation and behaviour. Unless things got nasty it was a good laugh, though there was always an undercurrent in pubs like The Unity, though The Hide was worse, with regular punch-ups and now and then someone getting glassed. That place was a tinderbox, packed with geezers ready to start tearing up. He didn't like the place. It was ugly. But The Unity was fine. And it was a nice evening. He was really going to enjoy this summer.

Will, Karen and Balti turned off the high street, sharing some of the short journey home. Televisions created patterns through net curtains and men and women sat watching life pass by. Everything was fine. Business was picking up after a slack period and Will was in love with Karen. They'd even told each other as much. She was going to move in with him soon. Will felt the best about life he had done for years. The streets were quiet and he could think straight, a couple of pints enough during hot weather like this. Now and then a car passed, and when Karen bent down to stroke a white cat it made a noise then hurried off.

They came to their street and Balti turned down the chance to watch the football round Will's. He was knackered and didn't want to move again that night.

Balti checked his watch. He was pissed but the air was clearing his head. He breathed in deeply and enjoyed the oxygen. As he was beginning to exhale he felt himself spun round and for a second thought he was a kid's top and wanted to laugh seeing the flash of a familiar face from five months back, his last memory of the working world, five months for someone to pick his moment and bring his head into contact with the space between Balti's eyes, that spot where there was supposed to be a secret gland that told the future and everything there was to know about everything else, he'd heard about that from some Indian at work, but the pain wasn't mystical, just a dagger through his skull rattling the brain's suspension and that moment of happiness, of breathing in and out in silence, shot out the hole, though maybe the drink had dimmed the sensation a bit but not enough, he should have had a couple more down the pub with his mates who were back there enjoying themselves, and he was bouncing back and that cunt McDonald was there in the flesh with big black eyes, where was the fucking blue, that's what they said about Paddies, their blue eyes and tin whistles and Balti was spinning remembering in slow motion his own headbutt down in Tooting, putting a man on his arse all that time ago, another world now where you got a pay packet at the end of the week and didn't have to search supermarket shelves looking for special offers and could have a pint whenever you wanted not worrying about pounds and pence rather than saving it up, and he reckoned the kicking was going to be a bit of lynch mob justice for the five car stereos he'd nicked for some pocket money that's what happened when you got fuck all off the social the only way to survive was to start acting like a juvenile again, thieving small time, McDonald something he'd forgotten about after the night the Irishman came calling knowing that revenge was going to take an exact course and waiting for the kick but trying to pull himself into shape, swinging a punch that didn't connect then feeling his arms pulled behind him up tight in the base of his back with a

388

heavy smell of tobacco and McDonald was saying something that he didn't get and there were another couple of shapes, one on either side like birds on his shoulders, massive fucking vultures waiting to pick at the remains of the dead, the dustmen, nature's bin men those Orangemen, waiting for the kick thinking about the old stretched scrotum and then it dug in deep with the pain jetting up through his body sending his balls racing in pure agony and he was sinking down and felt his arms released and they were kicking him on a patch of grass and he was wide open and he saw these legs in the air as one of the cunts, he wasn't sure which one, it didn't really matter, tried to stamp on his head and connected with the side of his face and they were sticking the boot in, stretched out, and he was in and out of it thinking about everything taken back knowing now why he was on the dole surviving on forty-six quid unable to live like a human being while the world around him insisted he was a sponger, politicians who spent that much on their breakfasts, that's what they did, they hired prostitutes and the prostitutes got you on the floor and kicked the shit out of you, stuck the boot in good and proper, and it was just being work shy that stopped him getting a job and those who lived by the sword died by the sword except that it wasn't a sword and he was shouting some kind of insult at the four men around him like they were vivisectionists or something, and he remembered that conversation with Karen saying what would it be like to have your arms and legs nailed down while some old cunt, no, she didn't use that word because she'd said once that it was insulting to women, some old sod with a scalpel half blind drooling into his tea not using the anaesthetic right trying to slit the rabbit open, carve it up, and Balti had no sympathy for himself because you had to have personal responsibility and everything and there was no forgiveness from your enemies, the fucking Belfast cunt and his scum mates, for the first time in his life he wished the IRA would blow the fuckers away because he saw the heavy hammer coming and he knew his legs were going, but then it all stopped for some reason and he heard shouting and the running of feet, one last kick in the head and a laugh saying the score's settled you fat cunt and then there were slamming doors exhaust fumes burning rubber and there was this black face right up against him with Ruud Gullit dreadlocks tight to the scalp and a thick West Indian voice, but he was alright, still conscious, and he sat up against a wall and tried to see straight trying to work things out, but bollocks, it was fine now though he was probably concussed and the three men around Balti were helping him up saying they'd call an ambulance on their mobile, but he said he was alright, he could look after himself and stand on his own two feet, and there were more strangers around him talking among themselves and now and then asking him if he was okay, so he stood up a bit unsteady feeling embarrassed getting a spanking on his own manor, but they were bad odds four or five on to one, and he was angry with himself getting slack thinking things like that would fade away and he was going to get the bastards, the first reaction was revenge, living the nightmare, fucking right, no surrender, no turning the other cheek, who the fuck did they think they were, and then he went down on the pavement and sat there for a long time getting his strength back.

SCUM OF TOYTOWN

HAMMERS ECHOED DEEP inside Churchill Mansion, the dull thud of steel on concrete filtering along tunnels and walkways, through broken security gates and across the common to where Balti sat on a park bench. By the time the vibration reached him it carried little of its original force. Music sounded further inside the building, thumping bass matching the hammers. Consciously he heard nothing. Just felt the gradually dimming pain in his skull and the sun on bare arms. The lion tattoo was worn and tired, a faded ghost of its original glory. The ink had been ground down over the past fifteen years and the Union Jack wrapped around the king of the Stamford Bridge savannah had lost the defining edges of its red, white and blue grooves. The skin had healed and absorbed the graffiti. It was two weeks since Balti had been on the receiving end of McDonald's anger and the breaks and bruises were still mending.

'Mind if I sit with you for a while son?' the man asked.

Balti shook his head. The old boy with the trolley had turned up at the same time the past couple of days. At first Balti was annoyed, but kept his mouth shut. It was a free world and they lived in a democratic society. One of the oldest on the planet. With the best judiciary and finest armed services, a sense of fair play and profound love of decency.

George wasn't as barmy as he first seemed. He was in his fifties with bleary labrador eyes and creased clothes. This morning he was clean-shaven. It was something the younger man had let slip. Normally he wouldn't go more than a day without a shave. He made sure he got his money's worth from the plastic razors. But the last couple of months he'd been going two, three, four days. His best mate had even accused him of turning into a hippy, a long-haired wanker who needed a good scrub. His hair needed seeing to, the number 2 crop filling out a bit. He was pushing past grade 4 and pissed off with his own laziness. He would visit the barber soon. But four quid was four quid and not to be thrown about when you were hard up.

That's what happened. You let your standards slip. Yet it didn't matter. Not really. That's what you realised. It changed your ideas being on the dole for months on end. Single mothers took a battering from politicians who screamed they were sponging off the state. You wondered if there was a bit of truth in the official hate campaign when you were in work looking after number one, no smoke without fire mentality. Like a kid would get herself up the duff for an extra tenner a week. The politicians got you thinking their way. Constant assault and battery. Assaulting your intelligence and battering you about the head soon as you hit the deck. But it brought you back to reality. Opened your eyes again. Got rid of the selfishness. Those cunts down the social, some useless but well-meaning, the others arrogant scum who only escaped a good kicking because you needed the button on the computer punched so you'd get your cheque on time.

'It's a fine day,' the man said. 'Feel that heat on your head. Nothing can beat a sunny day. It's easy to understand why they used to worship it on a day like today. There were sun-worshippers all over the world you know, and I'm not talking about boys and girls sitting on a beach trying to turn themselves into darkies. We make fun of the sun-worshippers now, but it's understandable really. Without that ball of burning gas none of this would exist. No photosynthesis, no energy, no life. We'd live in a world without colour if the sun ever burnt out. Think of that. Just consider it for a moment, won't you? We wouldn't last very long. We'd be nothing more than notions. Undeveloped ideas floating through the universe. That's all we boil down to at the end of the day anyway. Energy and notions. Some we call good, some we call bad. You have to take your pick, that's all. Make your choice and claim your reward. Please consider what I have just said.'

Balti raised his head and shaded his eyes. He was sweating and it was running under his eyelids. He couldn't get near the sun. George wore cheap sunglasses. Balti wasn't bothered. He knew the sun was up there and didn't need to burn a hole in his eyeball to prove the point. There was no need to blur your vision. He leant back on the bench. It had been dedicated to a Mrs Someone Or Other, the name of the dead woman cut by kids with no respect for memories.

It was easier having nothing to do when the weather was like this. In the winter you stayed in and kept your head down, a hedgehog buried in leaves, waiting for better days. Staying patient. Now Balti was outside making the most of the sun. It would've been nicer being on a beach somewhere, like the old boy said, but beggars couldn't choose. You took what you got and were grateful. What would the point be anyway, without a bit of cash in your pocket to go and have a drink now and then? He didn't want to listen to George wax lyrical about the nature of the cosmos, rambling on about the beauties of nature and the sheer wonderment of it all. He was on a different frequency. Probably didn't even hear the hammers. Balti wasn't slagging him off, because it was fair enough if he was on some head trip. It was just he'd rather enjoy the sun without a lecture, before a cloud came along and blocked the fucker out.

'Did you get down the bookies in time yesterday?' he asked.

'I lost a tenner,' George admitted. 'I lose a tenner a week. It's worth the expense and it's a hobby, getting to know the nags and the form. If I'd won I'd have been fifty quid better off. It's a chance you take, but it means you've always got something to look forward to. It gives you a stake in society. If it doesn't happen then that's fine by me. I could as easily spend it in the pub. The money's dead then. You piss it out half an hour later. With a horse you have a chance of getting something back.'

He moved his trolley level with the end of the bench. The contents rattled. He took out his pipe and tin and prepared a smoke. The smell of tobacco reminded Balti of McDonald. He looked at the trolley. The mesh was precisely sectioned and ordered. The old man lit up. He deserved a reward for his efforts. A patrol car slid along on the opposite side of the common, then turned into the flats. The banging stopped. Balti had noticed the old bill a lot since he'd been signing on. Like he was a crook. True, he nicked some car stereos now and then, just to tide himself over, when he was short of cash, but he wasn't making a habit of it. Breaking into cars was kid's stuff. If you were going thieving you should do it properly. If things got really tight, then he wasn't going to sit back and think of England while he got shafted by the exchange mechanism. He'd line something up and fight back good and proper. He was being looked down on. An expectation of guilt fired his way, that he didn't feel, not really, but which was force-fed and stuck in his throat.

'You have to have an aim,' George said, revelling in the contents of his pipe. 'That's what's wrong with the world today. Too many people drifting. There's no point coasting along hoping things will get better. They never do. That's one thing I've learnt from life. You have to go out and grab the opportunities. Spend to accumulate. It's important to try and better your situation, while at the same time doing something worthwhile for the community. Above all, though, it's vital to remember your place and your limitations. There's no point getting too big for your boots. Leave the more complicated problems to those with specialist skills.'

George was moving into a speech. Like he was on a platform. Balti waited in silence. It had been the same the last two days. He was worth listening to for a bit before he started losing the thread of what he was saying. It helped pass the time.

'Look at my situation, for instance. Not that I'm blowing my own trumpet. Far from it in fact. That's not my style. Anyone who knows me will back me up on this. It never has been and never will. I'm an average man of average means. I've suffered from severe depression and been treated by psychiatrists. They've fed me with drugs and recommended various therapies, but I feel no guilt. It happens to everyone at one time or another. Mental collapse. It's part of the human condition. I refuse to feel guilt. But that's because I have a purpose. And I also have hope. Always remember that young man. Whatever you might hear, I have a purpose and I have hope.'

Balti smiled as George leant forward, looking for the go-ahead. He sucked on his pipe and let his gaze scan the common, surveying the land stretching before him. There wasn't a great deal to see. The kid's playground and a few trees. Rows of houses to the left, flats to the right. The sound of hammers once more.

'People look at someone like me and what do they see? What do they imagine? I'll tell you. A well-turned out man of middle-age pushing a trolley around. What do they think? An eccentric perhaps. An environmentalist maybe. But I don't care about the labels people pin on me. I have a purpose. My own agenda. Simple in itself but a purpose nonetheless. My goal each morning is to fill my trolley with cans, as you can see. This goal has been achieved. Coca Cola, Pepsi, 7-Up, Fanta, Lucozade; whatever the name of the corporation involved, I will collect its cans and take them to be recycled, thereby saving resources and avoiding unnecessary exploitation of the planet's resources. You see, it's nothing dramatic when compared to famine and war, but it fills my time and if everyone was the same as me, doing their bit, then many of the problems of our society would be solved. Extend this attitude on to a global scale and the world would be at ease with itself. We would have an everlasting peace. I have my reasons. I move from A to B and follow a path. If everyone followed after me, what a society we could create. Just try and imagine it for a minute.'

Balti tried. He saw men in expensive suits pushing supermarket trolleys across the common. He imagined the Pope and other European leaders, mullahs and naked fakirs heaving their cargoes past the adventure playground. The dictators and owners of the multinationals were there as the kids on the slide took the piss raising their right hands in wanker signs. The arms manufacturers and monarchy. They were all there. Thousands of them. Following some nutter across the common, dodging the dog shit and squeezing over Mugger's Bridge, on their way to the recycling bins in the swimming pool car park.

'Serving the common good is not enough. I have learnt that. A man must have hope. Women also, in this age of equality between the sexes. One day I will strike gold. A nice winner on the ponies which is only the first part of my plan. I will spend this jackpot on the Lottery. This in turn will increase my probabilities of ultimate success. It is a simple mathematical equation. The more I spend on the Lottery, the better chance I have of becoming a winner. One day my number will come up. It is a simple chain reaction. I have calculated my chances of becoming a millionaire in this way. It is many millions to one, yet it remains a real possibility. It is a chance not to be spurned. The more I try, the shorter the odds. When the cheque is deposited in my account I will be satisfied. I will be comfortable for the rest of my life. That is how democracy works. I think you will agree that it is a fair system. We all have a chance to make a claim. There's no need to become angry and bitter at the system. After all, we are nothing in comparison.'

Balti thought George was a sad bastard. It was true what he said, in a roundabout way. Balti had been putting more than he should into the Lottery. It did give you something to dream about. That moment when the phone rang and there was some bingo master on the other end insisting you were no longer eligible for unemployment benefit, some smarmy showbiz cunt talking through clenched dentures clogged up on jealousy. Saying that you were a multi-millionaire with the tabloids hot on your trail. Would he want to remain anonymous? Fucking right he would. A cool ten million wouldn't make everything perfect, at least that's what they said, but it would certainly help. If news filtered out somehow, then bollocks, Balti had what it took to handle the pressure. It wound him up hearing people who'd come into a fortune moaning that the winning millions were making their lives a nightmare. Whoever said something like that had obviously never lived on forty-six quid a week. He was ready to be a winner. No problem. But George was a nutter. He really was. Balti wouldn't end up like that. He'd top himself first. Pushing a trolley around trying to save the world.

Balti thought about the first thing he'd do once the cheque was in his hand. He'd be straight down the bank to deposit his winnings. Wait for the expression on the face of the clerk. Next he'd be down the social to tell them he was signing off. It wouldn't piss him off standing in line wasting time because he'd make sure he got that cunt who'd forgotten to punch the button on the computer. The cheque hadn't come through and when he'd gone to find out where it was there was no respect, no apology, no nothing. This was with him being a customer now as well. A client. With a set of aims on the wall telling him how much they wanted to help you. One day he'd work out how much he'd paid into the system. He'd get the same person. See if he could get a bit of respect that way. It wouldn't matter how he became a millionaire, as long as he had the readies. Nobody thought that far. It was like if you had the money then there was some kind of divine justice about it all. Put a fiver in the collection bowl and you were away.

'I tell you this in confidence,' George shifted nearer, looking round and holding his pipe away from Balti so that the smoke from the burning tobacco didn't get in his eyes.

'When I was made redundant I pocketed a few bob. A couple of thousand pounds if you're interested. This is between you and me and mustn't go any further, because the kids round here, they'd be through the window and murder me in my bed for a tenner. Anyway, with careful management, using one light at a time at night and keeping the heating bills down to a minimum, even in the middle of winter, I've been able to hang on to a few hundred pounds. It's for a rainy day you understand. It's good to have a few hundred behind you in case of emergencies. You never know what's waiting around the corner. Plan ahead, that's my motto.'

Balti admired the self-discipline. George had been told by the doctors that his mood swings were related to the seasons. He'd talked quite openly about this on the first time they'd shared the bench. With the shorter daylight hours and overcast skies, he went into himself. He spoke little and remained indoors. When spring came he began to stir, his mood shifting full throttle when summer arrived. He was pure energy. Following the sun. The doctors had given their opinion. He was like the Aztecs, but without great pyramids and a need for human sacrifice. It was official.

'Well,' George said abruptly, after they'd been sitting in silence for five minutes watching the kids in the playground. 'I can't hang around here all day. There's work to be done. Must press on. I have to deliver these cans. I've given myself a deadline and it must be kept. Goodbye.'

Balti watched him go. He was a squat character with a balding head that would burn if he didn't get a hat sorted out. The sunglasses didn't match the overall impression. Balti thought about what he'd said about energy and sunlight. It was common sense really. You always felt better when the sun was shining. You had to have a bit of hope as well. Worshipping the sun was probably the obvious thing if you lived thousands of years ago out in the country and depended on the seasons for your food. In London all you needed was money in your pocket and a bit of respect. God was redundant these days. Signing on.

He stretched his arms and wiped the sweat from his face. He was losing weight. It was cutting down on the drink that did it. Not getting pissed as much as before. He was only able to manage thanks to the stereos. He wasn't going to hit rock bottom. If his Lottery numbers came up he'd be laughing the last five months off. Like George said, you had to invest to accumulate. He hadn't thought it would take this long to get work. He was bored. Well hacked off. Having all that time during the day got you thinking. It got you down and his motivation had gone. Dumped on his arse by four slags from South London. He'd thought it was the IRA that specialised in hammers, not Protestant militiamen. Time to think. It was deadly. You had to keep busy. Will slipped Balti a bit of blow now and then, specially after that night. It helped keep the lid on things. It had done him a lot of good if he was honest. But Balti wasn't going to get all emotional. He was logical. Holding back. Doing the right thing. Keeping his dignity.

Except when they got you down knocked off balance then there was no such thing as dignity because once your legs went you were another piece of shit just one more animal without a name without any say-so no tears no nothing just the violence that showed you up and when you thought about something like that like when you were tipped on your arse on your own manor round the corner from where you lived your whole life where you fucking grew up and walked and played when you were a kid so near home that if the telly was turned up loud enough or the music on it would've drained out the sound of the kicks and breaking bones the thud of hammers so near home kids getting murdered on the news youths going missing Pete never came home did he and it was mostly in the summer every year it seemed like it was more regular now living in the technological age when more and more you were plugged into the mains and pumped up with all that voltage pulsing through the skeleton up the backbone into the brain cracking across the room and all that radiation was deadly what was it Karen had said the other day about there being no strength in the unions any more telling him to think about the word union when they were arguing about Scargill and that and how the mines had been closed down just like Arthur had said part of a bigger plan maybe even worked out in advance a blueprint for a Britain where nobody knew their neighbours and there were no organisations to fight for your rights no solidarity with everyone scratching out their own boundaries even the street markets were being sterilised because the authorities wanted to erase community and turf the stalls off the street and they built shitty little shops and charged high rent selling mass-produced shit from China where the slave labour was cheaper free in fact so the capitalists were in bed with the communists and it was impossible to know who was shagging who and it all tied up because there was no such thing as unions in China and you weren't safe to walk down your own streets in London because they could do you any time they wanted the outsiders waiting late at night down a side street picking their moment when you were pissed and unable to fight back and the old bill could come into your home and the bailiffs would be banging on the door because that's what happened when you failed when you couldn't pay your way and it wasn't the old family firms and new-age gangsters and nutters who lost their furniture no fucking way like would the paper shufflers and magistrates put themselves out that was a laugh they were shitters who preferred the easy targets the honest people with their defences down not ready to fight just wanting to live quiet lives and it was always the small people the trolley-pushers of the world who did what they were told and swallowed their tablets and wanted to do something worthwhile give something back grateful for a bit of analysis from some stuck-up cunt who treated you like shit as he mended you but the sad old bastards never got the chance of a bit of dignity and it was the old and the young and the sick who got hammered because like Karen said it's those cunts in the cattle trucks were the ones who ended up stripped and naked because they couldn't fight back and Mango was right in that respect because he'd have been in with the guards looking after himself fuck everyone else like he was fucked and Balti wasn't going to be one of the losers even if it meant doing a bank one day and he could reason the thing out play the white man and say that McDonald was out of order with the verbal but he'd been more out of order kicking the cunt in the balls head gut a bit naughty that McDonald was working for a boss higher up and had a family to support and his own pressures getting his ear chewed job on the line investment and all that nonsense and if he was honest really straight with himself and there were times to be honest and times to lie and now Balti was being honest as honest as anyone ever could be but it didn't matter because he was telling the simple truth when he reminded himself that the thing wasn't over, not yet, no fucking chance pal.

Balti stopped walking and looked in the window of Will's shop. There was a picture of Jesus in a black frame. The face was dark, Arabic-looking, Jewish probably, but he knew it was Jesus because there were thorns in his head and blood gushing from the wounds. It was an ugly picture. There was no beauty. No warmth. It was cold pain and misery. Self-sacrifice the vicar would say. Balti couldn't imagine anyone paying good money for something like that. Especially seeing as how Jesus looked different. You had to be able to connect. There was a bowl full of cheap jewellery, odds and sods, and some bronze ornaments that were a bit more up-market with price tags turned the wrong way so he couldn't see what they said. He saw Will in the shop serving someone. When the woman turned to leave Balti entered. She carried a picture under her arm and he stood aside to let her pass. It was another Jesus. An identical twin in an identical black frame. They must've come from the same egg.

'Religion selling well?' Balti asked.

Will looked puzzled, then understood. He pointed to a row of frames. The first showed the same picture. They were part of a batch. He'd bought fifteen at a car boot sale in Wimbledon. Against the odds, they were selling. Once he sold two he started making a profit. He'd sold three already. It must've been the novelty value of seeing Jesus looking like that.

'You always think of Jesus as a white man, don't you,' Balti said, sitting down in an old armchair next to the big desk from which Will ran his business.

Will went to the chair behind the desk. It was worn wood but quality all the same. One day he would sand it down and give it a varnish. There was a big mixture of gear in the shop, something to satisfy most local tastes. It was junk with a touch of quality, according to the owner. The inside of the shop was musty and warm.

'That's because they make the pictures in their own image,' Will said. 'Jesus would've been dark, maybe black. Who knows. He wouldn't be Anglo-Saxon, that's for sure. No blond hair and blue eyes for someone from the desert.'

'Still looks odd though, seeing Jesus H looking like an Arab or yiddo.'

'The Nazis used to teach their kids that Jesus was part of an Aryan tribe that took civilisation to the Middle East and that they were slaughtered by the Jews. If you're taught that you're going to believe it, aren't you? We always believe what we're told, just depends on who does the telling. But we think like that any way. Make everything fit in. Draw him like he's a Viking or something.'

'It doesn't matter, does it,' Balti said. 'I mean, whatever he looked like it's what he said that counts. I know it's supposed to be history and all that, but a lot of it's made up isn't it, to suit the kings and the censors. Mind you, I don't know what he had to say anyway. There was the Good Samaritan. Dead man laying at the side of the road. Hartlepool fan comes along and eats the heart. Liverpool fan turns up and eats the liver. Arsenal fan arrives, but he's not hungry. Remember that one?'

'I remember. You still wouldn't go thieving from a church though, would you?'

'Don't know really. Probably would if you were desperate. I was thinking that walking over. If I was really skint, right down the bottom, I'd do a bank. I think I would anyway. Maybe not. Probably bottle it. No-one wants to go down do they? Don't suppose I'd do a church. No reason why I shouldn't. Don't suppose they've got anything worth nicking. I'll stick to petty crime, breaking windows and thieving stereos.'

'Most people wouldn't rob a church. It's a built-in fear of retribution.'

'Fear of getting nicked more like.'

'The magistrates would make sure you paid the penalty. They're all in on it. The old bill, vicars, magistrates, lawyers, judges, journalists, big business, politicians, necrophiliacs. It's a self-help club.'

'Divine retribution.'

'I reckon you can play at being God in two major ways,' Will said, putting his feet on the desk and skinning up. 'Either you use chemicals to get up there with the superhumans, or you're born with a silver spoon up your arse. Trouble is, the chemicals are mostly man-made so you end up with the after effects, whereas in the old days you could find something natural and, provided there were no witch-hunts on, you could get into the flow. Now it's different. More mechanical. Material society with a materialist religion. Trick is, you get the power, with the old bill backing you up, and you can play God that way. A certain kind of God. Lots of wrath and indignation. One that likes healthy profit margins.'

'You were alright with the old witch-hunts if you were a bloke though, weren't you?' Balti said. 'It was the women that got burnt and drowned. Like, which way do you want to die, darling?'

Balti thought about it for a minute as Will concentrated on his task. When he was young he'd wanted to be part of a midfield trio that had included Ray Wilkins and Garry Stanley. That was as near as he wanted to get to immortality. To be on the pitch bossing the game with Ray and Garry. He thought about that sort of stuff even now. He supposed most blokes did. In that world it didn't matter how old you were, or how unfit. It didn't matter if you couldn't kick a ball straight or you were the same age as those players approaching the end of their careers. He wondered what Harry thought about. He'd have to ask him later when he got back from work. Probably playing up front with Steve Finnieston keeping Kenny Swain out of the side. If Eddie McCreadie hadn't been forced out of the club then who knows? Balti remembered how upset he'd been when McCreadie left. He'd heard that Eddie was somewhere in the States. A great man.

It was the glamorous way out of the gutter. Running round kicking a ball. Either that or doing a Frank Bruno. Keeping yourself fit and building up for the big fights. Nobody pushed Big Frank about. He demanded respect. And if you were in that midfield with Wilkins and Stanley, then you were major as well. He didn't know what career he'd choose if he had his time again. Midfield genius or heavyweight champion. Probably the football. There was less chance of brain damage that way, though he'd read something about footballers who headed the ball a lot, how it rocked the brain on its suspension. In midfield you could keep your head and play it on the deck. That's what everyone wanted to see. Creative football. Seeing The Dutchman in action showed how far the English game had to go. The young kids coming through were lucky to work with someone like that. Funny, you got past a certain age and suddenly you looked at the young lads, the nutters and that, or the footballers, that's what he was thinking about, and they were like school kids, all wound up doing things wrong, getting booked, getting nicked.

Mind you, it was all in the hormones. He thought science had proved something along those lines. Birds didn't cause the problems that men did. If women were in charge things would be a lot better. Mango was always going on about the first female prime minister. How she'd done the business, in the Falklands and for the economy. But for blokes it was a time of life. He had to admit they'd been a bit naughty till their late twenties. Then they'd slowed down and the new talent came through all larey and tearing up. But you still had respect because you'd been there already. Nobody was going to give you unnecessary aggro. That's what it had been like at football. Things had changed a lot and the new mobs coming through were smaller in number but more vicious. He couldn't work people like that out really. Having a punch-up at football had just been part of the Saturday landscape till the politicians got involved. The new era was fine by Balti. He wanted to watch the football again. His second childhood had come around, though he didn't mind the odd punch-up for a classic fixture. But using knives, that was out of order. It was only a bit of fun, after all.

When you had time on your hands you thought about the past, but he also found himself shooting off into the future. It was easy to reinvent the past, but it wasn't so good somehow. There was always the truth nagging at you, or at least a version of that truth, telling you it wasn't that great. It was okay playing about with history, but when you planned the future you could be anything you wanted. The more you thought, the more unreal you could become. That's probably what was happening with that sad old cunt with the trolley. One minute he was stuck in the past ready to top himself, all the missed opportunities, dead loves, whatever, the next the sun starts shining and he's off, making plans and marching forward. But the thing was, whatever extreme he was into, there was always the chance of a controller in a white coat lining up an upper or downer trying to bring him back into the middle. It was like Harry was saying about the colour in his dreams. The past was usually black and white but confused, whereas the future was all about new technology and crystal clear vision. It was mind games. You went through life keeping busy, getting pissed and that, doing a few substances, but once you had time to kill your mind was straight into one.

Balti had a puff. Sweet as a nut. Carefree whoever he may be. With Will shutting up shop for a while so they could relax. They sat buried in old furniture and prints, a kid's doll sitting on a shelf, horse brasses and rows of yellowing books. There was some good gear knocking about. If you knew what you were doing and had ambition you could make a packet. Balti wondered if his mate needed an assistant. He doubted it. Kept quiet. Business was slack. Enough for Will to keep ticking over but that was all. Will was a diamond now Balti came to think about it. He'd always had that bit extra with the music and slower pace, and now he had Karen as well. They were made for each other. He wondered if one day he'd find someone like that. It would be nice. Harry was a sound bloke, another diamond, but he didn't want to spend the rest of his life shacked up with the cunt. There came a time when you had to move on. Find a woman and that.

Harry had been acting a bit strange. Balti couldn't work it out. At first he'd thought it was to do with him signing on, but reasoned it out and had even asked his mate up front. It wasn't that. Why should it be? He wasn't a beggar. He stood on his own two feet. There was something though. He couldn't work it out. Maybe he was going through a change. Everyone had slow periods. It would be alright. He was better than a brother.

'Me and Karen are moving in together,' Will said, after they'd decided to go down Andy's Cafe, the door locked behind them as they walked down the street.

'You leaving the flat then?' Balti asked, Will nodding. 'Why doesn't she move in with you. It's big enough for both of you. Just clear out some of the shit round there and you could turn it into a barracks, you've got so much room.'

'She wants to start somewhere fresh. You know. A new beginning. Something of our own. You know how women are. They get their minds set and they like the romance. I can see her point. I mean I wouldn't want to move in somewhere she's lived. You'd always feel like the lodger. It's better off starting together, then everything's equal. Nobody's in charge.'

'Do me a favour. She wears the trousers. Not that I'm slagging it off or anything, but Karen's in charge. Everyone knows that. You've got to put your foot down or the woman will run the show.'

'It's half each.'

'Alright, whatever you say. But someone's going to be the boss, aren't they? It's only natural.'

Will shook his head. Balti was winding him up. He did tend to go along with what Karen said a lot of the time, but that was because he wasn't bothered. She was sharper than he was. He hated the idea of being hen-pecked.

They ordered at the counter and sat by the window. The fruit and veg market was busy, Phil from The Unity on his stall outside. He waved when he noticed them, serving a couple of old women. Balti could never understand the bloke. He was one of the old-time Cockney Reds, born and bred in West London but choosing to follow Man United around the country. Where was the sense in that? His main day had been in the Seventies when Tommy Docherty had been the manager with crowds near-enough sixty thousand. There'd been regular aggro between the Cockney Reds and other sections of the Stretford End. He didn't go much these days, being older and everything, a time and a place. He preferred remembering Old Trafford how it had been in its heyday, rather than the satellite accessory he felt it had become. He went to a few aways and slagged off the club for making the ground a home for part-timers. When the club messed up then the thousands like him wouldn't be going back to fill the gaps.

Two teas arrived and Balti thought of the 4–0 Cup Final. It was funny, because they'd been gutted after the game, but it didn't bother him now. Just getting to a Cup Final had been a bonus, seeing the teams come out and everything, even though Wembley was a shit ground and thirty-five quid for a length of plastic with no back was a lot to pay. They saw you coming and shafted your loyalty. And there was no Vaseline on hand to ease the pain. At the end of the day though Chelsea had given Man U a good hiding outside the ground before the game. They'd been coming up the hill lobbing bottles at United who legged it, hid inside the pubs, or tried to have a go back but ended up getting a kicking. It was a good day out, Harry smacking some cunt with a flag, Tommy Johnson and his mates going mental. Balti was honest enough to say he'd rather Chelsea were in charge outside the ground than on the pitch. Getting a pasting off someone was the end of the world. You didn't want people taking the piss. Chelsea had a reputation to maintain. Balti had his self-respect. That fucking cunt McDonald.

'You hungry then?' Will asked, when the food arrived, Balti's plate loaded with sausage, bacon, beans, chips, toast.

'I'm getting too thin. I'm down to fourteen stone. People will start thinking I'm dying of Aids if I'm not careful.'

'Not for a while they won't,' Will said as he put ketchup on his plate only for the top to come off and half cover his chips. He put the lid back on and did his best to use it up.

'So what are you going to do about Slaughter then?' Will asked, once they'd finished and ordered more tea.

'What do you mean?'

'About the work he's offering,' Will said, seeing the expression on Balti's face. 'You told me Friday night when you were pissed. Dangerous talk costs lives.'

'I don't know,' Balti admitted. 'I mean on the one hand it's a chance to make the kind of money I'm not going to get anywhere else. On the other, I don't fancy ten years banged up. Depends on what it is, but once he tells me I'm going to have to say yes, aren't I? I mean, Slaughter's not going to want too many people knowing what he's doing.'

'You should leave it alone. That's what I reckon. Anything he does is going to be dodgy. He could tell you one thing, then the next minute you're too far in, stuck in some bank with Slaughter waving a shooter around. It's not worth the risk. Being skint's not as bad as killing some bank clerk.'

'I don't know. Maybe it's worth taking a chance sometimes.'

'What if he does that though. Takes his machete along and does someone. Or he gets a shotgun and the old bill turn up. It's not just him is it? Everyone goes down. ABH, murder, who knows. Nothing's worth going down for.'

'Say I made a couple of grand, maybe more. I'd be able to live well in the summer till I get something sorted out. Maybe it's worth it.'

'You go down and you'll crack up. What are you going to do for five years, maybe twenty, who knows. You go in and come out an old man. Eat, sleep, shit, piss, wank, get a bruising. What sort of life is that? You'd be better off dead.'

Balti thought about it as he sipped the hot tea. He might be a bit out of order now and then, but he wasn't a robber. Not that it was the rights and wrongs or anything like that, but Slaughter stunk of trouble. There was a kind of justice about it in a way, doing a bank or building society, because they were the system that ground you down, everyone wanting their share. They charged high interest and milked people. Going in there with a shooter would be alright. Then he thought straight. It was like McDonald. He was the small man. The representative. Those behind the counter weren't getting anything out of the interest rates and repossessions. Just earning a crust. It wasn't their fault. Why should they get their heads shot off? Why should McDonald get a kicking? Balti knew why. Because he didn't show respect. There was no excuse for that. The same as the cocky bastards behind the window in a bank. Except most of them were alright. And that cunt down the social. The one who'd forgotten to punch the button. He deserved a slap but there again he was nothing. Earnt fuck all for a boring job. But he was stroppy. That was the problem. It was the arrogance that got to you. Who the fuck were these little people holding the purse strings? But he would listen to his old mate Will.

'You look at the crack dealers and the bank robbers and everything,' Will said, 'and they're just small-time Mangoes, except that they operate in a different field. You get caught selling crack and they'll do you. The courts won't hang about. There's no glory.'

'But you do a bank or something like that and you're getting at those bastards, aren't you?' Balti said.

'You could even dress up in green tights and pretend you're Robin Hood. It's not worth it. Leave it. If you want to borrow five hundred quid till you're set up again, ask. Behave yourself in the meantime, that's all. Poor's in the head.'

When they left the cafe the sunlight had faded. Will went back to work and Balti headed home. He stopped in The Unity for a pint. He was surprised to see Carter sitting at the bar talking with Denise. She gave him a free pint with Len out for the day and he pulled up a stool. Carter was pissed, his eyes following her arse down the bar.

'She's a good-looking woman,' he said, lowering his voice. 'Looks better naked, I can tell you.'

He winked and Balti put two and two together. The silly cunt was taking a risk. Slaughter would kill them both. Maybe start on the rest of the Sex Division as well, if he thought they knew.

'Three points, but don't tell the others. I don't want word getting round. I put it down as that bird from Blues last week. She wasn't interested. But I counted her as Denise. No need to let points go to waste, is there?'

Balti agreed. Smiled. Said nothing.

'She wants me to take pictures of her. You know what I mean. But what's the point. Who am I going to show them to? I reckon she's pushing it. Send one to Slaughter in the post. She's dangerous. One word out of place and I'm dead. We're both dead. You're the only person I've told, so keep your mouth shut.'

Balti nodded. Slaughter was a headcase. There was no way he was doing a job with the bloke. There were more important things in life. You could be poor but have respect. It depended how you looked at things. Will understood that, though there were the basics to contend with. It was the fear of going down that made up his mind. You had to be a nutter to go that far. Those were the real hard men. He had respect for blokes who could push things. You had to be a bit mental and not give a fuck what the old bill did to you. That was how they kept you in line. Sheer violence kept the thing going. The old bastards who ran the show were nothing without the army, police, secret service. Take them away and any cunt could walk in, have his say, blow them in half. You were better off sticking to small scale thieving. Nobody cared about that. He'd work. Sooner or later. Earn a living and take his place in the scheme of things.

He tried to think how long it was since he'd last had sex. Must've been about eight months. He had to get his leg over soon. That would do him good. Maybe he'd borrow the cash off Will and go with the rest of the lads to Amsterdam. That's what he'd do. They said they'd chip in and pay his way, but he had his pride. At least taking a loan made the money his own.

Carter was off to Spain for a couple of weeks in the summer, but whispered to Balti that it was only half a holiday. You might as well be at home, and the birds weren't all that. Amsterdam was really going overseas, though they might have to put it off for a while because Mango reckoned the most he could get through his card was a trip to the seaside. They'd decided on Blackpool. Not Amsterdam. But it was better than nothing. Next year they'd go to Amsterdam. Next year Balti my old mate.

Denise came back down the bar and after she'd had a quick glance over her shoulder at the old boys at the other end of the counter, involved in some argument about the number of Asians who'd died building the Burma-Thailand railway, she refilled Balti's pint. She was more friendly now, with nobody about, and even if Carter hadn't let him in on the secret Balti would probably have guessed from the way she looked at him. Balti settled into his seat and started thinking about Blackpool as Denise told them how Slaughter had got himself nicked the night before for drunk driving. It was lucky he'd left his machete at home. Otherwise he'd be getting done for murder as well.

BEANO

THE JAG WAS spotless. Cleaned in one of those valet efforts staffed by Eyeties. It was a flash motor, nobody would argue about that, but there was nothing flash about Mango's CD collection. A right pile of shit. Luckily there was a cassette player and Will had done them proud, saving their souls and delivering a decent soundtrack. They were humming north with Harry's electric soup doing its duty, fucking up their heads, the man himself in the back seat with Balti and Carter, half-asleep.

Will was up front next to Captain Mango, playing the selector, and it was classics all the way. The Jam were stuck on the Underground as the Sex Division ran a bombing mission over Birmingham, the throb of the engine racing straight up Mango's right leg and tickling his bollocks. Will waited for the song to fade and slipped in a collection that included the Blaggers ITA, bringing the tradition forward with a bang. This Jag was no ramraider special though, not the kind of Made In Britain topnotch precision engineering model some hip-hop cunt was going to drive through the off-licence window. Not with the anti-theft gear Mango had splashed out on anyway. No fucking way.

The lads in the back were getting pissed quick enough on the electric soup, food of the people, Mango a bit nervous in case one of those mugs behind him decided to puke up, and Harry thought he'd have a laugh telling the cocky cunt at the controls, Captain Scarlet, that he felt sick, with his guts about to do the old heave-ho. He didn't know whether he could control those saveloys from last night, the pickled onions, wally and chips, that he might have to spread his breakfast over the upholstery as well, a bacon and eggs special.

411

Mango looked in the mirror and caught the fat boy's eye and told him, all serious like, with a cutting edge Harry and the rest of the lads hadn't heard before, real Jack The Ripper stuff, bit spastic, a tang that made them sit up and take notice – Mango saying that if Harry messed up the Jag he'd pull on to the hard shoulder and leave you behind you tart, this is my fucking car and I'm paying the fucking petrol. I'll drop you off and keep going and there's no U-turns on the motorway so I won't be coming back. I'm doing you a favour and there's no second chance. Behave yourself.

Harry wanted to get to Blackpool in comfort, enjoy the ride, the suspension and everything, not hitch-hike on the hard shoulder choking to death. He wanted to enjoy the weekend. Have a laugh. Maybe get his end away. That was only natural. I was joking Mango mate, where's your sense of humour you miserable git. To play things safe Mango pulled into the next services and parked up, the lads going for a piss, in another world now, an outpost in the wilderness.

This was the real England, not London, that was full of blacks and browns and yellows and all the colours in the rainbow, with every food and type of music, a cockney bazaar where the cockneys were a minority from Bengal. No, this was flat-cap land. Up North. Where they fancied their pigeons and shagged their whippets, five pence a pint and mushy-pea butties for dinner, four-bedroom houses that cost five grand and mining villages living with a hundred per cent unemployment. Balti nicked a couple of CDs from one of the shops for a laugh. He bought himself a chocolate bar that he scoffed in the car park, then got back in the Jag with the others, Mango sweet again, back in command, commander of his jet fighter – precision machine.

They quickly picked up speed filtering back on to the M6, putting his foot down knowing he could do naught-to-sixty in 7.9 seconds, six in-line cylinders, thirty grand's worth of XJ6 3.2 Sport sex on wheels, hardcore British technology second to none. And it was patriotic to buy British. Fly the flag. He was laughing again enjoying some old-time pre-revolution Ted Heath generosity, helping people out, the kindly benefactor,

Will skinning up sitting back soothing things, Balti in the back taking the CDs from inside his jacket, one a Country and Western greatest hits effort with a Dolly Parton lookalike on the front. Look at the lungs on that lads. The other a marching band with soldiers in busbies and red tunics, lots of brass on display. Must be hot, the silly sods, walking to slaughter.

Will was coming under pressure from the Bollock Brothers and Carter, the sex machine wide awake now and knocking back a can of Fosters, telling Harry that the electric soup would do him no favours. They wanted to listen to Land Of Hope And Glory, but Will said in a minute, hang about, and they soon forgot about the marching band because Carter was telling the lads that if they didn't service something this weekend he was giving up on them. Non-believers you lot.

Northern birds were alright and didn't pose like the women down south. Salt-of-the-earth, high-heeled tarts hunting in mobs twenty and thirty strong, inflated tits out on the counter. Girls who were ready for a good time, and all Northerners were like you saw on *Coronation Street*. But it wasn't a patch on *EastEnders*, though Carter reckoned the Mitchells were bottle merchants because you never saw them getting stuck in, not really, it was all front, and they were always mouthing off. Said it was like West Ham used to be, remember that time they came in Gate 13 and Chelsea gave them a pasting, and Balti asked the shag machine if that was the time he got his nose broken when some ICF cunt nutted him, and Carter shut up because it was and West Ham had the nous to get up the ground early and buy tickets for that area of the East Stand where they knew Chelsea's main faces would be.

Harry weighed in saying leave it out, I hate West Ham as well but you wouldn't have seen the Mitchells anywhere near the ICF, and Will was passing the puff round, Mango shaking his head keeping himself on the straight and narrow because he was doing the driving and the Jag was thirty grand's worth of sheer automobile heaven, cruising at ninety miles per hour, working himself into the machine, feeling the energy. The rest of the chaps should show a bit of respect for the power and the glory, a

Best Of British factory working overtime turning out the purest kind of machine.

They gave wanker salutes to the Liverpool and Manchester signs, all those games at Anfield and Goodison, Old Trafford and Maine Road, ice-cold Saturdays playing Oldham, on their way to Blackpool Friday afternoon. It wasn't much further now as the miles clocked up and then they were pulling off the motorway rolling towards the town centre where Mango had lined up a place on the seafront. He was fiddling it on his expenses, feeding the accounts department a line. Amsterdam would have to wait. He could only do so much. And the rest of the Sex Division wondered where they'd end up, whether Mango was just giving it the big one again flashing his credit card around, if he really had the say-so, but the bloke was a con artist of sorts and they had to agree that he was a good bloke sharing the wealth around like that. Not his own, mind, but ready to use WorldView for his old mates.

They were watching the streets. Houses plastered in bed and breakfast signs. Polished toytown brickwork. Wondering if they were going to end up buried in one of the terraces. Blue-rinse grannies and Glasgow bouncers sick on candyfloss. Then Mango was pulling up outside a smart hotel. A real quality effort it was too, and they were standing in the entrance, the foyer, whatever the fuck it was called. Mango steamed right in with his WorldView confidence, no problem, and the staff even wore uniforms.

None of the lads had stayed in a place like this before, except Mango of course, but they didn't feel out of place because corporate cards counted and made you something with the weight of a major firm behind you. Numbers mattered. They were going up in the lift with some spotty Lancashire youth showing them the way. They had two rooms side by side. Carter was in with Mango, and Will was sharing with Harry and Balti.

They dumped their gear and Mango went into the attached bathroom to wash his face in the sink, taking his time with the hot water and soap. Leaving the door open, Carter throwing his bag on to the bed nearest the window. The old sex machine magic was bound to rub off. Mango was tired. Carter sticking his head round the door – you fucking ponce, what's the matter with you, wasting time when we could be down the bar having a few sherbets. Mango was brushing his teeth – don't worry about your breath you slag, because you won't get near a bird tonight – and he laughed it off, but Mango was hoping he'd pull.

It was alright knocking off pros, a simple business transaction with both parties happy, but he'd like something for free once in a while. A bird who didn't need a backhander to open her legs. Genuine affection, or at least attraction. Shafting whores all the time made him feel ugly. As though he was rotten inside. He was in the mood, with WorldView left behind for a few days, but in a strange way he wasn't too bothered about sex, there wasn't the same frantic need to dip his winkie, because once you got out of the City, outside London, things eased and you could do whatever you fucking wanted. Blackpool was his first decent break for ages and he wanted to forget everything and relax.

The Sex Division were soon back in the lift on their way downstairs, piling into a bar that was nicely done up with big old paintings on the walls and a new carpet on the floor. There was some greasy scouser behind the bar pouring pints. They all hated scousers, because you had to if you came from London. It was written down somewhere in the rules. Everyone except Will that was, because he didn't hate anyone. But the scouser was alright when he came over and started talking. He had a sense of humour to go with his Terry McDermott tash, because they asked him where Kevin Keegan was and he said upstairs clearing one of the bogs that was blocked, making the most of the dodgy haircut. There was no preferential treatment in Blackpool. That fucking toilet needed clearing and King Kev was the man for the job.

They liked the barman straight off, so that meant they hated all scousers except the one they'd spoken to, and that was probably in the rules somewhere as well. They moved over to a table by the window, looking out to sea. The waves were grey and white in the drizzle that had started, the sun bright through grey clouds, a slow-motion strobe effect, the wind kicking-up and battering a tram carrying a fucking great Goofy cut-out. They all laughed. There was a word for it. They sat back and watched Goofy vanish.

This was the life. A chance to have a drink and breathe in healthy air, even if it was in the bar. The first round went down quick enough, Will ordering more lager. The prices were cheaper than in London even though this was a hotel so fuck knows what it's going to be like down the town lads, Carter lifting the glass to his lips. These Northerners are thick as shit, don't forget we're going back in time, that Jag's a fucking time machine.

They were kids on a beano, Will telling the others he was going to phone Karen to let her know they'd arrived safe and sound. They started taking the piss as he went to the end of the bar, Terry Mac moving the phone over so he could sit on a stool and take his time and have a bit of privacy. Will talked for a bit and Carter, Harry, Balti, Mango were having a good laugh, taking the piss something chronic, ball and chain and all the normal stuff. Who the fuck is it wearing the trousers? Look at that thumb print between his eyes. His head's nodding like he's giving Mango a blow job. Fuck off you cunt. Karen was a cracker though. Shame she didn't have any sisters. What about her mates? That was one to think about when they got back. Nice one Balti. Fuck off Carter, it was my idea, you keep your hands off. Don't want you infecting her with a tropical disease.

Will came back and took his glass, keeping up, and one or two older couples were coming into the bar and ordering from Macca and his dodgy tash. A husband and wife sat by the window, nodding as they passed, and the Sex Division had to admit that Northerners were friendly.

It wasn't just the mobbed-up brass either. They admitted this on the quiet, because you had to maintain the pecking order. An old geezer, a right northern slaphead, and his wife, a big postcard woman rabbiting on the whole time, sat at the next table. The slaphead took a shine to Carter and asked him who they supported. Were they into the football? When he heard Chelsea he laughed and called them a bunch of hooligans, because he read his papers and stereotypes were essential to the nation's well-being.

He was a Leeds man himself and had never forgiven Chelsea for beating them in the Cup Final in 1970. Will chipped in, saying Webby's at Brentford now, and the old boy went into one about Tony Yeboah and how Leeds hated Man United. Leeds were Yorkshire and Man U Lancashire. That was enough. It would've been interesting to know some of the history, but that kind of thing just kept going century after century, and then it was ingrained, and then it was all down to Eric Cantona.

When the Sex Division membership left the hotel they were on a roll. The electric soup had worn off, but the lager gave them a kick. They laughed at Goofy, the silly cunt, back and forward all day, and went in a big fish shop on the seafront. It was full of Jock tattoos and families, but there was enough room for everyone. The batter was crisp and the chips well done. They ordered and ate quickly, ready for a decent drink.

They had a couple of pints in a pub full of old-timers, then went for a wander along the front, legs eleven and intergalactic shoot-em-ups booming from speakers, the Sex Division standing back laughing as a mob of youths pegged it round the corner, a bit of a row going on, followed by a bigger mob, blokes done up in suits and ties like Northerners dress when they're out for the night, the dozy cunts. They were well thick the old Yorkshiremen, or were they from Lancashire, it was one of the two, and the locals would've been well pissed off if they'd heard that one, because there was the Wars Of The Roses to think about. Pikes and axes thick with blood. Men had died in the fields fighting for their county, and there were a few bottles flying without much chance of contact, a lot of shouting, the sound of breaking glass, and then it was all over and it was more than Leeds against Man U. Will would ask the Leeds man if they saw him again. Get some details.

It was like they didn't belong. Just spectators watching someone else's battle. But they didn't give a toss either way, with a gentle breeze blowing in off the sea, quite nice really, and

Balti said Ireland was straight ahead over the horizon some-where in the dark, and McDonald would be on his way home for a bit of rehabilitation in his Belfast slum soon enough. That was the best place for him with ten pounds of semtex shoved up his arse.

The Blackpool Tower was in front of them now, and there were crowds of people everywhere, a bingo town full of grannies. There was a bit of crumpet about as well, but so many Jocks you could've been in Scotland. Big extended families wandering around loaded up with donuts and the smell of chips in the air mixing with candyfloss.

They saw a decent-looking pub that was packed solid and were soon inside on their way to the bar, right off the Bollock Brothers chatting up a couple of birds, blondes done up very nice thank you with their tits stuffed tight inside boob tubes, heavily painted faces and sparkling eyes. They were friendly with it. Well fucking friendly. Drinking pints. And the rest of the lads were talking with some of King Billy's boys when Carter mentioned Chelsea, and the Rangers boys were sound enough, well fucking pissed, singing some battle hymn telling Will how much they hated the Fenian bastards, how Bobby Sands could do with a chicken supper, the dirty Fenian fucker, and Will wasn't going to argue the toss. He wouldn't get involved in a discussion on Ireland because he didn't fancy getting glassed.

A DJ sat in the shadows at the far end of the pub, togged-up bouncers on the door, a view through the bodies and glass to the sea, and Will was gagging for a decent drink, the same as Mango who was smiling and looking all laid back. Even Carter didn't seem that bothered about pulling, and the time was going fast, getting stuck into the lager-lager-lager, and before they knew it the fat northern cunt behind the bar was calling last orders, just like the fat London cunts at home, no fucking difference. They were tired, rolling back to the hotel with the two birds who'd linked arms with Balti and Harry on the seafront, drunks wandering around talking to themselves, people shouting and laughing at each other, laughing at two drunks trying to smack each other but swinging and missing and ending up on the ground.

. They piled into the hotel bar lining up the drinks and Carter was apologising to Terry behind the counter for that game when Newcastle got thumped 6–0 at the Bridge and every time McDermott went near Gate 13 they'd been offering him ciggies and it was like Gazza and the Mars bars, winding them up, they earnt a decent enough wage to suffer a bit of verbal, and Terry said not to worry, it was all part of the game, he'd laughed all the way to the bank, and they were back by the window, same table, getting stuck into the drink, and then Mango asked where the Bollock Brothers had gone and the lads realised they'd pissed off upstairs.

Who cared anyway? That geezer from Leeds had appeared and was winding them up, and his wife was howling, red in the face, such a dark red that Will thought she was ready to pop but kept quiet, at least he hoped he did, he could feel the hangover coming, and above them Balti was turning off the light, with the door locked – Will would have to sleep next door – and he took off his trainers and jeans and was between the sheets and he could hear Harry and the other girl whispering in the next bed.

The bird Balti was with had his knob out and he hoped he wasn't too pissed, too drunk to fuck, so he ran his hand back from her pants and made sure, the old confidence returning, and then he hoped he wasn't going to blurt before he got inside because it had been a long time, too fucking long, and he had her pants down, bra off, naked now except for her stockings, and Harry was taking his time, his head spinning round and round the mulberry bush and the same ideas were there, and then he heard his mate in the next bed banging away and the bird moaning, the cunt didn't waste any time, and the girl was whispering about using a rubber, just my fucking luck to pull a sensible bird, and then she was sitting up and the curtains were so thick they couldn't see a thing, so she turned on the lamp by the bed and the first thing Harry saw was Balti on the job.

It was a right royal turn off that, and the dream came back, hitting in a massive rush, and the thought of that flabby arse made him laugh because he was relieved. He'd been wondering about that dream of his, why he'd dreamt of his mate's arse. The experts on the telly said that you didn't even know sometimes if you were a bum bandit. They said that social pressures made you keep that kind of thing buried. It had been on his mind for a while. Imagine that, Harry a shirt-lifter. Horrible. It had been worrying him, and Balti had even asked if there was something wrong, and now he knew it was just a premonition of this very moment.

Everything emptied from Harry's mind. He was in the clear and wasn't going to end up a queer. Thank fuck for that. But Balti didn't like performing in public; what the fuck are you doing the fat cunt said and the bird underneath him pulled the covers up, the one with Harry saying sorry, but there's no need to swear is there love, reaching for her handbag and then turning off the light.

She pushed Harry back on to the bed and he heard her messing about and then felt her slipping the rubber on his knob, and before he could sing IF SHE DON'T COME, I'LL TICKLE HER BUM, WITH A LUMP OF CELERY, she was on top of him doing the work, hanging her tits in his face and he reckoned that if he was going to die then this was the way he wanted to go. Her body was so warm and she smelt good, smelt of rum and perfume, pure heaven, this was the kind of dream that was better than real life.

Downstairs in the bar Leeds was telling Carter what a great player Eddie Gray had been. A couple of younger men came over with Leeds crests cut into their arms. They were the same age. Big bastards who asked if the London boys were at the 5–0 thrashing Leeds got that year they smashed up the scoreboard and Chelsea tried to get in the North Stand. Carter remembered well enough, with the old bill steaming into the Leeds mob, Chelsea on the pitch at the final whistle trying to get in as well but forced back by the truncheons, then that time up at Elland Road when Chelsea had gone mental outside, but Mango was turning off the football.

One of them was a mechanic and somehow they were talking about Mercs, and everything was sweet, having a good laugh, with Will getting chatted up by the old woman wondering again how a face could get that red. She loved Elvis and she'd been to Graceland in Memphis with her husband. Did he know that you could buy an Elvis model that was battery-operated and would move around? It's true dear. Her husband leant forward and said Memphis was alright, but the black areas were very poor, the younger Leeds saying it sounded like Chapel-town because there were too many niggers in Leeds, and you went to Bradford and you might as well be in Mecca. Combat 18 would sort things out, and they asked Carter about the C18 presence at Chelsea, Carter saying he didn't know about all that political stuff.

Will felt sick from the drink and went to the bogs. He stuck his fingers down his throat. Nothing happened. Back in the bar he got the keys off Mango and went upstairs, banging into walls, falling into Mango and Carter's room, nicking a pillow off one of the beds. He crashed out on the floor, felt himself spinning for a while and then everything went blank.

Next morning when Will woke up his head was fine, and there was a narrow ray of light hitting the wall next to him, a laser threatening to burn through to the next room for a view of Harry and Balti, the sound of Mango snoring, Will turning his head and going back to sleep. A second later the curtains were open and Carter was scrubbed and ready for the day ahead, telling Will it was eleven and Mango wouldn't budge, wanted to sleep a bit longer. Mango said he was fucked, and Carter said fair enough mate, I'm going down for breakfast. Will said he'd catch him up.

Carter walked into the restaurant and found the others half way through a quality breakfast with two women opposite. He remembered last night, sitting down ordering orange juice, bacon, sausages, eggs, tomatoes, toast, coffee. The birds were scousers. He hadn't realised they were from Liverpool. They weren't bad either, the one with Harry carrying a healthy pair of lungs if he was honest. They were having a laugh going on about some techno club they'd been to a couple of nights before where they'd done well, five Es each and the neurotransmitters rioting, and maybe they'd see the lads later down the same pub tonight, about nine, because they had to meet a friend.

They left money for the food and pissed off, and Carter wanted to know the scores. It was about time the Sex Division got into gear again, with the boys off the mark and looking well pleased with themselves, well fucking pleased. Two points each. But more than that it was a good feeling after so long wanking, and there was Carter on thirty-eight points with Mango on fifteen, or was it sixteen, they'd have to check that one, but at least they were off the mark. Carter said they should get down that boozer tonight and pick up a bonus point, who knows, maybe two, and Balti smiled and knocked back the coffee, sweet as a nut, out of the chicken run, away from London, free as the proverbial.

Harry had slept a deep sleep without the sniff of a dream, and it was great sitting there listening to Carter, thinking how that bird had ridden him last night. She'd wanted it another couple of times as well, and he was tired. He fancied a kip. But then Will arrived looking fresh and raring, and if that cunt could do it then so could Harry, Will ordering and going to the phone again with the others taking the piss, again, coming back happy enough telling them Terry was behind the bar. Newcastle obviously weren't paying him enough if he had to work here as well. You'd think they would've worked something out wouldn't you? Next thing you knew you'd have Les Ferdinand and Peter Beardsley in black mini-skirts serving tables. Will ordered Cornflakes and toast from a bored teenage girl with chubby legs and black slacks.

At twelve there was still no Mango so they left the hotel and walked along the seafront. The sun was sizzling and Blackpool was burning up. They went down the pier for a go in the arcade. Mango was the one for space games but the sloppy cunt was probably wanking as they spoke. Thinking of England. They'd go get him later. When he'd finished.

There were a few anoraks at the end of the pier with their fishing rods out and Carter led the way into some dome effort where you stood holding crash barriers and an aerial film of forests in Canada passed by and the idea was you felt like a bird, an eagle or hawk maybe, fucking daft this, the sex machine said, but they were serious forests. Think of the amount of bear shit there must be in that wood, he said. It was his only comment. The others had been impressed by the size and beauty of the landscape.

They went down the beach, strolling along taking their time, past white flab turning a deep tandoori red and kids building castles and kicking balls. With the pier and beach done they fancied a pint and found a pub further along the front, ordering four lagers. It tasted different, the water heavier, or lighter, noticing it more now without the electric soup. They should really go and get Mango, though, and Will said he'd do it and left quickly. Balti and Harry were going on about the two scouse birds like they were in love or something and Carter was telling them to leave it out, it was getting right up his nose. The Bollock Brothers laughed at him saying that's a bit rich coming from you, all you ever think about is fanny.

They'd finished their drinks when Mango arrived with Will, so they bought him a pint seeing's how he'd seen them alright with the transport and accommodation. He screwed up his face. This lager tastes different, have you noticed, we should stick to bottles, you know what you're getting, and the others told him it was the water. They had a few more with men coming in and out, one or two women, and they hadn't heard another London accent yet which they didn't mind really, seeing as they were on holiday.

Mango showed them a postcard he'd bought on the way to the pub, so stupid it was funny, some fat old boy going through a tunnel on a train with a dolly bird in a short white skirt next to him, a misunderstanding involving a couple of geese, and they asked him who he was going to send it to. That bird from his work? Penny? He said no, he didn't have her address with him, he'd keep it for himself. She was above all that, a class act. Everyone smiled and nodded their heads.

Mango had to admit he was the happiest he'd been for ages, having a drink with his mates, a long way from home. They could do anything they wanted to you in this world, but if you had a few good mates you'd always get through. People you'd known for years. Grown up with. Got pissed and kicked to fuck with as juveniles. Three Brummie birds came over from the bar and sat nearby, Carter giving them a line of chat and two were into the old jungle, the other preferring punk, and the jungle girls shifted over and were chatting up the Bollock Brothers, which was a turn up. Carter wondered if he was losing his touch, and before Will knew it he was the music expert and the third girl was sitting next to him as he told her how he'd seen The Jam at The Rainbow and The Clash at the Electric Ballroom.

She was younger and well impressed, and he was tempted and knew he should stop drinking otherwise he was going to do something he'd regret. It looked like the afternoon was going to end up in another session, which seemed to suit everyone, but then Mango said he wanted to see a bit of Blackpool and off he went. Carter told the girls to get a round in, which they did, and the Sex Division were on their sixth pints already. Things were going very nicely, no cares in the world, even Carter wasn't that bothered because, after all, even though the Brummies were fit enough, three right little ravers if he was honest, they were right old slappers. They had to be, blanking him like that. If the rest of them wanted to fuck pigs, then that was their problem. It was a free world. They all had a vote.

Eventually the lads decided to go for some food at a curry house they'd seen earlier. They'd stopped to check the menu and it seemed alright. They left Will in the pub with the girl he was chatting with, while the other two Brummies went to the pier, saying they'd be back later after they'd been over the forest.

Will was more pissed than he'd thought. He was giving the woman the once over and he knew he was in if he wanted. He couldn't help playing the thing through his mind. Taking her back to the hotel. Up in the lift. A bed to himself. Stripped off and having a good time together. He wanted her, but fought hard and said he had to get back and meet Mango. He'd see her later maybe, if she was around. She looked disappointed, a bit hurt even, which made him feel bad, but said that would be nice. They walked some of the way back and he shot off and found the lads in the Blackpool Tandoori, sitting in the back near the bar with the waiters.

The Sex Division members present stood up and clapped him in, because they knew he'd been on for a shag but had come through the test in one piece. None of them wanted to see him do the dirty on Karen. It was easy saying yes, so fucking easy to just say yes all the time. It was much harder saying no. Will had shown quality and self-discipline, controlling the beautiful game and keeping possession, showing patience and reserve, choosing the highest footballing values above kick-and-rush. It was just what they had expected, though Carter, Harry and Balti would have taken the easy option and gone for a great big yes please darling, if you could just go easy with the teeth on the helmet, but Will was his own man. He wouldn't meet her later, even though he wanted to. It made Harry and Balti happy because it showed there were people around with morals. Not many, mind, but one or two. It was temptation and all that.

They were single men, and Balti and Harry were interested in the Brummies, Carter reminding them of their responsibilities with the scousers, and he had a point. Bollocks did he. He just didn't want them getting cocky and scoring too many points. Look who it was giving it all that. But it was fucking typical. You wanked yourself silly for near enough a year and when a shag came along, right away it was followed by another portion, by more sex on a plate. Like tube trains. Why couldn't it be spaced out a bit? It wasn't right. Did they go back to the scousers, or try and knob the Brummies? A difficult decision.

They were soon into a feast, filling up nicely, the tikkas and vindaloos washed down with Carlsberg, and the waiters all had northern accents which was fair enough really, telling them Bradford was the curry capital of Britain. Maybe even the world. The owner had moved over to Blackpool, extending the family business, and Mango emptied the chutney dish leaving the lime pickle and onions to the others. It had started raining heavily outside so they had another pint and when it stopped they paid up, left a tip, and went back to the hotel.

Will left for a few zeds, and the others joined Mango in the bar. The drink was making them a bit tired, delayed reactions, but Terry was pleased to see the boys, the afternoon floating past easy enough, and next thing Will knew he was being kicked awake by Mango and Carter who'd both had a bath and a shave, and were looking spick and span ready for a decent night out. Next door Harry and Balti were still trying to decide whether they should service the scousers again or go for the Brummies. Harry was thinking of the warmth of the scouser, a million miles from his dream's harsh moorland. They were unable to make their minds up, but bollocks anyway, they just fancied a laugh. No need to take life so serious.

They turned off the light and went next door, banging to be let in, sat on Carter's bed waiting for Mango to hand out the Buddhas. It was pure stuff, or so he said. They were downstairs for a drink and Terry Mac was there behind the bar. Waiting patiently with his selection of lagers and beers at the ready.

They had a couple of lagers and, giving Macca a wave, were outside in the night air, a real buzz to Blackpool now – and they watched the colours and heard the sounds and stood in a pub bumping into the Brummies more by chance than anything, having fun enjoying themselves, not expecting anything, not bothered, and they had a thirst on, Will ordering, then they were off down the road paying their money and taking their chance indoors, lights popping, everyone together in the dark and there was no North or South now and the music made sense getting inside the feel of the bass and football was a beautiful game – it really was – and there was no hatred because you realised that everyone was part of the same thing and even something as naff as sex meant nothing – what was the difference? – mostly a bird could carry a sprog in her belly, there didn't have to be rules and regulations because slagging people off because of what they were was a nonsense – they were part of the same thing – and you could feel it now, like what was a Scot except someone who lived in another part of the country and had a different accent, a few different customs, a history that was all in the past, and if any one of them had been born in Glasgow, say, rather than London, then they'd have been Jocks as well, it was so simple, but sometimes you couldn't see things clearly because you were in this multi-storey car park looking for the ticket machine watching the clock all the time because you had to spend your money, but when you came out into the light then it was there waiting, because it made some kind of sense that everything was connected somehow – a long line of DNA that went back to Java Man – back to Lucy in Africa – some Stone Age primitive world – and when you listened to Aboriginal music it could've been made in a factory so there was a connection there and they looked at the birds around them and there was no need for sex or points there was no difference now and it was all decoration like lucky charms and jewellery something to play with and pass your time and it didn't matter if you died tomorrow or if you were dirt poor because when you got into the clearing with the lights and everything – right inside the fucking dream, that was just like life – then you could do what you wanted – if you wanted to drop your kegs – but what was the point, you could never escape the conditioning that was part of what you became and it was like the wild children you read about who lived like the apes that raised them so if someone dumped you on your arse then what was the point of killing them for it because they were the same as you (deep down inside) and there was no reason to stitch people up and use prostitutes because every porn actor was a human being as well and money meant something but not everything (it was worth remembering, it would be forgotten) and the dreams made sense (perfect sense) now they were all in the clearing together with the jungle in the background – Big Frank on the door checking tickets – and time didn't matter with Karen back home and punk and reggae black vinyl relics of the past, everything was how it should be.

The connection was obvious, but the women were tasty, maybe he (Carter) was losing his touch, they were in shorts and bra straps, something like that, but they weren't that game, must be the effect of the Buddha, and you couldn't be bothered talking let alone talking shit and even the Bollock Brothers were tapping their feet, big men with cropped heads, the volume seemed to be moving through the ceiling shaking the foundations but the house stayed standing no problem there with the scousers of last night and the Brummies as well, the whole of Blackpool in one place and London seemed a long long way away.

The Buddha was breaking down their attachments and that was what it was all about really because you didn't want to suffer and all life was suffering because you were going to die, so you did something about it and considered the problem with the pulse running through the building and there could be no regrets because history was rewritten, but for the individual it wasn't going to matter, and who knew what would happen, only Harry the dreamer, they all had a glimpse, he was no saint no prophet, religion was a mug's game the Buddha made that clear enough and they could've been in a crowd on a Saturday thinking of The Shed singing together with a rougher edge, but there were similarities, some kind of fanaticism, and where were the fascists and where were the communists?

It was like time flashed past outside in the street with the music shut off but still echoing through their skulls, fading away, ears toasting, the lads wandering home, buying chips with curry sauce, sitting down on the beach, looking out to sea, with the Brummies and the scousers, nobody talking much, it wasn't that cold, five o'clock, they were shagged out, wandering off home, the lads alone back in the hotel, Terry McDermott nowhere to be seen, none of them fancied a drink, sitting around having a smoke, eventually fading off to sleep.

Carter opened the curtains and walked back across the room. He went into the hall and banged on the next door. Come on you lazy bastards, it's time to get up, we've only got half a day left. The rest of them were taking their time getting sorted out so the shag man went for a walk along the seafront, breathing in the air and watching the gulls hover. He found himself thinking that it would be nice to live by the sea one day, when he was older. Maybe run a little shop. He shook his head. That was a soft way to think. He'd been born in London and that was where he'd die.

When he got back to the hotel, the others had almost finished breakfast and the papers. They were quiet and thoughtful. Two days wasn't long enough. They went down the pier and played the arcade, then down the pubs of the last couple of days for one or two civilised Sunday pints. Everything was different now. It was a bit of a disappointment.

Mango unlocked the doors and the Jag purred. They were on the move, leaving Blackpool behind. It was the warmest day so far and no-one thought to put any music on. They were dozing or thinking their thoughts, with the driver back inside the machine enjoying the smooth ride, doing a ton in the outside lane. He pulled into the middle to let the cowboys past. Usually he'd blow them away. Thirty grand was a lot of money for a car. He couldn't be bothered right now.

The countryside flashed past and you could understand the road protesters, even though motorways made life a lot easier. They were early enough to miss the major jams, two and a half hours later at the Watford Gap approaching London. Nobody was saying a thing, the lads in the back asleep with Will looking forward to seeing Karen again because it was nice to have someone waiting for you. He was glad he'd had enough sense to leave that girl alone. The traffic got heavy around Brent Cross and it was a slow haul down to Hanger Lane and on to the Uxbridge Road.

BALHAM ON TOUR

BALTI SAT IN The Unity with Harry and Carter. Mango had refused point blank. He had too much to lose getting involved in petty squabbles, scratching around in the gutter getting his hands cut. It was bad news Balti getting a kicking like that, but he should pay someone to do the job on his behalf. Get a whip-round going in the pub and send some hard-up headcase down to Balham. A spanking by proxy. If it came to money, simple pounds and pence, then he'd be first to dip into his wallet. There was no problem there. He was willing to back his old mate with cold hard cash, putting his money where his mouth was. Now he couldn't do better than that, could he? But Mango was missing the point. And Balti had been spending a lot of time slagging him off.

Will tried to talk them out of the idea. They were making a big mistake in his opinion, picking his words carefully, because he understood the logic well enough. This was fair enough in Balti's eyes, because Will was no bottle merchant and had always been a peace-lover, though not the kind of pacifist wanker who'd lay down on the pavement and let some psycho jump on his head for fun. Will reckoned bad blood had to settle sooner or later, otherwise everyone involved would bleed to death. That it took a stronger man to walk away from trouble than it did to keep the thing going. Will was true to his nature. They couldn't fault him, that was his belief, and though Balti and the others disagreed, thought it was bollocks if they were honest, that was his genuine view so fair dues. Mango, though, was always giving it the big one and now he was counting job opportunities instead of friendship.

Carter and Harry sat with Balti, Slaughter staring into his glass examining the fizzy reflection, near enough care in the community that bloke, a liability in his combat fatigues. But it was better not to wind up a bloke who had a glint in his eye and a machete under his pillow.

Mark, Rod and Tom sat at the next table. The Sex Division knew the younger men from football and the pub, and the news that it was an Irishman, a season ticket holder at Millwall no less, who'd given Balti a pasting had got them interested. Johnson owed Balti one, an incident that went back years to when he'd been a kid and Balti, Harry, Carter and the crew they'd knocked about with at the time had saved him from a kicking in Cardiff. It had been a good day out, with Chelsea going mental before, during and after the game. They'd even gone in the Cardiff seats where their main mob had been and the Taffs had needed a police escort back to the terraces. Talk about getting your noses rubbed in it, and it had made things worse when it went off outside. Balti had helped him out in the town centre.

'I'm the only bloke drinking am I?' Slaughter asked, as he necked his fourth pint, fed up with the ugly mug staring back.

He'd been having a hard time lately and looked towards Denise serving behind the bar, raising his empty glass. She didn't notice. She was demanding sex all the time and he'd had a lot of overtime and was shagged out. Denise was killing him, treating him like a dildo on legs. Not that he was complaining mind, but he was going to ask her to marry him and wanted to get into a conversation where he could lead up to the big question nice and easy, without having to perform like a speeding chimp. He hadn't got the proposal worked out yet. It took a lot of bottle doing something like that. It was funny, really, because he'd kick someone's head in but wouldn't propose to the woman he knew and loved and trusted with his life. She was getting a bit kinky as well. Wanting him to use cucumbers and carrots. He had to be up at six-thirty in the morning and wasn't a fucking market trader. If she wanted cucumbers and carrots she should go down the market to one of the fruit and veg stalls. Mind you, if he caught her shagging some barrow boy she was dead. Denise and the cunt giving her a portion. Slaughter loved Denise. Wanted her to be happy. But only with him. Anyone else started sniffing round her and they were history. He knew he shouldn't complain about the sex, but he really was worn out. Least she wasn't some old slapper though, and he wasn't pumping his right hand like a lot of blokes he could mention. Denise was classy alright, though he didn't think much of the cucumbers and carrots. He was a lucky man.

'Right, drink up lads, and we'll get going. Me and Harry in the motor, you lot in the van.'

Balti knew McDonald's habits. You didn't work with someone like that year in, year out, listening to the non-stop patter, without learning how he lived. The habits and everything. That's why the Irish toerag had been able to bushwhack him. Just showed up at the right time and place. The car was slow starting, but Balti pumped the accelerator and it fired up. Just his luck, the fucker. He set off for South London keeping an eye in his rearview mirror so Carter could stay with them.

Balti was looking forward to the trip. You could say what you liked, about turning the other cheek and letting things go, that the needle had to end somewhere so why not with you, but that kind of thinking was shit. It was like at school and the first sign of trouble from another kid and you hit him hard. That way you were left alone. Show weakness and you became a punch-bag. Let McDonald get away with it, and the next thing he knew Balti would be getting a slap everywhere he went. It would take his self-respect away. It was inside him. Self-respect was even more important than respect you got from others, and the people who tried to persuade him otherwise would still think he was a bit of a wanker if he didn't hit back.

There was nothing you could do about it. Alright, Will was different, but that was nature and genes talking and, fair enough anyway, he didn't want to go on about his views. Will spoke his mind and was straight. Mango, though, was nothing. He'd shag some kid and take the piss in King's Cross, but drew the line at helping a mate. That's where sex and violence got mixed up. It was another kind of violence, taking advantage of runaways like that, treating women like shit. It was worse than giving a bloke a kicking, shafting a frightened kid. He'd sort Mango out onc day. Priorities – that's what it was all about. Look at the blokes in the van behind. They were up for it. You didn't hear them whining about jobs and the old bill. They understood what it was about, or at least Carter did, the others along for the ride. Never mind, you needed numbers.

It was almost ten and the roads weren't too bad. It didn't take long getting down to Balham, taking the South Circular to Clapham Common then off down the High Road. Carter was tight behind them all the way keeping himself happy getting right up the car's arse. The memories came back, Balti shovelling shit for slave wages, blood on his hands and the smell of concrete, dust in his eyes and pennies in his pocket, though even that was better than what he got on the social. At least you had pride at the end of the week and the hard graft stopped you thinking. He'd sell the car if he could get anything for it, but truth be told it needed an MOT and tax, and the clutch was starting to slip. Another week or two and his acceleration would be fucked. Maybe he'd torch it and pick up on the insurance. He'd take a chance and spend fifty quid on the Lottery. He'd done a tenner of his forty-six quid last weekend on the numbers game. Mental really, but the fever was everywhere. Everywhere you looked there was some poor cunt standing in line. You had to wait ages just to get a paper in the morning there were so many no-hopers going without their protein.

Ten million in his account and Balti was taking a week to think things through. He'd sit back and laugh himself sick. Delivery pizzas and crates of Fosters straight to the front door. Enough to keep him and Harry happy till he decided on the next move. Keep the cunts waiting. Carter could come round for a big slice of the extra-large deep pan Hawaiian and a couple of chilled cans, Will too with Karen, but Mango would have to stand outside with the scum from the papers. His old girl would be there with his sister later on, aunts and uncles, everyone he knew and trusted, and when they were stuffed and went home happy he'd let the dolly birds in. Blondes, brunettes, redheads. He'd have the lot queueing up down to the end of the street and round the corner. Put Harry on the door checking tickets. In bikinis next to the telly. They'd flock to Balti with his ten million in the bank. Anything he wanted they'd do it for him. They'd be stunners, no down-and-out street girls dying from the cold and malnutrition and Aids. He wasn't taking those girls for a ride, no way.

'Run the bath for me, will you darling?'

'Right away big boy,' Pamela Anderson said, shifting herself from the cushions by his feet, collecting the clipped toe nails and scurrying away.

'Make us a cup of tea, will you love?'

'Milk and two sugars, beautiful?' Liz Hurley asked, stroking his tired brow one more time and hurrying to fill the kettle.

'Get us some chocolate biscuits would you? When you've finished.'

'My pleasure,' beamed that scouse bird from Blackpool, speaking with her mouth full.

Ten minutes later, when he'd fully recovered from the sheer pleasure of expertly performed oral sex, Balti tied his dressing gown together and went for his bath. He sat in the middle of the bubbles with his mug of tea while Pam shaved the stubble from his face, Lizzie massaged his shoulders, and the scouser operated the taps, making sure the bath was kept at the right temperature. He'd put on his new jeans and shirt, call a cab and steam down to Balti Heaven, leaving the crumpet at home to keep his bed warm. The lads would be there waiting and he'd get the Kashmiri boys sitting down to enjoy the feast and have Mango serving. He'd send the wanker back to warm up his kulcha nan as well. Make the big-shot bangra bastard work for his tip. Serve the flash sod right. His mouth watered. They'd drink and eat till they couldn't move, and when Mango came round with the mints and Buddhas he'd buy the fucking lot.

They said the Lottery was a bad thing. The old queens in their gold-crusted churches banging the holy book and the bishop, denouncing gambling as evil. But Balti didn't see them signing on. Didn't see them going through the rotting carrots and mushrooms on the special-offer table down the supermarket. Moral guardians said the Lottery was a sign of a society in serious decline, a culture with the threading picked bare spilling its guts, well, everybody knew that was the truth, too obvious even to talk about really, but it was still freedom of choice. You couldn't argue with that. At least it offered you one chance in sixty million or whatever it was. He didn't know a person who didn't want to win a fortune. It was something to look forward to. You had to have your dreams. What else was there? Without dreams all you were left with was the reality.

'Deeper, Balti, deeper,' Pam screamed, legs wrapped round his shoulders.

'Harder, Balti, harder,' Liz begged, head banging into the wall.

'Shut up will you, I'm trying to get some fucking sleep in here,' Harry shouted from the next room, covering his head with his pillow to get rid of the horrible sound of Balti servicing the entertainment industry.

Balti had taken the Carter crown and was an unstoppable sex machine with an industrial drill for a penis, standing on the side of the M4 by Heston Services flashing the cars in the inside lane laughing his head off, catching the startled look on the faces of the blondes in their Jags as they realised he was that multi-millionaire Balti Heaven Playboy on the front of all the papers, the one that scouse bird had found in bed with Pam and Liz but even so stood by her man and forgave him his sins, face plastered over billboards, a wealthy man who didn't give a toss if the neighbours knew he was loaded. According to the grudging editorials, he was a winner with a heart, ploughing a cool million into homes for the homeless. It added to the attraction. He had conscience as well as soul.

Carter had lost his way, unable to compete with the new boy, but Balti knew it could never be as good as with that scouse bird in Blackpool. He was seeing her regular now he'd got a private detective to track her down and put him in touch. It was a shame it would never happen. Mango with his Buddhas had messed things up. The chance was there for another portion and it had turned to spit with the vague image of some bald guru with big ears sitting in the full lotus position, taking sex out of the equation. It was nature. The birds and the bees. And with ten million quid you owned the fucking hive.

When Balti calmed down a bit, he knew his ideal woman.

Ingrid Bergman would meet him in Copenhagen. Everything would be crystal clear. The air would be pure and the food healthy. Even the lager would taste different. They'd sit outside by the harbour, surrounded by classic buildings, holding hands across the table. Ingrid would tell him about her life and times, and listen fascinated as Balti revealed his hopes for the future. It was a shame she was dead. But you never knew. With ten million you could achieve a lot.

'Mind out.'

Balti hit the brake just in time. Harry laughed. Balti was back in Balham doing a right and a left and pulling up thirty yards from The Carpenter's Hammer. It was a small pub with blind windows and a dark interior. McDonald was down there most nights. Sometimes for a session, usually for a few quiet pints. He'd sat in back streets with his mates waiting for Balti, hiding in the shadows like a nonce, so Balti was going to do this in style. There was no need turning the pub over. That was asking for publicity, lining up witnesses. It would be quiet, Tuesday night, and it should be easy enough to shift things outside. He was marching straight in. Carter was behind them under a big, overhanging tree. There was nobody about. The street was dead.

'Right, when I come out, you lot steam in.'

Harry walked back to the van, everyone on the pavement. Slaughter was standing there like Action Man, having a slash. Mark was giving him a wanker sign behind his back. Carter shook his head sadly. They had a nice collection of cricket and baseball bats, Slaughter told to leave the machete at home. As Johnson had pointed out, they weren't a posse of fucking niggers, were they? No need to go overboard. If McDonald was in there with a few mates they'd need the numbers. If not, then Balti would do the cunt on his own. Harry watched Balti walk over to the Hammer, then disappear inside. It was a shame you had to grow up. Things were easier when you were kids.

It wasn't long till Balti was out in the street again moving fast along the pavement, away from the light. The only sound was the bang of the pub door. There was a short pause then the door swung open and three men came running out. Balti was twenty yards off now, on a bit of wasteland, and he had an iron bar out from under his jacket slapping it into his hand like he was in some budget gangster production, cheap video rental, third-generation video nasty. McDonald and his mates were concentrating on the silly bastard who'd strolled in, given them the come-on, then walked out again like he owned the place. Didn't the cunt understand? A bit slow in the head was he? The boy hadn't learnt his lesson. He was going to get some homework for his trouble. He should be locked up, but if that's what he wanted then that's what he was going to get. The punches and kicks couldn't have registered first time. It was those jungle bunnies spoiling things.

Bill Docherty was a Glaswegian and had known Roy McDonald for more than twenty years. They were good Protestants, though Bill was more dedicated to the politics than Roy. They'd been working in Highbury and dossing along the Holloway Road when they first met up. It was a hard life and there were enough Fenians around to make you nervous, but when you were trying to earn a crust you had to put your differences on hold. They'd eaten in the Archway Cafe after work, then drunk till closing in the local boozers, many of which did lock-ins. They'd stayed mates after Bill saved his nest egg and moved into the car trade. He was an alert bloke, his eyes keen and his mind ticking, but he was getting on and the five pints of bitter dimmed his awareness, the first thing he knew about the West London boys the thud of Slaughter's cricket bat against the side of his head. He wouldn't feel the kicks till the next morning and then it would be aches more than pain. Alcohol was a great anaesthetic.

'You and me, come on you cunt,' Balti shouted, lunging at McDonald who stopped dead and shifted back, the bottle in his hand still in one piece but ready to make its mark.

McDonald heard the noise behind. He turned but only partially. There was little light and he could see something crashing down. Doc stumbled forward and Roy tried to hold him up. Balti caught McDonald a beaut across the bridge of his nose, misting his eyes and smashing the bone. Slaughter was after the bloke he'd just hit, cracking McDonald in the balls in passing, Balti pulling his old foreman forward and dumped him in the rubble. There was the stink of rotting paper and wet mud taking Balti back to the reek of shit he remembered so well. Now it was his turn. Tit for tat. Hide and seek. Throwing the dice, one after the other playing the game of chance. They had the numbers and the Balham lot were getting a hiding. Balti kicked McDonald, then kept going, again and again, continuing till long after the Irishman had stopped moving. The others had backed off and were standing around waiting in silence. Not a bad result. Piece of piss in fact.

There was no colour to the scene and the whole thing had lasted a couple of minutes. Still there was nobody about. It was a dead part of the world. Balti felt empty. The tension gone. There was no pleasure kicking McDonald now. It was just something needed doing. Everything was still as a graveyard. He didn't feel good or bad. It was over. McDonald was one more bit of rubbish. He wasn't a person.

Balti remembered going down the Hammer a few years back. He'd forgotten about that. It was after work and Roy had taken a few of the boys along to celebrate the birth of his first grandson. Bought them drinks till closing. Funny how he'd forgotten that. The kid had died. Leukaemia or something. It all came rushing back, how McDonald had gone sour, but Balti couldn't let himself think like that. He was on top again and had to stay unemotional. Everyone suffered. You couldn't waste time on other people's problems. You still deserved some kind of respect. He stopped kicking. The kid had only lived a year and then they'd buried him. Given him back to his maker. What a waste, the poor little bastard.

McDonald didn't groan or move. He was very still. Maybe Balti had killed him. Kick a bloke in the head like that enough times and they could go under. He bent down and shook the figure. There was a moan. He'd live.

Balti noticed a wedding ring. It was a darker outline and he didn't know whether it was silver or gold. He pulled it off and was about to throw it as far as he could into the distance. Send it into orbit. But he stopped and thought and then dropped it next to McDonald. If the others hadn't been there he'd have put it back on his finger. Enough was enough. It was personal and had nothing to do with family. He was in a street full of ghosts, a sad world south of the river. Balti turned and the others were hurrying back to the van now, Harry telling him to come on and stop pissing about, that they shouldn't hang about riding their luck. Only Slaughter remained. Pissing on one of the unconscious men.

'I saved a bit,' the headcase laughed. Balti looked at him and was glad Carter was shagging his missus.

Back in the car and Balti hoped it would start. No problem. God was on his side alright. A just God who understood revenge and retribution. An eye for an eye and a tooth for a tooth. It was so easy he wanted to laugh. Balti had the last word and from now on he was going to be careful where he walked, wouldn't get careless like before. He'd take precautions and look after himself. As long as you were smart you were in the clear. It was when you got cocky and thought you were special that you suffered. It was God said the meek would inherit the earth. Or was it Jesus? One of those Bible boys. They'd done it in school. Why was he thinking of God anyway? And Balti was meek and mild and signing on, and McDonald would let it go now. Balti knew he would. He had a wife and kids. He'd taught the man a lesson. Best yet. That was it. Top of the totem. Finished. There had to be a winning line and he was the one drawing it here in Balham. End of story. Nobody took the piss out of Balti. Maybe the other two they'd done had been with McDonald before, maybe not. Who fucking cared anyway? They were up for a bit of five-onto-one so deserved everything they got. It was a neat package, wrapped and sealed with a kiss.

It was strange though, because the thing had been eating away at Balti and then when the pegs were put in place he felt empty. Not in a bad way, but like something was over and there was nothing to take its place. He felt that for a bit, then he was a man again, with mates to back him up. He was worth something. He might have to sign on and talk nice to some tart with a computer button to punch, but when it came to the crunch it was your fists and feet that counted. That and an iron bar. See, the thing was that nobody listened to you unless you showed a bit of violence. They talked about the ballot box and the great democratic experiment, about putting your cross on a piece of paper once every five years or so, giving you the chance to vote for some tosser from Oxford or Cambridge, Tory or Labour, it didn't make much difference, they were all the same, but the thing was that they never listened to anyone but their own kind.

Balti was riding high, crest of a wave, somewhere off a Gold Coast beach skimming thirty-footers trimmed down with the beer gut tight and under control, pizza under his arm, thinking the thing through, not listening to Harry talking about the aggro. Because it was only the violence of the old bill that kept you in line and some kind of idea that there was justice in the legal system which everybody who had ever dealt with the law knew was shit, so when it came down to it, if you had the front to use your fists then you could get things done. It was like the IRA and that, and he hated them like most people, but they wouldn't have got anywhere doing things peacefully. Or like the Poll Tax riot in Trafalgar Square tearing up the West End and scaring the tourists. That was the only way you could ever change things, but most people were scared shitless. He'd been listening to Karen and Will, though they talked ideas and weren't about to go out and plant a bomb to back them up. They were alright those two. It must be nice to kick back and not give a toss, but still know what was going on, get wound up in your head but be able to control things. Turn it all round somehow and make sense from the chaos. But that was them and Balti was Balti and fuck it, he'd had enough of South London, a right shithole, crossing Wandsworth Bridge returning to the civilised world. Bollocks, he fancied a pint.

'Your round then?' Harry laughed as they entered The Unity.

Carter was at the bar with Slaughter. The sex machine was sharing a joke with the machete man, Denise filling glasses with extra strong refreshment. There were minutes till last orders, but they were on for afters. Balti muscled in with a tenner and Denise completed the round. Slaughter blew his special girl a kiss as she went to the till, winking at Carter, who was thinking about the night before with that old scrubber in her red gear wanting him to stay longer. He'd had to get going, with work in the morning, and didn't like hanging about in case Slaughter turned up. He was a bit nervous about it all, because though Slaughter looked a joke, with the fatigues and everything, he was seriously off his head and Carter didn't fancy having his balls hacked off and shoved down his throat. It was well dodgy, shagging that mad woman behind the bar, but he was in too deep and, anyway, she was a great ride, rough as fuck taking it like a trouper.

Carter had to be careful. That was all. Denise hadn't been too pleased when he'd left, her face twisting around and in on itself so he wondered if she was a nutter as well, which when he thought about her and Slaughter made sense, a marriage arranged in hell, acid bringing out the toxins, leaving purple scars. It was a shock when he put two and two together because he could deal with most things, missing limbs and pictures of lepers rotting away on the other side of the world, but mental illness was different. He couldn't handle that sort of stuff and Denise had enjoyed telling him before they'd gone down Balham how she rang Slaughter and he'd come straight round to take Terry's place. Fair enough, Carter wasn't complaining, but he couldn't look the bloke straight in the eye with the fresh image of his bride-to-be naked with a cucumber up her fanny.

'You see that film last night?' Harry asked. 'It was about this bloke who came back from beyond the grave. This witchdoctor jets over from Haiti, takes the shekels, digs up the coffin and gives this mug the zombie treatment, blowing some kind of angel dust in his face. Then the zombie kills the witchdoctor for interrupting his beauty sleep and goes on the rampage. Steams this pub full of yokels and wipes them out.'

'When did you watch that then?' Balti asked, enjoying the lager and good company.

'About three. I woke up and couldn't get back to sleep. But I was thinking, imagine being dead like that granny the other day on the news who the doctors sent to the morgue and it was only luck that they saw her varicose vein twitching and realised she

441

was still alive. I mean, how many people do you reckon that happens to? Bit naughty, isn't it? Waking up six foot down.'

The lads shook their heads. It was shocking. A sign of the times. The failure of the state to protect its citizens from premature burial. They paid their taxes and were entitled to accurate diagnosis.

'This zombie, big fucker he was, and it only took a bit of the dust. It's supposed to be true. They use that kind of magic in Haiti. They say voodoo can bring you back to life.'

'That's a load of shit,' Carter said. 'Once you're dead, you're dead. That's the end. Heaven and hell is here. There's nothing afterwards. You've got to enjoy yourself right now.'

'You think though, if you could live forever. You wouldn't be bothered about anything, would you? It's only the thought that you're running out of time, that your best years are flashing past and you're going to end up with a shit pension, freezing to death, that does your head in most of the time.'

Harry stopped to think. If you could dream then it showed there was something more. It was imagination that made it all click into place. If you were asleep, but the brain was still ticking over, then there had to be something extra. It was the same with instinct. That had to come from somewhere. It was alright saying it was built-in, but that didn't explain anything. If you could get a good dream going then why wasn't that real in its own way? If you were pissed or charged-up, then you saw things different, and that was real as well. There'd been a few times when he was stoned that he knew what the others were thinking, and they agreed, so how did anyone explain that? Nobody really tried. Maybe they knew deep down. In their dreams.

'The only zombie round here is Slaughter,' Carter said when the nutter had gone for a piss.

'He's alright. Just a bit sad.'

Harry thought about it. Even Slaughter must have dreams. He wondered what he dreamt about. Whether he took them seriously. Maybe he didn't remember anything the next morning.

'And dangerous,' Carter mumbled.

'You should leave his woman alone then,' Harry grinned.

'Why don't you shout it out,' Carter snarled. 'Let the whole fucking pub know.'

'Calm down girls,' Balti said.

They moved over to an empty table once Carter had got a round in, leaving Slaughter talking to Denise at the bar. Balti stretched his legs out and noticed blood on his trainers. There wasn't much. Just a black smudge that had congealed. He'd wash it off later. But he wasn't thinking about all that now. It was history, and the image of ambulances and nurses was fantasy.

'My granddad had one of those out-of-body experiences when I was a kid,' Balti said. 'He snuffed it and next thing he knows he's looking down on his body laid out with this nurse banging his heart. He said first off he saw his mum and dad standing there waiting for him, all his old mates, his gran and granddad, everyone who was dead, outlines he recognised against this brilliant light. Then the next thing he knows he's off down this tunnel and finds himself floating around the ceiling like a balloon. Except he didn't feel like a balloon because there was no feeling at all. He was there, but not there, if you know what I mean. An out-of-body experience.'

'Leave it out,' Carter said. 'You're winding us up. Dead is dead. There's no second chance.'

'Straight up. He told me. He's not going to lie about something like that, is he?'

'You never told me about that,' Harry said, interested.

'You don't like to, do you? People would just take the piss.'

'So what happened next?'

'He was up there looking down watching this nurse trying to revive him and he said he felt the best he'd ever felt. Really happy and everything seemed perfect and it was like he understood why his life had gone the way it had, even though it wasn't the details so much as one big hit. None of it mattered any more. He said everything was suddenly alright. There was nothing to worry about. Then he was sucked back into his body and he was alive and felt like shit for months after. Once that was over, he was sweet as a nut because he knew there was something waiting for him and he could go to sleep one day and see everyone again. He knew there was a happy ending.'

The lads sipped their drinks and thought about this for a while. Carter knew it was nonsense. It was a nice enough idea, but impossible to believe. Still, he wasn't saying anything. After all, it was Balti's family and you didn't slag off a mate's family. Harry was amazed and trying to get his head round it all.

Balti wondered why he had come out with that story about his granddad. That's right, it was the zombie film Harry mentioned. Word association. Football association. And for some reason he was in the dark on a patch of wasteland with these three men laying in the mud and there was a big flash of light like a bomb going off, except it was more like a searchlight because it wasn't doing any harm. It was so bright it made him blink, but there was no sound because someone must have pulled the plug, and when he looked around the banks of speakers had been removed and there was just dark concrete lit up by this light that came from nowhere. He could see his foreman floating about, or at least some kind of ghost outline, and there was this Ulster accent telling everyone that it was alright and that there had to be peace because they were just acting their parts and keep that nurse away and send the ambulance back to the hospital because there's this little boy waiting for me and we're going to have all those football games we missed because of bad blood.

'Alright Will?' Balti asked as his mate pushed through the doors looking a bit nervous.

'You did it then?'

'No problem.'

Carter watched Eileen pouring pints. She wouldn't cause the kind of grief Denise was capable of bringing down on his head. He saw Slaughter lean over and kiss his woman on the cheek. Carter wondered what she would say when he popped the question. He had to laugh. Slaughter with his hair longer and styled, the tattoos removed and bitten fingernails grown and manicured, a five-hundred quid suit and shiny new shoes, down on one knee with a close shave and quality aftershave swamping the pores, a fine speech prepared in front of the mirror and not a drug in his system, seeing things clearly, ice cool, down on his knee with a bouquet personally selected from that expensive flower shop on the high street, building up to the big moment, a subtle line of chat, four-grand diamond ring in his breast pocket and a suite lined up at the Mayfair Hilton, dinner at the Savoy, the vintage champagne chilled, asking for the hand of the queen of West London barmaids, the look on Denise's face as she realises what's going on, that gold-plated machete in a shoulder-holster, James Bond making a comeback.

More like a tab of acid to get his night vision focused on the job in hand, a few pints and a couple of burgers on the way home, giving her a take-it-or-leave-it offer just as he was about to dump his load. Because that was something birds forgot. That sex was personal, even with strangers, though no bloke was going to admit as much. It was better than talking shit for hours on end, girls lined up in the bogs applying their make-up and discussing the men they'd shagged, giggling like they were back in the playground, the stupid fucking slags. Carter wouldn't get caught out. Not like Slaughter. Not like Will. Not like before.

'You heard, Chelsea are trying to sign Gazza,' Will said.

'They're always going on about Gazza,' Harry replied.

'He couldn't play in the same team as the Dutchman,' Carter insisted. 'You can only have one major play-maker in a team. It's like me and you lot. There's only room for one shag machine.'

'Mango's still within striking distance,' Balti said. 'At least mathematically anyway.'

'What about when Osgood, Hudson and Cooke played in the same side?' Harry asked. 'They were all quality players.'

'That was different,' Carter insisted. 'They were out on the piss night after night and didn't have to worry so much about their fitness levels. Football's more athletic now and there's so much money at stake nobody's going to go out and let themselves go when they've got ten years at the top creaming it.'

'I don't see you sitting at home keeping fit,' Will laughed.

'I'm different. A throwback to a golden age. When footballers were men and the crumpet down the King's Road was well fucking nervous.'

'I bet you The Dutchman isn't getting hammered every night. It's not like he can't afford a pint. He earns more in a week than us lot do in a year.'

'It's good work if you can get it.'

Harry was thinking about the death trip. It sounded like the old boy had been at the Buddhas. Burning away the weeds and leaving the ground clean and full of carbon. There was no pressure weighing you down and everything seemed perfect, though you couldn't work out why. There was no reason or rhyme, you just felt good. He'd have to have a word with Mango. It had been a good night out. The memory was still there and it was easy back-pedalling, but it was different. Strange how Blackpool and the jungle dream had come together, walking into the clearing where the lights were brighter and Frank Bruno was keeping things in order. Maybe they were nothing more than chemical reactions. He didn't know if it was a good thing or not. None of them had been raised with any kind of religion.

Harry knew from the telly that the Mayans had been into peyote and mushrooms thousands of years before the righteous majority stood up in Parliament and pointed the finger. Most places in the world had their own version. Like the Christians getting pissed on blood. No wonder they feared vampires in the Middle Ages. But they were all at it, all over the planet, whether it was magic mushrooms in the shires or sweat lodges on the American plains. Everybody needed a holiday. The brain had to loosen up sometimes and he reckoned the old witchdoctors understood these things, picking plants and mixing potions, collecting the fungus and reaping the harvest. They fixed up the strobe lights and created ceremonies, added a bit of music and some costumes and away you went. That's why they got pissed sitting in The Unity. Easing the tension, though Karen was right when she said lager was a violent drug. But they lived in that kind of world, so it was natural enough.

It was the fucking hippies that got acid banned, with their

long hair and noncy dress code. The Sex Division came from a punk/herbert generation that identified hippies as sell-out merchants. Until they started making a big noise acid had been legal. It was before their time anyway, and the Christians lived a material life without visions or imagination, so nowdays it was all synthetic stuff. Pills and powder. Badly brewed lager shifted down the assembly line. Scientists in backrooms juggling formulas, creating reactions, maximising profits. But mention death experiences or dreams too loudly and you were in trouble. There was always some cunt around ready to slap your wrist. Telling you to get back in line and stand up straight.

'Did you hear about the new sports centre they're going to build?' Will asked. 'There's going to be a swimming pool, weights room, sauna, squash courts.'

'Where's that going to be then?' Harry asked, fed up with mind games.

'Over by the library.'

'What about the swimming pool down the road then?'

'They're knocking it down and building a DIY shop.'

'Bit daft, isn't it?'

'You know what they're like. It never makes much sense. Suppose the swimming pool's a better site for a shop. The sports centre isn't definite yet, but the finance is more or less in place. They reckon it will be a luxury effort.'

'Probably one of those fun pools. Plastic dinosaurs slides and a maximum depth of two feet.'

Denise was in charge of the pub with Len away and had called last orders. Before long, the pub had emptied, leaving Carter, Harry, Balti and Will at their table. Slaughter passed them on the way out, knackered.

'See you lads.'

'Thanks Slaughter.'

Eileen and Denise came and sat at the table once they'd cleaned up. Denise sat next to Terry and slipped her hand between his legs under the cover of the table. Eileen was beside Will. He'd noticed her looking at him the last few times he was in the pub. Ever since he'd started bringing Karen along. Maybe she was interested, or perhaps it was his imagination. He thought hard about Karen as Eileen started going into one about the hard evening she'd had.

'Have a nice night out then?' Denise asked.

'Great,' Harry said.

'Where did you go?'

'Nice little pub in South London.'

'Anywhere's better than here. I'm fed up with this place.'

'It's alright,' Balti said. 'Free beer after closing-time then?'

'In your dreams,' but Denise hadn't charged them for the last round.

Will wondered if Carter was getting to grips with Denise. She was sitting quite close to him and there seemed to be something between them. Carter kept looking away and Denise seemed cocky. He'd ask him later on. He didn't like her much. She was a real turn-off. Not so much the looks, but the attitude. Eileen was different, but he had Karen and was a one-woman man. Like Balti and Harry, probably, if they had the chance.

Will had had a good day. It was a bit morbid sometimes going round the houses of old people who'd just died, making offers for their furniture and various odds and ends. The stuff had to be shifted, though, and it made things easy on the relatives. The house he'd visited that morning had been full of good stuff. The furniture was old and sturdy, built to last. Nowdays it was pinned together and the wood was cheap and cheerless. He'd told the son and daughter they could get more than he could offer them, if they sold items on merit and went to a bit of trouble, but they didn't care because they were in mourning and he'd done well for himself. Will believed in being up front with those kind of things.

Karen had come round the shop later on, admiring the furniture and china. He had to find space to display the stuff and he'd been wrapped up in the thing, not really listening to her, then picking up on what she was saying, about how they could use the furniture and he should put it aside.

'Anyone want another drink?' Denise asked, and Will was sure she was touching Carter up.

'Go on then,' Balti said.

He watched Denise as she went to the bar, Eileen following.

'That Eileen's gagging for it, Will,' he said.

'Leave it out. I'm a married man.'

Balti watched the girls behind the bar, then turned and looked down the street. The wind had picked up. He wondered how McDonald was doing. Getting stitched up as he sat there enjoying a free pint. Sitting in Emergency while Balti sat in The Unity. The bright light of a sterilised hospital and the warmth of a friendly pub. Life was good sometimes. Taking the pint Denise placed in front of him. Tipping the magic liquid down his throat. Letting the lager take the strain.

DEATH TRIPPING

THE VICAR WAS consulting the holy book and delivering his words of comfort. The mourners listened in silence. Mango sat next to his dad. To his right was Debbie, to the other side of the old man Jackie, who was holding a tissue to her eyes. Now and then she lowered it tentatively, but never for longer than a few seconds. Mango looked at his sister with a dull throb of irritation. Her hair was freshly dyed and the roots that normally showed through and annoyed him were gone. At least she wasn't sobbing out loud, sending echoes into the rafters, embarrassing him.

The Wilsons were together in their grief. Mango had bought a new suit. The material smelt good. The cut was perfect and elevated his already heightened sense of worth. His gear was new and alive and boasted prosperity and success, in a church that was old and musty and stunk of death. Flowers added colour to the dark interior, but were doomed to wilt in the next couple of days and only served to increase the morbid atmosphere. The best thing was the stained-glass windows.

The scenes incorporated the usual classic imagery – Christ as a child with his mother and father, Christ as a young man drinking with the saints, Christ dying nailed to a crucifix bleeding from his head and chest, myth and history rolled in together, promoting self-sacrifice and resurrection. The heart and lungs had been crushed by the weight of the dying man, the sadism of the Romans right there above the congregation, detailed in black and white, red and yellow. It was the colour that dominated. The images melted as clouds shifted outside. Glass trapped sunlight and filtered it through a prism, thousands of precious stones converging in raking shafts of light that cut through and highlighted floating dust, illuminating the epitaphs carved into grey stone walls.

Margaret was the beloved wife of Nicholas Young, and the loving mother of Emily and Patricia Young. She had died in child birth in 1847, and though she was greatly missed by her husband and children, they were content in the knowledge that she sat with God in a kingdom of eternal light, surrounded by angels and saints, with their son James who had died with his mother, an unborn spirit that would rest forever in the heavenly realm, a celestial world where there was nothing but love and eternal joy.

Mango tried to ignore the effects of the stained glass and concentrate on the vicar. He didn't want to read the memorials. They were depressing. He'd never seen the vicar before because, after all, the Wilsons weren't exactly a churchgoing family, but even so, this was the correct ending. Having a man of the cloth, someone trained and educated in the Christian mysteries, delivering the final tribute made things official. But Mango was finding it hard following the vicar. He was lecturing them about blind material values and a new spiritual order, about good and evil and the bliss that followed the long, hard struggle. Materialism had swamped humanity and at times like these it was important to remember that there was a spirit that needed nurturing, that death should be seen not so much as an end but as a new beginning. Mango wondered whether the vicar had ever heard of shares and bonds and the profits available when a man with business acumen invested wisely? The vicar had obviously never felt the tug of a brand new Jag eager to soar past the hundred mark. Now that was living.

Mango concentrated on the sky behind the Christ Child, keeping his eye on the shepherds and all the other potential animal-worriers in the background going about their hopefully legitimate business. There was straw for bedding and no room at the inn, which wasn't surprising when, even today, with technology racing ahead and the materialist ethic firmly established, thousands slept on the streets of London. Mango was glad he hadn't been in Bethlehem at the time, because he would have put his foot down and passed the pregnant mother roaming alleyways, heading for the orphans that the priests sold to men of means. Because, when you had a hard-on and listened to the priests in charge, it wasn't really prostitution if the girls were cared for by holy men and protected by God. And the girls remained virgins in the eyes of the creator. The synagogues were charging through the nose, and those shepherds caught his attention again. He had to keep them under constant surveillance. Never turn your back on a sheep shagger. He was back with the light losing the images. Back inside a grey church. A religious sanctuary where his most private thoughts were no longer his own.

Mango's dad leant forward and his son started. Was it a heart attack? A stroke or something? The shock of realisation? No, he was smiling, the old sod. He was actually smiling in the middle of a funeral service. Maybe not. No. He was sitting up again. It was a trick of the light. Because Mr Wilson was a decent citizen who, though he never went to church, nevertheless respected the sanctity of religion. The church may no longer have been a focus for the community, but Mr Wilson would have been shocked by its destruction. It was an old building that went back hundreds of years and there had to be something like that around, even if the congregation was tiny. Birth, marriage and death were all worth celebrating. It was something that had to be done. And done properly. Speaking of which, they were going to have a good drink after. Destroy a few brain cells and do it in style. It was what the deceased would have wanted. It was a chance to wash away the sadness.

The light in the sky over Bethlehem consisted of various shades of purple and the star marking the occasion was a brilliant yellow that left an impression. Mango saw the spaceship hovering, recording the miracle birth for later study. A peephole through time and all you had to do was lift your head and blank the words fired by the cross-dresser in the pulpit. No, that was out of order. He couldn't think like that in God's house, bringing everything down to the gutter. He had to keep his mind focused. He was fine at WorldView because his attention was centred and he could listen to his colleagues and the clean thoughts and cleaner language rubbed off. It was true that some of his colleagues were far from angelic, but it didn't matter really because they were proper and confident. There was pure colour and light flooding through the window, a focal point within the church. He should be able to appreciate the place for what it was, rather than wondering how much it cost to enter, or whether the smile on a dodgy-looking shepherd's face was genuine, or what kind of benefits Mary could expect as a single mum.

Mango was tired. He wished he was alone and able to enjoy the sunlight. Just sit in total silence for a few minutes, with all the radios and TVs turned off, the cars still, everyone deep asleep minding their own business. Nobody preaching, telling you what to think and what to do. He wasn't hearing much of the service, now and then returning to the vicar's words, making an effort, and then he was off again. Moving from the colour to the pictures and back to the colour. He had to pay attention. A small boy at school with the teacher shouting that if he didn't pay attention to the mathematical equation on the blackboard he'd end up stupid and on the dole and never do anything with his life. But the coffin the Wilsons had chosen was top of the range and Mango felt proud putting it on his credit card. His old man and uncle nodded their heads solemnly and thanked Jimmy, the kid they'd seen grow to be a man and make his fortune. They were proud of the boy. Mango smiled and looked at the mouth moving in time.

The vicar had a kind face and seemed sincere enough. Mango made a last effort and realised the vicar was telling a story. Something personal from his own life. An event that had come to pass a few days earlier. At seven in the morning in fact, because, you see, the vicar was an early riser. Every day was a new beginning. He was walking his dog around the common when he'd found a purse belonging to one of his parishioners. An elderly lady with little money, who was a regular at the church – it would be nice to see some of the people here today come again because religion had an important part to play in everyday life – and he had made a detour. This wasn't a problem. He'd tucked the purse through the woman's letterbox as he didn't want to bother her. Maybe she was still asleep or valued her solitude. The curtain twitched and before he knew where he was he'd been invited inside for tea and biscuits, and Reggie the labrador sat at his feet and was patted on the head and given a Digestive. That was the most important thing in life, fellowship. Everyone gathered here today should rest assured that this feeling of unity and giving continued beyond the grave and in to the next world. This was truly the greatest comfort.

Mango agreed, but had been distracted as the story drew to its happy conclusion.

He saw a new face in the stained glass. The mouth was moving and filled with a pulsating red light. It was a young mouth drowning in blood and wine, and sometimes the edges curved up, then down. Mango recognised features in the face. It had been in the window for hundreds of years and the expression was changing all the time, clouds covering the sun before relenting and letting the light through. He understood why it was so dark inside the church, and why the atmosphere was sombre and why stained glass had been invented. It forced you to lift your head and look towards the sky, towards the sun, like plants that always found a way towards the energy source. At WorldView the layout of the office meant he was without sunlight during the day, the windows a mark of seniority and superiority reserved for his betters.

When the vicar concluded the service the mourners left the church and trouped into the graveyard. The earth was freshly dug and black against moist green grass, the yew tree still in the wind and the bark rock hard and bleeding. Mango looked around and the stones were older to his left, chipped and touched by moss, the inscriptions battered by rain and pollution, the dates more recent where they stood.

Mango breathed in deeply and smelt the richness of the soil, studying the earth, the shades of stones and white roots ripped and exposed. He watched a worm. It was thick and juicy and trying to dig back down under the surface, hurrying to escape predators. There were more words and tears, the vicar a good man at heart who was respectful towards the deceased, helping family and friends find solace in this dark hour. As the box was lowered Mango felt another flush of pride in the fine wood and quality handles. The first handful of earth that hit the lid of the coffin made a crisp sound that gradually dulled as people came forward to take their turn.

Will stood at the gate watching from a distance. He could see Mango and the rest of the Wilsons. Mango stood out in his new suit. Will hadn't known the dead woman very well, but she'd been friendly to him when he was a kid and that was enough. He wouldn't stay long because it was a family occasion and he didn't want to get in the way. Will wondered where Mrs Mango was. He looked at his watch and left, leaving the Wilsons to get on with it.

'Do you want lager or bitter, son?' Mr Mango asked, when they were back home.

'Lemonade's fine,' Jimmy smiled.

The old man was looking sharp. His eyes were shining and he was standing tall. Jimmy Boy watched him pour the lemonade from a two-litre All White's bottle. It was quality stuff. None of your own-brand rubbish today. His old man was standing straight and fighting the sadness he felt at losing his sister.

'Thanks Dad.'

Mango went over to the table his sisters and cousins had filled with food and took a sausage roll. He wondered what it would be like when it came time to bury his own sisters. How would he feel? Jackie an old woman carted off to the morgue for the butchers to prod and cut up. Youth drained and replaced with whatever it was they put in your veins once you were dead. Top of the head sliced open. Inspecting the brain of a little girl playing in the street in summer, skipping with Debbie. He couldn't think about it right now.

'Your aunt was a fine woman,' Uncle Ken said, standing next to Mango.

'She was Ken. She was.'

'Shame your mother couldn't be with us at the church.'

'I know. She was upset. It hit her hard.'

Ken lifted his tankard to his mouth and gulped down three healthy mouthfuls of the Chiswick bitter. It was a bit of an expensive drink, but Jimmy had been more than generous. The lad had certainly done well for himself and didn't mind sharing his wealth around. Uncle Ken smiled at Mango and patted his nephew's shoulder with a huge hand.

'You're a good lad Jimmy.'

Auntie Stella came over.

'I've just seen your mum Jimmy, and she'll be out in a minute. I gave her something for her headache. She feels guilty not turning up for the funeral, but I told her she shouldn't worry. It's only the ceremony. We're family.'

Mango smiled.

'You can't beat family,' Ken said, putting his arm around Mango's neck. 'Family values, Jimmy. Look after your own and you won't go far wrong. That's the problem with this country. Too many selfish bastards only thinking about themselves.'

Mango nodded. His uncle was right. He'd finished his sausage roll and leant forward for a couple of egg sandwiches. Stella had her head on Ken's shoulder. Mango smiled at Ken and Stella and said he was going outside for some fresh air. Ken asked whether he was okay, because he was very quiet, are you alright son, except Ken was Jimmy's uncle, not his son. He was fine. Just sad. It was natural enough. Mango went out and sat with his back against the wall, by the door, below a slightly-open window. Someone had put on a CD. Irene always said she wanted music after her funeral. That she didn't want people to be sad.

'Irene loved John Lee Hooker. We should put some of his stuff on instead of this rubbish. She was mad about his music. She never could stand Elvis you know.'

'Strange that. I thought everyone loved Elvis.'

'Not Irene. John Lee Hooker was her favourite. Sonny Terry and Brownie McGhee were up there as well. Muddy Waters and Blind Lemon Jefferson. She loved the blues.'

'She didn't like Elvis at all? What about Gene Vincent and Jerry Lee Lewis?'

'No. None of them. She said it was watered down English folk music. She'd go to a session in an Irish pub if she wanted to listen to native music, but she preferred the blues.'

'Why do you think that was then? We all liked Elvis when we were young.'

'Wasn't black enough.'

'Elvis wasn't black at all. He was a white boy. A truck driver who loved his mother and decided to surprise her with a record.'

'I know Elvis wasn't black, it's the voice I was talking about. He sounded black but his face was white. That's why Irene never liked him.'

'But if he sounded black then why didn't she listen to him.'

'Because he wasn't black enough. He was copying the originals and Irene didn't like that. She thought it was wrong nobody would listen to black music unless it was sung by a white boy.'

'Everyone likes Elvis.'

'Irene didn't.'

'Everyone except Irene then.'

'Pete didn't. He hated Elvis.'

'I don't remember that. Did he really?'

'All the kids his age did. The ones who liked punk hated Elvis and the Rolling Stones and the Beatles.'

'I can understand the Rolling Stones and the Beatles, but Elvis? How could they hate a dead man?'

'He wasn't dead then, was he? Not at first anyway. They said he was fat and old and that his money was as bad as how he looked.'

'That's a shame. I liked Elvis. Still do in fact. I was playing that Twenty Best collection I got for Christmas last night. You know, I never think of him as being old or fat. I always see him as a good old boy. Some kid in his pick-up truck driving along just minding his own business eating peanut-butter-and-jam sandwiches.'

'I don't suppose they cared once he died.'

'Who's that?'

'Punks.'

'They died, did they?'

'I suppose so, or at least the ones with spiky hair, but I mean the punks, or at least some of them, probably wouldn't have cared about Elvis if he'd been dead at the time, but then he died and they forgot about him I suppose. Now all you see is pictures of Elvis when he was young. It's like Marilyn Monroe. Once they're gone, you want to remember them at their best, don't you? No kid's going to pay good money for a picture of Elvis with a massive beer gut and side burns. You can go down The George if that's what you want.'

'Why do you think Irene liked blues so much then? I always found it too slow.'

'It was in her blood maybe. I don't know. Everybody has their own tastes. Human nature. Suppose it would be a bit sad for right now, when I think about it.'

Mango listened to the conversation. He could smell cigarette smoke and hear a pop tune he didn't recognise. The voices drifted away and he found himself listening to the song. When it stopped there was a lull, the sound of people talking rising up to fill the gap. The music restarted, this time low and respectful. Mood music that was trying to shift everyone sideways. Irene had told her family they should have a party and get pissed when she died. That's what everyone was going to do.

'I remember when we were kids. When the school got bombed and Irene was upset about it and started crying. She was the only one who did that you know, because the rest of us were chuffed. She loved her lessons. Especially geography and art.'

The voices had returned.

'It's a shame they closed it down, isn't it?'

'No they didn't, they repaired the school. It didn't take the teachers long to get us back in our classrooms again. They were dedicated.'

'They closed it last year and shifted the pupils. A cost-cutting measure.'

'Do you remember when Irene and Ted got married? I'll never forget that day. She was so drunk by the end of the reception that he had to carry her to the taxi, never mind through the front door. Mind you, Irene did like a drink. She lived life to the full, didn't she? Always laughing and enjoying herself. Nothing was ever too much trouble.'

'Salt of the earth, Irene. She had a good run, though sixty-nine's still a bit young.'

'At least she lived that long. Some don't, you know. She's alright where she's going. She was a believer. Mind out, here comes Ted.'

'You two alright?'

'Fine, Ted, fine. How about yourself?'

'Bearing up.'

There was a silence and Mango leant his head back straining to hear what was being said.

'Poor old Irene. She was the best woman ever walked the earth. We had a lot of good times and that's something to look back on and smile at I suppose. I've got lots of memories and everything, but God knows what I'm going to do without her. I can't believe she's dead. It's like this person is with you most of your life and then she's gone. And there's nothing you can do about it. I'm going to miss her so much.'

There was another silence and Mango felt awkward. He wanted to move away from the window but was stuck. It wasn't right sitting there listening to other people's conversations.

'Come on Ted. It's alright. I'll get you another drink. Come on mate.'

Someone seemed to have turned up the music. Not a lot, but enough. Mango could feel the vibration moving up his spine. The walls of the flat were thin. Right along the nerve endings into his skull. He tried to concentrate on the good and the positive. He thought about his car, the power and the glory of the Jaguar. Named after a wild cat, a killer, fleet of foot and lithe of form. It was the first time he'd made the connection. Of course, the jaguar was covered in fur and had a mind of its own, while his Jag was a brainless machine built to obey orders. Jaguars could shift a bit, because he'd seen wildlife programmes on the telly with all kinds of big cats running down gazelles, or whatever it was they ate.

'Give her another half hour and I'll get her up,' Mango's dad said. 'She's gone back to sleep again. She's had a bad shock. We all have. Except with her she just goes and get pissed.'

'Never mind. Let her sleep.'

459

Mango couldn't place the voice. It was a man. That was all he knew. It was the music distorting things.

'I don't know what to do sometimes. I mean, the boy's gone, but there isn't a day goes by that I don't think about Pete. Where he is and whether he's still alive. Sometimes I think he'll turn up one day, and the next moment I know there's no chance. She's been drinking all these years and it doesn't do any good. It doesn't solve anything and she only feels worse the next day.'

'Maybe she'd drink anyway. You don't know. Everyone has their crutch. She must get something out of it, otherwise she wouldn't do it, would she?'

'I know all that, but it makes her unhappy. The more you have, the more you want.'

There was silence and Mango reckoned the two men had moved away from the window. Maybe he should talk to his dad about Pete. Funny thing was, he'd never really gone into it with the old man. At least not for a good few years. He couldn't remember. The door opened and Jackie came outside, surprised to see her brother sitting there on his own. She shut the door and lowered herself down next to him. She was average-looking and a bit shabby the way she dressed. Her appearance was okay now, but she needed to take more pride in herself. She wore cheap clothes and cheap perfume. Everything about his sister made Mango think of cheapness.

'You alright, Jimmy? You're very quiet. That's a nice suit you've got. Irene liked black suits.'

Poor old Jackie. Working in the baker's earning three quid an hour.

'I'll miss Irene. We used to meet up every Thursday dinner-time in The Bull for a drink and a chat. We took turns buying each other sandwiches. She was so happy all the time. Whenever I was feeling miserable she'd cheer me up. Just being around her made you feel better somehow. She never seemed to worry about anything. Not that she didn't think, but she never let things bother her. She always told me that life was too short. That one day we would all be dead. Now she is.'

Mango had never known Irene and Jackie were close, though

she went along with Irene and his mum to the bingo sometimes. He didn't know a lot about his sisters really. He'd never liked them much. He stopped himself. It wasn't that he didn't like them, it was something else. He didn't know them. At least not as grown-ups. It was his fault. They'd done nothing to him. But he remembered them going on and on when Pete went missing, crying and worrying, while he suffered in silence. They were common as well. He hated the thin walls of the flat and the cheap perfume they wore.

'Auntie Irene was one of the best. It's strange how it's always the good people who die, isn't it? You'd think it would be the other way round. It's like Pete. He was a good person, what I can remember about him. Not that he's dead. I don't mean that at all, but, well, you know what I mean don't you? I didn't mean he's dead. I know he's not.'

Mango knew what Jackie meant. She was right as well. Maybe she wasn't as thick as he'd thought. Just because she worked in a baker's. Perhaps she enjoyed it. He'd ask her.

'I always liked baking. Mum will tell you that. It's fine. They're good to me there and I can walk to work. I know everyone who comes in and we have a laugh. The pay could be better, but that's the same for most people. At least I've got a job and that's more than a lot of people can say. You've got to be grateful for what you've got. There's no point wishing for things you know you'll never have.'

It wasn't the same for her brother. Her poor, hard-working, loaded brother. He knew that the pressure was on and if he messed up one day he'd be out on his ear. There was no generosity at WorldView. There was no real happiness there because you were only as good as your last deal, and there was a balance sheet in operation that once it shifted away from the black spelt trouble. There was no room for passengers because the rewards at the top were good so you didn't want to fall off and you gave more and more of yourself. Every morning Mango had to haul himself out of bed and get dressed, and drive through the greatest city in the world to the greatest multinational, in his eyes anyway, and the best reward he had (and he almost wanted to grab one of his colleagues and shout it in their face), the best reward was that he'd sent Irene off in a top-of-the-range box and paid for the drink and spread afterwards. It was the first time he'd put decent money into his family, and it was all for a woman who he'd never really known, not properly, not like poor old Jackie who was rich in a way because she got to go down The Bull with her aunt who made her happy. Mango had never known that his chubby aunt with the dyed hair had gone to a school that had been bombed during the war and had grown up liking John Lee Hooker, that old blues man in the beer adverts.

'I didn't tell you, Jimmy,' Jackie was saying, looking away from her brother, then staring into his eyes. 'I've been seeing this bloke for three months and he wants us to get engaged.'

There was a silence. He had never really seen his sister's eyes properly and they were brilliant blue and sparkled as though made from stained glass, burning with a light that seemed to come from inside her skull. It was frightening. He wanted to look away. Mango thought he should say something, but didn't know what. Why was she looking at him like that, as though she could read his mind but still wanted approval?

'What do you think, Jimmy? I mean it's not a long time, is it, three months, but we get on well and he treats me like I'm special, which I know I'm not. I mean I'm not good-looking and I'm not clever – I don't think I'm thick, but not really smart. Thing is, he treats me like I'm special and he makes me feel good. That seems like enough for me. What do you think?'

'I don't know.'

Mango was confused. Why was she talking like this? Why was she slagging herself off? Why had he never noticed the blue eyes that swamped her clothes and perfume and made a three-quid-an-hour job in the baker's unimportant? He slagged her and Debbie off in his head, he knew he did, but that was because he was a wanker and those kind of values rubbed off after a while working at WorldView. You couldn't help but be affected. It was the price you had to pay, selling yourself, a prostitute in an Italian suit. It didn't mean Jackie had to think like that as well.

'I mean, yes, I do know. Give it a few more months and see

how things go and then, why not? If that's what you want then get engaged, or don't waste any time, go and get married now. You don't have to ask me. What do I know about it?'

'I just wondered what you thought,' Jackie said, smiling and holding her brother's hand, and Mango was so surprised that he didn't even have time to feel awkward.

Jackie was off on a marathon sprint telling Mango how she'd met Dave when she'd been out in the West End one night with her mates and he'd been very polite and he'd phoned her up and they'd gone to the pictures together and he was very proper and they went out again to a pub in Ladbroke Grove and then for a pizza and he lived in Westbourne Park and was a mechanic and did alright for himself, and everything had gone on from there. They got on fine and he was very respectful and he reminded her a bit of Will because he was thoughtful and kind but not poofy or anything like that, and would you meet him one day? Of course I will, and Jackie threw her arms around Mango and gave him a hug and he felt a tear in his eye but luckily she didn't see because she was on her feet and going inside saying she was going to tell Dad about Dave now she'd told Jimmy, and Mango felt honoured that he was the first to know. Or at least the first of the two men.

Mango closed his eyes and leant his head back. He dozed a bit, but it was a shallow rest, thinking about his sisters. Family was important. He felt sad and happy at the same time. He was glad Jackie had spoken to him. Pete was gone but Debbie and Jackie remained.

It was getting dark. Mango wondered how long he'd been sitting outside. Nobody bothered him. He thought logically about the girl last night and tried to work out why he'd gone back to King's Cross. It was far easier picking up the phone and calling for home delivery. The girls were women and in far better shape, though they had a confidence about them that put him off a little, but there again, they weren't as stroppy. He felt better with call girls because somehow it all seemed more above board and business-like, and they came recommended by the chaps at WorldView. Their bodies were often tanned and usually toned, and the extra he paid for his sex was made up for by the gear they wore. They were clean. The street-walkers were full of disease, but he'd gone back to King's Cross because the girls made him feel important. His car was better than those of most of the other punters and he could be generous. He was helping put food in their mouths while the call girls were earning big money and probably servicing far more important clients than the likes of James Wilson. But never again. He was finished with all that. He was second in the Sex Division, but if the proper rules were applied he still had to get off the mark. The others didn't know so it would never really matter, but in this brief moment of clarity he admitted that it was pretty sad finding himself behind Balti and Harry. They couldn't even be bothered, not really anyway, preferring to dedicate their attention to the finer things in life.

'Why don't you come inside Jimmy?' his dad said, standing over him. 'You'll catch a cold out here. Come in and have something to eat and a proper drink. You've been out here on your own for ages.'

'Alright. I was having a think, that's all.'

'You know what they say about too much thinking. It's not good for your health. Look at me. Never had a thought in my life and it hasn't done me any harm.'

They both laughed.

'Here love, fill a plate for Jimmy will you?'

Mango watched Debbie load a paper plate. He was feeling better. It had done him good being on his own.

'You heard about Jackie's bloke then?' his dad asked.

'Sounds alright.'

'You think so? Good. That's what I thought. As long as she's happy. That's what's important.'

'A bit early to get engaged, but give it a few months and why not? Suppose you've got to let yourself go sometimes.'

'Exactly what I thought. She told me you'd said that. Sound advice. Get him round and see what we think. If he fits the bill fine, if not we'll sort him out. Only the best is good enough for my daughters.'

Mango saw Jackie and Dave sitting on the Wilson couch, lights dimmed and a spotlight shining into their eyes. The interrogation team wanted to know about Dave's background. His schooling and certificates. Whether he'd done well at university and served his country. How he would develop the family estates and his views on the encroaching environmental lobby threatening the local hunt. There would have to be blood tests and a line of heredity drawn back at least two hundred years. After all, the Wilsons didn't want poisoned blood seeping into the family line. They themselves didn't have certificates, medals, estates, and like every normal human being they hated bloodsports. They had fuck all in fact. But that didn't mean they lacked breeding. Far from it. They were keen on breeding. At least Mango was.

'It's funny having kids, Jimmy. One minute they're babies and it's almost like you blink and there they are all grown up living separate lives, threatening to have kids of their own. I'd be a granddad. Imagine that. Jackie will be getting married and getting pregnant and sitting around thinking of names for her kids just like me and your mum used to do.'

Mango bit into egg and bread. He thought of the name Jackie Wilson and how his sister shared it with a singer. He wondered if Irene had been involved. So close and yet he had never realised. Jackie had soul, he knew that now. He supposed there was a link between blues and soul. He'd ask his old girl.

'You okay Mum?' he said, when the old man had gone for a piss and he'd spotted her across the room. She was sitting in a chair with a glass of Coke in her hand.

'Of course I am. Just a bit tired. Me and Irene were close.'

Mango sat next to his mum on a hard chair that rocked on unsteady legs. Her skin was pale and she was getting old. There was no colour in the face, but she was a tough woman all the same. She would live forever. He knew she'd never die and felt sad trying to imagine himself as a baby in her arms, wrapped up in the white blanket he'd seen in the photos. He hadn't had much hair and looked like a chimp. He thought of the ape in the zoo and how Pete had got angry when that kid started winding it up. Pete was always ready to help the underdog. He missed his brother more and more. You'd think things like that would dim with time, but they didn't. Pete had been close to his Auntie Irene as well.

Jimmy listened to his mum as she told various stories about his aunt. She emphasised the fact that she hadn't been feeling well and that was why she hadn't gone to the funeral. It had nothing to do with drink. Mango nodded his head and offered a few encouraging words, while around him everyone drank and told stories, voices merging together into a wall of noise that grew louder and louder. He saw Ted patting his eyes, trying not to cry. Mango's cousins stood together pouring lager down their throats, the language straying now, and he hoped they'd remember where they were. There was no reason starting a punch-up at their mum's funeral.

Mango stayed till after eleven, feeling more sober as those around him slurred their words and spilt their drink on the carpet. Debbie came to talk with him. His other sister didn't have anything amazing to say, no coming marriage, but as they spoke he realised she was okay as well. He smiled and she seemed happy enough given the circumstances. He looked at her eyes, and though they were blue like Jackie's he couldn't find the fire. That's what love did for you. He felt bad for Debbie. Everyone should have that fire. Something extra. He thought about that bloke she'd been set to marry. Years ago now. He'd let her down. A week to go and he called it off. Joined the merchant navy. Wanted to see the world. She never heard from him again, or at least not as far as Mango knew. He wanted to hug Debbie and tell her it was alright. He wondered if it still bothered her. He couldn't ask.

When Mango left he did the rounds and was hugged and breathed on, his hand shaken by the men and his cheek kissed by the women. Jackie hugged him and said thanks.

Outside he was alive and free. The sky was heavy and the glare of the city meant the stars were invisible, but he felt happy. He was suddenly relieved to be away from everyone, yet glad he'd spent time with his family and spoken with Jackie and Debbie. Somehow everything had worked out fine. He walked towards the car juggling keys, flicking the electronic lock and buckling his belt. The engine started first go and Mango

466

marvelled at the smoothness of the Jag as he reversed and then straightened up. The interior smelt clean and was revitalising after the smoke and alcohol. He was moving in different circles now.

It was a short drive back to Fulham and he watched the drunks on their way home stumbling over broken pavements, kebab houses full of customers, a tall woman in black leather trousers and a red jacket standing at a bus stop. Her hair was swept back and she had thick lipstick that matched the jacket. She was a real cracker and shouldn't be hanging around late at night on her own. He pulled over and reversed. The window opened automatically. He leant across the passenger's seat and asked her if she wanted a lift.

'No thanks.'

He asked her if she was sure. It was late at night and London was full of muggers with their eyes on her handbag and men who would follow a woman home and cut her to ribbons.

'I said no thanks.'

Mango wanted to help and told her that it was okay, he'd just been to a funeral, and did she understand that there were some very sick people around. She shouldn't be travelling by public transport because it was dangerous and the buses were full of perverts with skinning knives tucked into their coats.

'Why don't you just fuck off,' the woman shouted, her face contorted.

He was shocked by the strong language and about to respond when he noticed a bus approaching in his mirror. The Jag eased forward and Mango shook his head sadly. Perhaps he was being a little naive, because after all the woman didn't know who to trust. She didn't know that he was an upright citizen who earnt a decent wage and had helped pay for a first-class funeral. How could she know? But the language really was a bit much and the woman needed a lesson in manners, though he blamed it on the parents really, because if sound values were applied early enough in life children grew up to be decent citizens able to contribute to society. It was too late for the woman, and he mustn't really blame her because he read the papers every day and there were so many cases of people going missing and unprovoked assaults on ordinary men and women just trying to live honest lives, on the way to the cornershop for a carton of milk when they suddenly found themselves covered in blood, slashed across the face, cut to the bone. It should have been obvious from the suit and car that he was safe.

Pete should have been more cautious. If he'd been determined like that woman then perhaps he'd still be alive. It was a fine line between trust and plain rudeness. It was better not to take chances and they'd had a great day at the zoo. Pete had been amazed by the polar bears. A man standing next to them said the bears loved to travel big distances. They roamed for thousands of miles through freezing conditions. It must've been hard for such a proud and powerful creature to be confined in such a small artificial world.

Back in the flat Mango turned on the TV and moved through the channels. There was a documentary he'd seen before. Johnny Rotten was snarling through the screen and then Joe Strummer was talking to the camera. It was old footage and the narrator was telling the story of punk. Mango wondered whether Pete was in one of the crowd scenes. He'd never shared his brother's interest in the music, and it was a shame really because Pete had taken Will along to quite a few gigs. Maybe he'd missed out, but he'd still been close to his brother. He missed him so much. It was like Jackie said. It was always the good people that died, or went missing. Everyone had their story. Those kids up in King's Cross had their lives and he knew he was a bad man and wanted to do something to make things right, but didn't know what, and soon the natural chemical balance would shift and he'd be working to another agenda.

He made up his mind that he'd give Pete the best send off possible if they found the bones. He'd spend thousands of pounds. People said it was a waste splashing out on funerals, because the person who'd died was gone, but ceremony was important. If you couldn't do things properly then, when could you? It made him feel better and he was listening to a girl with jet black hair and heavy mascara and she seemed very young and sincere, so he switched channels to a mindless Miami cocaine-smuggling story where the men carried Uzis and wore pigtails and all the women were blonde-haired beauty queens in tiny

bikinis that showed off their perfect figures and their sparkling
dead eyes.

PART THREE

PART THREE

SKIN-BONE-DRUM-BASS

THE BROWN SAUCE bottle was empty, so Balti leant over the back of the chair to the table behind. Nice and full, he squeezed the plastic container and added a generous helping to his plate. A full English breakfast with chips for two-pound twenty, and Andy the Turk always gave his regulars an extra cup of tea on the house. You couldn't beat it for value. Balti only came in two or three times a week, but it filled him up for the rest of the day and probably saved a few bob in the long run. It was tasty food as well. Freshly cooked and served with a chat and a smile. Sausage, bacon, beans, egg, two slices and the chips he always ordered on top. Andy's was a good place to start the day, watching the world yawn and stretch and get itself in gear as he sat on his arse going nowhere. Least he could let his breakfast sit. He was in no hurry watching that Cockney Red bastard outside selling tomatoes and peppers on a fine August morning.

Balti's paper stayed at the back page as he got stuck into his breakfast. Funny thing was, not working he thought he'd be eating less, but found he was as hungry as when he was grafting for McDonald. It was the boredom that did it. He'd never realised how much he relied on work to fill the gaps. Going home knackered had its benefits. When he finished he leant back and savoured the warm glow in his gut, reaching for the tea. He sipped the magic brew and turned from the back page focus on an Italian international who'd reportedly soon be earning twenty grand a week in England. The star striker was said to be collecting an undisclosed signing-on fee, moving expenses and a loyalty bonus if he could be bothered to stay with the club for more than two years. His agent was earning his cut and the player a crust. More like the fucking bakery. It was

473

crazy money. He flicked through sports pages filled with cricket reports and athletics meeting results. When he hit the racing results he flipped to the front page and another sex murder. They all came out in the summer. All the nutters and pervs. He skimmed through outraged tales of sexual violence and violent sex, past the saucy photos featuring well-endowed blondes who loved holidaying in the sun, looking for something to get his teeth into.

When he was working he wanted a paper he could flick through and laugh at, but signing on he was looking for a bit more. A few articles that would hold his attention longer than five minutes and help pass the time. There was fuck all here. He gave up and stared out the window waiting for something to happen, Phil the Man U fan rearranging his yams and cabbages. After another slow cup of tea Balti paid Andy and left. He walked through the market and turned down a side street, past the construction yard towards the common. He'd sit in the sun for a while. It was going to be another scorcher and Balti was already sweating. It was the car fumes that did him in. Down a back street it was better. When he came out of the shadows he was hit by the fumes. He waited for the lights to turn red and crossed with the mums, kids, pensioners, unemployed men and women using up time.

The billboard overlooking the zebra crossing was new and boasted a blonde in a short red skirt. She was young, or at least made up to look young. She must be ill. Almost a child when he concentrated on the picture. The advertising industry seemed obsessed with thin, pale-skinned girls as it flirted with anorexic child-sex. The girl was so skinny that at first he thought it was part of an Aids warning. It took him the length of the crossing to see that the billboard was promoting a fashion house. Fucking horrible. Aids and bulimia. Like shagging a fucking skeleton.

The girl reminded him of the kids you saw in TV documentaries on child prostitution in the Philippines, Thailand, Cambodia. All around the world. Virgin life-savers. Anywhere but England. Nepalese girls drugged and shipped to the knocking shops of Bombay, and the television crews went

474

undercover and recorded eight- and nine-year-olds on sale to sick old cunts on their way home from work. The yanks were another favourite target, because though they filled up the viewing schedules with shit sitcoms and the music charts with middle-of-the road tunes, the researchers still liked having a go. The big shock, apparently, was that *middle-class* kids were on the streets, lining up outside the shopping malls and drive-in takeaways. It was a big bad horror show and there was a happy, warm feeling that England was in the clear. That it didn't happen at home. Until a crew zoomed in on Bradford and Leeds and even London itself.

Balti thought about Mango. It made him sick, all that sort of thing. Undercover video shots of small girls in a windowless Bombay whorehouse. He didn't know how a bloke could fancy girls that young. It was unnatural somehow. You had to have standards.

Balti sat on his usual bench and skinned up. Will had passed a bit of blow his way the week before and he was making it last. Taking things nice and slow; clock ticking, detonator disconnected. Mind you, he'd nicked five car stereos and sold them down Audio 5 the week before. This was an easy place to dump nicked gear. He was thinking ahead and hitting the jackpot. Fifty quid on the Lottery and he was a winner. He'd soon be laughing. No more sitting on park benches rotting away. No more haggling with that slimy old cunt Stan in Audio 5. He'd be straight down Heathrow and into the departure lounge, sitting at the bar sipping a bottle of Becks waiting for take-off. A month in the sun and when he got back he'd hire some posh financial adviser and invest wisely. A month in the sun at a classy resort. None of your everyday Ibiza packages. Fuck that. No, he'd go somewhere in the Caribbean. A real luxury hotel that looked after your every need. He fancied Jamaica. One of those paradise hotels in the brochures where you could eat and drink as much as you wanted and then swim it off in a crystal-clear ocean. There'd be no radioactivity or sewage eating into his skin. No candyfloss and processed chips to weigh him down. He'd trudge back up the beach and crash out on a sun bed. He saw the massage girl rubbing coconut oil into his back, easing the tension and getting rid of the knots in his shoulders. Heaven on earth with nothing to worry about. No dole queue, bills or loonies. Pam and Liz would have to wait till later. Maybe he'd blow them out. Fuck it, he had the readies so he could do whatever he wanted.

Balti inhaled deeply and watched George on the far side of the common pushing his trolley. The old boy had a goal in life and was serving the community, but Balti was no mug. He was playing the numbers game and confident of his chances. He deserved a bit of luck. It would make a change. Life had to get better and when he was in the West Indies he'd be strolling along golden sand and turning off into the jungle. Through the palm trees to a natural waterfall where he'd buy best quality herb from a local rasta. A day in the jungle wandering back to the hotel for his evening meal of lobster and sweet potatoes. A few chilled Red Stripes to wash it down. He'd sit on the verandah and get talking with the massage girl. A Kingston woman training to be a doctor, using her knowledge to earn a living. She'd sit on the porch and they'd talk till midnight and then she'd leave. They'd meet the next day and romance would blossom. Maybe he'd invite her back to England when he returned to face the press. No, he didn't want to spoil things bringing her to London. He could see the scene now. Pam and Liz at the airport throwing themselves at his feet. He didn't need it. What would she think seeing him in Jamaica and then back in London? It would spoil the image. He'd get things sorted at home and move to JA. Spend the rest of his life in wedded bliss growing pumpkins and sitting on his porch. Natural respect and no aggro.

Balti inhaled again. Will was a good man. So was Karen. A good woman. They were good people. Diamonds. It was all about people. Men and women were from the same egg. Different chromosomes and he would've been a bird. He laughed at the thought. That was all it came down to, the difference between X and Y. He was glad he wasn't a bird. It had been a narrow escape. It was bad enough being a bloke, let alone a bird. Or a black woman from Kingston fighting the prejudice. That would be harder. He'd move to Jamaica and tell them all to fuck off, McDonald and the social and the old bill in their crawling patrol car watching George on the other side of the common, but he wouldn't forget his mates. He'd set up in business with Will and Karen. They'd come over and get into the import-export game. Shifting old reggae and ska over to London. They'd fucking love it. And he wouldn't forget Harry. He could come over as well. He'd buy him a nice little place on the beach, something with a swimming pool, a couple of miles away so Balti had a bit of breathing space. Carter could visit, but he couldn't have him staying, because he wanted to get away from all that competitive football, the dog-eat-dog of it all. Strictly for fun in Jamaica, and anyway, he was a married man now with pumpkins and responsibilities. Sitting on the porch breathing fresh air, a different world to London.

He'd come back regular. Especially for the big games. He could see it easy enough, a sixth round Cup game against Spurs. Land at Heathrow at ten, meet the lads by eleven, a few beers and then turn the bastards over 5–0, with Ruud at the controls and Johnny Spencer scoring a hat-trick. Chase the yids down the Fulham Road after the game, then round off the day with a full session and a curry down Balti Heaven. England at its best. Welcome home Balti. But he knew the reality was different. Tony down the pub had been back and forward between Kingston and London since he was a kid and he reckoned it was well rough. That the poverty made England look rich. It could be a violent place and even music-wise ragga and jungle were more important than reggae and rocksteady these days. So maybe he'd have to go somewhere else. How could he know? He was waiting for pay day, when the numbers would rack up right and give him his due. He saw George catch sight of him and change direction, glad he'd found someone to talk to, and Balti didn't mind his company these days. With an Andy special tucked away and a nice bit of blow, everything was sweet. He had his dreams and the chance to make those dreams come true. He was used to George now. He was a sound enough bloke, even if he *was* a nutter. Least he was harmless. The world was full of nutters.

'Hello son,' George called, his trolley packed tight.

'Alright George? You've been busy. It's only ten.'

George sat down and wiped his face with a rag. There were wet patches under his arms and a strong smell of sweat. He needed a bath. You had to look after yourself.

'I woke up at five and felt like I'd been given an electric shock. I was raring to go and was up and out by half-past. It was such a beautiful morning, walking through empty streets with just the cats for company. One or two cars, but otherwise a city empty of life. The air was cooler and the engines hadn't started up yet. I was ready for the big push and here I am with a heavy cargo and an early finish. I'm going to dump this lot and start again. See if I can do two loads before midday. I won't stop long. There's work needs doing. Why don't you give it a go? We could work together. We'd make a fine team.'

Balti tried to imagine himself working the bins with George. He didn't fancy it somehow. The bloke was speeding and Balti was taking things nice and slow. George needed to hit the brakes. He shook his head. He didn't like the idea that George saw this younger man as similar to himself. Balti was passing through. He wasn't a dosser.

'Is that drugs you're smoking?' George asked, looking over his shoulder and then back at Balti, lowering his voice.

'Sort of.'

'Can I have a go? It won't get me hooked, will it? I don't want to end up an addict with no idea of what's going on around me, living in a fantasy world.'

Balti laughed.

'It's harmless. Drink and fags do more damage.'

'What about that ecstasy stuff you read about then? Now that's a real killer. Kids dropping dead like flies. I've heard that their brains explode. I wouldn't want any of that, though the way I'm feeling now I don't think I need it. I've got so much energy I could shoot off into space. I feel like Superman.'

George inhaled and sat back. They were silent for a while. Balti looked towards Churchill Mansion. He was thinking of that scouse bird up in Blackpool. He wondered what she was doing now. She was alright.

'That helped,' George eventually said. 'It happens like this. I don't feel like doing much for months and then I'm off when the sun comes out. I have to slow down a little. Did I tell you that once I was out walking early and I saw a fox coming down the road. He was big as well. Probably thought he had the streets to himself, but he didn't mind that I was there. He kept going on his way. I shouldn't sit around talking though. I know what people think. They think the old man is eccentric, a bit of a character, maybe a little strange. But I have a purpose. I have an aim. I have ambition. That drug helped. I'll give myself till twelve and have a nap maybe, if I get another trolley done. I'll be off now.'

Balti watched George struggle with his load. The poor bloke needed to knock himself out, but sometimes you didn't get the chance. It was easier being sedated than trying to fight back. Balti thought about fighting back but wouldn't have known where to start. There was nowhere to go. Nothing that could be done. He was white trash like they said. Scorned by both the Right and Left. Judged by silver-spoon commentators who didn't understand the complexities of English culture. The behaviour and use of language. You couldn't win. Whatever you said or did was going to be wrong. So you gave up instead.

He hung around for ages, watching people pass and the pure white clouds above play kiss chase with the sun. He was hot and fancied a pint. A cold pint of lager. Maybe he'd treat himself, seeing as he had the money from the stereos. Just the one though. He didn't want to end up getting pissed every day like the winos you saw year in year out, rotting their livers and brains. He'd top himself before he ended up like that. He was a social drinker. He had to keep a firm hold on things.

Will sifted through the racks, searching for the vinyl that would give him that special kick, the intense feeling that discovery brought. He was meeting Karen in half an hour for a drink during her break, and using the time wisely. It was funny to think that eight months ago he'd been in this same shop and had first spoken to her a few feet from where he was now standing. It was pure romance, a mutual interest in good music bringing them to the record shop at the same moment. Now they were living together and he couldn't imagine anything coming between them. They were made for each other. It was one of those things you know is right the moment it happens. It was a fresh start for a new year and it had all happened so fast. Now they were sharing a bed and that was perfect as well. Will was happy. More happy than he'd ever been. The balance was just right.

A Blackbeard album passed under Will's fast-moving fingers and he paused over Two Sevens Clash. Now that was real culture. The Clash had understood. He flicked the yellow cardboard and stopped dead. From One Extreme to Another by Keith Hudson, and the sticker said it was in mint condition. Will was well chuffed and lifted the album from its polythene sleeve. He inspected the cover and hovered for a while, before half-heartedly completing his inspection of the rack. The bloke behind the counter had just put on a ragga track. Will hated ragga. All that macho guns-and-bitches bollocks. He hated violence. He paid for Keith Hudson and hurried out into the street. He couldn't wait to play the album. Maybe he could make it home before he met Karen. He checked his watch. He didn't have time. There was a small record player at work that he sometimes used, so he'd give it a spin there. Better still, he'd shoot off home after he'd met Karen. He'd just have to open the shop a bit later. The punters could wait. He wanted to hear the record on some proper gear. Usually he listened to tapes at work, only using the dodgy record player when a customer wanted to hear one of the shitty old albums he kept by the door.

'You're early,' he said, walking into The Crown and finding Karen already sitting at the bar.

'I punched out a quarter of an hour ahead of time. I thought I'd find you here already. I've really missed you today.'

'I saw you this morning.'

'I know, but I still missed you. Silly isn't it?'

'No, it's nice. I missed you too. Do you want a half in that, or another pint?'

Will paid for two pints and ordered a couple of Ploughmans. They went to a table and worked their way into the corner. The Crown was a steady kind of pub and didn't get flooded during the day. It was a hard-drinking, middle-aged pub at night and they must've been coining it behind the bar.

'Look what I found,' Will said, opening the plastic bag and pulling out the album he'd just bought.

Karen smiled and kissed his cheek. He was like a school kid with his enthusiasm for music. It was a quality she found attractive. It meant their life together would never be sad. They were solid and there was an understanding she'd never known before with a man. He was as open as anyone she'd known and it meant they could live together. She was happy with Will. They were great together. It had been love at first sight, though that wasn't strictly true, because she'd known him when she was a kid, but then it had only been a childish crush. She'd met the family, her old friend Ruth, and it was natural and easy-going. Will had his shop and mates and interests, and she had her job with the council and her friends and interests. They were into a lot of the same things, while their friends were separate, which was healthy. They both hated the idea of happy couples going out in groups of six and eight and any even number under the sun. It gave them room to breathe. Independence was important. So were the Ploughmans coming their way, because Karen was starving. That last case had built up her appetite. If she could change anything, it would be the amount of dope Will smoked, but he was a laid-back bloke and it was only an extension of his character.

'What do you want to do this evening?' Karen asked.

'Listen to this record.'

'Nothing else?'

'That's enough.'

'I thought I could make us something special for dinner. Don't look surprised. There's no reason, I just thought it would be nice.'

It was fine by Will. Sometimes it seemed unreal how he'd met Karen and how everything had gone so well for them both. He'd start thinking that it couldn't last, that she was too good for him, but then Karen was with him again and everything really was fine. It would be something to look forward to while he was in the shop. There was nothing better than a good bit of music, a decent smoke, a drink or two, some home cooking, and quality time with a quality woman. That's what love and comradeship was all about. That's the way men and women should be. You couldn't ask for more.

Balti had only planned on the one, but he'd got the taste and was on his fourth pint. He'd had a chat with Len behind the bar and Eileen had said hello, but The Unity was near enough empty except for a few pensioners sipping halves of stout and bitter. He sat at the bar and Len asked if he'd ever met up with those Paddies who'd come in that time looking for him. Balti smiled. It was a couple of weeks since he'd thought about McDonald. He shook his head. It was funny, but something happened and it was important for a while, and then it was sorted, and before you knew where you were it was forgotten. It was months ago when they'd gone down Balham. Balti tried to remember the details, but it was blurred now. An old video ready to be recorded over. It was history. When Len went out back he moved to the window. He'd been on his toes for ages, but nothing had happened. McDonald had learnt his lesson. Don't fuck with Balti. Even so, he shouldn't get sloppy even now. He saw the van speeding down the street, indicate right and park up outside. Carter jumped out and came into the pub.

'Alright Balti?' he asked, looking toward the counter.

Balti watched Carter go to the bar. He said something to Eileen and she shook her head. Balti liked Eileen, but knew he didn't stand a chance. Maybe he'd take her over to Jamaica. She could work in the bar at the hotel while he sat on the beach getting oil rubbed into his back. At the moment she wouldn't look at him. Birds expected you to be doing well. It was a power trip. Whatever you said, it was the law of the jungle. Most of them looked at blokes as a provider, the old lion-out-on-the-prowl-hunting routine. It was in the fucking genes. You never saw a dead-end bloke with a quality bird. No chance. You needed to be flash and drive a convertible to pull the models. The real hundred-carat crumpet. You had to have something to offer. They weren't interested in your mind. They wanted to be looked after. Not when it came to one-nighters, but long term. Slags were like blokes, just wanted a good fuck. The best you could hope for was someone on your own level, though if you accepted that yourself then maybe it wasn't surprising others looked at you the same way.

Balti couldn't be bothered about it all now. There was no way out. More jobs lugging bricks. Sitting on his own drowning his sorrows staring into a glass. He'd finish this drink and go see his mum. He couldn't remember the last time he'd been round the old girl's. Carter came over, said a few words, and went back to work. He seemed wound up. Balti finished his drink, took the glass to the bar, and left.

It was a fifteen-minute walk to his mum's. As he went he started thinking about her and how he should go round more often. His dad had run off when he was fifteen and they'd never heard from the cunt again. For the last five years his mum had been living with a retired copper. It was hard to take at first. A fucking copper. Everyone hated the old bill. They were fucking scum. It had been a few years ago when she met him, and once he got talking with the bloke he'd found that he wasn't that bad. He would never forget he'd been old bill, but you had to go along with things sometimes. Bob treated his mum well. That was the most important thing.

Bob could tell a story. With his tales about the Krays and Richardsons. Mad Frankie Fraser who was on the telly these days. Now there was a bloke who'd never given up, no matter what the system did to him. You had to admire people like that. Balti never knew if Bob was telling porkies or had really been involved with the top gangsters of the day. When he reminisced he spoke of the Met as though he and the force were one. After serving his time he'd set up in the security business, made a packet to go with his pension, and was willing to share it with his new love. Balti's old girl had peace at last and a four-bedroom house, money in her purse and all her old friends. She'd done well for herself and Balti realised that he was thinking the same way, that he was seeing her as a woman who needed looking after. But it was different, because his old man was a cunt and he loved his mum. His dad had knocked her about and treated them like shit. It wasn't even like he was an alkie, and he'd made good money on the trains. Till he lost his job. There were no excuses. He was a cunt pure and simple. If Balti ever saw him again he'd give him a good kicking. The old man had slapped him around enough when he was a kid. A fucking sadist. Slapped the old girl. Black eyes and missing teeth. Crying children. A mother's love and sobs. No wonder some women hated men. Maybe he was little better. He didn't know.

Balti stopped outside the house. He didn't like thinking about the past. At least not that part of it. You moved on. He opened the gate and walked between flowers lining the path. The grass was cut and the beds weeded. It was a nice house. His mum had done alright and she deserved her happiness. Everyone deserved to have some kind of happiness. Who cared if Bob was a former copper? None of it mattered when you got old because you should have your bit of peace and quiet. It showed there was justice in the world and gave everyone else something to look forward to, knowing that things could turn around.

He flashed back to his mum battered and bruised, and when the old man left Balti remembered her sitting in silence, and he remembered thinking that she had turned into a witch. The expression on her face said it all. Her face cracked in half and she went all spastic. She'd been like that for a year, not looking after herself and crying all the time. She began to smell and he was ashamed of her. Didn't invite his mates round any more.

Then she suddenly goes back to being his mum. Has her hair cut and buys some new clothes. Just like that. She said she was a better person for it because she'd been through the mill and got rid of old rubbish. Sometimes he wished the old man would stroll up cocky as fuck and Balti would put him in Emergency along with McDonald and all the other cunts who didn't show respect. He was big enough. All grown up and filled out, through the courts when he was a kid for all that juvenile nonsense. He smiled. When you had fuck all else going for you then blokes like him were better off than most, because at least you had your fists. That was something.

Up down, up down, making sure the paint covered evenly and

filled in the odd crack, maintaining a steady flow. A big oblong of pure matt white with a cut of gloss to frame the south side of the room. The wall was straight and the work steady. The ceiling might be a bit tricky because it was covered in small shards of hanging plaster, but he'd take his time and dip the brush into all the nooks and crannies. Harry was into the rhythm listening to a DJ crack half-funny jokes in between a blend of lightweight guitar sounds and classic semi-hard rock. There was a cassette Will had lent him and he would play it when he finished the wall. The paint was going on a treat and the minutes slipping past. The room would look smart once it was finished. He was going with the motion of the roller. These were the best days, when everything went to plan.

His only regret was that his old mate Balti couldn't seem to sort out his head. He'd been signing on for months now, and while he felt bad for him, Balti needed to get his finger out. When you went back to nicking stereos from cars you were playing a loser's game. He was no snotty-nosed hooligan sciving off school. If he was going thieving, then he should be thinking big. Either that or find a job. Breaking into cars was for kids and junkies.

Harry laughed and wondered if his dream of last night would come true. They'd been back on that Mexican beach and it seemed they'd settled in for a long stay. They were living a lazy life swinging back and forward in their hammocks and had given up on the all-night raves. That last bit of aggro with the riot police had been well out of order. You went abroad to get away from all that. Balti had been spending a lot of time in front of the small mirror he carried in his rucksack. He seemed lovesick. The focus of this interest was the village school teacher. Harry hadn't noticed her before and was surprised to realise she looked like Karen. It wasn't Karen, he knew that well enough because Will was a mate and Balti wouldn't shaft his mates, but when he'd been on the psychedelics he looked across the beach and saw her there talking with the kids, her face shifting shape, and for a few seconds she was the spitting image. He wondered where Will was. Over the sea in Jamaica sitting in a shanty town with Scratch Perry blowing his mind, leaving Karen to educate the people.

It was late and Harry was walking home alone, stopping when he saw a light on the front porch of their hut. Karen was swinging back and forward in his hammock talking politics with Balti. He closed his eyes and listened. He was floating gently. She was telling Balti that he should fight back. Look at the Zapatistas and what they had achieved. Nobody could say they weren't real men. Maybe the real men were the men who spoke up and didn't get conned the whole time. Balti was nodding his head and Harry smiled. It was all words and his friend was like a kid in the classroom with a crush on the teacher. He waited for his best mate, his old friend the Balti king of West London, to reach over and hand Karen an apple. Standing in front of the class grinning at the blackboard. Karen was giving a lesson on English rebels, from the Diggers to the Suffragettes, to the streetfighters of Cable Street and the Poll Tax Rebellion, rows of skinny kids in the background asking whether it was true that Henry VIII had died of the clap.

Harry was carving his name into the desk with a clasp knife as Balti dozed next to him, head in his hands. His old man had been rioting the night before and his mate had a black eye. The history teacher was telling them about the Industrial Revolution and factory conditions before the formation of unions. They weren't interested. They were kids in The Shed, packed in tight so you could take your feet off the ground and let the mass of people carry you up and down the terrace. Every so often the old bill would form a wedge and try and get into the middle of The Shed and chuck a few of the young herberts out, but when the place was full they didn't have a chance. The whole end was having a knees up as it piled down the terrace taking the coppers with them. Nipple helmets bobbed over the heads of the crowd and were thrown towards the dog track.

Balti walked out of Stamford Bridge and bought himself a burger. He stood in a pub doorway waiting for the revolutionaries to arrive and together they were heading for the hills. Harry went back to the hut. He heard the sound of hooves and knew Balti was gone. He wasn't bothered because he wanted some time on his own. He felt no panic at the dangers facing his mate as he had realised he was inside a dream and because he had the knowledge he was able to turn the tables. He was lucid. Fucking right he was. Not only could he see the future, but he could take control. A whole new world was there for the taking and he understood that the argument about control was about to start all over again. He opened the paper and read about the Lottery win. The high court had decreed it valid, so Balti was in the clear. Balti had issued a statement saying he was going to settle down and marry a scouser he'd met in Blackpool. The hunt was on. She had to be found.

It was an easy, stupid sort of dream. Up down, up down, applying a nice even coat. Waiting for the DJ to tell a joke he thought was funny. It was the first time he'd been inside a dream and really known what was going on. Even then, though, there was some confusion, as he'd seemed to wake up, but was still asleep. He didn't know how often it would happen in the future, but it really did open all sorts of windows. If he could take charge of his dreams he could do whatever he wanted. There would be no more limits and no more boundaries. Roller applying an even coat.

Carter slammed his foot down and yanked the hand brake into position. He jumped out of the van and ran back to the Sierra. The driver was getting out as well, but the dozy cunt was too slow. Flash him, would he, the fucking cunt. Carter hit him with the sawn-off snooker cue he kept under the driver's seat. He felt the hatred surge. There was blood splattered across the bastard's face and the man staggered back. Carter pulled the door towards him and rammed it home, brought the cue down on the back of the cunt's head. He fell into the car. His eyes were rolling. Carter looked around and hurried back to the van. He released the hand brake and shot off. Who did the cunt think he was? He'd had it coming. Flashing him like that. The fucking cunt.

Sometimes you had to be hard as well as skilful. With women you had to show your good side, pile on the charm and avoid aggravation. The goal was the most important thing. Flatter a bird and eventually she'd let you in. This constructive approach to the beautiful game rarely failed. If you could show them you were open to things they'd keep an eye on you. Find their interests and then connect up and you had it made. The next thing you knew you were slapping your balls against some bird's chin, chalking up points as you shot a wad of salty duff over their tonsils. Stroll in the pub and the rest of the Sex Division wondered how the old charmer had scored yet again. It was simple when you knew how.

When it came to cunts like that getting up your arse and flashing his lights just because you'd cut him up, then you couldn't fuck about with pretty talk. That was a mug's option. You had to get stuck in. All the great teams were like that. They could knock the ball around sweetly, but they were also able to stick a foot in when they needed. It made sense. Compete at the physical level and then let the imagination flow. You had to have a plan. The more straightforward the better. That's why the rest of the lads didn't get their leg over more. They were too busy with other things. You had to focus your attention.

Balti and Harry. A couple of fucking donuts. If they made the effort they'd be alright. Balti sitting in the pub on his own like that. He'd have to have a word. Shame he couldn't get him a job on the vans, but there was nothing going. You never knew. But he couldn't let him sink down like that. It was all in the head. Harry was doing alright, but how long since he'd done the business? Carter couldn't live like that. Fucking Will shacked up. Fair enough. As for Mango, he didn't know how much of what he said was true. All those points and nobody ever saw him with a bird. Still, he was way out in front so why should he bother? No complications. That was the way he lived. The trouble with blokes like Harry and Balti, though, was that they didn't care enough. Give them a few pints and they were happy just having a laugh. Where was the sense in that? They thought they were letting themselves down talking shit. They'd lost sight of the goal. With the points in the bag you could relax. The Sex Division was important. Carter loved women. He wanted them all the time. He loved the chat and the sex. It was like being a salesman really, giving them a line and reeling the catch in. Except it was all friendly. Nobody got hurt. Except cunts who tried to shove their bumper up your fucking arse.

Balti's mum poured two cups of tea. These cups sat on a tray. This tray rested on the coffee table. She sat on the sofa. Her son was in the chair on the opposite side of the table. The furniture was new and smelt fresh. She knew that her son had been drinking. Not a lot, mind, but he'd been drinking all the same. He wasn't drunk. She could smell the drink. She felt sorry for him being out of work, but felt that it was simply a case of him hanging on. Things changed. She had an optimistic approach to life. She handed her son his tea. He was a lovely boy. She thought of him as he was seconds after she had given birth. Smacked into the world. Opening his lungs to cry out and choking on the air. Covered in slime. A nearly-bald, peanut head. Pure virgin skin and frail little bones she could have crushed with too strong a hug. His eyes saw nothing. She held him tight against her chest. She tried to feel his tiny heart beating against her, but her own heart was like a drum deep inside and they blended together. A rhythmic pounding. Her son. A beautiful boy who would grow and be anything that he wanted. The possibilities were endless. Floating on a cloud. She was a mother. He was so fine and honest and totally dependent, how could anything bad ever happen to him? Nursing her little boy, changing his nappies and wiping his nose, seeing her son grow, happy-go-lucky as a little boy kicking a football around, wanting to be an engine driver. He wasn't that much different now. Not really. She wished she could turn the clock back and her kids could stay six years old for ever. That had been the best age. Old enough to talk and communicate but still innocent and excited by life. He was all grown up. Her baby had become a man. She wondered if the boy's father had ruined it all. Seeing the violence and unhappiness. How could anyone know. The man had turned and she hoped her boy wouldn't go the same way. Something in the genes. But her boy seemed fine. He made jokes sometimes like all the men felt they had to, but inside he was still pure. She knew he was clean. But she wished he'd settle down with a nice girl. If he could find a decent job and a woman who would love and cherish him, then Balti's mum would be able to rest easy. She worried about her son. Every mother worried about her children. It was natural. She knew him like nobody else in the world. Drunk or sober, he was always her child. Things would get better. She knew things would get better. They called it a woman's intuition, but it seemed obvious enough. Things always got better eventually.

RENT BOY

James wilson left WorldView early, his hasty departure causing a few raised eyebrows and a great deal of whispered comment among his colleagues. The excuse was vague, a mumbled line concerning family matters. A doctor's appointment for work-related insomnia, or perhaps long-delayed dentistry would have sufficed, but no, Wilson had spoken of family matters in a broken delivery that, while comforting in the weakness it revealed, had also shown a peculiar forcefulness. His fellow workers didn't expect this from such a dedicated employee as, of course, the corporation came first, but he was determined and the surprise lasted at most a few minutes. It was out of the ordinary, but his colleagues were more concerned with the various tasks facing them. Time was most definitely money. When he disappeared through the door, James Wilson was neatly indexed.

Jimmy sat in the front room, his Rest-Easy chair pulled across to the window where he could watch the street below. He sucked the leather's treated fragrance deep into his lungs, held it for a few seconds, and then slowly let it go. He felt the air tickle the end of his nose. He shut his eyes and repeated the process. This time white light crossed his eyelids. A tingle remained in his throat and he felt calmer. He had changed into smart but casual clothes, and had taken twenty minutes in the shower, liberally dowsing himself with his most expensive aftershave and deodorant. He had been to Dino's Delicatessen on the Fulham Road and purchased two types of fresh tea, caffeinated and decaffeinated coffee, skimmed and full milk, four kinds of biscuits. But perhaps they would go to the pub. Or maybe for a meal. Fulham was packed with up-market restaurants, though Mango rarely visited them. Italian, French, Greek, Thai. Whatever money demanded there was always a well-bred entrepreneur on hand to supply the goods.

His mum had phoned and told him the news. Her words were warped as they passed along the line linking two very separate worlds. It was the first time she had called him at WorldView. It had taken Mango several seconds to tune in properly and realise he hadn't drifted over the edge. The words filtered through and were distorted by the receiver, the message trapped and disjointed, turning to a fuzzy echo. It had taken him those vital seconds to understand the sense of his mother's message. Then he was asking questions and receiving answers, finally putting the phone down and going to collect his coat in a daze. The details of the office were of little consequence, his direct superior no longer a key player in the thrilling game of international finance but a small-minded wanker with BO, dandruff and a boring tendency to transfer *The Times* editorial into self-aggrandising lectures. WorldView melted into the background, the people around him shadows. He went to the lift and waited for the doors to open, unaware of his noiseless descent. He drove home at a relaxed speed, the radio silent.

Jimmy strained his eyes and sipped a glass of mineral water. He was nervous. The deep breathing exercises the doctor had suggested worked up to a point, but his brain refused to be totally sedated. It was more than nervousness. That was natural enough. He was alone in his flat and terrified. Actually terrified. Of what he wasn't sure. Expectations. That's what it was. He tapped his foot against the skirting board and looked around the room quickly, making sure everything was in place, trying to distract his attention, fear coming again, flicking back to the street. He could have stayed on at work for a few more hours, but knew he wouldn't have been able to concentrate. He had wanted to leave immediately his mother's words kicked home. Property, wealth, status; what did it matter when your brother was coming to see you after eighteen years buried in a field? What did any of it mean? His head was buzzing. His brain playing games again.

He thought of the churned field, thick black mud and thick brown worms. An ancient battlefield filled with the corpses of Danes and Saxons and all the tribes who had ever landed in England and fought over the land, artery blood absorbed by the soil. Men had been hacked and chopped into ragged pieces, shining gold axes rusted and blunted from the constant hack hack hacking of Jack The Ripper and M25 murderers with their vans and cars and razor-wire erections. Jump on the ring road and observe the speed limit. Dump the evidence. Spade in the boot. Silver clean. Fresh from the superstore. Brand new wellies. Green rubber padding. Out for a stroll bird-watching on Sunday morning listening for woodpeckers in the copse in the distance but only ever hearing crows and seeing ravens with their jet black feathers and peck peck pecking beaks sharp and merciless ripping the heads off smaller birds, pulling the neck tight, cutting into the skin, decapitation headless bodies rotting blue from the rain thunder lightening flooded England, draught-stricken England. Black soil, black birds, black mummified hand pushing through the soil reaching out for Jimmy, grabbing him around the neck feeling the pressure of finger bones on his throat making him want to throw up, gasping for air, inhalation/exhalation restricted, muddy fist pulling him down into the mud, into the sewer, into the sordid backstreets of homelessness and psychiatric disorder, care in the community beyond the streetlife blockbuster romances showing at a five-screen deluxe cinema, popcorn backseat masturbation as a kid spunking up over the velvet chairs and black stockings and suspenders of a girl from school. Back from the dead. Back from the grave. Back from heaven and hell on earth, high-rise office blocks and high-rise flats where the views are the same. Clogged earth reeking of insecticide, washed away by acid rain, burnt off by sun, watered again until it's clean and rich and ready to give up its dead in some kind of resurrection. And classroom history lessons forget the men in the field, content with kings and queens and their sons and daughters, ignoring the raped sons and daughters of the peasants buried alive.

Seven o'clock his mum had said.

Pete Wilson had been hit by guilt. It connected with the bridge of his nose sending blood over a bare-breasted Snow White. His guilt was natural rather than something conditioned or manufactured, an ingrained notion of justice. Looking straight ahead he'd ended up in bed with Jill Smart, and his biggest mistake was that he kept going round knowing full well she was living with a boy who loved her and would be heart-broken if he ever found out about her infidelity. But he didn't care. Didn't give it a second thought. It was help yourself time and everyone out for themselves.

Then one day they were unlucky. Playing with people's emotions. All so he could have it off with a fucking soulgirl. Kev Bennett walking in and finding them on the job, naturally enough going off his rocker as he took in the scene, Pete behind Jill, the woman Kev loved on all fours, turning her head to see her fiance in the doorway snapped in half, snapshot disaster, faces registering shock and a stark realisation of what the moment meant. All because of glands. Natural urges. Then there'd been the inevitable punch-up, Pete's head racing from the speed and his reason wired as he stumbled out of an unhappy home with his clothes tucked under his arm. He'd left Jill to sort out the mess. He dressed in a doorway hoping it wouldn't be opened by a middle-aged bodybuilder who hated flashers. With his clothes on he'd hurried home to hide. A bottle job, but he hadn't known what to do. Couldn't think straight. Just didn't want Bennett banging his head on the bedroom wall or passersby seeing him naked, laughing their heads off. Jill had been game enough and he didn't want any aggro with Bennett because Kev was the one getting stitched up. Pete didn't blame him. Anyway, Bennett would've slaughtered him if he hadn't got away, Kev turning back towards Jill looking for some kind of explanation, something that would make everything alright. He was waiting for the magic excuse knowing there was nothing left to say. Actions were more honest than words. Pete rolling home and waiting for sleep to come and turn the engine off, willing his brain to close down, tapping his fingers impatiently with a pillow burying his head. It was a long, tormenting wait and when he finally slept he didn't wake until the next morning.

Pete had a bath and washed away the filth. Stared at his face and into battered eyes – red veins and stunned pupils. Dressed slowly feeling sore where Bennett had punched him in the ribs and head. A kick in the back as he legged it out of the bedroom. He was walking into a nightmare as he sat down and took the Cornflakes box. Filled his bowl, pouring milk from the bottle. Sat silently with Mum and Dad talking excitedly about the police siege of Kevin Bennett and Jill Smart's flat. Young Kevin holding Jill hostage with a shotgun, pissed up threatening to blow her away and then top himself.

He'd made no demands, that was the strange thing. There seemed no reason for the madness. No request for a fast car to the airport, a suitcase full of cash and a private jet to a mystery destination. Nobody could understand why he'd gone mental like that. What else could the police do when they arrived and tried to talk him into handing over the gun? After hours of patient, logical discussion things were getting worse, with Bennett swigging from a bottle of whisky. The reason they were trying to apply only wound him up. Mr Wilson wished he knew what was behind it all. Then Kev fired a barrel into the wall and the old bill had taken him out. Blown his head in half according to heresay. Splattered spirit-pickled brains all over the new wallpaper Kevin and Jill had put up together, laughing and joking as the paper peeled and the paste stuck to their hands. Imagine that, Mr Wilson said – being the marksman with Kevin Bennett in your sights. He remembered Kevin when he was a young lad, a nice enough kid who loved motorbikes. He shook his head sadly and wondered how his family felt. Didn't know what the world was coming to. Wondered what Kevin was doing with a shotgun in the first place.

It was a sin, playing with people's emotions. Pete returned to his room and laid on his bed until midday before venturing out. He felt as though people were staring at him, but in truth nobody knew why Bennett had gone off his head like that. It was just one of those things, now and again someone cracking under the pressures of living. Thing was, he was only nineteen and had the whole of his life ahead of him. He had a good job as an apprentice electrician and a nice fiancé who'd done a typing course, and it wasn't like they didn't have anywhere to live. It was a crying shame, it really was, and when Pete went into the newsagents they all seemed to be talking about the shooting and he wondered where Jill was, the first time he'd thought about her properly. His skull was creaking and he had to sort things out. He needed to justify himself, but was unable.

He tried to imagine Bennett's face after the marksman had done his job. Did he get it between the eyes like the Westerns, those spaghetti efforts where the eyes stayed open and blood covered the walls, or did the bullet go straight through an eye and leave a neat wound in the socket, exploding deep inside the brain. An earthquake sending tremors down the spine. A police horror show. More likely half the head was blown over Jill. He wondered if Bennett had let her get dressed. Whether she had stood there screaming, naked, with grey matter plastering her hair. He went home without buying anything and sat on his bed, everyone out. He hung his Snow White T-shirt on the door, watching the sick midgets go about their business, Snow White with a big smile on her face enjoying the attention of her seven lovers. He propped the pillows behind his head and stretched out. What would Snow White's prince think when he walked in after a hard day finding the love of his life on all fours with a spiky-haired freak banging in and out of her? Only Bennett knew the answer to that one.

Later that day he heard that Jill was staying with her mum and dad in Uxbridge, and after a week sitting around wondering what to do he looked up the family name in the phone book and took the tube to the end of the Metropolitan Line. He found the Smart house and sat on a wall down the road waiting. It was a warm day and he was conscious of being on his own, but eventually he saw Jill come outside, a bent, wrecked version of her old self. He followed for a while and then caught up with her. Jill's eyes took time to focus and it was obvious she was sedated, the bruising on her face only now beginning to fade. It took a little longer for her to register who he was and then she was scratching his face with blunt fingers, long red nails bitten down and the skin ripped to threads. She was screaming that they were murderers. Why hadn't Pete stayed and taken his punishment like a man? He'd shifted his share of the blame and left her to die.

She ran home and when Pete phoned a couple of weeks later a harsh male voice said she'd slashed her wrists and been cremated, that her ashes were in the rose garden where Kevin was at rest. Then the line went dead.

Mango went to the cupboard in his bedroom and took out a box of photos. He'd had the doors specially made, hardwood from an Asian forest. He ran his hand over the surface. Strong and beautiful with centuries of life ahead, until a chainsaw brought the tree back down to earth. The doors were built to last. You only lived once and he wanted the best. You had to look out for number one because that was the first law of nature and England was a nature-loving country, where the land had been deforested and carved up for the various business interests guarding the nation's heritage.

He held a picture of Pete in front of him and studied the face. Thin and pale with black hair and bright eyes dominating the face. He was smiling and wearing a Harrington, T-shirt, moleskin army surplus trousers and DMs. He seemed happy enough, though who really knew what went on inside someone's head. It was hard enough working out what went on inside your own at times. The next photo showed Pete juggling a football in a pair of shorts. Winter and summer images. Dark skies and bright sunshine.

Mango sifted through the snaps stopping at a family photo of all the Wilsons together. Mum and Dad in the middle with their four children. Two on either side – boy girl, boy girl. He looked at the faces, how they had gradually changed so you never noticed. Then he was staring across the room unfocused trying to imagine what Pete looked like now. It was something he often found himself doing. All his family admitted to doing the same thing. Now his mum said he'd become a farmer in East Anglia.

Mango laughed out loud. A farmer? The dream had been a

top international financier riding the high seas in a luxury yacht and the nightmare a smack-addled boy prostitute. For some reason a farmer seemed about right. How could any of them have guessed something like that? The imagination took you to the far corners. The best and worst options. Extremes always seemed more attractive somehow, as though there was no middle way. How the fuck had he ended up in East Anglia turning earth? Mango pictured a broad character in wellies and overalls, with a ruddy complexion and cow shit under his nails carrying a pitchfork. He laughed again despite himself. Pete the farm hand building a scarecrow and then hanging his old Harrington around its shoulders. A head full of straw for nesting birds. Squire Wilson.

He thought of thick English soil again, but this time he was away from the ring road, the M25 overgrown and reclaimed. Rich earth and healthy crops. None of that intensive farming shit. Pete living a clean life away from London on an organic smallholding, and what would his big brother think of Jimmy in a flash office block in the City, taking the lift to the ground and then slipping into his £30,000 XJ6 3.2 Sport, foot down, naught to 60 in 7.9 seconds, six in-line cylinders humming, rolling through King's Cross picking up runaways. The bloke was driving a tractor home while Jimmy lowered his window and solicited juveniles. Moving on to call girls shifting up-market while his brother strolled through the fields on his way to the local. A Green Man sign over the door and East Anglian ales lining an oak bar. Pipe loaded with tobacco. Country and Western on a jukebox that was rarely used because it broke the calm. Watching stars burn in a clear sky as he walked home.

On the one hand, vast wealth would have offered some kind of justification for the family's loss, while the role of victim would've allowed Mango to condemn the exploitative system which he himself had so successfully embraced. But a farmer? It didn't suggest success or failure, just everyday life away from London and the satellite towns. It meant that Pete could have walked away without a care in the world, unbothered by the misery he was causing. That would be worst of all. The final insult. It would mean that he hadn't given a toss about the rest of the Wilsons, leaving his brother to fend for himself and his mum, dad, sisters to grieve. Year in, year out. All that wasted time. All those Christmas presents hidden away waiting for Pete's return.

Pete Wilson walked slowly. After so many years in East Anglia, the tight London air was a shock but at the same time so familiar. It brought everything roaring back, adding colour and movement to dreamtime imagery. There was less wind and the same artificial, carbonised warmth with which he had grown up. The concrete beneath his feet was harsh and unforgiving with none of the softness and flexibility he had found in Norfolk. Buildings smothered the sun and blocked the wind to which he had become so accustomed. A deep chill had long since worked its way into his bones and would stay there till the day they lowered him down. It was part of him now. The dark soil and barren winters, when the flatness of the land made his ears ring and his mind twist in on itself, when the days shortened and he had time to sit alone and remember Kate. He had spent almost as much time in the country as the city, but eighteen years of his life was compressed as soon as he got off the train at Liverpool Street and stood on the escalator taking him underground to the tube home. It seemed a month since he ran off. He still called London home despite everything that had happened.

Pete had met Kate two months before leaving. She was twice his age and had grown up outside King's Lynn. She had a bumpkin accent and the worn features of someone born and raised on a farm. Her hair was frizzy red and she had a straight, slightly mocking manner. She also had cancer.

He first spoke to her at a Clash gig at the Electric Ballroom in Camden Town. He'd been to see the band the previous night as well. Mickey Dread on stage beforehand toasting, while Joe and the boys had been at their best. The first night he'd gone with a mate and Will. The second time he was on his own standing at the bar listening to the records the DJ was playing. Reggae and punk. Minding his own business. Then this woman had started talking to him in an accent he could hardly hear above the music, let alone identify. He found it hard to understand what she was saying at first and had to lean in close, noticing the way her perfume and sweat mixed in together. The Electric Ballroom was baking hot and she was also there on her own.

Kate was in London for a month enjoying the bright lights, because she might've been in her late thirties but she loved the music and ideas, and had been a mod when she was younger, going on the runs and living the life. But punk was better because of the strength of the music, the Jamaican-inspired bass and the everyday political lyrics. She was staying with her cousin in Greenford, and then The Clash were on stage and Pete forgot about everything else. The place was full of dehydrating bodies and the thud of Topper Headon's drums and Paul Simonon's bass, Joe Strummer in control of the microphone and Mick Jones doing his guitar hero bit. It was one of the best gigs he'd ever seen. He noticed Kate again at the end as they came down the steps into the street, a line of police helmets through the sweaty mist and a young skinhead in a sheepskin standing on a white Merc. He got the tube some of the way with Kate and he was conscious of her age at first because he'd been told age was a bad thing and something to be sneered at, old and boring, all that stuff that he soon labelled as another brand of prejudice.

He'd seen Kate again, a week later. They'd gone to The Ship in Soho and found a corner in the busy pub. Chelsea were playing at the Marquee and they'd thought to go along and see Gene October's Right To Work encore, but started getting into a conversation and when it was time to leave they stayed behind as three-quarters of the pub filtered away. They got pissed and took the tube towards West London together, but there'd been nothing sexual. She was attractive, that was all. They enjoyed talking about bands they'd seen and records they liked and anything at all really. He'd got off the train and said goodbye and it didn't seem strange not going home with her. Anyway, he had Jill Smart on the go and there were no complications there. Love didn't come into it and they were both satisfying themselves with easy sex.

He had nothing in common with Jill, a soulgirl into the

bargain, and punks and soulgirls weren't supposed to mix. All those tribes that made up England in the late Seventies. Jill was the opposite to Kate. They didn't talk much. Just went to bed and had the sex which was good and uncomplicated and that was all there was to it. No emotion or feeling except for what happened between their legs, and when it was over Jill always wanted to put some twelve-inch American import on the record player and talk about her Kevin and their plans for the future. That was a real turn-off because it made Pete think of the silly sod working and trusting her, and he started telling himself he shouldn't be there in someone else's bed taking their place. It wasn't right, but he'd been so into his music and sulphate that he went along with everything and dismissed any kind of morality as old-fashioned.

He saw Kate a few more times and then the nightmare began. Kate told him she was going back to Norfolk and invited him round for a goodbye drink, that she knew of a job if he was interested because he couldn't stay on the dole for the rest of his life. They'd gone down that pub in Greenford and drunk till closing and ended up in bed together. Watching the older woman striptease in front of him throwing her bra in his face and peeling off her panties. It had been different. Another kind of sex. More warm and human. The next morning she told him there was work on the farm if he wanted it, that she would have to hire someone anyway now she had inherited the place. It wasn't big, but too much for Kate on her own. She also told him that she had cancer. She didn't want to hide anything away and didn't want Pete feeling sorry for her either, because maybe she would live to be an old country lady, or if she was unlucky she would last a few more years. She was being upfront. There were no ties. He could come and work for a couple of months and save a bit of cash and then leave without any hassle. He should know about the cancer though. Just in case.

Pete wanted to ask questions but was embarrassed searching for details. So he left with her. Just like that. His head getting to grips with the sex and the work and the illness that would kill her one day. Just like that. Because he needed the money and because he liked her.

Sin and retribution they called it. He didn't believe in the dogma, but he had been guilty. If you were able to pay for your sins and achieve some kind of redemption, then he was in there with a claim. If there was a God responsible for everything, and if he operated how the preachers insisted, then he would be there with gold stars next to his name. The idea of justice had to come from somewhere. Natural justice. And he felt these things free from any kind of indoctrination because he had only ever been to church a couple of times in his life and didn't come from anything near a religious family. Maybe it was built into his culture. Your everyday person had a greater morality about them than the rich and powerful. It was natural to feel remorse and guilt. There weren't enough people learning from their mistakes. But he had suffered. Nothing but cancer eating Kate away for the last year, the visits to the hospital and treatment, the hopelessness. Making arrangements. The years spent mourning. Then the obsession with death. Kevin Bennett, Jill Smart and now Kate. He was paying his dues. For all the good and bad sex and endless attempts at procreation, there was only ever going to be one end to the affair.

Finally it got to the point when he had to push himself, with Kate dead for four years. He decided to phone his Uncle Ted and ask about the family. He wanted to test the ground. He became scared when he couldn't find his old address book, digging through cupboards and finding it wrapped up in a decaying Snow White T-shirt. He held the shirt up in front of him. Snow White enjoying an orgy with the seven dwarfs. He couldn't believe he was the same person who used to wear that shirt. He threw it across the room and opened the address book, sat down on his bed. Pete flicked through the pages that had turned yellow with the passing years. He saw Jill's number in among the names of people he'd once known. The reality hit home, making him realise that eighteen years was a lifetime for some people. His mother could be dead. Or his dad. Perhaps both of them. His sisters. And what about Jimmy who would've been waiting for his big brother to come home. How could he do that to the boy who'd looked up to and admired him? He was a selfish bastard wrapped up in his own misery. Self-centred and full of himself, and that was what had gone wrong in the first place. He'd had no sense of responsibility, following his knob straight up Jill and then running away. But living with a dying woman had taught him respect and humility. He appreciated the world now. Working on a farm brought you back to some kind of starting-point. He was disciplined and had picked up Kate's honesty. She had changed him for the better.

Pete ran through the book again and finally phoned his uncle, found out that his aunt was dead. His mind was made up. He had to go back. He had shut that other world away in a cell pretending it didn't exist. He'd exhausted himself working the land, pushing his body through the hard, miserable winters and busy summers. He'd spent his days either shivering from the cold or sweating in the sun. His muscles ached yet he pushed himself. His body was healthy but at the expense of his head which he wanted to keep numb. Others would have turned to drink, but Pete worked until he was too exhausted even to get pissed. Now and then he would have a pint, but more for the walk than the alcohol. In the evenings he mostly sat in front of the fire thinking of how the woman who had sat opposite him gradually lost her grip on life and faded away, tortured by chemotherapy. When she died East Anglia seemed alien. For four years he had kept going until the worst was over and he had to move again.

He started looking back, examining where it had gone wrong. First there'd been the guilt of Kev Bennett and Jill Smart, that was obvious, and he had submerged it caring for Kate, but with her death any sense of atonement had been replaced by guilt for what he'd done to his family and friends. The longer it went on the worse it became. He hurt everyone he came into contact with. He was a disaster and wasting time. His uncle was so excited to hear from him that it filled Pete with shame, explaining that their greatest fear was that he'd been murdered. If only they'd had some news that he was alive and well. Why hadn't he phoned? Written a letter. Got in touch. But now he was alive. Back from the grave. Some kind of resurrection. Ted said it was a miracle. When was he coming home? He couldn't wait to see him again. Everybody would be excited.

Pete phoned his parents. Amnesia was the excuse, the only explanation with which he could come up. It would cope with the bitterness and prevent him having to explain things in too much detail. Sickness had claimed him one day and he had drifted away and become a farmer in the country. He wasn't sure of all the details. Then his memory had gradually returned. Very slowly over the years till one morning he woke up and remembered his life in London. Imagine that. Without memory you didn't exist. You were nothing. Amnesia would make everything much easier to handle. All those years away and it was sex that had led to his downfall and the guilt that came with the consequences of fucking people about. Kev Bennett and Jill Smart, forever together.

Mango checked his watch again. It was a quarter to seven. Normally he would be hard at work burrowing into rows of letters and numbers pushing himself to identify a good investment. Instead he was hurrying to the bathroom and arriving just in time. He leant over the toilet and was sick into the bowl.

That girl last night. A woman. Sophisticated with exotic eyes and eyebrows that stretched up and away towards her temples. She was beautiful, with a nice voice and a slight tilt to her head. Black hair cut in a bob like thousands of Cleopatra office girls. Except she was no office girl this one. Hetherington at WorldView had recommended her personally. Mango sat in awe as she drank the gin he'd poured, her gaze wandering around the flat. Her legs were long and shapely and he imagined Hetherington with the whip turning her back into a mass of lacerations. He had paid heavily for the privilege, the sight of blood costing extra. After all, she would need a few days to recover and it wasn't as if Hetherington didn't have cash to throw around. His colleague had explained it to James. That it was the desire for power that drove people to the top of the pecking order and that once you joined the march you had to crush everything in your path. Sex was nothing but a display of

504

power. Hard sex. Wilson should think of his pecker as a weapon. Women loved it. They really did.

When Monica arrived Mango sat there wondering what would happen next. Whether he would chop off her head in a fit of free expression or merely thrash her to within an inch of her life. He had never been interested in sadism, but Hetherington and Ridley from WorldView were always encouraging their colleague to give it a go. They had painstakingly explained the mechanics of power, and how sex could be inverted. He had ended up with all that class in front of him and what had Mango done? Bottled it. That's what. He could remember the look of scorn on the woman's face as he asked her to leave. It withered him and he was sure the chaps from the office would find out that he didn't have what it took.

The water stopped spinning and he remembered Hetherington telling him to thrash her but treat her with respect, telling him about a cheap whore he'd picked up with a friend, how they'd fucked her both ends and how Hetherington had lubricated her and tried pushing his fist up the slut's arse. She'd screamed and his friend had helped secure her, Hetherington stretching her sphincter until he had three, four fingers inside, easing the pressure, then inserted a full fist. The dirty fucking whore. His eyes and smile widened as he explained things to Wilson. The only way to treat the workers was to bend them over a barrel and fuck them rigid, then shove your fist in and pull out their guts. The women were the easy targets, but they'd do the men as well, but in a roundabout sort of way so half the time they didn't even know what was happening to them. That was the beauty of democratic politics and people like Wilson were there to be educated.

Mango was lonely. To be reduced to sadism was the end point as far as he was concerned. He knew he had been thinking mental thoughts with under-age kids and that he was scum taking advantage of them, but faced with a willing victim he didn't want to know. Loneliness must have driven thousands to perversion. He was sure of this. He understood the difference between right and wrong. He wasn't some misfit freak without morals or decency. He wasn't like Hetherington and Ridley, however much he tried and listened to their bragging, because he understood what it was like to be part of the majority. He knew what it was to struggle and have those you loved taken away. But he'd been taught to respect his betters. He couldn't hurt the woman with the clipped tones. He needed his own kind because they were rubbish and he was rubbish.

Mango puked again until the tears stung his eyes. He was sorry for everything wicked he had done in the name of his brother, in the name of himself. He could blame things on Pete but it was a con. He was okay. He would be alright soon. With his brother back everything would be like it was when he went away. Life would be simple and bursting with youth and vitality. It didn't matter if he was rich. Mango could open up again. He flushed the toilet and watched the water twist away with the sickness. He straightened himself up and brushed his teeth, rinsed his mouth with mouthwash. He was fine. And when he went back to the chair by the window for some reason he thought of his first serious curry with the rest of the lads when they were teenagers and how he'd been cocky and ordered a prawn vindaloo. He was pissed and went straight into the food and was halfway through when his mouth caught fire. He'd knocked back a pint but it only worked for a while and then he'd steamed into the mango pickle and emptied the tray trying to cool the fire in his mouth. He still had the nickname today, after everything that had happened. He had a good job in the City, a posh flat in Fulham, and he drove a £30,000 XJ6 3.2 Sport with six in-line cylinders, which did naught to 60 in 7.9 seconds, yet his mates still called him Mango after a night in the long-closed Ganges. His mouth had tasted of curry and mango for a couple of days after. Now mouthwash and toothpaste masked the sickness.

Pete stood at the end of the road and prepared himself. So far everything had gone according to plan. He had spent the afternoon with his mum and dad, and then his sisters when they arrived. There had been tears and kisses from his mum and arms thrown around his neck, squeezing him tight, and then a firm handshake and watery eyes from his old man. Debbie and Jackie ran at him and almost knocked him down they were so excited, crying and laughing at the same time. He felt the tears in his eyes, but men didn't cry. The words came fast and he sat everyone down and slowly explained the amnesia. It made all the difference. He knew he was doing the right thing. He was letting himself off the hook, true, but at the same time sparing them the truth. They didn't want to know that he was shit. Lies were important sometimes. They kept things going. Pete wanted to see his brother alone. After all, it was Jimmy who he'd been supposed to meet in the playground.

What did the kid think as the minutes and hours passed and night began to draw in? Why hadn't he returned? Pete knew why well enough, the drink he'd shared with Kate and a heavy mating session that took them well into the night. It was easy to run away in the short term, but long term he had made things worse for everyone. He had hated himself, and maybe deep down he still did, but he couldn't think that way any more. He had to make amends. Had to see his kid brother on his own and try to put things right. Just thinking of Jimmy on the swings, going up and down the slide, getting worried by his brother's absence, looking into the shadows as the darkness came down, scared as he ran home. What had his mum and dad told Jimmy when he got in? That maybe Pete was out with a girl or had met someone and gone down the pub? His dad would've told Jimmy not to worry, that Pete was a growing lad who was late for everything.

Pete didn't want to think about it now. There was a stack of Christmas presents that his mum had brought out and she said that tomorrow they'd have Jimmy round as well and they'd all sit down and have a proper dinner together. Pete could open them then and Jimmy could watch with the rest of the family because every Christmas that boy had wanted to know what his brother was getting. He was a big kid at heart, though he'd done well for himself. He'd done them proud. Pete sat with his cup of tea and listened and didn't really notice how much his parents had aged, though his sisters were women now rather than kids.

He walked down the Fulham street with its precisely spaced

trees and top-of-the-range, polished cars. The pavements were clean and small patches of grass well maintained. He was hot and the fumes filled his head. He stopped outside the address he'd written down and looked up to the floor where his brother lived. He thought he saw a face move back from the window, but couldn't be sure.

The Wilson brothers sat in a corner of the pub. They were on their fourth pints. Mango drank Fosters, while Pete had opted for London Pride. He found the prices high and the beer lacked the flavour he was used to in Norfolk. Still, he wasn't concentrating on the quality of the drink. He had avoided his brother's eyes at first, but with the Pride inside him he was able to look Jimmy in the face. His kid brother was all grown up and filled out, and while it was obviously going to be the case the reality took time to absorb. It was the same with Debbie and Jackie. They were adults. Jimmy's features had filled out but the bone structure was how he remembered. He certainly dressed well. Pete felt scruffy, despite the new shirt he was wearing. But it was good to see Jimmy again. Pete was glad he had decided to meet him on his own.

Jimmy was floating above the clouds. Amnesia meant there had been no rejection and his brother was a victim without the degradation he had feared. They were together again. Pete was late coming home, but had made it in the end. One more pint and maybe they'd go for something to eat. Anything his brother wanted was going on the Gold Card. Life was good. Life was fucking brilliant. Feeling the drink at the back of his throat and studying his brother's face. He had really aged. Looked older than his years with a bit of a receding hairline, creases in his skin, and a weathered face. He looked healthy enough, but tired. Exhausted more like. It must be the hard living. That and the strain of not knowing who you are.

Pete wasn't bothered about food so they stayed in the pub. The more they drank the more the barriers faded and it could have been yesterday when they'd seen each other. Even so, Mango couldn't ask too many questions. He was pissed but still bottling things up. The details would come later. They drank until closing and were the last to leave the pub, swaying as they walked back to the flat. Pissed-up brothers strolling home at peace with the world on a perfect summer's evening. Mango's thoughts were jumbled and simmering while the Pride that had at first made Pete confident now kicked back and made him ashamed. Their emotions had been chopped up and put through a liquidiser.

Pete couldn't get over at how much Fulham had changed. It was really posh now. Not how he remembered it when he was a kid. He heard his name.

Mango hit his brother in the side of the face and Pete rocked back against a parked car. His kid brother followed up with a kick that bounced off his thigh, then a flurry of drunken punches that either missed their target or half-connected. They staggered in and out of the cars. A wing-mirror smashed. Pete didn't respond, just staggered back from the impact. He wasn't even that surprised. It seemed right somehow. There was nothing he could do. He faced up to Jimmy and the London Pride made him keep eye contact as he felt the fist connect with his nose. The punch was straight and it hurt. He wondered if his nose was broken. There was a lot of blood. It pumped from his nostrils and spilled over his shirt. A white Fred Perry he'd been given by his mum as a Christmas present. She'd even got the size right. She'd let him pick one present to open now, but the rest would wait for Jimmy. It fitted him, but there was no way of knowing when she'd bought it. She hadn't bothered putting dates on the tags. He would have to ask. It would need a good wash. He hoped the blood wouldn't stain.

'Mum gave me this shirt,' he said.

Mango stopped. He blinked as he focused on the shirt, his vision hazy. He saw the red pattern covering his brother's chest. Pete had always liked Fred Perrys, but they were expensive.

'Mum gave it to me before I came round. It fits perfect. She let me open one present without you and this was it. All the rest I've got to open when you come round for dinner.'

Mango stared at the shirt. It was a good fit. His mum was a smart woman. He started laughing. Shook his head. Looked at

the pavement for a bit and turned. The brothers continued
walking back to the flat, Pete laughing as well.

BURNING RUBBER

WILL HAD SAID little all night and the rest of the lads were starting to notice, though Carter had been keeping their attention as he entertained the Sex Division with his latest exploits. It was hot and humid and he was talking as much to himself as the others, trying to forget about the aggro he'd had with Denise the previous week. He'd been looking to wind things down, regular sex breeding contempt and an appreciation of the finer things in life – such as freedom from hunger, poverty and the fear of Slaughter's machete. But Denise wasn't taking hints. She was acting strange and Carter was worried. There was something about sickness in a woman that turned him right off. All that pervy sex stuff was okay, something you had to laugh about otherwise you looked soft, but insanity he didn't even want to consider.

Slaughter had asked Denise to marry him and it had done something to her head seeing the bloke on one knee acting the poet, with a bunch of roses in his hand and a tear in his eye. She told him she'd consider the proposal and seemed to think Carter was planning something similar, as though she had a choice to make between the two men. A decision that was going to stay with her the rest of her life. That moment when she'd reached the crossroads and had to go one way or the other, all that destiny nonsense. He was shitting it because she kept telling him she was a single girl and staying that way, that life was too short for major attachments, which was fine by Carter, but he didn't like the new way she was looking at him. He'd turn his head and her eyes would be drilling into him full of possession. It was like she was trying to convince herself. Then there'd been that business when she'd gone off her trolley, smashing plates in his kitchen and punching him in the mouth. For no reason. Well out of order. He'd pulled his fist back ready to drive that pretty little nose into the slag's brain, then stopped. He'd never hit a bird before and wasn't starting now. End up like that and they'd done you good and proper. Made you into a prize wanker. It was a load of bollocks and he was bailing out soon as he saw his chance. These things needed timing and tact, especially when you were dealing with a headcase who could put a word in the wrong ear and cause you some serious grief. Women were dangerous. Never mind all that weaker sex propaganda.

He must've been mad getting involved in the first place. He was a relaxed bloke and wanted a simple life. But that's what happened. You followed your knob and ignored the messages coming through from the brain, and then it ended in tears. His fucking tears. Even so, he'd given her one up against the fridge for good luck after she'd calmed down and said how sorry she was about hitting him, that she'd replace the plates and was his lip alright? She was mad enough to get the hump and tell Slaughter. He had to be careful. If he wanted Denise then he'd be up front with Slaughter and get it over with, but the thing was he just didn't care. All he wanted was to get his leg over. He felt no guilt about shagging Slaughter's woman. He didn't give a toss. Guilt was for wankers.

'That bird last night was pure class,' Carter said, trying to wash away the problem of Denise and concentrate on the football. 'She worked as a bouncer for a while in King's Cross, but you wouldn't believe it looking at her. She's tall, but not exactly made of muscle. At least she doesn't look that way. She's got a black belt in karate and keeps herself fit. I met her down Blues when I lost you lot. Very nice. Anyway, we had a good chat and everything and then she invites me back, and there I was with a smile on my face lining up a few more points. That's the mark of a champion, the ability to keep churning out results even when faced by quality opposition. I only managed a swift one off the wrist though, because she doesn't drink and eats healthy and doesn't put poison in her body unless she knows where it's coming from. That's her words, not mine. Like my duff's toxic or something. Still, can't blame her I suppose.

Anyway, I'm on for another point tomorrow. I've got these curry-flavoured rubbers from The Hide. I'll be unstoppable with these beauties.'

Carter dipped his hand in the right pocket of his jeans and held the condoms up for inspection. The pack was a mass of colours and Balti leant over to sniff the wrapping.

'Doesn't smell of anything to me. What kind of curry is it?'

'It just says curry flavour.'

'What one though.'

'How do I fucking know? What do you expect, a recipe on the back and a couple of chappatis chucked in for free? It's the thought that counts.'

'It could be a jalfrezi or something. She might not like jalfrezi, all that chilli up her snatch. Or what if it's vindaloo? She's not going to want a chicken vindaloo tickling her clit is she?'

'It's not going to be a jalfrezi or vindaloo,' Harry said. 'It's not like they dip it in a cauldron. It's more likely a korma. It's all fake anyway. Like crisps. I mean, you bite into a bacon crisp and all you're getting is a load of Es.'

'Can't be bad, can it? Fried MDMA for less than a quid. What do you mean fake?'

'It's chemicals mixed up to taste like bacon. It's cheaper.'

'Fuck off. You telling me there's no pork in a bacon crisp?'

'That's right.'

'You're winding me up. No pork in a bacon crisp?'

'God's truth.'

'Fuck off.'

'Swear on the old girl's life.'

'Really?'

'Straight up.'

'Bunch of cunts. They should do them for that. Trade's Description Act.'

'Fucking hell lads,' Carter was getting wound up, with Denise on his mind and Slaughter coming towards the table, and the boys going into one about a packet of fucking crisps. 'These rubbers aren't going to burn a hole in her. It's just a laugh. That's all. A bit of fun. And what's the matter with you,

Will? You look like you've just had your bollocks coated in pharl sauce and found that Mango's been at the pickle tray again. Smile, for fuck's sake.'

Slaughter nodded on his way to the bogs and Carter felt the tightness in his gut ease. His balls were lighter as well. No additives there. Hundred per cent quality. They'd been given room to expand now the danger had passed. It was like he was in the ocean with a shark circling not sure whether he was there or not, knowing that once its brain made the connection he was going to be dragged down and would have to be ready to go the distance. But he was getting to the best part and needed the distraction of story-telling to help him forgot about nutters and their psycho birds. And what was Slaughter doing walking around in his leather coat in the middle of summer? It was a hot night and he had his coat on. Mental that bloke. Fucking mental. Should be locked up where he couldn't do any harm.

'The best bit was when we'd got off the night bus going round her place, coming out of this kebab house with a bit of pre-sex nourishment. There's this big bastard standing there eyeballing us and I ask him what the fuck he's looking at. There was another geezer with him who I didn't see I was so pissed and he hits me and I was so fucking surprised I went straight down like I was Arsenal. Right embarrassment it was, though the cunt was dead once I got up.'

Eileen came to the table, picked up the dead glasses and emptied the ashtray. Carter stopped talking and asked her how she was. Even Will took a bit of notice, because Eileen was looking good, full of herself off on holiday to Ibiza the next day. Then for some reason he thought of her flat on her back with the rest of the girls who trooped over to Spain and Greece, and he was hacked off by women in general and Karen in particular, and all that respect and everything seemed like just more bollocks.

'So there's this freeze-frame moment,' Carter continued, after Eileen had moved on to the next table, 'when I'm on my arse and there's kebab meat and chillies in the air and some wanker coming through to shove his trainers down my throat . . . and then it happens.'

He paused for silence and Will raised his eyes into his head. Carter was so fucking dramatic. He belonged on a stage as he prepared to deliver the punchline. He got right up Will's nose at times like this. Why didn't he get on with the story?

'I'm on my arse and this bird just piles in. Doesn't say a word. A couple of kicks and the first bloke is crouched over, then finished off. Another one and the other bloke's down. Fucking magic. She wasn't screaming or carrying on, just did the business. Hauled me up and there's these two cowboys moaning on the pavement. Never seen anything like it. Cold and calculated and at that moment she was the most beautiful woman in London. No grannying around. Everything in one: good looking, interesting conversation and a minder as well.'

The rest of the lads took their time digesting the story. Even Will was impressed. They tried to imagine the possibilities such a woman offered. It was like something from an old black-and-white sci-fi film, where space travellers land on a distant planet and find it populated by brainy Scandinavian beauty queens ready to treat the new arrivals as though they're kings. Fighting off the dinosaur population and then feeding them with cold bottled lager and the finest burgers.

'A single point was a bonus,' Carter admitted. 'Thing was, I woke up next morning and she was still beautiful. Seeing her in action like that, fucking deadly so you wouldn't get on the wrong side of her, but somehow it didn't make her any less a woman. It wasn't like she was cocky and going on about how fucking hard she was. She did it because it had to be done and maybe that's what a strong bird is all about. A strong bloke as well when you stop and think about it. Did what was necessary.'

The Sex Division sat in respectful silence for a while sipping their drinks and contemplating the wonders of the world. All of them were running the scene through their minds, a mild dose of confusion easily swamped by honest admiration. Will thought harder than most, shifting images through his head and matching them with the argument he'd had with Karen, her words and tears, and Karen off to see her dad leaving him to go down the pub alone and think about the news that she was pregnant and planning an abortion.

The thing that got him was that she didn't even ask what he thought. She announced she was pregnant and then hardly stopped for breath before telling him she was going to get rid of it. All that bollocks about talking to each other was just that – bollocks. It was her body, her life, her decision. Will was expected to do the decent thing and behave himself, say nothing and nod his head in time to the music, a eunuch without an opinion, a toy dog in the back of a Ford Cortina, head banging up and down. He didn't have a chance to think about the thing before she was telling him what she was going to do. He knew all the logic – women suppressed for thousands of years, the right to choose, bodies turned into intensive factory farms, the pill the great liberator giving women a stake in their own destiny, that men thought with their pricks and were incapable of emotion and feeling, that men were monsters and rapists and the scum of creation.

Thing was, he agreed with the bit about women being treated like shit, but where did that leave him? He didn't see why he had to pay the penalty for long-dead politicians who refused to let women vote and the sick bastards who raped women. It wasn't his fault. Sitting in the pub with his mates Will had time to go over it all, and the more he drank the more angry he became. He was being treated like shit. All that stuff about seeing the other person's point of view. Karen didn't give a toss what he thought. She was one more con-artist. When it came down to it, a bloke was supposed to behave according to a certain agenda and listen to a woman's problems and worries, but when it came to a bit of give they didn't want to know.

He started imagining himself as a dad and how it would mean giving up things, freedom and that, but he knew you got something in return. It would be a laugh. There wasn't one bloke he knew with a kid who didn't love it and put it up there on a pedestal and think the world of the little snot machine. They said it was hard work but worth the effort. Something to focus on and love without the complications that came along after a while with a woman. All that history and posturing. The endless need to justify and assert independence. It would be something pure and new, and while he would never be able to plan something like a kid, if it came along then maybe it was meant to be. Like fate or chance. He didn't know all the answers. Didn't pretend he did.

'What would you do if that bird with the black belt turned out to be a two-pointer, and then she got you in a neck lock a few weeks later and told you she was in the club?' Will asked.

Carter almost choked on his lager and everyone turned to the silent one in the corner. Birds you picked up in Blues didn't get pregnant. They were pumped full of chemicals and knew the score, and anyway, it wasn't their role in life. Women you pulled in Blues and shagged an hour or two later were different to mothers. After all, nobody wanted a kid off some old slapper who'd been servicing three or four different blokes a week for the last ten years. If you were planting a seed you wanted to know that the soil was in topnotch condition. It was nature's way.

'You're still with us then?' Carter replied. 'I thought you'd died over there and your right hand was on remote control, lifting the glass to your mouth every twenty seconds. What made you think of that one?'

'I was just wondering. What would you do?'

'It would just be a bit of sex. Nothing serious. Anyway, she'd be on the pill so there's no need to worry, and I'd have a condom massala on the end of my knob.'

'Suppose the spices burnt a hole in the rubber and she'd forgotten to take her pill. Or gone to pop it in her mouth and seen the face of Mango winking up at her. What then?'

Will was getting all serious on them and it made the rest of the Sex Division nervous. They came down the pub for a laugh, not a serious discussion on the state of the universe. The miserable cunt was in one of those moods. Every now and then all that common sense came crashing down.

'She'd have to get rid of it, wouldn't she,' Carter laughed. 'Give it the old coat hanger treatment. Either that or I'd have to take a loan and get it seen to so the NHS don't mess up.'

As Carter made his joke, Will understood why fundamentalists were able to get away with labelling blokes like him, why
your ordinary herbert ended up tarred and feathered by the
thought police. Thing was, it was a knee-jerk reaction, and
Carter wasn't getting off so easy. It was the same kind of
approach that Karen had used. It wasn't good enough. No
fucking way. The lager was going to his head, exaggerating his
thoughts, just like pills with Buddha, Mango and every other
takeaway king decorating the surface, but bollocks anyway. He
was narked.

'Seriously though,' Will said, keeping his voice level. 'You go
out and shag a bird, any one of us, not just you, and what's it all
about? What's the reason? I mean, I know we don't waste as
much time talking about them as they do about us, because we
have more important things in life like football, drink, curries,
music and all that. But why do we go after them at all? What's it
all about?'

'What do you mean,' Balti asked, confused.

'Stop and think about it,' Will continued. 'Look at the
mechanics of the situation. It's like those toys you have when
you're a kid. Plastic shapes and holes to put them in.
Something's empty and then it's filled, but what makes you do
it? I mean, sex is all about having kids, isn't it? That's the real
function when you turn on the lights and switch off the music.
It's just about kids.'

'Course it fucking isn't,' Carter laughed. 'Sex is about getting
your end away. That's all sex is. A bit of fun.'

'But why? What's the point.'

'What do you mean what's the point? You going queer on us
or something,' Carter asked, puzzled, looking to the others for
support. 'Birds are there for blokes like me to service. I'm here
for their enjoyment. It feels good. They're happy and I'm
happy. A simple business transaction. A bit of give and take.
That's what it's about you dozy cunt. Fuck me, Will, you
should give the blow a rest. What do you reckon Harry, has he
been touching your leg under the table?'

The rest of the Sex Division laughed and Will knew he
wasn't getting his ideas across. They were coming out wrong.

That's what too much spliff, too much lager, too much anything did to you. Made you talk gibberish like some sad case wandering the streets. Everyone was laughing except Harry, who'd clicked back to last night's dream.

Harry had been minding his own business on the seafront in Blackpool – watching the waves crash in as a storm built up, jagged lightning far away on the horizon, eating chips from a polystyrene plate – when he'd found half a pill in his ketchup. There was enough of the embossed image left to tell him what was coming next, the face of Michael Portillo leering up at him. It was too late to do anything about it, though, and he was hungry, so he finished the chips and went back to the hotel where he'd arranged to meet that scouse bird. He was looking forward to seeing her again and went to his room, waving to Terry McDermott behind the bar. He noticed Kevin Keegan sitting at the counter with his head in his hands mourning a lost championship. Harry opened the door and was hit by a bright light, suddenly finding himself in an operating theatre. He was in the wrong room and tried to turn back, but a steel door had slammed tight behind him.

He went to a sink and washed his hands, then put on surgical gloves and a mask. He was on automatic and watching his actions as though they belonged to someone else. The Portillo had flooded his brain and for a few seconds he wanted to stand on a stage and point a finger at the sponging single mothers who were single-handedly responsible for the decline of the British Empire. Thankfully he'd only had half the stated dose and was able to fight against the righteous indignation threatening to destroy his soul. It was a battle against superior odds. An expensive education had given the politician the vocabulary and arrogance to effectively deliver his message, hope anaesthetised as the light turned and focused on a scrawny teenage girl strapped down to an operating table. Her accent was pure St-Mary-le-Bow cockney and she was clearly terrified, the skin on her face broken by acne and an Income Support diet. Harry fought against the influence and understood the sickness of such a bitter pill. He knew what was coming. He recognised the wickedness of the Portillo.

He heard the whispered mantra from the pulpit – ALL DRUGS ARE EVIL, ALL DRUGS ARE EVIL . . . EXCEPT THOSE THAT WE TAX – and he saw the posters in the spectator's gallery promoting family values. He wanted nothing to do with the operation that was about to take place and battled harder, relieved to find himself joining the spectators. His personal resistance was too strong for the chemicals, pride replaced by disgust when he realised that he had somehow been tricked and was strapped to a padded chair. He was surrounded by various royals and upright members of the establishment. Hooded sadists and shaven-headed child molesters were well represented, the faces of the latter rotting and leering and pointed towards the operating table with unconcealed excitement.

A deep, official voice filled the room. Single mothers were ruining the nation. They conceived so that they could claim extra benefits. Family life was being eradicated by their antics. It was disgusting. Worse than this, some were prepared to abort their children rather than bring them up in poverty and sickness. They didn't want the stigma and sense of shame the government was imposing. They understood that they were wicked and wasting finite resources. Abortion was evil. But necessary. Sorry – he shouldn't have said that, it went against the Christian ethics of the shire electorate. But it just showed how depraved these little girls were and how the Conservatives loved small children, how they wanted the best for the little ones, and Harry was shouting out that it was the poverty and fear of poor mothers that led to their kids being terminated, but his accent was strange and common like the girl on the table and nobody could understand what he was saying. The hand of a liberal baroness reached out to pat his head. He was a quirk of nature who might one day be allowed to work with the terrier men, if he behaved himself and came to her boudoir that same night. He must perform, though, and satisfy her darkest desires. She wanted him to fuck her in front of The Baron. Very hard, please, young man. Otherwise he was ignored. Like a woman. Like a lump of meat.

The grey-haired surgeon wore a plastic Portillo mask. He

moved towards the girl on the table. Her legs were secured in stirrups and she had been sedated. Her hands were nailed to the table, stretched above her head. The blood running from childlike palms was thin and anaemic. Cables had been attached to her ears. A tape relayed messages and created a climate of terror in the core of her brain. The scientists knew best. They would save the girl the misery of child birth and the tax-payer many tens of thousands of pounds. Another hungry mouth to feed. And then the surgeon was plugging in an old industrial vacuum cleaner and positioning it in front of his groin, strapping it into position before moving forward to push the tube attachment into the girl's vagina. He tried several times but without success. Finally a gentleman in a Peter Lilley mask had to move forward from the shadows and place his hand over the girl's mouth to stifle the agonised screams, smiling as he administered the sacred amyl nitrate. A mysterious figure disguised as Michael Howard stepped forward, greasing the nozzle with lubricant and helping the surgeon insert the tube. The girl fainted and the crowd cheered. Harry tried to shout out, but was unable. At first he thought he was pissed, but then realised that his lips had been stapled together. He was struggling, unable to break free.

A junior civil servant plugged the vacuum in and the surgeon switched the machine on. There was a screen on the far wall and a miniature camera had been inserted in the tip of the nozzle. Harry tried to shut his eyes on what was about to happen, but his eyelids had been sewn open. His heart was pumping and he felt sick. The heartbeat of the foetus became a throbbing pain in the side of his head. He had to hold back the bile rising in his throat otherwise he would drown in his own vomit. He could see the foetus stretching and struggling to hold on to the walls of its mother's womb. It was screaming. It was fucking screaming. He couldn't believe what was happening. It was screaming that it was alive and didn't want to die, that it wanted its mother, but only Harry could understand what it was saying and then the screen turned a dark red and there was a scientist's face superimposed over the gore explaining that life only began when he and other scientists decreed, that there was no God apart from the God of science. The abortionists were nodding their heads in sad agreement and, although they swore hatred for the Tory politicians and their men of the cloth, they were in total agreement, because, after all, they were two sides of the same materialistic coin.

Harry wanted to feel what the foetus felt. He wanted to know the truth. How could a lump of meat feel pain? It didn't make sense and yet he had seen it with his own eyes. All he really understood was that the kid was dead and the girl on the table was haemorrhaging and there was some kind of debate going on as to whether such a worthless creature deserved hospital treatment. Because anyone who aborted their children like that was below sympathy and NHS resources were better spent on educating doctors for the private health sector. Harry saw the foetus floating in a corner of the room waiting for some kind of ceremony. He looked at the partially formed features and wondered what it would have become, all that potential, and then there were other spirits around it, one with a clipped accent explaining that mother was big in advertising with a sparkling career ahead of her and wasn't ready yet . . . give it another few years and then she would have a family and a nanny . . . when she was good and ready . . . on her own terms thank you very much, darling . . . and the foetus said that it understood but Harry knew it didn't, not really, and the newly dead foetus, baby, child was alone again, watching its blood and guts being popped into a jar and handed over to a paedophile who passed back a thick brown envelope in return for the chance to fulfil his fantasies.

It seemed like hours and Harry understood that it was merely seconds as the girl left her body and the machine next to the bed showed that her heartbeat was finished. He saw the spirit of the girl with the child, but there was no happy ending because he was waking up and realising it was a dream, all that emotional blackmail, fucking pile of shit, a fucking nightmare, and he pushed himself to forget. There'd been nothing lucid about that one. A fucking horror show. The last image was of the surgeons and spectators leaving by a neon-lit back exit as the nurses were allowed in to mourn the dead and clean up the mess. He watched the politicians and upright citizens vanish down an alleyway lined by private-sector abortionists who cheered and shouted and slapped their fellow businessmen on the back, applauding the promotion of cottage-industry terminations and the continued state of mental siege that drove customers into their welcoming arms. Freedom of choice. That was the crux.

Harry sat up in bed feeling sick. The sun filled the room but it didn't make any difference. He wanted to erase the dream, though this time it wouldn't fade away. He went to the bathroom and sat on the toilet. Nothing happened.

'I dreamt of this kid having an abortion last night,' Harry volunteered. 'It wasn't funny. It was the worst dream I've ever had. Or at least since I was a kid. Will's right when you think about it. That's what sex was originally invented for, to have babies. It's not just coincidence, is it? That's why you get morals and everything. I suppose if you were religious in the old days then that was the nearest you ever got to playing God. It's creation pure and simple.'

'Creating havoc more like,' Carter said. 'Forget all that. It's fun. Nothing more, nothing less. You get in there, do the business, spill your beans, notch up a few points, and that's the end of the story. You've got to be a mug to end up getting a bird up the duff these days.'

'Harry knows what I was trying to say,' Will said. 'You wouldn't ever plan to have a kid, or at least most people wouldn't in their right mind. But then whatever invented men and women saw that logically the race wasn't going to continue so they built in the pleasure side of things. Orgasms and everything. That way you forget the reality, a screaming brat shitting itself and dribbling all over the place, and just look to get your leg over. Then you end up planting your seed.'

'You sound like a gardener,' Balti said.

'Why worry about it anyway?' Carter said. 'That bird Sherry I went out with had an abortion and a fucking good job too. It's just a ball of blood and veins before it's born. It doesn't matter, does it? If she hadn't got rid of the thing then I'd still have to go round and see her and pay for it. She didn't want it either so everyone's happy. It's not alive, is it.'

'Don't you ever wonder what would've happened if it had been born?' Will asked. 'Don't you think whether it would've been a boy or a girl, or what the kid would've become?'

'No. Why should I? It's done. End of story. It's your round as well. There's only half an hour till closing so get your finger out. I'm fed up with all this. If I wanted a fucking lecture I'd have stayed home and watched the telly. Listened to the religious nutters.'

Will went to the bar and ordered. Eileen served him saying how happy she was to be getting away for a bit of fresh air and sun. It was hot in London now and the place smelt like the inside of a garage there was so much pollution. She couldn't wait to spread her towel on the sand and relax. He wished he was going with her. Carter had a point. It wasn't worth worrying about things, but Will could never escape because it was in his nature. He watched Eileen's bum moving along the bar, and the curve of her breasts when she turned around. There was no escape. It was hormones that drove you on. Chemical warfare.

It was the first time he'd really argued with Karen and it hadn't even been a proper row. Not really. She'd said her piece and left. He saw her in a different light now, but hoped it was the drink making things worse than they really were. Maybe he'd wake up tomorrow morning and everything would be alright. Perhaps it would all turn out to be a bad dream.

He looked at Slaughter at the end of the bar sitting on a stool rocking forward talking with Denise. There was a kind of glow about the bloke and he was stroking her hand. Will knew he was a nasty bit of work, but underneath it all he was a big kid. They all were. They'd started as a cell somewhere and what made someone like Slaughter turn out the way he did? A good woman could bring a bloke like that back to the starting-line. Maybe all of them wanted that deep down. Even Carter. It was just that the women they usually met were acting like blokes giving it the big one all the time. Maybe he'd been wrong acting soppy with Karen. He wondered whether Carter was right and you had to hold something back the whole time so they respected you, because if men expected things from a woman then it followed they thought the same way. Carter had it sussed. He was the happiest one out of all of them. But Will was what he was. He couldn't pretend to be anything else, however much he wanted.

'Will, you remember that game against Leicester you came to with us a few years back?' Balti asked, when his mate had brought the drinks over in two shifts. 'Well, that bloke who came up with us on the train who you were talking music with, Gary, I saw him the other day and he was asking after you. Asked if I still knocked around with that Brentford record collector. He's a DJ and wanted to have a chat about borrowing some vinyl off you. He's got a plum spot in the West End.'

'That's where the money is,' Harry said. 'Keeping the kids supplied. A lot of the old boys do that now. We should go into business, though the West End's going to be sown up, and Smiler and his mob have started doing Blues and a few places round here as a sideline. There again, it's class A if you're doing Es, and the roof'll fall in sooner or later. Always does. We're not really drug dealers are we? Pissheads more like.'

Balti had an interview the next day for something a bit more legit than flogging ecstasy, but was keeping quiet till he knew the result. It sounded alright as well, Mango coming through with a job selling insurance. It might be a doddle, following up leads and trying to persuade people to part with their hard-earnt pennies. The money sounded good as well. Mango was the only one of the Sex Division missing and had been reborn since his brother returned. He was like the old positive kid they'd known and this was reflected in him coming up with the interview.

'Give me his number and I'll give him a bell,' Will said. 'It'll be nice to see Pete again when Mango finally brings him out and play a few records. He was a good bloke. Imagine that. Farming in Norfolk. Well out of order, though, not getting in touch. Mind you, Mango said he'd been ill.'

'When do you reckon we'll get to see him?' Balti asked. 'Now that's like a rebirth. All those years and he turns up with everyone thinking he was dead. Mango's well chuffed.'

Will forgot about Karen and thought of Pete. Balti was right, it was like he was newborn, in adult form. He wondered if he'd be the same, or at least similar. Maybe they wouldn't even recognise the bloke. It was a long time. He was pleased for Mango. A minor miracle. Pleased for all the Wilsons. Most of all Mr and Mrs Wilson. Their flesh and blood. It must be the worst thing in the world losing a kid.

He thought of Pete in his Snow White T-shirt and how silly it all seemed now. Childish really. His last gig with Pete had been The Clash at the Electric Ballroom. Will remembered it so clearly. The air conditioning or whatever wasn't working, and people were sweating buckets, dropping with the heat. He thought of Strummer there with the mic. All the great lyrics and commentary that fitted in with what was going on around them at the time. Another life and yet that education was the best education. Johnny Rotten's attitude that showed you could do whatever you wanted in life never mind what the wankers and controllers told you. Poor old Pete. It would be funny seeing him again. Suddenly Will was hungry and went back to the bar for some crisps.

'You know,' Eileen said, leaning across the counter, 'everyone thinks that because you're going to Ibiza you're just going for the sex. Like that changes because you get on an airplane. It's cheap and I can't afford expensive holidays. Two weeks sitting in the sun will do me fine.'

Will thought about the time he'd gone to Magaluf with the rest of the lads. Ten thousand or so British between the ages of eighteen and thirty-five living in a town of high-rise hotels and Watneys pubs. Chicken and chips and clubs full of DJs celebrating the Leeds Service Crew and Huddersfield Soul Patrol on tour. He remembered the holiday league. There'd been books run for sex, wanks and the amount of times they'd had to shit. Carter won the Sex League, Mango the Masturbation Conference, and when Harry had come down with food-poisoning he'd cleaned up in the Shit Series. If there'd been some decent music and drink, and a few nice women around, Will wouldn't have minded so much, but after two days and nights it was boring. They stood on Psycho Street watched by the Spanish riot police out in full force after, rumour had it, a

Spaniard had been glassed and killed a month before. Packed in tight, hundreds of them drinking their Chelsea Aggro cocktails, with a Union Jack hanging from Balti and Harry's balcony. Up there on the ninth floor and one night at five in the morning a girl from Barnsley forgot the acid and thought she was a bird, attempting lift-off and falling to her death. Rockets exploded in the sky and van loads of police waited tooled-up looking for trouble, mopping up the mess.

That reminded him, Carter and Harry had booked up this year. Once in Spain the league would be blown apart. The season was drifting.

'What's going to happen when you two go to Spain?' Will asked, back at the table. 'You'll get so many points over there it'll mess up the Sex Division.'

The others looked at him and laughed. Now he was with Karen, Will's ground had been shut down and the gates barricaded with barbed wire. He was right all the same.

'We'll have a league of our own over there,' Carter said.

'No more leagues,' Harry moaned. 'You're always on top. We should finish the season the night before we go away. Get it ended. Like Will said, it's going to throw the whole thing out and we'll only end up even further behind. It's the same as using prostitutes over there. There's no competition. Mind you, I might get into second position.'

'It's alright with me,' Carter said. 'Funny, isn't it, how birds go mad when they go abroad. It's like because they're outside England they think they can do whatever they want, though they could do it here as well. It's the same when England play in Europe. Everyone goes on the rampage. There's no respect. The laws don't count any more and the chains are removed. It's like nothing really exists outside England. We obey the law here, but once we're over the channel we don't give a fuck.'

The Sex Division laughed because they knew Carter was right. Nail-on-the-head job. They were an island race and the laws of the land only applied at home. It was fucking mental when you thought about it. They'd left the Amsterdam trip because they were planning to see England play away and wanted to pass through Holland. That way they could make the money stretch further. Blackpool hadn't exactly been a replacement, but it had been a good laugh. The beer tasted like shit but you got used to it, and the Buddhas made for a good night out.

When the bell went for last orders, they'd all had enough and there was no last-minute rush for refills. Slaughter sat with them for a bit slagging off some bloke who'd said something to someone that he didn't like, and Carter's heart shot into his mouth as he saw a machete handle inside the nutter's coat. So that was why he was wearing it in the heat. Carter wanted to ask why he was tooled-up on a beautiful summer's evening, but reasoned that if Slaughter knew anything he wouldn't be sitting there swapping idle chit-chat. It was better to leave well alone and get moving.

The Sex Division walked out of the pub together and Will left the others in the Caribbean takeaway. He walked slowly home, turning the key in the door to the flat and noticing that the lamp in the hall was on. That meant Karen had come back. He was relieved. He stripped off, went for a piss, and then climbed into bed. She was asleep and hadn't heard him come in.

Will watched the patterns of the streetlights on the curtains. It was a game he'd played as a kid, trying to create shapes and then scenes out of the curved and ragged lines. Between the ages of nine and twelve he'd had a lot of trouble sleeping, with all the wonders of life racing through his head. He'd lie there for hours wishing he could drift off. Once he became a teenager he was fine. It was funny how those things worked. Like Harry and his dreams. The bloke was wasted. He'd dreamt about an abortion before Will even knew what Karen was planning. Harry had a gift. He should be dealing with psychiatric cases, honing his skills. Balti, too. He had a lot to offer but instead he was wasted on the social. Mango was out on his own and that was understandable considering what had happened with Pete, while he'd never really known what Carter was thinking. He didn't worry about anything. Nothing that had happened in the past could be changed, and the future was a lottery. He was right, but somehow Will didn't think it was enough. It was incomplete. If you had no sense of the past or future, then maybe you didn't really exist.

Forget the philosophy. He had work the next day and was going to have to face Karen. He looked at her back and regretted the way he slipped into the familiar pattern. Blaming her and thinking of Eileen like that.

Will remembered Balti telling them years ago that 'the only real difference between a man and a woman is that a bird can have a baby. That's it.' Of course they'd laughed, Will as well, because women were different in a lot of other ways, physically and psychologically, but on a bigger level Balti was right. Divide and rule. The ordinary men and women in The Unity and the streets around, in the clubs and markets and the rest of London, England, Britain, the world, had more in common with each other than with the tiny band of financiers who kept them at each other's throats. Women blamed men and men blamed women, but unless you were gay you couldn't really live a proper life without the opposite sex. It wasn't about having sex either, it was something else. You needed the balance. On their own they were just men; half-human almost. A man without a woman ended up in the Sex Division.

Will got up and walked to the curtains, pulling them aside. The window was open and a breeze picking up. He pictured Bev as she'd looked the last time he saw her. Was she awake or asleep at that moment? Did she ever stop and remember him? He often wondered. What she looked like. What she thought about. Whether she had a man and kids. He tried to imagine her sitting in front of the TV watching a film, or deep asleep with the blankets pushed back struggling against the heat. Did she remember that New Year's Eve they'd gone to Trafalgar Square and got pissed in a pub in Soho, just the two of them, and she had a balloon but it was popped by someone and she was so drunk she started crying. But she was happy. He couldn't remember hearing Big Ben. They took the night bus home after a long wait that gave the drink time to wear off, stopping at every stop like night buses did, with the windows misted up and an above-average ratio of nutters aboard. What happened next? He wasn't sure, but maybe they'd had a row. A nice way to start the new year. It was a long time ago now so it didn't matter any more.

No music, no blow, no nothing but the empty street outside and the heat that sent sweat trickling down his back. He stayed there for a long time, thinking, until the breeze got stronger and cooled him down a bit. Eventually he went and laid on the bed and started running through names for their baby. First he thought of girl's names because he knew it was going to be a girl. Then boy's names, because what if it was a boy? And he wondered if Carter ever thought about the kid he could have had, just the once. He must, now and then.

Will rolled against Karen's back and looped his arms around her, moving his left hand down her body until it was over her belly, resting his open palm on the warm skin, wondering what was happening inside her womb.

NORTHERN LIGHTS

BALTI WAS WELL into his second day with West London Decoration. He was top of the world. Running with Jimmy Cagney as he moved the extension-fitted roller up and down the wall. Cagney on a black-and-white time bomb going mental with bullets popping off all round him, calling for his old girl, counting down till the whole place went up. Top of the world? Top of the slide more like. Sitting in the adventure playground looking down at the sad fuckers roaming the streets pushing supermarket trolleys packed with tin cans and their heads stuffed full of green politics. Sad fuckers like Balti hanging around with spaced-out care-in-the-community gents. Sweating with Lottery fever. Playing the numbers game loading his basket with cheap tins of butter beans. Standing in line handing over saved pounds, juggling balls, a clown in the circus. Helping to build West End opera houses and art galleries. Not that Balti was giving up the Lottery. There was no chance of that because he'd put a fair bit in already and had to keep going till he won. It would be easier now. He was a winner. Knew it deep down. With a wage coming in he could afford a flutter and it wouldn't mean going without. It was goodbye to the butter beans and welcome back BSE. He'd been working two days and it was great how everything raced away. It had been the worst time of his life with nothing to do during the day – bored out of his skull and fuck all in his pocket.

He kept thinking about all those blokes who had families. He didn't know how they survived. Thing was, a lot of them didn't, and then you got some Parliament cunt on the box saying how the government was paying out too much in welfare. That they were going to crack down on benefits fraud while their mates in industry pocketed hundreds of thousands in privatisation deals. It made you feel like shit. Like there was going to be a knock on the door and then a sledgehammer following through. It was the lowest trick in the politician's book. Pinpointing the weakest people in society and redirecting the rest of the nation's bitterness their way. MPs with outside interests sitting on advisory boards earning more in a week than most people did in a year. It made Balti sick. At least he was on his own. No small kids to explain things to when all they saw in the shops and on the telly was the endless stream of consumer goods. Made to look bad in front of their mates. There was no union of the unemployed to state the case. No sense of comradeship. You were on your own. The opposition had been either crushed or paid off. Taking the shilling. The gloss applied insisted there was nothing wrong. They were all in it together and you were isolated, and Balti knew he would move on now he was working and look after number one. He didn't have the guts to do anything else. Wouldn't have known where to start.

'Come on lads, tea up,' Paul shouted from downstairs.

Balti stopped work, propped his brush in the paint tray and went into the bathroom to wash his hands. There was a massive glass mirror that reflected the size of the room. Everything was oversized. The bath, shower, sink, even the drugs cabinet. The taps were ornate brass and there was one of those French things for cleaning your arse. They were going to put in a cork floor once it had been painted.

'It's too nice to be working,' Harry said as Balti sat down next to him in the garden.

'Should be on a beach somewhere watching the girls,' Paul replied, passing Balti's tea over. 'Sitting by the pool with a bottle of lager in my hand.'

'You expect me to drink it out of this?' the Balti man laughed, holding the West Ham mug up in front of him and staring at the crest. 'You cheeky cunt. What's the matter with Mickey Mouse?'

'I want Mickey,' Harry said. 'I'm not drinking out of a West Ham mug.'

'Well what about yours, Paul. What's wrong with Goofy.'

'I've already put three sugars in. I like the Goofy one.'

Paul was West Ham, even though he came from Acton. He shrugged his shoulders and passed the biscuits. Balti took four custard creams and put them on the iron garden table they were sitting around. The chairs were uncomfortable if you sat on them too long, but the garden was smart – long and wide with old brick walls decorated with flowering clematis and Russian vine. There were ceramic pots and several small trees. It was great, having a tea break in the garden, feeling the sun. Better than some scabby common smothered in dog shit.

Balti dunked a biscuit and looked back at the house. It was amazing the money some people had. It must've cost four-hundred grand minimum and hadn't been in bad nick to start with. Even so, the family wanted the whole place redecorated and were having an extension added to the back. The builders had finished most of the work and now it was West London's job to give the house a going over. Turn it into a palace. Balti would have thought that a six-bedroom house was big enough for a couple with two children, but figured they must be used to bigger and better things. They could use the extension as a greenhouse. There was enough glass and it faced south. Grow some of the old herb. Something like that. But Balti wasn't complaining. No chance. He was glad of the work. If the owners didn't want the place done up they'd all be signing on. It was an eye-opener, that's all. The house prices in Barnes were right up with the best of them, though he didn't know if he'd fancy living there. Too far from home and there didn't seem much in the way of decent pubs and curry houses. He wouldn't mind the garden though.

The house was detached with a garage to the side and there was a taller wall at the bottom of the garden with a thick layer of ivy eating into the bricks. It was high enough to shut out the house behind, though you'd need binoculars to see in, it was so far away. A retired colonel scanning the windows for action. The lawn nearest the house was feeling the strain of the extension work. Sand, bricks and concrete slabs had destroyed the grass, a cement mixer standing idle, its work done. It was hard work building and he was glad to be out of it. Painting and decorating was better. You really felt like you achieved something. You were putting the finishing touches to the final picture. Get stuck in listening to the radio and watch the room come back to life. Balti was well into his new job and the money was alright as well. Things were looking up.

He'd lasted two days selling insurance before one of the blokes at Harry's firm left and he was straight in the door. He didn't have to think twice. Talking shit was no way to make a living. He'd hated the insurance game from the beginning, talking out of his arse trying to con people who weren't much better off than himself. The interview had been a doddle because most of his earnings were based on commission and the firm wasn't taking a risk. The rest of the blokes were wide boys who didn't give a toss about anyone, while the few women there tried to out-male the males. Not that Balti was a social worker, but he still felt like a cunt trying to worm his way into someone's wallet, a working man or woman struggling to make ends meet worried enough by the crumbling welfare state to want to buy some kind of private protection. They were trying to think ahead and he was expected to prey on their fears, the same fears he'd had signing on.

Like there was nothing to look forward to, just the skip in the street stacked with broken concrete and rotting rubbish, because everyone knew the country was being stripped bare. It was like Karen said, the more the rich got the more they wanted. They ground you into the gutter and then pissed on you as you laid there drunk on supermarket lager. It was dog-eat-dog philosophy and it set people fighting each other. Kicking and punching, trying to get something for themselves so they could switch off and pretend there was nothing wrong. Balti wanted an easy life. He was like everyone else. Cash in his pocket and a job. He wanted to be left alone. Didn't want to think about the unfairness of it all. Karen was a diamond though. She knew what it was all about, but the way he saw it things were never going to change. It was human nature to be selfish, but with time on your hands it made you feel worse knowing the truth. He didn't want to be a victim that everyone felt sorry for. He wanted respect. A job gave you that. Without money you were fuck all. You couldn't do anything and you walked with your head down. You felt different. Birds weren't interested if you were hard up. It didn't fit in with the power trip. If you acted hard then it filled in some of the gap. That was the pecking order for you.

'Remember that time in Magaluf?' Harry asked. 'We walk in the room and Carter's doing the business with those two birds taking turns sucking his knob.'

'Should have got in there as well,' Paul said. 'Me and this mate of mine did a two-ender with some bird over in Hornchurch. I unloaded down her throat and he gave her one from behind. Right filthy old slapper she was. Fucking slag.'

'These birds in Magaluf were alright,' Harry said. 'I'm not into that kind of thing myself. I mean, you don't want to see your mate on the job do you.'

'Suppose not,' said the Happy Hammer. 'But it was dark and this bird fucking loved it, the dirty cow. Back of a fucking transit van as well.'

Balti remembered the holiday snapshot. Opening the door and finding the sex machine on the job. One of the girls turned and gave them the once over, then told them it was a private party and they weren't invited. Obviously didn't think they were up to scratch. They'd gone down the bar. Five in the morning and they were knackered, forced to sit around with the whizz kids waiting for that greedy cunt upstairs to finish. They hung around patiently sipping their bottles of piss water moaning about Carter lying back with a blonde between his legs and a redhead sitting on his face. Pure heaven. That was Magaluf for you.

'It's a bit out of order, isn't it?' Balti said. 'I mean, the girl looks after you both and then you slag her off. Like if they do the business right off then they're tarts, and if they keep their legs closed they're fucking lesbians. Least she was game for a laugh.'

He was mimicking Karen on double standards, trying to get a rise out of Paul for lumbering him with the West Ham mug. Balti told him it was a divide-and-rule plan pushed by the government and promoted through the media. Something to keep the people in line. Keep them fighting among themselves so they wouldn't get organised and have a pop at the scum in charge. They had fuck all in common with some bloke who drove a Roller and lived in Hampstead, or some bistro trendy in Kensington. It was right what Karen said. She made you think about things like that, but it was hard working it all out. It wound you up something chronic when you realised you were being shafted the whole time. It was the same with blacks and that. Another way to break you down and keep you fighting each other.

It was funny, because even though the months signing on had been hard and driven him round the bend, he'd slowed down and not been so knackered all the time. Sitting on the common wasn't how he wanted to spend his life, but it made him think about things. True, it only made him more hacked off, but it was good to know he could reason things a bit. Usually he was just working and going home to sit in front of the telly, or going out and getting pissed, but without the hard graft his mind was all over the shop. He didn't like thinking too much. That's what did you in. There was no way out that he could see, whatever Karen said. Life was a struggle. You were born, grew up, fought for everything, and then you lived on a shitty pension and became a burden on the economy. Then you died. That was it for people like him. Pure and simple. He wasn't complaining. The facts of life.

'Suppose it's a bit unfair, but so what?' said Paul. 'It's just a laugh. You wouldn't want to end up with that transit van bird though. Walking down the aisle knowing she was into threesomes. No bloke would. I mean, your trendies and that, they say they wouldn't care, that they'd fall in love with gang-bangers, but they don't. They say it doesn't matter what colour you are, or where you work, but you don't see the knobs marrying black girls from Woolies do you? They still stick with their own kind.'

'I wouldn't be that bothered,' Balti said. 'Doesn't worry me at all. Means she's a goer and that's only going to be good for me, isn't it?'

'You'd mind,' Harry said. 'Even though you say you

wouldn't, you would. It's only natural. I'm not saying it's right, but that's the way we are. Birds are the same.'

Being out of work might have got Balti's brain going, but it had also started him thinking about sex more than normal. Specially in the summer when anything between twenty and fifty started to look good, in their short skirts and tight tops. All the gear coming out of the wardrobe. Fucking heaven, and if you weren't wearing yourself out you had time to start thinking about how you weren't getting the business. He'd spent a good few afternoons in front of the telly plugging into the old porn videos. Watching the Germans and Dutch doing their O and A levels. Jeans round his ankles with a hard-on as Wanda with the thirty-eight-inch bust took everything her three admirers could shove into her. She was getting every hole filled and when the grunting and groaning reached its climax the camera zoomed in for a close-up of the blokes withdrawing and shooting over her face, belly, arse – and there Balti was sitting with spunk over his T-shirt and the video rolling on to another scene in another house with another blonde bird getting another length off another headless junky with a sagging knob. He always felt let down after he'd come and wondered how he got so worked up, turning the video off and going to wash away the mess. He still went back for more, though, because London was hot and steaming and he wasn't getting the real thing.

That's how it went, unless you were Carter who didn't need magazines and films. Running through the contact mags he'd got his bottle together and written off to three women whose masked photos showed them in all the regulation gear. Flicking through pages of glossy pictures and lines of ads he knew they weren't going to be stunners, but so what. Balti didn't care. They must be desperate to advertise. Either that or nymphos. Nutters even, but he wouldn't know till he tried. The phone-lines cracked him up, beautiful models with big tits plastered with slogans – BORED HOUSEWIVES TALK DIRTY ...CLIMB ABOARD AND I'LL BRING YOU OFF ... SHOOT ALL OVER MY HOT TITS – with the tiny type giving the phone rates. He wasn't a mug. And some of the videos they sold. Fair enough, everyone liked watching a bit of oral and anal and double pleasure, but it was stretching things selling videos of freaks and all that dominatrix stuff. Mango had some of those videos, but Balti wasn't interested in spanking birds or sitting in a fucking cage. That was comedy stuff. Balti didn't mind a bit of rubber, but birds with whips was a right turn off. He'd leave that to the Tory MPs. It made you wonder when they sold freak videos of twenty-five stone women shagging blokes half their weight. The pictures made him feel sick, the rippling flesh and collapsed bodies. That really was taking the piss. Then there'd been the midget getting it off a couple of nice-looking birds who should've known better. Fucking horrible. You had to have standards.

Then last week this bird from Archway phones. Suzie says she's got his letter in her hand and that she loves the content and the handwriting. A couple of words spelt wrong and it looks like it's been written by an artist, all spikes and tatty edges. At first Balti thought she was taking the piss, and he didn't remember spelling anything wrong, but she said she meant it in the nicest way because she'd been dyslexic at school and had a bad time of things till she finally got some proper help. Most of the time it had been teachers telling her she was stupid and wasting their time. They started talking and it seemed easy enough so they lined it up and tonight was the night. She sounded alright and he'd been up front saying he was no oil-painting, but she wasn't bothered because as far as she was concerned it was the imagination that counted and she liked solid men. Hated skinny runts with their ribs sticking through hollow skin, pale hairless bodies and a serious lack of blood flow. As long as he remembered that a woman had a clitoris then they'd get on fine. It was a right turn on that and her voice went husky asking him how he wanted her to dress. For a couple of seconds he'd been tongue-tied knowing this was a test of imagination and that Suzie liked men with imagination. He had to come up with something fast so went for a red basque and high heels. It wasn't very original and he held his breath because he thought he must've fucked it up, but it seemed to do the trick.

Best of all Suzie could accommodate. That was important. He

didn't want Harry on the scene. He'd take the tube up after work. It was all a bit sad, but exciting as well. She could be okay or a fucking headcase. Either way he was in for an interesting night. North London on tour.

'Look at this sick cunt,' Paul said, flicking through the paper. 'They should take the bastard out and hang him. Every other day there's a fucking nonce in the paper.'

There was the blown-up face of a child-killer, his brow heavy and face unshaven. He looked like a nonce. Maybe it was the way the picture had been taken looking up. The headline condemned the monster who had dragged off a six-year-old girl during a hot summer's night, sodomised her and then set fire to the body. The report said that the police believed the maniac had planned the attack, stashing a can of petrol in a blackberry bush. Hard eyes stared straight ahead. The previous day Babs had smiled and pouted and pushed her full breasts forward, nipples ice-cubed erect. Babs liked watersports in the Caribbean (especially jet skiing) as well as quiet Italian meals for two and dancing the night away in Stringfellows. She had a big future ahead of her. The paper had been in no doubt of that. But today the message had changed. The fun was on hold with outrage filling the gap. Paul finished the report and turned to the editorial with its subhead SCUM.

'What's the point letting people like that waste our money in the nick?' Paul asked when he'd finished the editorial. 'Nonces should be strung up. Them and terrorists who put bombs in shopping centres and murder innocent women and children.'

Balti nodded. There was no point arguing. He didn't believe in the death penalty simply because he knew what the old bill were like. They'd fit you up for stupid little things, so what would they do when they were faced with a crime that had to be solved fast because the media was breathing down their necks demanding instant retribution?'

He finished his tea and took three more biscuits to keep him going. He wanted to get back to work. It was too hot and he needed some shade. It was cool indoors and he didn't mind getting back into the painting. There was a steady motion working the roller and his brain got into the rhythm. He ran his hand along the polished banister leading upstairs. Right the way up and no chance of a splinter. Into the room he was painting with the radio playing Oasis quietly in the background.

The rest of the afternoon passed quickly and they were soon knocking off. Balti stayed behind and ran a bath. He had a bag with him and clean clothes. He stripped off and got in, spread out. Bubble bath hit the rim of the tub. Fucking lovely. It was amazing what a bit of luxury could do. He dried off and put on a clean pair of jeans and a new-breed Ben Sherman. He let himself out the back and walked to the BR station. It didn't feel like London in Barnes. He could've been at the seaside or in some market town. He felt relaxed. He didn't have to wait long for a train and he was on-board cruising through South-West London and up to Clapham Junction, past Asda, New Covent Garden and Sainsburys. The sun lit up the MI6 building opposite Vauxhall BR, with its flash design and glass panelling. The carriage was nearly empty, a kid with some kind of drum n bass playing in his earphones and an upright elderly woman reading a gardening book. Everyone was going in the opposite direction. The train pulled into Waterloo, the international terminal to his left.

He pushed through the crowds watching the departure board and went underground, buying his ticket and checking the adverts lining the escalator, West End tourist shows and dodgy soul albums. Fucking typical – the board on the northbound Northern Line platform said the next train was in seven minutes and the cunt was going the wrong way. The one after went through Archway, but it was twelve minutes. He'd go up to Camden and change. The platform started to fill up and he wasted the time watching mice play under the lines. The Northern Line had to be the worst line in London. Nothing but hassle. The waiting made him think about where he was going, the woman at the end of the trip. He had to phone Suzie when he got to Archway as she wasn't that keen on giving out her address. Fair dues. A girl couldn't be too careful. For all she knew he might be some serial killer. When the tube finally arrived he was pressed against the door between the carriages, where at least there was air rushing in when the train was moving.

Balti didn't like being packed in tight. He'd heard the horror stories of the tube going down because the wiring was so out of date. Thousands stuck underground and he didn't fancy it in a packed carriage. He didn't fancy being pressed up against the office girls in front of him either. Felt like a right perv trying to think of something apart from Suzie. He tried counting sheep but he wasn't a farm hand like Pete Wilson. Mango hadn't brought his brother out yet and wanted to go up to Norfolk to stay on the farm. He'd miss the luxury of his flat and wouldn't like getting the Jag covered in cow shit. But he was pleased for the bloke. Mango got on his wick at times, but he'd been through a lot and now maybe he'd ease up.

Balti relaxed when a good chunk of the passengers got off at Leicester Square. Camden came up soon enough and a short wait later he was passing through Kentish Town and Tufnell Park, walking up the out-of-order escalator at Archway past the puffing old-timers. When he reached the top he was out of breath himself. Torrential rain pounded the concrete outside. He was sweating from the train, straight out of the sauna so he shouldn't have bothered about the bath. He hoped he didn't smell too bad. He found a phone and made the call.

'Hello.' A man's voice.

Balti hesitated. Must be the wrong number.

'Is Suzie there?'

'Hold on.'

He didn't expect this. She said she could accommodate.

'Hello.' A woman's voice.

'Suzie?'

'You made it. You're a bit late. I'll come down and get you. We can go for a drink.'

Balti walked outside and waited by the railings. The rain had stopped. Short and to the point, steam rising from the pavement. A man answering the phone, meeting at tube stations, off down the pub. It wasn't what he expected. Wasn't like the films. He had the script in his head. The easy run up to Archway, round to a nice little flat where the sex goddess

opened the door in some silky gear, ushered into a nicely laid-
out living room. Sitting on the designer couch. The pouring of
drinks. A couple of sips. Suzie downing hers in one. Rushing
towards him. Off her head with lust. Sex mad. Balti carried out
on a stretcher, with an intravenous drip in his arm and a big
smile on his face. Something like that anyway.

'Hello.'

He turned round. The surprise must've shown. He'd never
realised eyes were so important to a person's face. The photo in
the magazine showed her in stockings and suspenders, with the
main part of her face covered in one of those digital masks they
used on the telly when they were showing police video footage
of a crime. Hiding the identity of the man in custody so as not
to prejudice the case. All fair and square.

'The train took ages. Sorry I'm late.'

Suzie had big blue eyes. They were massive. She was a
cracker. What the fuck was she doing in magazines with the
losers? He was a bit stuck for words. He hadn't expected much,
just a good shag with a clapped-out nutter who had enough
passion to make up for a wrecked body. Bit like him really. But
Suzie could've been a model.

'It's alright. My brother was round so I had someone to talk
to. He's gone now. Bet you wondered who it was answering
the phone. Thought I had someone else there. Lining them up
on a conveyor belt. I'm not that bad you know.'

Suzie started to talk as she took Balti by the arm and led him
back through the station towards a pub she knew. She was
going to be upfront with him and said that she used the contacts
columns to avoid complications. She was an actress, a proper
actress, and she didn't want men becoming attached. But she
needed sex as much as the next person. Could Balti understand
that? He nodded and opened his mouth to say something. That
it was fine by him. But she asked him did he really understand,
because men were pretty thick when it came to working
women out. They had to understand that women had the same
needs as men. They had a sexuality that could be just as material
and unemotional as that of a man. What really pissed her off was
all that hippy earth mother propaganda that said a woman was

full of intuition and creativity. Now she was an actress, and that was something creative in itself, but she was no earth mother. She liked sex. Pure and simple. Nothing wrong with that was there? And Balti said no, of course not. She was only being honest and how was the new job going that he'd been talking about, she'd been out of work a lot and one thing she would never do was appear in porno mags. That wasn't acting. It was demeaning to the women who were forced into those roles. Women posing for men to dribble over. It made her very angry. Dirty old men in their old age masturbating over pin-ups. It was exploitative. That was the difference. She could do whatever she wanted with her body and didn't have to do what men told her. She was taking what she wanted. Suzie was no prostitute. She hoped he understood and she wouldn't go on about it any more. It was better to get things out in the open. She wasn't mad. She didn't think Balti was a failure with women because he had to hunt them down in magazines.

They walked up the hill and Balti was knackered already. His head was spinning. He wanted an easy life. An easy shag.

'That's a beautiful pint,' he said, feeling a bit better as they sat in the Whittington with Dick's cat on the wall behind glass.

It looked like something squashed they'd just scraped off the road. He concentrated on the Guinness.

'It's a nice little pub,' Suzie said. 'They have diddly-daddly on Thursday nights. Session musicians with fiddles and bodhrans and pipes and banjos who just turn up and sit around playing. There's no stage and no sense of being an audience. I like it in here. It's very natural. I often thought that plays should be performed in that way with no sense of Us and Them, but it's a visual medium so it wouldn't be much good if you can't see what's happening.'

Balti looked around the pub. It was a small Irish boozer with a central bar and the atmosphere of a pub where the quality of the drink came first. It had the mark of class most London pubs used to boast before the craze to gut them and turn the inside into imitation spit-and-sawdust barns. Thing was, it was all decoration and the drink was usually overpriced and the lager flat.

The Whittington wasn't busy. Not what he'd expected at all. He was looking to get his leg over. Nothing more. But the Guinness was worth the trip and Suzie was something else. Long blonde hair and a fit body. She wore dangling earrings and tapped her short nails on the table. She'd stopped rabbiting now so he could get a word in. It was nice having a second's pause between sentences. She spoke sense he supposed, though she went on a bit. She was another strong woman. Karen was strong. His old girl was strong. They were all different though. Most of the women he knew were strong. But it was strange because he'd had the thing fixed in his head. A wham-bam-thank-you-darling session then out the door. He hadn't planned on a pint and idle conversation. He couldn't get his head round it. There had to be something else going on. There had to be a problem. Simple as that. She didn't seem like a nutter. Went on a bit, but that could be nerves, because fuck knows he was nervous enough now.

He liked Suzie straight off. The eyes and face and rest of her body. Big warm pools of colour. He lifted the glass and took a long drink. Just the one, then he'd get things moving.

Balti knew his place in the scheme of things. He wasn't in good shape and had been out of work. He didn't expect anything other than a shag and was prepared to scrape the barrel. Suzie wasn't the barrel. It had to be inside her head. He tried to picture the basque and high heels waiting at home. Started thinking of the videos under his bed. The Germans and Dutch taking it down the throat and up the arse. False groans as some wanker with a half-erect knob rubbed KY up a Filipino's arse and drove it home. Three-onto-one wasn't nice. The girl on all fours getting it rammed down her throat. A bloke underneath who she was riding and then the third bloke arrives and climbs aboard. Camera zooming in as the bloke giving it the A treatment rubs balls with the man below. Switching angles, changing cameras to show the expression on the girl's face. He could tell she was feeling the pressure even though she tried smiling for the camcorder, but with some junky's knob halfway down your throat it was difficult.

Suzie was off again telling him all about the Archway and

how she'd moved there from the south coast. She'd grown up in Brighton and would return there one day, but she was waitressing in London now and things were going well for her. He smiled and nodded and wondered what made people appear in porn videos. Maybe they didn't care, but more likely needed the money. The bird doing the threesome couldn't get much out of it, so it had to be the cash. They all looked scabby. The blokes well dodgy and the girls all worn out. Maybe some of them got off on it. Difficult to say really. Not the kind of people you met down the pub. He remembered that story about Barry Walters a couple of years back. He sits down to watch a dirty video and there's his girlfriend on the screen. Two weeks before the wedding as well. Packs her in. It made the lads laugh because the hypocrisy was so obvious. What was he doing watching in the first place? You had to apply the rules to yourself as well. You couldn't judge. But you did. Strip off the personality with the clothes. Blow up dolls. You couldn't escape it and Suzie went for the public health warning straight off and it didn't do a lot of good. He couldn't work out if she was a headcase or what.

'Do you want another?' she asked.

Balti looked at his pint. It was empty. He watched her walk to the bar. She was wearing dungarees and a T-shirt. He watched her joking with the barmaid as the Guinness settled. She drank pints as well.

'I could drink this stuff all day,' she said, raising her glass to her mouth. 'Drink too much though and it sets your heart racing. It's the iron content.'

Balti noticed she wasn't wearing make-up. He couldn't smell perfume either. Suzie was obviously a natural girl.

'That letter you wrote was great,' Suzie said. 'The way the letters mash up together and all the spikes. It had character. I'm into shapes you see. Odd shapes. Outlines and angles. I love fractals, the way they expand and trail off into the distance. Do you know what I mean?'

Balti nodded his head. He didn't have a clue. He'd never thought about his writing before, but he liked fractals.

'You made a few mistakes in your spelling as well.'

'I was never very good with spelling.'

'I got left behind at school because the teachers didn't know I was dyslexic. Funny, really, but they get the chance to set you up for life and if you struggle then they get on your back. Not all of them, but too many. It's like life when you grow up. If you're no good at your job then people take it personally, as though you're lacking something in your personality. It's like you're doing it on purpose.'

'I'm not dyslexic. Never had much interest really. We were always mucking about. They don't get hold of you and make you want to learn. Just tell you you're a problem. I couldn't wait to leave and get a job.'

'It was acting that made it alright for me,' Suzie said. 'Nothing classical. I didn't have any formal training. The local youth club did something and then I joined an amateur group. I don't make very much, but it's fun, and you can always pick up bar or restaurant work. I've had a couple of bit parts on the TV as well. That helps. Acting you get to be anything you want. You can get lost in a role and then say it's someone else. Nobody knows how much is inside you. Depends on the part of course. They only ever see the outline. It's all shapes isn't it? I mean, you look at a woman and you see her figure. Whether she's got nice breasts and legs. How much she weighs. The height and proportions. That's fair enough. The shapes and sizes. Weights and measures. What's inside though?'

Balti smiled. He didn't know. The Guinness was slipping down a treat. He pointed at the dead cat on the wall.

'Dick Whittington's cat's been knocked out of shape a bit. Looks like he was run over by a lorry.'

Suzie laughed and looked at the cat.

'There's a bridge up the hill where the suicides go. They jump off on to the road. It's a bit unlucky if you're driving along and a face bursts through the windscreen. I can't understand how someone could be so depressed they could go and kill themselves. Life shouldn't be taken so seriously. We live forever so why worry about anything. We should go out and get what we want. That's why I use the magazines. What's the point in hanging around expensive clubs trying to pick someone up when all you want is sex?'

'I don't know,' Balti said, looking towards the barmaid who was talking to an old boy on the opposite side of the bar.

Suzie moved closer and lowered her voice for his benefit.

'I got fed up with all that. Standing around waiting for some idiot to get enough drink down his throat so he has the courage to come over and chat me up. All that mating ritual and you don't have a clue what you're going to get. You could pick up a psycho who's going to come home and kill you. The amount of boring bastards I've had in the past. All the shitty one-liners. It really gets on your nerves and then they last a couple of minutes and fall asleep. Next morning they don't have anything worth saying and you want to get them out the door as fast as possible. The pretty boys are worst. All shape and no substance. So I've given all that up now. I use the adverts. There's no hassle that way. I want sex. You want sex. Straightforward and honest and I get to talk to my partners beforehand. I get a lot of wankers mind. We're all the same you know. Everyone on the planet. There's no individuals. There's no point being pinned down with one person because then it becomes boring and miserable and you end up tearing each other's hair out. We're going to live forever even when we die, so who cares. It's a great feeling, don't you think? Now that's real freedom.'

Balti nodded. As long as Suzie was happy. He existed. He was an individual. And while it was true enough that he would be in another situation and probably quite different if the Queen was his mum, he reckoned there would still be something that was his own. There again, he didn't know what he thought about life after death. If it wasn't for his granddad telling him about that out-of-body experience then he'd say death was just an appointment with the furnace. Nothing to look forward to after the flames had burnt you to a cinder. He knew the old boy wouldn't have lied, but he didn't have the faith. He wouldn't mind believing, because like Suzie said, it would make everything a lot easier, but you couldn't make yourself believe something if you didn't really feel it. But bollocks, he'd come up to Archway for a bit of creation, not all this talk about death.

'So what are you doing now?' he asked.

'It's a play about the Wigan Casino,' Suzie said. 'It's about these four people who have been going to the Casino for years listening to northern soul and now the Casino's closing down. There's three songs the DJs always played. Long After Tonight Is All Over by Jimmy Radcliffe, Time Will Pass You By by Tobi Legend and I'm On My Way by Dean Parish. The play centres around the songs and what the characters are going to do with the rest of their lives. Whether they'll give up on northern soul because the Casino is the best there'll ever be, or whether they'll move on to another kind of music. Where will they go next? We're still rehearsing. It's going to be good. I'm enjoying my role.'

'What do you do?'

'I'm going to settle down and get married because nothing will ever be that good again. The Wigan Casino is the ultimate and I'm going to stop dead and start leading a very mundane, everyday life and find love and happiness. It's a good part.'

'It's a bit unfair on the bloke you end up marrying. If he's just a shape to fill the gap. He's going to have feelings as well.'

'That's the kind of character she's going to be. Decisive and working to a plan.'

Balti felt sorry for the man involved, but it was only a poxy play so it didn't matter. The time passed and he forgot what he'd come up to North London for after four pints. They were having a good old chat and before he knew what was happening it was ten o'clock and Suzie was drinking up and telling him it was time to go. He carried the glasses to the bar and followed her outside. Down the hill and through a multi-coloured, piss-soaked subway. He watched the mugging mirrors and saw their bent reflections approaching. The curl of hip-hop graffiti formed a giant snake through the passage. A bottle rolled in the breeze. Reds and greens and yellows rushed past.

He walked up the ramp and felt Suzie next to him, talking a mile-a-minute. He'd had eight pints of Guinness and was feeling heavy. He was hungry as well. They cut through the flats. He needed a piss and went behind a wall. Suzie waited under a light. Having a slash in a dark corner turning his head to find she'd come over and was standing next to him watching. He felt awkward as he shook himself dry. He felt her hand drift down and work him erect. Moving back and forward slowly, then faster.

Suzie pushed Balti back into the shadows, faint light from the Archway roundabout filtering through the trees. Balti was hot and the sound of traffic died down with a red light. He could hear Irish music from the Archway Tavern, the doors wide open for fresh air. Suzie pulling his jeans wide open and reaching inside his pants for his balls, grabbing and yanking them forward. He tried to pull her into him but she shrugged him off, moving her hand back to his cock. He had a stonker right enough and tried to kiss her but she turned her head.

'When we get back.'

Suzie was reaching into her dungaree pocket and taking out some kind of gel, undoing the top with her teeth and then lining the lubricant along his knob. She replaced it and started working harder, in total silence, bringing Balti off in a machine-gun succession of spurts that disappeared into the darkness.

'Come on,' she said. 'Let's get back.'

Balti did up his jeans and tried to catch up, following her through a small estate and up a street lined with rundown but still impressive houses. His knob was sticky. He'd been looking forward to a good bit of sex, not a quick hand job in a dark corner. Fuck that for a game of soldiers. But he'd have time to recover, though Suzie had gone all quiet on him now. Just his luck. He would need a piss again soon. The Guinness felt bad in his gut. It was the wrong drink in this kind of weather. He was sweating like a pig and the gel was uncomfortable in the front of his jeans.

A door opened and Balti followed Suzie up a flight of stairs. Another door and she was having trouble with the lock, finally inside turning on the light, walls lined with posters of famous actresses. All the big names from the past were there. Marilyn Monroe, Doris Day, Bette Davis. The pictures were big and framed and leading into the living room, where smaller glossy photos took over.

Suzie led Balti to the couch, sat him down and put on a CD. A song he didn't recognise.

'Jimmy Radcliffe,' she said. 'What do you want to drink?'

'A bit of that whisky would be alright. No water thanks.'

She handed Balti the drink and leant over. She kissed him on the lips. Her mouth was warm and friendly. She walked to the door and disappeared, leaving Balti to look around the room. It was nicely decorated, full of plants and the photographs. She must be doing okay, though it wasn't an expensive set-up. A bit of imagination had obviously been applied. This was better.

He turned his head as Suzie returned. She was wearing a long see-through number. She looked great. Her body was perfect. The light was dimmed and she walked over towards him. There had to be something wrong. It was a dream. She was a film star in the making. Wrapping those arms around his neck and pulling him in close, whispering romance in his ear. His bladder was full. He needed a piss but didn't want to break the spell.

'You'll last longer after what I did outside,' Suzie whispered. 'You won't let me down will you?'

Balti hoped not. She led him towards the bedroom and he managed to get into the bathroom for a piss. He leant over the bog and hung his head. It was a dream come true. Like the films. He flushed the toilet and washed his face in the sink, a quick wipe under his arms. So what, she'd been drinking as well. He was more Sid James than Humphrey Bogart. You had to have a laugh. He pulled the string and hurried towards the bedroom.

HAPPY HOUSE

It was a nightmare. A fucking nightmare. Worse than anything so far and Harry was taking it seriously. He was paying attention because he had the gift. He could see the future and prophesise events. It had happened so many times before that he couldn't bottle out and dismiss last night's dream as meaningless. He was walking up and down, stopping halfway, sitting in the condemned cell waiting for the hangman to arrive, handcuff his hands and slip a hood over his head, string him up from the gallows, cut him down in the nick of time. Dragged screaming to a club full of clones with Saddam tashes. He felt like topping himself. Why him? Why? Bath houses full of queers taking turns banging out the primitive four-bar beat of the swamps on his arse. No fucking way. He'd rather die. No way was he living the life of a shirt-lifter.

'You coming or what,' his best mate Balti shouted. 'What are you doing in there, having a wank?'

Like a fucking wife.

'I'm having a piss. That alright with you?'

Harry finished brushing his teeth and left the bathroom. Thing was, looking in the mirror, he didn't look like a bum bandit. Maybe you didn't. Ken Davies, now, he didn't look like an iron, but he was bent as the proverbial. A nice enough bloke who kept his interests to himself and never got any grief. Thing was, everyone knew the bloke. That was the difference. It wasn't like he was some stereotype off the telly emerging from the bushes in a G-string.

'My knob's still sore from that bird up in Archway,' Balti said, once they'd left the flat and were walking down the street. 'What a night. Don't think I'll ever be the same again.'

'Where'd you say you met her?'

'I didn't.'

'Well, where'd you meet her then?'

'On the tube.'

'On the tube? What were you doing, touching up office girls in the rush hour?'

'She asked me what platform she was on and we got talking, went for a drink, and before I know what's happening she's inviting me back to listen to her CDs.'

'Those three points you got mean I'm bottom of the league. I'm not even joint bottom now that Will's given up.'

'Relegation mate. You've still got tonight and then you're off on holiday and the season ends. You'll get your end away over there no problem. Unless you're a pillow biter. But it won't count will it? Birds don't count in Spain. You could still catch up tonight. Never know, I might get lucky and give Carter a run-in myself. I can feel the old confidence returning. Surging back more like. What a fucking night. First wage packet in my pocket and three points in the bag. Dear oh dear, she didn't just swallow, she fucking gargled first like she was on the Listerine. I'm back in the land of the living and showing some form.'

Balti was full of himself and Harry couldn't help laughing at the thought of his mate making up the massive points difference in a single night. He'd have more than a sore knob the amount of work he had to do. They'd be carting him off in an ambulance, but at least he'd die happy, which was more than Harry could say for himself. They didn't bother with calculations as they turned on to the high street and hurried towards the pub. Carter was the undisputed champion waiting to be crowned. The shag machine was pure Dutch quality and had played the game as it should be played, using the wings and knocking the ball through the midfield with a deft touch born of practice.

It was Friday night and Balti had money to burn. It was going to be a good one. His first week's wage and it was a great feeling. Welcome back to the human race and all the bother and mind games were over. He could feel the tingle in his bones, even though his knob was aching. That Suzie was a right goer.

She couldn't get enough. She fucking loved it and was moaning her head off all night. It made him feel big. He'd made her happy. Things were definitely looking up. It was just a shame it was a one off. She'd made up her mind and he knew there was no going back for seconds. She'd taken what she wanted without complications. But Balti was grateful. It wasn't every day a bloke like him ended up in bed with a bird like that. Northern soul. Catchy songs, though he'd never been into that sort of music. Truth be told, he'd always found it a bit weedy. Suzie was making the effort playing the part and said northern soul was a much rawer version of the weak stuff that you usually heard. It was soul mingled with RnB. Wigan Casino hadn't served alcohol and the all-nighters had functioned on speed. It was part of a culture that had eventually progressed to acid house, techno, jungle and all the other strands of a basic theme. Suzie said she'd always preferred old platters though. Frank Sinatra, Ella Fitzgerald, Dean Martin. Silver-screen Hollywood romance and kiss-and-cuddle music, and while it was a mechanical kind of sex she enjoyed he could understand her reasoning. She was a romantic, whatever he'd first thought about her being a nutter decked out like that posing for contacts columns. The songs were sad though. Love didn't seem to exist, however much the soul singers tried to persuade you otherwise.

Balti went into the newsagent's while Harry waited outside with his head down staring at the pavement. The bloke had a far-off look that Balti couldn't work out. He bought fifteen quid's worth of Lottery tickets. His woman was waiting over the Atlantic and she didn't appear in dodgy magazines. He could feel the oil soaking into tired muscles and see the fireflies dancing near enough to grab. A coal black night on the verandah with the perfect woman skinning up. He was on his way to paradise while Carter and Harry were jetting off to The Coast Of A Thousand Slappers.

'It's a mug's game you know,' Harry said when Balti came out of the shop waving his investment in the air. 'A fiver's alright now and then, but fifteen quid's throwing it away. You think how much that adds up to if you do it every week. You're a fucking junky.'

'I'll remember that when they come knocking on the door with the cheque. I wish you'd cheer up you miserable cunt. Fuck me, you're going on holiday tomorrow.'

Harry wasn't bothered about getting rich. Last night was enough for him. Tossing and turning unable to breathe half the time let alone sleep, with the window wide open wishing it would rain. A nice electrical storm would have done him. Thunderbolts and lightning and a monsoon downfall to break the spell. A terrible night. The atmosphere heavy and sky overcast blocking the moon, drifting in and out of his dreamworld dungeon and the steaming concrete of a Turkish bath. Sweat on his skin brushing against the sheets sitting on his own back to the wall, dripping water running down from the ceiling following his spine. His rucksack was in the corner and Balti sat by a pool. Five fat Arabs in white towels were sipping mint tea. The mist was thick like he was back on the moors and then it began thinning, swirling and vanishing so he could see the room clearly, a thin masseur with a skull on his neck working an old man's back and shoulders, thumping white flesh. There was a faint hum in Harry's ears, Turkish music drifting in from outside. From a London roundabout, mixing Irish and Turkish strings along the echo of a spraycanned tunnel. He could see through walls and into the street outside. It was dark, drab, depressing; full of lepers and orphans. Beggars sat outside a tube station. There was a faint smell of hashish in the subway.

Balti was with a beauty queen tapping his foot to the dull thud of a rapper calling for respect, red cap pulled over his mate's bloodshot eyes. The kebab house on the corner serving closing-time drunks. The mosque with its blue dome and sound system broadcasting white noise. Balti led into a doorway by the she-man actress-actor humming sweet soul music, just a sex machine James Brown, sex machine Carter, big blue eyes and dungarees playing a role, travelling on the Northern Line with the pissheads and bandits heading for Hampstead Heath. Harry shaking his head and blocking out the vision, calling for a cup of PG Tips, making a stand for the English way of life, leaning his head back against the wall and allowing the heat to melt his gut, sweating out the poison, cleaning his pores and clearing his head.

The smell of shit. Ancient sewers breaking down and flooding the tube. The radio said that tens of thousands were feared dead. Buried alive deep underground. Quick-drying sewage clogging the system as dancing girls danced around their handbags. Shit flowing from the telly, from the mouths of preaching hypocrites, their faces outraged and purple as they held court, theatrically running from the studio to a waiting Rolls that rushed them to Ms Party Discipline in Mayfair, a special kind of lady who would make them obey the whip. The fuzzy logic of the Turkish bath fizzing and splashing piss over tiles. Harry feeling sweat in his eyes, salt poisoning the blue pools. Travelling the planet with Balti only to find himself back in London, watching his mate drop his jeans and flash his arse, all the time the words SEX SEX SEX beating out from a red neon display above the toilet door.

'Fucking hell,' Harry said out loud, shaking his head.

'What?' Balti asked, turning as they entered The Unity. 'What's the matter now?'

'Nothing. It's alright.'

'What's wrong with you? You look like you're sick or something. Come on, have a drink. Life's not that bad. You've been miserable all day. I wish you'd cheer up.'

Carter and Will were sitting at the bar. Balti eased his way through the packed pub and ordered, flashing a twenty. Denise took one for herself and handed back the change. Balti was rolling, with money to spend and his balls well and truly emptied of the pressure that had built up over the last eight months. He'd wanked himself silly while he was signing on, but it was more than that. Porno mags and dirty videos were alright, but there wasn't a lot of variation once you'd gone through the various combinations. The tension had to come out some way. A few more days and he'd probably be sniffing again, but for now he was satisfied to get pissed out of his head. Harry and Carter were off tomorrow but he didn't care. He was back in the swing of things. London was the best city in the world. Who wanted to go to Spain? London pissed all over Paris and

Rome and Berlin, even though he'd never been to any of those places. If you were happy inside your head then you'd be happy wherever you were. West London was the place to be. Centre of the universe. Hammersmith, Shepherd's Bush, Acton. Home was where the heart was. West London was top of the tree. Fucking class as the lager-lager-lager soundtrack on the jukebox belted out and the Chelsea boys drifted further West through Hounslow and Feltham and Hayes and Harlington, out to the satellite towns burning bright on the horizon. He felt brilliant, dipping his finger in the whizz Carter offered.

Will was smiling and making the announcement that he was going to be a dad. Him and Karen were going to get married and he wanted the rest of the lads to be ushers. His brother would be best man. Nothing too flash mind, but they'd do it nice. They'd get a decent band for the reception and someone who'd play their favourite records. He wanted his daughter, or son if it was a boy, to have the best start in life. It would give the kid security. He asked whether the rest of them understood and they nodded their heads. They were pleased for Will. Karen was a fine woman. They all loved the opposite sex, Harry especially as the lager soothed his fears. His reaction to the nightmare was healthy enough. The sheer horror he'd felt was reassuring. He was happy like the rest of the Sex Division because Will would make a good father and who knows, maybe one day Harry would have kids of his own and get a place somewhere further out where the property was cheap and you could buy yourself a bit of space.

Balti looked at Will and knew he'd make his own dad look like the scum he was, but he was doing okay now and there was even room for a few seconds of understanding. Times had been hard and his old man had taken the easy way out blaming his nearest and dearest, like all cowards, picking on those who couldn't defend themselves. Balti supposed he understood why the old man had been a cunt. He understood but would never forgive. Everything around you was geared up towards competition, and there always had to be a scapegoat. Some blokes hammered their women and kids. Others kicked the shit out of strangers. He wondered how much of it rubbed off, how much you could decide things for yourself. At least he was sound, and so were his mates. The real scum, the wife batterers and child abusers were usually out of sight, round the corner. When you found one you kicked seven shades of shit out of the cunt. Them and the rapists and muggers and other perverts. That's why his old man deserved a kicking. He'd brought the headlines home with him. He didn't care. Not now. Of course he didn't care. The Sex Division drank up and Harry ordered.

Will and Karen had sat down and talked the thing through. Will said he was sorry. Karen said she was sorry. It was a tense time full of surprises. Karen told Will that she had decided to have the child. She had been scared at first, but now she was used to the idea she didn't want an abortion. It would be okay. After all, they would be together for the rest of their lives. She said it was their decision. Will didn't think this was strictly true, but the result was what he wanted so he kept quiet. Everything was sweet. The important thing was that they were going to have a baby. They would be happy after all. It showed that stories could have a happy ending, even if it was really the beginning. They hugged each other for a while and then Will asked Karen to marry him in a rush of excitement. He was surprised when she agreed. In the end, he supposed, you all ended up just like your mum and dad. So it was agreed, and they'd plan the marriage and wait for the birth. Will felt a deep sense of relief. The rest of his life was mapped out and the security erased any self-doubt or irrational fear. He knew exactly where he was going.

The Sex Division raised their glasses and toasted the father to be, and then Carter was asking Will if he wanted to sit down, or did he have any strange cravings. Maybe he wanted some coal to eat or deep friend soap because, after all, that's what happened when you were in the club, and Balti reached over and placed his hand on Will's stomach and said he could feel kicks, and Harry fell into the joke and asked Will when he'd start showing. And Will was as happy as he'd ever been, thinking for a second or two about Bev and how lucky he'd been to find Karen because it showed there really was something called love. He couldn't have had this with anyone else. He didn't care what the cynics said. Love could be personal.

There was family love, where you didn't have much choice, and then you had the kind of love you had to discover, more down to luck than anything. A lot of people never found that. Will thought about Mango last night on the phone telling him he'd taken a couple of weeks off work and was leaving at midday to stay on Pete's farm. The brothers were driving up together and the rest of the Wilsons were going up on the train the following Friday night for the weekend. Pete wasn't sure what he'd do yet, but they'd been getting on well – apart from a couple of pissed punches that didn't mean anything – and there was a good chance he'd move back to London. Pete was older, but the same person. A diamond. The bloke had suffered, like the rest of them. It wasn't his fault. Mango was amazed how the years had fallen away so quickly. Family love rarely died, whatever happened. Mango said everything had changed. His mum and dad were born again, sisters crying all the time, but he wasn't bothered as they were crying because they were happy. Mango said life couldn't be better.

Will knew he was the other extreme from Mango in many ways, but they'd both found something special. The bloke sounded good, and though Pete hadn't been seen by Mango's mates yet it was something that would come. Will thought about the amnesia. It was as though for all those years the real Pete hadn't existed, but had been left dangling. Then he returned and that time didn't matter any more because the relief and happiness outweighed the sadness, and the happiness was current and the sadness in the past, another memory. He hoped Mango and Pete would get on alright in Norfolk. Somehow he knew it would work out. He told the rest of the Sex Division what was happening with Mango and how it was a good idea getting away. They all drank thoughtfully, not exactly toasting the Wilsons, but pleased all the same.

'Wait till we get over to Spain,' Carter shouted, trying to make himself heard over the noise of the Friday night drinkers and the music which had suddenly cranked up, easing the emotion. 'Me and Harry are going on the pull big-style when we get over there. Stick with me Harry my son and you can have the leftovers, all the old heifers I don't want. The Sex Division king is off on tour and the birds are in for a treat.'

'You haven't won yet,' Balti said.

'I'm on fifty-seven points and you're my nearest challenger with five. Will's given up, Mango's down on the farm building scarecrows with his brother, and Harry there's fallen in love with his right hand. I'm the winner. All fair and square.'

'There's still tonight. It's not over until the ref blows the final whistle. Till you take off tomorrow there's still a chance for one of the outsiders to come through with a late surge. That's the problem with the big clubs, they get too cocky. It's a funny old game, shagging.'

Carter smiled indulgently, but he'd lost interest and was watching Denise at the other end of the bar serving Slaughter. He was looking forward to the two-week break. She'd come round last night and it had all got a bit serious, when after giving her a good servicing he'd told her she should make an honest man of Slaughter. She couldn't keep the bloke hanging on forever. Denise said she knew she had to tell him something. She would miss Terry when he was away and she started going into one about how she could piss all over Slaughter any time she wanted because she had him eating out of her hand, but with Terry it was different because he would go his own way and she had to understand that. She would think of him when he was on holiday with all those randy girls chasing after him and she hoped he'd behave himself. He looked at her a bit surprised and said nothing.

'We going down The Hide then?' Harry asked. 'Let's have a drink down there.'

'In a bit,' Carter said, watching Denise and Slaughter.

The perfect couple and the imperfect twosome walking down the aisle in a double marriage. Will and Karen with a bun in the oven dressed in a white wedding gown with pink flowers in her hair, followed a minute or two later by Slaughter and Denise in a short skirt and high heels. Will would be in top hat and tails, while Slaughter would be wearing his leather coat with a specially-designed secret-agent holster for his favourite machete. The two couples would stand side by side as the vicar struggled with their names and rambled about sickness, health and obedience. The reception would be a laugh and end in a punch-up between the good, bad and ugly.

Carter didn't care if Denise married Slaughter or not. He'd still be able to give her a portion whenever he wanted. But those birds at the bar were alright and he felt the familiar urge. He couldn't wait to get away. It was going to be good. He needed a holiday, though tonight he was going to rub the Sex Division's nose in it and pull something classy to round off a successful season. It had been a good campaign and he'd had a few results along the way, irrespective of the opposition. He'd had his share of pigs, but a few crackers as well. Carter reckoned he deserved a lap of honour. Maybe later. There was a party tonight and it would be stacked with crumpet. A few beers in The Unity, down The Hide, maybe Blues, then the party. It would be a good warm-up. They'd be knackered tomorrow getting down to Gatwick, but a drink in the bar and a few sherbets on the flight over and they'd be raring to go. Carter was going to shag himself silly. He always did when he went away. He was looking forward to the sand, sun and low prices. He'd come home with a dose on a couple of occasions so this time he was taking a big supply of rubbers. Not being able to drink while he took the cure fucked him right off.

'You heard about that queer march they're planning,' Balti asked. 'They should ban it. Who wants a bunch of poofs walking through the streets upsetting everyone? It's not like they even come from round here.'

'They're dirty bastards,' Carter agreed. 'Fuck anything that moves. They should line them up against the wall and shoot the lot of them. They're full of disease. Just the blokes though. I don't mind the lesbians, because you can see their point of view. There's nothing wrong with that and I like a good lesbian video like the next man. It's only natural. Queers, though. Fucking horrible.'

'I'll tell you who's full of disease,' Harry said, shifting the conversation, 'and that's Slaughter. I heard he did some bloke down the newsagent's yesterday because he leant across him to grab a paper. Went fucking mental right there in the shop, dragged the cunt outside, and gave him a right pasting. He's got a fractured skull. The old bill were down but they didn't get anywhere. I would never, ever want to get on the wrong side of that bloke. He's a fucking killer.'

Harry was looking at Carter as he said this, but the sex machine brushed the warning aside. What did he care, he was going on holiday and didn't give a toss. He watched the birds he'd been eyeing move across the pub. They weren't all that, now he thought about it, and they'd seen him and not shown any interest. The Hide would be better.

'Come on then, let's fuck off,' he said. 'It's all blokes in here tonight except for those birds over there, and just our luck they're probably lesbians. Lets go down The Hide.'

The Sex Division drank up and were soon following the familiar run from The Unity to The Hide, a golden path that led on to Blues. They were following Children's Ward painted footprints through sterile hospital corridors, straight past Pathology concentrating on those red and blue cartoon toes and heels. The only Sex Division member missing was Mango, the rest of the lads pounding the same pavements they'd been pushed through as babies and run along as kids. Balti saw them as family men treading the rutted path, grey hair sprouting and baldness spreading, finally pensioners hunched over standing on the corner watching a demolition crew rip down The Unity, a Space Age amusement arcade planned for the site. He looked at his mates and tried to picture them with kids, because it always happened that way. It was the fucking domino effect, and he wasn't talking about the spread of communism. Will was expecting and getting married. He was the first one to go. Planting a seed in Karen's belly and the rest of their heads. It only needed one person to break the pattern and those left would eventually follow. Bollocks. Now they were following the leader into The Hide.

'That's a bit better,' Carter shouted, once they'd settled in. 'I prefer drinking surrounded by beautiful women rather than a pub full of pissed-up geezers.'

Harry pointed out the birds they'd entertained earlier in the year with tales of stretched scrotums. Balti was up for another go, because after all they were the Bollock Brothers, or was it the Lager Twins, he couldn't remember because it had been a while back and they'd been well pissed. He bounced forward as someone bumped into him, turning to look the bloke in the eye. He could feel the violence rush up from nowhere and a split-second temptation to glass the cunt was cut short as a fist connected with the man's face. It was kicking off behind them between two headbangers and Balti could afford to smile and take a step sideways, watching the cabaret. It was only half-nine and already the muppets were performing as three bouncers steamed through from the door and separated the two men, kicking them back through the pub and bouncing their heads off the brickwork in the doorway, sending them on their way. Glass and lager covered the floor and there was a pool of blood that looked worse than it was because blood had mixed in with the drink, but the show went on and the jukebox kept playing as it moved through the tunes of the moment, the incident quickly forgotten, Balti laughing and turning his head to find that Carter had moved over to the women with pierced tits and lips. The flash cunt didn't waste any time, he'd give him that, and Harry was telling the boys old Carter's on the pull tonight, and Balti knew what he meant because he was back in the groove himself.

A bit of respect. He'd come through in one piece. And after all these months he knew what was going to make it a perfect night. He was going down Balti Heaven, because it was in the name and he'd been a regular there until the beginning of the year when he made a resolution to lose weight and that was followed by a lack of cash, so tonight he was going down there even if the rest of the lads fucked off down Blues. He wasn't bothered because there was that party round Julie Jones' later and she had some nice mates. It would be heaving. Funny what the drink and a bit of whizz could do for you because when he'd come out he wasn't thinking about getting his leg over after his night with Suzie in Archway, but now he was plugged in again. It was more about the Sex Division really, because Carter was such a cocky bastard thinking it was all over just because he was fifty-two points ahead. It was the arrogance that got him. You had to believe in miracles, even if the Virgin Birth was impossible. You had to think things like that could happen. The Sex Division was supposed to be a laugh, but Carter was taking it seriously like it mattered or something and Balti was moving up the social scale. He had self-respect. Julie Jones really did have some tasty mates, and Julie herself wasn't bad and had a bit of a reputation. It would be a rave up, Harry shouting in his ear that it was time for the Nutcracking Nephews to get into top gear because Carter was bringing those posers over, the ones in the trendy clobber, the fucking lesbians who'd blown them out last time.

'Alright girls?' Harry asked, back in the swing of things, forgetting all about dodgy dreams.

The girls smiled but didn't say much, and if they had it would've been hard to hear them because the music was thumping out, tapping eardrums. Harry had to hold back from giving it the old stretched bollocks routine, while Balti was thinking how it didn't matter that all those months had passed because here they were in The Hide again with the music drowning the conversation, with the same birds.

He fancied a curry. He couldn't be bothered shouting to make himself heard over the drums, though Will was leaning into one of them going on about something. Probably telling them he was going to be a dad, and though he wouldn't be thinking anything, birds liked that, because women were soft and sentimental and Balti loved them, and he'd like to fuck the arse off every female on the planet he was feeling so good. They all loved women. Certainly Harry did, and he was keeping away from the speed because otherwise he wouldn't be able to sleep and he had to pack tomorrow. More than his rest, he didn't want his dreams scrambled. He was beginning to feel better about last night and was ignoring the possible interpretation of the Turkish bath and all the rest of the gibberish. That's what happened when you got into all that psychic stuff. How could you know what was going on in your head? They could put men on the moon and genetically manipulate life, but the scientists never worked out what was going on inside the brain of your everyday herbert. Harry wouldn't have minded a bit of help now and then, some kind of explanation.

It was all shit really, and just because he'd had a few dreams that came true, maybe it didn't mean he had a special gift. It had to be down to chance. Maybe it was a bottle job, because if you took the glory then you had to take the stick as well, but there were no rules and without rules you drifted. One thing was certain, he was no queer, because he wouldn't have minded these birds and he was looking forward to going to Spain and getting stuck in. Women made the world go round and your head spin. So fucking what anyway. If he was a bum bandit, he'd come out and say so. He wouldn't hide away. No matter what the lads said, it wouldn't make any difference. Not really. He just wanted things straight in his head and put in their proper place. He was alright.

'I was talking to this bloke I do business with,' Will said, standing next to Harry now. 'He's had three kids and been there when each of them was born. Can you imagine that, seeing your child being born. He says there's nothing like it. Says it's a bit messy and the woman suffers, but it really is a miracle. I still can't get my head round it, that I'm going to be a father. Can't believe me and Karen have created a life out of nothing. When you really think about it, it's unbelievable.'

Harry smiled and nodded. Something like that must take you back to the beginning. It was where they'd all come from. The lust of their mothers and fathers. None of them wanted to think of their parents doing the business. It was a disgusting thought and the old folk had to remain sexless, beyond frantic mating sessions. The mask had to stay in place because it gave you a foundation. Kids made you think. Took you back to the meaning behind the action. Men and women creating life. Something from the Bible or a mushy film. Sperm and eggs working to a hidden plan. Harry felt very unimportant. He dreamt all kinds of things and it was beyond his control. Every time one of them took a shine to a bird, there was another pattern working under the surface. It was one big mating ritual really, the use of language to show you didn't care, the pisstake and humour, the pubs and clubs and clothes and music, and the need for drink and drugs to loosen the restraints. Behind it all, the eggs and sperm were waging war, demanding action, eating into you the whole time, pushing you forward. A drunken shag and the glands were sober and efficient and working fast. You were nothing more than a messenger, a slave to the almighty DNA. But you had the last laugh because the birds were all on the pill, and it was that forward planning that kept you in charge.

'This bloke even videoed one of his kids being born,' Will said. 'When that kid grows up it'll be able to see its first second of life. Think of that.'

Harry thought about it, but wouldn't have fancied sitting down in front of the VCR watching his head emerge from between his old girl's legs. He didn't like the idea at all. He thought about Chelsea's first game in Europe after more than twenty years when they played Viktoria Zizkov in the Cup Winners Cup. It was a big match for the Blues and at half-time the announcements were made over the tannoy and three Chelsea boys were informed that their wives had given birth, while another was told his girlfriend was in labour. That showed dedication. Respect was definitely due, putting Chelsea first. Talking to Will, he wondered about the ways of the world.

'Karen's got a video of her mum,' Will said, going on a bit now, enjoying the drink and the course his life was taking. 'I watched it once. I saw the past frozen and when I think of it now I reckon I've seen the future as well. A bit like you and your dreams, though this was just a machine. It was towards the end of her life. Cradle to grave and you can catch it all on video.'

'What's the point though?' Harry asked. 'If you get a rerun when you snuff it then the video's in your head already so why waste money on VCRs? It's all a bit sad. There's no point thinking about the past too much.'

'If you don't think about the past, then you don't learn, do you? If that happens then you keep on making the same old mistakes.'

Harry wasn't bothered. The more he thought about things, the more it seemed his dreams were starting to bleed in with reality. Until recently he'd have insisted the two things were separate, but since his lucid dream, and the recent blurred lines, he saw the two worlds merging. He didn't know if this was a good or bad thing, though of course generally speaking he liked everything in its proper place. Without order you ended up in the nut house. That lucid dream had been a one-off. He'd like to dream like that again and take control. Before that dream he'd been at the mercy of the controller sitting deep in his skull directing operations. It was like a computer with one of those viruses loaded for fun, to cause disruption, fucking up the circuits. It was all this digital music that was making him think about machinery, because the nightmare was up in the air and he needed order. He also needed another pint. A couple more and he was going to fuck off home. No curry, no Blues, no pierced birds, no Julie Jones. He was going home to bed. Tomorrow he was off on holiday and starting fresh. Early swims and orange juice for breakfast. Civilised living asleep by the pool. Last time hadn't been all that civilised, but that was then. He'd get himself some nice slow sex with a half-decent bird. He wished Will would shut up for a while. He was doing his head in going on about placentas and afterbirth and umbilical cords. It was making him feel sick. Will said it was amazing, and he was right, but Harry still felt ill.

Standing outside The Hide at closing, Will said he was off and left Carter, Harry and Balti with the three posers. In the lit-up street and with a few lagers and a bit of whizz they were alright. They started walking towards Julie Jones' place, Balti forgetting about his curry with the three women showing a lot of interest, while Harry reckoned he'd go along and see what happened. It was a ten-minute walk and they were soon hammering on the door to make themselves heard, a three-bedroom house that Julie shared with a couple of other women. Slaughter opened the door, and going inside they found a lot of regulars from the pub, as well as Denise and Eileen. As promised the place was stacked out, and the three remaining Sex Division members rubbed their hands and found some cans. Carter and Balti were at the whizz again and Harry knew that some unfortunate was going to get their ear bent. He looked for the three birds who'd come with them, and for a moment reckoned they'd blown the Sex Division out, but there they were coming through from the kitchen, helping themselves when Carter offered the speed.

Harry soon found himself cornered by one of the girls. He was sipping from a can of supermarket lager. It tasted like shit. It wasn't cold enough, and it was going to be one of those nights because the woman chatting him up was racing to keep up with her thoughts and it was doing his head in, but then he felt her brushing against him and the whole thing was changing because he knew he was in. He adjusted his hearing and forgot about the music, because whoever had chosen the CDs had done a good job, and the bird was only going on about blokes stretching their bollocks, and did he remember that time when him and his mate had been going on about being the Bollock Brothers? Harry smiled and was trying to think of a smart one-liner not knowing whether to play the game or take the piss, part of him wanting to feed her another line, but the sensible voice inside telling him not to be a mug because she was dying for it, fucking gagging, couldn't he see that? So he kept quiet and the girl, whose name he found out was Jo, was saying that his mate Terry had told them it was just a wind up. She was laughing because it hadn't been much of a turn on imagining a bloke with balls round his knees, and it was her mate who had the pierced lip, she couldn't do that to herself, what did Harry think about it all?

Harry didn't know really, and fuck it anyway, it didn't matter what he thought because he was drunk enough and before long he was going upstairs for a piss, standing in line with a couple of boneheads and several birds in white leather mini skirts, taking his time, finally giving up and going downstairs and outside, pissing round the back of the house. He was a cunt sometimes, because everyone was using the garden, and when he went inside Jo was sitting at the top of the stairs calling him back up. He worked his way through the people talking in an orange glow and he was sitting next to her, feeling her mouth against his, the taste of fags and drink, a fine mixture, the best kind of perfume, and then he was walking with her along the landing to one of the bedrooms.

Harry was back in the saddle. Jo was game and wasn't bothered by the couple in the next bed grunting and groaning in the blackness. They were soon stripped off and she was tugging his bollocks, laughing quietly, moving now to his cock. Harry brought her off and she was telling him to come inside her, which he was only too pleased to do. She was digging her fingernails into his hips spreading her legs as wide as they'd go, and before long he collapsed and pulled the sheets over them. He laid his head back against the pillow and the next bed was quiet and the music far off in the distance, a gentle thud through the bricks and plaster. There were no words now, just the soundtrack, and he felt himself drifting a bit because he was knackered, and the drink was wearing off leaving a dull ache between the eyes. He felt sad, post-sex reality coming through fast and chilling. He thought about the Sex Division and realised he'd picked up two valuable points in the relegation battle. If Balti missed out tonight then he was equal bottom. Harry was well pleased. No he wasn't, Balti had picked up three points in Archway. He looked at the body next to him and wondered if she was up for giving him a blow job? Probably not. He'd leave it a while. That was the difference between someone like him and Carter. He wasn't planning ahead. He hoped he hadn't missed out. If he was Carter he'd try and slip her one up the jacksie and send Balti down, but Harry was no bum bandit. Still, he'd made a last ditch effort, but the way Balti was getting on with her mate the fat cunt would be doing himself some good as well. Harry didn't care. He could hear Jo's breathing. He wondered what she was like sober. He started drifting.

Harry was walking across a moor following the sun. He saw a farmhouse in the distance. He was tired and the weather was turning. He saw smoke from the chimney of the house and knew somebody must be at home. The inhabitants could be friends or enemies, he had no way of really knowing. He hurried towards the house prepared to take a chance. It wasn't as far as he'd thought and when he knocked on the heavy oak door he was surprised to find it answered by Mango. They shook hands and Harry was invited inside. Pete sat in a big chair in front of a roaring fire. Mango told Harry to sit down. He'd bring some brandy to warm him up. Harry sat down and looked at Pete. The missing brother smiled. He said he'd heard the news about Will. Things were working out. Carter was top of the league, Balti was working and Harry was safe from the elements. Everyone was happy.

Harry jolted awake. He was on the floor and pulling himself upright. There was a sack on his back. He was covered in soot from head to toe, and there was a fire in the next bed. He could see charcoal figures in the flames. There was no sound. It was a terrible sight, but Harry was in charge. He was inside the dream. He was lucid. He knew it was only a dream.

Harry jolted awake. Jo had disappeared. The house was silent. He needed a piss. He fumbled around on the floor looking for his pants and jeans. Where had Jo gone? Obviously not impressed by his fine love-making skills. A shame really. He felt movement under the sheets. He'd missed her somehow. He pulled his pants on and stepped into his jeans, moving slowly through the room. The landing was lit by a street light. He went into the bathroom and stood over the bowl. The room stunk. Someone had thrown up in the sink. You expected that when you were a teenager. Some people never grew up. He flushed the toilet and headed back towards the bedroom. His throat was dry and he stopped. He went downstairs looking for a drink. There were sleeping bodies in the living room. He trod quietly. He didn't want to wake anyone. In the kitchen Harry went to the fridge and found some orange juice. He washed a glass and poured the juice. It tasted alright, a bit sharp.

The kitchen opened on to a small room, which in turn led to the garden. Harry could hear something or someone moving around. He went to look. Balti was hitching up his jeans. Six open handbags were lined up on the floor. It took Harry a moment to understand the deeper significance.

The dirty bastard. He couldn't believe what his old mate had done. Harry was filled with disgust. Shit splattered the handbags. Despite himself, Harry was totting up the points. Six times ten points. Fuck, that was an extra sixty points and with the five he already had Balti was on a grand total of sixty-five. He'd roared past Carter. The sick fucking cunt. Balti was out of order, and Harry was just about to give him a bit of stick when the reality kicked in. It was a result for Harry as well as for Balti. The old magic hadn't let him down. Harry was in the clear. The dream of last night fell into place. He was a one-hundred-percent Anglo-Saxon heterosexual. He was also a Protestant, but he wasn't bothered about that right now. He was holding his head up high, part of the majority. There would be no bushy tashes and greased fists, no amyl nitrate and Vaseline standing orders. He was saved. Tomorrow he'd be on his way.

Harry was happy. Everything was in its place. Everything was as it should be. There were no corners in need of lighting, no hidden secrets. There was logic and understanding. He was a simple man with simple needs. And Jo was still upstairs.

Balti turned and saw his best mate standing in the doorway. His thoughts were racing and he couldn't slow down. Carter had pissed off with one of the posers and he'd been blown out, the unstoppable shag machine giving it the big one as he hurried outside to a taxi. Balti wasn't taking it laying down, even though he'd found a place on the floor and a smelly old blanket. It was a laugh, collecting the handbags, lining them up, and letting nature take its course, coming from behind to clinch the championship. Now with Harry standing there like a plum Balti felt a twinge of embarrassment, even regret, but fuck all that.

Balti told Harry that he was the witness. The Sex Division champion was going home and he'd see him later, Harry nodding and going back upstairs. He stopped by the window at the end of the landing and saw Balti walking down the street. A chill passed through him. He thought he should call out, but didn't know why. Everything had been sorted out. There were no looses ends. The sun was coming up and a warm orange glow dusted the rooftops. Harry saw his best mate getting smaller, turning the corner, out of sight now as he walked through the empty streets, Balti's head racing knowing it was going to be hard sleeping once he was back at the flat. But bollocks, he'd put a video on or something, and he had a bit of blow left. Everything came rushing towards him in one big wave, all those days and weeks and months signing on, rotting away, getting older and heading for the grave, it was all there in your genes, everything you said and did was programmed from an early age, and if you had a helping hand maybe you'd go another way, but the thing was, the people supposed to give you a hand hadn't grown up themselves.

Balti wanted to go round and see Will and Karen and have a bit of a smoke, enjoy their company, but he was together enough to know they'd be asleep. He thought of his fortune and a four-poster bed packed with Lottery supermodels. He turned into his street and slowed down. He was almost home. Safe and sound. Maybe he shouldn't have done the handbags, but it was a laugh. It didn't matter. Not really. He hoped Denise's handbag hadn't been in there though. Slaughter wouldn't like that. No, he remembered them leaving. His legs were aching. Maybe he'd have a bath with some salts and wash it all away. Scrub away his sins and start all over again. It was a new beginning and everyone was happy. Balti was back. He'd learnt his lessons. You came out of the hard times stronger. Sex Division champion and a job painting houses with his best mate. Life was there to be lived and experienced. He was the happiest he'd been for years.

Balti heard the car door and turned his head. McDonald stood behind him with a shotgun wedged into his shoulder. Pulled the trigger.

ENGLAND AWAY

FOR MY DAD, MIKE KING

'The English don't kill people,
unless they fucking have to'

Steve Thorman, *The night of Heysel*

ISLAND RACE

ISLAND RACE

A STROPPY CUNT in a grey uniform stands in front of me, acting cocky – standing there like a plum. He's looking at my passport. Inspecting the photo but not raising his head to check if Tom Johnson is one and the same. He's waiting for something to happen. Waiting for the face in the picture to lean forward and the mouth to tell him to fuck off. Pull the skull back and nut him on the bridge of the nose. Sending blood down that nice official jacket, running along sharp creases. He's searching inside the lines of my forehead. Reading the script and playing his part. Holding that shitty red passport close, the proud old British version ripped up and burnt by the invisible scum in Brussels. Manky old cunts busy working through the night, nailing us with the European tag. Claiming triple time. No identity and a crisp ironed suit; sagging sweaty skin and pockmarked cheeks. Customs cunt saying nothing, just hanging there, a fucking tart inspecting the photo. Staring into space, the slag. And I can feel my foot tapping and fingers itching, fists clenched, holding back and keeping the violence down. Does he remember something from his hooligan database, or is it a routine piss-take? He raises his head with a blank expression and cardboard stance. Sucking air down so it rattles in his throat. Gagging on bad manners and the smell of a Fisherman's Friend. Giving it the big one. Giving me grief.

– What are you planning to do in Holland then, Mr Johnson? he asks, all curious and suspicious. Full of himself. Full of shit.

I smile my best friendly smile.

(Well, I'm passing through Holland on my way to Berlin, Mr Customs Cunt, where I'm going to see England play Germany and hopefully help turn the place over. That's what. But first

I'm going to stop in Amsterdam and get pissed, then service some of those Dutch birds you hear so much about. Not the whores, mind, though I might give them a seeing to as well. Reduced rates for a classic English gentleman. No, I want some of those Dutch beauty queens, with their blonde hair, black armpits and never-say-no attitude to sex. Maybe have a row with the Dutch for a warm-up. Then we're going to do the Germans outside the Reichstag. That's what. And by the way, mate, that wife of yours, she's a right little raver. She fucking loves it, the dirty cow. Last I saw of her, round about nine this morning, after you'd had a wank over the ferry timetable and left for work, she was seeing the England boys off in style. Talk about catching a train. You want to keep your eye on that one.)

– I'm going to Amsterdam for a few days to stay with friends and have a holiday. Visit some of Holland maybe. See the sights and relax.

I watch the rest of the chaps moving away, turning the corner. Acting innocent as new-born babies. Looking at the floor, the walls, finally the ceiling. Makes me laugh how they can waltz through so easy. Blokes like Facelift and Billy Bright who look the part. Bright Spark with his Cross of St George flag under his arm tied together with a thick length of rope and covered in black plastic so it doesn't get wet. These colours don't run. Mark hanging back waving, smiling, laughing. Waiting for me to sort things out and catch him up. Enjoying the show.

I go back to this wanker in front of me. Smile again. A big yellow ball with black strips for the mouth and eyes. Cartoon gun-runner, going the wrong way. Why's he chosen me? Luck of the draw or something more serious?

– Going to test some of the drugs in Amsterdam are we, Mr Johnson? Is that the reason for the trip?

So that's it. Cartoon drug-smuggler. You have to laugh.

(Don't know about you mate, but d'you really think I'd spend the fare just for that? Wise up, giving me hassle when you've let the others through. I should kick you in the bollocks. Kick you so hard your balls jam in your gut and you spend the rest of your life sounding like you've been on the helium. Like we don't have enough drugs at home. But I'll let you off because then I'd miss the fun and games, and your mates would be pissing themselves when I get six months for castrating a member of the civil service. I'm on the move. Amsterdam, Berlin and the Germany-England game. I don't plan on getting nicked before I'm even out of the country. Fuck that. Don't plan on getting nicked at all. It's worth behaving because once we're across the Channel there's no more of your petty rules and regulations. No more Mr Nice Guy. Get to the Continent and that's it. The laws don't count over there because they're made by foreigners. Get out of England and you can do what you want.)

I smile some more. Cheek muscles starting to ache with the effort. Haven't smiled so much since that time me, Rod and Mark got done for a bit of puff he had in the car. Talk about taking the piss. The old bill stopped us because they said Rod didn't indicate. Load of bollocks. Luckily Rod was sober, and we're coming back from a Sunday drink and the old bill tug us because they want the easy life. Can't be bothered raiding Brixton crackhouses and tracking down serial rapists when everyone else is sitting down for their Sunday dinner or on their eighth pint in front of the pub satellite. Maybe they checked us on the computer or something, found out we all had previous, because they only go and charge us. I couldn't fucking believe it. Rod says we have to walk in the magistrate's court stoned. Take the piss. And that's what we did. I was grinning like I'd won the fucking lottery while this old boy's going on about the threat drugs pose to society – 'a very real and tangible threat, because what we must remember is that soft drugs can lead to harder drugs, and before society knows what's happening large sections of the community become ecstasy and heroin addicts, and that means a lowering of moral standards, inevitably resulting in unwanted pregnancies and a rapid increase in lawlessness'. The wanker in the pulpit stops for a breather and tells me to wipe that grin off my face or he'll charge me with contempt. You're not even allowed to smile these days. They take your taxes and all you get back is aggro.

But I'm being polite, that's all. Don't want to wind this

Customs bloke up. He's just doing his job. Flexing dead muscles as he drives the train to Auschwitz. No need for a row. I want to keep him sweet and get moving again. Enjoy myself and see the world. Because travelling with England is always a laugh, no matter who you're playing. Add a friendly in Berlin and the stage is set. I remember the man in front of me and his natural concern at the drugs waiting in Holland, all those unnatural substances pushed by subversive elements within the clog authorities.

– I'm not really into that sort of thing. I mean, each to their own and that, but I prefer a drink.

– A nice pint of real ale always goes down a treat.

– I drink lager myself.

He glares at the passport for a few seconds, then raises his head. He looks me in the eye all hurt, like he's about to burst out crying.

– Of course you do, Mr Johnson.

The man looks hurt. Real ale's the true English drink he says. Lager's just European gas and water mixed through EC filters.

I smile, all innocent. Not a care in the world. Chugging along. Wishing he'd give it a rest. Wishing he'd fuck off and bother some other cunt. His eyes are mean and there's sleep in the corner of the left socket. He's one of those sick sperms that should've been flushed away with the rubber, but instead hangs on under the rim growing in slime. Ends up in a uniform causing trouble. No wonder his missus spends her spare time getting gang-banged by football hooligans on the living-room carpet.

I hear the renegades from the train coming along behind me. Pissed on bottles of fuck-knows-what singing their heads off on the train from Liverpool Street. I don't reckon they'll get out of Harwich the way they're carrying on. Been at the cider probably. They look the sort. We could hear them in the next carriage and Brighty reckoned they were Black Country boys with their farmhand look. Facelift wanted to go and have a word because they were making a racket and he wasn't in the mood, a hangover lingering from last night. We laugh it off telling him to calm down. Take it easy. This is England on tour and you have to know your enemy. All that club stuff goes out the window – most of it, some of it – but it's his first time travelling with England so he's not to know. He's got a few things to sort out and it was the same for me first time I saw England play abroad. You turn up at Liverpool Street or wherever all lairy, but then you get moving and there's other clubs around, and you realise that it's all about people, that you're all basically the same but doing it in different places, that you're all English and patriotic and standing under the same flag. Somehow it works. Give it ten minutes and it makes sense. England, united, we'll never be defeated.

One of the Bully boys is wearing an England shirt. Asking for trouble. Big red face puffed up on the cider and a bottle of spirits, tattoos right up his arms. Covered thick so you can't make out the details. A Union Jack, young Noddy Holder face and several snakes mixing together under a layer of matted hair. He can't wait to get stuck into the duty-free this one. We only left London two hours ago and I'll be surprised if we see him in Berlin. The old bill will be on the look-out for English hooligans, and though we're a few days early the shirt gives the game away. But they're farmhands from the piggery and we're Chelsea boys and that bit smarter. We're taking it slow and easy. The old bill can do what they want and not let you on the ferry. Rights and wrongs don't come into it. Just keep your head down and think of those fräuleins waiting over the Channel. Legs wide open. I can't wait to get away and have some fun. To be honest, I'm sick of working in the warehouse day in, day out. The same old boozers and clubs. All the familiar faces. Same old birds. The football season's over and it gets boring when Chelsea aren't playing. I need a break from London and England, because then when you get back you love your life even better than before.

Some more coppers and Customs appear; smiling and rubbing their hands together. Thank you very much, thank you very very very much. Hurrying now towards Strongbow and his Steve Bull mates, so fucking excited they're almost running to the ice-cream van filling their trousers. Mr Drugs looks over my shoulder and he's not interested in Tom Johnson any more because he knows what to expect from the drunken scum coming his way. He reads his papers and studies his cartoons, and the sad fucker's probably even gone out and bought the fucking video. Replayed it a thousand times with his knob out and the missus banging him off – because here they come . . .

THE FAMOUS FOOTBALL HOOLIGANS.

He hands back my passport and says thank you Mr Johnson. Sorry to have bothered you sir. Enjoy your stay in Holland. He says Amsterdam is a beautiful city with canals and barges and tasty continental breakfasts. They serve fresh bread, ham, cheese and various jams. There's fine architecture that escaped the kind of bombing that wrecked the East End and levelled Coventry. That's what being pacifist does for you. The same goes for Paris. That's what cowardice does. Bunch of wankers the French. It's a private joke that shows unity. Before moving on to the pissheads he laughs and warns me not to overdo things in the bars. Watch those women of the night as well. He starts rambling suddenly saying those darkies are pure filth, getting worked up, pure jungle filth even though they come from Surinam and Indonesia, they'll do anything for a price, and I'm looking at the bloke and have to hold it back. I don't need this. Leave me alone. Just fuck off and leave me alone. He's doing my head in so I push past the cunt. Say nothing and hurry to catch up with Mark and the others. Fucking slag.

The old bill and Customs don't care about me now because they're moving in on the cider drinkers. These men in uniform are all self-important because they know what's what and they've got the intelligence, know their hooligans. Just shows you how intelligent these wankers really are because it's all boot boy vintage recordings. Black and white tabloid snapshots and archive news reels. Customs picking on a few drunks who, if they don't watch their step, are going to be spending their time in the local nick sobering up while the Expeditionary Force filters through and assembles in the half-lit skunk bars of Amsterdam. Hands forming Bomber Command goggles over our eyes, humming the *Dam Busters* tune. Have to laugh. Customs and the old bill. Stroppy cunts the lot of them.

* * *

Bob 'Harry' Roberts hated ferries and hated the sea. Thank fuck he lived in London and not some grim seaside town like Grimsby, where you went to school in clogs till you were eight then the elders sent you to work strapped to the mast of a ten-foot-long fishing boat. He saw himself standing there unable to move, frozen in time and a block of ice, brought back to life by Long John Silver. The captain was hobbling through the rigging with a blowtorch, the one-legged sea dog slicing Harry's ropes with his cutlass, the ancient mariner telling the young land-lubber he was free to go – stuck on a tug miles from shore. He was in the middle of a Force 10 gale helping the fisher folk drag in nets of mutant fish, a North Sea catch of three-eyed monsters, lights pulsating through orange scales, chemical stew boiling under the waves. The young Harry was working through the night to earn enough for a loaf of Hovis. He hummed the tune from the commercial all the way up the fucking hill, past rows of cobbled streets and steaming horse shit. He didn't fancy life in a northern fishing community. It was grim in the North. Give him London any day.

Harry went back to the day Chelsea travelled to Grimsby and won the Second Division championship with a 1–0 victory, Kerry Dixon scoring the goal. They hadn't seen many fishing boats that particular Saturday, and maybe there weren't any steep hills, but never mind, because he'd been pissed like everyone else after a session in Lincoln. Pissed or sober, it was a day he'd never forget. They'd had tickets for the seats, but ended up on the terraces as the organisation inside the ground broke down, Chelsea mobbing the place. No-one was com-plaining, because Dixon, Nevin and Speedie were leading the charge back to the First Division and it looked like they had a team that was going to bring back the glory days, though the old bill had to go and bring on the horses at the end to show how fucking clever they were. Silly cunts almost started a riot. It was magic, getting promoted to the First Division after nearly going broke and down to the Third. They'd spent the night in Chesterfield, in a big pub packed with Chelsea drinking the place dry. There was no aggro, because the coaches often stopped there on the way back from games and everything was friendly enough. They'd had a good laugh chatting up the local girls, Harry and Balti and those Slough boys, the two Garys, Benny with his Crossroads hat. The pub had a late licence and turned into a disco, and they'd had their guts out on the dancefloor like some select firm as the DJ played old singalong Gary Glitter and Slade numbers. There must've been two or three hundred Chelsea in that pub alone and not so much as a broken glass. Funny how it worked. Mind you, there'd been a big punch-up on Morecambe Pier that night, so it was luck of the draw.

They'd had a drink with some striking Chesterfield miners, and he remembered being surprised they were so different from the tabloid pin-ups. He'd always pictured the miners in hobnailed boots and red crash helmets, and there they were, ordinary everyday blokes out for a pint on Saturday night, having a laugh. He'd got talking with these two punks and they were giving him the story on what was happening in the coalfields. He'd listened but not really heard what they were saying. Harry laughed. They were so pissed they'd got the wrong coach back to London and ended up on the North Circular somewhere around Willesden. It was a long trek home at four in the morning because no cab was going to pick them up with their cropped hair and green flight-jackets. Now he was older and wiser and enjoying an easy life in the Premiership. Wreck the old rundown grounds and the club chairmen rewarded you with brand new seats, burger bars and sponsor's lager on tap. Crime definitely paid.

The crossing to the Hook was going to be a nightmare. Harry could feel it in his gut. It was going to be six hours of pure fucking misery. Six hours crouched over a shit-stained bog with the boat rocking from side to side, piss running along the floor soaking his jeans. There was never any paper and always some wanker who had to start banging on the door. He needed a drink to settle his nerves, so broke off from the rest of the boys and headed for the bar, telling Carter to hurry up before the place was packed. He needed some Dutch courage, some Heineken, heading down the steps but stopping in his tracks when Carter said the bar wouldn't open till the ferry was out to sea. It was written down in the rules somewhere, so sorry Harry you fat bastard, you'll have to wait.

Harry shrugged and they went out on deck to get some fresh air and watch the ferry load. He was beginning to wish he'd gone the long way round and taken Eurostar, but then he'd be travelling alone and that wouldn't be much fun. If you were going to be on your own you might as well stay at home in front of the telly. He didn't fancy the tunnel and it would probably be more expensive. He didn't fancy an IRA bomb under his carriage or another fire. Whatever way he got to Europe, though, it was worth the aggravation. Harry had been to Spain, Portugal, Belgium and France, and he'd liked them all. He enjoyed the extended drinking and the food, the clean streets and laid-back manner. There was a different attitude somehow, even if it was only what you saw as an outsider. Probably if he lived in Lisbon or somewhere similar and he was decorating houses like he did in London, then the fumes would smell the same and there'd be all the usual problems, but that was why you went away in the first place. If the language was different it meant you had a breather from all the propaganda being pumped your way through the media. It was a break from the non-stop doom and gloom. A big plate of paella and a nice jug of sangria and Harry was happy. That's all you needed in life. Food and drink and a decent shag every so often.

The European birds were sound as well, though the Spanish and Portuguese didn't seem to get out much. Mind you, the Belgians were a bit scruffy and the French stuck-up, but he liked the accents all the same. That's what made them attractive, the accents. Give a half-decent bird a European accent and he could feel his knob stirring before she'd finished the first sentence. He was turning over a new leaf on this trip and going back to square one. He was sticking with Carter the unstoppable sex machine, and picking up a few tips. Carter would be dabbling non-stop and Harry reasoned that if he followed the bloke like a shadow he could pick up the leftovers. He was the apprentice boy marching with the grand master. He'd learn from Carter and shag his way across Europe. The rest of the lads, Tom and Mark and that, they were more into the aggro side of things, but while Harry didn't mind that part of the national identity, he needed some sex. His bollocks were aching, down round his knees. If he stuck close to Carter he'd be alright. Holland and Germany wouldn't know what hit them and the girls had better be ready for the road show. He was looking forward to Europe, but London would always be his home.

Thinking of London, Harry felt the first tingle of homesickness. He couldn't believe it. They hadn't even set sail. Right now he'd be coming in from work, running the bath, putting the kettle on, sticking his kebab and chips in the oven, getting in the water and washing the paint and wallpaper paste off, out and dry, putting clean clothes on and stacking his work gear in the corner of his bedroom. Then with his mouth watering he'd be back in the kitchen buttering the bread and pouring boiling water into his Chelsea mug, covering the tea bag, adding milk and sugar and taking everything into the living room with the kebab and chips on a plate, using a knife to push the chilli sauce back over the meat and salad, sitting there all ready to go with his mouth watering and his arms feeling good from the roller, fucking starving after a long day grafting for West London Decoration, the kebab meat steaming with the chilli sauce and peppers, the chips piping hot, salt and vinegar on the tray ready to go, a beautiful mix of smells, sitting there ready to go and – FUCKING HELL – the remote was on the telly. So Harry would put everything aside and go for the remote control, hitting the On button and running through the channels till he found the news for some easy entertainment. He'd sit back at last and enjoy the full experience, getting stuck into the food with TV images of Protestants and Catholics in Belfast, Spanish fishermen nicking the English catch, and finally, just before the sport, news of a ferry sinking off the Philippines. Harry was digging into the kebab, sipping his tea, waiting for the football slot and a couple of minutes of gossip before the weather. The new weatherman was a weatherwoman with a nice pair of tits ruined by a BBC accent that promised a violent storm at sea. Ferries were sailing at their own risk. He almost choked on the kebab and swore. He should've guessed.

* * *

I catch up with Mark and he wants to know what Customs were on about. I tell him it's nothing personal. He wants to know if they've got me on record as part of some Dutch porno ring, dealing in kids and freaks. Rumanian orphans and drugged English teenyboppers. Limbless grannies and two-headed pygmies. I hate all that stuff and tell him he's a sick cunt. Tell him to fuck off. Child-molesters are the lowest brand of scum and I know Mark agrees, because when he was inside he gave this nonce a serious hiding. Wouldn't have cared if he'd killed the bloke. Long as he didn't get done for the murder. The telly says all the nonces are working overtime on their computers, hiding in Amsterdam wanking over the Internet. Dregs of Europe pulled to the magnet of a liberal society. Maybe the England boys will wreck the place as a taster and show the Dutch that it's worth maintaining standards. That it pays to fight back now and again. Stand up for what you believe in. An eye for an eye and a tooth for a tooth. There's no need to stand around trying to analyse scum like that.

Harris is already in Amsterdam and the word going round is that Berlin is going to be major. It's all there at the right time because you're not going to find many blokes on this trip who agree with the way England's being ripped apart by Europe. None of us wants to be ordered about by Berlin. That's what the last war was about. It's all big business and laws coming in through the back door. Not that I believe in our legal system being the best in the world, because that's bollocks. Anyone who's dealt with the English legal system knows it's run by the rich, for the rich. The only ones who believe that shit about being innocent till proven guilty are the people who never go outside their front door. Upbringing decides your fate. Commit the same crime and your accent says whether you get ten years or an apology. It's fucking mental thinking, though, that some cunt in another country can tell us what to do. It's bad enough having some jumped-up wanker telling you what to do in your own language, but who wants the lecture in German and French as well?

The politicians are all traitors. Keeping us in the dark, doing what they want. Just like they've always done. Berlin is pulling a lot of things in at the same time and when we get over to Europe nobody's telling us lot anything. We don't need an excuse for a riot. Don't need an excuse to go on a two-day bender in Amsterdam. We'll see if the Dutch can get a mob together. Don't know much about them to be honest, but Ajax have the F-Side and there's some Chelsea boys who've added Feyenoord to Glasgow Rangers as an extra interest. Widening their scope with things so tight in England these days.

Mind you, the idea of Amsterdam is more about sitting back and watching the world pass. It's not so much that the dope's legal, I mean that's common sense, but there's this atmosphere about the place that can calm you right down if you're not careful. Suppose we shouldn't stay around too long or we'll lose the edge. But that goes to show you what's wrong at home. Imagine us getting nicked for a bit of blow on a Sunday afternoon down the Great West Road when we're minding our own business, not hurting anyone. Thing is, the cunts in charge have got no bollocks. Those Crown Court duffers you can understand, because they live in another world – another fucking planet – with their livers burnt out on gin and tonic and their brains rotting from heavy-duty clap. Diseases they picked up in Asia and Africa during the days of the Empire. Filling all the hospital beds and demanding hanging for some fifteen-year-old kid flogging Es down the local youth club. Hang the boy and cut him down, then hang him again while the judge spurts off. All because the boy's selling some happiness that doesn't come in a bottle. Heavy drinking Empire administrators propped up in their hospital beds, packed in with heavy-smoking cancer victims. I mean, I don't care either way if they want to kill themselves, but it makes you think. It's all double standards. Let us drink twenty-four hours a day, take whatever other drugs we want, turn off the surveillance cameras, and England's the perfect place to raise kids. It's the best country in the world.

– What do you reckon on them over there, Mark asks, when we've caught up with the others. Look like West Ham to me.

I clock the blokes queueing for food. They look like West Ham well enough. Can spot them a mile off. The badge the tall one's wearing gives the game away. I know Mark holds a grudge when it comes to West Ham, his old man getting a slap outside Upton Park when he was a kid. They were fucking wankers doing that to a bloke taking his boy across London to watch a game of football.

– I've seen them at England games before. Outside The Globe before Holland during Euro 96.

Not that we spent much time down Baker Street. The place gets too packed and then everyone goes for the tube at the same time. The trains can't handle the crush and there's always some wanker who pulls the emergency lever, starts fucking about with the doors or mouthing off at the old bill. You're standing there waiting to move and the old bill aren't going to take any verbal off some pisshead when they've got the numbers and are on overtime. This is their big day out, so reinforcements are called in and they make everyone suffer for The Bad Old Days when the hooligans made their lives hell. No, we prefer drinking round St John's Wood and Kilburn. If we're playing someone fruity then we might even go down the ground and use one of the pubs there if the old bill are all over the trains. But the foreigners never bring a firm over. Where were the Dutch and Germans during Euro 96?

It's funny, though, because in the build-up the papers, radio and television were crying over the security situation, creaming themselves like the Customs and judges. Bunch of wankers the media. Mindless cunts saying how they couldn't understand the mentality of the men who were going to defend their country. They couldn't understand it, but fucking loved the idea all the same. Right-wing, left-wing and no-wing, every social commentator was earning a crust writing stupid articles and presenting self-righteous reports. Preaching double standards. Bleating through the airwaves while we were laughing at them, because everyone knew the Europeans wouldn't show. Just send their mums and dads and happy families over. Keep their own heads down. Makes you laugh sitting there reading the articles about the media's major love, Nazis. They can't leave it alone. The ignorance is unbelievable. And then you've got the old bill raring to go, because we don't want any nasty business, do we son? Everyone has to have an enemy.

– I fucking hate West Ham, Facelift says, nice and loud.

I look at the Dagenham cockneys again, but they don't react. Didn't hear or don't want to know. Too busy drinking in Barking and making plans in Gant's Hill, telling everyone how wonderful East London is now they're living in Essex. Chelsea always have a bit more class, tying up Kent, Surrey, Berks. Knowing the Happy Hammers, Facelift was out of range, because there's enough of them for a row. Fair enough. But Facelift has to realise the rules are different. You can't go away with England if you're kicking seven shades of shit out of each other the whole way. And another thing, we're on a ferry and you've got to behave when you're on a boat. If it kicks off on the ferry we'll be turning round and going straight back to Harwich. It's simple really. Doesn't take a lot of brains to work that one out. You're a sitting duck waiting for the Luftwaffe to blow you out of the water. Thing is, you get all these blokes who're ready to go, been looking forward to the trip for months, and they get on the boat and they can't fucking wait. Soon as they get on the train the cans come out and they're on the piss. We haven't even got out of the port yet and Facelift is acting the cunt. Could be a liability and I've never been sure about the bloke. You have to watch someone who glasses his own brother-in-law over a game of fucking snooker.

I can just see Customs and the old bill lining the pier ready to welcome us home after the ferry gets wrecked. The media circus tipped off for some special-edition moral outrage, running on about the English Disease and our rich history. Harping back to The Good Old Days when hooligans ruled the waves and sunk their ferries before they'd thought about getting off. That's the way those wankers see things anyway. You have to grin and carry on regardless. Work your way round things these days instead of going straight through the middle. I don't want to eat, so me and Mark piss off to the bar. Leave Facelift to make his own decisions.

– I'll have a word with Facelift, Mark says on the way. He's got to wait till we're in Holland before he starts anything.

I nod and we're thinking the same way. Great minds. We pass through the ranks of the brain dead. Guidebook tourists and confused travellers walking round in small circles. Hands on the shoulders of the zapped-out zombie in front. Worrying about their luggage. Bothered by the exchange rate and rip-off commission. They can't wait for the single currency to arrive so they can save a few pence changing their pounds to guilders, and then watch the price rocket on everything else. We have to skirt past these people and I wonder why they don't go and jump over the side. Hundreds of lemmings following the basket case in front all the way to the till. Follow the leader over the rails and into the deep blue sea.

– It's shut, Mark says. The fucking bar's shut.

The grille's pulled down and there's no sign of a barman. There's a few old boys standing around with light in their eyes and a hurt look on their faces. They need a drink after the coach down from Macclesfield.

– Let's go outside and have a wander.

– Like kids on a school outing, crossing the Channel and seeing the foreign port and supermarket, then coming straight back home again. Back in time for tea.

– I don't remember that.

– We never went on those trips, but that's what the kids get now. They get all the privileges.

We work our way through another herd of passengers moving at one mile an hour, out of their heads on Prozac, dumping our bags in the luggage store as we go. Squeezing through spotty teenagers and arguing couples. A baby starts crying. We push through the doors and get a face full of fresh sea breeze mixed in with what smells like oil. We pass along the side of the ferry and up some steps to a deck where we can see the port better. Pulling on the rails, feeling old rain on flaked paint. The Unity boys are there already and we go over. We drink in the same pub, and every time I'm in there these blokes are sitting by the window with their mates, on the piss. I know them from football so it's a double barrel. Fat Harry and Terry.

– I don't think those Brummies are going to get on, Harry says.

– Serves them right, Mark laughs, looking over to where a police van stands with its light rolling. You can't expect to arrive pissed like that and not attract some attention. Definitely not these days. It's up to them how they handle it, whether they behave and keep their mouths shut or start pissing about.

Harry laughs and nods. I like the bloke. He's alright. A big bastard with a heart. Terry too. Less heart, but sharper. They're a few years older and wiser. Terry's a bit of a Romeo as well and always on the pull. Listen to Harry and the others, and they reckon it's all dog meat, but I've seen him with some nice enough fanny through the years. Harry can drink any of us under the table and he's got the gut to prove it. He hasn't really been the same since his best mate got murdered. Another Chelsea boy from the pub. Head blown off by his old foreman. We went down to Balham and helped sort the cunt out several months before the killing. You never know where those things are going to end I suppose.

– It's manners, says Harry. It's the new way. Never mind, though, because it means there's more room for the rest of us. There'll be more Dutch birds going spare.

We see the Brummies being dragged along by the old bill. Another van arrives with its siren off so's not to upset the happy tourists. But it's hurrying all the same. Can just see the driver all pumped up at the thought of battering some football hooligans. The Brummies have probably got mouthy with the coppers and that's all the excuse the old bill need. It's honest in a way, telling the police to fuck off, but it only gets you in trouble. Where's the sense in that? There again, the old bill don't need an excuse. Strongbow is struggling like only a drunk struggles and he's got four coppers on him. They pull him into the van and crack his head on the door, the Bully boy bouncing back and the old bill trying again. A little harder this time. Head thumping metal panels and the body spilling into the van. All accidental of course, the fucking wankers.

– Fucking scum, says Terry. There's no need for that.

The back door slams shut and a tall copper thumps the side of the van. He's tall and thin and loves the power. The brown dirt cowboy at the controls puts his foot down and speeds off. It's pathetic. Thinks he's in The Bill or something. Things like that make you hate the cunts.

– Don't worry, we'll make up for all that when we get to Holland, says Mark.

Everyone nods. We all want the holiday and the chance to take out some frustration on the Europeans. We want the trip abroad. A nice break from the daily grind. Change as good as a rest.

Mark and Tom hung around for a while watching Harwich grind along, hung about till they got bored and said they were going inside to wait for the bar to open. Carter fancied a drink and went with them. There was nothing new to see on deck and he'd rather be watching the crumpet pass than a load of sweaty sailors. Harry was settled into his seat and enjoying the view. The others didn't understand, didn't appreciate the finer points. He wanted to stay where he was until they set sail. He wanted the full holiday experience and maximum value for money. There was some drizzle falling and the wind was picking up, but Harry liked the idea of sitting on deck till they got out to sea. It was good to be alone sometimes. He watched the lads walk away, heads turning for a girl in a short skirt and plastic mac. She was well dirty and Harry wondered if he was being clever letting the sex machine out of his sight.

Carter was probably off to pick up some sort and give her a portion in the luggage room, while the other two would get hold of one of the satellite town pearly kings in the canteen and set him on fire. They'd chuck the burning Iron over the side for the port authorities to fish out, killing time till the bar opened and they could have a decent drink, Carter in the top rack behind the bags of tea and I ♥ LONDON T-shirts servicing some Danish au pair who'd come to England and fallen in love with the bulldog breed. Fucked off with Copenhagen she'd gone to London looking for adventure. She was searching for the bulldog spirit, with Carter breeding in the top rack doing her doggy style, keeping their voices down so they didn't upset the other passengers. Imagine that. Mr and Mrs Rotterdam pulling a bag of dildos down and seeing a wide-eyed English hooligan shafting a Danish beauty queen. They probably wouldn't be all that bothered and take it in their stride, select a Dark Destroyer from the bag and disappear into the Ladies. The Dutch were a funny lot. Not like your Middle England couple who'd be narked they were missing out on the fun and call someone in a uniform to break things up. Pull those two apart steward and give them a good caning.

Harry turned and looked over the cars and lorries waiting to load, drivers held back by the barriers getting impatient, juggernauts narked they were losing precious time, all of them wanting to get on a free stretch of road and accelerate into the sunset. Funny how they called it Harwich International, like it was going to compete with Heathrow. He scanned dead grey buildings and oversized ships, passing through stacked containers and packed coaches. The containers were packed with rockets, and the coaches held rows of holiday-makers dreaming of Stockholm and Venice and Prague. Harry was glad of the break, but wouldn't really start enjoying himself till touch down in Holland. This was the worst part of the journey, crossing the English Channel, because Harry had a problem with ferries. He always got sick when he went to sea.

Joking apart, he was glad he wasn't in the Grimsby fleet or the Royal Navy. He wouldn't have lasted ten minutes. Those blokes in the old days who popped out for a pint and got lumbered with twenty years on the high seas definitely lived at the wrong time. The poor bastards put their coats on and went down the pub to meet their mates, and then when they're wandering home feeling good about life, glad to see the missus and check the kids, maybe get their leg over, then the fucking press-gang steams in and gives them a kicking, and next thing they're waking up on the way to Jamaica. That kind of thing was bang out of order and it made you think about how the men themselves felt. Wife and kids left to get on with things while Dad was forced into a life of rum, sodomy and the lash, but because it was so long ago it became some sort of joke. Nobody cared about the feelings of those men. You could put up gravestones and carve names and dates to last five hundred years, write books about the admirals even, but Joe Public was history as well. The difference was the unmarked grave. Another skeleton at the bottom of the ocean.

Harry had been a dreamer most of his life, rolling along and trying to work out the future, and it had taken the death of his mate Balti to bring home a few truths. It made him stop and look at the world. There was no place for dreams and soppy ideas. The bloke had been dead less than two years and already people were forgetting him. Not really forgetting him, it was more like he now belonged to some other story. The memory wasn't alive. That's what it was. The memory was stacked away with all the others. It was like it didn't make any difference whether Balti had ever lived. He was now known as that geezer from the pub who liked his drink, football and curries, and who'd got his head blown off by some mad old Paddy from South London. If that was all there was to show for all those years of life, then it was seriously fucking sad. It wasn't the drink, football and curries, because that was fair enough, but those were the things he did, not what he thought. Everyone said he was a good bloke, and that was important, but the memory had to stay alive. They'd forget he was a decent bloke and go back to the drink, football, curries line. That's what everyone did in the end.

Harry could hear the crew shouting to each other. The ferry was getting ready to leave and a lot of people were going to be left behind. They were impatient and angry because the system was failing them. The boat was full and the electronic board was passing on the message. Digital displays relayed the information in thin streaks of light. It was too bad. He watched the passengers around him, most of them leaning over the railings. They spoke different languages and this brought back his first thrill of going over the Channel. The boat was moving slowly and he realised the sheer size of the hull, looking back over the railyard and storage zones. Harwich did its job and nothing more. It was a gateway and didn't have time to sit still. The worker ants came and did their jobs, some of them getting to go to sea on the boats, while Customs looked out for drug smugglers and vans full of hardcore porn, checking the containers coming in from all over Europe and parts of the

Middle East, looking for that major heroin haul, the illegal guns and explosives, unwanted immigrants and asylum seekers.

There was no beauty in the place and Harry looked further along the coast, past half-hidden pubs and hotels, noticing the change of scene, the boat slow to move then gathering speed, the English coastline broadening fast as the people and buildings on the shore got smaller, shrinking as the view widened, the incredible shrinking nation, cities spilling into green fields, the ferry pushing out to sea until the first proper waves came through, deeper troughs that told you it was real, that the Channel was deep and dangerous, Harry hearing somewhere that the seas around Britain had claimed more than a million lives since records began. He tried to get his head round the figure. He wanted to make the most of this trip and had forgotten about being sick. He tried thinking of a million skeletons under the water without the headstone Balti's mum had put on her son's grave. The island race buried at sea.

Harry was looking forward and leaving Balti in the past, dead and at peace. He was crossing the Channel and when he came back it was going to be a fresh start. He wanted to get stuck into the birds in Amsterdam and hoped he could pull something nice, but if not he was straight down the red light and splashing out. With Carter at his side he was feeling lucky. He would watch and learn and try to repeat the bullshit the sex machine used. Everyone who ever went to Holland always came back with stories of the blow they'd smoked and the whores they'd fucked. It sounded good to Harry, because he hadn't got his leg over since Balti was killed. He'd been drinking more than usual and things were building up. He'd been getting so pissed when they went out that he couldn't speak halfway through the night, let alone chat up a woman. When he got to Amsterdam he'd get himself a right little cracker and fuck the arse off her. If it was a prossie he'd give her the best shag she'd get that night.

He started feeling better already. Mind you, he didn't really want to pay for the business. He'd prefer a nice Dutch bird who worked in a shop selling clothes rather than sex. Someone who wanted him for his personality – well, not his personality, but maybe a drink and a laugh. It didn't matter. He had to be realistic because the future was never going to be that rosy and he'd have to make sure he didn't get too pissed. He'd take a rubber along and remember to protect himself in the red light district. He didn't want to die young. He wanted to see what happened next. Get everything in order and see where things were leading.

Balti hadn't left a will, though in truth there wasn't much to leave. There were his clothes, and those went to the jumble, because no way was Harry walking about in a dead man's jeans and trainers. There were some odds and ends, a few records and CDs, a broken record player, a small pile of Chelsea programmes from when Balti was a kid. There wasn't a lot really, but then Balti hadn't had much, and towards the end he'd been skint and signing on. Just playing the lottery trying to get a lucky break, and imagine that . . . if he'd won and left Harry a fortune. He'd pocket the millions and buy himself the best whorehouse in Holland. He'd be Harry the Pimp and get himself a zoot suit and smoke Havana cigars, do his old mate proud. He was feeling positive. He used to dream at nights but now he was sleeping straight through. Death had blown everything away. What was the point of mights and maybes when you could die in the street in a pool of blood? He was going to live his life right and stick with Carter. Terry didn't bother thinking too much. He got on with the job and concentrated his attention on getting his end away.

There's different kinds of holidays. Different away days. Different ways to go. Following England is all about pride and history. Our place in the pecking order. For centuries we've been kicking shit out of the Europeans. They start something and we finish it. We're standing on the White Cliffs of Dover singing COME AND HAVE A GO IF YOU THINK YOU'RE HARD ENOUGH. Waiting for the Germans to get the bottle together and cross the Channel. Fifty English will run two hundred or more Europeans no problem. A thousand if you're talking Italians or Spanish. I'm proud to be English and proud to say so. This Germany game is a chance to escape the prison football at home and flex some muscle, because however hard the foreigners try to control us when we get on their soil they don't have a chance.

It's all in the head. In the genes. We've got this stubborn streak. We hang on and don't let go. They can't beat us. We know it and they know it as well, deep down inside. Where it hurts. We're winners. They can send in their riot squads and fire their tear gas and, if it's Luxembourg, they can even call out the army, but we just don't care. We're English, and if there's any slack then our drunks will walk through foreign borders with their jeans round their ankles, taking the piss. Flashing the forty-inch bust at the passport desk. The Europeans don't know how to handle us. They can do the mass arrests and that, try it on, corner someone in a back street and batter the fuck out of them. Try and crack your spine and open your skull. But still the English carry on, full steam ahead. That kind of pain's skin deep, though now and then they go overboard and you have to watch yourself. They take things too seriously and target someone. Try to cripple him. It comes with the landscape.

Thing is, they pull out all the stops, give it their best shot, and what happens? If they're waiting at the border we tread lightly because we're no mugs. We pick our spot and then when it goes off we keep coming back for more. The English have been rioting in Europe for well over twenty years, and that's just the football. Your Italian and Spanish old bill can't get their heads round it. They're used to dealing with the ultras of Juventus and Real Madrid. Holding seminars and printing scarves. That's why we won the war. No surrender. Get beaten to a pulp by a mob of spics and back you come before the wounds have healed. And because of what's happened you're worse than before. The mad dogs just get meaner.

If this game wasn't on I'd be spending my time somewhere else. In a Spanish or Greek resort taking things easy after the domestic season. On the pull shagging anything that moves. Cutting through the stereotypes servicing every brand of decent-looking English woman available. No-nonsense spunk-lovers from London and the Home Counties; the factory workers from Liverpool and barmaids from Newcastle; the officer girls from Leeds and johnny-sellers from Bristol; the shop

598

assistants from Manchester and unemployed goths from Norwich. Then I'll be showing a healthy interest in foreign culture with the roving Morvern nutters of Scotland, the religious Orange Order girls of Northern Ireland and the Merthyr miners' daughters of Wales. Showing no prejudice and moving forward to the fish-slicers of Oslo and strippers of Munich and nurses of Vienna. Women are the best thing God invented. His greatest idea letting me sit on a Spanish beach watching the girls pass by during the afternoon, then slipping them a length at three in the morning. Now that's another kind of holiday.

It's an easy break where you don't have to do much work. Give it some bollocks and empty them inside the hour. Wander the clubs and bars putting up with the tinny music they play. Weaving in and out of the wankers lining the pavement talking through their arses. No need to go overboard. Taking things nice and steady. Keeping yourself together. Maintaining standards. Looking to get some bird on your knob by the end of the night. At first keeping a tab, but losing track when it gets boring. The same old words and the same old cunts. No challenge and no danger. Still, what else is there, because then you start looking forward to the mornings when you get up early and have a swim. The weather's fine and there's a buffet breakfast waiting, and you're having a laugh with Pedro the Barcelona fan. Tell him you know his brother Manuel. You do your duty and get your money's worth. Along to the pool for a couple of hours in the sun watching the bird you shagged last night up against the back wall of Del Boy's London Bar try and stroll past, too embarrassed to say hello. So you yell out alright Kim? She turns and goes red but seems keen. You give her the once over and she's not as fresh as last night. You've shot your wad up her so you let the small talk fade. She goes her way, you go yours. Straight in the pool. Have a swim. Mark and Rod awake now. Same old stories. Gets more boring day by day. Concrete blocks and formation palms. Chicken dinners and flat lager. Everyone pissing in the pool.

Then you've been there nearly a week and you're cranking up inside. You see the Munich boys in a bar across the road and start getting lairy. Feel the energy coming up. Keeping it back.

Taking your time. Those wankers across the road in their shitty megastore gear. You know it's going to kick off because you look at your mates standing around fucked off by the routine and they're feeling the same way. Want to take it easy, but need some excitement. The Munich boys aren't the real Munich. They're not your old-time Stretford Enders, just Premiership playboys. More into their club-sponsored clothes than a cold midweek game in Leeds. You have some respect for the Red Army, but these wankers make you laugh. Getting wound up looking at the slags giving it the big one with the women. Their own little world. Don't go to games half these cunts even though they've got all the gear and mouth.

But before you get anywhere there's a row on your own doorstep with some fucking yids at the bar. Can't believe it. Tottenham right next to you and you didn't even see the cunts. Taking the piss or what? Looking at the bloke two feet away with the side of his face sliced open, a neat cut from the bottle Mark's holding with blood spouting out of his face and you stand back looking at the fountain and, to be honest, it's not pretty. Bit naughty really. The Spurs holiday-makers come through and you don't have time to think about the ifs and buts, because you dodge back and smack some cunt in the head as he swings pissed and out of control on the old dodgems of life. Kick him in the top of the head twice and stroll away singing HE GOES TO THE BAR, TO BUY A LAGER, AND ONLY BUYS ONE FOR HIMSELF, leaving one cut, one twitching, and three more bruised and helping their mates. Nothing personal you fucking cunts, passing the Munich fashion dolls hiding now inside the bar. Cunts. Give us some Cockney Reds and we might even let them buy us a drink.

Different holidays for different things. Go to a resort and you're looking for a nice line of slappers flat on their backs. Leaning forward over the railings of the tenth floor balcony as you give that Nottingham bird with the tiny nipple-sized tits an oil change. Watching rockets explode, flashing orange and red sparks over the tourist tower blocks. Looking over the landscape of Cliff Richard's summer holiday nightmare. Cheap food and drink. Forget the music because it's shit and you take your own.

Play the cassettes in your room or by the pool. Wind the wankers up. That's the seaside in Spain, but go away with England and the whole thing's ten times better. Resorts are more sex and football's more violence. England away's sex and violence if you play your cards right, but the aggro comes first. Least that's how I see things, though Carter and Harry would list the birds first. Sex and violence are what we're good at. Right through England, from top to bottom, through the centuries, it's sex and violence all the way. The Cross of St George drenched in blood and spunk. Putting some bollocks in the Union Jack.

Look at your politicians and it's all there. It's the power trip. Sex gives them the power because they can pay some poor girl to do anything they want. They're in charge. Even the old cunts you read about who want to get whipped and tied up with barbed wire. They're still paying for the service, letting the tension run loose. It's their big treat. The violence, though, that's a bit different, because when they're mixing it up with the sex they can pay for that as well, but when there's no sex angle they don't fancy getting involved. Not personally anyway. They want the thrill but have to pay someone on their behalf, so fork out for their men in uniforms – the old bill, army, what have you. They want the control. Violence is allowed when they say so. Pass a law and it's on their terms, mixing in the power, while the trendy cunts want it in their films and documentaries. They want to sit in a circle discussing it through the night, throwing in their minority views and filling it with meaning, never going anywhere. Trying to settle their own grievances. Boring fuckers clogging the channels when you want a good horror film.

Sex and violence. Everyone loves it, because that's where the excitement comes. You don't have to confuse the two. It's what made us great. We move in on the women and they can't resist. We kick fuck out of anyone who has a go at us. The English are fair and square, and by English I mean your everyday bloke like me and Mark, and Rod as well if he wasn't a sad married cunt. People like Harry and Carter and Brighty and Facelift. Don't know about Facelift. We're hard but fair. That's the English. No pretence or pissing about, because what you see is what you get, standing outside the duty-free talking with a couple of Man City fans, old-time Kippax we know from before. They're eyeing up the rows of fags, spirits, choccies, wondering out loud whether there's any scousers on board, or maybe ICJ. Looking to fill their pockets. Mark tells them it's the yids who'd go for the instant thieving even though they're stuck on a ferry. Can't wait. We all laugh. Funny how it works.

We were in this bar in Paris one trip, making do paying over the odds drinking frog piss water, real shitty drink. Makes you wonder why all the Latin countries have piss for beer. They're all the same. I've been to Italy, Spain, France and all these cunts are the same, serving shit bottled lager. The more you pay the worse it is, and some of the England boys even end up drinking the local wine it's so bad. There's always one or two blokes who get stuck into the wine like it's lager. Drink gallons of the stuff and go mental. But in Paris there was over a hundred English from all over the country packed into this one bar doing their best to force the piss down. Lots of different clubs drinking and having a sing-song, making the most of life because the French were nowhere to be seen. Then out of nothing the bar starts singing SPURS ARE ON THEIR WAY TO AUSCHWITZ. We were cracking up laughing because it shows how everyone hates Spurs. Thing was, there was this big skinhead looking a bit embarrassed and the bloke's only a fucking yid. Well, not a yid as in Jew, but yid as in Tottenham. Harris was patting him on the head telling him not to worry, and the Stevenage skin was saying you've got it wrong, it's not all yiddos at White Hart Lane, I hate those Star of Davids like the rest of you, I'm an Anglo-Saxon. World turned upside down with nothing in its right place.

We go for a wander and catch up with Billy and Facelift. We spot some of the Pompey boys and have a chat. Old faces from England trips. Original 657 Crew with a few younger lads tagging along. Everything's mush and Millwall and scummers. Wonder who they hate most, Millwall or Southampton? They've got their ensign flag with them and it seems everyone's plotting the same route through Amsterdam. This is the early arrivals on the ferry, because give it a day or two and the boats will be packed with England. We're getting the march on the rest of the boys and it's going to be a good turn out. We head for the bar. At least the Dutch and Germans know how to brew decent lager.

Bill Farrell ordered a pint of bitter and walked over to his usual seat. He lowered himself into the chair and, once he was settled, took a mouthful of beer. He was drinking Directors and savoured the taste. Two or three pints was his limit these days. His legs were a little stiff, but apart from that he was fit for his age. His working life in a local park had served him well. He'd always drunk bitter and The Unity served a decent pint. He'd used the pub for the last three years since moving up the road from Hounslow to be nearer his daughter, and the beer was always good. He'd drunk in The Unity years ago, when visiting his brother who had lived locally. It was strange to think they'd drunk in this same pub as young men. He'd been coming in The Unity, on and off, for more than half a century. The secret of a good pint of bitter was clean pipes, and successive landlords had maintained standards.

He put the jug down, opened his paper and began reading. He was soon lost in one of the main features, only raising his head when Bob West entered the pub. The younger man nodded, checked Mr Farrell's glass, and went to the bar, ordering a pint of Tennent's from Denise. She smiled as she poured and asked Bob whether he wanted his usual plain crisps, or perhaps he fancied cheese and onion today. It was a joke they shared and Bob said he'd wait. He asked Denise if she'd like a drink and she said thanks, but it was okay. She knew he wasn't flush and appreciated the offer. She didn't normally drink when she was working anyway. Bob paid and went over to Farrell, asking if he could share the table.

– Of course you can, Farrell smiled. There's plenty of room.

Bill Farrell didn't mind the company one way or the other. He'd only become friendly with Bob West over the last few months. He'd known who Bob was, of course, and that the younger man had served as a pilot in the Gulf, but until recently they'd never spoken. He'd assumed Bob was keeping himself to himself, but the younger man had turned out to be a friendly enough character. He wasn't well, and it was only recently the Government had admitted there could possibly be something called Gulf War Syndrome. Bob had problems with his breathing and suffered from mood swings. He'd be down in the dumps and told Farrell he felt he was falling into a hole, where his part in the conflict no longer seemed real. His memory was becoming distorted and sometimes he imagined he was nothing more than one of the graphic air-force rangers flashing on the games machine in the corner of the pub. He had fought and most certainly killed, yet felt removed from the experience. He was imagining all sorts of things these days. His brain was running wild and he didn't enjoy the faces it was conjuring up. There was an initial excitement and blazing colour, but this soon vanished and was replaced by a prolonged, numbing horror. The faces were black and charred, the skulls clearly visible.

Coming back to London and signing on had been a huge culture shock for West. He'd dedicated his life to the RAF, thereby fulfilling his childhood dream and following in the footsteps of the Spitfire pilots who'd saved the country during the Battle of Britain. These men were his heroes and he'd tried to match their achievements. He passed the tests, trained hard and travelled the world. It had been a good life, disciplined and exciting, but now he'd come full circle and was back in London living three streets from where he was born. Every morning on his way to the cornershop for a carton of milk he passed the school he went to as a kid. He had been one of the élite and now he was a dole queue number. From the steak dinners and post-raid comradeship of Saudi to beans on toast and life in a lonely flat. He'd experienced the glory of the Gulf and come down with a thud. It seemed so unreal, part of someone else's life. His mood sank and then rushed back as he tried to recall the thrill he felt soaring over an Arab desert with his finger on the trigger and millions of pounds of precision technology at his command. He could wipe out entire streets with the press of a button and had felt like a god riding through the sky, dealing out death and destruction as he saw fit. Now he was powerless.

His moods were up and down. One minute he was a silver-screen hero with an orchestra roaring him on, the next he was sucked along with the missiles and forced to witness the aftermath.

Farrell had quickly become used to Bob West and let the younger man do the talking. If he was silent, Farrell concentrated on his paper or the street outside. Bob was sitting quietly now, so Farrell went with the bitter. He had time on his hands, drifting through the window to a wartime London of blackouts and air-raid shelters, where incendiaries set the streets burning and kids watched doodlebugs splutter to a halt, then fall silently to earth. Everyone waited for the explosion. It was high-tech warfare. The ranks of Nazi bombers, the V-1 buzzbombs and V-2 ballistic missiles. After the bombs and rockets, men and women scraped through charred rubble searching for survivors, full of hatred for the men in the clouds who killed and maimed while hiding in the darkness. Farrell remembered the bombing and thought of the time he'd spent billeted in camps waiting for the Allied invasion of Europe to begin, training and retraining. When the time came, they were ready and willing. There were a lot of debts to repay.

Farrell had played his part and was intensely proud of what he'd done. He'd gone across the Channel with the invasion force and helped defeat Hitler and the Nazis. Now he was back in the same old pubs. He didn't mind at all. He was happy to sit in The Unity. Very happy indeed. He liked the pub and he liked London. Many men never made it back. He was lucky to go full circle. He had survived and was proud to have got through the slaughter. Young people didn't appreciate just how precious continuity and community were. They wanted excitement and adventure, but you had to put things in perspective. He was thankful to drink a pint of Directors and enjoy the moment. Of course he had his memories, but the strongest memories were often the ones you never shared. The history of the English working class was buried in coffins and burnt in incinerators. From cradle to grave the details were often kept private, and if you did share the knowledge it was verbally, and this in turn meant that eventually it was lost. Nothing was written down. It was the English way. It some ways it gave you a dignity no-one could steal, but in another it was a cop out, letting the rich claim history along with everything else.

For a while after the war Farrell was withdrawn. Once demobbed, everything seemed trivial, and it was only the presence of his wife that stopped him becoming bitter. His wife had seen and experienced something far worse in the camp, and this in turn taught him humility. But he didn't like to remember those things. Before the war, he'd been a bit of a tearaway. It was part of growing up. After the war it had taken him time to adjust as he ran the pictures through and tried to make some sense of everything that had happened. Maybe that's what Bob was doing now, but he didn't think it was exactly the same. Farrell had seen the unimaginable, while from what Bob said it seemed he'd seen very little from the cockpit of his plane. Farrell didn't like to go back and remember the horror, but it was there and he'd kept the lid on things for over half a century. Bob had troubles Farrell didn't understand. Maybe it was weakness, because the younger man was from a different generation. There seemed to be more and more weak people around these days.

Perhaps it was the way West had fought or maybe it was this Gulf War Syndrome the papers were talking about. Perhaps – and this was just his own theory – perhaps it was the nature of the war itself. Maybe it was the justification for war that mattered more than anything else. War was a blend of excitement at what was to come and sickness when it arrived. The end had to justify the means. Farrell had thought about this a lot when he was younger. War was sold on glory and colour, while the fighting itself was repetitive and vicious. Farrell knew he was right fighting the Nazis, but wasn't so sure about Bob fighting Iraq on behalf of Kuwait and the oil industry. You had to feel justified in your actions, because there came a time when you had to think about these things. Bob was struggling with the reality. In the old days people put this off, and many managed to ignore such questions for the rest of their lives, but the younger generation was different. Farrell had done a good job keeping his memories in line. Most people didn't have the mental discipline and self-control. Bob West was back home on the dole with time to waste so his mind was bound to wander. Whatever the reason for his moods, the man was sick. His skin was patchy and his eyes glazed. There was sweat on West's forehead and the man didn't look well. Farrell sipped his drink. He didn't look well at all.

Harry leant over the railings and let the sickness go, his gut exploding as a full cooked breakfast roared back up at a hundred miles an hour, straight through his mouth in a hurricane twister. Gulls picked up the scent and turned their heads, rolling their eyes at the coming feast. There was a moment of calm, a freeze-frame second or so when the rolling green waves were solid rock and the motion of the ferry stuck, rudder jammed tight, a magic moment when Harry could blink and watch the sickness hover in front of him, a chance to understand the power of the sea. Then wallop. The video rushed away as he lost control, leaning over the railings and looking down. Bull's-eye.

He couldn't help laughing as the Spice Girl schoolkids on the deck below stopped their shrieking and realised the truth. There was another second of silence before the storm, when the waves rolled again and the ferry rocked, ducking and diving through the Channel, pushing against the elements dipping its bow into the wind. There was a second's pause on the video nasty and the thirteen-year-old girls looked at each other and understood what had happened. They understood that they'd just been soaked in a bacon-and-eggs English-breakfast £2.99 special, home delivered by the big fat bastard bent over the railings above looking down on them, laughing his head off. The head was square and shaved, and the man didn't care about their clothes and hair, everything ruined. There were bits in the sick as well. Pieces of what seemed liked bacon. It was horrible. The vomit and the man above who was laughing like something off The X Files. The mechanism clicked and the kids started howling.

Harry heard their screams rising through the thrashing of the wind, the flapping throb in his ears chopped away by teenage hysteria. A vicious cocktail of greasy cafe cooking and too much ketchup had ruined expensive haircuts and girl-power fashion. A mob of kids ran off crying their eyes out, all flashing lycra and long blonde curls trailing in the wind.

– Fucking slags, was all Harry could mumble, acid in his throat and tears in his eyes.

Harry pushed himself up on the rail, thinking of England and trying to keep his guts in. You had to see the funny side of things, though, because there was the future down below coated in the sick of the last two decades. The pretty young things that would shape the England to come soaked in the bile of the nutters who'd rampaged through the past. Well, not really the past, but someone twenty years older who should've known better. Together they represented the present, but the consumer kids were feeling the effects. No amount of ecstasy could save you when England mobbed up. Mind you, like the rest of the country he wouldn't have said no to a proper Spice Girl knocking on his door with a takeaway at three in the morning. It didn't have to be a Spice mind. He'd make do with some old slapper on her way home from Blues who fancied ten solid inches of BSE up her arse. But he couldn't be bothered with that sort of thinking right now because the wind was getting stronger and he had to sit down, moving away from the crime scene before Cracker appeared to go through his reasons, finding an empty bench where he could put his back to the wall and watch the English coastline disappear in the haze. Gulls followed the ferry the whole way, tracking the trawler from Grimsby with the press-ganged Harry on board, panicking fish thrashing on the deck, hungry gulls following Eric Cantona all the way back to Europe.

– You were sick all over those young girls, a voice said, appearing from nowhere.

Harry looked to his right and noticed the mini-skirt and mac sitting next to him. He hadn't seen the woman come over. She had to be a Scandinavian. A Danish beauty queen maybe. Someone to take along to the storage room and knob in the racks. No, she was Swedish. He was certain this bird was a Swede. A fucking lovely bit of skirt.

– It was not a nice thing to do, the woman said, laughing.

Harry felt awkward. It wasn't the ideal way to a bird's heart, puking on a bunch of school kids. He wasn't sure how to answer that one. What was he supposed to say? That it didn't matter?

– Can you understand me? You are English, aren't you?

– Yes, I'm English.

– Only an Englishman would do that to such young girls and then laugh. It is the English sense of humour I guess.

Harry was struggling now. Was she taking the piss? He didn't think so. Yes, the English sense of humour was alive and well and doing the business on the high seas. He wondered what Terry Thomas would do in this situation. Give it the sophisticated approach and use the old English gentleman routine, though Harry didn't think he could pull that off. But he was missing the point, because this bird had just seen him in action and she was still coming over for a chat. He was in, no fucking problem. They loved it, the Scandinavians, because their blokes were so fucking serious the girls flocked to any English cock going spare. The English knew how to enjoy themselves. That's what it was. They wanted a bit of that olde English magic. The blood, sweat and spunk of an English hooligan. Forget the wankers tucking into their health food and sipping low-alcohol lager, not wanting to lose control. The Swedish birds wanted some excitement. This girl was crying out for a night on the town, moving through the pubs of West London and filling up on a cheap Indian, then back to Harry's unmade bed for a quick shag, those ten pints of lager making sure his performance was up to the usual standard. It was the hooligan element making its mark, putting England on the map.

– My name is Ingrid, from Berlin, said the Swede.

– Harry. From London.

– Nice to meet you Harry.

– Likewise Ingrid.

The wind picked up and they were silent for half a minute or so. Harry was gagging for it and so was this bird. But he still had the taste of sick in his mouth and had to get his breath back. He needed a shag and was going to ask Ingrid what the chances were of climbing into that luggage rack when Carter had finished servicing the Dane. They fucking loved it, the old fräuleins. Dirty slag had probably been shagging her way through all the London clubs, taking her pick of the ICF boys in Mile End and the Bushwhackers down in South London, the Gooners in North London, but missing out on the full experience. Shame he hadn't met her down Blues and given her the usual patter, shown her the local sites, but there again, reasoning the things through, she'd probably never got out of the West End, spending her time getting chased by trendy wankers and long queues of greasy Italians. What a waste.

– I have just spent two weeks in London. I enjoyed it very much. I am on holiday with my boyfriend.

Harry nodded.

Just his fucking luck. Nice-looking bird like that, with a mini-skirt and a plastic mac, sitting on deck flashing it about, and she's only travelling with some goose-stepping cunt who probably didn't realise what he was getting. Fucking gorgeous she was. Mind you, Ingrid was flirting and you never knew. Maybe the cunt she was knobbing worked part-time for the Gestapo and was bringing his work home. Handcuffing her to the bedposts and pulling out her fingernails. Ingrid had long, red nails that would pop out of her fingers easy enough. Poor old Ingrid shagging some Aryan superman in a full-length leather coat and jackboots. Pliers under the pillow and industrial voltage pulsing through the electric blanket. What she needed was a change of scene. She needed Harry to show her the way forward. Forget the Germans and kneel down for the England boys.

– I work in a bar called Bang in East Berlin, Ingrid said, handing Harry a card. You should visit me and bring your friends along.

Harry saw the boyfriend approach and Ingrid was up and running to some scruffy anarchist-communist cunt with one of those haircuts that stuck up like a bog brush on top of his head, small eyes shut away behind the regulation round glasses. Harry watched them go. First thing he was going to do in Amsterdam was get himself a bird. Ingrid was fucking lovely. He needed something like that and put the card in his pocket. You never knew. Stranger things happened.

Harry saw himself walking into Bang. He was looking good, with his head freshly shaved and a new Ben Sherman ironed by some bird at the luxury hotel. He'd been swimming in the hotel pool and then had a massage and blow job off a blonde number in silk stockings. She didn't even try to charge. He'd gone back to his room and eaten steak and chips and drunk a nice pint of lager delivered by an old boy who'd served in the war. He'd even given the man a tip. Now he was out and about, calling a taxi from reception, surrounded by wealthy American business-men, ten minutes later racing through the Berlin streets to Bang. He was walking into Ingrid's club with his head held high and straight into her arms, the Green cunt with the bog brush old news, Harry sitting at the bar enjoying the chat and flavour of the place. He would drink till closing and follow Ingrid upstairs for a night of non-stop sex.

– Who was that bird you were talking to? Billy Bright asked, sitting down next to Harry.

– She's German. Works in a bar in Berlin.

Harry showed Brighty the card.

– Sounds like a fucking queer bar, he said, sneering. What kind of name is Bang. Must be full of shirt-lifters. We'll wreck the place.

– Never thought of that. Suppose she looks a bit trendy.

– Nice arse on it.

– Bit flat-chested.

Billy laughed.

– It's probably alright. We should go down there and see if she's got any mates.

Harry didn't fancy Brighty coming along. He was planning a private party. He wanted to get out and about on his own. It was a killer that, going along hoping to get your leg over and taking a fucking mob as well. If Carter turned up, he'd be in there before Harry finished his first drink, and the rest of the boys would have a couple of lagers, rob the till and put all the windows through.

– I'll take some tapes along, Billy said. I spent last week

getting them together. Marching bands, Oi! and some modern stuff. A patriotic soundtrack for the trip. You know what these bars are like over in Europe. It's all poppy shit. You need some decent sounds to keep you happy.

Harry nodded. He looked at DJ Bright the bulldog mixmaster. It was a good idea. Billy opened the bag he was carrying and showed Harry the cassette player and ten or so tapes. It made sense, because you never got to listen to the music you wanted as the radio had its own ideas on what to play. The wind started pushing harder and Billy closed the bag quickly so the spitting rain didn't get in and ruin his music.

– Where have the others gone? he asked, looking around the empty deck.

– They're in the bar.

– I think I'll follow them. It's getting rough up here. You coming?

Harry was staying a bit longer. He'd always liked the rain; it was the rocking of the sea that did him in. DJ Bright looked at Harry as though he was mad and nodded, showing he understood.

It was still early, but with two pints of Director's in his belly it was the right time for Farrell to go home. He said goodnight to Bob and put his mug on the bar for Denise. She was a sweet girl and smiled at the pensioner. It was a fine summer's evening and he hoped Bob would be able to sort himself out, or if it was this Gulf War Syndrome then he hoped the Government would do its duty. He wasn't optimistic about the official angle, and it was odd how events constantly replayed. He thought of the mustard gas used on the Somme, the shell-shock and executions that were nothing short of murder, the madness of traumatised men brushed under the carpet and left to fester. He pushed this away. The memories had been coming back recently, rising more and more frequently. He thought he'd buried those things deep. He knew the reason of course. There was a decision to make, but it would have to wait for another day. Farrell wanted to enjoy the evening air. It was a strange world and one of the benefits of age was that you became more reflective and less angry. Life was unfair and it was cruel, but your moment passed and there was nothing more you could do.

Bill Farrell imagined life had been more innocent when he was young, but at the same time tougher, and once the bombing started people began living for the moment. There was little planning. You didn't know what was going to happen, whether you'd live or die. His time billeted in camps had been dull and repetitive and morale was low early in the war, with Doenitz's U-boats creating havoc in the Atlantic, the mass bombing, the defeats at Dunkirk and Dieppe. Conditions were basic in the camps and there was some bad feeling towards those in charge and resentment at the pay being so low. There'd been a class-consciousness among the men that didn't exist today, and the officers had to prove themselves. The Americanisation of English culture over the past thirty years had seen a crass materialism take hold, and this had allowed the establishment to sweeten the population without really giving them anything substantial in return. Farrell had watched this happen and it was the ease with which money had bought England's soul that he found most depressing.

The soldiers of the Second World War had learnt from the experience of those in the First. They'd been raised by men who'd served on the Western Front and seen hell on earth. There was a closeness between the two experiences, and Farrell was always amazed at the way the ordinary soldier was portrayed years after the event. In reality, they'd spoken their minds and not suffered fools gladly. The thousands of working-class men slaughtered on the Western Front due to the incompetence of upper-class officers hadn't been forgotten. Even now he felt the anger of his youth simmering, something that happened when he considered these things. He was disappointed that the gains made by his generation had been squandered by a superficial élite, but knew he had to let go. It didn't matter when you were old. He'd moved on and kept telling himself he didn't care until he almost believed it himself. He'd done his bit for England and there was little reward from the state. He'd learnt the hard way. But he hadn't fought for the politicians and businessmen, and the politicians and businessmen didn't think about old men living out their years in one-bedroom council flats. He remembered the VE Day celebrations and how the Tories had even wanted to march German troops through Central London. It really was unbelievable.

Farrell thought of the two pints he'd drunk and smiled. Two pints was a lot these days, and it wasn't just the price. In the old days he'd liked a drink, and so did his mates. It was his life and his culture and he'd had fun. The Unity always had a piano in those days, and there was one bloke who'd played boogie-woogie along with the more traditional London singalongs. He thought of his brother standing at the bar ordering all those years ago. The White Horse in Hounslow had been his local and they were bitter drinkers, though some of his mates drank mild. Beer was cheap and the pubs were packed. Lager didn't take over till years later. They'd had a few punch-ups too, though it wasn't something he ever talked about. It was foolish. They'd never used knives or bottles, just fists. It was good-natured and brief, caused by drink. The cuts and bruises healed and all that was left were vague memories doctored by time.

Farrell pulled himself up and knew he could remember if he really wanted, if he pushed himself. If he was completely honest with himself, age hadn't destroyed his memory. At least not yet. He thought about it some more and let his mind go back. It was hard to remember things how they were rather than how you wanted them to appear. This especially applied to the war. There were so many impressions and sights he'd pushed down, applying a gloss finish. It was the only way to survive such a thing. West had to learn this. It was the English way of dealing with things. Sometimes it worked, sometimes it failed. He thought he'd done okay. It was about self-discipline and control.

When he reached his flat, Farrell brewed a small pot of tea and went to sit by the window. He could see the buildings around him and the light was starting to dim. It was a nice time of day and the weather was fine. He liked hot weather and so had his wife. He looked at her picture on the wall. He saw her with the shaved head and broken ribs, raped and beaten and destined for the Nazi ovens. But he wouldn't think of that, because he preferred looking at the lights coming on outside and the peace of the evening. He'd left their old flat and started fresh. It was a good decision, though he'd been pushed by his daughter and would rather have stayed where he was. After all, the flat had been his home, but it was for the best. You had to leave things behind eventually. He could hear the thump of bass and the tinkle of people laughing. He felt happy with his lot.

There'd been some real tearaways in the old days, of course. He'd thought this last week when he heard about Johnny Bates dying. He was a hard case, old Johnny, always drunk and fighting with the police. There were unwritten rules and if you hit a copper then the biggest one in the station would pay you a visit in the cells. It was the way they kept order and most people went quietly. You never heard about men getting kicked to death like you did today. He wondered if it happened all those years ago, or whether the difference was that murder was more easily hidden. He couldn't imagine it happening. Today things were out in the open and that wasn't bad, it just depended how far it went, but England was a more violent place. There was greater freedom in many ways, but what they gave you with one hand they took back with the other.

Johnny Bates had lived in the next street to Farrell in Hounslow and they'd been close. Johnny was a few years older and Farrell admired him. He'd got Farrell interested in boxing and it was something the younger man kept up and developed in the army. Johnny's old man had fought in the Great War and some of the local boys said that the shells had damaged more than just his ears. They said his brain was scrambled by shrapnel, because there was a big scar across his temple and he often sat in his bedroom in the dark for hours on end with the curtains shut. Old man Bates was supposed to have a fancy woman in Chiswick, and this was while his wife was still alive, before the house was bombed out. People talked about Bates's madness and his mistress as if the two were linked. There was a lot of gossip before they invented television and there was even a story that Bates sat in the dark crying, proof enough that the Kaiser had driven him insane.

Maybe that's what made Johnny such a hard bastard. Maybe

he heard the talk and decided to put a stop to it. He didn't want to hear that sort of stuff about his dad, a brave soldier who'd fought for England and deserved better. Johnny loved a fight and Farrell reasoned it was more than the old man bruising his knuckles. Johnny used to tell Bill that he was a champion in waiting, teaching the big mouths some bare-knuckle manners. His nose was flat by the time he was fifteen. The two youths hung around together, but when Johnny joined the army they lost touch. After the war things weren't the same. Johnny was out every night living the life of Riley, while Farrell would go for a drink sometimes but spent most nights in with his new wife. They still saw each other, and it was Johnny who'd got Farrell to join the TA. Eventually they drifted apart. It was hard for Farrell's wife when she came to England, with everything that had happened, living in a strange city and dealing with her past. He'd done his best and had always treated her right. They'd had a good marriage. That was one thing he was certain about.

London was very different after the war. When he looked back he could remember so much, how things were, but this could turn a man inside out and he didn't want to end up like some ex-soldiers who thought everything today was rubbish and that the rest of the country was in their debt. Everyone wanted respect, and when you'd been through a war you wanted it even more than normal. It became a need. But things didn't work like that. It was impossible to ever get across the reality, and how could anyone know who wasn't there? So it was all buried and gaps appeared between people. He'd got along and his wife had helped. They'd never had much money but had made do and enjoyed life. Expectations were lower, and after the war it was enough to be alive. This was the important thing, and they realised how precious life was and this had given them a great sense of fulfilment.

A pint of beer had been an essential part of life and the pubs were happy places. There was music and laughter after the war ended, a massive sigh of relief. During the war it had been lively, but in a different, more frantic way. Farrell was young and grabbed his chances and it made the camps so boring because you felt you were missing out. Farrell looked at the young girls today and even though there was so much more money about and a lot more choice when it came to fashion, they couldn't compare with the girls of his day. There'd been some real beauties around. Farrell remembered that one Johnny had liked and somehow Farrell had ended up taking her to the pictures when he was on leave. Her name was Angie. Farrell was going right back now and found he could remember her with a clarity that was almost embarrassing. She really had been a beauty and she'd worn stockings that night as well. The back row was always full of couples because there wasn't the housing and most kids lived with their mums and dads. You had to get it where you could. It was only natural, after all.

If someone had gone into business recycling rubbers they could've made a fortune just going round the parks. That's where the young people went for sex. Once the war got going there was much more sex about. At least that was Farrell's impression, though he was a soldier so maybe it was just him and his mates and their time of life. It made sense, because the population was under threat and nature would take its own action. All he knew for sure was that he was on the job regularly. He'd had lots of sex in those days. He was careful and used a rubber. There was no pill and maybe men had a greater sense of responsibility. He knew that if he got a girl pregnant he'd most likely end up marrying her. You were both in on the thing together. Maybe they'd had greater respect for women, even if there was more chauvinism. It had been a good life in spite of everything. At least until he went to Europe and saw the other side of human nature. He hated the old Second World War films and the way they romanticised everything. They were propaganda really. Still, *Gone With The Wind* had been a good film to take a girl to see.

They'd gone for a drink afterwards. Come to think of it, Farrell probably took Angie to The Unity. He was amazed to remember this and wondered what they were doing away from Hounslow, remembering the film was showing in Hammersmith. What did Angie drink? He didn't have a clue. It was more than fifty years ago, but he could see them leaving the pub. They'd taken the bus and walked the last bit. The night had been much the same as now. The weather was warm and they'd gone to the park. He could feel the texture of Angie's stockings. It was so long ago, another world. For him at least. Because he was an old man and sex didn't matter. It did then, of course, and he'd peeled her knickers off and stuffed them in his pocket. He'd had her in the long grass by the hedge. He used a rubber and they'd had a fag afterwards and stayed there for ages talking. He'd seen Angie for a while after and they'd had a lot of sex before going their separate ways.

Drink and women were what counted when you were a young lad sowing your oats and he'd never thought badly of the girl. You didn't really consider the future. Now he was thinking about the past, something he normally tried to avoid.

We get ourselves a table and Billy hangs his Cross of St George over the windows behind. Nice little backdrop that says it all. The flag is England and the white letters Chelsea. His girlfriend cut up a sheet and did it special for the trip. It's a good-size flag as well, nicked from a five-star hotel in Victoria. Midnight job with a knife. Boot of the car and Billy's cruising home listening to his radio, tuned into a phone-in about law and order when he spies the old bill coming up behind. Lights flashing and siren screaming. He pulls over wondering about the bald tyres and out-of-date tax disc, the insurance he doesn't have and the Cross of St George tucked under the spare tyre. They keep going. Through a red light and on to something more exciting. After someone else. Says imagine that, they'll be putting electronic tags on our flag one day.

I can believe it as well. See, it's okay for the Spice Girls to wear Union Jack dresses and for magazines to put it on their covers, and for the knobs who go to the last night of the proms, but if it's us lot with the Union Jack or Cross of St George, then we're automatically Nazis. Imagine that. The fucking mentality of those media cunts. We're patriotic Englishmen and that's the truth. Some of the blokes on this ferry might not particularly like blacks and Pakis, but if you're white and working class then you're automatically labelled scum by the likes of the Anti-Nazi

League. Being patriotic doesn't mean we follow an Austrian. Our pride is in our history and culture. That's the way things are and one day the thought police will be tagging the flags and only selling them to pop stars and the upper classes. There's no politics here, but that doesn't mean we don't have views and opinions. Everyone's a patriot. How can there be anything wrong in loving your country? It doesn't make any sense at all.

Mark and Facelift come back from the bar carrying a tray each, balancing drinks, the ferry dipping suddenly so they spill some of the lager. Mark smiles but Facelift's face stiffens. The ferry evens itself and they're lining the glasses up on the table. Drop crisps in the middle of the glasses. They're some of the first ones to get served. I'm looking round the bar and it's starting to fill up, seeing what's what. A normal ferry mixture. Coachloads of pensioners off to see the sights, European students and travellers, English versions of the same thing, one or two half-decent birds, and quite a few youths and men who are probably on their way to Berlin. West Ham haven't turned up yet. Still having their tea. We're waiting for things to get going because the only way to get through the boredom of crossing to the Hook is to have a decent drink. That's what it's all about. A few lagers, a tasty bird or two, and you're set. The time flies when you're on the piss with some half-decent sort sitting across the way flashing her gash.

I look back round the table and Mark's going into one about how Rod couldn't come along, seeing as how he's a married man and has to behave himself. Facelift and Brighty lean back enjoying the lager and looking into space. Carter listens to Mark, nodding, with Bob Roberts nowhere to be seen. Harry Roberts everyone calls him. Nice one that. He's our friend, kills coppers. Carter and Roberts are blokes I remember looking up to when I was a kid. They're alright. Ready for a laugh, though they want the peaceful life most of the time. They're the kind who if something happens then they're ready and willing, but who don't go looking for trouble. Not these days anyway. England is different and they'll be up for it. Wouldn't be knocking about with us if they weren't. It's a special occasion, like getting Millwall in the Cup. I think back four years to that kicking I got down in South London. Everyone comes out of the woodwork for the big games, whether it's club or country. Then there's Biggs and High Street Ken, a couple of herberts from the pub back home, tagging along picking up scraps.

Have to laugh thinking about Biggs and High Street. You talk about scousers and how they're robbers and that, and the Mancs have their thieves as well, but fucking Biggs is the original tea-leaf. He's no juvenile and still loves nicking cars and running them through shop windows. He's a speed freak, fresh out of the nick. Did six months for thieving some drink. Imagine that. Six months for ramraiding a shop. It was the previous convictions that did him. Biggs and Ken are cousins and watch each other's backs. They're okay and they've been to football through the years. Not hundred-per-cent, but turn up for the big games. Now they're on their way to Berlin and that makes eight of us. We'll get to Amsterdam and meet up with Harris and the others. We're all Chelsea. All England. With the Cross of St George blocking out the night as the waves get deeper and the Channel heavier. We're on our way and it's going to be a good one. I finish my drink and push it towards Ken. His turn.

I watch High Street going over to the bar with the tray in his hand, Biggs following. It's getting deeper there as everyone starts crowding in, waiting their turn patiently because it's still early. Give it a couple of hours and the barmen will have to get their fingers out. We need our lager and we need it now. Have to keep the blood flowing at the right temperature and thickness. They're starting to earn their living and probably wish they were on another shift. I'm watching the men in their white shirts and black trousers, lager bubbling, taking those plastic scrapers and cutting off the head. It's a con because you end up with a glass that's a quarter froth. Fucking typical. Going metric and losing out in the translation. That's the power of the exchange rate mechanism for you. Forced to sit there like a mug for hours waiting for the fucking thing to sink down so you can have a sip of lager. It's like drinking candyfloss. Trying to drink candyfloss. You need a straw to fight your way through and taste the lager.

– This is the way to travel, says Mark, enjoying himself. We all nod.

– No Eurostar bollocks for us.

We nod some more.

– Fuck me, talk about giving a drink some head. This is all fucking froth, the fucking Dutch cunts.

– You wouldn't get a bar like this on the train would you? Carter says, blowing the white top to the side.

I think about this. He's got a point.

– I tell you what, and Mark leans in, warming up. If those IRA cunts don't blow the tunnel up, then we should do it. I hate that fucking tunnel. We should get a squad together, have a whip round and buy some Semtex. The sea would soon flood it once we've opened a hole. You think of the money they wasted building it, and for what? So they can drive the ferry companies out of business and make us part of Europe. That's what they're trying to do. Fucking slags.

Mark's right. What's the point? Fuck knows what's going to go wrong with the tunnel in the future but, more important, it's symbolic. In truth, it should make long crossings like this unnecessary and one day you won't have to deal with every wanker who works for Customs, but it's missing the point. Thing is, we shouldn't have all that hassle in the first place. It's only small-minded cunts with the rule book jammed up their arses and let loose on the general population who cause the problems. Those people will just go and find a job somewhere else. They're not going to disappear.

Another thing with the Channel Tunnel is the rabies they're going to let in. You might as well put up a sign inviting all the diseased dogs of the East to come over and milk the benefits. Every other cunt is taking their share, and we're a nation of animal lovers. I know it's the future and they're not exactly going to turn round and fill it in, but it's unnatural. One day they'll probably build a bridge as well. Everyone will be forced to speak a new language and there'll be tunnels boring in from every angle. Even the Vikings will be at it, tunnelling in from Sweden and Norway. Taking the fast train through to the new shopping precincts of Central London. Looking for the excitement of football mobs, punk rockers and traditional London boozers. But all the Londoners will have been forced out to the new towns by then, the city overrun by Britain's yuppies and the world's rich tourists. You can't afford to buy a house where you grew up, so if you want to get ahead you have to move down the arterial roads. Maybe it's always been like that, but the way everyone sits back and lets the rich of Britain sell the silver to the rich of the world makes you wonder. They might as well not have bothered fighting the war, while our part in beating the Germans is dismissed by do-nothing intellectuals with no pride or culture of their own.

Even the East End is changing and that was a fucking bomb site not so long ago. Every time you pick up the paper there's some tale of rich-son-and-daughter artists in Hackney and Hoxton, or football-loving yuppies who've just discovered the game even though they're in their thirties. None of this reflects what you see around you day-in, day-out. There's no-one telling the truth, so you make do with the tabloid piss-take. By the time the Swedes get through there'll be nothing left but a maze of empty galleries, Jack The Ripper tours and coach trips out to the shires to view the natives. Europe is one more attempt to crush England. London run by some faceless wanker in Brussels banning bitter because it's a different colour to lager, insisting that everyone raises their metric measure at exactly the same time.

Europe's a plot by big business to centralise power and create a super-state with a super economy. Hitler had the same idea, though he was a nationalist who saw Germany at the heart of the union, controlling things from Berlin. Now the financiers are doing the same, but without the publicity. Everything is through the back door. Endless regulations piled on the already top-heavy stack of English laws. I just don't fancy some fat German or French businessman ramming Deutschmarks down my throat and telling me my vegetables are illegal because they haven't been genetically engineered by Dr Frankenstein. Fuck that for a game of soldiers. Could be worse I suppose. Could be the Spanish getting control. That would be a disaster. Least the Germans like their football and drink. None of your Real

Madrid, red wine bollocks. It's going to be a meeting of old enemies in Berlin. Time to put them in their place. They can have their penalty shoot-outs, because it's the fighting that counts. Someone starts singing TWO WORLD WARS AND ONE WORLD CUP at the bar and we all join in.

—You're an English tommy fighting the Nazis wondering what's coming next. You can feel the breath of the men surrounding you and the thump of the sea below. You're bobbing up and down on a waiting graveyard. The sea is cold and powerful and will pull you under if it gets the chance. Maybe there's a special smell, that's what they say, but you don't notice anything because you're struggling down the rigging and into the landing craft. The waves are big and you feel sick. You're scared because this is the real thing. You don't hear the breathing of your mates because you're too busy thinking of your mum, and if you're old enough or married young, then your wife and kids as well, making sure you don't lose your grip and fall into the sea. You don't look at the others because you're more concerned with keeping your dinner down. You don't want to get sick in front of the other lads, but you can feel the breathing inside your head and the landing craft keeps jumping in and out of the waves.

You're pressed in with everyone else and you keep quiet. You bide your time, not that there's much choice. Once you've been loaded onto the landing craft you start moving. The sea is rough and choppy and dangerous. There's thousands of men going the same way. Thousands of men are on the way to their deaths and everyone thinks about this. You don't say anything, of course, because that's how things are. You resist the fear and this makes you stronger. You want to fight and are a tiny part of a machine, but to you and yours the most important part. The years of waiting mean you're glad things are moving at last, but part of you wishes you could go home. Nobody wants to be one of the unlucky ones lost in the Channel. You keep your fingers crossed as the landing craft moves away from the ship and hope God will watch over you. Before going to Europe most men believed in God, but a lot were probably unsure after it was all over. One of the boys, a big man from the East End, passes some gum around and winks as the landing craft starts to plough through the waves. He's flash and makes you feel better, pulls everyone together with some hard cockney humour and disrespect for the sergeant.

We grew up around men who'd fought in the First World War and heard the stories. We were raised with the aftermath. Those men were part of our childhood and we saw the leftovers. They were treated badly and, what's more important in some ways, everyone knew what the upper class had done. It doesn't matter what anyone says now, because in the forties there was an impatience with the officers. They had to prove themselves and earn our respect. The mistakes of the trenches cost the ordinary man dear and the stupid games of the politicians were despised. We were fighting a different kind of war, but it wasn't until we got into Europe that we understood just *how* different. There was a spirit that said there was a job needed doing. We weren't blind and Kitchener's boys were pitied for their faith. We knew what was what. We got on with the job and made do. It wasn't like us to complain about things for the sake of it, but nobody was pushing us around. Once the landing craft started moving we were more of a unit, knowing we only had each other. Our minds were working fast, but we were strong and knew there was no turning back.

It's a terrible thing. The sergeant behind you with a machine gun pointing at your back and the Germans ahead waiting above the beaches with their guns trained on the Channel. If you don't go when the door opens the sergeant will shoot you and when you get on the sand the enemy will do their best to blow you to smithereens. There's no real choice when the moment comes, but at least you've finally got the chance to pay the bastards back for Dunkirk, the Blitz and the whole bloody war. It really is a terrible thing and you don't want to remember it too often. You want to keep the memories under control. You have to battle with time and your own mind if you want to find the reality. You don't want to make a fuss. That's not the English way.

* * *

It was time to move. The coast had vanished, the waves were rougher and the drizzle had turned to rain. Harry wasn't exactly soaked, and it wasn't a storm, but he was feeling left out, sitting there on his own with everyone inside having a laugh. He could fall over the side and no-one would notice. The rest of the lads wouldn't miss him till they arrived in Holland. Maybe they'd be so pissed it would be Amsterdam but, knowing that lot, it would probably be Berlin. They'd be enjoying a stein or two and Carter would suddenly look round all surprised and ask where the fat cunt was, looking left and right and then losing the thread as he focused on some Nordic tart strutting past in a G-string.

Harry had been miserable the last year, since Balti was killed, but this trip was going to put the past in its proper place. He felt better since he'd puked up over those girls. Fucking hell, he felt bad about that, and laughing didn't help, but there again, bollocks, those screaming teenage brats got right up his nose, with their repeat fashion and too-loud chatter, screaming so everyone could hear them, fucking and blinding their way through life. He didn't need to get sick in their hair, it wasn't nice, not really, but that's the way it was, and if a cooked breakfast was all they had to worry about in life then they were lucky. The same went for all of them, because you could moan about how the country was going to the dogs and everything, but you could also cross the wrong person and end up getting your fucking head blown off.

Harry hurried along the walkway. He opened the door and the light hit his eyes. It took a couple of seconds for him to adjust and take in the warmth and artificial smells of the ferry, the cheap carpet and blank faces. He could've murdered a pint an hour ago, but now he didn't fancy it. He turned left and walked through the passages, having a scout. He passed the canteen and the smells hit home, the counter doing a roaring trade in bangers and mash. One hour out of England and it was like everyone had to get in there and have a good feed, because they knew what was coming. The older ones were the worst, because for most of their lives they'd never had much choice in what they ate, making do, controlled by price and availability, so now they were faced with a couple of weeks eating foreign muck they were going to make a stand and go out with a bang. They were building up a supply of starch to see them through the coming ordeal. Harry smiled, because it was worse coming the other way.

When you got on a ferry from Calais to Dover, say, you could tell the English who'd been away for more than a few days – and it was the Scots and Welsh as well, he wasn't being prejudiced here. It was mental, because as soon as the boys and girls from Doncaster and Dorking and Derby were off the coaches and up the stairs it was a race to the canteen. Big queues formed and the kitchen had to work hard to keep up with the demand for pies, sausages, chips and bacon-eggs-beans, all the gourmet cuisine that made you what you were. Harry liked all that grub, who didn't, but he liked the other stuff as well. The paella in Spain and the fish dishes he'd had in Portugal. French food was shit, he had to be honest, unless you found an Arab cafe doing couscous. When everyone had had their feed and felt better, the strength back after starving for two weeks, they were straight in the bar looking for a pint of bitter or at least a decent pint of lager, sitting happy with their guts back to normal and the relaxing simmer of alcohol, feeling the sunburn ease as they looked forward to developing the holiday snaps.

Best of all was sitting on deck when the Dover cliffs appeared. He remembered one time and it was like a reverse of now, because he'd gone out when the sun was just coming up, the air cold and biting, and he'd sat there as the cliffs got bigger and whiter, sailing back to Kent really putting a lump in his throat. He'd been glad to get home. Even after a week away he couldn't believe how different everything seemed. The approach was the best bit, because back in England there was the slow grind of Customs, waiting for the coach to London, passing through the countryside, which was fair enough, but then you came into London, through Deptford and New Cross, Millwall territory, with the run-down estates and broken roads, the hustle and bustle which was fine if you were in the mood but shit when you were knackered and all you wanted to do was get back to Victoria and catch the tube home, have a bath and read the paper. A nice cup of tea and a wank over Page 3. Time to spill your beans over a pure English rose.

There he was again, missing home before he'd even made it to Holland. He was a right donut sometimes, but smart as well because there was a cinema on board and he didn't fancy getting pissed with the rest of the boys. There was enough time for that later. He didn't fancy meeting those girls again either, and at least in the dark he could keep his head down. It wasn't nice, but there you go, so he paid his money and went in, fumbling through the blackness to an aisle seat where he could stretch his legs out. The last advert was ending and he was ready for the main feature.

Harry had been raised on Second World War films, a wide-eyed kid taking in the dramatic music and exciting stories of bravery and self-sacrifice. The Second World War didn't get as much of a show now because the new enemies were vague and far away in the East, over the horizon where they couldn't be seen. There was a new agenda and nobody wanted to remember the bad times, for a variety of reasons. When he was a kid he'd got his history from *Battle of Britain* and *Dam Busters*. Everyone his age did. Ask any of the England boys on the ferry and they'd mention films like *The Longest Day*. He laughed when he thought of Nigger the dog. Fucking hell, you wouldn't get away with that now. Come here Nigger, there's a good boy. No Nigger, don't piss on Bomber's staff car. No fucking chance.

The stories were real as well, because you were surrounded by family and friends who'd grown up in London during the Blitz, people who'd had their houses burnt down and fought in Europe, Africa and the Far East. Civilians lost people overseas and suffered along with the soldiers. Most people were touched somehow. It was a simple thing to say, but to understand it was harder. The businessmen said it was better to sweep things under the carpet and not hold a grudge, because everyone wanted peace and prosperity, but maybe they went too far sometimes. You had to learn lessons. Even so, Harry liked Europe and counted England in with the Continent. True, the

English were different, but it was silly slaughtering each other like they'd done during the war. He preferred an easy life.

Harry was soon daydreaming his way through the film. It was the same old futuristic special effects for the sake of special effects. With the money and freedom these film cunts had you'd think they'd make something with a bit of soul. At least classic films had decent dialogue, even if the squaddies were generally thick as shit, either Alright-Me-Old-Cocker southerners or Ee-By-Gum northerners. The Scots were all red-haired little alkies called Jock who died early, and the Welsh had all been christened Taff and sang for their suppers, rolling dark eyes in the back of pixie heads. The stars were upper-crust and well-spoken, their superior accents naturally enough reflecting superior intelligence. The stereotypes were a load of bollocks, but Harry loved the heroes he saw on the screen, because everywhere you went there were people with stories to tell who didn't want to talk, keeping the details to themselves. It was how the English, the British, did things. Now they were dying as the years caught up, but that war experience was still deep inside everyone, young and old, whether first-, second-, or third-hand. Even the cunts who tried to walk all over the memories and laugh off the war years spirit did so because they knew how deep-rooted these things were. They couldn't get in and dictate like they did with everything else, so instead they sneered.

The Yanks often had big parts in the films because Hollywood was where the money was, and they said that if you went up Piccadilly during the war it was a knocking shop, with the GIs loaded and the English girls wanting a share. He found that hard to believe because there were higher standards in those days, but he didn't think too much about it because he was watching a battle between two semi-human machines firing off lasers and kicking each other in the head. He wondered what the soldiers thought, but nobody asked those sorts of questions. The officers wrote their memoirs and the squaddies signed on.

Harry was sitting there in the dark surrounded by strangers. Their fathers and grandfathers could've been the cunts in the pill boxes mowing down English tommies. It made you think, though you weren't supposed to think like that, because bygones were bygones, and that was right in its way, but Harry didn't feel guilty about the Empire and the slave traders because he wasn't even born then. Everyone had to get on, but he'd still like to see one of those old war films shown on the ferry, just for a laugh.

He'd like to sit back and watch *The Longest Day* and see what happened. He saw *Battle of Britain* at the pictures when it came out as a kid, and he'd loved the RAF dog-fights and the way Good had overcome superior odds and defeated Evil. What he remembered most was a bomber gunner getting his face shot up. The mask was splattered with blood and as a child it had hit Harry hard. It made him feel ill, the blood on the glass, and it had almost spoiled the film. The pomp and circumstance of the music soon took over and he was able to appreciate how a small number of brave men had saved the country. He thought of the burns many of them suffered and how one bloke's wife asked an officer what it was like to have a husband without a face. It stuck in his mind. A man without a face. Or was it another film? The details merged with time. All Harry had to do was drive down the Western Avenue a few miles and he could see the RAF bases at Northolt, Harefield and Uxbridge, right there, near enough on his doorstep.

It would be brilliant to sit in the cinema with all these Dutch and Germans and watch *Dam Busters*. He'd sit there with his popcorn and Coke and enjoy the show. The Dutch would cheer and the Germans would look embarrassed. The England boys in the bar would probably come along if *Dam Busters* was on. He loved the bit where they were using the bombs on the dams and they kept missing, then one of the fuckers got a bull's-eye. Those pilots had steel bollocks cruising through enemy flak. It wasn't going to happen in this particular cinema, so he made do with the bloodbath in front of him, except there wasn't any blood. The killing was clean and efficient and the semi-humans fought without thinking. There were no entry and exit points, and no mess. Everything was clear cut. It was an action-adventure and easy entertainment for the masses. Harry wasn't really taking it in, smiling as he imagined the trouble there'd be if they put on *Das Boot* and gave the passengers some U-boat action.

The bar's full and Bright Spark's got his cassette player out. Thinks he's on the World Service pumping out his own Radio Hooligan Roadshow as he places the machine on the table and starts fucking about with his tapes. He puts in this cassette of military music. The sort of songs the poor bastards played as they trooped off to the slaughter in the good old days. Red shirts so they couldn't see the blood and busbies so they couldn't feel their brains explode. The music's strong and patriotic and it must've helped the boys along. Play some loud music and you can't hear the guns up ahead and the pissed laughter of the generals miles behind. Beat the drum and stir the emotions. We have our own songs right here. Our own set of explanations. West Ham are on the other side of the bar drinking among themselves, looking over and smiling at the band. Music brings England together. There's a truce and everything's sweet. We do our thing and they do theirs. Same goes for the other clubs. We're not exactly going to start swapping stories with West Ham, but there's no need for aggravation, not here anyway.

There's a lot of England on board now that they're in the bar and we can see who's who. Strongbow and his mates are missing in action. Mugs are back in Harwich sobering up, the big man himself charged with something a bit more serious than drunk and disorderly. Looks likely seeing the way they were banging his head on the van door and the way he was trying to stop them. Something the old bill call resisting arrest. Stop us cracking your head open and we'll do you for that as well. There's other people in here, not just the England boys – middle-aged men and women in groups lining up the lager and shorts, a few made-up couples, solo travellers enjoying a bottle of lager and checking their passports. There's also three tasty birds nearby. Well nice in fact. Carter says he fancies a shag and might go and have a word, but I don't reckon he's got much chance on the ferry. Suppose he's got his reputation to consider.

I try to work out where they're from. Obviously not English.

Not tarty enough. That's the problem with English birds. They're a load of old brasses compared to some of the Europeans. Mind you, the Europeans are boring, even the dirty ones in their expensive designer jeans and sweaters. That's why the stuck-up birds at home like everything European, because they're thick and boring in one. Don't be fooled by the posh accent, because education doesn't mean intelligent. Your average English bird down the pub though, she's alright. Likes a laugh and doesn't waste her time posing. Best of all are the blondes, and then it doesn't matter where they come from. Everyone loves blondes. It's the Aryan ideal. Blondes have more fun and you can understand why. Every generation has its blonde pin-up on the screen doing the business.

There's more English coming in all the time, with one or two in colours, everyone else without. Can never get my head round grown men wearing replica shirts. There's a few flags and we get a couple of looks, but this is an easing-in period as everyone clocks everyone else, seeing if they recognise faces from previous trips. There's probably sixty or so English in the bar now, and there's another Chelsea crew who we know well enough. Doesn't take long for them to start singing ONE BOMBER HARRIS. All the English join in straight off because this is what it's all about. It winds up the Germans, and it upsets the trendy wankers and all that scum who are always trying to pick holes in everything to do with England and English pride. None of us is seriously laughing about Dresden, but why should Arthur take the blame? It was a fucking war and the Luftwaffe was flattening our cities, but there again the cunts slagging off Bomber Command are quick enough to laugh off the spirit of the Blitz. We sing deep in our throats. THERE'S ONLY ONE BOMBER HARRIS. It's a nice little ice-breaker and Billy turns the volume on the cassette down, then turns it off. Nice one Billy, showing respect for tradition.

I hate the musical accompaniment one or two clubs take along to football. Sheffield Wednesday have that brass band that plays some kind of lobotomy trance. It's some nothing Dutch tune and it goes on for hours. Like we don't have enough songs of our own. It kills the atmosphere. Don't know how Tango puts up with that whining in his ear game after game. The yids had a fucking drum last season at White Hart Lane as well, though the atmosphere there's fucked anyway. The drummer starts tapping out his rhythm and Chelsea fill in THE YIDS. It was like Euro 96 and all those years of football songs and humour were forgotten as the game was sold off to the corporations and you ended up with Fantasy Football supplying the soundtrack. That's what the businessmen are doing to football. The architects have made the grounds sterile and the seats have killed the atmosphere. They say yuppies have taken over football, but that's bollocks, because I never see them in the pubs where we drink, but they've mixed everyone in together and you're not going to be singing your songs if you're next to a granny or some bloke with his kids. It's in the media and business side of things that the trendies have cashed in. Football's expensive and most ordinary people spend the game recovering from the shagging they've just had at the turnstile. But Billy's songs are good. It's the humour and the situation. ONE BOMBER HARRIS.

I think of Dave Harris who's already in Amsterdam. Harris has been getting worse over the last few years and I hope he never gets sent down because I wouldn't want to share a cell with him. Nice enough bloke mind, but he's gone a bit mental recently. There's always respect for the big characters. You run through the main faces at Chelsea through the last thirty years and they've got massive respect. They're the ones everyone secretly wishes they could be, but know they just aren't that kind of material. It's the character that does the trick. Leadership qualities. These people are the real culture.

Everyone's loosening up in the bar and I can see the Red Hand of Ulster badge on Gary Davison's jacket as he raises his fist in the air and goes into No Surrender. Some of the younger element in their early twenties are catching on and beginning to see what's what, while the more peaceful people in the bar smile to themselves and pour extra alcohol down their throats. England games are interesting because there's always blokes who travel on their own. You get a lot of these characters. If you take the amount of men into football and then chop it down to those who go away with England, we're a fairly small percentage. It means that not everyone's going to have mates who want to go to the likes of Germany and Italy. These solo characters don't care about the reception committee. Just pack their bags and go. After the first trip they find out how easy it is to fit in. If you're sound then there's no problem. Sometimes you get a wanker or two, but that's life. The English can always sniff out a wanker. NO SURRENDER, NO SURRENDER, NO SURRENDER TO THE IRA.

I see the three birds a couple of tables away looking around and talking among themselves. As the drink eases in I start eyeing up the one with the shoulder length hair. Brown and pulled back from her face. She's wearing faded jeans and a thin top. Fucking beautiful. I'm trying to work out whether she's German, Dutch or something else. It's a game all the boys play. Her skin's too light to be an Italian or anything like that, and anyway, if she lived in Rome she'd be on a plane. No dirty ferry travel for the spaghetti princess. I'm putting my money on Dutch. Don't know why. Instinct probably. It's like working out where a firm comes from. You can usually suss them out by the clothes or faces. Same with the birds when you go overseas. I see her jump when Carter arrives, failing with the smooth approach. Sex machine leaning over the back of the seat. You have to laugh because the bloke's got more front than most people I could mention.

He's there for a while and the girls seem interested enough. Least they haven't blanked him. Three into one shouldn't really go, but you never know with Carter. He's going to have to share the catch with the rest of the boys. I'm watching him in action when I recognise an ugly mug from the past. A big geezer from Shropshire. Been watching England for donkey's years. Started in Spain in 1982 and has seen all the World Cups since. One of the original Man United boys who kept the club going before the Stretford End was sold off to the living dead. Have to feel sorry for them because the Stretford End was a major end and the Red Army a massive away support. Funny thing is, they still get huge crowds but the place is a morgue. They've still got a proper crew, but tucked out of sight. Old

Trafford's almost as bad as the Highbury Library. It's a load of bollocks what they've done to the game back in England and that's why getting over to Europe is a tonic. It's like clicking back to when you could do whatever the fuck you wanted.

– Alright bud? Kev asks, shaking hands, followed by a couple of other blokes I don't know who he introduces by name and says he met on the train down to London. Crewe and Bolton fans.

– Alright Munich?

Shouldn't really use the Munich tag, but he's okay long as I don't do it more than once. I know him well enough. Wouldn't want to try and take liberties. He still carries a scar down his face from when he steamed into a carriage-load of Brighton single-handed at Finchley Road, on his way to Wembley.

– Careful, he smiles. Or I'll have to do the helicopter.

Don't like that. Have to admit it gets right up my nose. When we played Forest some of them were doing chopper impressions, winding us up about Matthew Harding. Man U were doing it as well up at Old Trafford. Only a few of them, but I suppose we used to sing WHO'S THAT BURNING ON THE RUNWAY enough times. Chelsea sorted Forest out after the game. Can still see Facelift stamping on some cunt's face. Shouldn't take the piss though. Specially about something like that. Right out of order. Makes you wonder what's going on in the Midlands. Leicester is a grudge game, some kind of Baby Squad revival. Doesn't matter now. We're all England.

I start thinking about Matthew Harding, the respect the man had from everyone in football. Couldn't believe it when he died. Why did it have to be someone like that? It's always the good ones who die. If it wasn't for Harding then we'd still be scratching around in the dirt. Thing is, he was Chelsea right through, and even though he was a multi-millionaire he was still down The Imperial having a pint with your everyday fan. Real diamond. The sort who only comes along once a lifetime. That's why you get us singing MATTHEW HARDING'S BLUE AND WHITE ARMY. Matthew should've been there to see Wise go up to lift the FA Cup after all he'd done.

We were standing outside the old Beer Engine after the Cup Final and there was a line of knobs coming though in their cars. The kind of stuck-up cunts who've overrun the area around Stamford Bridge. The old bill had sent them down the wrong street. The younger element were jumping on the bonnets, roofs, right over the top, while further down the road everyone was enjoying themselves having a drink outside The Adelaide and Imperial. Don't know about The Palmerston. It was all good natured. Then the old bill come down the road with their riot horses and vans and a fucking helicopter with a spotlight. Ruining the fun. Saying four pubs had already been turned over. Wrecked and looted as Chelsea celebrated the Cup win in style. Everyone in a good mood because we've won the FA Cup at last.

Now it's England and we're still Chelsea but putting everything in its right place. It's all a game really. It's the same for soldiers, though they'd never admit as much, because they like to feel more important than they really are. They sign their name and do as they're told. There's none of that bollocks here, because we're a volunteer army with a set of rules that are basic common sense. It's a good laugh, based in the English way of life. We're here because we're here. Because we want to be.

Bill Farrell couldn't sleep. He got out of bed and went to the kitchen, where he made another cup of tea. There were two biscuits left so he polished those off. He had this decision to make and it was gnawing away, demanding an answer. He was an old man now and had his routine. The only time he'd been out of the country was in a uniform. He'd gone across the Channel, fought, killed and come back. Since then he'd never been outside England. Now his nephew wanted him to travel across the world for a holiday in Australia. It was a long way and he felt he was too old, but didn't want to let the boy down, especially when he'd supplied the ticket and Farrell's daughter had arranged the visa. The family told him to go, but he didn't want to leave. London was his life. What if he died over there? He didn't want to end up with his ashes floating around in a bloody billabong.

He'd always been close to his nephew. He didn't know why really. Farrell's dad had died when he was one, from TB. He'd never known him. He'd looked to his uncles instead. Everyone needed a role model. Maybe that's why him and Vince were so close, the boy bypassing a generation. Boys needed men to set an example. They pointed you in the direction you'd follow the rest of your life. He thought of his uncles and looked at the picture on the wall, a drawing of a nun with a lamp. He hadn't thought of his uncles for a long time. He sipped the tea and wished he had some more biscuits. He was glad he'd thought of them now.

He'd had three uncles on his mum's side and all had served in the Great War. They were in his mind as he approached Normandy and he'd told himself that nothing that was to come could possibly be as bad as what they had experienced. He remembered those thoughts clearly. But he'd had no idea what was ahead of him. It was the First World War but they called it Great because of the number of people killed and maimed. Men, women and children. Animals too, thousands of dead, rotting horses with maggots eating into their guts. It wasn't so great for those who signed up for this War To End All Wars. There were the words and the music of the recruiting sergeant and his band, urging the boys to take the King's shilling and kiss the book.

There must've been a lot of excitement when the army started recruiting, the Kaiser an evil monster on the horizon threatening the English way of life, a traditional Prussian enemy far off in the East. The sergeant would have smiled and slapped the English boys on the back, pushing the comradeship and unity in fighting a common enemy. He would've drawn on English history and exploited youth's love of adventure, the atmosphere of the time created by the men in control and a compliant media. Farrell guessed it sounded good, and his uncles had admitted as much. They were simple boys and knew nothing of the world.

Farrell's uncles were Stan, Gill and Nolan. They lived in Hounslow, but their mum, Farrell's gran, ran a pub in Great Bedwyn, a village in Wiltshire. When he was a boy he'd looked up to his uncles because they were grown men and he wanted to be like them. They were kind to him and even now he smiled when he thought about them, how they talked and acted. When he was older he got to know about the Great War. He found out Gill and Nolan had fought on the Somme, and Stan in German East Africa, though they never went into details about their experiences. They never talked about things much, and Farrell had to piece their histories together later. He was told stories by his aunts, and after he'd been away himself and come home, they answered some of his questions. He supposed he became like them, that they shared something. Much of it he never learnt, but at least some information was passed down. He never knew what they thought or really felt, just that the Somme had been hell on earth. Farrell knew some of the facts, the bones of their stories, but could never feel what they felt. He wished he could now, all these years later, and he had tried in the landing craft. At least it kept him quiet as they headed for Europe.

Stan was the Jack-the-Lad of the family. Farrell smiled thinking of the story his mum told him, that she was at school sitting in her classroom when there was a loud bang on the door. The teacher went to see who was there, but only found a rotten potato on the ground. She turned and looked at Farrell's mum and asked if her brother Stan was home. It was the first she knew of it, but it was him alright. He'd been away fighting in an African jungle and still threw potatoes at classroom doors.

Stan was a bit of a rebel, even though he was a career soldier. He was a Royal Marine who wanted to travel and see the world. It was a way to discover things, signing up and broadening horizons. But Stan caught malaria and was forced out. The illness affected Stan and made him very unhappy. He wasn't going to be defeated, though, because he wanted to cure himself of the malaria and get back in the Marines. He drank a bottle of quinine and spent two days in a coma. He swore he'd either die or make himself well again. When he came round, when he survived his do-or-die treatment, he was cured. Nobody could understand it. The doctors were amazed. Stan went back to the Marines and they agreed he was cured, but because he'd had malaria the regulations said he couldn't return. And because he didn't have malaria, he was no longer eligible for his disability pension.

All Farrell's three uncles were changed by the war, sitting in the mud with the rotting bodies of their mates, the rats chewing through dead skin, the blood, shit and mutilation of the trenches, or in Stan's case the hardship of fighting in the jungle. Thousands were blinded by chemical weapons. Every man who served was mentally scarred, and Farrell knew deep down that the same applied to him. When he was a boy they knew the men who had suffered most, men like Bates. Their minds must have been racked by the horror of what they'd seen and done.

Nolan was upset by the war and upset by the brothels. He believed in God and was a spiritualist, something Farrell's friend Albert Moss had practised before his death. The sight of the English soldiers queueing for the whorehouses stuck in Nolan's mind for the rest of his life. He thought of the women in the brothels on their backs with queues of laughing-drunk squaddies waiting their turn, reduced to production line, last-gasp sex before the German guns blew them to kingdom come, filling the girls with syphilis. He wouldn't have used the prostitutes. Nolan was a quiet man who loved the country and suggested Farrell tried for the parks after the war.

Nolan was accused of theft while in France and spent six months in the glasshouse. It would've been hard in a military prison and there weren't the same rights in those days. This was a time when the officers were having soldiers shot for shell shock and barely-proven offences. Legalised murder it was, and even today they wouldn't grant pardons. It was a disgrace and showed the contempt the establishment had for those doing its dirty work. Eventually someone else was found to be responsible. Nolan was released without any kind of apology. Six months in the glasshouse for something you didn't do and you were treated like that. Stan and Nolan always felt they were badly treated by the armed forces.

When their mum, Farrell's gran, died, they took her coffin to the cemetery on a hand cart and lined the grave with wildflowers. They didn't have money for a gravestone. Farrell wondered whether if someone dug the grave up they'd find the flowers. As a boy he'd tried to imagine the colours. Even now he wished he knew. It was in his head again, trying to picture the unmarked grave. A blanket of colour and the smell of wet earth. The vicar would've stood over the hole and said the right words, and there she'd stay unseen but remembered, till her children died and the generations went on, and one day she would be forgotten.

Gill drew a picture in 1915, shortly before he went to war. Now it was on the wall of Farrell's living room. The frame was cheap and coming apart, but the drawing stood out. The paper was yellow, yet the sharp pencil lines and foggy shaded areas made an impression. Gill had drawn a nun with her head bowed, a lantern in her hand. The head was covered by a hood and he'd drawn her from the side. It was a thoughtful, sad picture, and he signed his name and added the date. Farrell was sitting in his flat in the early hours suffering from insomnia, looking at the picture. He wondered whether it was drawn from memory or imagination. Maybe Gill saw his death and the figure was coming to lead him to the light, but it was more to do with survival. Gill didn't fall in the Great War.

Years later Gill did two paintings. They were watercolours and Farrell had them there next to the nun. Each painting was of a vase, and each of the vases was full of flowers. There were different shapes and colours, and the paintings were more childlike, more happy. Gill painted these in 1933, years after the war when peace had returned. Six years later, of course, there was another world war and his nephew was sent to fight the Germans again, the new enemy on the horizon coming from the same place. Farrell loved the nun and the flowers.

The next generation who went off to war were again fresh-faced youths such as Bill Farrell, again ready for adventure. They say nothing is learnt from history and he agreed, but the monster on the horizon really was a monster this time. The Second World War was different. When Farrell saw that concentration camp he knew it was different. His uncles sat in miles of trenches as the machine guns rattled and shells shattered human bodies. They would never forget and they'd never be able to share the feeling. Maybe that's why they never really tried. Farrell knew it was the way things were. He could never share what he felt. He could never make Bob West understand. That's why his wife had been special. One of the reasons anyway. She'd seen the horror and been through much worse than her husband. Both of them knew something. Even now, Farrell felt sorry for his uncles and the mates they'd lost. Maybe it was worse for them, because there was no real reason for the slaughter.

Stan had told Farrell he'd either be rich or hang. He said Farrell was a lot like him and Farrell's mum agreed. Farrell never got rich and he'd obviously never hung. He'd lived his life best he could. There were hard times, but mostly they were good.

He remembered the food and drink of the spread they'd done for him when he came back from Europe. It was a good time and he had to struggle to see the landing craft. It came back, the way the guns pounded the shore and the knowledge that the Beach Master would be in there first with the commandos who'd pave the way. They admired those men because they were brave enough to take the initial flak and would suffer the first losses. But they were all in the thing together. The troops rolling in were ready to fight. There were a lot of blokes who'd been evacuated from Dunkirk and their pride was at stake. They were going to give the Germans a going over.

Farrell didn't want the details, but they were there in his head. The sea was rough and there was a smell of shit. Farrell wasn't disgusted and it made him feel stronger because it wasn't him. The man behind him was praying quietly and he heard a couple of deep sobs from further back. Some of the rougher men were shouting and swearing and telling everyone what they were going to do to the Germans when they got hold of them. There was one they called Mangler, a villain who hung around the racetracks and was well known to the police, a bad man to know but worth having on your side. He wanted to kill and maim Germans, he told the lads he was looking forward to it, and despite what they put in the films there were men like that around. The films painted the English as naïve virgins, but they were men like other men.

There was sex and drink. There were fights and there were drugs. Mostly opium dens in the East End. It was in the background, and those interested kept their business to themselves. Around Piccadilly and into Soho there were prostitutes – painted dollies – and sex clubs. There were said to be sex parties with people twisted by the war. There were poofs, but they were looked down on and kept themselves to themselves. You just knew these things existed. There was no need to talk about it too much. It wasn't the English way.

Harry had forgotten the film and he'd only been out of the cinema for a few minutes. He wasn't thinking of vintage war films because they'd be arriving in the Hook soon enough and he was in the duty-free looking for a bargain. He caught sight of a couple of the Spice kids he'd showered with sick and moved behind a rack. They were washed and scrubbed and back to their giggling best, and didn't see him. It was the roll of the dice and he checked the Toblerone and Yorkie prices. His mouth watered as he considered the options, a heavy hand on his shoulder the hand of an arresting officer telling him he was nicked. He turned round fast and faced the wide boys themselves, the toy-shop gangland bosses thieving gin and vodka, thinking big and acting small. High Street and Biggs were helping themselves. Both were pissed and getting their money's worth.

– The bar's packed and there must be at least two hundred England in there, Biggs shouted. They're on the piss and there's going to be trouble before we get off this boat. I can see it boiling up.

– If this is the warm-up, what's the rest of the trip going to be like? Ken wanted to know. This ferry's full of headcases.

Before Harry had time to reply they were stumbling off round the aisles pushing each other back and forward, behaving like a couple of snotty-nosed juveniles. Harry decided to leave the chocolate till the return leg. He looked towards the woman on the till but she didn't seem bothered, yawning as she served a man with a stack of fag cartons and a hacking cough. The way High Street and Biggs were acting they were going to get themselves nicked. There were cameras and there'd probably be a security guard. Harry was sober and going down the bar. He wanted to get off the ferry and didn't fancy knocking about with a couple of shoplifters. He was bored as fuck. That film was shit. Why hadn't they put on the *The Cruel Sea* or something? Jack Hawkins doing the business in the North Atlantic. This was the worst bit, getting across the Channel without being torpedoed by a fucking U-boat, or sunk because the doors weren't shut properly.

The ferry was a mess of people and it smelt scabby. The flavours were all blending together now – sausages and bacon in the canteen, car fumes in the hold, drink from the bar, perfume from the duty-free, piss and sick from the bogs, plus the sweat of all these men and women packed in together. He clanked through the turnstyle and hurried towards the bar to find Carter and the others. It shouldn't take them too long to get to Amsterdam and they had a hotel lined up not far from the red light. Harry was looking forward to a couple of days sitting back having a good smoke, a chilled lager or two, with a nice Dutch model on the end of his knob. Not tonight though. He wanted to dump his bag in the hotel, find a bar and have a drink or two, then a few zeds.

WHO THE FUCK, WHO THE FUCK, WHO THE FUCKING HELL ARE YOU... WHO THE FUCKING HELL ARE YOU?

Harry could hear the singing right down the hall and noticed that a lot of passengers were looking nervous and going in the opposite direction. He'd seen the faces before. The shocked, stunned, half-disgusted faces of honest Middle Europeans coming face to face with the flower of English manhood. They'd caught a glimpse of the Expeditionary Force and didn't like what they saw. The invaders were drunk and noisy and turning nasty. The cropped hair, tattoos, jeans, jackets, broken glass, songs, Union Jacks and Crosses of St George made Franz Foreigner nervous. Harry had to laugh. Maybe it was just good humour, but the singing didn't sound too friendly, and he wondered who was asking who the question.

HELLO, HELLO, WE ARE THE PORTSMOUTH BOYS.

Harry had his answer.

HELLO, HELLO, WE ARE THE PORTSMOUTH BOYS.

He nodded.

AND IF YOU ARE A SOUTHAMPTON FAN, SURRENDER OR YOU'LL DIE, WE WILL FOLLOW THE PORTSMOUTH.

Portsmouth always travelled with England. If there was a Millwall or Southampton mob on board there was a very good chance the crossing would end in tears. He wondered if it would be Millwall or Southampton, heard the bells chime.

FUCK OFF POMPEY, POMPEY FUCK OFF.

Harry arrived as Southampton and Portsmouth met on the small area that acted as a temporary dancefloor. It was roughly ten a side and those non-football people still in the bar were running past him, getting out of the firing line. Several lager bottles landed behind the counter, lobbed by other drunk English further back simply enjoying the film, and the bartenders were pulling the shutters down. Another bottle hit a row of spirit bottles, drink and glass exploding with a hollow popping sound. He saw Gary Davison and a couple of his mob taking advantage and unloading the cash register, moving in from the side. In and out like scousers. Harry clocked all this in a second because walking in on the scene sober was mental, a laugh and a half seeing the funny side of life, even if Southampton and Pompey were going at each other full of the kind of hate that's personal and built on history and endless derby battles, bad blood frothing with the lager, spat out and kicked back twice as hard. He stood aside as one bloke went through a table and a couple of men started kicking him in the ribs and head, the man's mates piling in, tables and chairs cracking as some of the other English started wrecking a corner of the bar, building a splintered bonfire for Guy Fawkes and the Pope.

In the background Harry could see Billy Bright's flag with its CHELSEA headline and the man himself fucking about with his cassette player, laughing his head off trying to add a soundtrack, but he couldn't find what he wanted and gave up. When Harry looked left there were similar flags hanging over windows with SWINDON and ARSENAL and WEST BROM along the horizontal bar of the red crosses, a huge Union Jack with KENT LOYALISTS blaring out, Harry taking all this in fast as the battle spilled through the bar, the rest of the English drunk and backing off to let the South Coast rivals sort out their differences, harbour town clubs used to fighting at sea, more tables turned over and the sound of smashing glass mixing with the violence of the punches and kicks, a youth with short shiny hair and a stained leather jacket stumbling past with a wicked-looking cut along his cheek, blood all over the shop, standing there shocked as a couple of spectators gave him a hanky to stop the flood. Harry looked at the gash and shook his head.

Southampton and Pompey were taking no prisoners and there were enough cuts and bruises on the two sides, neither running the other, a stand-off as they battered the fuck out of each other, having a breather shouting insults, and then it kicked off with stewards coming in between the two sides trying to calm things down. The rest of the English hung about waiting to see what would happen next, knowing it was personal and daft somehow, because if you couldn't get it together for the battle in Europe you had no chance. They had to be united. Harry saw it clearly, that it was the stress and strain of crossing the water, and for a minute he wondered if the English would mob together and do the stewards, these men in white shirts, sinking the ferry for a laugh and swimming to shore. The moment passed and some kind of calm returned.

Tommy Johnson and the rest of the boys came over and Tom was laughing, telling them they'd better move down the boat otherwise they'd be there for hours in the Hook while the old bill tugged the sailors and anyone stupid enough to hang around watching. No fucking idea, he was saying to Harry, no fucking idea, and they started filtering down the ferry. Harry looked back and the bar was wrecked, the flags down and packed away. Tom was pulling a pissed Facelift back because he was eyeballing the West Ham boys and one of them was a Romford

644

mirror of the Hayes man, pulled back by an Essex version of Tom.

Harry followed the rest of the lads. They were pulling into the Hook and the Dutch old bill would be waiting. They didn't need the grief. Holland might be a laid-back country, but not when it came to the old bill. They had enough hooligans of their own not to treat it like a circus, and they no longer thought of the English as good-natured eccentrics. You had to get across the Channel in one piece, but Harry understood. It was part of being an island race. The English Channel was built into everyone. It was a natural barrier that set Britain apart. If Hitler could've taken out the RAF he'd have crossed the Channel. The Luftwaffe couldn't do it and that bit of water kept England free. Harry had seen the films. There were no borders other than those with Scotland and Wales. No wonder the Europeans invented fascism, because they had to fight to preserve their identity the whole time inside man-made boundaries.

It was hard for the England boys going across the Channel, and naturally they needed a drink to ease things along, and naturally people could get out of hand, and naturally the continental lagers were that bit stronger and fucked your head up, but it didn't matter. Old rivalries came into the open and discipline was bound to go out the window. They were crossing the line and it was an emotional time, hanging on to the last link with home before they entered a strange, dangerous land, full of people who hated the English. Harry saw it differently, but then he liked Europe more than the others. He understood what the boys were going through and hoped they would relax in Amsterdam. Foreign travel helped broaden the mind and Harry couldn't wait.

—The English way of getting through something is to close our eyes and jump in at the deep end. When the front of the landing craft went down everything moved very fast. Our thoughts were confused as we approached the shore so I did my best to keep my mind on my uncles. For the first time in my life I was really trying to imagine how they felt. It was an impossible task, but it kept me calm. I breathed deep and it worked. I imagined I was the weak one, but I suppose most of the boys felt the same way. Being brave is being scared but conquering the fear. Even now, I find it hard to admit I was a scared young man. We did what had to be done. The noise was terrible and I tried to block it out. There was a man screaming, but he wasn't in our landing craft. I blocked this out as well, glancing at the pale white faces packed shoulder to shoulder. I didn't want to think about what had happened to him. I was trying to dig a hole in my head and bury myself. I wanted to be brave and I was going to be brave, bracing myself for the moment, because the front of the landing craft crashed down and there was a thud that snapped us into action. At that moment I was the most pointed I'd ever been in my life. The metal shield fell forward and we were faced with the reality, a beach crisscrossed with wire and barricades, explosions churning up great holes and the sea chopping about. We knew we had to get out of the landing craft fast and now I discovered that I actually wanted to get to the sand and feel my boots sink in. We were sitting ducks in the landing craft. We were exposed and the realisation was a massive electrical current through our bodies. One shell would wipe us out. The sergeant knew this better than anyone. We were angry now and wanted to kill. We wanted to wipe these Nazis off the face of the earth. Suddenly I wasn't scared because as we moved forward all our energy was centred on getting to the sand and from there fighting our way to the enemy. We wanted to kill these men and get the job done. I shouted and my hate made me hard. I was trained to channel this anger and my boxing helped. We surged forward and the feeling was incredible. It was the adrenalin that comes to save you when your life is threatened. There was an injection of the drug as a shell exploded in the water and rocked the craft. We stumbled and fought to stay standing. It's a chemical in the body that fights for your survival because surviving is everything, the survival of the individual and survival of the tribe. The sergeant didn't need his machine gun because we moved quickly as a unit, tramping through the water, and the next thing we knew we were knee deep in the sea. It must have felt good to touch the bottom, though I don't remember clearly. I was looking to my left and right briefly and the beach ahead was sandy and covered in obstacles, but the sea was packed with assault craft and the shapes of men battling against the water and the rattling of German guns, exploding mortars and shells creating havoc with the sea and sand. A shell whistled to my right and blew a man's head clean off his neck, blood pumping into the air and staining the Channel, and I could feel the bile in my mouth but somehow I swallowed it again, and for a couple of seconds I slowed up to look and try to understand what had happened. I was pushed forward by the man behind, my eyes locked to the body of the decapitated soldier which moved forward one or two steps before falling to the water and floating front down with the back hunched like a rock. I felt myself falling with the dead soldier. I stumbled towards the sea and my hands went out and under the water, a wave backing up from the shore and filling my mouth with salt, water flushing through my nose with the snot and covering my head. For a moment I thought the salt was the taste of blood and that I'd been hit by a bullet or shell. I was still and then pushed my head above the sea. I was choking on the water and the image of the soldier was confused in my head. I saw myself blown to bits before I'd even had a chance to fight the enemy and this made me angrier, thinking of my mum and family, the bombed out London streets and stories of Dunkirk, the suffering of my uncles fighting these Germans who were always stirring up trouble, Johnny Bates's old man alone in a dark room whimpering like a dog. I wasn't going to be one of the countless war dead filed on a church monument and forgotten. There was no way I was going to die in the Channel, sucked into the depths and left to rot. I had a life at home and I wanted to get back in one piece. I hauled myself up and someone gave me a hand. I was moving forward. The front of my uniform was soaked but I didn't feel the wetness, it was just the water made me heavier. I was determined and hurried to the beach. Getting to firm land reassured me. I was one of thousands of other men and just a name on a churchyard monument, but I was all I had right now and I wanted to see my mum again because she'd made me promise I'd come back. She didn't want to lose me to a stupid war. Why did this keep happening to her, because she'd spent years worrying about her brothers and I had to come back just as they'd done. Everything was precious on that beach, my memories kept me sharp. I was walking into a nightmare, but I had good mates with me. We were united together against a common enemy. All these boys would help me out. I wasn't really thinking this at the time, I just knew it was true, because if there is a hell on earth then this was near enough. The Germans were killing the English and it wasn't clean, bloodless bullet wounds. There were no rules. There was little mercy. It was bloody fighting and killing. Men were blown in half, their arms and legs torn in every direction. Teenagers took wounds in their guts and one boy saw his intestines spill into the sand, a mass of bloated worms. The blood was red and black. I was down on the sand and there was a man's arm under my chest. I moved forward quickly and we started working our way up the beach firing at the enemy. I couldn't see them but I could see what they were doing. Planes were screaming over as the RAF attacked the German fortifications, the boom of the big guns off-shore already established in our heads. The air force and the navy gave us hope because for the first time we really believed we were going to sort these bastards out. We were moving towards the enemy when Billy Walsh next to me took a round in his groin. It was in his balls, and he was leaning into me screaming blue murder. I could see the front of his uniform had turned black and the material was ripped. The Germans had blown his balls and dick off. There was nothing left. There was just gristle and I needed help. I called out but nobody came. There were wounded everywhere and I was cradling his head, because Billy was in shock and I didn't know if he was bleeding to death. I tried to stop the blood with my hands, but then someone with a cross took over. I held Billy's hand for a moment and I wondered what his life was going to be like, forced to live without his manhood. I wondered if he was better off dead and what I would do in his position. Maybe I should've smothered him there and then, put a bullet in his head, but there was no time to think with the sergeant yelling at us to go forward. I squeezed Billy's hand and let go. We shared the same name, but I was the lucky one, rubbing my bloody hands in the sand, bits sticking. He was screaming above the sound of the guns. We moved forward slowly and stopped. There was a long line of soldiers firing and I stayed for a while. I don't know how long, but I know my ears were numb from the sound. I might've pissed myself. I'm not sure. It could've been the sea. I hope I didn't piss myself. I'd never admit as much. Stopping wasn't good for you because it gave you time to think and look around at the mutilated bodies, the body parts cold and shapeless. There was a lot of blood where I was. I'll always remember that. The smell of blood is with me today. Sickly, rich, sweet and dead. I looked back and knew this was me gone now. I would never be the boy in the pub who liked a drink and a laugh. I wasn't made for this. None of us were made for this, but we were men and we conquered our fear and controlled ourselves, and then we were charging the enemy and working our way through defences opened up by professional, specialist commando units, the mob charging through shouting and swearing, a rabble of men tight and controlled somehow, pumping blood and ready for murder. I ripped my arm on the wire but felt nothing, kept moving with the rest of the boys.

I don't know how long we were fighting. It was slow and dirty. Eventually we were off the beach. There were German soldiers waiting for us, moving back from their burning pill-boxes as flames licked through the cracks incinerating their mates. I suppose they must've been more terrified than we were. They didn't scare me much individually. It was better hand-to-hand. Better than being picked off in the open. Hand-to-hand fighting suited me fine. I really wanted to fight now with the actual landing behind us and people I knew ripped apart. For years we'd been pinned down in our own country fearing invasion while Hitler killed our women and children, and now we were fresh from another assault with the chance to make amends. I felt brilliant. For the first time I felt great, though it wouldn't last long. I was concentrated and all my fury came through. This is what we'd been waiting for. Without uniforms the Germans would've looked like us, I suppose, but I didn't think of this at the time. There was an older German turning towards me and before he could fire I stuck him with my bayonet. The steel jammed into his heart and I had trouble pulling it out. He was a murdering kraut bastard and when the bayonet sprung out it was red and gleaming. His blood suited the steel and I enjoyed the kill. Not like a sadist, but like a soldier killing the enemy. It was me or him. It was us or them. I cut him across the neck and he dropped. I shot two Germans running towards me. One I killed and the other looked as though he was dying. Other Germans started to run and we followed. I was with Mangler and some others. There were fires everywhere and the burnt wrecks of cars and trucks. The smell was incredible and it was hard to breathe as we passed one burnt-out wreck. Mangler was shouting at the Germans and some other English soldiers cornered them. The Germans stopped and threw down their guns. They put up their hands. Mangler hit one in the face with his rifle butt and forced his bayonet against the man's balls, pushing him against a wall. He laughed in the German's face and said he was going to castrate him for Billy Walsh. The German was shaking. A sergeant intervened and, with some difficulty, pushed Mangler away. Maybe I wouldn't have cared if Mangler had done it at the time because I was mad. I don't know for sure. I think we were all a bit mad because you have to be mad to fight in a war. To kill people and see your friends butchered. Every normal value is forgotten. Afterwards they try and patch things up and apply a nice coat of paint, hand out some medals and compose tunes, but I know how I felt. I'm being honest with myself. We left the Germans and I suppose they were lucky. I like to think I would have stopped Mangler if he'd ripped the bloke's trousers and started cutting. I'm sure I would. Maybe he wouldn't have gone through with it and was trying to scare the man. That's what it was. It worked because the German started crying and his mates looked at him with disgust. We moved forward and the fighting continued. The killing went on. The German soldiers eventually surrendered. Men died and it became dull and repetitive as the killing on the beach was repeated, but more deliberately. Our senses were shattered. The noise and smell were sharp for a while, then disappeared. My ears were ringing and smoke made my eyes sting. I saw things I'd never forget, maybe because they were new, but the man having his head blown off and Billy Walsh losing his genitals, and shortly after, his life, stuck. The same things happened many times during my time in Europe and after a while I stopped feeling sick and there was a dull throb in my head that passed right through me. It was inside now and when we'd taken the beach we were able to stop for a while. Someone gave me a fag and even though I didn't smoke I took it and enjoyed the taste. It showed I was alive. I have to try and remember what I felt at that moment because it's over half a century away. Some things you never forget, and landing in Europe is one of them. I knew it was something I never wanted to experience again, but this was naïve. This was the beginning. I would see other things that would affect me, but this was where the liberation began. The men from Dunkirk had been through a lot already, but they seemed stunned. I sat there and smoked the cigarette and looked around for Mangler. I was glad now the sergeant had arrived and saved the German soldier. I wondered what Mangler was doing, because the sergeant had struggled to stop him. I thought of the beach and how the smell and colour of the blood had got inside my head. It's hard to be honest about those twenty or so minutes immediately after we knew we'd secured the bridge-head. I can't remember any of our mob cheering, and no-one seemed over happy. What did I do? How did I feel? Even though it would be unmanly, I'd like to say I shed a quiet tear or two. But I didn't. I think I just sat there and didn't feel anything at all.

NO-MAN'S LAND

IT TOOK HARRY a few seconds to remember he was in an Amsterdam hotel and not back home in London. The room was dark, but a beam of light had broken under the curtains and created a spotlight effect on the floor. He looked at the clock on the bedside table, at the glowing digits swearing it was nine o'clock, and realised he felt fine after the ferry crossing. He hadn't slept long, but that childhood excitement of going on holiday was coming through with a vengeance. The sheets were crisp and the room airy, everything smelling clean and new. He definitely wasn't in London.

Once his eyes had adjusted he could see the shape of Carter under the duvet in the second bed, the sex machine snoring like a pig. The old hog-fucker was doing what pigs do best and he'd let the bloke sleep. The sex machine needed his energy for the girls running their way, and Harry would be spending enough time with him later when the action began. Once the lights went down and the birds started stirring, he'd stick closer than a shadow. He was learning some overdue lessons and could taste those red ruby lips already. He'd woken up with half a hard-on and thinking of the girls they'd be knobbing finished the job. He thought about banging off a quick one, but resisted the temptation. He wanted to be at his best. The lucky woman he was destined to meet later that day was going to get the back of her fucking head blown off.

Ten past and Harry was off down the hall for a shit, shower and shave. He stood under a full-throttle nozzle generous with the hot water, using a brand new Bic to remove the stubble on his face. He was impressed, because in England the hot water would've run out after five minutes they were so tight. People went on about Jocks and yiddos being mean, but the English even counted the peas on your plate to make sure you weren't getting one too many. He dabbed aftershave on his cheeks and checked himself in the mirror. He looked the part and went back down the hall with a towel around his waist, a middle-aged woman passing and not taking any notice. This was Holland and they didn't give a toss. Do that in a bed and breakfast in Bournemouth and they'd have the Tactical Support Group battering down your door.

Carter was still snoring and Harry got dressed quickly, selecting yesterday's Levi's, trainers and a crumpled shirt, running his hands over the material to try and get rid of the creases. He left Carter well alone, closing the door quietly and going down a narrow wooden staircase to the reception. He almost fell arse over tit it was so tight. Hank behind the counter was a middle-aged man with a balding head and a cup of coffee on the go. A typical Dutchman, he spoke perfect English.

– Did you sleep okay? he asked, radio low in the background and the smell of fresh coffee rising from the mug. You boys were tired when you got here and still you went out for a drink.

– Slept like a baby, Harry said.

He wanted to add that he'd done it without a nappy and hadn't wet the bed, but knew the joke would probably get lost in the translation. He didn't want Hank sniffing the sheets while he was out.

– Best night's rest I've had for a long time.

It was gone three by the time they arrived in Amsterdam. They'd had a few cans while they fucked about with the trains from the Hook, done the fifteen-minute walk from Centraal, dumped their gear, and then found a bar down the road. They'd lined the hotel up ahead of time, otherwise they'd have been fucking about all night banging on doors. Tom had stayed there before and got them a bulk discount.

The bar was quiet and they'd had a couple of lagers to wash away the dust before turning in for the night. Four in the morning and they were fucked. When they arrived in the Hook, the Dutch old bill had turned up in force decked out in riot helmets and backed up by dogs, and the Pompey and

Southampton boys were identified by members of the ferry crew. With a few whacks from the truncheons the seasiders were rounded up ready for deportation. They'd gone through the rest of the English and Facelift was sent home along with High Street and Biggs, both caught with their nicked gear. Facelift was pissed and mouthy and started sieg heiling the coppers. He was a thick cunt, because this didn't go down too well with the Dutch. They didn't fancy the Union Jack tattoos and the beer bottle in his hand, but worst of all the Gestapo routine wasn't too clever in a country where the Germans were hated for what they'd done during the war. Harry didn't know Facelift that well, he was Mark and Tom's mate, but though it got a laugh from the rest of the chaps, Facelift was a mug.

The rest of the lads kept quiet and did their boy scout routine, and Tom, Mark, Carter, Billy and Harry had got the train along with Gary Davison and his mob, plus Kevin and the lads from Crewe and Bolton, the rest of the English scattered through the carriages. There were probably a good twenty English kicked out for fighting, being pissed, thieving, or because the old bill just didn't like the look of them. The papers would have a field day back in England and there was bound to be some wanker on the boat ready to tip them off. Thank fuck that was over. Harry hated ferries.

– Breakfast is along the corridor, Hank said, shifting his head. It's not your traditional English food, but there is ham and cheese. The coffee is very good. It is an Italian blend I buy specially for my guests.

Harry went down the hall to a small room. He was the only one there and Mrs Hank brought him his food right away. The coffee smelt fucking brilliant, while the breakfast looked so-so. It was on the light side, and though he loved a good fry-up like the next man, there was more to England than greasy spoons. Harry started running through his favourites: jam donuts and bacon rolls from the baker's where Mango's sister worked, cod and chips from the chippy, chicken jalfrezi down Balti Heaven, spare ribs from the chinky, a double egg burger from the Istanbul Kebab House, patties and dumplings from the Jamaican, Heinz tomato soup and crusty rolls with a ton of butter in front of the telly. He could go on, but his mouth was watering and he wanted to forget London, that's why he was on holiday. Even the biggest food snob had to agree that England had its own fair share of decent grub. Or scran as Kevin would say when he came in and sat down.

– Alright bud? he asked.

– Not bad, Harry replied, feeling brilliant inside.

This was what it was all about. Going walkabout and seeing the world. Sitting in Holland with the sun shining through the window, stuffing cheese and ham inside his bread roll, eyeing up the croissant. He took a bite and had to admit it wasn't bad.

– That Hank who runs this place, Kevin said, once Mrs Hank had been and gone. He's a bit of a perv that one. You look behind the counter and he's got the wank mags piled right up for the nightshift. We probably interrupted him when we came in this morning. That's his on-duty reading by the looks of things. Big motorbike mamas with huge tits covered in tattoos, the dirty bastard.

– They're all like that over here, Harry reasoned. They don't care, do they? Anything goes in Amsterdam.

– You wouldn't want those women out on show if there were kids about, Kevin observed, looking at the thin ham and cheese with a worried expression. Not much chance of putting on any weight with this, is there?

– The coffee's alright.

– You take a young boy and he sees those monsters with fifty-inch tits and tattooed nipples, and it'll put him off birds for life. Could even turn him funny. I'm going to need a bit more than this to eat.

Harry had to agree with the northerner. He had a hole in his gut and the food was already gone. He polished off his drink and left Kev to eat his breakfast, asking Hank which way he should turn when he got outside. He tried to sneak a look and see the owner's magazines, but there was only a couple of phone books and the register they'd signed last night. Hank was thinking hard and asked Harry what he was looking for, suggesting left, right, left for the busier areas.

Outside Harry was reborn. The ferry crossing hadn't been as

bad as he'd predicted. He laughed thinking about the school-kids and how he'd covered them in sick. It was all in the past now, a story to tell the rest of the boys over a few pints, and something the girls would learn to laugh about. It might take a few years, but they'd get there in the end. He was in Holland and determined to make the most of his time away from England. He wasn't thinking back any more. Looking at the buildings and the canal and the bikes on the railings, a clean sky above and happy people passing, Harry couldn't be bothered with the arguments against Europe. If this was Europe then he couldn't wait till England was fully signed up. All he got the whole time was propaganda shoved down his throat, but from now on he was going with what he saw. Imagine thinking of baked beans when there was a stall selling chips and mayonnaise. He went over and ordered his cone. He was served by a man with an Ajax badge on his shirt. The chips tasted good, the mayonnaise even better. This was the life. He'd crossed the Channel and left his sickness on the lower deck, in the curled hair of some Home Counties teenyboppers. It had done Harry the world of good. At night he was sticking with the sex machine on his hunting trips, but during the day he was off on his own.

The hotel was on a canal and Harry did as Hank suggested, turning left and strolling next to the slow-moving water, passing painted houseboats moored along tree-lined streets, cobbles clicking on the heels of pedestrians. He didn't fancy the dog shit he almost stepped in, but there was always someone acting the cunt. On the corners there were stacks of bikes locked together, the big windows at the top of the buildings beaming back leaves and clouds. The air was fresh for a city, the canal-side streets free from traffic. There weren't a lot of people around and that suited him fine, because it gave you space to breathe. It was a lot different to London, where everyone was packed in tight and the car fumes and traffic grinding along the high street stuck in your head.

Harry followed Hank's directions and after passing through a small square he ended up in a market stacked with flowers. It seemed right and he wandered along, turning back towards

Centraal. He spent the next three hours walking, looking at canals and dodging trams. His feet had started to ache, he needed a piss and he fancied a rest. He also fancied a drink and Rudi's Bar looked okay, so he went inside. There were twenty or so people scattered around, talking among themselves, a couple of birds at the bar, the barman fucking about with some glasses. He looked at the names chalked on a big blackboard and chose a Belgian beer made from wheat. He paid his guilders and shot off to the bog.

He stood over the toilet and the piss blew out of him. He was pissing for England and stopped to read the graffiti, a mixture of Ajax and Feyenoord football and drug-happy nursery rhymes. Something in his head made him think about adding his signature to the wall, but why bother? He was too old for graffiti. He could hear someone shitting in the cubicle and didn't hang around once he'd finished.

Harry went back to the bar and picked up his drink. It was a strange taste, a lot different to the lager he was used to drinking. You had to give these things a go, so he wasn't complaining. The two women next to him stopped to look when he made a face and he gave them his best smile. They nodded back and did what the Dutch do best, acting nice and friendly, asking him if he was English. Harry nodded and sat down on the bar stool. They were eating something that smelt of peanut sauce and looked like kebabs on skewers. He was hungry. The girls said they were satays and came from Indonesia. They said Indonesia had been a Dutch colony and this surprised Harry because he didn't know that the old clogs were into empires same as the English and Spanish. It was like the Indian food at home. The satays smelt good and Harry ordered some for himself, chatting with the girls as the Rolling Stones played quietly in the background and the barman boiled a plastic bag behind the counter.

This was living, finding a hideaway and chatting with a couple of nice-looking locals, a bit hippyish but more biker than smelly crusties, in their thirties with long hair and red and green trousers, but he wouldn't say no if they offered him a blow job, and their tits were a lot tighter than fifty inches. He could smell dope in the air, everyone in their own worlds.

– So why are you in Amsterdam? Hairy 1 asked.

– I'm just here for a couple of days, having a holiday, Harry said. I'm on my way to Berlin with a few friends.

– Have you been there before? Hairy 2 asked. Do you know people in Berlin?

Harry felt like he was on Mastermind, but without any light in his eyes. Either that or he'd been lined up by two undercover coppers sniffing for titbits. He was going to say he was off to a football match, but thought better of it, because the papers were the same wherever you went and they'd get the wrong idea. Long-hairs didn't understand these things. He didn't want to put them off, though he wasn't really looking to get his leg over right now. There was a time and place for everything. Maybe later.

– Not yet, but I think we're going to meet a lot of Germans when we get there.

A couple of greasers wandered in and sat down with the girls. They were big fuckers. Must've weighed twenty stone each. They weren't greasers either. More like Hell's Angels. Harry waited for the smell to hit him. He'd heard the Angels wore originals covered in the shit and piss of their mates. It was supposed to be some kind of initiation ceremony. It wasn't nice, but what did you expect from hairies? Maybe he was wrong about the shit and piss, because it sounded like something a bunch of queers would get up to, and the Angels definitely weren't bum bandits, no fucking way would he accuse these two of crimes against nature. He'd heard they were into gang-bangs as well, which he didn't fancy at all. He didn't know much about the Hell's Angels, just stories, and he knew from his time going to football that the way these things were written up was usually a load of bollocks. But they were big cunts, covered with tattoos and must've been forty if they were a day, and they even bought him a drink when they saw he was friendly with the girls.

Harry settled in for a couple of lagers and one of the Angels skinned up and passed him some blow. This was the life, but he had to laugh, because you wouldn't get this at home. If a couple of nutters walked in and found some bloke chatting with their girlfriends he'd get more than a drink and a smoke. The Dutch were classy people and Harry reckoned he could get used to this. Stroll on Europe.

We don't have to look far to find Harris because there he is at the end of the bar sitting on a stool, the wall behind him acting as a screen. There's a blonde bird worked into the lining of the plaster, flickering light showing off a nice pair of medium-sized tits and a cropped cunt. You can tell she's a good-looking girl and deserves better than the skinny ginger cock shooting spunk over her face. Ginger pumps a couple of gallons of mutant seed over an appreciative Blondie, somehow managing it in slow-motion. Talk about self-control. Blondie throws her head back and licks her lips as Ginger follows through with another better-placed spurt. I'm half expecting Andy Gray to start spouting a commentary, except this isn't something you'd get on satellite. There's no sound and the film drifts into shades of grey before bouncing back full-frontal. It's an early afternoon matinee with ten or so English sitting at the tables watching the show, Amstel and Heineken bottles in their right hands. One bloke isn't bothered. Head down on the table sleeping. Blondie's smearing spunk into her cheeks and taking it down to her tits. The camera moves closer so the whole bar can see her working the congealed mess into upright nipples. Ginger has disappeared and this other bird arrives with a massive black dildo strapped to her cunt. Apart from this and a pair of red stilettoes, she's naked. The dildo has a gold tip and is greased in a glistening cream. Blondie assumes the position. The camera moves in again and gives the punters a close-up of her fanny and then backs out so we can get a good look at this Black Dick Dyke moving in for the kill. The new girl doesn't hang about and we get to see Blondie's ecstasy as the creases of her moaning face crack the fast-hardening spunk. Mark's going fucking hell, you wouldn't get this down The Unity, looking at Carter in particular who's been poking Denise the barmaid and could well have been doing something similar in the cellar. Can't see any pub at home showing this sort of stuff, but now it seems the girl getting serviced by Black Dick isn't getting off so easy. Ginger's back for a second helping and this time he means business. He's back with a vengeance. The production crew's been busy behind the camera, sticking a needle in his knob and injecting some muscle. Ginger's frothing at the mouth and doing the stallion routine. Blondie opens her mouth and gets a genuine length rammed down her throat. The film settles and the cameraman moves back out for a long-shot of the happy threesome, probably having a wank himself. But the bird on the receiving is well nice and you have to wonder how much she's getting paid. It takes all of twenty seconds for Ginger to get bored with this oral pleasure, pull out and move aside for some Arab who's appeared out of thin air. A couple of the boys aren't too pleased about this, seeing a white slave girl getting abused by a camel-shagger. Ginger goes up behind Black Dick, moves her aside, greases Blondie's arse, and slips in, buried to the hilt. We get a close look at her face and she winces as Ginger enters. Now she shows her acting ability. The kind of talent that would go down a treat in Hollywood. Showing the boys in the bar she loves nothing more than a good six inches of ginger cock up the dirt box. The Dirty Arab is wide-eyed at the other end as he gets his first blow-job off a bird. A blonde as well. Can't believe his luck. Years spent in the desert humping young boys and geriatric camels and now he's getting stuck into the opposite sex.

– Move over Ginger, Carter laughs. It's my turn next.

There's an old grey-blonde woman sitting at a table with a glass of red wine. She's watching the film with a funny look on her face. Probably Blondie's mum. I wonder how she feels seeing her daughter on the silver screen, the wall of a bar.

– That bird's going to have trouble sitting down when Ginger's finished, Mark says, as we finally get to the bar. You wouldn't want to go in after Ginger. I reckon old Ginger's a bit ginger himself.

– He's not a shirt-lifter. He wouldn't be able to get it up, would he?

Harris turns round and has a look. Turns back.

– They had that one on last night, he says. There's worse to come.

Carter leans in and orders from the barman.

– This is Johan, Harris says, introducing the skinhead serving the drink. He lives in Amsterdam but supports Feyenoord.

Johan nods and pours the drinks. Says they're on the house.

– Did you read this? Harris asks, handing over an English paper. This should stir up a few people.

We have a look and run through the front-page story. The basic line is that the Germans have organised a truce between rival firms for what the paper is touting as the Hooligan Battle Of The Century. The Germans are supposed to be warning the English not to turn up because they're going to send us home in coffins. The paper doesn't know who to slag off, the Germans or the English, so goes for both sides. On the one hand they're warning of neo-Nazi English hooligans wrecking Berlin and terrorising innocent Germans, and on the other of neo-Nazi German hooligans killing innocent English football supporters. Don't know what they're talking about, basically, but in typical journalist tradition they're going to blame everything on Nazis. You have to laugh. They've been getting away with this for years. The word Nazi sells. Doesn't matter what kind of paper or magazine it is, Left or Right they all love the mysterious Nazi threat arriving from the shadows then vanishing again. To add some extra spice they've got a photo of a skinhead snarling at the camera. Except he's got a bonehead crop and isn't a skinhead. But they don't know the difference. Don't have a fucking clue. Surprised they haven't drawn a swastika on his forehead for good luck. It's mental the way they stick to stereotypes all the time. The tabloids set the agenda and everyone else in the media follows.

I've never been into politics because all the wankers in charge are the same. A bunch of cunts. None of them gives a toss about the ordinary man and woman struggling along. They'll all sell you down the drain. Berlin's the wannabe leader of the new Europe and this is going to add extra friction. It's got nothing to do with Nazis. Thing is, we've all done it, standing there singing No Surrender with a Union Jack behind us, right hand in the air, taking the piss. Or like that Dublin riot. They say it was just politics, but the situation in Ulster added an edge. Obviously nobody following England overseas is going to support the IRA, and naturally their sympathies are going to be with the Loyalists in Northern Ireland, and of course there was going to be some C18 doing the business, but it was more of a football mob making a point. To say it was one or two blokes stirring things up is nonsense, because it was a riot waiting to happen. England having their say.

I'm thinking about all this because there's enough old soldiers who say we fought on the wrong side during the war. That the Germans are just like us, brave fighters, and they're right. I mean, not that I want Hitler in Buckingham Palace instead of the Queen, but the Germans are okay. So are the Dutch come to think of it, because we're all Saxon blood. The Dutch and Germans are well into the English way of life. Look at Johan behind the bar with his Fred Perry and number one crop. He's got his Feyenoord pendant next to pictures of Judge Dread and Prince Buster. There's a big stack of CDs. The Cockney Rejects, 4-Skins, Business, Last Resort and various Oi! compilations. And then there's the ska of Madness and Bad Manners. Now that's the real skinhead there, plus some original Jamaican ska. They love our football and music and pubs and gear. The Dutch and Germans have their football mobs and they're going to have a go at us when we come over and take the piss. That's natural enough. Under the surface, though, we're similar. They have a lot of respect for the English. For our hooligan element.

It's the fucking spics and dagos most Englishmen really hate. Slimy cunts with their flick knives and expensive clothes. Always up for it when the odds are stacked in their favour, then run like shit when they're faced by an equal numbers mob of English. I've seen it enough times. Heard the stories. We hate them because they're cowards and flash. You watch a football game on the telly nowdays and every time the cameras look at the crowd they pin-point well-dressed women and kids. Or crying Newcastle fans in spanking new club shirts who never went near St James' Park when the club was struggling. The media ignores the real culture surrounding football because the cameras are part of the system that's squeezed the atmosphere from our grounds. When they show the Spanish and Italians it's all this Latin culture routine, dropping libero terms and playing opera, zooming in on their so-called ultras for some flavour. The media laps it up because these ultras are a nice little oddity, but look into our own crowds and they don't want to know. It's too near home and something they're not part of, so they pretend it doesn't exist. It's not just football. This comes across in everything. The media is controlled by class. They want everything to reflect themselves and forget the rest of us. Go to Italy and the England boys walk through the piazza with their underpants on their heads taking the piss while the locals stand around all confused.

Mind you, when I was at Wembley and Di Matteo went piling through the middle and smacked that ball past Roberts he was the greatest man on the planet. For a few seconds greater than Zola and Vialli, so there you go. What can you say? Zola's the best player I've ever seen in a Chelsea shirt and Vialli's the business with his shaved bonce, strolling along the touchline looking like Mussolini. Every Chelsea boy in the country, whether they were in the ground or down the pub in front of the telly, loved that Italian. So what does that say? Thing is, you have to have an enemy. There's no point spending good money and taking time off work just to go over to Europe and stand around shaking hands with the locals. What's the point of that? Where's the excitement? Playing happy families like a bunch of wankers. You have to have an edge. It makes things more fun. Football's a game so you need some opposition.

Like this time we played in Denmark and, truth be told, the Danes were friendly as well, though they knew what to expect. Every nutter in Denmark had made the pilgrimage to Copenhagen to see the English in action. First copper we come across walks up and asks when the fighting's going to start. Not long, pal. We were down this square in Copenhagen with shopping precincts running off from a market. The English were having a sing-song. The Danes were peaceful and you're not going to smack blokes who don't want to know. Then they have a couple of lagers and start taking the piss. You feel like a cunt letting them in. We piled into the cunts, and those who didn't leg it got a pasting. The whole thing turns because these wankers couldn't take their drink. England go on the rampage and everyone says how bad we are. We go through the shops and cafés smashing the place up, doing anyone who wants to have a go, the scousers tagging along on the side doing some shopping. It was ages before the old bill arrived and they didn't have a clue how to handle the situation. They were shitting it, trying to nick people who didn't want to get nicked. Trying to hush everything up. Calm it all down. Trying to get their heads round what was happening. We walked off as the riot vans arrived. Flagged down a couple of cabs and went straight to the ground.

The Scandinavians and Danes are too fucking honest. They're too nice. They don't realise what's happening and think we're all gentlemen with monocles and bowlers. That Gary Lineker rules the waves. So we just walk into their supermarkets and help ourselves. Go through the Tivoli Gardens and enjoy everything for free. Load up on cases of Elephant lager and lob bottles at shop windows for fun. We can drink in their bars then rob the till and smash the place up if we fancy it. We can do whatever we fucking well want because we're England and nothing can stop us. It's a massive beano. The Scandinavian old bill haven't got it worked out properly, though the Dutch and Belgians know what they're doing now, and the Germans don't fuck about. They've got the tradition. The Stasi and the Gestapo. When it comes to the Italians and Spanish, they hate the English and are straight in hammering anything that moves. The papers try and blame it on Heysel, but it was going on long before that. They fucking love it because they're scum. Look at Man U in Portugal. Women and kids trying to watch a football match and the old bill think they're on a firing range. We hate the Latins but they hate us more. Their police are always having a go at the English. Makes you laugh, seeing the reaction to Rome. The media gets a glimpse of the real world and doesn't have a clue what's going on.

It's great when you're in these northern countries though. Whistle at the girls and they love it. Big smiles on their faces giving us the nod. Suppose you feel bad for the decent people for a few minutes because you do get some English who go overboard, getting so pissed they don't know what they're doing. Feel sorry till you come round the corner and the local nutters have mobbed up. Trying to pick you off and do you through sheer weight of numbers. That's what it's all about. But eventually everyone learns and now when we go overseas the old bill are ready and waiting. It gives them the chance to batter a few Englishmen without any come back. The embassies don't want to know, because they hate us like all the rest. Bunch of cunts the lot of them.

– You have to smile, says Harris. The newspapers really wind things up. There's going to be enough soldiers going over to Berlin anyway, and now they're organising a recruitment drive for us.

None of us is bothered because the more English come over the better. It's a load of shit what these papers do though. They've probably given some unemployed kid from East Berlin fifty quid to spout off. During the build-up to Euro 96 they had this bloke from Derby boasting on the radio about how the Turks were going to get murdered. The media like stirring things up, and then when they've got people listening they deliver a lecture. I'm sitting there on the forklift at work listening to this radio programme and everyone's laughing because they've disguised the bloke's voice so he sounds like a poof.

– The Germans will give it a go with or without these stories, says Harris. Their papers will make sure of that. It'll be a fucking good laugh. It's going to be a classic in Berlin. It's been quiet here so far. We went down to Rotterdam and met up with some of the Feyenoord crew last night. There was a row in this club, but nothing major. How was the crossing?

We fill him in. How the seasiders went to war. He laughs and shakes his head.

– We'll see them again, Harris says. I know that Portsmouth mob and they'll be back. It's typical Facelift as well. He won't bother giving it another go. All you've got to do is go to a different port and the old bill are so fucking thick they won't get you a second time. I've done it before. They wouldn't let me go to Turkey one time. I had the ticket and they wouldn't let me out of Heathrow, so I got a coach to Gatwick and bought a standby and ended up having three days in Istanbul. That was mental. The Turks are dangerous. There's fucking thousands of the cunts and a lot of them are tooled-up. We did alright. You're in the Third World over there and there's none of these bars showing porn films. Istanbul's dirt poor. Shitty food and drink. At least over here you can have some fun. Decent food, drink, music and the women are sitting in the windows gagging for some English cock.

Harris has been following England for donkey's years. I've been at least fifteen times now and it's always been lively. Mark usually comes, and Rod's done a few.

– Yes, lads, Amsterdam is as good as it gets, Harris laughs. We're in the centre of the civilised world here. You can drink as much as you want, do some drugs, and then go and fight and fuck your way through the tourist attractions. This is European civilisation at its best.

Harry caught up with the others early evening. He found them easy enough because they were still in the bar where they'd planned to meet Harris at twelve. They started telling him about some film with a blonde bird and a William Hague lookalike who had a Rottweiler on a lead, but he didn't understand what they were on about. There was a big skinhead behind the bar playing a Madness tape. The sound was clear and he liked the bar, and he wouldn't have minded a drink, but the others were going for some food. Harris had been to a good place the night before and there were six of them following the leader. Harry could stay and have a beer or go with the rest of the boys. Harris said it was an Indonesian and the food was tasty and cheap. Harry thought of the satays and made up his mind.

The sunny weather had been replaced by a dark sky and it was spitting, but Harry was still in a good mood. His head was light but he was together. He had a bit of blow in his pocket from one of the girls in Rudi's Bar, a nice gesture making visitors welcome. It showed how it didn't pay to slag people off just because they had long hair. It worked both ways. He was going with popular opinion now and following Harris and Carter and Tom and Mark and a couple of other Chelsea boys he didn't know towards the Indonesian. The colours had changed from this morning, but the drizzle livened things up and made the streets smell fresh.

The man nearest the door didn't seem too pleased when seven half-cut Englishmen stumbled in, but then he recognised Harris and his face cracked into a grin. Suddenly he couldn't do enough for them, leading the lads to the best table in the house and getting the waiters to pull an extra table up so there was room for the customers to spread out.

– He likes you, Mark said. You could be in there.

– He's alright, Harris replied. Left Jakarta ten years ago after some problems with the government. Until two days ago I'd never had any Indonesian food. Knew fuck all about the place to be honest. I had a satay in Johan's and yesterday I came in here.

Harris joked with the owner and ordered seven bottles of lager. Harry was enjoying himself. There was a lot of bamboo and wood carvings were scattered around. It was great how it worked. Inside a day they'd set up in Hank's, had found themselves a local, and were sitting down for some cheap and tasty food. In each place they were in with the owners. They'd got their base sorted out and everything was ticking over nicely.

Mark seemed more pissed than the others and started going on about how Amsterdam was alright, but that didn't mean he wanted to be part of Europe. Tom joined in and Harry was listening to them going on about England and Europe and how it was all a load of bollocks, how they were going into the centre of the conspiracy and planning to wreck Berlin, that it was the master plan of big business and the financial institutions, and suddenly he was sitting there, minding his own business, and it was a line he went along with – most people did when you stopped and thought about it – but then he started thinking that they were talking shit. Sure, he'd come over and seen the Channel as the big barrier, those pirate crews from Southampton and Portsmouth feeling it more than most, but he was mellow after the blow and didn't really give a toss. That was the problem with blokes like Tom and Mark. They were too wound up, like they were on speed the whole time. There was too much of the geezer about them. They needed to calm down.

Harry had been in enough bother when he was young, but was a peaceful man at heart. You had to grow out of those things. If he got the chance he'd rather be a lover than a fighter. He didn't go looking for trouble like the others did. Thing was, now he was lost in the tangle of Amsterdam's canals and side streets he didn't give a fuck about all the usual nonsense. That's what the place did to you. It showed you there didn't have to be all that mental bulldog stuff, crunching his eyes to peer through the smoke, watching those two nutters across the table turning their heads and eyeing up the classy Dutch birds passing outside who smiled through the window but kept going, taking everything nice and easy, nice and mellow, Harry sipping his lager and thinking about his mate Will at home, a big influence with his outlook on life, and how he'd helped Balti through the bad times, signing on and everything.

– Those Germans won't know what's hit them, Mark said.

Maybe Europe wasn't such a bad idea after all. Look what you got in return – civilised drinking so you could go out any time you wanted and have a few sherbets; soft drugs legally available so you could sit back listening to old Stones songs playing in the background, taking things easy; and there were the birds as well. He was watching the two girls at the other end of the restaurant ordering, full of confidence. There were no small-minded wankers shouting for everyone to get a move on please, drink up gentlemen, get outside in the rain and piss off till tomorrow. There was none of the corruption and short-term thinking that turned your streets into traffic jams and meant you rarely got a say in what was going on around you. Look at the football. Everyone rated the Dutch. A small country like Holland had produced so much world-class talent over the last twenty years it was unbelievable. They played football for football's sake, and it was only the peso and lira that saw the talent leave. They were class, but couldn't compete with the finance of the Spanish and Italians. Now the English game was going the way of the Latins, with money dominating everything.

Harry wasn't bothered, because he had more interesting things running through his head than football. If he lived here he didn't think he'd ever see a game. What was the point when you could drop into a warm friendly bar and sit around with good people enjoying life, floating on a cloud like some zapped-out old hippy. That's what the herb had done to him. It had made Harry relaxed and happy. If this was Europe then it made perfect sense. Just lie back and let the world get on with things. The drug got rid of the need to fight back in a battle you were never going to win. If you didn't care what was going on outside the window, it didn't matter. The politicians and businessmen could do whatever they fucking well wanted, carve everything up between themselves, so Harry could see how it was better to have a smoke and let them get on with it.

– You remember that league we had? Carter asked, bringing Harry back out of Rudi's and into the Indonesian.

He had to think and didn't have a clue what the sex machine was on about.

– That Sex Division we had, Carter laughed. You haven't forgotten already, have you? It wasn't that long ago. I was playing total football, like the Dutch.

Harry remembered. He'd been relegated. But he didn't think of that any more because it tied in with Balti. He didn't want those kind of memories. Things had to be good. He just smiled.

– We had this league, Carter said. You got ten points for shitting in a bird's handbag.

Harry pictured Balti and wished Carter would leave it alone. It had been a bad time. Shortly after that Denise had married Slaughter and two weeks after they'd come back from the honeymoon someone told Slaughter that Carter had been servicing his blushing bride. Slaughter was a psycho, went mental and had gone after Carter with a machete. Denise was lucky, because she'd gone to Guildford for the night with her mum and dad. Carter had told Harry down The Unity soon after the event, hand shaking as he lifted his pint.

It was a Sunday morning and Carter was coming home after a hectic night with some half-decent tart from Blues. He was feeling pleased with himself because he'd been after this bird for a while. He'd got home and there was Slaughter standing in a doorway and the headcase had come and jammed the machete against his neck. Slaughter pushed Carter back against the wall and pushed hard on his jugular. It was sideways on but the blade was cutting his skin. Carter kept still. He saw his throat sliced open and the blood drained. He told Harry he'd been shitting it. Fucking shitting his load. He was about to die like a pig. Slaughter was crying and telling Carter he was going to kill him for fucking Denise. Did he understand that he was in love with the woman. The thought of you, you cunt, fucking my Denise makes me fucking sick. It makes me want to slit your throat and cut your bollocks off and that's what I'm going to do because they call you Carter and you think you're a sex machine but to me you're just a cunt, a fucking piece of shit who fucks up people's lives and you don't do that to me, you don't fuck me about you fucking slag, you don't take liberties and think you can walk away, you fucking cunt.

Carter was quick to think and said it wasn't true. It's not true. Someone's taking the piss. Who told you that? Someone's telling lies about me. I'm not that sort of bloke – yes I am, of course I am, Slaughter's a stupid cunt but he's not that stupid, he's never going to believe that – she's not that kind of girl. Denise isn't some old slapper is she? Do you really think Denise would do that to you? She fucking loves you. Denise would go out and top herself if she thought you had her down as a slag, just some whore who goes round fucking anything that moves. Do me a favour. Do Denise a favour. More than that, do yourself a favour Slaughter. Denise is a classy lady. It's just not true. I swear on my mother's life, there's nothing between me and Denise and there never has been (and even faced with having his throat cut Carter thought of the day after the newly weds came back from their honeymoon, and while Slaughter was at work he'd gone round the flat and Dirty Denise was up to her old tricks, fucking gagging for it, the dirty talk and everything).

People heard what they wanted to hear and that was the thing to remember. It worked in everyday life and it worked in the long term. That was why he was the sex machine and got the women. He told them what they wanted to hear and made them feel good about themselves. He was doing them a service talking shit. The shit made them feel good and he got his reward. The shit smelt good. Shit smelt like Chanel for these birds, and that's how he lived to shag again. He applied logic in a near death situation and simply treated Slaughter like a bird and told him what he wanted to hear, that his wife was a good, clean woman who was honest as the day was long. Carter told Harry he was standing there with that machete ready to cut his throat and Slaughter's face changed and he thought about what he was being told so Carter could almost hear the gears clanking. After a couple of minutes Slaughter told Carter he liked him, and that maybe he was wrong, jumping to conclusions.

Slaughter gave himself some more time to think about this and then he backed away and apologised. He even begged Carter not to say anything to Denise about what had happened. He felt really bad about all this now. What was he thinking of? It was the overtime he was doing. It was hard getting by sometimes. Everything was so expensive and they'd had the honeymoon in Greece. That hadn't been cheap. Sorry Terry. And Carter's first thought was to lay into the cunt and give him a kicking because the whole time he'd been thinking of Balti and how the poor cunt died on a Sunday morning in the street outside his home, and how it was all going to happen again. But he held back because he'd have to kill Slaughter and he wasn't going that far – don't worry Slaughter, just make sure you get the cunt telling lies about me, this wanker slagging off your wife, making out she's a slag.

Slaughter nodded and walked away. Next day Carter heard one of the regulars in The Unity had been found sitting at a bus stop with his face slashed. It had taken thirty stitches to sew the cunt back together. The bloke told the old bill he didn't recognise his attacker, even though the attack had happened during the day. Carter had a quiet word with Denise and she started shitting herself. She was happily married and didn't want to die. They knocked it on the head, at least for a while.

– Shitting in a bird's handbag? one of the blokes with Harris asked. Did anyone do it?

– This mate of ours managed it, Carter said, looking to Harry in apology. Did six of them. Lined them up and filled the lot.

– That's brave of him. He was lucky they didn't kill him. No bird likes getting shat on.

Harry thought of the kids on the boat, with sick in their hair and clothes. It could've been worse. He wished Carter hadn't brought all that up now, when he'd been on the puff and was feeling mellow.

– You can get all that kind of porn here, Harris said. You can get birds covered in the stuff like they're auditioning for some rap film. Birds getting golden showers, birds with midgets, birds with horses.

Everyone laughed and Harry relaxed again.

– You go round these sex shops and you wouldn't believe some of the stuff they've got here, Harris said. First time I came to Amsterdam was more than ten years ago and I went in one shop, picked up this magazine, and there was this fucking kid in there. Stark-bollock naked wrapped in barbed wire. Little boy of about nine. On the opposite page was a girl even younger. I couldn't believe it and had a go at the bloke behind the counter. I don't think they let that sort of stuff go any more. Makes you think though, the kind of scum there is in this world.

– Do you think they've really got rid of that stuff? Mark asked. Because if they haven't we should go and do the cunts selling it. Make it a righteous Christian crusade. You can be Richard the Lionheart.

– Must be underground now, Harris said. I don't know. Amsterdam's a good place and they're laid back, but you get the rubbish coming here and taking advantage. They know things are loose and they can get away with murder. Most of the nonces go to Asia, places like Thailand and the Philippines where they're poorer than in Europe. They can do what they want over there, but that'll change one day as well.

Harry didn't want to hear about all this. He was in a positive

675

frame of mind and wished the others would ease up. He didn't want to think about nonces. You got enough of the child-killers, rapists and all that at home. When you were abroad you couldn't understand the language, so it was hear no evil, see no evil as far as he was concerned.

– That's the only thing wrong with Amsterdam, Harris said. The nonces and Ajax. They've got a good youth system and that's probably why the nonces come here in the first place.

– What's wrong with Ajax? Carter asked, coming awake.

After all, he believed in total football. In filling a bird any way you wanted. That's what it was all about. He thought Ajax were a respected outfit.

– They're a fucking yid team, Harris said. They're the Spurs of Holland.

– I thought Hitler gassed them all? Carter said.

– Doesn't seem like it. No, they're the yiddos of Holland. You wouldn't catch me going to see them play. It would be like going and spending your afternoons at White Hart Lane. You look the next time they're on the telly. They've got Stars of Davids on their flags. They're Tottenham alright.

Carter sat in silence for a while. That was a turn-up for the books. Ajax a yiddo team. As Chelsea boys they all had a natural hatred for Spurs that went back a good thirty years to the original skinhead era.

– So what are we having? Harry asked, studying the menu.

Harry had been talking with the hairies about the things to see in Amsterdam, and they told him about the Docker statue with its inscription: 'keep your filthy hands off our filthy Jews'. The Angels laughed and it showed a few things about the Dutch. One of the women said the Dutch starved under the Nazis and that there was still a lot of bitterness towards the Germans, which these days usually came out at football matches. Harry didn't want to think about that right now because he was starving as well, or at least hungry, and the owner was hovering in the background. They left Harris to order. They got seven more bottles of lager and waited for their food.

– Suppose this is like an Indian at home, Tom said, and Harry laughed. It was exactly what he was thinking.

– Funny how everywhere you go there's the same things. There's Ajax and Tottenham, and then there's Feyenoord and Chelsea, and there's this Indonesian same as a curry house. Mind you, walking into a bar and seeing Blondie getting one up the arse is different. You'd only get that at a serious sex club or on a stag night. You wouldn't get it on a screen down the pub before a game would you?

– I wouldn't mind a pint of Fosters, Carter pointed out.

– And a pack of English crisps, Mark added.

– A nice pint of Fosters in a pint glass.

Harry wondered sometimes. They'd just spent a bomb getting over here and Carter was moaning because he wanted a pint of Fosters. It was just lager and not exactly pure English heritage. Harris, now, he was a bit more together. He had a taste for Europe. The bloke had certain leadership qualities and needed room to manoeuvre, some extra living space. He was looking at bigger horizons and Harry wondered if he would stay in England all his life. No, he wouldn't be able to live without going to see Chelsea. After a while somewhere like Amsterdam would be too quiet. England was in his blood.

With some decent grub inside us, we're ready for a wander. The bill's cheap and we've done the place proud, paying and not doing a runner. Even leave a generous tip. Suppose the Dutch leg it often enough, but I remember when the yids played here a few years back and the Dutch were popping off shots at the English. Someone even got killed. Outside the rain's stopped and we walk slowly. Turn across another canal that could even be a river. There's not a lot of people about as we cross, and we turn a couple of corners. Dam Square's up ahead with a funfair buzzing away. Buildings tower over the commotion, all flashing lights and blaring music. Organ tunes and Abba pop favourites competing. We stand on the outside looking in. It's happy families and tourists, but I don't think any of us are interested in the rides. We're standing with the husbands and wives and kiddies having fun. Simple pleasures. We're just hanging about and seeing the sights. Not bothering anyone. I'm an ordinary bloke having a look and glad the kids are enjoying themselves. Laughing and screaming. Singing their heads off. I'm just standing around when this fucking cunt comes up to me and asks me if I want to buy some smack.

This pisses me off. First off, this is a family event. Second, he's a stroppy black bastard slurring his words with some wank street slang. Third, he's talking down like he's drug sussed and I'm shit. Fourth, and this is the one that gets right up my nose, the thing that does my fucking head in, is that he thinks I look like a fucking dosser. He's out of order and he's hit the chord. My hair's short and I wash my clothes. I shave my face and have a bath. I look like what I am. I don't look like a smackhead. I don't mind junkies, because that's their problem. Each to their own. But I work for my money. I pay my rent and get along. I work hard and keep my life in order. I don't like cunts I don't know coming along and telling me they think I'm a fucking loser.

This wanker stands there bouncing from foot to foot. I ask him if he's a Harlem Globetrotter. He looks at me half-sneering with this stroppy attitude that gets me where it hurts. I punch the cunt full in the face. He's not ready for this because he's used to dealing with scrawny wankers and hippy scum. I reckon I bust his nose. He stumbles back into a candyfloss stall. Luckily we're still on the outskirts of the fair and only the candyfloss man sees what's happening. The dealer goes inside his jacket, but before I can kick the cunt Harris pushes past and knifes him in the leg. He doesn't go deep but cuts the bastard and the cunt staggers sideways. Drops a razor. Harris goes to cut him down the back and rip his expensive top, but Mark clocks a couple of coppers and we move away. The old bill haven't seen us, and this wanker's not going to start screaming with his pockets full of a class A drug, or however they classify it over here. We filter towards a side street and disappear.

– What did you go and hit him for? Mark asks, as we go back over the river towards the red light and a drink. He only asked a question and you go straight into him.

– He wound me up, I say.

– He only asked. This is fucking Amsterdam. What do you expect?

Mark laughs.

– It's a fucking drugs town and they sell drugs. What's the matter with you, you silly cunt? You'll end up nicked with the old bill right there.

– Just didn't like the way he was muscling in. He was rude. I didn't see the coppers. It was bad manners. I didn't see the old bill.

– Neither did he, Harris says. He was a fucking wanker. Lucky for him they were around. Did you see the razor? I hate people who go round tooled-up like that.

Me and Mark look at each other and smile. Harris doesn't care. Old age is making him worse than ever. He's always been a nutter, but we're in the middle of Dam Square and he knifes someone. Mind you, I shouldn't have hit the bloke right there on stage. Lights shining in my eyes. I don't care now, but it was open and asking for trouble. It's the drink makes you careless. They've probably got video cameras like back home, but we're passing through so it doesn't really count. At least Harris didn't dig in like he could've done. He could've made the cunt scream. Thing is, you get the scent and now we're walking with a spring in our steps. Everything was nice and quiet and now it's turned round.

We keep moving and Mark says come on, let's go and have a look at the whores, we haven't seen the prossies yet. He's got a point. We all know about Amsterdam and the whores. I've seen them before but suppose we'll have to go and see them again. We follow the street back into the centre of the red light. The pavements are busy and we're away from Dam Square. A good percentage of the people who visit Amsterdam come down for a look, and you see enough Dutch as well. Always remember how bored the girls look, till you get near and they smell money. The sultry look comes out and they're better actresses than Blondie filling the wall of Johan's bar. Just keeps smiling as another queer junky actor corks her arse. A girl's got to work.

Amsterdam doesn't have things all its own way, because tourism and over-exposure destroys every good set-up in the end. We were on our way to Denmark that time when England played in Copenhagen, and we stopped in Hamburg for a night out. I'd never heard of the Reeperbahn but some of the older blokes who'd been that way before showed us where to go. There was England everywhere and the girls were legal. Logic is, it keeps them in order. There were girls on corners and in doorways, and there was this underground car park as well. It was fucking massive, with a big door and huge painted legs doing the splits. The girls were on little stages. Real crackers as well. Standing on platforms giving the shoppers a twirl. Mirrors in the background for an all over view. The England boys were on the prowl. When I think of it, most times I've been away with England we've ended up staying in or near the red light zones. Never really planned it that way, but it's true all the same. Maybe it's where the cheap accommodation is, but probably it shows how the English like to mingle and experience the local culture. Give us a choice of bars and drink, throw in some half-decent birds, and we're happy. And there's always going to be a punch-up somewhere along the line. Put all these things together and you've got the perfect package tour.

There was a bar in Hamburg where this big mob of English were drinking. We were watching these girls working from a doorway. There were three of them and none was a pig. Rod was eyeing up this blonde number. Couldn't have been more than twenty. Long hair down to her arse. Short white skirt. I can still see her. Rod was watching her for what must've been at least an hour. She was a German girl from the country who'd gone to the city to make her fortune. That's how we were telling the story. He kept saying he was going over but never did. Just stood there in the bar watching her approach passing men. Back and forward offering her services. Don't know why Rod didn't go and shag her. There weren't many punters around and none of the girls was getting anywhere. Rod was thinking big. Going over in a minute. Any minute now he was going to fuck the arse off her. Wrap that long blonde hair round his bollocks.

He started wondering why she was on the game. We gave him the fräulein story. Kept repeating it till he got bored. We were looking at Rod. He was going on and on about this blonde. What was she doing chatting to strangers in the street like that when he was ready and willing? We were pissing ourselves laughing. So was Rod after a while. Something stopped him going over. As soon as he finished his drink he was going over. He slammed his sixth or seventh bottle down and was on his way. This was it. He'd see us later. Big smile on his face. Hitching up his jeans. Except he had to stop and watch as the girl approached an old man. They started chatting. A sad old man in a saggy flea-bitten suit. Must've been at least sixty years old. The blonde's mate joined in. Licking her lips. There was some laughing and whispering, and then the two girls linked arms with the man and led him away. Down the street to a door and off inside. We told Rod that the girls were taking the old git to a big double bed and were going to give him the best heart attack he'd ever had. They'd give the man a line of coke and blow his brains out. Rod didn't know what to do or what to say. He'd missed out on a treat. He told us she was a fucking whore. A dirty old slag. A fucking scrubber. Couldn't we see she was a bad woman. We were all laughing. Me, Mark and Rod and a few others. He nodded his head all serious like a preacher and said she was a harlot. Rod was making the most of his missed opportunity. Taking the piss.

But we started rubbing it in. Telling him he'd taken too long and now he'd just have to make do with his imagination. Think of it, Rod, those two birds taking turns sucking that old codger's knob. First they'd have to clear away the cobwebs, and then they'd have to smooth out the wrinkles, but then he'd get the scent and be humping away for hours trying to dig up some fluid. Rod's bird would be leaning over the bed with that centurion behind her while her assistant offered encouragement. Trying to get a result. Rubbing his arse and those fossilised balls. And that dirty fucker would be beavering away for at least an hour with his dentures chattering and dribble falling on the girl's back. Heart racing and brain bulging. Finally reaching Go and giving her a bellyful just as the old ticker explodes. Could've been you Rod. But you missed out because you'd rather spend quality time with your mates. Rod just stood there. Stood there in silence before going back to the bar for another bottle of lager. Shaking his head.

I tell Harry this as we're walking along. He laughs.

– Maybe that's why he got married young. He wanted something more than tarts bending over a bed. Must be good if you fall in love with a decent woman, settle down and have some kids. It's hard to find anyone worthwhile. Most birds just want to grind you down, and if you haven't got money they don't want to know.

Don't know why he's getting all romantic. A fuck's a fuck as far as I can see.

– Married life's a life of misery, Mark says, overhearing Harry. You look at Rod, stuck at home with the wife. Mandy wants her cut and they've got bills to pay. He'd love to be in Berlin for the football. He'd love being in Amsterdam smoking some herb, but no, he's stuck at home like a fucking cunt. He's lucky as well, because he still gets out. Some blokes get married and you never see them again. I don't like Mandy much, because she nicked our mate, but she doesn't tell him what to do all the time like a lot of people I could mention.

Don't know what Harry's thinking. Must be age. He's a few years older than me and Mark. Suppose things change. Maybe that's what he wants. Some of that romantic nonsense. It's bollocks though, because there's plenty of birds around so why get stuck with one? It doesn't make any sense. Suppose it's in all of us, just depends on how much you're willing to change your life for a woman. Maybe it's his nature, though, because Carter's the same age and he's not exactly saving up for a white wedding.

I notice a shop that's still open. Selling all the usual tourist shit. There's a rack of cards and I stop to have a look. The others hang about waiting. The owner's standing there and I buy a card off him. He gives me the stamp. It's a scene from the red light district. Welcome to Amsterdam. There's black buildings and a row of lit windows. Girls behind plate glass in stockings and suspenders. Red neons glow. There's signs promising live sex. Live action. Promising the world. This one's for Rod and we'll think up a good message while we're pissed, and send it before we're sober. That'll wind the poor cunt up even more.

We turn down another street and look at the girls. Most are black. There's one or two Orientals and a few white girls. They look shagged out, and there's groups of wankers waving and making stupid jokes. Welcome to the show. We're spectators staring at the prostitutes lit up nice and pretty. There's this group of wankers nearby and they push a young lad forward. He goes to a black girl and has a word, then disappears inside. The men stand there not knowing what to do next. It's fucked them up, knowing he's in there getting his knob inspected. They move along quietly. The authorities are keeping it off the street and supplying an extra tourist attraction. Something to go with the art galleries and churches. Can't be bad. Might even splash out myself, but not with any of these.

– Anyone having a go? Harris asks.

We all shake our heads. Later on maybe.

– Come on then, let's have a drink. You can get a whore anywhere.

You can get a bottle of lager anywhere. But I know what he means.

Harry stayed with the girls in the windows. He watched Carter and the rest of the boys walking off, pissing about, and no-one even noticed he'd been left behind. It was the same as the ferry coming over, and if he'd fallen overboard they wouldn't have missed him till they got to Berlin, Carter sitting there in the room they were sharing talking to himself, but it gave him some space so he wasn't complaining. They'd been drinking all day and it was fair enough. They were starting to get edgy, with Tom and that wanker in the square, Harris doing his bit for Chelsea and England, but Harry wasn't interested in roaming the streets of Amsterdam looking for people to slap, not right now anyway. He was inspecting the girls on the meat racks and had to be honest and say there wasn't anything better than he'd find down Blues back in London. He didn't know whether to be glad or sad, so he headed in the opposite direction to the others, putting some extra distance between them in case Carter came back looking. Harry did some window shopping, checking the sex shop displays and sex club line-ups.

There was a big queue outside one club in particular and he couldn't help laughing how ordered and proper everyone was. He thought the English were the only ones who could be bothered queueing, but the hundred or so people outside were in a rigid two-by-two formation, gagging for a bed in the ark, handing their rubbers in at the door. They were people as well: men and women of all ages, shapes and sizes, and though he knew the clogs were open-minded he still didn't expect to see whole families chatting as they waited for the advertised live sex. It was mostly couples and small groups, but there were grey-haired parents with grown-up children, in-laws, cousins, all waiting patiently. He couldn't get his head round that at all. It was sick. Somehow perverted. It just wasn't right. He looked at the masked photos outside the club a bit closer and they were going to get some hardcore sex for their guilders.

Harry couldn't sit through something like that knowing he was surrounded by happy families. It was almost the same as incest. He turned away and passed a couple of smaller, dodgy-looking clip joints where the champagne was a hundred quid a bottle and the bouncers big bastards in tuxedos. He turned down a smaller side street lined with glass. This was more like it. There was a better mix of girls and the street's quieter atmosphere gave him confidence. He stood back and took his time because his balls were heavy and he wanted to make the right choice. There was a blonde who looked alright, with red stockings, suspenders and basque. She was a big girl with a healthy figure. Harry breathed deep and moved in for the kill. He was halfway there when he spotted a smaller brown girl. He stopped and looked her over. Now he'd spotted her, she stood out. She had short black hair and was dressed like a European tart, which didn't seem natural, a bit artificial somehow. The stockings and that looked right on white birds, but on black and brown girls it didn't work. He'd never find something like this down Blues. No fucking way.

He turned towards the girl and thought hard about what she saw coming. A big white man with a shaved head and drink on his breath, the smell of smoke on his clothes and half-stoned eyes, who in a few minutes would have his jeans on the floor and his knob racing in and out of her, his big white gut bouncing against her flat brown belly, arching his back as he finished in a pool of sweat. She probably saw one more pissed geezer from England swaggering towards her, on holiday looking for something dirty he couldn't get off the wife back home. Maybe she'd had a drink and was resting after that last wanker from France who'd given it three quick thrusts and finished, then started moaning about how he hadn't got his money's worth, causing trouble so she'd called her minder in to turf the ungrateful cunt out into the street, leaving a bad taste on both sides. Harry guessed it was something like that and hesitated, but then he was right in there talking to her and she was almost too friendly, inviting him inside after he'd agreed to her price. He didn't know what the going rate was, but went along with what the girl said. It was all about money in the end. He wasn't going to argue over a few guilders. He was Chelsea, not Tottenham.

The room was small and warm and the girl laughed a lot as she invited him to come and stand in front of her so she could have a look at his cock. She was professional, but friendly. She opened his jeans and did a quick check. There wasn't much of the Orient about her room and she put on a Sting CD for some flavour. He didn't like the music, but it was in the background and soon faded off. The girl had a way about her that put him at ease, but there she was handling his knob doing her clap-clinic routine and he was limp. He wasn't bothered because this was the preliminaries and she knew what she was doing. He started taking his trainers and jeans off and she was getting ready arranging the cushions, and to pass the time he asked her where she came from.

She said her name was Nicky and that she came from a Thai village near to the border with Laos. He stripped off his pants and she kept talking. She'd wanted to see the world and get away from Thailand, so she'd come to Amsterdam with a Dutchman she met in Pettaya. She was twenty at the time and he was in his forties. He'd treated her good for a couple of years and she'd got her residency, but then things changed. He started going with boys and wasn't interested in her any more. She didn't mind because he was old and she was young, and she wanted to be free. She'd been in Pettaya since she was sixteen and was determined to stay in Europe. All the girls dreamed of moving to Europe. Her village was poor and the resorts were full of Western men who paid good money, but she wanted to get ahead. European men usually treated the girls better than the Thais, and they had a lot more money.

She smiled this mental smile and Harry nodded not knowing what to say. She had a perfect body without any trace of fat, and she was still soft despite an adult life on the game. Nicky loved Amsterdam and hated Thailand with a vengeance he couldn't understand, because to him it sounded like a tropical paradise. Her Dutchman had given her enough money to keep going for a couple of months and then she'd had to find work. They'd had two years together and it had worked out okay, but now she was free and could have some fun. She'd done everything for him, and he'd looked after her. He'd bought her clothes and took her to restaurants. She'd never been in love with him, and he'd only loved her youth and body. Her life had improved.

Nicky made a good living and she liked white men, the colour of their skin. For Thais white skin was attractive. She hated Arabs. Harry liked the way she spoke and the way she moved. He couldn't help himself and asked how she'd ended up as a prostitute, even though he felt like a mug soon as the words came out of his mouth. He expected her to tell him to mind his own business and get on with it, because time was money, that stupid lines lifted from shit films would cost him extra, but she wasn't bothered and started going into one so he wished he'd kept his mouth shut. She was a fucking beauty and he wanted to get stuck in, to fuck the girl's brains out, to squeeze inside the tightest cunt on the planet and dump his load, but the way she started carrying on was killing his passion dead.

Because Nicky was telling him all about her village, set in the jungle but poorer than anything he would see in Europe, about the hunger and illness. She had three brothers and two sisters who'd survived infancy and the money she sent home helped the family survive. It didn't matter if she was a prostitute because she was getting along and helping other people. She wasn't just surviving either, she was enjoying herself in Amsterdam. She had clothes and went to clubs where she could take ecstasy and dance till early morning. She would never live in Thailand again. One day she would get married and settle down. Nobody really chose to have sex with people for money, it was something that was forced on you by karma, but she was lucky. She was glad to have a face and body that men desired, because otherwise she would be working in the paddy fields, and did he think she was pretty?

Harry nodded, because he did, but all this talk about brothers and sisters and extended families scratching around in the dirt and kids dying early was putting him right off. Everyone knew Thailand was a knocking shop. He'd made the mistake of treating her as a human being, but that was him all over, making mistakes Carter would never dream of making. Carter would've mumbled a few words and had the fucking slag over the bed inside thirty seconds, giving her one from behind as he planned his next move. More than that, he wouldn't bother with prostitutes in the first place. He didn't need to pay for sex. Bollocks, though, because Harry was his own man and he was riding the crest of a wave, seeing the world and meeting exotic tarts, getting wasted with hairies and on the piss with his mates.

Nicky pulled him to the bed but Harry was thinking about the girls in Rudi's and the blow, and his head was floating imagining a Thai village and a ready supply of poppy seed. He saw himself going from one opium den to another, surrounded by hippies and Siamese princesses, the prince in his harem spaced out on sex and drugs, no fucking rock-n-roll or even music as he turned off the CD. Nicky dimmed the lights and he was in this little palace somewhere in Bangkok, down by a river with the bustle of sticky-rice street vendors, while really he was in Amsterdam following the train of tourists shagging for their photo albums. He moved in on Nicky but when her hand went down to his knob he was sorry to say there was nothing there for her to get hold of. She looked at him and smiled, and started playing around, and then she pushed him back on the bed and went down and started using her mouth.

Harry laid back and thought of England. He thought of The Unity and Rod missing out, about the rest of the boys alive and well, his mate Balti dead and gone, a red ball of gristle at the top of his neck, brains seeping into the sewer. He stopped and tried to concentrate on Nicky. Here he was with the golden chance to shag a real cracker, even if she was a tart, and he was trying to will some steel into his cock but still nothing happened. The more he tried conjuring up a hard-on, the limper he got, shrinking from those Thai teeth as his brain drifted off again. He raised his head and could see this girl with small tits and a tight cunt, a suction pair of lips and perfect body, with years of training doing her best for her customer and not getting anywhere. Harry wished he'd stayed with the rest of the boys and given all this a miss. It was that fucking hippy smoke that had done him. Never trust a hippy. He had to admit there was no point going on, because the more he thought about what was happening the worse he got. He was thinking of England, but just couldn't get it up.

Harry moved away and started putting on his pants. He said sorry about that, bit too much drink, bit too much dope, and Nicky said it didn't matter, that he'd be surprised how often it happened. He told her to keep the money, that it was down to him, but he didn't look at the girl and she wasn't exactly going to hand it back. Fucking hell, if he couldn't shag something like that then he was in serious trouble. She had the rubber ready and everything. Nicky ran through a list of limp knobs, premature ejaculations and general rubbish sex that made him feel a bit better. She was trying to cheer him up and he supposed she didn't mind either way. It was probably better for her not having to lay down under yet another fat cunt. She was probably pleased.

She asked him where he was from and when he said England she asked if he liked the Queen. Everyone liked the Queen, and Nicky started going into one again as though nothing had happened, saying the Thais had a king who they loved as well. He sat down for a minute doing up his trainers and she was rambling on and offered him a drink, pouring two glasses of whisky. She had a small container of ice and for some reason she wasn't in a hurry to get rid of him. She asked him what London was like and what he did for a living and where he was going after Amsterdam. When he said Berlin she told him of a man she'd known in Thailand who came from Berlin. She'd stayed with him for two months on Ko Samui before he went home, leaving her pregnant when she was eighteen. She'd hoped he'd take her away from Thailand but he'd left suddenly and she'd found someone else. All the bar girls in Thailand wanted to get out, to go to Europe and America.

She said she was finished for the night. She'd been working hard and was tired. She aimed at ten men a night and Harry was number ten. He nodded and got up to leave and was surprised when she suggested he come with her for a drink. She pulled the hair on his arms and pinched his gut. Harry wasn't sure what she was doing. He wondered if it was a con, if she had an ambush lined up, but she said she had some whisky and hashish in her flat. She lived a couple of miles away in the flat her ex-friend had rented for her. He'd been good to her. She looked up at Harry and he could feel his knob stirring. He couldn't believe he'd paid good money and hadn't poked her, and though he was confused he thought why not, because what else was he going to do tonight?

They were soon walking out of the red light district, and once over the Amstel River everything seemed different. He was wondering where it was leading, but enjoying himself and this woman next to him. She had her arm through his and he had to remind himself she was a tart. She was fucking lovely, and it seemed unreal somehow. He felt like he was in a video. He remembered Mango saying how the girls in Thailand didn't see it so much as a shag as a possible introduction, but Harry was smart enough to know that Amsterdam would've changed some of that. He was looking for an angle and half-expected a couple of pimps to arrive and start slicing him up. But Nicky was talking about whisky and hashish and how she loved going out to buy clothes and music and how shit Thailand was, that he couldn't help wondering if Mango was right.

They took a cab the short journey to her flat. It was small but well done up and Harry sat down on the couch as Nicky brought out a bottle of Jack Daniels. She was asking about London and he found himself telling her about the pubs he used, about Blues and how he liked going to football. She rolled a chunky spliff and after a while he was even telling her about his mate Balti who'd been murdered in the street, her hand going to her mouth in shock. He told her how they'd grown up together and shared a flat, and how they'd been closer than brothers. Funny thing was, he didn't mind talking and didn't feel too bad about the memory. He couldn't smoke a lot and the hairies had already set him up, so maybe that was the reason, though it could've been because she was a stranger and, more than that, she was a whore who didn't really count.

That wasn't true, though, because Harry had to keep reminding himself that this woman sitting next to him was a prostitute. She had sex with ten men a night. Fuck knows what kind of diseases she was carrying. She was a fucking prostitute, and whores were supposed to turn their mouths away from you if you tried to kiss them, and they were supposed to be professional and blunt with their services, showing the punter who was in charge, and then if he was pissed he was going to get narked by this lack of respect and start having a go and fuck knows what could happen. No, Nicky was talking to him like he was a person rather than some sleazy cunt off the street. He found it hard remembering she was a pro, and with some of the old herb he soon forgot altogether.

Nicky got up and went for a piss as Harry poured himself another glass of whisky. He fancied a bottle of Heineken, but the Jack Daniels was fine for now, till she came back. He wondered what the rest of the boys were up to, but was happy enough here. It wasn't that late, and Nicky said she liked to finish early and avoid the worst of the drunks. He was in Amsterdam, but could've been anywhere in the world. This place was international, because you went for a simple shag with a whore and ended up sitting on a couch getting stoned with some Thai all the way from the Laos border. You didn't get this kind of thing down Blues.

Harry had never been outside Europe. One day he'd go to the States and, who knows, one day he might even go to the Far East. It would be hard, because the poverty would get you down, but there were a lot of places to see in the world. When England joined up with Europe they'd be getting all the influences and this would liven things up. Harry sipped his drink and put his feet on a stool. He looked up and saw Nicky walk into the room naked and this time he was ready.

We're standing by one of the humped-back bridges that arc over the canals enjoying the scenery, wondering where Harry's disappeared to. Little knots of English are scattered around. Sitting on cars and railings. A bottle lands in the water and ripples catch the sex club neons. The water's a burnt-out stretch of black in between brightly-lit buildings. There's clubs, restaurants and bars rubbing shoulders. Enough drink to keep us going and one or two shops still open selling stuff to the locals. We're outside two bars sitting side by side, having a drink and watching the show. It's after ten now and it's nice knowing the bars will be serving late. These two are packed. One with English and the other with a mixture of English and locals. Might not be local to the red light, but they're Dutch. The English bar is singing RULE BRITANNIA while the other has the music blaring out. Rule Britannia on one side and The Prodigy's Firestarter on the other. The songs mix together and somehow sound perfect.

– Did you see those sand niggers run? Carter asks, rocking back on the parked scooter he's sitting on. I've never seen men run that fast. I thought the Italians were nippy, but those blokes were greased lightning. Should sign those cunts up, give them passports and get them to run in the athletics team. You'd never get an Englishman moving like that.

Carter starts carving CFC and ENGLAND into the scooter with his keys, talking about the pimps we smacked on the way here.

– They knew their time was up, Mark says. Makes me sick seeing white girls getting used by those cunts. What were they? They weren't Turks, were they?

– Moroccans, Carter says. Moroccans, Tunisians, Algerians. Something like that. Fucking sand niggers. Fresh from the Sahara. You go down Bayswater and you'll find enough of them round there running the shops and kebab houses. They're not poor. How do you think they get out in the first place?

– Couldn't believe it when that cunt hit the girl in the gut like that, Mark says. Just punches her in the belly as if that's how we all behave. Fuck me, what kind of cunt is that? Still, I did him alright. Straight in the bollocks, and Tom slapped his mate. Couple of shitters.

I nod and agree. I mean prostitution's a natural enough business, but there's no need to hit the workers. I thought the Dutch had all this stuff sorted out. That's what they say. That's the impression you get back home. But they've only gone so far. It's the soft drugs that are legal and only so much in certain places. There's enough pushers around selling smack and what have you. As for the tarts, you'd think the shop windows would get rid of the pimps, but there they are. Scum always floats back. Suppose there's always going to be girls selling themselves, and that's the way it should be, because we live in a free-market economy. The girls get their money and the bloke gets his end away. Everyone's happy. Till some fucking sand nigger comes along and starts knocking them about. There's no excuse for those wankers. Pimps are fucking scum. They're always these fucking greaseballs as well. Either that or blacks That Turk or whatever he was won't be hitting anyone for a while. Never mind his sore bollocks, his hand's going to take some stitching after Harris slashed his knuckles. That's what those cunts believe in anyway. Chopping off hands. They treat their women like shit. An eye for an eye and a hand for a hand. Instant justice. Harris doing his good deed for the night.

– I had that bird down to ten guilders for a blow job when they turned up, Carter says. That's about three quid. Imagine a blow job for three quid. She wasn't bad was she? She wasn't Dutch though. Said she was from Russia. Blondie was well nice. Ten guilders for a blow job. I'm going to have to get in somewhere tonight.

– Don't look at me, Harris says, laughing, the old humour coming through again.

– I can't spend too much time thinking about that bird, Carter says. She had rubber lips as well. Ten fucking guilders. That's three quid.

– Fuck off, Mark says. She never said ten guilders.

– Straight up. Ten guilders. I gave her a line and she told me business is shit tonight because there's so many English about. Said the local news has been going on about the English hooligans drinking in the red light district. The office workers are too scared to come down here because they reckon there's going to be trouble. There seems to be enough punters around, but she said there's not a lot of work tonight. The girls are starving.

– You're telling me that bird was going to suck you off for ten guilders? You'd spend more than that on a round.

– Honest. Ten's better than nothing for a working girl. Thanks to that pimp I've got lover's balls. Just the thought of that old slag's doing my head in. If I don't pull anything later I'll go down and have one of those girls in the windows. Mind you, they're not going to be ten guilders. Maybe there was something wrong with those girls. Ten guilders. Fucking hell.

You have to laugh because it's pure justice seeing Carter getting let down. Thought he was supposed to be this big sex machine. It's early yet I suppose. Surprised he's going to pay for it though. A man of his talent and reputation should click his fingers and have the women come running.

The England bar starts up again. There's faces pressed against the glass, skulls coloured by red and blue light. There must be a hundred of them in there. Should move outside where they can breathe. The glass sweats and every now and then a hand comes through the bodies and wipes it clean. Big hand clearing a view of the street outside. I don't know about the punters being put off. There's tourists and that, but Dutch as well. Mind you, no middle-aged men in raincoats. The England boys by the windows watch Amsterdam pass in a pissed daze. Their eyes are glazed and they bang on the glass whenever something half-decent strolls past. It's funny watching the girls jump and look into that bar. Must be a horror show for the Dutch. Out for a walk looking in on a cave packed with drunk Englishmen. All tattoos and shaved heads, laughing and shouting faces, one or two wrapped in Union Jacks and Crosses of St George.

The window's almost popping, the multi-coloured lights opposite flashing on and off creating a strobe effect. Fucking mental how the skulls flash. The bar's singing NO SURREN- DER and we all join in outside showing solidarity with the soldiers fighting for England. The window vibrates as that big love-and-hate hand comes through the crowd, banging out a Loyalist rhythm. There's England right outside and stretching down the road, and they all look round at the same moment in case the glass comes crashing down. The red hand disappears in the crowd and they go back to their singing.

– Why don't we go and find that bird? Mark says. She'll do us all for three quid after we saved them from the sand niggers. She'll do me for free because I kicked that bloke in the balls. St George riding across the desert saving white women from slavery.

– You're joking, aren't you? Carter asks. They'll be keeping their heads down because those cunts have been put in their place. They'll probably take it out on the girl and her mate once they've finished at the hospital.

– You think so?

– It's not like there's anyone around to stop them, is there? I don't suppose the old bill can be bothered because you're only talking about a couple of tarts, and you never know, they could be illegal immigrants or something.

– We should've cut that bloke's throat, Mark says.

I can see him getting wound up and tell him not to worry. She probably had broken teeth and would've ripped Carter's foreskin off. He laughs and Carter looks worried.

– We'll get something better later, Carter says. Blow jobs all round for five guilders. Don't worry, we'll get our legs over before we leave Amsterdam, and it won't be whores.

I look sideways to the music bar and there's enough England in there as well, mixed in with the locals having a laugh. There's a few birds, but nothing special from where I'm standing. The window in the England bar bounces again. The red hand of Ulster appears as the song ends and we're into ONE BOMBER HARRIS. I wait for the hand, but someone's had a word and the blokes outside can relax. THERE'S ONLY ONE BOMBER HARRIS, ONE BOMBER HARRIS. There's a few scousers, who you can always tell by the shape of their faces and style of dress, a small group of Leeds who look like Yorkshiremen, and I bet when they look at us they know we're from London. Probably know we're Chelsea as well.

Billy Bright comes outside and Harris goes over, and they start talking to the Pompey boys next door, the ones from the ferry who've arrived as Harris predicted. The scousers wander off taking their bottles with them, and then one of the Leeds mob starts chatting to Harris. Suppose he knows who he is and Harris starts laughing at something, and there you have Portsmouth, Chelsea and Leeds having a chat and that's something a lot of people who don't go away with England wouldn't understand or even believe.

That's what happens. A perfect example. Go back a few years and think of the rows we've had with Portsmouth and Leeds. But you get over here with England and all that filters away. Some things can never be smoothed out, and certain faces are remembered. Things can get personal. But with this lot it's okay. I see the scousers wandering back. I turn my head because Mark's banging me on the shoulder.

– Come on, it's your round, he says.

I nod and go towards the England bar, then think again and go in next door. It'll be easier to get served, and anyway, there's a few women in here. I lean over the counter and order three bottles. I look around the bar. There's not much on offer. Mostly small groups of boring-looking birds getting chatted up by pissed English. I go outside and talk with Harris and the others, but see Mark and Carter waiting for their drinks. I get to the bridge and hand the bottles over, turning to see a man with a Union Jack around his shoulders fall over in the street pissed. He's one of the Leeds lot and he stays there. A couple of blokes pull him over to a wall and leave him to sleep.

– Why don't we go to a club? Carter asks.

– You can see a sex show anywhere, Mark says.

– A proper club. Somewhere we can find some women. It's all tarts and tourists down here.

We look at each other and it makes sense. We're not going to meet any Dutch birds when there's hundreds of us hanging about, half the blokes pissed out of their heads. Move down the streets a bit and there's more English. We're everywhere. Harris and Brighty have gone inside the bar so we just leave. Halfway down the road I start wondering where we're going, but Carter says he sussed out a couple of places before leaving England.

It's a fair old hike so we stop a cab. Carter passes the address to the driver, a big friendly bloke who acts like he's known us all his life. He's a Norsk giant with a deep laugh. Says he knows the club and puts his foot down, cutting across tram lines. The air's hot inside the car and we roll down the windows. He tells us the climate's changing. It's June and there's rain. The air's turned muggy and we could do with another drink. Five minutes later he drops us off at the end of this pedestrian zone. We pay our money and we're lining up outside the club, but when we get to the door there's none of the hassle you get off the bouncers back in London. Blues is fine because we know the blokes on the door. I'm talking about the West End clubs. We're inside quick enough and there's a decent mixture of music. It's not really a club in the normal sense.

Carter doesn't waste any time and gets the drinks. Starts talking with these three birds at the bar. Piece of piss and we're straight in. Have to keep hold of things. Hanging about with a bunch of nutters all day can lead you astray. Have to be nice and polite. Luckily these girls are pissed as well so there's no chance of them storming off because they can't stand the drunk bollocks coming out of our mouths. They seem happy enough. Listening to everything from Block Rocking Beats to Babylon's Burning.

– It's my birthday tomorrow, this bird Monica says in my ear. I'm going to be thirty years old.

She looks younger but I'm not complaining.

– My friends are older. She smiles. How old do you think?

How the fuck should I know? Don't say it though. I have a guess and she laughs and whispers in their ears. They all laugh some more then piss off to dance around to Smack My Bitch Up. Nice one that. Mark nods and says those sand niggers must drink in here. I move over to the wall with Mark and Carter.

– No problem here lads, Carter says. We're all going back to Monica's. It's her birthday party and the girls are sleeping with her tonight. This is our night boys.

Carter is enjoying himself, doing what he does best.

– The blow jobs are on the house tonight, he shouts, trying to be heard. We owe those pimps a favour. Instead of these three we'd have been making do with those mangy old slappers down a back alley, throwing away good money.

I watch the dancefloor bouncing. I can see the girls dancing and looking over. They keep going through Nirvana, Oasis and Black Grape. When they come back Monica's leaning in heavy, asking if I want some ecstasy or speed? I go for the whizz with Mark and Carter. It gives me a pick-up and the strength returns. I have that dedicated feeling now. Dedicated to getting this bird's G-string off and in my pocket. Fuck the arse off this bird. Give her the perfect birthday present. She's full of life and it's a couple of hours later when we get around to leaving.

There's six of us walking near empty streets. The girls are singing a song in Dutch that sounds like shit. Some languages fit music, others don't. English is the perfect example where it works. French the worst. The song they're singing means nothing to us. It's a short walk and we climb these cold stone stairs to Monica's flat. It's a big place, and one of her mates goes and takes out a punk compilation. There's old stuff from Stiff Little Fingers, X-Ray Spex and the Pistols, and newer material from the likes of Leatherface, Fugazi and the Blaggers. She puts the CD on and music fills the flat, Monica going over and turning it down. In the light they look dirtier than down the club. Their make-up's blurred and Monica just stands there and takes off her black jeans. She laughs and says it's too hot, one of the girls opening a window. I want to get stuck in right away but hang on, because they're acting coy with Monica half-naked.

One of the girls brings in a pack of lager. It's nice and cold. Monica puts a lamp on and turns the main light off. Carter laughs and says Harry will be angry he missed out. Probably got lost and is back in the hotel right now fast asleep. I have a long swig of lager and my mind is racing trying to keep up with my tongue. I'm going on about Blues back home and talking about the Dutch-German border for some reason. Fuck knows what I'm on about. I stop talking and sit listening. Can still hear my voice somewhere.

Don't know how much longer it is but Carter and one of the girls has gone. The sex machine is doing his duty. I look at the chair opposite and Mark's got this bird on his lap. Her top's up and her tits are out. They're kissing and so am I, but it's not Monica. She must be with Carter. Or maybe she's with Mark. Fuck knows and who cares, because I'm up and following this bird to a small box room. We go inside and I'm thinking of that film in Johan's bar. Blondie getting serviced by Ginger. This isn't Blondie, but it's a blonde bird. I don't follow what's happening but I know what has to be done. I can't come for ages and this gives the girl the kind of sex she wants. Eventually I finish and lie there next to her. She promises me a blow job first thing in the morning. Starts snoring. I spend the next hour trying to shut down and get to sleep. I hope she keeps her word.

Nicky was down between Harry's legs when he woke, and it took him a couple of seconds to realise where he was and what was going on. It wasn't London and if it had been the hotel with Carter he'd have topped himself. When he realised where he was Harry was king of the castle. He looked down and saw the Thai dealing with a serious hard-on. This was the life, leaning back and admiring the wonders of the East, and it wasn't long till he filled her mouth with some fine English seed. He shut his eyes and rested with Nicky's head against his shoulder and next thing he knew he was waking up with a cup of coffee next to the bed and Nicky parading a dress she'd just bought. It was bright yellow and showed off her brown skin. She showed him a pair of matching open shoes and he didn't really know what to say, telling her they were very nice. This did the trick and she seemed pleased. She laughed and skipped across the room and Harry wondered what the fuck was going on.

Last night his brain had been working overtime as he drifted in and out of sleep. He was walking into a Saigon hotel and falling down on the bed, playing a star role in *Apocalypse Now*. Then he was in *The Deer Hunter*, falling from a helicopter. From being a cocky bastard firing into ancient rainforest, he was a scared little man on his own, hated by the people he was helping to slaughter. When Harry was a kid Vietnam had been on the telly more than the war in Northern Ireland. He remembered the images – the man getting shot at point blank range and the girl running down a road, back burnt by napalm. The Vietnamese didn't count because the coverage was all about the number of American soldiers getting killed by Ho Chi Minh.

– This is my son, Nicky said, stripping off the dress and shoes and getting in bed next to Harry.

She propped a picture album on his lap.

– This is my son. He lives with the monks in a monastery outside Surat Thani in Southern Thailand. There is a school near the monastery and that is where he lives. The nuns and monks teach him.

Harry looked at the first picture. A short-haired boy of four or five stood by two cross-legged Buddhist monks. He was wearing brown shorts and a white shirt. The monks wore orange robes. It was the brightest orange he'd ever seen. Their heads were shaved in number one crops, and Nicky laughed, ran her hand over Harry's head and said their skinheads were even better. Harry said he wasn't a skinhead, but it didn't matter. He got the joke. The kid was smiling and Harry wondered if he thought about his mum. One of the monks had tattoos around his neck and on his arms, and when he asked what they meant Nicky said there was a tradition of tattooing in many Thai monasteries. The necklace was for protection and the monks did the tattoos themselves, using swords. She hoped that one day her son would come and live with her in Europe. One day in the future when she had enough money.

Nicky was sitting close with her legs drawn up to her chest.

Her tits were perfect, pressed against scar-free knees. Small but perfect. He left it alone and went back to the photos. She was keen and wanted to show them off. There were pictures of the school and the monastery. Some were slightly blurred and showed two golden Buddhas, various buildings, a collection of monks and nuns and kids, some ordinary Thais, and a forest of tightly-packed trees and big shiny plants. There were lots of photos of the boy and Harry looked sideways at Nicky's face. She seemed proud of her son and he imagined it must be hard being separated.

Harry felt like a cunt sitting there. What did she expect from him? What did she think about her son growing up in an orphanage thousands of miles away? How often did she get to see him? Thing was, you never thought about prostitutes making mistakes. He imagined they just had abortions if anything went wrong, but maybe things were different in Asia. Maybe they didn't have the same birth control and hospital treatment. He wasn't looking for answers. He wanted a good time and should skim the photos and piss off, but he couldn't brush it away. He tried to think what the rest of the boys would do. Fuck off and never think about her again. He was just like Balti. They were too fat and slow. They didn't work things out ahead of time, so hung about and got lumbered with photo albums and sob stories.

He sipped his coffee and the caffeine helped. Nicky jumped out of bed and went to skin up. She was quick and efficient, struck a match and inhaled. Harry didn't know how she did it first thing in the morning. The coffee gave him a kick because he was slow and tired, but she was jumping around and trying to slow herself down. Fuck knows what else she was on, because when he forgot about her laughter and smiles it had to be a fucking hard life. She had to have something to get her through. She came back to the bed and sucked smoke down her lungs, not caring about her nakedness as she leant over Harry and pointed him back to the photos.

– This is Marc, she said.

Harry thought he looked like any other everyday European. There was nothing to say he hung around massage parlours and go-go bars in Pettaya worrying young girls, and then ended up turning his attention to blokes. He just seemed ordinary.

– This is when we stayed at Chaweng on Ko Samui, Nicky said, running through various beaches and temples.

She looked happy in the pictures. She was wearing sunglasses and her skin was a shade darker. He pointed this out.

– In Thailand it is better to have white skin. The lighter my skin, the better I am considered by Thai people. Western men like dark-skinned girls. Europeans want to sit in the sun and turn brown, Thais want to stay indoors and become white. We both want what the other has.

Harry laughed at this because it was true. People were like that wherever you went, always wanting what the other person had but didn't value. It was the same in the old days. Dark skin in England showed you were a peasant, while pale skin belonged to the rich who didn't have to work outdoors. Things had changed, but it was interesting what Nicky said about Thailand, and he supposed it was the same in other countries as well. She was dark in the photo from her time on the beach behaving like a Westerner. Other Thais would've looked down on her skin colour, but in the photos she was happy and almost cocky, walking with the European and not caring what the small-minded cunts thought. It wasn't because he was European, but because he had money, and money was important for both the peasants and rich snobs. They fucking hated it when someone they considered below them came racing through the ranks. He thought of Mango, who'd gone for the shilling and done himself proud, but there was always going to be jealousy from those he worked with who had a massive head start yet found themselves trailing behind.

Harry respected Nicky for the photos, because her pride was obvious as she showed off her victories. Life had been a struggle, but she hadn't given up. She pointed to a picture that showed her sitting in a posh restaurant.

– This is in Bangkok, before we came to Holland.

She looked happy and sad in the photo, but was making her mark and he laughed at the light-skinned waiters forced to serve this whore and treat her with respect. Harry saw it clearly. She was coming through from a poor village, coming up from the go-go bars of Bangkok and the two-on-one massage parlours of Pettaya, walking tall after years of getting the white man's spunk drilled into her belly. Nicky was getting out on the last helicopter gunship, leaving the entrepreneurs behind to cut each other's throats. The pimps and hustlers couldn't touch her sitting in the Bangkok Continental. She was eating tom yum soup that cost more than she usually got for sucking off a dirty old slob who wanted to stick three fingers up her arse while she worked. She'd surrendered everything physical and come through the other side. He thought of Vietnam and the ability of the Viet Cong to take everything the Yanks could drop on them and still come back for more. Peasants in tiny villages brought down B52s with vintage rifles. All the high-tech killing power of the industrialised world failed. He'd seen it so many times on the television and now he was seeing it played back here. Nicky was fighting her own war and she'd survived. The restaurant was her medal.

Nicky was fighting back against the foreigners taking advantage of her poverty, but more than that against the traitors who kept her poor and sold her to the highest bidder. Harry was getting a bit emotional. There was no respect, but she had used the system to escape. He saw this but what could anyone do? Thailand was a good friend of the West because its politicians accepted the new imperialism, and while the men in suits didn't bend over personally, they were quite happy for others to do so on their behalf. Funny thing was, Harry understood what was going on, but as a kid he'd always wanted to be the gunner in one of those helicopters, the man with the machinery at his command. It was natural, really, because everyone wanted the glory and none of the mess. But you had to look on the bright side. At least she'd had the chance to work her passage out.

– Here is our home in Amsterdam, Nicky said, pointing out the rooms of a three-bedroomed flat.

She went through the apartment in detail, like she was shopping for furniture. She was house proud, but Harry wasn't interested. He had to move on and fancied something to eat. He listened but didn't hear what she was saying, and when she finished he asked if she had any food. Nicky jumped up again and put on a T-shirt. She went to the kitchen and fucked about in the fridge, coming back with some cheese and bread. He ate this and then went for a shower. He fancied a shag but Nicky was dressed now and he couldn't insist. It wasn't like he was the punter any more. He didn't know whether to leg it or go down this bar she was talking about. Harry dressed quickly and had some coffee. If he went back he'd just be hanging about with the others, so he might as well see some of Amsterdam with the girl. It didn't mean anything. She'd be off to work in a few hours and that would be that. She was skinning up again and he noticed a glass of Jack Daniels. It was eleven o'clock. He sat down and had a puff. He felt okay. He was seeing the world and wondered if they'd make it outside as Nicky came and sat next to him on the couch, coming close, fishing the rubbers out of his pocket and dropping them in his lap.

The tour boat chugs along and gives us a different view of the city. It's one of those things that's shit, but you end up doing it anyway. An hour and a half to see the sights. I've left the others behind and paid my money. Taken a chance on the hostess pointing to bricks and mortar. Telling us about Amsterdam's rich history. It's the same as taking a train is some ways. On a train you pass through the back of a city and see the place with its trousers down. There's no development-zone plastic coating. Pass through on a train and you get empty warehouses and rusted railway sidings. Terraced houses spilling into overgrown nettles. Stacked rubbish and burnt-out sheds. Derelict factories and steaming wasteland. It's the best way to travel, though I suppose this boat's not going to major on that sort of thing. But it's interesting going through the back door. Don't care what anyone says. Playing tourists.

There's a couple of stuck-up English in front talking down their noses about the Van Gogh Museum. I remember seeing the film on telly. The silly cunt wanted to be with the poor. Wanted to do something to help the peasants but his old man told him to get a career. He lived with a prostitute and cut off his ear. He was a fucking nutter who did his own thing, but now he's dead the sort of scum who made his life hell when he was alive come back and claim the glory. It's all fame and fortune and who can pay the most for his paintings.

We pass the warehouse where Anne Frank lived. The tour guide fills us in. Gently rocking on the canal. Fat tourists with cameras and travel books. On holiday, having fun. Tickling emotions. The woman tells us Anne Frank was a Jewish girl who lived in the back of the warehouse, in what they called the back annexe, for two years with her family and friends, hiding from the Gestapo. They were helped by non-Jewish friends and survived for two years. Their spirits were getting better because the Allies were starting to win the war. Then they were betrayed by a collaborator. The families were discovered and the eight people there were shipped off to the concentration camps. Otto Frank, Anne Frank's dad, was the only one to survive. Anne Frank and her sister died from typhus one week before the Germans surrendered.

I remember that film as well. It was hard to watch and made me sad. The tour guide is silent for a few seconds.

I wonder what happened to Otto Frank. What would you think after going through that? Must be millions of people alive still in the same situation. More than that, I wonder about the collaborator. The wanker who grassed them up. Out of Amsterdam's 80,000 Jews, 75,000 were killed. The tour guide says there's a statue erected to mark the spot where, in 1941, 400 Jewish men were shipped off to Mauthausen concentration camp after a Nazi sympathiser was killed following fights between members of the Jewish Resistance and the Dutch Nazi party. Didn't know the Dutch had a Nazi party. They were killed in retaliation for the Nazi's death. Following this there was a strike led by the dockers and transport workers. She says it was arranged by the communist party, illegal at the time. It lasted two days before it was broken. She says it was unusual in Holland, where people did little to protest against the treatment of Jews. An old Dutch couple tut and shake their heads. The guide says that most European countries under German rule did little to save the Jews.

I wonder what England would've done. Would people have stood up and tried to save the women and children? Can't imagine the English standing aside. We're just not like that. I know we call Spurs yids and that, but it's different. There's no real feeling because we're not religious. No, the English don't kill women and kids. We're hard, but fair.

The boat picks up speed and we move to more cheerful subjects. Snips of information are fed through the microphone. Anne Frank is forgotten as the water parts and tourists click their cameras. There's camcorders recording life. Picking up on moving boats and still buildings. Eventually the tour ends and we troop off. I see Kevin and catch him up. Tap him on the shoulder.

– Didn't see you there, he says. Were you on the boat as well? Bit boring wasn't it? Do you fancy a bevvy?

We walk for a few minutes and I sit at an outdoor table while he goes inside for a piss. When he comes back we order a couple of draught lagers.

– The only interesting thing was that girl dying one week before she was going to be free, Kevin says, emptying half the glass in one swig. Imagine being so close to freedom. They were wankers the Germans. Fucking scum of the earth. A bunch of child-molesting poofs.

Don't know about that, but no-one's going to agree with killing kids. Imagine what her old man must've felt like when he found out what had happened. It seems unreal somehow. You can't imagine that sort of thing actually happening.

– I went to Dachau, Kevin says, finishing his drink and ordering another.

He looks at my glass because it's still two-thirds full. For some reason I finish it in one go so he can't take the piss and call me a soft southern wanker. It's hot now and knocking about in Amsterdam is thirsty work. He's a big bastard and takes his shirt off. The waiter minces back and looks at the Man U crest on his arm. Takes the money and pisses off. Kevin has another swig and leans forward to continue his story. Just as he's about to fill me in on Dachau this executive-type cunt leans over and asks

Kevin to put his shirt back on because he's causing offence. He says this is a decent bar.

– Fuck off, Kevin says.

The executive is with a couple of other wankers and doesn't move, so Kevin pulls him by his collar and topples him half off the chair. He brings his fist up and holds it in front of the bloke's face.

– Fuck off bud. I'm trying to have a conversation I come in peace. Understand?

He lets go and the businessman goes inside with his chums looking shaken. Kevin finishes his beer and tells me to come on, we'll go round the corner in case the cunt calls the old bill. You never know with these Europeans, there might be a law against taking your shirt off. He says there was this time in Oslo when some of them were sitting in the park having a drink and the old bill pulled up in a van.

– They were a bunch of wankers, he says. They stood there and poured our cans away. It was illegal to drink in a public place. They even said they were being generous, because if they wanted they could put us in the cells. They're mad about their laws in Europe.

He leads the way to another bar and we go inside. We get our drinks and sit in among a mixture of office workers, labourers and one or two tourists. It's a clean bar but without the petty attitude of the last place.

– I was in Munich for the beer festival, he continues, and we got the train out to Dachau. I was expecting something like you see on the telly, something like Auschwitz with the wire and hair and glasses. All the buildings where the prisoners were kept had been knocked down and there was this big, flat space. We went to the furnaces but it was hard to imagine that people were killed in them. The thing that made the biggest impression was the museum.

He leans forward.

– There were these pictures of experiments. Altitude experiments and things like that. Outside was where these things happened, but I couldn't feel anything. Inside it was a museum and it showed you what went on. Thing was, there were all these German kids on school trips and they just looked bored. A few of them were laughing and the teachers had to tell them off. There we all were in this place where they killed political prisoners and Jews and anyone else they wanted to get rid of, and it wasn't what we'd expected. It was like we were let down. We couldn't imagine what had happened. You just couldn't get a feeling. We took the train back and that night we were on the piss surrounded by big German women singing along with this small cunt dressed in shorts and squeezing an accordion. It was as though nothing had happened. We knew it had, but it didn't feel like it. I suppose you had to be there.

Harry said goodbye to Nicky and she kissed him on the mouth. He even thought he saw a small tear in her eye as they went their separate ways. He turned his head briefly and saw her disappear down a side street, a frail little thing in among the beating neon and dead corners. She kept going and he admired her, because she'd been through a lot and was positive. It had been a good day, and he'd promised to see her on his way back from Berlin. He meant it when he said it but now, walking towards Johan's bar, he knew he was acting soft. He probably wouldn't bother. He was asking for trouble getting involved and feeling sorry for her. She was nice enough, and had a fit body, and she knew how to look after him, but she was a fucking whore, he had to remember that she was a prostitute who sucked blokes dry for the price of a four-star meal. Nothing more and nothing less, and he had to apply standards. He'd keep it quiet because he remembered the story of Rod in the Reeperbahn, when they were in Hamburg, and he didn't want everyone taking the piss out of him.

Harry turned his head for another look, but Nicky was gone, off to sit in a window for the tourists cruising the streets adding some spice to their holidays. Nicky was off to service her ten men, sucking and shagging her way to rest and recreation, an inflatable doll for a troop of drunks and dirty old men. She was a tart and he had to look after himself. He was over here to enjoy himself without any hassle and now he was getting wound up

707

about a whore. She'd done an E before leaving the flat and would be feeling good.

He could stop for a shag on his way back, but shouldn't look for anything else. He felt sorry for her when she didn't feel sorry for herself. It was the photo album. Leaving the crowd ogling the fanny and walking over to the pin-ups, then making conversation, was dangerous. You were better off in the crowd. He had to pull on a human-size condom and protect himself. Start fucking about with birds like that and it would bring you down. It was all a game and he had to think what Carter would do in the same situation, but then Carter had got himself in enough bother sniffing round that nutter Denise. They were leaving for Berlin tomorrow morning and tonight he was going to get pissed. You were better off sticking with the rest of the boys and having a good old-fashioned punch-up.

Entering the bar Harry felt like he was walking into a major convention, where the dope had been replaced by lager and the Eastern magic of a Buddhist peasant by the solid Christian realism of a select football firm. He moved through the faces – some familiar, others new – and tapped Carter on the shoulder. The sex machine turned with a drunk grin and Tom moved aside to let him through. They didn't ask any questions, which was how things should be, and Harry looked around and saw that a good mob was already forming – Tom and Mark, Billy Bright and Dave Harris, Martin Howe, Gary Davison and his mates, plus some older faces who showed up for the high-profile games, preferring European travel to domestic games. Don Wright and some of the Slough mob were there, along with small firms from Feltham, Battersea and Camberley. There was an assortment of other English picked up along the way, but it was mostly London and the Home Counties in the bar, which was fair enough, and of those it was mainly Chelsea. Harry settled down with a bottle of lager, picking up on the conversation at the table.

– It's Garry Bushell, said Billy. He was the bloke who gave Oi! a chance when he was at *Sounds*. He was the one who ignored the middle-class wankers in the music press and gave working-class punk its chance.

Harry asked Carter what they were on about, and the sex machine said they were arguing over who was the greatest ever Englishman.

– I thought he wrote a television column, Mark said.

– He does, but before that he was into music. Bands saying what nobody was allowed to say, that it was alright to be white and working class, and that it didn't make you a fascist if you carried the Union Jack. The bands were saying that because you were proud to be English didn't mean you hated blacks.

– Everyone knows that, Mark said.

– We do, but he was standing up for what normal people think against the media.

– Those cunts aren't real anyway, Harris laughed. Who cares what they think.

– But the thing was, he took stick for what he did and it was a brave thing to do.

– Maybe it was, but it doesn't make him the greatest ever Englishman, does it? Harris said. It's just because you like the music. Do us a favour. No, it's got to be someone from history. Richard the Lionheart or Oliver Cromwell. They gave the Arabs and the Irish a good slap, didn't they?

A few of the lads laughed at that one. Harris might've been going a bit over the top recently, but he still had his sense of humour intact. There was a short silence then, because suddenly nobody knew if he was serious or not. Richard the Lionheart and Cromwell were going right back.

– What about Churchill? Harry asked. He has to be one of the top boys.

– You can't have a politician, can you? Tom said. I mean, he did the job and that, but you want someone like Montgomery.

– Winston did alright, Billy said, but I know what you mean. He was safe at home when they were going through Europe. How about Bomber Harris?

A few people nodded. The stick Bomber Harris had been getting off the trendy press gave him added attraction. It always worked like that.

– What about Maggie Thatcher? She did the Falklands.

– Politician again. Anyway, look what she did to football. All the undercover operations and the all-seater grounds. No football fan can vote for Thatcher.

Harry sipped his drink and looked around. People were moving away from the conversation. It was losing its humour.

– It has to be someone with a sense of humour, he said. That's what makes the greatest Englishman.

– Charlie Chaplin?

– Too far back.

– What about Black Adder?

They thought about this one for a while. He was funny and Harry thought Rowan Atkinson was the choice. He was fucking brilliant in the First World War sketches, the way he took the piss out of the generals and everything. All those series were good, getting under the skin.

– We're not a bunch of comedians, Harris said, putting his foot down. It was Churchill, whatever Tom says. Churchill was the main man. It doesn't matter if he was a politician. He was an exception.

They didn't want to argue with Harris and he had a point. They all agreed that Churchill had been there in the country's hour of need, and that he represented all the soldiers who'd died. Harry could handle the choice, because he wanted a drink and a laugh and didn't care about titles.

To be honest, his head was a bit spaced out from the blow. He couldn't smoke a lot of the stuff, and it seemed like Amsterdam grew some strong weed. He supposed it helped Nicky get through life. There he went again, being all paranoid and making her out to be unhappy. It suited him to see her as carefree and loving her work. The ecstasy helped. He didn't know, his brain slipping in with the humour of those around him. He looked at the faces and Tom and Carter and Mark were all laughing at something. For a moment he thought it was him, that they were taking the piss, but it was something else. They were happy and the feeling spread to Harry.

The bar was a good place to be and Tom leant over and said Johan had put that film they'd told him about on again, you'd think he'd get another one the tight cunt. Harry looked through the mass of faces packed in and there, playing on the wall where

Brighty's Cross of St George hung, was some blonde bint on the go with this weedy-looking bloke. Harry didn't watch much of the film but he got the idea. He was feeling sick suddenly and got up to go outside. He struggled through the crowd and went over by the railings lining the canal. He leant over the water and saw a vague reflection, then threw up into the water. He could see the schoolkids from the ferry and he could see this kid sent from a Thai village to Sex City. Fucking hell, he should've left the dope to Nicky and stuck to the drink. It was doing his head in and he could feel the ground heaving.

– You alright? Carter asked, standing next to him.

Harry stood up, the sickness finished.

– Just felt sick, that's all. Had a hard night.

– So how come you ended up with this bird then? Carter asked. You said on the phone it was a whore you'd knobbed.

Harry wasn't going to admit he couldn't get it up. Specially not when he'd paid good money. He'd phoned Carter earlier at the hotel to check where they'd be.

– Suppose she enjoyed what she got and wanted some more. She was knocking off for the night and just fancied having a drink and a chat. She had this blow and it's done my head in. I'm fucked.

– You stayed with her all day then?

– We went out and had something to eat at a café and then a couple of beers. We went back to her place. Fucking hell, Carter, that girl gives the best blow job I've ever had. She's fucking beautiful as well.

Carter looked at Harry in a strange way.

– She's a tart though. That's her job. She's probably shagged ten thousand blokes and had ten gallons of the stuff down her throat. I hope you were careful. You know what those girls get up to.

– I know all that.

– Long as you do.

– I was careful. She said she was clean anyway, but I made sure I used a rubber. So did she. I mean, she doesn't know where I've been either, does she? It works both ways.

Carter laughed.

– You haven't been anywhere recently. No, that's a result getting a whore for nothing. Shows you stood out from the rest of the blokes standing in line. If she was good-looking, all the better. Some of those prossies are right old boilers. I was surprised there's so many ugly ones sitting in the windows all banged out and full of the clap and Aids. Suppose they get worn down before their time. Cunts like concrete.

Harry nodded, trying to imagine Nicky as some wrinkled peasant woman sitting in the jungle with an opium pipe and a handful of sticky rice, watching the patrols burn her village and kill the pigs. His head was fucked. He was sweet as a nut on his own, but this stuff was getting him confused. He had to sort himself out and told Carter he was going back to the hotel.

– See you later on, Carter said, slapping him on the shoulder. Mind how you go and leave those girls alone.

Harry laughed and headed towards the hotel, but instead of turning into the street he kept going, working his way through the clubs and bars to the street where Nicky worked. He found a doorway and stood there for an hour before sitting down in the shadows with his back against the wood. He stayed for another hour and a half. People came with roars of laughter. There was every kind of male and a lot of females just having a laugh. He saw a few pervs and a lot of drunk men in small gangs, but most were just decent citizens. They came and stared and pointed. These were the little people. Men and women who wouldn't say boo to a goose. They came and looked at the spectacle, leaving their living rooms and filling up on sleaze. They were window-shopping for memories and tales to tell their mates. A lot of them laughed and some pushed men forward.

Harry could see Nicky in her window. He counted five men who disappeared inside before reappearing after varying lengths of time. There were two drunk tourists, an older man, a business type and a couple. Strangely, he didn't think about what was happening on the other side of the curtain. He was simply counting. After five he saw the light shut off and he imagined she must've done five before he got there. For the first time he thought of the reality. He saw her taking a mouthful of spunk and tying up a succession of condoms. He saw the gel by the side of the bed next to the mouthwash and could smell the sweat of the men and the perfume of the girl. He could taste the lager on the men's breath and the sweetness of Nicky's mouth. He remembered Nicky saying how she didn't like Arabs because they always wanted to give her one up the bum and he laughed at that, because she always said no. The Thai girls got pissed off at the Arabs because they only wanted the girls up the arse. Them and the boys. Then it was all gone and it was numbers and meant nothing, the rubbers putting up a barrier and her kisses something private.

He stood up and moved down the road. He waited for Nicky to come outside. She closed the side door behind her and she was alone. Harry thought she would be because he'd been counting properly, but he wanted to see it with his own eyes. He saw Nicky hurry down the street, a jungle spirit nipping through the city, so small she passed inside the cracks. He followed her a short way, feelings of being a spy replaced by those of a bodyguard. He saw her cross the Amstel River and jump in a taxi. She was home and dry. Harry turned and aimed for the hotel, his head a little clearer now. He'd seen her alright. More than that, he'd seen her leave work on her own. For some reason that was important.

When he got back to the hotel Hank was sitting at the night desk reading a magazine. He made no attempt to hide it away and it was like Kev had said, full of big flabby mamas with big flabby tits. Hank winked and remarked that Harry hadn't been home last night. He had a flask and offered his guest a cup of coffee. Harry said no thanks and hauled himself up the stairs. He was tired but happy. Sheets had never felt better and a minute after hitting the pillow he was asleep.

More English have arrived in Amsterdam and everyone's got together in a small square on the edge of the red light district. It's getting late and things are starting to liven up. If the Dutch are going to have a go then now's the time, because tomorrow we're on our way to Germany. Word's gone round that there's a mob of Dutch by Centraal Station. They know where we are, but shouldn't leave it too late. We're in the middle of Amsterdam taking the piss and it's up to them to approach us. This isn't going to be about pimps and drug dealers, but a mixture of Ajax and other local hooligans. Probably some travelling football fans from Rotterdam, the Hague and Utrecht. Who knows and who cares where they come from. Give us a few hundred punch-bags and we'll batter the fuck out of them.

There must be at least three hundred English drinking around the square and there's a buzz going because this could be the start, the Charity Shield warm-up for the big kick-off in Berlin. Up till now it's all been nice and quiet. The Dutch have got to make an appearance otherwise they're going to look like shit. They've had snippets on the local news. The Dutch have to know there's a big English presence in Amsterdam so it's up to them to make an appearance. We're standing in the middle of the city, ready and willing, waiting for the cunts to live up to this reputation we're always hearing so much about. They've got to show sooner or later.

There's blokes from all over England mobbed up in the square. There's all the firms you'd normally expect and it's amazing what a cross-section you get. There's a new enemy and the club stuff is frozen. It's all a game. It's a game with something extra to get the adrenalin going. That's how I feel now seeing all the England together with three riot vans parked down the road. The old bill obviously know there's got to be a riot of some kind before we move on. Just depends how bad it gets and whether they can get a handle on things.

There's some Bolton lads who have been drinking all day and they go into NO SURRENDER, pissed out of their heads, and everyone else joins in. We're hanging about seeing the numbers grow as different English find out where everyone is, and though it's not hard to guess we'll be down the red light district where all the whores and bars are, they still have to find the main England mob. Now they know because you can't miss this square full of Englishmen waiting for something to happen. It's only a matter of time, because with this many men knocking about some kind of disturbance is guaranteed. In a way I'm surprised the old bill haven't moved in already and closed the bars. The bomb's packed and the detonator's ticking. We're having a drink behaving ourselves. If the Dutch come down looking for trouble then naturally enough we'll respond. Nothing more than self-defence. We're minding our own business. Keeping our noses clean. Conducting ourselves with dignity and restraint. Working hard to please our masters at home. We're doing the decent thing. Turning the other cheek. Promising we'll walk away from provocation. Making the most of the local culture. Doing our best to avoid aggravation. And when the Dutch appear at the other end of the street a massive hit of patriotism swamps everything else. The energy comes through and this is what we're here for.

We're off and running up the street towards the Dutch who are lobbing bottles and a couple of firebombs. We're all united now steaming into the battle and you know you're with some of the most dedicated here. Everything is forgotten. The drink and drugs and whores vanish. Any lingering club grudges disappear. We're England, united, we'll never be defeated. We're England and run towards the Dutch who've pulled a decent mob together and are raining bottles and bricks at us, hitting a couple of blokes who slow down with cut heads, but the rest of us keep going and the Dutch manage to stand firm and we go straight through them like a fucking rocket. They do their best but it's more or less equal numbers and we kick the fuck out of them. There's some hard cunts but they don't have a chance. They haven't got the history. We run them over the canal and do a few of the big boys brave enough to stand and proud enough to take a hiding for Holland. There's a few stragglers paying the penalty, but the main mob are back down the road.

The old bill are the ones to worry about because there's a good hundred of the cunts appearing from a couple of side streets. They're the business this lot, decked out in the height of riot control fashion, like machines off another planet with their body suits and air-force helmets. It's the same at home and probably right through Europe now, with coppers everywhere looking the same and sharing their information down the computer lines. They go for the high-tech paramilitary look these days and it's a long way from those seventies riots in Lewisham and Southall and all the other inner cities that used to burn in the summer, because in those days the coppers were defending themselves with fucking dustbin lids. That's how it should be. Coppers digging around in bins looking for scraps. Not these days. They spend a fucking fortune on the right gear and weapons. They've got everything they need to fight a war. The old bill are all over the nearest people and doing whoever they can get their hands on. They go straight towards the bars where we were drinking and start laying into the English fans still there, the tiny number who weren't interested in steaming the Dutch. Not many have stayed behind and they don't have a chance.

All that wishy-washy liberalism is forgotten by the Dutch as their police force fights back. They've had their hands tied behind their backs by faggot politicians who've flooded their country with immigrants and drugs and perverts, so when they get the chance they want to make up for lost time. A few blokes get battered, and once the old bill have finished there they start moving our way.

We're already on the move ourselves, smashing every bit of glass we can see. Wouldn't bother with this sort of vandalism normally, but for some reason it's different when England go away. Takes you back. There's Dutch tourists and workers standing back watching the spectacle and none of the English bothers them. The police come so far and then stop as the bottles rain in. We start rocking a car and turn it on its roof. A couple of youths stuff a ripped T-shirt into a Renault's petrol tank and set it alight. Everyone moves out of the way and the fucker explodes. White and red fire shatters the darkness and it starts to burn. A column of flame rises and the old bill back off as more bottles are lobbed their way. The faces in the glow are sort of mesmerised by the flames, and the same blokes start doing a Saab. We back off again and after a delay that explodes as well. The old bill don't move, using some kind of tactic they haven't told us about. There's a mob wrecking the shops and a couple of Dutch blokes get a slap for protesting, and then Harris is over by this big sex shop with vibrators and bodies in the window, and there's this scouse lad saying that the cunt who runs it was selling kiddie porn when they were looking at the merchandise earlier in the day. There's a load of England boys gathered round and they smash the windows. There's a mixture of shoppers and hiding Dutch inside and they filter out, the dodgy ones getting a kick and punch, and then the fucking owner comes out with a baseball bat.

Harris takes him out and the English pile in because the bloke's a cunt doing the paedophile stuff and he's getting done badly like he deserves. The scouser and a few other lads run in the shop and they must be after the till. The police have moved forward and we all walk back a bit further leaving the nonce on the ground unconscious in a small pool of blood. We stand there along two streets and on a bridge going over one of the canals. Brighty's flag is out on show hanging over the rails and I can see a couple of flash bulbs popping behind the old bill. A few of the lads have cameras and take their own pictures. There's another car, a Volkswagen, and we rock this over. Ten or so English sit on the upside-down car and have their photos taken against a line of coppers in the distance. It's easy this and it's a show with a mob of three hundred English standing here in the middle of Amsterdam fronting up the old bill who've got all the paramilitary gear in the world, and even they're keeping their distance.

We're singing ONE BOMBER HARRIS, THERE'S ONLY ONE BOMBER HARRIS, ONE BOMBER HARRIS as the Volkswagen explodes, singing as the cars burn bright and the flames light up the splintered glass lining the street. There's a bar with the windows done and everyone's helping themselves to bottles of spirits inside, having a drink and a laugh, and it's a mad scene and I don't understand why the old bill don't charge. There's a lot of England around so that must be the reason, but I start thinking, then look inside and there's Kev pouring drinks and a load of blokes ordering draught lager. Outside the bottles are still flying at the police. We're getting our money's worth. Nice stretch of the muscles. The riot police are behind their shields and they've got to get stuck in soon. They must be gagging for a row with the commander playing his own game. The English old bill would be straight over the space between the two sides, but maybe the Dutch are that bit more intelligent.

We're into RULE BRITANNIA and GOD SAVE THE QUEEN when Harris comes round and says we should shift, because the old bill will be closing the area off right now and we shouldn't get cocky. They're not standing there for their health. This clicks home and the Chelsea boys get together and start moving in the same direction as the Dutch mob because they're not just going to disappear. Most of the English follow. It's a stroll this one with a few windows getting kicked in as we go and the English split up gradually, smaller mobs patrolling the streets. A sort of search-and-destroy operation that happens without anything being said. The streets are smaller and darker and we've already made our mark. I look back as we leave the canal, see the burning cars and the wreckage. It's like a bomb's gone off. It's fucking brilliant and a taster for Berlin. Getting everyone in the mood. Now it's a case of working through the streets looking for the Dutch, but the area will be mobbed soon with old bill, like Harris says, so we've got to watch our step.

The riot police have started moving forward. There's dogs barking and we move further away from the lights. We've made our point. I see the riot police pass over the sex shop owner lying there in the street. They don't even look at the cunt. The coppers take back the main street. Leave him face down in his own blood, a piece of scum in the mud of no-man's land.

GATES OF THE WEST

THE TELEVISION SET in The Unity was showing video footage from Holland. There were three cars burning in the middle of the screen and a thick line of riot police dodging a hail of bottles thrown by a big group of English football fans. The film had been shot the night before and rushed to various news studios around the country. It had also been sold abroad. The camera was steady and the black silhouettes of the rioters contrasted with the vivid colours of the burning cars. The soundtrack mixed human voices, barking dogs, smashing glass and the well-chosen clichés of a disgusted reporter. There was also an alarm ringing. When a car exploded there was a loud cheer from the English.

Bill Farrell and Bob West watched the images and heard the outraged moralising of a politician demanding instant cat-o'-nine-tails retribution. National Service was mentioned. The politician's message was followed by the ecstatic self-congratulation of a social commentator. Farrell wasn't exactly impressed, but his nephew Vince had gone to football when he was younger so he knew something of what happened. West, though, was shocked and angry at the behaviour of the thugs. They were nothing more than a lawless bunch of vandals dragging the good name of England through the mud.

The barmaid Denise was talking with her husband, a local man with a reputation for extreme violence, and didn't seem too upset by the burning cars, looted shops and flying bottles. The man was known as Slaughter and was encouraging the rioters. He was telling them to 'do the old bill' and 'kill the fucking cunts', while his wife shushed him and tried to pick out the faces of people they knew. Another man, who they called

721

Rod, was moaning about how he was missing all the fun stuck at home with the wife. He wished he was over in Europe with the rest of the boys and bet they were having the time of their lives. Just to wind up Denise he said Carter would be chasing everything that moved. He'd be doing two or three girls a night down the red light, not to mention the ones he didn't have to pay for in the bars and clubs.

Slaughter laughed and Rod told him that Tom, Mark and the rest of the English would be running the Dutch mobs ragged. Rod had heard that Carter had been servicing Denise behind her husband's back and threw the red light comment in for fun, acting ignorant. Slaughter said it wouldn't just be Carter, because all the lads would be shagging and rioting right through to Berlin. Rod nodded, because he was never going to live this down. He noticed Denise making herself busy washing glasses and he was sure her cheeks were red.

West was starting to seethe, hearing the men at the bar and seeing the hooligans on the screen. Moral disgust at the disturbances swamped his own uncertainties. He was surprised at Denise. She was a nice, decent girl and he expected her to show some shock at this stain on the country's reputation. Instead she was looking for people she knew as though it was a game of I-spy.

Farrell finished his pint and said his goodbyes as the presenter shook her head sadly and bemoaned the state of the nation before moving on to the happier news that an English firm had secured a multi-million pound contract to help build a new state-of-the-art prison in the Middle East. There was a short discussion about the gallows the company was going to include, with a civil servant pointing out that this was a question of democracy rather than morality. With a dismissive laugh he said that just because the gallows were built for executions didn't mean they would necessarily be used. Anyway, it wasn't the manufacturer's responsibility what went on in another country. The report faded inconclusively and the programme continued.

Farrell put his empty glass on the bar and Denise told him to have a nice time. She was a sweet girl and said Farrell looked smart in his jacket and tie. She'd forgotten Terry and was glowing with the knowledge she only had another week behind the bar before she was off on holiday – a two-week last-minute package in Greece. Denise was looking forward to some sun, sand and sangria. Her husband and the other man smiled and nodded, and Farrell left the pub as the midday news moved to a story of bravery in the Solent, a teenager saving a young boy from drowning just off Hirst Castle. The shaky hand-held film showed a skinhead with a red rose tattoo on his arm and a surfing towel around his shoulders explaining what had happened. The youth was shivering but happy he'd saved a life, while the presenter had adopted a condescending tone in the voice-over as the event was relegated to an amusing happy ending.

With a double whisky inside him Farrell felt confident. He was glad to leave the pub and the news behind. He could see West boiling up inside and didn't know why he got so upset. Maybe he was trying to shift his own feelings of blame, clutching at the righteous citizen angle. Farrell knew West had to sink or swim by himself. There was nothing anyone could do for him in his situation. He had to sort things out himself.

Farrell was leaving West behind and going into the unknown. It was all a game with the reassuring Teacher's warming his blood and giving him courage. There was a nice breeze and he felt good about his decision. He turned right and walked towards the station, passing through shoppers and skiving children, past the amusement arcade with its napalm graphics and man-animal-machine super-heroes, on to the dirty chimes of London Underground. He heard the rattling of a train but didn't rush. He was early and too old to run for the tube. There'd be another one along soon enough. He bought his ticket and went through the barrier, down the steps to the platform. He sat on a bench and waited. The man explaining the gallows situation came into his head. It was hard to understand his logic.

I stick my head in the next compartment and Kev passes over a bottle of vodka. I have a swig and hand it back. It's cheap and tastes like shit but washes away the dryness. You have to be

723

friendly. There's eight Northerners packed in playing cards and laughing about last night – Kevin, Crewe, Bolton, three Blackburn lads and two younger boys from Birmingham. They're having a sociable drink and playing for guilders as we hurry towards Berlin and our meeting with the Hun. The train is packed with every kind of Englishman, with a few rivals naturally enough keeping their distance – Man U and Leeds, the two Bristol clubs.

– I wonder how that nonce's head is today, Kevin wonders. It was the scousers who pointed him out. I hope we got the right bloke. You never know with scousers. I fucking hate scallies.

Man U and Liverpool is another war zone and I can't imagine Burnley and Blackburn sharing the same cards. I continue along the carriage and go back to my seat, squeezing past this long-haired Arsenal man who's already been nicknamed Student because it's rumoured he did a night course in engineering. The long hair seals his fate.

We've got this old boy in the middle of our compartment. Fuck knows where he turned up from, but he must be fifty if he's a day. This bloke's glad to be travelling overseas and experiencing foreign cultures. He works on a sewage plant somewhere outside Swindon and keeps reminding us that it's only the condoms that survive. Says it gives a man like him confidence knowing the rubber he buys in the pub can stand the toughest battering. He could tell us a few stories about the married women of Swindon and the surrounding countryside. He's a tall man with bottle-top glasses. Drinks from a duty-free bottle of Gordon's. He's told us five times now that he deals in shit. That he hasn't slept since he left Swindon for Paddington. And that last night he was stuck in a carriage full of Dutch who were so fucking boring he had to take some kind of action.

He smiles and says there wasn't any room to stretch out and they were so clean-living and healthy he decided on some chemical warfare. He was silent but effective. He laughs and tells us younger lads that nothing upsets the Europeans more than being stuck in a confined space with someone who's got rotten guts. Says they hate it when the smell starts leaking out. But these health-food nutters weren't to know he dealt in shit. Yes, he deals in shit. Sixth time. We should've seen their faces when he shifted his arse and eased another one out. At first they tried to ignore his bombing runs, but fifth raid in they were struggling. Naturally they looked his way, because he was the outsider and the English are barbarians in their eyes, but he acted innocent and continued with the assault. We laugh and look at him in a different way.

Mr Shit says that a couple of minutes after he started farting the compartment was clear of foreigners. He was scorching the earth and clearing the land. The Dutch went and stood in the corridor muttering to themselves, so he shrugged his shoulders and tried to look hurt. He told this woman there must be something wrong with the bog, but winks and says that really it was the baked beans on the ferry. That beans means Heinz and the krauts wouldn't even have noticed. You'd need a vindaloo for those Germans. The woman didn't believe him, but with space to stretch out he was able to relax and take his shoes off. Still couldn't get to sleep he was that excited about seeing England play. He loves upsetting foreigners and says you have to do it the right way. Says he stopped in Amsterdam for a few hours. Just enough time to have a drink and a meal, then knob this big black girl in the red light district. He paid her well and got her to lick his arse. He deals in shit. Mark calls him a dirty cunt, half with humour and half fed up listening to the bumpkin voice. Tells him that if he does his baked beans routine in here he'll be doing a flying header off the train. Mr Shit nods and smiles back, but a few minutes later he goes into the corridor himself and starts talking with Student. Then when Student eventually blanks him he fucks off to another carriage.

– Thank fuck that cunt's gone, Mark says. He was doing my head in. I haven't come over here to spend my time listening to some mangy old fucker going on about his guts.

– I wonder how much he paid that whore to lick his arse, Harry slurs.

– You'd do it for half the price, wouldn't you? Carter says.

We all laugh and Harry tells him to fuck off. He just wondered, that's all.

I open a bottle of lager and have a drink, washing away the vodka. Look outside and watch a village flash past. Small column of Nissans and Volkswagens waiting for the train to pass. The Japanese and German industries did well out of the war. Lose against the Yanks and they'll rebuild your economy for you in return for some fast-food outlets. These decent German citizens are living well and not bothered by the contents of the carriages heading East. Not bothered by the glazed eyes of Fat Harry looking their way, getting stuck into the drink like there's no tomorrow. I look at him as he asks us to imagine a poor little prostitute having that lanky Swindon cunt standing there in his birthday suit, making her kneel down and tickle his bum. We nod, but what does he expect? That's what they do for a living. It's their role in life. Paid to service the menfolk and keep them happy. Mr Shit gets to play the big hard master for fifteen minutes. She only has to say no and keep her tongue clean.

Harry nods and moves on. Starts winding Carter up asking the sex machine why he's only got his leg over once so far. Has his big end gone or is it just the rust? Carter the rust bucket runaround clanking to a halt on the Great West Road. Carter ignores this best he can, but Harry's in one of those moods. He's pissed as a cunt and I watch Carter steer him away from sex and onto something a bit more healthy.

– Remember that time we were coming back from Bristol and the coach broke down at the services, he says. Don't know if the big end had gone, but we were stuck outside Swindon. Do you remember, fat boy?

– What were we doing in Bristol? Harry asks.

– Coming back from that Cup game against City. We were at the services and that Tottenham coach arrived and we were going to kick them off and hijack the driver.

– The time when Chelsea did that pub and you got bitten by some farmer with rabies.

Carter goes red. It must be the one. I ask Carter what happened.

– There was this pub full of City and Chelsea steamed in, Harry says. We were fighting them out in the back of the pub in a car park and this scrawny little cunt jumped on Carter and bit his arm. The bloke dug in and wouldn't let go. Must've held on for at least a minute. We thought he had rabies. He was a fucking wild man. Nobody went near the cunt after he let go. He was spitting and dribbling and walked through us. He was a fucking dangerous man. He's probably still around, in a farm-worker's cottage baying at the moon then going along to Bristol to see City play. I wouldn't want to be a Rovers fan with that loony around.

– Forget the fucking Wolf Man, Carter says. I was thinking about that Spurs coach right behind us. Remember we all piled off and queued up waiting for the yids to come and get it, but they wouldn't get off. They were sitting there shitting themselves. We wanted their transport but they wouldn't open the fucking door.

– That's right, they wouldn't get off, Harry laughs. They were dying for a piss and some bagels and then they finally get to a kosher services blessed by the rabbi and there's this mob of Chelsea in the middle of Wiltshire waiting for them, eating bacon rolls. Balti put a bottle through the back window and Martin Howe was trying to open the emergency door when the yiddo driving said enough's enough and went back on the M4.

– The best bit was these younger lads on the coach nicked all the ice-creams from the shop and the old bill turned up. The silly cunts got done for robbing lollies.

– The services usually got robbed of something, Harry says, getting all nostalgic. There used to be a lot of trouble at the motorway stops. You wouldn't get away with it now.

– You can't get away with anything today, Mark sighs.

– We always had a good time in the West Country, Carter tells Tom. There was this stampede years ago when we played Reading in the League Cup. All these Reading wankers were down the side of the ground behind their fence mouthing off and there was this steward or something fucking about with a gate.

– I remember that, Harry says. Chelsea jumped him. The gate swung open and they piled through.

– Never seen anything like it. It was the same as one of those wildlife documentaries studying buffalo on the plains of Africa. There was probably fifty Chelsea who got through the gate and the whole of the Reading side started running. It was like they were bouncing in the air. It was fucking brilliant. The Chelsea end was pissing themselves.

– It was the same at Burnley when we lost 3–0. There'd always be a crew who left the ground ten minutes from the end and tried to get in with the home fans. The old bill were busy changing positions preparing for crowd control outside and in they'd go. It was seeing so many run from so few that made you laugh.

Go back ten or so years and a mob went in the Stretford End at the end of a midweek game. The United crew down the side were going mental seeing Chelsea doing damage in the home end. We were kept in and filled the ground with WHAT'S IT LIKE TO RUN AT HOME? Shift forward through the years and Kevin could've been a kid as well in the streets around Old Trafford trying to do the cockneys, while there could even be a Reading fan on the train. None of that matters right now and the memories don't include faces, just shapes. Everyone gets lost in the crowd. Travelling through Holland and Germany we see the features and name tags. Picking up speed and getting tighter as Germany closes in.

The train was racing and they'd crossed the border into Germany an hour before, a Doctor Mengele ticket inspector coming along and sneering at the English until Mark asked him what the problem was, do you think you're Goering you German cunt, and because Mark was on his feet Mengele backed away and bottled it, then pissed off down the carriage. Harry took a long drink from his bottle of lager and laughed. Mark and Tom didn't stand for any nonsense, and it was a good job the death-camp doctor had decided to fuck off. Nobody liked people who experimented on children. The Angel of Death was a fucking nonce. Harry would've let it go with some verbal because, after all, the world was full of cunts in uniform searching for a plum position where they could unload their frustration and tell every other cunt what to do, tie them down

728

and start experimenting, sharpening the scalpel and playing God with mice and rabbits and dogs, playing Frankenstein with Jews, pikeys, queers – doing the vivisection routine with whatever came off the conveyor belt. Now they got rabbits and pigs. This week's special offer on items that nobody cared about. But Mark and Tom, they didn't fuck about and Harry could see Mengele joining the sewers cunt on the road running along next to the railway track.

Harry made his point and Tom was agreeing, forgetting his story of Chelsea and Leicester's Baby Squad to tell the boys that the world was full of wankers, and how much he hated small-minded cunts trying to tell you what to do all the time, and did they see that wanker at Harwich, the Customs cunt questioning him about his drug use? He couldn't fucking believe the bloke. Only Mark remembered and he didn't seem to care, and as far as Harry could make out it was a small incident not worth its weight, just part of the everyday routine. The old bill, ticket wardens, security guards, bouncers, all of them only obeying orders. Tom said he'd been on the verge of nutting that wanker at Customs and had to use all his self-discipline, and Harry had to admit that was a bit over the top because after all, they may have been small-minded little cunts – the world, like Tom said, was full of small-minded little cunts; in fact when you really stopped and thought about it, being a small-minded cunt had to be one of the main qualifications for getting a job in politics, the police, whatever; all you had to be was be a small-minded, petty little fucking cunt – but every cunt had a job to do. Fucking hell, how many bottles had he drunk, because he was well pissed and they were still a few hours from Berlin.

Harry sat back and listened to the others laughing and joking and enjoying the journey, Carter punching him playfully on the shoulder and saying remember that time when we played Sunderland in the League Cup semi-final, the game when Dale Jasper thought it was a basketball tournament and gave away two penalties. That was a mad night and did he remember how that copper had come up to Balti and smacked him in the bollocks with his truncheon. Stroppy little cunt hit him right in the balls and somehow Balti had done the iron nuts routine and stood there and told the wanker to come on, let's see how fucking hard you are. He never showed the pain, and it had hurt, but he wasn't giving the copper the satisfaction. Carter laughed and explained to the rest of them that this small-minded little cunt looked at this nutter in front of him who could take a truncheon in the bollocks and feel no pain, and he'd just bottled out and legged it. There was no way the old bill could deal with that. They'd nicknamed Balti Iron Bollocks for a while, but eventually he'd got a new name because of the amount of Indian he was eating.

Then Carter was telling Tom and Mark and Gary, and Billy Bright and Harris and a few others who were hanging around the door, how after the game when everything was kicking off and Chelsea were fighting the old bill and Sunderland, how Harry had walked right up to this copper and nutted him, then disappeared into the darkness. Tom said nice one and Harry could tell they were impressed, because the way Carter explained it the head butt was perfect and the copper went straight down. But it was a long time ago and Harry didn't think of those days very often, had forgotten a lot of what went on and saw himself in a different light to the person Carter was describing. Carter asked Harris if he remembered that night, and Bomber said of course he did. Sunderland had their coaches done with baseball bats back at the Bridge, the benches had come out as Chelsea went on the pitch, and then they'd had a go at the old bill outside. Harry was listening and wondered if there were any Sunderland on board and Tom must've been on the same wavelength because he was saying how funny it was being on this train with all these different clubs who Chelsea had probably done at some point over the past ten years.

Harry stood and opened the window, pulled the sheet of glass right down and lobbed his empty bottle onto the road, aiming at a shiny red Porsche with some wanker in a cravat breaking the English speed limit, credit cards to burn, the bottle just missing the Porsche and smashing on the tarmac. The driver fought for control as he veered away and back again, shitting himself and slowing down like a good little cunt. Harry laughed and his right hand trembled in a wanker sign as he pushed his head through the gap. That would teach Jurgen a lesson for taking the piss. The train pulled away from the Porsche which had decided to keep its distance, the carriages fluttering Union Jacks and Crosses of St George, the red, white and blue of the Crusaders steaming towards the German heartland with Harry Roberts feeling the rush of air against his skull and the warm beer in his blood.

Bill Farrell had been abroad once in his life, to Europe during the war. More than half a century later he was considering a second trip, this time to Australia. His nephew Vince had saved his money and gone off to see the world. He'd returned to England for a short time, but then emigrated to Australia. Now he was settled in New South Wales and had bought a small farm.

Vince had a house and a hundred acres of land. His plot was in a valley, with aboriginal rock drawings in the caves on one side, and a forest on the other. There was a billabong and rows of fast-growing Japanese trees Vince was raising and selling to farmers, who in turn used them as shade for their cattle. He also had a woman, a Sydney girl whose family went back to the prison ships sent over from Mother England. There was a small caravan under a tarpaulin cover for visitors and a garden where they grew food. When Farrell thought about it, Vince sounded like a hippy, but knew his nephew would have been upset by the term. He was a farmer pure and simple, working the land and waiting for the rains to come.

Every Saturday night Vince drove to the nearest town and had a drink. Some traditions never changed. It was a small place with wooden buildings and a population of under a thousand. It was a twenty-mile drive and the people were mostly descended from the English. There was a Chinese restaurant and a Greek shop. Vince promised his granddad he'd take him as well, the pub like something from the lager commercials, the difference being the Chelsea team photograph behind the bar. There was a pendant and another photo of Ruud Gullit and the FA Cup winners on the pitch at Wembley. Vince had flown back for the final and paid three hundred quid for a ticket. On the other side of the world there was a little outpost that would forever be Chelsea and England. He said it was a decent pub with lots of things that reminded him of home. The lad had always liked his football and Farrell flashed back to Vince as a child, excited by life and the world around him. Farrell was pleased he'd done something different, even if it meant he was a long way from his family.

Farrell had thought about going to Australia when he was young. He'd had a mate from the army who went over and wanted Farrell to go as well. It was as though Vince was doing it on his behalf. Vince knew his granddad was reluctant to accept what he saw as charity, so he'd bought the ticket and sent it over, while his mum had arranged the visa.

Farrell was weighing it all up in his head. He would sleep in the caravan and have to get used to the spiders. Vince wrote regularly and said they were big and silent, with long legs and small bodies, but most weren't poisonous. Farrell thought of Albert Moss, who'd fought in Asia and been stuck with these things for years. Farrell had lived in London all his life and was used to the hustle and bustle of ten million people arguing and treading on each other's toes. London was in his head and his memories of travelling abroad weren't good. On his return, he'd jumped back into everything English for protection. He was in two minds about Australia, unable to make a decision.

Vince had written about the Anzac Day celebrations he'd seen in Sydney. Even in the scorching heat they marched and remembered. There was a platform at the end of the parade with various dignitaries giving speeches as a small group of Aborigines stood silently on the margins, ragged men, women and kids transported to a city of shining towers and tarmac paths. The dignitaries spoke about Gallipoli and how the slaughter of Australians had helped put the country on the map. It had gained them respect in the eyes of the English. They sang God Save The Queen and Waltzing Matilda.

The country was big and Vince felt free. The sheer size of the place put things in perspective. In England everyone was on top of everyone else, and events seemed more important than they were. He'd always liked the sun and found things to do away from the endless work ethic. He'd slowed right down. At first he thought it was the heat and the slow pace of life, but after a while he realised it was the lack of pressure. At home everything was pumped up the whole time. It wasn't the people so much as the establishment urging them on. There was a constant bombardment, whether it was from the media, politicians or advertisers. Everything had to keep expanding for them to feel content. The media, politicians and advertisers eventually blurred in together until people couldn't tell the difference. There was little difference in reality, because all three were run for personal advancement. Principles didn't matter any more, though the ordinary man and woman in the street was still basically decent, trying to scratch a living against the odds. Coming back for the Cup Final, Vince was amazed by the pace of everything.

He kept on at his granddad that they'd go to the Great Barrier Reef. The old man could come for as long as his visa allowed. The Reef was fantastic, something you'd never know existed unless you dipped your head under the water. The Pacific had always seemed dangerous to Farrell. From the photos it looked like a beautiful place, but the war there had been violent and bloody. The sharks knew that a bang in the water meant food, a drowning pilot or a ship's human cargo. It made him sick thinking of hundreds of men struggling in the water thousands of miles from home. He thought of the water thick with blood as sharks pulled the men below the surface and ripped them to threads. Vince had reminded him of the time they spent in Kew Gardens after Albert's funeral, about the pictures they'd seen. Anyone could travel, you just needed the will. Farrell thought of the Pacific and how for him the name conjured up dark images.

Farrell saw the colour of the Barrier Reef. It really was fantastic in the photos. That was what a holiday was about and he was lucky to have the chance, but it could only ever be a holiday. He was English and his home was in London. Vince had gone away, but he was the exception. The boy had the spark to do something different with his life. Not that Farrell was complaining. Everyone did their own thing and he'd been blessed. His wife was a fantastic woman. She was the only woman he'd ever loved and even though she'd been gone all these years, there wasn't a day went by when he didn't think about her. She'd never wanted to go back to Hungary. She hated the place and became more English than her husband in some ways. Like a lot of refugees who settled in England after the war, she adopted the country without reservations. She saw things differently to the cynics. What she went through was terrible, yet she survived with so much strength she'd put him to shame.

Farrell was on the platform waiting for his train to pull in. It was the middle of the day and quiet. He heard a couple of Australian voices and thought of Vince again, except this time he imagined that Anzac Day parade. The temperature was way up and the marchers kept in time along the road, their collars done up and shirts smart. They were sweating, but despite their English skin they'd lived with the climate all their lives and adapted. Australia was their country, yet they had a sense of belonging to England. They couldn't shake it off. Farrell laughed at how the Aussies called the English poms, Prisoners of Mother England. That's what he was, a Prisoner of Mother England. He nodded his head and smiled.

The tube arrived and Farrell found a seat. There was an American couple at the other end of the carriage with three suitcases, travelling up from Heathrow to see Big Ben and the Tower of London. Farrell imagined the man as a young boy in the Philippines. Maybe he'd been one of the Marines taking Manila or under the ridge at Iwo Jima, held down by Japanese guns. The Yanks had suffered at Utah beach during the D-Day landings and had a worse time of things than the British and Canadians at Sword, Juno and Gold, which had been bad enough. That bloke at the end of the carriage would've been making the most of London in the forties, hanging around Piccadilly where the prostitutes helped themselves to the GI pay-packets. But there were plenty of other girls interested and Soho offered a lot of life. Funny how everything went around, but when he looked more closely the man wasn't old enough for the war.

The tube started moving and Farrell forgot the tourists. He looked at the black and brown faces around him reflecting the Commonwealth troops who'd fought and died for Britain. He felt that the Commonwealth had been sold out as multinationals pushed for European union. If some of these kids today saw the troops gathered in the south of England for the D-Day invasion they'd be surprised. When they saw a Polish name did they understand what had happened in Poland, how the Free Poles had fought and died? Did they know Bomber Command was forty per cent non-British? In his own lifetime he'd seen history rewritten so many times. They didn't even have the decency to wait till you were dead.

It was a line of thought Farrell couldn't resist, because sitting in The Unity he'd heard one of the men at the bar laughing about the newsflash from Holland, saying how the English would be marching back into Berlin again. That they'd be taking it for a second time and rubbing salt in the wound. Farrell was amazed this man didn't know it was the Red Army who'd captured Berlin. It was incredible they didn't get taught these things in school. It wasn't that long ago either. Not really.

Of course, the Allies went in later, but it was the Russians who fought their way through the city, street by street, with the loss of 100,000 men. Not that it was solely men, because women fought with the Soviets and it was a woman who'd lifted the flag over the Reich Chancellory. It made him smile when pop shows talked about girl power. Was that all it had become? Maybe it was part of Hitler's downfall, because Stalin had his women working next to the men and fighting for victory, while Hitler saw women as there to mother children and build a super-race.

Farrell had met some Russian soldiers in Germany. They couldn't really talk, of course, but they'd toasted each other. They were allies. The Germans and Russians called each other fascists and communists, but in England it was different. When Stalin and Hitler fell out after the invasion of Poland, and when Hitler went on to attack the Soviet Union, the people in London had looked to the Russians and admired their bravery. This comradeship had been promoted by the Government. It would be hard for people raised in the post-war years to believe, but Stalin was Uncle Joe and the Russians brave allies much admired by ordinary English people. Politics didn't come into it. The Russians were allies and their resistance gave Farrell and the people around him hope. Many people forgot this under a post-war propaganda offensive, while Stalin closed up shop and tried to crush the people of Eastern Europe.

When Vince was a child Farrell had played soldiers with him. He only did it when his wife wasn't around, because it seemed wrong. But he played because boys were interested in these things, and the Action Men were either English, American or German. He didn't remember any Russian uniforms. But the kids today, their soldiers were different. The enemy was distant and imaginary and the weapons more complicated. Animals and machines merged with men. Now the boys preferred Power Rangers to Action Man. He supposed it was a good thing, but imagined they'd learn little about, and from, the Second World War. His own uncles, men he admired as a young boy, were already lost in the distant past. If the memories faded so quickly, why had they bothered? He knew the answer, but it was always a battle, and one many people his age lost. People's moods swung this way and that. For years after the war the Russians had been promoted as cruel tyrants who wanted to turn England into a dour communist slave state, while now they were confused criminals and drunks who craved Western-style democracy.

Farrell's memory was clear as the train rolled along. The Russians had suffered like nobody else. Twenty million had died. When the Germans attacked it was a blitzkreig, but the Russians destroyed everything as they retreated. Farrell knew what the Germans were capable of, having seen a concentration camp first hand. During the war five million Soviet soldiers were taken prisoner, but less than two million survived. That left over three million who had died. The Germans treated the Russians like scum and it was no surprise that a couple of years later, following the seige of Leningrad, when the Russians had recovered and were ready to attack, they wanted to wipe the Germans off the face of the earth. The soldiers who survived would never forget and would pass the hatred on. It was the same on both sides.

Bill Farrell was on his way to a meeting of old soldiers. He didn't usually go in for this sort of thing. He had never been that interested in ceremonies and reunions, but today he was sitting on the tube with a clear head. It didn't seem to matter now. Before, when his wife had been alive, it was enough to live with her and enjoy their time together. His own experiences were insignificant after what she'd been through. He never thought too hard about this, but following her death he'd started trawling through the past. The more time passed the more he went back. He didn't see anything glorious in the war. He tried to forget but it was impossible. Fifty-five million people had died in the Second World War. Whenever a politician came on the television screen and said the old days were less violent he knew they were insane. It was like the newsflash about the football. Three cars exploded and these reporters were describing it as a war zone. It really was ridiculous and Bob West shouldn't have got upset. There was no perspective, just sensationalism and hypocrisy.

Farrell's sip of whisky had put him in a positive frame of mind but had loosened his self-control. He looked at the other passengers and wondered how many knew what things had been like, how many even guessed or cared. Even now, all these years after the war had ended, everyday life could seem very trivial. He tried not to think this, but it was inevitable really. It had been much worse after he'd returned from Europe, but he'd fought back and won the mental battle. When Farrell watched these idiots on the television and read their editorials in the papers he couldn't take them seriously. The war had made him immune. It was a strength, he thought, as his stop arrived.

—After the landing we started moving forward. Once we were on shore and off the beach, we had to consolidate our positions and begin fighting our way out of the bridgehead. We did this, but it was a slow, bitter advance. Neither side was going to give up. I don't believe in the all-comrades-under-the-uniform view because the Germans caused a great deal of pain and were

737

killers, but they were brave men. The same is true of the Russians, British, Poles, Canadians and Americans. In fact, anyone you care to mention. We all believed in what we were doing and fought to the death. Once we were through the initial defences things changed. It was the expectation and build-up to the landing that was hard to handle, but once we were through that and had killed it was different. It's a hard thing to admit but we had more confidence. We were closer with our mates and we were harder now than the Germans. We were going to win. We were afraid we'd die when we were in the landing crafts because we had too much time to think, but now we believed we were going to come through the fighting. The idea that an Englishman couldn't be beaten was built into us from an early age, and when the killing started we found this belief made us tough enough for the job. We had this confidence, which when the waiting was over made us strong. We had the determination to win and went forward. The Germans would fight us all the way and there was a lot of killing. It was terrible seeing the bodies, and Billy Walsh and the soldier with his head blown off were right there in our heads. We didn't think we could see worse. Death became common. The Mulberrys did their job and troops and tanks were pouring into France. The countryside was tight with hedges so we had to move slowly. It was all very much within our group and our space. The speeches of Monty were nice but didn't really mean anything. We saw what was in front of us and watched each other's backs. Mangler was nearby and a bloke from Bolton called Charlie Williams. He was a smiling lad with red hair who'd worked in a textile factory before the war. He was married with a baby and carried a picture of his wife and son in his wallet. Billy Walsh was dead, but this North London lad Tiny Dodds was a good mate and of course Jeff Morrison from Hounslow. We were on the move now, getting stronger all the time. We knew each other from training and the camps, but now there was a stronger feeling. We needed the unity as we faced the enemy. You never have friends in quite the same way because all the little prejudices and stereotypes vanish and it's basic survival. There's a link with men who've lived the same life, something that goes unsaid and lasts through the years. It doesn't matter how old you are, it never fades.

Harry kicks my trainers as he goes for a piss, slamming the compartment door open and stumbling into the corridor. Surprised he didn't break the glass. Stops to say sorry then fucks off. Born in a barn that cunt. There's some English singing CAN I TELL YOU THE STORY OF A POOR BOY. Must be scousers. Their history goes back to the Boer War and the Battle of Spion Kop, the old Anfield terrace named in memory of the men who died there. Wonder what Kev makes of it. Quietly impressed because it was Englishmen fighting for England. Mark leans over and pulls the door shut, turning down the volume. He gives me a fresh bottle. Hands lager to Harris, Billy and Carter. Gary Davison and Martin Howe are looking down the corridor, talking to some other English. The train keeps moving. The lager's getting warmer, but it's still cold enough to drink. Passing the time.

Chelsea and England go together. We've always supplied a good chunk of the England away support. We fly the flag no matter how many foreigners the club pulls in. It changes nothing, because we're the ones paying their wages. The Europeans work for us. We pay for their expensive apartments and designer gear. You need the class foreigners, but English football doesn't get the credit it deserves. In Rome it was another story, the English pulling together a big mob in a dangerous city. England will always do the Italians. It's been going on for years. It's in the blood.

Germany is a blur through the window with none of us taking much notice of the towns, villages and countryside. I sit back listening to Harris talking about Berlin and the Germans. I lean my head on the rest. It's a great feeling being on the move with something to look forward to at the end of the journey. That trouble in Amsterdam firmed up the travelling English. People talk about the trouble and that, but it's the whole thing that makes following England worthwhile. Going overseas is another step on from club football. It's more exciting, especially these days with the cameras and everything.

It feels like my eyes have just closed when I bang forward. At first I think it's Harry back from the bog, but then I see him in the far corner. The others are looking around and I realise the train isn't moving. Harris is up and opening the door, looking for a reason for the delay. We go into the corridor and someone says the emergency chord has been pulled. Mengele's coming along with a couple of SS guards, and he has to squeeze through the English. He's a lot more polite now and doesn't look Mark in the eye, but he's got the same attitude. Cunt in a uniform who thinks he's the fucking business. We want to know what's happening, stopping in the middle of nowhere. Maybe the train's been set on fire by juvenile delinquents, or the engine blown apart by that dirty old Swindon geezer. Can't see him anywhere. Gary leans through the window and starts laughing. We try to get a view of what's happening. The Hooligan Express is at a standstill and if he's not careful Mengele's going to have to deal with several hundred unhappy customers. The least these German cunts can do is make sure the fucking trains run on time.

Then we see this figure running from the train. Someone says it's a scouser bunking the fare, but Gary says no, he's a Geordie. A northern voice says it's a cockney. Could be anyone, but the youth is young and fit and heading for some nearby woods. He's got a head start on the guards trying to keep up. Big fat krauts tempting a heart attack. The English start cheering and banging on the side of the train, and the bloke keeps running, increasing his lead over the Gestapo. Something's gone wrong. Bunking the train without a passport. Fuck knows. But he's getting nearer the trees and finally turns and raises his fist towards the train, gives the guards a wanker sign, then disappears into the woods. When the Germans get there they lean forward with their hands on their knees, knackered. They peer into the trees, shrug their shoulders and walk back to the train, the English packing the corridors, hanging out of the windows and putting their hands around their eyes in imitation RAF goggles, humming the tune from *Dam Busters*. Don't know if the Germans understand, but they must know we're taking the piss. They don't look happy.

After a short delay the train starts moving again and we settle down. Don't know where the bloke's gone, but it shouldn't be too hard for him to find his way to Berlin. Mind you, stuck in the German countryside, who knows. Bailing out behind enemy lines. I suppose we'll find him in a Berlin bar sooner or later, and if he's smart he'll live off the story for the rest of the trip. Everyone has a story to tell. The train picks up speed and we have another drink.

Bill Farrell stood outside Sloane Square tube waiting for the traffic lights to change colour. He was in another world now, surrounded by expensive shops and wealthy people. The faces were different from those of working-class London. They were tanned and manicured, and even the features seemed different. He smiled at all these stern men and women who'd probably never done a hard day's graft in their lives. There was nothing new under the sun, and the English squaddie wasn't looking for a revolution after the war, just something better. Demobbed soldiers wanted work and a future, and he couldn't remember any of his mates being interested in party politics or ideology.

The northern lads were different because they had a strong union and industrial tradition, though a lot of East Londoners knew all about Jack Dash and the London dockers. Ulster had its own thing going on, but London and the South were different again. He'd never known any Northerners before the war threw everyone together, and they were good people like anyone else, a long way from the stereotypes. They had their own view of Londoners as well. They thought Londoners were all cockney wide boys and flash harrys, spivs and cosh boys with a soft belly. Cheeky chappies, barrow boys and racetrack wheeler-dealers. But the barriers were ripped down during the war and they'd all got on fine. The same went for the Welsh and Scots, while Farrell had never realised there were so many Catholics fighting for England in the Irish Guards. It was a mixed up world where nothing was ever what it seemed. And anyone who had trouble adapting soon sorted themselves out when the bullets started to fly.

People wanted something better after VE Day and Churchill

wasn't re-elected despite his role as a wartime leader. They were looking for peace and stability and social change. The soldiers had self-respect and wanted the understanding of those at home. Beveridge made his famous report and if the country got anything out of the Second World War it had been a welfare state. As a young man fighting in Europe, Farrell wanted the things that had been denied his uncles. He knew how they felt about the war and its aftermath, and had expected better. At least Farrell's generation got the NHS and a welfare system, but it had suffered badly under the Tories, while New Labour saw socialism as a dirty word. Farrell tried not to get angry, but it was unbelievable. Even during the war there'd been a few strikes, and Churchill had respected Bevin enough to give him a role in the cabinet. People seemed to have no long-term memory of where their benefits began. Either they forgot or reinvented the past to fit in with what they were told. The young ones weren't even told.

When the lights changed he crossed and started down the King's Road. He was on his way to a TA meeting in the Duke of York's HQ. He'd joined the Territorials after the war, when it had consisted of old soldiers, and had made some good friends. He'd lost track of them, just like the boys he'd actually fought with in Europe, those that survived, but had met up with Ted at Johnny Bates's funeral and been persuaded to come along today. It was just a chat and a drink and a cheap meal. Farrell had never gone in for these things, but Ted was enthusiastic and he didn't see why not. With his wife dead maybe it was time to look back and find some comradeship. It was something he'd only get from a shared experience. She'd always wanted him to go along and show off his medals at the Cenotaph because she'd been proud of him, but it had seemed pointless somehow. He was a man and she was a woman, and she'd been raped and brutalised by the scum of Europe while he'd killed German boys like himself who had no choice whether they fought. He wanted to forget, but you could never forget. At least he didn't want to forget the reality. Anyway, the bar was subsidised and he'd have a laugh with some of his old mates.

Farrell passed the gates of the Duke of York's HQ and found the pub they were meeting in beforehand. He took a deep breath and went inside. It was one o'clock and fairly busy, but Ted said they'd meet on the left as he went in and Farrell spotted him straight away. He was sitting with Eddie Wicks and Barry James They jumped up and pumped his hand and almost fell over themselves offering to buy him a pint. Farrell was embarrassed by the attention, but Ted was already doing the honours so he sat at the table in the corner with the others. He'd seen Eddie and Barry at Johnny Bates's cremation and they'd exchanged a few words, but it had been very brief. Now the circumstances were different and it was okay to show some pleasure at meeting again They were good lads and Ted put a pint of London Pride in front of Farrell. Eddie had been a corporal in the Paras and had jumped at Arnhem and swum the Rhine to escape capture. The Germans fired at him as he went but Eddie made it to safety and went back to fight again. He'd also been at Dunkirk and was a big man with a handlebar moustache who immediately took control. He got the others to raise their glasses and drink to Johnny Bates.

– You came along then, Billy boy, Ted said, slapping Farrell on the back after he'd tasted the Pride We wondered if you'd make it. Not that we doubted your word, but things crop up when you get older.

– I'm glad you came, Barry said These things are much less formal than you'd think. The bar's subsidised and the food's good. A fiver for as much as you can eat NAAFI conditions, but there's chicken curry today.

Farrell had another sip of the Pride and savoured the taste. The pub wasn't as professional as The Unity, but that was often the case with high-street boozers Those pubs tucked down back streets had to satisfy the locals while pubs like this could pull in enough passers-by to keep ticking over no matter what. Not that Farrell was complaining, because he liked a pint of London Pride. Chiswick was another decent West London beer. The whisky had got him through the journey and now he was sitting in this pub he had no second thoughts. Eddie was 'a big character and they'd had a good few sessions when they were in the TA. Eddie and Farrell had both fought in Europe, while Barry had been a merchant seaman and Ted had served in North Africa. They all had their stories but never said much. There were things that filtered through as the years passed so it was possible to build a picture. When they'd been in the TA and drinking they tended to open up and tell individual stories. Afterwards life continued as normal.

– Not a bad pint for Chelsea, Eddie said. You pay extra, but it can't be helped. Have to keep the blood flowing.

Eddie had done well after the war. He'd stayed in the army before eventually leaving and running a pub. He'd served in Palestine and seen members of his regiment killed by the Jewish resistance, which had turned him against Israel. He knew Mrs Farrell's history, but separated Judaism and Zionism. Eddie was a strong royalist and felt England had been betrayed, that socialism had eaten away at the backbone of the country. Bill and Eddie had different views and once, when they were young and drunk, had even come to blows. But it was in the past, and time and old age had blurred the edges of Eddie's resentment. Like a lot of people, though, he felt let down.

Eddie had run a drinker's pub in Brentford and done okay. He could always handle himself and wasn't someone to muck about. He'd pulled in a lot of the local hardcases, and they liked a pint or ten. Civvy street had treated him well and he had five sons, all of them following in his footsteps. He was big on army tradition and loved the comradeship. He was a good man, and in some ways a pussy cat. Farrell remembered the time he'd taken his wife to Eddie's pub and she'd been treated like a queen. He used to talk rubbish sometimes when he was pissed, but it was just talk. Eddie respected Bill and his views and the fact that he'd married a woman from a concentration camp and helped her recover. Eddie's right-wing sympathies didn't extend to genocide. Farrell was a hard man, in some ways harder than Eddie, but he had a softer shell. Eddie was the reverse. Farrell had put Eddie on his arse when they argued all those years ago, and Eddie had got up and done the same to Farrell. He was a soldier to the bone and respected a good fighter. Add Farrell's dignity and convictions and he considered the man a class apart.

– Look at the arse on that, Ted said, indicating a well-dressed executive-type woman at the bar.

– She's too old for you, Eddie laughed. She must be all of forty-five.

– Do you think she's that old? Ted asked. Oh well, not to worry. She's still young enough to be my daughter.

– You want something nearer your own age, Bill remarked.

– You must be joking, Ted said. What do I want with a horrible old granny. All dried up and wrinkled with soggy gums. Give me a youngster any day. A nice forty-five-year-old will do me fine. Look at those legs and arse. She can sit on my lap and rustle up some life any time she wants.

– She'd have to work hard to get any life out of you, Eddie said.

Ted was a confirmed bachelor. He'd never married and always been one for the women. Farrell remembered him as a young man with slicked back hair and more than his share of charm. He'd served in North Africa with the Western Desert Force and fought Rommel and the Afrika Korps. Before that he'd been one of the 30,000 who took 200,000 Italians prisoner. He'd been under the command of O'Connor and later Montgomery, and been involved in Operation Lightfoot and the battle at El Alamein. Farrell recalled how much Tobruk and El Alamein had raised his and the country's spirits.

Ted preferred talking about the time he'd spent on leave in Cairo than the dysentery, flies and bully beef of the desert. The fighting had been bloody when the British finally pushed Rommel back. He always said victory in war owed more to nature than strategy. England had survived because of the Channel, the Russians had defeated the Germans because their winters were so harsh, while the victory at El Alamein owed a massive debt to the Qattara Depression. The salt marshes and quicksand of the Depression had prevented the Germans using the usual desert tactic of outflanking the enemy. His favourite line about the desert was that both the English and Germans sung along to Lili Marlene. They were fighting and killing each other, but both sides fancied the woman in the lamplight. It was odd, but proved music had always crossed borders. At least they'd had their leave in Cairo, and those Egyptian girls were special. The English didn't appreciate the fine features of Arab women.

– I can still get it up, don't you worry about that, Ted said. She could do worse than come and sit on my knee. There's life in the old codger yet. There's nothing better than a fine pair of stockings and she's wearing some sheer heaven.

– Calm down, Eddie laughed. You'll give yourself a stroke.

– I'm younger than I look, Ted replied, indignantly. When I got to sixty-five I started going backwards. I'm getting younger year by year. I've turned time on its head. It's the after effects of serving in the desert and spending your time with Egyptian girls.

– You might be getting younger, but I'm feeling the years, Barry said, moaning. If the desert made you younger then the sea aged me. It's my foot giving me gip.

– You've got a bad foot because you were pissed and fell off the pavement, Eddie pointed out. You never could drink. Four pints and you're falling down in the street.

Farrell thought of Bob West soaring over the Iraqi desert. Ted had told him there was no place to hide in the desert. Air superiority was vital because any movement stirred up clouds of dust and gave the game away. Nothing could move on the ground that wasn't seen in the air. The same would've happened in the Gulf, though West had also attacked cities. They said the war in North Africa was the last war where chivalry survived and maybe it was true to a certain extent, but Ted insisted it was brutal. It was always brutal, whether there were rules or not. There was no such thing as humane killing. In the Gulf the scale had been massive and West was paying the penalty. Farrell would rather have died in the desert than at sea.

Even though Barry had been a merchant seaman, Farrell wouldn't have wanted his job for anything in the world. Barry had helped keep England alive sailing back and forward across the Atlantic bringing food and supplies from North America. Crossing the Channel for the invasion had been bad enough, but to be torpedoed in the ice-cold mountains of the Atlantic would've been terrible. Barry had been sunk twice during the war. He hated Doenitz and his Wolf Pack U-boat crews. The second time he'd been sunk a U-boat had come up close and the sailors had laughed at the English in their lifeboat hundreds of miles from land. They just laughed and left them to die.

Farrell remembered Barry telling him about the U-boat, more than thirty years ago in a pub in Salisbury when they were away training with the TA. He'd got really angry about it, but Farrell understood. To be left to die was bad enough, but the Germans laughing made it worse somehow. Barry could never forgive that. It was personal. The U-boats' silhouettes were low and the hunters killed tens of thousands of merchant seamen. Without the merchant navy the country would have starved. Barry was an unsung hero in many ways, but Bill, Eddie and Ted recognised his value. He was a good man, but liked a moan, which when you'd been sunk once and then gone back for more, then been sunk again and still returned, was maybe something to which you were entitled.

– I'd had five pints when I went off the kerb, Barry insisted. I can still manage six.

– No you can't, Eddie roared. What do you think, Bill?

Farrell was thinking of the U-boats and how it had taken the idiots in Whitehall time to sort out a common policy to deal with the problem. He wondered how many seamen had died because the RAF and navy commanders were playing games with each other. These things were brushed away and you ended up convincing yourself they didn't matter, because otherwise you'd go mad with the injustice of it all. Nobody else cared, so why should an old man at the end of his life? It was something Farrell could never mention to Barry because, especially in his case, maybe it really was better to forget.

– What's that? Bill asked.

– Wake up boy, Eddie said. You've only just got here and you're nodding off. I was asking how many pints you think Barry can drink before he falls down drunk in the street.

– Five or six, Bill ventured. Four's enough for me these days.

– You're having more than that today, Eddie insisted. You're out of practice, that's all. You're a soldier and you'll do better than four bloody pints today, mate. You can't let the squad down.

Bill smiled. Eddie hadn't changed a bit and his light-hearted bully boy routine never failed. Eddie would always be the corporal and take charge. He pointed you in the right direction and made sure you didn't stray. There was no time to feel sorry for yourself when this man was sitting there with a pint in his hand. They were all in their seventies and Eddie was still doing the I-can-drink-more-than-you routine. Thing was, he knew he was doing it and loved winding Barry up, because the old sea dog took life too seriously. Eddie was acting like a young man because behind the wrinkles that's what he was.

Bill nodded and knew he was on for a session. He didn't mind. It would do him good to get pissed and forget the cost for once. Even though he hadn't served with these blokes during the war he felt a strong bond he couldn't get from someone who'd never been involved. He felt no link with Bob West, despite the fact that he'd met Spitfire pilots and Lancaster crew men in the past and felt a connection. They'd flown nailed-together buckets, while West was part of a minimal-risk machine. He'd told Farrell about the controllers urging him on, telling him to kill the Iraqis. Farrell remembered the song the RAF sang in the Second World War – 'the controller said how can you miss them, and I heed you to guess what I said, bring back, bring back, oh bring back my bomber and me, and me, bring back, bring back, bring back my bomber and me'. Farrell hummed it in his head. Same old story. And Eddie still drank more than his fair share.

– We've got to make the most of these pint glasses while we can, Eddie said, snorting now. Before you know it those wankers in Brussels will be replacing them with some metric rubbish. Then you'll end up with even less for your money.

– It makes you sick what they're doing, Barry moaned. They're giving England up without a fight. Put one of those politicians in the front line and they'd run a mile before the shooting starts.

– Nobody wants this Union, Eddie said, warming up. The German banks want to control Europe but the people themselves don't care. Even the French don't want to be part of the Union while the Scandinavians are showing some national pride for once. If every country admitted to their patriotism we wouldn't have to worry. They want to crush our identity. They couldn't do it during the war.

– It's the right-wing businessmen, Barry said.

– It's the fucking communists and socialists, Eddie insisted. They can't stand us having an identity. All through the seventies they were trying to run down the economy, the unions going on strike over nothing. The Russians always had their eye on England. They knew that if they could get in and subvert us they could take over Europe. It's the Bolshevik plan. International communism.

Farrell doubted the Soviets had been that concerned with England. They had other problems and were busy crushing their own people, but it was true that the atmosphere in England had been very heavy during the seventies. That was how Thatcher managed to get a foothold. She'd promised the good old days and the chance for working people to better themselves, but at the same time had sold them short. She adopted policies which owed everything to rampant capitalism and nothing to the more casual, traditional approach. Farrell believed in a mixed economy. The Tories had set out to dismantle everything and sell it off to the highest bidder, thinking short term. He let Eddie go on, because although they disagreed on certain things, it was only talk. At least they both recognised the dangers of the EU.

The end feeling was the same, and while he agreed with Eddie that there was an attempt to eradicate individual cultures and replace them with a bland shopping-mall-type society, he felt the biggest danger was the centralising of power. At the moment unelected bureaucrats were easing themselves into well-paid positions of power with smooth-talking liberal policies, but if the structure was in place that allowed this to happen then what was to stop the extreme right taking advantage? But he wasn't going to get drawn into the argument. He had his views and that was enough.

– The best sex I ever had was with a Japanese woman, Ted pointed out, blocking Eddie's rant. I was sixty at the time and I met her at the car showroom. She was under fifty and well preserved. Bloody brilliant it was. I wonder what happened to her?

Eddie stopped and looked at the Desert Rat.

– Great, isn't it? he said, laughing. Ted never changes. You try and get the boy thinking about how England is being destroyed from within and he's rambling on about a Jap he had sex with a thousand years ago. He'll die with a hard-on. There's too many people thinking about women and having fun when they should be thinking about England. Come on Ted, it's your round.

– You're the only one who's finished.

– Well hurry up then. We've still got time.

– Alright, Eddie. I don't know how you managed five children the amount you drink. You must have been pissed the whole time.

Eddie frowned, wondering if Ted was taking the piss.

– Every one's a winner.

– They're good kids, Ted said. You did well there, Eddie.

Farrell liked Ted. He was a decent man and had always been a sharp dresser. Farrell could see why women fell for his charm. He was like Leslie Phillips or Terry Thomas, but without the accent. He'd made money selling cars right after the war before running through a variety of vague jobs, eventually returning to cars. It was money in his pocket, but his big love was music. He loved jazz and spent his cash at Ronnie Scott's and various other London clubs. He'd knocked around Eel Pie Island in the old days with Eddie. He could name all the jazz masters and knew a lot of London musicians. Alexis Korner was someone he admired. Ted was a smooth talker. He was wearing well and didn't want any problems. He had no interest in politics. He said the sun in North Africa had burnt all that out of him. It was a time and a place and he'd answer any question thrown at him about Monty and Rommel. He lived in Shepherd's Bush now and had developed an interest in pool. He played regularly in his local and earnt a few pounds extra from the kids hanging around the tables. Ted knew how to handle Eddie.

– Come on, Eddie. Let's get going. We're paying too much

in here. We should be drinking cheaply, at the army's expense. They'll serve a better pint in the club.

Eddie nodded and the others saw their chance and drank up. You couldn't argue with reasoning like that. Ted had a point. The army would do the business.

Everything's quiet now, heading east, the youth in the woods forgotten. Probably flagging down a tractor at this very moment. I see these blokes from Blackburn pass and go back a few years to the time we had a go at this club up there. We were travelling by train and after a brief row by the station the old bill made sure we got on the service back to London. Thing was, the train stopped ten minutes later, so we jumped off, had a drink, and caught another one straight back. It was easy enough to filter off and mob up in this pub. A shitty boozer with ten or so brain-dead punters dribbling into their bitter. They soon fucked off. The landlord didn't care if he was serving cockneys or Pakis, because this was pay day and he wasn't about to phone the old bill and complain about the tenners filling his till. He didn't give a fuck and we drank in peace and quiet, then headed to this club Harris knew about. There were fifty of us and it was early for a club, but we knew there'd be some chaps there as this was supposed to be where this particular firm drank.

We didn't bother paying. Facelift took out one bouncer, and a combination of Harris and Black John did the other. The rest of the lads smashed the big glass windows, nodded to the girl taking money, asking how much for a blow job love, and we were straight down the corridor and onto the dancefloor. We slapped anyone who didn't shift and it didn't take long for Blackburn to sort themselves out. It was a disco with fairy lights, but was playing the same fire-alarm techno all these places run on. Don't imagine there was much ecstasy in this place though. These Blackburn were game enough and it was more or less equal numbers. Thing was, we didn't want to stay too late because we still had a train to catch and we were making the most of our surprise visit. Harris checked his watch and was running things like it was a commando raid. Don't think they could believe their eyes. They've relaxed and kicked back, and suddenly there's a Chelsea mob in their front garden. We had to work fast and get back to the station for the London service.

It was fucking great because the drumbeats kept going and the lights continued flashing, and after working through the nearest blokes and announcing our presence we went into the bar where all these fat cunts were getting pissed. They were worse off than Chelsea and though they gave it a go they didn't have a chance. We'd kept our heads and were acting sober. Turned over the bar, robbed the till, and Harris even let off some tear gas as we made our withdrawal. It was a clean operation and looked like a good result, but things don't always run to plan. When we went back to the station there was a pub full of locals and the snotty-nosed kids begging crisps outside filled them in. The drinkers inside piled out and there was this battle through to the station. There were a few black eyes and cuts on the platform, but nothing too serious, because this was Saturday night on the piss and just like any other Saturday night punch-up. The old bill had turned up by now and everything quietened down as BR pulled in and took us home in comfort.

Every club tells a story. Like that time at Southampton before the grounds were all-seater. There were nine or ten nutters who went in the Southampton end and just piled in five minutes before kick-off. Knew they were going to get battered but didn't give a fuck. Went in the home end, stood nice and quiet, then bang. Just went mental. Now those blokes were hard as nails, and it's always stuck in my mind. Never knew who they were, but that's Casualty behaviour. Knowing you're going to get done. Zero life expectancy. Southampton were nothing special, but doing something like that right against the odds shows how serious some blokes can be. It takes a lot of courage. The old bill waded in and these Chelsea boys trotted back down the middle of the pitch to a standing ovation from the four thousand Chelsea at the opposite end.

Back in the sixties and seventies the main aim was to take the home end, but it died out in the eighties with better policing and the nineties has seen the whole thing shift again. Those blokes were left to jog down the middle of the pitch whereas today they'd be filmed and indexed and banged up for six months. Every paper in the country would run their pictures and every wanker with a column or slot on the telly would be coining it on their behalf. We were young hooligans singing LOYAL SUPPORTERS while down the side there was what passed for a Southampton crew, and these Chelsea boys saw them, ran over and piled in. This set the main mob of Chelsea trying to get over the fences, but the old bill were ready. Somehow those blokes came out alive and it set the tone for the day.

After the game Chelsea went for the old bill. One of the funniest things I ever saw was this copper getting a kicking and this bonehead went over and pulled a plank from the remains of a wooden fence that Chelsea had demolished and been using for ammunition. He worked the plank out and checked the weight. Made sure it felt right. Ran over to the copper who was alone now and trying to get up, and broke it over his head. Real silent movie routine with a Keystone Cop getting his skull bruised. The bloke got ready for a second swing but this woman in a club scarf ran over and slapped him. Told him to fuck off and leave the policeman alone. The bonehead shrugged and walked back into the main Chelsea mob which was busy throwing everything they could at the line of coppers behind the copper on the ground. Chelsea were mad that day and the old bill couldn't cope. It must've gone on for half an hour before we moved towards the town centre.

I think about the carriage and the people travelling with England. There's so many stories to tell. The major rows, small-time vandalism and peaceful Saturday afternoon football. It all merges together eventually. But that's domestic. This is England on tour and the English know how to enjoy themselves. We're living in the moment, rooted in the past. A volunteer army marching into the sunset.

Eddie lined the boys up and did a quick head count. One, two, three, four. All present and correct and no-one forgotten in the pub bogs. When the traffic stalled he led them across the road. Eddie believed in leading from the front and Ted pointed out that this was the route Charles II took when he rode down to ride Nell Gwyn. The rest of the troops laughed as he pointed out that royalty knew how to have a good time with the nags. They were all enjoying themselves, and that included Barry. Once safely across the street, Eddie peeled away towards the Duke of York's. Bill had the others line up behind Eddie and get in step with their leader. The men were marching in a column now – left, right, left, right – with the corporal at the front unaware of the battalion behind. All he needed was a Union Jack or some bagpipes to pipe the boys through the gate.

Eddie was leading the lads to the Battle of the Bulge, with his bulging beer gut out in front doing the job of the sappers. He was defeating the last great German offensive – the war of attrition lager was waging against the great English pint – with a jug of best bitter. Eddie gave his full support to the Ulstermen resisting union with the Papists, and fully believed that the Apprentice Boys should be allowed to march whenever and wherever they wished, but in the war against lager he was even prepared to stretch to a Fenian pint, whether it was Guinness or Murphy's. He didn't care about religion and had mates who were Catholic, but where there was a Union Jack flying Eddie would stand shoulder to shoulder with its defenders. They were all patriots, but Eddie wore his flag on his sleeve. As they approached the Duke of York's he looked behind and saw the boys mucking about. He fell in with the joke and told them to break rank and prepare for some well-deserved leave. Ted would organise the Egyptian girls.

The police at the gate checked their names and let the four ex-soldiers through, and when they turned left in the car park the noise of the King's Road faded away. It was a short walk over an empty square to their destination. There were some cars and a couple of army jeeps, but otherwise the runway was clear. Eddie pointed out his old Rover and carried on. The rest of the boys were impressed by the way the car had been maintained, and were mindful of the fact that they'd arrived by public transport. Eddie had the officer mentality and it was only his working-class origins that had stopped him progressing through the ranks.

Farrell knew Eddie would laugh such a remark off. He

believed in the status quo and the honesty of the establishment. There was no point arguing with Eddie, trying to tell him that if it hadn't been for blatant class prejudice he could have become a major, or better. What was the point anyway? Eddie was happy and had no sense of injustice. He accepted his place in the pecking order and was content.

– Hurry up, you lazy buggers, a voice boomed. The bar's almost dry.

Farrell looked up and saw a grey head leaning out of a second floor window. Sunlight caught the glass and lit the skin, the man's hair turning white. The head looked as though it was glistening and for some reason Bill contrasted it with a youthful Barry struggling in the Atlantic, hanging onto a mast in an oil slick, skin peeled from his back, the oil burning. He thought of Barry's legs dangling under the surface and saw the Great Barrier Reef, Vince reassuring his granddad that the sharks wouldn't come across the coral. No wonder Barry was miserable, torpedoed and left in the sea thousands of miles from home. The thing was, he'd gone back. Then Farrell saw Bob West and imagined him leaving The Unity and returning home. He saw the RAF pilot rigging up a noose and standing there thinking the thing through. Cold and methodical he kicked the chair away. His legs started to jerk. Piss ran down his skin as he struggled, limbs under the water, eventually sucked through space and into some kind of nightmare. Farrell saw West in limbo, Christian and Muslim war dead manoeuvring for space reinventing themselves to fit in with the new order. But West was young and had so much to live for once he sorted himself out. Farrell knew you had no control over other people. He could listen and offer an opinion, but everyone went their own way in the end.

– That's the bar, Ted told him. They'll all be in there, making their pensions stretch and enjoying the company. That's one of the best things about these get-togethers. When you're younger everyone else is young as well, but now we're on our own. Get inside that bar and the outside world vanishes. It's like going home in a way. That's the bar for you.

– And that's Dave Horning, Barry said. He's probably drunk

already. He can't drink as much as Eddie, but he can hold his beer. Me, I can't keep up any more. I spend too much time recovering. It's not like the old days. When you don't know whether the next day's your last you want to make sure you feel your best if you wake up in the morning.

– Shut up, you bloody misery, Ted said. You're the same as you were when I met you. You've always been old.

Barry smiled because he knew Ted had a point, whereas Ted had always been young. Farrell smiled as well, but was thinking hard because he recognised Horning from somewhere. He looked again and saw the grey head disappear inside, window swinging back against the brick and losing the sun. The name came back suddenly and it was a shock that slowed him down. They'd called Horning something else all those years ago. His name was Mangler then. It was a turn up for the books, and Farrell felt uneasy.

He flashed back to Mangler charging across the sand calling the men facing them every name under the sun. They'd lived and fought together for a long time, but Mangler had always been separate from the others. He thought about the bayonet and the German prisoner Mangler had threatened to castrate. It was so long ago now and Farrell had to push his memory to remember the look on the German's face. He could see the scene but for a few seconds the face was blank, then it returned, full of terror. Somehow mutilation and torture seemed worse than death. Poor old Billy Walsh. The worst thing that could happen to a man was to have his balls blown off, or taken by a bayonet. War was a sickness and Farrell had to remind himself he was here for the drink, food and company. He hadn't seen Mangler since they'd been demobbed. No, he told a lie. He'd seen him once.

It was the only get-together Farrell had ever been to and he'd hated every minute of the evening. Farrell had a wife at home trying to recover from the chicken-farmer Himmler's Final Solution, and he found himself sitting at a table with chicken bones on his plate and three idiots moaning about the communists and how England had fought on the wrong side. He almost blushed remembering how he'd argued with one of the men and pulled him outside and into the car park. Everyone at the event was drunk and they were on their own, left to sort out their differences. Farrell might have been drinking, but his boxing moves came through and he dumped Donald Smith on his arse, then kicked him several times to make sure he didn't get up in a hurry.

Farrell went back inside as everyone raised their glasses for a toast. Smith was outside propped against a wall, his nose full of blood and two of his teeth on the ground. Half an hour later, Farrell went back out and pulled him to his feet. He dusted him down and apologised. They went into the toilets and Smith washed up. They were drunk and disorderly. Farrell felt he shouldn't have really done that, but idle talk cost lives. Maybe he'd over-reacted, because Smith was mirroring a growing hatred for communism. Farrell explained things and the man was embarrassed and ashamed. He told Farrell he'd been right to stand up for his wife and knock him down. Smith said he'd forgotten what had happened a few years before. He felt like a fool because he'd seen the same things as Farrell. It ended with a handshake and they went back to their table. Next morning Farrell had a hangover and his wife took him his breakfast in bed. He never went to an army dinner again.

Farrell wondered if Mangler would recognise him. They were so much older now. Rock-n-roll had come and gone and they were still plodding along. Mangler would look at him and see an old man, not the young squaddie fighting his way through Europe. It had been a mad time. He wouldn't know what to say to Mangler. There was nothing needed saying. None of them could ever experience life in the same way again. What did the chaplain say? In life we are in death. Something like that.

– Come on, no slacking, Eddie called, and Ted, Barry and Bill caught up, entering the building and going up the stairs.

– Left, right, left, right, Ted said, taking the piss.

He'd always been the comedian, making fun of the tradition and regimentation, a thorn in Eddie's side.

– I hate stairs, Eddie confided. It does something to my right knee. I'm a fucking para, not a mountain climber. I'm used to dropping straight in among the enemy and getting stuck in.

There was the hum of voices coming from the bar to their left, and a couple of men at the entrance to a small museum on their right. Bill looked in and saw various pictures, the first one showing English soldiers sitting on a jeep in the Sahara. Further back there were several tunics. It was a funny thing, but he still had his Uncle Stan's tunic at home. It was a small red Royal Marine jacket that he'd kept all these years. He would get it out again when he went home. There were some medals as well, and he thought of his own decorations, but he'd leave them in the drawer. He remembered how his wife had loved his medals. It was silly really, but he'd just kept quiet. He didn't want to upset her too.

The bar was busy with eighty or so men standing in small groups talking. Several welcomed Eddie, and Farrell looked around for Mangler but couldn't see him. He went to the bar and ordered, pleasantly surprised by the price. It was another kind of working-man's club, with a central location and framed pictures on the walls. It was nothing particularly grand, but there was a sense of history and a friendly atmosphere. The men in the bar were mainly around his own age, give or take a few years, and he had to admit that it was a nice feeling. He felt at ease. This surprised him as well, because he'd expected something different. He couldn't really put his finger on what he'd expected. The woman pouring was very nice and handed him his change as she took another order. A couple of men next to him were a lot younger than the rest and probably serving soldiers. They moved and nodded as he passed the drinks back.

He stood next to Ted and Barry and looked around. There were several well-padded armchairs and a couch, some tables with newspapers, and a club feel to the place. It wasn't posh at all, but felt right somehow. He sipped his pint. Farrell stood with Ted and Barry because Eddie was a big, sociable character and had gone over to talk with some grey-haired men in blazers.

– Not bad, Ted said. Not bad at all. Certainly gets the blood flowing.

Farrell thought he was referring to the pint, but saw that Ted's eyes were focused on the middle-aged woman behind the bar. She was opening a bottle of light ale and Ted was admiring her action. Farrell supposed she wasn't bad-looking and had made the effort with her clothes and make-up. He had no desire in that direction, though he of course appreciated beauty, but Ted would always have an eye for the women.

– She's sagging a bit around the jaw, Barry said. She's showing her age I'm afraid, and you're showing yours as well Ted, just by fancying her.

Farrell looked at this man in his seventies and there was no hint of self-mockery. Men were like that. Even when they were old and grey, they still judged women as though they were in the prime of life.

– I hear she speaks highly of you, Ted replied.

Barry nodded and understood.

– So how's your new place, Bill? Ted asked. You're nearer me now. You should jump on a bus and come round. It's nice meeting old mates after so long.

– It's fine, Farrell replied. I'm nearer the family and I know people locally. It's okay. It was good to move really. It's a new start and I cleared through a lot of stuff. It was a new beginning. Not that I was unhappy before, I wasn't. It's good to have a change, even when you're old.

– I've lived in the same place since the beginning of time, Barry moaned.

Ted spluttered in his pint.

– You miserable old git, he said. You were there in the Garden of Eden spying on Eve. You're like one of those vampires lurking in the ivy of the churchyard looking for victims. Barry Dracula all the way from Transylvania.

Bill laughed and Barry nodded, shrugging his shoulders, playing along with his image.

– Come on boys, Ted continued. There's a world of women waiting for blokes like us. There's a cheap bar as well.

Farrell spotted Mangler. He looked smaller and less dangerous than he remembered. He watched him through the crowd, talking with another man. Mangler was Dave Horning. He wondered what he'd been doing all these years, but wasn't drunk enough to go and find out. What if Mangler didn't recognise him? Worse than that, what if he started talking about D-Day and the advance through Europe? What if he talked about the killing? Farrell tried to remember where Mangler was and when. His head was fuzzy. He knew Mangler wasn't there when he killed the boy. But he'd had to do it, there was no choice. It was him or the German soldier. He was nervous suddenly, because if he had a view and memory of Mangler then it followed that the same was true for both of them. Farrell saw his medals. The clean ribbons and shining surfaces. The King's head gleaming. Blood on the ribbons and sweat on his hands. Farrell lifted his pint and took a long drink. He asked Barry how his wife was doing.

– Very well thanks, Bill, Barry said, reviving. We're going down to Selsey this summer for a couple of weeks in a caravan. We always took the boys to the caravans when they were young. We've been going there for years and know people locally now. It's a lot of fun, and Dick and Bernie are coming down with the kids for a few days.

– How many grandchildren have you got?

– Nine now, Barry said, smiling. Three kids of my own and nine grandchildren. Five boys and four girls.

– Sounds like your kids take after Eddie, Ted noted.

– I don't mind. The more the merrier, and at least I don't have to put food in their mouths.

Farrell nodded and wondered what it was like for Ted not having kids. It made all the difference, but he knew Ted liked the ladies too much to settle down. He'd always had his wits about him, ducking and diving and listening to jazz. When they'd been in the TA together there'd been stories about Ted, told in jest but with an undercurrent of truth. Stories about gun-running and semi-precious stones, and something about a gambling ring. Farrell didn't remember exactly, but if Eddie was the up-front English patriot with the bluster, and Barry the moaning family man, then Ted was the slicked back wide boy with a deep soul. Farrell had to admit they were all a bit special somehow.

— I had a child, Ted said, lowering his voice. I was living with this woman for a while and we had a boy. Lovely little thing he was. It didn't last between us and she took him with her when she left. I found out later that she gave him away.

There was silence and Farrell could see the sadness in Ted's face.

— What happened to him? Barry asked. Did you ever find out?

Ted's face brightened again.

— He looked me up a few years ago. I searched for both of them and then when I found out he'd been adopted I put my name down so I was there if he ever wanted to contact me. He's a great lad. We see each other every couple of weeks. Funny thing is, he was taken in by this family in Neasden and was never very far from me. I didn't think too much about it at first, because I knew he was with his mum, and I was out and about. It was a time of life when I wasn't thinking about anyone else but myself. She had problems later with drink and even went on the game for a while. I could've done a lot more and she did what she thought was best I suppose. She was always highly-strung, a boozer. My son ended up with a good family, and his new mum and dad loved kids. Those sort of people love children for what they are, not just because they're related by blood. It worked out in the end.

There was another silence and Farrell didn't know what to say.

— What happened to his mum? Barry asked.

— She's dead. Her life got better as she got older. She married a man who looked after her better than the other blokes she'd known. He treated her with respect. She had another twenty-five years until she died of cancer. I haven't told the boy that his mum was a drunk who went on the game, because it's a long time ago and it just doesn't matter. I've known working girls through the years and they love and suffer like anyone else. It's funny, because you look back and think of all the problems you've had, and you wonder what all the fuss was about. Whatever I say about her is his truth. Why give the boy sad memories?

Ted stopped and looked at the others. He was a chatty, funny man and didn't usually open up like this. It was the mention of his son, his pride and joy, that had made him break the carefree image.

— Me and the boy get on a treat. He's like a mate really. We go and get drunk together and have a meal. He likes the women. Just like his dad. So I'm not the lonely old sod you think.

They laughed now and Eddie came back through the crowd at just the right moment, showing his officer potential. He took charge again and told the boys to drink up. Were they turning into a bunch of poofs? Ted was standing like a fucking teapot. He went straight to the bar and even now he was a big man with a big presence. He ordered and swapped a joke with the barmaid, then started talking to the squaddies nearby. He was exchanging stories and Farrell could see that the soldiers appreciated this former para, one of the Arnhem mob. Eddie was living history. He was a living, drinking, fighting man who'd gone into enemy territory and fought against the odds. Eddie was a one-off and wouldn't let the sentimentality of old age get a foothold.

— Come on, Eddie, Ted shouted.

Eddie nodded and the younger men laughed.

— We're dying of thirst over here.

There was a lot of genuine affection among these men that Farrell hadn't expected. They were all drinking a lot and Barry said they'd be going in soon for the meeting. It was routine stuff and didn't last too long. Farrell needed a piss and Barry gave him directions to the Gents. He went into a big room, split between a changing area with showers and pegs, and the actual toilets. He saw himself in the mirror and knew he looked a great deal different to how he felt. The years might have passed, but with these blokes he felt like a young man again. It was being with people your own age, who had all the same reference points, just like Ted said. He walked across the empty room, his shoes echoing.

Farrell was almost finished when another man came in. Farrell shook, zipped up and went to wash his hands, then filled the sink and splashed his face with cold water. He was happy and looking forward to the curry, drying himself on a green paper towel. The other man started humming to himself and Farrell looked at him in the mirror. He started at the grey head and knew immediately that it was Mangler. Farrell had kept away from Mangler, knowing that he was safe in the crowd. He looked so different now that if Mangler did look his way he was unlikely to be recognised. Farrell briefly thought about saying hello, but then what, and anyway, he didn't want to talk about the old days. He hurried out of the Gents. He didn't want to get involved in all that right now. Maybe after the meeting and the food. Maybe later on he'd sit down with Mangler and have a chat, but he felt uneasy. Maybe another time.

It would be a rough trip through memories that were more than half a century old, the two men shadow-boxing, knowing they could say more. Farrell didn't want Mangler pulling things apart, didn't even like him. Mangler was always spoiling for a fight, stirring up trouble, and Farrell didn't want his ability to remember his own life questioned. With Eddie, Ted and Barry it was okay. He was secure with them. Mangler was different. He was too close.

– Where have you been? Eddie frowned, holding Farrell's pint.

– I went for a jimmy, Farrell said, taking the glass. Did you want to come as well and shake it dry?

– You haven't turned queer on us as well, have you? Eddie asked. If you've turned funny you'd better give us a warning.

– Eddie needs to know, Ted laughed. Don't you, Eddie?

– You behave yourself, the corporal growled. We don't want any poofs around here, do we?

– Barry might, Ted replied.

– Fuck off, Barry said. I'm happily married with children. I reckon Ted's the one you've got to watch.

Ted smiled and blew Barry a kiss. Bill and Eddie laughed as Barry threw a pretend punch at Ted, who made to grab Barry's balls. Eddie came between them and said no punching below the belt, and at that moment everyone was called to the meeting, Eddie leading his rioting troops towards the hall.

* * *

Sitting in the corner listening to the rest of the lads pissing about, Harry wasn't feeling too clever. He was sitting quiet as a mouse letting the rest of the boys babble away about nothing in particular, leaning his head against the window thinking of that Porsche and the flash cunt driving, about the autobahns of Germany and how Mussolini got the Italian trains to run on time. The countryside outside was green and starting to blur as he nodded his head. He was tired, drifting, thinking about Nicky. He was on a train heading east and she was stuck in Amsterdam listening to her CDs. It was the afternoon and she'd be getting ready to go to work.

It sounded strange putting it like that, Nicky on her way to the checkout. Yesterday he wasn't too bothered, because she was a prossie and that was her business, and even though she was nice enough he had to meet the lads later on, but now he had the chance to think, killing time. He saw Nicky sitting in her flat alone, with a cup of coffee and a slice of cake, while outside the bars and cafés and markets bustled with life. She was sitting there on the side of her bed stretching those beautiful legs and getting dressed. She'd go outside into the rain and wait for a tram to take her to work, getting off and crossing the river and taking her place with the rank and file. Maybe she'd go and have a drink first, sipping whisky with the other prostitutes, knocking back a double with the greasers and junkies and all the rest of Amsterdam society. She liked her ecstasy and he thought of the Buddha he'd done in Blackpool.

Nicky had a Buddha statue in the corner of her bedroom and a little shrine for the house spirits. She said it was a Thai tradition. The Buddha was sitting pretty, the gold paint on one of his ears chipped and revealing plastic. Harry saw the coffee and CDs and the bed where he'd sat like another, fatter Buddha. She said she liked big men. She told Harry he was a baby sumo wrestler, except he had hair on his body. She laughed and said she loved his hair. Thai men were hairless. She pulled at his arms and his chest. Nicky was natural and unscarred even though she'd been on the game for years. He'd heard about Thailand and Pettaya, and Pat Pong in Bangkok. He thought of Nicky as a teenager leaving her village and taking the bus south, working in the bars of boom-town Bangkok before moving down to the coast.

Harry was half asleep, with images playing in his head. Nicky was sitting on the lap of a sixty-year-old pharmaceutical executive enjoying a holiday from the wife and family, his pockets full of pills. A fatter bastard than Harry with a deep wallet and some unnatural things on his mind. This man was rich and liberated away from England, running his hands over Nicky's arse and rubbing her cunt in front of a gang of other men gathered from the civilised West, these decent gentlemen from London, Berlin, Paris, Rome, Vienna, Copenhagen, Washington DC rubbing shoulders with the more obvious nonces. Men from every corner of the civilised world in light cotton shirts and flip-flops watching the straining young boys and girls on stage fucking each other in time to elevator mood music more suited to the Hilton and Holiday Inn. Their crisp twenty-dollar bills were putting a nice commercial gloss on the oldest profession in the world. They were giving generously as the collection tray was passed from left to right. It was another kind of war and Harry was mixing his sex and violence, seeing Nicky as a casualty of war. It was a battle to survive, the East taking everything the West could fire its way. His head jolted and he heard Tom laugh and tell the others that Harry was sleeping like a baby, but then he was gone and Harry was alone with the pictures. He was sitting in a multiplex watching re-run Vietnam films, riding with Jesus Saves painted on his computerised helmet.

Along with Second World War stories, Harry and his generation were raised on Vietnam, the images big and exotic with hills burning in the distance, soldiers picking their way through tropical rainforests. They saw the scale of the bombing and the freedom of Hollywood gunships. It added something to *Dam Busters* and *The Longest Day*. It was better than Northern Ireland because that was bitter city street-fighting through British housing estates, and every now and then you heard about someone's older brother or cousin who'd been killed or wounded, almost every day a name announced on the news, blokes you didn't know personally but understood were a bit too near you and yours for comfort. Northern Ireland was grim and miserable, while Vietnam was the other side of the world, the enemy small and unseen, the news footage of childhood blending into the films of their youth. The squaddies listed on the news were young and white, their heads shaved and the faces familiar. They looked like you'd look when you grew up. They were English and counted. In the Far East it was jungles burning, not people. It seemed unreal, the difference between the Gulf and the Falklands.

It was the Yanks who'd turned Thailand into a knocking shop. Harry's mate Mango had been to Pettaya and said a lot of bars were run by former servicemen who'd gone back and set up in business. During the Vietnam War they were flown into Pettaya for some rest and recreation, and afterwards the place kept going. Tourists came to join the Gulf workers and soldiers. When the Gulf War ended Pettaya suffered what they called the mother of all hangovers. Along with the bombing raids went sex missions. Mango said it was a mental place, going on about the go-go bars, sex clubs, blow-job bars and so on. Harry imagined kids forced to work hard for their bowl of rice and felt sorry for Nicky.

He jolted when he wondered how she'd managed to avoid Aids. She said she was clean and he believed her, but had been careful anyway. It was chemical warfare, poison in the blood stream. You didn't have to bother with invasions and air strikes any more, just send over the rich holiday-makers and fat nonces to fuck the poor and the thin up the arse. Make them squeal and get girls like Nicky to lick the sewer clean. Harry sat up and had another drink. He had to get that woman out of his head. He was here to enjoy himself. What was the matter with him? He was part of the Expeditionary Force and they weren't taking any prisoners.

—I sit in the meeting but don't really listen to what's being said. I think of Europe and the way the English behaved. I believe we did what had to be done and compared to the Germans and the Russians we were decent and honest. I sit between Eddie and Barry. These two and Ted are good, decent men. They all have their experiences and their lives after the war. It is the same for me and for Dave Horning. I think of the men I killed now because I have it all laid out in some kind of formation. I have thought about what we did and it makes sense. Dave Horning is Mangler and he was with me in Normandy. He was in the same landing craft and he would have smelt the same shit and heard the same sobs. I don't know if he will remember things in the same way. I have my version of events and one thing I have learnt and observed through the years is how history is reinvented. It isn't just the people who make a living from the subject, because in some ways it is the people who were there as well. I hope I haven't done this myself. The thing is, sometimes I wonder. I have done my best to keep my mind clear and remember things clearly, but try as you will you can never fully escape your surroundings. Little things start to niggle. I think of the boy, the last German I killed. I shot him in the head. He was crawling away through the rubble but there was a gun in his hand. The village was a ruin and there were many corpses. I didn't want to come this far and die. It was more than that, because maybe I could have kicked the gun away. Would it have made a difference? I find it hard to know after all this time and I wonder how Mangler would see things. I remember him with his bayonet threatening to castrate a man. I remember other things I don't want to remember. It was war and you can do anything. I know what Mangler did in that village. I saw the woman with her dress up around her hips and the bloody cuts along her legs. His eyes were wild and he was mad. I wonder if he's mad now. There was more gunfire from the enemy. The woman could be alive today, but she'd be ancient. We were numb and I swore at him and asked him what he'd done. I could have turned my gun on him but there was another enemy. We fought on. I wonder if he saw me kill the boy, but I know he didn't. There's always a possibility. Mangler was elsewhere doing other things to other people. I think of the woman and I think of my wife who was raped in the concentration camp. I hate rapists. I don't want the bitterness and the anger, but I hate Mangler. I didn't see him rape the woman, but this is what I believe happened. I am not certain. I don't want to be a moral Christian because there's no God that would let these things happen. I prayed in the landing craft, but how can you trust God? It is bad enough that Mangler could have raped the woman, but I don't want him to think about the boy. Germany was in ruins, like the rest of Europe. We were monsters roaming the earth. There's music and flags and medals to cover the madness and make sure the means justify the ends. I think of the boy and the doubt goes. It was me or him, a battle for survival. A clean shot to kill an enemy soldier.

Bill Farrell found himself squeezed between Eddie and another man Ted introduced as Rai. The meal put on by the kitchen wasn't bad at all and Farrell was tucking into the curry, rice, bread and salad. The others said it was like being back in the army, but he'd never had all this when he was a soldier. The others were joking about something or other, but Farrell was concentrating on the food. He was hungry and had to agree with Rai when he said that it was well worth the fiver they'd paid. The meeting had been alright, but he wasn't involved in the running of the place so wasn't too concerned, his thoughts elsewhere. It was only when he'd cleared his plate and Rai mentioned something about Burma that Farrell started taking notice of his surroundings.

 − I had a mate who was in Asia, Farrell said, wiping his mouth. His name was Albert Moss. He fought in Burma. He's dead now, but he never forgot what the Japs did. He wasn't a prisoner of war there, but he saw some of what they left behind.

 − It was a hard place to fight, Rai nodded. Everywhere is hard in its own way. A lot of Indian boys died under the Japanese. I went back to see the graves in Thailand one year. The War Graves Commission looks after the cemeteries very well. There's a lot of respect from the local people.

Farrell knew the Commonwealth had fought with the British, and this was one of the things wrong about the European Union. He was no colonialist, but believed the Commonwealth had evolved into something positive. A lot of people felt this, and you only had to look at the young for confirmation. It was a union based on something other than race and geography. This was forgotten by the vested interests. He knew the Thailand–Burma Railway had been built from both ends, with the British dying at the Thai end of the route. Albert had seen the living skeletons and heard about the Japanese torturers. There was the malaria and the snakes and the tropical conditions Englishmen found hard to handle. Even more men died at the other end of the railway line, Asians who were largely forgotten.

Albert had been a good friend. He carried a dislike of the Japanese to the grave, however hard he tried to forgive and forget. It was something that didn't happen so much with the Germans. Farrell knew it was down to personal experience. Compared to the Russians, British POWs had been well-treated, while the Germans and Russians left millions of the other side's men to starve. The same happened with the Japs. It was personal, and Albert didn't like the Japanese selling their cars in England or their politicians shaking hands with the British. It was the same as Eddie and Palestine. It was natural enough.

– Are you having some more? Rai asked, looking at Farrell's plate.

Farrell was and so was Rai, so they went along the counter again, and then to a table for the bread and salad.

– I've got an allotment, Rai said. I grow a lot of this stuff so it's funny eating it when it's not my own. I'm still digging for victory.

Farrell laughed and said he'd worked in the parks. He missed grafting outdoors, but his years working manually with plants and the earth had given him good health.

– I've been there for thirty years now, and I've never felt better, Rai said. You get all sorts of people. There's no class or prejudice there. Mostly it's the retired people who keep their allotments up to scratch, but there's others. We've got a punk who can't be more than twenty-five. It's a haven.

It sounded good and Rai told Farrell about the vegetables he was growing. About the way the soil had to be looked after and allowed to develop. He told him about roots, brassicas and others, and about the bulbs he planted. He had some frogs who lived there and helped keep down the slug population. He was growing everything from potatoes and spinach to pumpkins and corn. He had a good crop of chillis coming up and this year his tomatoes were already flourishing.

– You watch that bastard, Eddie said, leaning over Farrell and jabbing his fork at Rai when they returned to the table.

– You bloody watch him, Billy boy. He'll have you down that allotment of his tomorrow working your bollocks off while he sits in his deckchair brewing tea. It's the tea that never brews. The teabags that never were. Just watch your step or he'll have you breaking your back for him.

– That's not true, Rai said. The tea just took a bit of time.

– A bit of time? Eddie roared, so Ted and Barry stopped and listened. It took hours. Am I lying, Ted?

– It was a nice cuppa though, Ted said. You've got to admit that, haven't you, Eddie?

– And Rai bought us all a pint afterwards as well.

– True, Eddie admitted, feeling better.

– I bought you two pints each, Rai insisted. Don't listen to them, Bill.

Farrell couldn't help but listen as Ted explained how Rai had been ill a few months back and needed to get his soil turned over. Eddie had assembled a crack commando unit and organised an assault plan. Farrell snuck a glance and saw Eddie settle back to enjoy the tale. Ted explained how they'd had to meet at Eddie's and then gone down in the Centurion, picked up Rai in Roehampton and continued to Putney Vale. The allotment was in a perfect site, on a slight hill but right at the top next to Wimbledon Common. Looking down you couldn't even see the M3, just trees and allotments on one side, and the woods of Richmond on the other. They'd gone four days in one week and suddenly Rai was back in business. His groin-strain had healed and everything was fine.

Eddie nodded and Farrell could imagine the big man bullying the others into action. He was all front, but would do anything for anyone. That's what made him special, and Bill thought about telling him, but it would sound soft and only be embarrassing.

– I've got some new potatoes for you all later, Rai said. They're in a bag behind the couch in the bar. Shall we have another drink? I need something to cool my mouth down after the curry. The English never learn, do they? They love their chillies too much. English curries are too bloody hot.

They went through to the bar, and as they were the first ones in they got the couch. It was a nice position. Farrell sat in a chair that could have been made for him. It was so comfortable he'd gladly have taken it home. Eddie had the other chair, while Ted, Barry and Rai sat on the couch. There were five pint jugs on the table. Four contained bitter and the other lager. Eddie was telling Rai off for drinking a girl's drink, but when he pointed out that the lager was chilled and that it was a hot day and they'd eaten hot food, the corporal graciously conceded defeat. He warned the others there could be no surrender. Exceptions could be made about everything, but in the end they had to maintain standards.

– I always maintain standards with the ladies, Ted pointed out.

– There must be standards when it comes to the fairer sex, Rai agreed. Men must guard themselves at all times against the power of the flesh.

The others laughed and explained to Farrell that Rai was a charmer from the same mould as Ted. The difference was that Rai was married, but had what he termed a modern relationship. He was a man of romance and thought rather than action, and had never been unfaithful to his wife. Farrell wondered if Ted was still having sex, or whether he'd also chosen love and romance without the physical side. Farrell hadn't had an erection for years and didn't think about women much these days. It was funny how it was so important when you were young and you spent so much time chasing the girls. He thought of Mary Peacock suddenly. He remembered having her when she was young, after a drink in The White Horse. Now that was a rough pub. He'd had his share of fights in the old days. Funny, because that had gone as well. No more sex and no more violence. It made life a lot less complicated.

* * *

Corporal Wicks led his squad to the staff car. Privates Farrell, James and Miller were pissed as newts. The corporal was drunk as well, but with a stripe on his arm had to set a good example. He was in charge of the transport and made sure the front-seat passenger was strapped in before starting the engine. Bill was next to Eddie and acting as navigator. He had his wits about him and was already looking for the enemy. Bill also had seven pints of bitter, a double whisky and a large brandy sharpening his senses. He was alert and invincible as he watched Rai stumble through the gates to a waiting mini-cab. Bill rolled down the window and shouted that he'd see him the day after tomorrow when they would blitz the nettles. Rai turned and waved and fell into the cab.

Bill could hear Ted and Barry laughing in the back telling Bill that they wanted to head west, not east. They were part of the West London Brigade and didn't want to die on the Mile End Road. Like the Germans, they wanted to be taken prisoner in the West. Ted and Barry were paralytic. He was the only one keeping up with Eddie. The corporal started crunching gears. It took him a couple of goes to find reverse, but he reassured Ted he was in total control. It was after eleven and they were the last to leave. He reversed and stalled. Eddie hit the brake hard to stop the car rolling and Ted and Barry swore. He turned the key and inched backwards.

– Fucking piece of shit, Eddie mumbled. I learnt to drive in the army, in lorries. You know where you are in a lorry. I wouldn't mind driving a tank right now. That would be fun.

Bill nodded and wondered if this was a good idea, but he was as pissed as Eddie and the alternative was trying to find a night bus or a tube. Corporal Wicks had always been the British bulldog at its best and nothing had changed in later life. He would see this operation through and clicked into action.

– Keep looking straight ahead, Eddie ordered, as they rolled towards the gate. We don't want the SS coming over and smelling our breath. Getting through the gates has to be perfect. We could dig a tunnel and crawl out like rats, but I'm going through the front door. If those wankers get a smell we're dead. We've got to stay calm. They'll smell the drink on our breath.

– We should've drunk lager so they thought we were Nazis, Ted pointed out. We've had it now, boys.

– Don't panic, Barry shouted.

– Come on Captain Mainwaring, Ted said. Sort it out, chief.

– They don't like it up them, Barry laughed, almost pissing himself. The fuzzy wuzzies don't like the cold steel of a bayonet up the jacksie. Who can blame them?

– Stupid boy, Eddie muttered, looking in the mirror at the drunks behind him. You lot can't hold your beer. No English now lads, we've got to be German for a couple of minutes to get past the guards.

The barrier was lifted without a problem and they were on the move. They all agreed that the King's Road was a funny old place. It wasn't really part of London at all. It was a strip of Occupied Europe transported to London, with Mussolini fashion, Vichy food and the kind of prices only a Swede could afford. The people were young as well and Bill honestly wondered how they ended up so wealthy. It didn't matter of course, and he advised turning right towards Earl's Court, but Eddie had his own plan, and carried on till they were passing Stamford Bridge. Ted had watched Chelsea play when he was a young man. He'd been been born in Fulham, but moved to Notting Hill in the fifties, before the teddy boy riots. In the sixties he'd gone to Shepherd's Bush and stayed there ever since. Fulham had changed since he was a boy and now the streets around the football ground were empty of life.

Ted got Eddie to slow down so they could look at the new stadium. The hotel was huge. Funny thing was, Ted had been a big football fan in his youth. He'd watched the club win the League in 1955 and gone on the pitch at the end to celebrate. He'd spent his pennies on Drake's Ducklings and Docherty's Diamonds, and had even been to Wembley and Old Trafford to watch the Cup Final games against Leeds in 1970. He remembered the mods and skinheads in the sixties and the time when Manchester United had gone into The Shed and there'd been a lot of trouble. He'd been to the League Cup defeat against Stoke City in 1972 and the FA Cup Final against Spurs in 1967. When they sold Osgood and Hudson he stopped going. Selling those two was unforgivable, and their loss plus his age meant he'd never been since. The wages some of these players were paid now was ridiculous and the football methodical and system-based. It was all money-motivated. He had lost interest, but was curious to have a look. He remembered the streets and the crowds of people. There'd been some rough pubs in the area, but it was the sixties when he remembered the first real hooliganism. It was annoying, but if you watched yourself you were okay. There were skinheads everywhere in those days. It was another era and he didn't care any more. There were better things in life than football.

Eddie veered right at Fulham Broadway and headed for Shepherd's Bush, planning to drop Ted off first. The corporal had worked out the best route back to Feltham, the boys bailing out on the way. Shepherd's Bush, Hammersmith, Isleworth and home. He was in control and soon on North End Road with its market litter and wandering drunks, on through the tower block estates at the back of Earl's Court. Two miles from the wine bars of Chelsea and the population could've been from a different planet. Farrell felt Eddie was taking an unnecessarily complicated route that invited the attentions of police patrols, but kept quiet. He knew his rank and Eddie wouldn't stand for insubordination. He was a brawler and used to getting his way. It was his car and the punishment for mutiny was a long walk home.

At a set of traffic lights Eddie reached over and pulled out a small box of tapes. There always had to be music when the troops marched into battle. He inserted one and punched the button on the cassette player. Bill was expecting a Royal Tournament collection, Vera Lynn or some old paratrooper sing-along, but instead there was a blast of sentimental ballad. He didn't have a clue who the singer was, but it wasn't anyone he'd heard before. Bill looked at the corporal, who was glaring straight ahead.

– What's all this shit then? Barry slurred from the back. Sounds like country-and-western to me.

– It's the Rolling Stones, Eddie said. An early track.

– Didn't take you for a Stones man, Barry remarked. I thought you'd prefer something off the parade ground.

– I saw the Stones years back, before they were famous, when they were starting off. I've always liked their music. Local lads as well. Ted knows my musical tastes.

Eddie pulled away from the lights and before long they were on a search-and-destroy mission through Shepherd's Bush with the music picking up and Sympathy For The Devil coming through the speakers. Bill Farrell had never listened to the Rolling Stones much but found himself pulled in by the rhythm. The words were good as well, talking about the Devil and how evil cropped up through the centuries, all over the planet at important moments in history. It was part of the human condition and no-one escaped. It was depressing but at the same time he felt uplifted. It made him understand the Lucifer mythology and the need for some kind of belief. He was drunk. He was an atheist.

– Turn it up will you, Ted called from the back. Do the next right, Eddie. It's quicker that way.

As they drove around W12, Farrell marvelled at how for years he'd avoided these drink-ups because he didn't want to sit around listening to old soldiers rambling on about the war all night. For some reason he thought it was going to be an endless post-mortem, both of their own actions and the aftermath, but today had been nothing like that at all. He hadn't laughed so much for ages. He knew these people from way back and it was easy company. It was a good laugh, like tapping into his youth. There was nothing to say about death and destruction, because they'd seen enough first hand. The thing they all appreciated was the comradeship they'd felt at the time. It was still there, and Farrell never thought he'd admit something like that. He supposed whatever side you fought on and whatever the battle it was the same. People needed to feel that unity. It was just a shame it took something like a war to make it happen.

The details of their army lives were buried below the surface and that's why he'd avoided Mangler. The man had been a few feet away, but Farrell had kept quiet. All that mattered in the bar was the funny stories and piss-taking that made the bloodshed somehow ridiculous. Fine details were bound to be blurred. They'd all stood their ground and that's what counted. How could any of them explain the war? They just wanted another pint and the chance to take the piss out of each other like they did when they were young. The drink made them forever young, not words on a headstone.

– Right here, Eddie, Ted said. Turn the music down will you, because the ravers across the road need their beauty sleep.

Ted jumped out and banged on the roof. Eddie pulled away with a screech of rubber, showing off, then slowed down when Bill reminded him that if they were stopped the corporal would face a ban.

– You sound like one of my sons, Eddie said, but he took notice. The old bill would have a fight trying to take me. You mark my words Bill, you too Barry if you're alive back there, I can still fight like a young man. I might not use this dragon between my legs much these days, but I can take anyone, young or old. I'll fight to the death and die in the carnage. Feel that muscle, Bill.

– What muscle?

– His prick, that's what he wants, Barry laughed from the back.

– The muscle in my arm, you cunt.

Private Farrell did as Corporal Wicks ordered.

– What do you think of that then? Eddie beamed.

– Police up ahead, Barry said.

Eddie concentrated on the driving. There was a patrol car coming the other way, moving slowly.

– Don't panic, Barry whispered in Eddie's ear, pretending to nibble the lobe.

– Fuck off will you, Eddie hissed. You'll make me swerve and then we'll have the SS after us.

The police car kept going and Eddie checked it in the mirror.

– That was lucky. You have to watch out for patrols when you're on a mission behind enemy lines, trying to get that miserable cunt Barry back to England in one piece. That's the most important thing. It doesn't matter what you do overseas as long as we all get home in one piece. You're next Bill, then Barry. Not far to go now.

– Put another tape on will you, Barry said, but Eddie just grinned.

It didn't take long before Eddie was dropping Farrell off in front of his flat. He staggered out of the car after they'd said their goodbyes, with the promise of a trip to Rai's on nettle detail and a drink. Farrell slammed the door hard and was soon indoors. He turned on the lights and put the kettle on. He was pissed, but didn't feel sick. He hadn't drunk this much for years. He kissed the picture of his wife and went to the bathroom for a piss, returning to the kitchen and making his cuppa. He stirred the brew and went into the living room, sitting in his favourite chair by the window. Farrell waited for the tea to cool, the stillness and silence calming him. He looked at the picture of the nun with the lantern, a council glow outside, the fuzz of a summer night taking over. He saw the nun calling him forward and the name of his Uncle Gill scribbled on yellow paper, a scared boy off to the trenches wondering if he'd ever see England again.

—I walk down the gangplank and look into an ocean of faces. There's a band playing and my head feels woolly. I can hear the drums and brass but can't name the tune. It could be God Save The King or a funeral march. I'm grateful I haven't been killed during the last few days of fighting and listed as missing in action, presumed dead. It was only a question of time before the Germans surrendered. We had them beat. I can't imagine how families feel when they discover their boy fell on the last day of war. To go through so much and die needlessly causes the sort of bitterness that gnaws at the mind for ever. A lot of people will never recover. The person who'd feel my death most is Mum. She'd never survive the shock. To carry a child and raise it, then see him shipped off and buried hundreds of miles from home would destroy any woman. To carry your child on the trains and have it ripped from your hands is beyond belief. Many men will never recover, but my mum brought me up after Dad died so I'm extra special to her. I'm a special boy and that's what she

777

told me when I was a nipper. I'm glad for myself but glad for her. She prays for me every night, begging God to watch over me and make sure I keep my head down. She says her prayers and will do whatever it takes to keep her boy alive. Nothing else matters when it comes to survival. Sailing back to England and walking down the gangplank is my biggest triumph. This is the real victory, coming back to English soil. If I drop dead now I'll be buried at home. That's important. I don't mind dying here. Flags don't matter in this new world. Coming home alive shows I'm a man and can look after myself. I'm happy and drunk, but I'm drifting. Coffins draped in Union Jacks belong somewhere else. The faces blend together in a vague pattern. The music is slurred and there's mist on the Channel. The sea is calm and I can hear it lapping against the dock, the voices of the other men fading into the background so I suddenly feel very alone. I know it's not true. There's thousands of faces out there waiting for the boys to come home. There's so many people waiting I hope there'll be someone for me. Nobody can live alone, shutting everything out. I can't see anyone in the crowd and slump forward. The surface under my feet is uneven. When I steady myself and finally set foot on firm ground again I walk slowly, floating in the clouds with sunlight beating against the mist, the lights ahead bright in my eyes. Suddenly I see them, even though the faces are still merged. They're small balls of white, but I can guess the rest. My mum is here. I see Stan and Gill and Nolan. For a minute I think I see my dad, but he's dead. He died when I was a baby. I see others behind them and know everyone is here. These are the first ones and they'll guide me home. I'm drifting and following the pattern. My uncles fought and sailed home more than a quarter of a century before me. They're pleased to see Billy breathing fresh air. London's at the end of the line. I have to remind myself where I am. My uncles are a surprise, but even now, so many years later as an old man myself, I can feel the pride I felt all those years before. I admired my uncles more than I knew. I wanted to be like them. I was the same blood. Pride swamps the relief, drowns the shock. I'm running through my life and the dates are lost. I'm going home. I see that clearly. I'm on my way and what's done is done. There's no turning back the clock. I dig my heels in and refuse to surrender. I'm a survivor and the survivors have more pride than the murderers and rapists. All my choices were right. I wouldn't be here if I'd done wrong. The spirits see everything. I made the right decisions.

Farrell shook off the ghosts and sat up straight. He'd never been the same since he left England and never been abroad since. He wouldn't admit it, but he was scared to leave. England was safe while the rest of the world represented danger. He'd seen enough. There was pain even now. Maybe his time had come and this was the heart attack that would kill him once and for all, but no, he was okay. It had been a fantastic feeling returning after the war. At first he was tired, but the nearer the ship got to England the stronger he became. He was excited and contrasted it to the fear of the invasion, but once they landed he forgot everything as his mum pushed through the crowd with a swagger and pulled him close. Everything went in a circle and he'd been right round.

He had a biscuit and sipped his tea. He felt good about his day out. He couldn't believe he'd drunk so much. He understood now why old soldiers kept in touch. It made sense. He felt at ease with Eddie, Barry, Ted and Rai. It would do him good to see them again. He'd renew these friendships and have some fun. He let himself go back.

He supposed Germany did well in the post-war years. It was rebuilt and the Western half of the country got democracy. The US became a true world power. Other countries regained their freedom. In some ways England had missed out. It was near enough in ruins and had to start again. Of course, the same old problems returned with the rich coming along to claim victory for themselves. Nobody took much notice and that was a problem, because it gave them a clear run. The ordinary man and woman in the street had something much more important. For that period following Germany's invasion of France, when Stalin still had his pact with Hitler and the Americans didn't want to get involved, Britain was the only one standing up to the Nazis. Farrell passionately believed this was something to be proud of, even if the view was often dismissed. Even now it made him proud and meant nothing could touch him, no matter what the Government did to his pension, heating allowance and health care. Farrell had the moral victory to go with the medals he never wore.

At first it had been pure relief to be back in England. They'd taken the train to London and the family had laid out a spread. Farrell got quite drunk and his uncles treated him differently. They were sensible men and Farrell had talked about the concentration camps. He told them what he'd seen but they found it hard to comprehend. The boy was a grown man and had seen something they could never know or understand. It was the same hearing about the First World War. They spoke of their experiences more now, though never fully opened up. They were English. They couldn't understand torture and experiments. Farrell remembered Gill saying that if he'd been a German standing in a queue and someone said they were making soap out of Jews, he'd think they were mad.

Farrell's uncles drank more than he'd ever seen them drink and everyone was happy. He'd wondered how Billy Walsh's wife and boy were feeling. Mrs Walsh would never see her husband again. She'd never see his body and would have to make do with a war grave. A part of France forever English. Her son would grow with a memory for a dad. The old man would be a hero figure, shaping his life from the grave. The boy would be bitter and pass the feeling on. There were millions of people in the same situation. Farrell had felt lucky at the time and he still did today. There were millions worse off. He'd prayed in the landing craft but couldn't say God had helped. How could he know?

He felt he was fortunate to have a roof over his head and be able to dunk biscuits in a cup of tea. It was a luxury he tried to make sure he always appreciated. The bitter, whisky and brandy was making him tired and emotional. Drink made him sentimental and he had to struggle to push his wife's face into the photos, holding back the nun coming with her lantern. For decades he had held out but now the past was right in front of his eyes. There were clips of stories fitted together and Farrell had to keep them in order. They said that when you died your whole life flashed in front of your eyes. They said you ran through every experience without any idea of time. He'd always heard it happened fast. Suddenly you were sitting on the bus and then you slumped sideways, and in the time it took to hit the window your life had raced past.

The rational world Farrell had created was fraying. He thought of Mangler, but told himself he was mistaken. He thought of his wife, but the memory was too sad. He thought of the bodies, and the boy returned. The last person he killed kept coming back into his head. The order was crumbling and new pictures appeared. He knew he must be dying, but the flashbacks were slow and cruel. He was being tortured slowly now, forced to fight harder to justify his actions. Farrell could see the lights through his window. The memories were too strong and he saw the faces. They'd say he was sleeping because it sounded better than death. He was in the ruins but fighting back, the earth black from a plague that had risen from the soil and destroyed civilisation. The buildings had been bombed and torched. Smoke hung over the earth. The English were fighting house to house, young men moving through towns and villages, flushing out the last remaining resistance. The ruins had no name. It was a German village crushed and burnt. Farrell had sworn he'd find out the name of the village one day, but he never did. The memory was pushed back, festered, rose up, and was pushed back again. There was the smell of burnt bodies and the reek of gasoline, flame-throwers turning men into screaming fireballs.

Farrell was tired and his head throbbed. He was dirty and hungry, but the strongest he'd ever been, charging through what was left of people's homes, possessions scattered and ruined by rain and mud and fire. The stink of death was in his nostrils and his skin coated in scum. He was moving automatically. German snipers were popping off shots and the soldier next to him was hit in the head. Farrell felt the tears as he looked at the man and saw a black hollow where his left eye should have been. Half a century later it was coming back, a dirty rush of horror. The smell was strong. The fear and hatred worked its way under his skin and pulsed through the lining. The only direction was forward, more slowly now, with every ounce of concentration focused on survival. The war had sent Farrell back to the wild as the English fought for their lives, knowing a mistake meant death. He didn't want to die overseas. He didn't want to end up in a foreign grave, buried poor like his gran, buried in a place where there were no wildflowers and no family.

Leaning forward in his chair Farrell thought of his mum. With the shock of bullets splintering bone he saw the woman crying when they came to break the news that her boy was dead. She'd heard enough stories from the first war to know that death was ugly and without honour. Despite this she would ask for a quick death, a painless death for a brave boy, a special boy, a small boy forever young in the photographs, a young man crawling on his belly seeing a nun with a lantern. It was better that way. She didn't need to know the details.

BLITZKRIEG

THERE'S THIS OLD dear sitting next to me bending my ear, really going into one. It's late morning in West Berlin and the English are starting to gather along the main street around the corner from the hotel where we're staying. Must be sixty or so here at the moment. We're drinking outside a small row of bars, in among white metal tables set out on a wide pavement. The sun is shining through a clear blue sky and we're settling in nicely. The journey's over and we're enjoying the scenery. Doing our own special sightseeing. The woman's got a good head of strong blonde hair, but reminds me of a witch. Don't know why, but there's something about her. The eyes are clear and blue, and she seems sane enough, but then she goes and mentions guardian angels. Maybe she's religious with some serious contacts. Better treat her right. She says that she's a decent German and knew nothing about the concentration camps. Says she was a child during the war but will never forget the horror that followed the German army's retreat from the Eastern Front.

Childhood shapes the rest of your life. Her life has been miserable, yet she was one of the lucky ones. Can I understand that? There were many Germans of her age who did not survive the war. Do I understand what she is saying? The point she is trying to make? That she was helped and looked after and cherished because she was young and innocent and destined to live. I nod and look towards the rest of the lads. They aren't taking much notice. They're enjoying their drink and keeping away from the loony. Avoiding the mad old girl sitting with Tom giving him a headache. I've done it myself enough times. Let some other cunt deal with the nutter wandering round tapping people for attention. They all want someone to talk to.

Someone to listen and understand. They just want to have their say.

I look at her powerful blue eyes and wonder. The strong bones and straight shoulders. She leans in close and I can smell the schnapps on her breath. It's hard but sweetened with fruit. Could be strawberry flavour. I wonder if those white teeth are her own. She asks me if I know what the Russians did to the Germans? I shake my head. Probably kicked fuck out of them, but I'll let her explain. Her eyes water as she starts telling me how thousands of German civilians were left behind by the army's retreat, the countryside around her village swamped by the communists. She says the Bolsheviks were worse than animals. Her voice trembles. They showed no mercy, raping the women and, when they'd finished, killing them along with their children. There were massacres everywhere as the Russians looted houses and exterminated innocent people, ransacking and burning whole villages. The land was thick with blood. It wasn't fair, because they were simple folk and none of the people she knew were members of the Nazi party. They were being made to pay a debt according to their nationality. So much for communist ideals. The communists were less than human. She hates communists and is glad the Soviet Union has collapsed.

She lowers her head and I feel bad for her, an old woman lost in a big city like Berlin. She raises her head and tells me she's a peasant forced to hide among cold towers. That she wanders through heartless office blocks watching strangers. Her father was a peasant forced to fight in the East when all he wanted to do was stay in his village and grow vegetables. He was a gentle man who died somewhere outside Stalingrad. Before she became a refugee and was forced towards Berlin, life was uncomplicated. The village would still be her home today and she would have married a local boy if it wasn't for the Soviets. They'd have had children. Lots of children with blond hair and blue eyes like their mother and father. But everything was destroyed by the communists and her life was never the same, her father frozen in ice and left for the wolves.

She holds her gaze steady and says she was very friendly with the British, French and American soldiers. She worked hard to survive and refused to give in. There's a swelling pride in her classic face and the water has cleared from eyes that stare into mine. I can imagine she was a good-looking woman when she was young. She puts her hand on my leg and smiles for the first time. The blue eyes sparkle and there's a hard, piss-taking humour. She runs her hand towards my bollocks but stops short. I don't know what to do and this old dear has put me in my place. Her eyes never leave mine and she's got the power of a woman who knows what's what. Her fingers are inches from my balls and she squeezes. Digging her nails in. She holds it for a few seconds then softens and starts stroking my leg. The worst thing that could happen now would be if I got a hard-on. Sitting in the street in front of the troops. It's a fucking nightmare and I shrug my shoulders. She nods and moves her hand back to the table – I was a good girl for you British boys and you've all forgotten me now my skin is wrinkled.

The woman is sad and serious, switching back and forward. She lowers her voice and turns her head quickly to the Englishmen nearby, making sure I'm the only one listening. She says that the people were running from the communist murderers gripped by a panic someone like me can never believe. It was an extermination of innocents, a holocaust. Stalin was a monster. She knows Hitler was a monster, everyone knows that now, but do they understand about Stalin? They were both monsters who never lived in her village and never knew she even existed, yet together they destroyed everything she held precious. The Soviets were out of control – hard, bitter men with no kindness in their hearts for German civilians. There were women too, fighting for the communists. Imagine that, tough peasant women matching the men. The Nazis started everything and then hid, buried in their bunkers. They left the ordinary people to pay the party's debt. Hitler didn't even evacuate her family. She was lucky to get out of her village before the Bolsheviks arrived.

She lowers her voice further. She seems uncertain for a moment and then tells her story. There were angels. She is telling the truth about this. There were angels who came at night to help the German people. Many Germans know about these angels. They were mysterious figures who appeared in areas invaded by the Soviets. Angels led the people back through enemy lines to safe German territory. She went through the woods as a child, heading for the magic city of Berlin where they hoped they would be safe. Where were the men when they were needed? The angels helped her reach Berlin and she stayed for the rest of her life. Her mother and brother died in the shelling. Their bodies were burnt in a street near where we're sitting now, drinking lager and feeling the sun, their corpses bruised and distorted. Everything was destroyed. God was on her side though, and she wants me to understand that God was with her because she was young and innocent.

She saw the Berlin Wall go up and she saw the Berlin Wall come down. Nature made her beautiful so she could work and survive. What happened to the ugly people? Did I ever think what happened to the ugly women with scarred faces and missing limbs? Who would care for these women? She grew quickly and was working when she was thirteen. She had been lucky because the soldiers liked blonde hair and blue eyes, and they liked her breasts and some of them liked her behind. She laughs.

– Yes, some of them liked my behind as well as the other places. Mostly it was the French boys who liked that kind of love. I was beautiful and they wanted my body. They paid and I saved and one day I bought an apartment. I worked hard and built a new life. My brother was nine when he died. My mother was twenty-eight and my father thirty-one. I was the only one left to continue.

Tears trickle down her face. I feel like shit and don't know what to say. I nod my head. I can see Carter behind the old woman with a bottle of lager in his mouth. Raising his eyes to the sky and laughing through the drink because I've got the nutter. Tom's got the fucking headcase. The mad old granny pissed on meths, schnapps, whatever. Brain rotting with the clap and dementia taking a grip. Mark shakes his head, glad it's not him. You can't tell old people to fuck off and leave you alone.

Doesn't matter where they come from and how bad they make you feel. You can't tell the old folk to fuck off and die.

Carter and Mark turn away and go back to their conversation, the England boys drinking and enjoying the day. Not a care in the world. Probably don't see anything in the old girl except decay and weakness. We're young and hard as nails. We don't care about anything except ourselves. Don't let the disease in. Stand together and have the dignity to fade away when your time's up instead of causing trouble for people with the sadness of age. It'll happen to all of us eventually. The ones who last that long. There's no story the young want to hear from this old dear. But I'm interested. Trying to imagine the panic of war. Must be a fucking nightmare for the women and kids. The weak left defenceless. Left to pay the tab for their men's behaviour. Mothers watching their kids bayoneted in the street. Young boys and girls seeing their mum gang-raped by Russians, Germans, whoever. Never the English. Suppose there's always someone left to pay in the end and it doesn't matter if it's your fault or not. All that bollocks about the meek inheriting the earth. The woman takes out a hanky and dabs her eyes. Focuses on the table. Lost in her memories.

I look down the main street and feel the rush of being in Berlin. Have to shut this old girl out and stop thinking. Don't know what it is, but Berlin is the place to be. Maybe it's the history lodged in our heads. All those pictures fed to you as a kid. It was the centre of the Cold War and a focus between East and West. Now we've got it off the communists, but the memory of the Wall is still fresh.

This woman is old and battered but has her pride. Maybe she's a nutter, I don't know. I'm not a fucking doctor. But she's glad she lived to tell the tale. One day she'll die and it'll be sooner rather than later. In some ways she's already gone because the financiers are rebuilding Berlin and the young girl sweating under a column of Allied soldiers doesn't count. As long as the boys pay in hard currency everyone's happy. There's no need for pride in the multinational equation. This might be Germany but the ordinary Germans in their run-down estates and rural hovels don't count either. None of these banker cunts know the name of a kid's village swallowed up by the Soviets. It's the new dictators who'll piss all over her and say she's better off – the bankers and industrialists, and every kind of cunt you can imagine. They're looking our way next, England in their sights.

The prossies in Amsterdam must've made a killing from the England boys and one day those girls will be touching up young men when their looks have gone, their blood riddled with tropical disease. But the latest wave of English hooligans don't give a fuck. I don't give a fuck about all that bollocks. You can't do anything about what happened half a century ago. At least we won the war and didn't do what the Red Army did. We've moved on and now we're on the piss in the middle of the same city the RAF bombed. It's sinking in. Where we are and what we're doing. Sitting in Berlin hearing an echo of a miserable past who'll piss off in a minute. Life is for the living.

Mark comes over to help out and tells me to forget the old grannies and feel sorry for all those sad wankers at home stuck in front of the box. Or if Rod's lucky he'll be wandering round Blockbuster trying to make the right choice. Keep the missus sweet. Rod trying to get the CD player to stop jumping. Mandy's disco compilation skipping while his mates are in Germany with some extra-strong Deutschelager in their hands. We're centre of the world. Maybe not the world, but the wannabe leader of a brave new reich. Berlin is a place you hear so much about as a kid that you form this strong image.

The Berlin Wall was right there as kids and we were raised on Cold War politics and the threat of nuclear disaster. We're packed full of anti-Soviet images, our papers matching KGB sadists to the trendy cunts on the council, all those pro-queer, pro-black, anti-white cunts chipping away at England. We've been taught to hate the scum in the East and the rubbish selling our culture down the drain. Listening to the woman brings it back. It's the real story and I can't imagine the English acting like the Russians in a war. Maybe if you've lost twenty million people you just don't care any more, but that's not the English way. We're not mass murderers like some of these cunts. We fight because we have to and have our honour. That's why the

Germans wanted to surrender to the English. That and the fact they'd killed so many Russians.

The woman looks at Mark and nods. She understands more than I think and I feel small. I've seen nothing compared to her. He's cut across her and the tears have stopped. Her pride is there for everyone to see, except I'm the only one looking. She says she has to go to the shops and stands up, and though part of me wants to hear her stories another part wants her to fuck off and leave me alone. Let me enjoy myself without all this misery. She has to be a headcase anyway. Talking about angels like that. Fucking nutters everywhere these days.

Football is serious, but it's still a game. We're doing our own thing without anyone shouting orders. I don't want to start thinking about women and kids getting butchered. It makes you sick, don't care who it is. So when the woman leaves I bury her in my head. It all becomes unreal again, something for the film-makers and soundtrack writers. I don't know. Her time has come and gone, I suppose, just like the pensioners who fought for us in the war. We respect them, of course we do, but respect doesn't pay the bills. The Government doesn't give a fuck, whether it's the Conservatives or Labour. It's all money to Parliament. People's names are just more statistics.

The old woman walks through this mob of English hooligans. Blonde teenager getting fucked rigid by the troops of the great democratic experiment. The boys move aside and let an old woman pass. A shadow filtering through the years. Tiny pin-prick face on the horizon waiting for the strategic missile to pass by and destroy the munitions dump. Designer explosives directing shrapnel in the opposite direction. I wonder if she's making it up about the angels. I try to imagine these figures in the wood. All I can think of is fat cherubs with wings, but know that's not what she means. I suddenly wonder if she ever got married and had kids. I wish I'd asked. A happy ending makes you feel better about things.

– What was she on about? Mark asks, sitting down, looking at my face and laughing. What's the matter you miserable cunt? Cheer up, you slag, you look like you've seen a ghost. She was a bit pale I suppose, but just another nutter like you get back home. They've all got the same story.

– She was talking about how the Russians killed the people in her village and how she escaped to Berlin through the woods.

– Couldn't have been much fun, Mark nods. Still, they did enough themselves didn't they, the old Germans and that. They slaughtered the Russians and Jews and anyone else they could get hold of without any problem, so what do they expect? Hitler didn't think about all that when he was bombing London did he? They killed enough of our boys. Bet she wasn't out there protesting when the bombers left for London or the yids were being hauled out of their homes. There were enough kids ripped from their parents then.

– She was a child. So it wasn't her fault, was it? I mean, how was she to know what was going on? It wasn't down to her personally.

Mark thinks for a moment and looks for the woman. She's gone.

– Suppose not. Don't worry about it anyway. It's all in the past.

– Those Russians were fucking scum, says Brighty, coming over. I heard what that granny said and she's right. Communists are the fucking scum of the earth. There's enough of the cunts over in East Berlin. Me and Harris are going over there later to have a look. There's some Germans he knows coming in from Leipzig. They're from the East, know what they're talking about because they had to grow up under the cunts. They know where to go. You want to come along. We should have a tidy firm together. There's a few card carriers, but they're mostly along for the ride. They're not into the football.

Football and politics are separate as far as I'm concerned. That's the way I see it anyway. Still, it's an excuse for a row I suppose and these things are always played up. Long as it's not against some hostel for women and kids. Harris comes over and a few other blokes seem game enough. The majority keep clear. Harris tells Billy he doesn't reckon it'll be up to much, because the area of East Berlin they're talking about is full of wankers. They're students and squatters, people like that, a few cracked hippies, white dreads and such-like. But we'll visit some of the sights because we're staying in West Berlin. A cheap hotel behind these bars and restaurants. Might as well see the rest of the town.

We were lucky getting the place when we arrived. We get off the train expecting a reception committee but the locals are sleeping. Ends up a few of us turn down this street where there's a flashing sign. Harris leads the Expeditionary Force into Reception. There's this old Turk sitting behind the desk reading his papers. He's finished the Arabic and is studying the German version. Looks tired and lifts his head. He's got the muddy remains of his Turkish coffee. I think of Hank in Amsterdam. A night-shift brotherhood hooked on caffeine. Abdul's peering through his glasses. Harris asks if there's any rooms going and the bloke can't be bothered. He's tired and probably doesn't fancy the look of the clientele. Men stinking of drink and a railway journey. Short hair, tattoos, jeans, trainers, small bags, a Cross of St George around the shoulders of the man with the missing hand. Can't say I blame him. Abdul says the place is full. Harris stares hard for a moment, then shrugs and turns. We head back to the door.

Suddenly something clicks. The caffeine kick-starts Abdul's brain.

– Hey, he says. You English?

Harris turns back again and nods. He's not impressed.

– That's right mate, we're English. You got a problem with that?

The man's face opens and his manner changes.

– You, he stammers. You hooligans?

There's a second's pause and we start laughing. Abdul seems excited for some reason.

– We've come for the football, Harris says.

Abdul frowns.

– But, you hooligan?

Harris shakes his head.

– We're good boys. We won't wreck the place if that's what you're worried about. We're the Society For Better Anglo-Kraut Relations.

The man doesn't get the joke and hurries around the front of the desk. He's short and chubby. He peers at Harris, then points to the Chelsea tattoo and Cross of St George. Points to the rest of the boys waiting to see what happens.

– No, he insists, you boys are hooligans.

– Is he taking the piss? Mark asks.

– You hooligans, the man half shouts. Come and sit down boys. I have rooms for hooligans.

Nobody knows what the fuck the bloke's on about, but he's obviously been reading his papers. We sit down and he starts rabbiting on about the English hooligans and how there's going to be a lot of fighting with the Germans. We go through the routine of signing the book and this takes ages, but Abdul's the owner and his hooligan prices are low. He calls some help for the bags. The bloke's suddenly a character instead of a grumpy old cunt. He's running around and can't do enough for us. It's a mad world. It's worked out well. The hotel's handy and cheap, and now we're pointing new arrivals in Abdul's direction.

– Tell your friends, he insisted when we went out this morning. Tell them that hooligans are welcome at the Hotel Kasbah.

I go over to a table where Carter and Harry are sitting with three Millwall boys. I sit down and listen to the conversation, running through names and dates and a Chelsea-Millwall connection. The South London blood ties of certain characters. Harry knows them through some contract West London Decoration was doing. One comes from Tooting and knows someone else and before you know what's happening there's marriage and mates arriving from every direction. Funny how it works. Wouldn't get that with West Ham, because they're miles out down the Commercial Road. As for Arsenal and Tottenham, you won't get any mixed blood there. No fucking chance.

We hang around enjoying the atmosphere, and when I get hungry I order some food off a poofy cunt in a white jacket and black dickie bow. He minces off and comes back with a plate of cold sausage and Hitler only knows what other type of spiced meat. I take a bite and it's not bad. Continental shit, but it'll do for now. The poof opens another bottle of lager and hands it over. Pisses off. This is the life, in the heart of the fatherland whistling at the reich-birds hurrying past. Bottle of ice-cold lager in my hand. I lean back and look around. There's more English drinking here now, with small groups coming along the street and seeing what's what and who's who. Popping in for a quiet drink. Being nice and sociable. Ticking over nicely.

The old stone church stood against a background of new developments. It was similar to the ones you got back in England and somehow it had come through the Allied bombing. Glass towers had replaced burnt-out homes, businesses rising from the devastation. Harry remembered a picture he'd seen of St Paul's in London, the dome rising through a wall of flames. Somehow St Paul's had survived the German bombs. Everyone said it was a miracle, and he bet the people of the time had taken it as a sign that God had a soft spot for the English. It was good to have God on your side, and it must be true whoever you were, whether it was the Muslims waging holy war against Allied infidels, or God-fearing Born Again pilots strafing unbelievers in the Iraqi desert. Everyone was always right, and as a kid that photo of St Paul's stuck in Harry's mind, proving that in England's and London's case, it really was true.

Here he was all these years later in the middle of Berlin seeing a mirror image. It was smaller because St Paul's was fucking massive, but he stood and stared at this Berlin church all the same. The only time he'd been to St Paul's was as a kid, but when you went overseas you looked at these things.

There was a square further forward, but Harry turned the other way and walked under the shelter of a jutting roof that shielded a selection of small food outlets and several amusement arcades. The fast-food places smelt like their equivalents in London, the grease and fried onions not making much of an impression after the satay sauce of Holland. He looked in the arcades and saw a familiar collection of kids and youths, with older men and women thrown into the war zone. He spotted a gang of boys standing around Smart Bomb Parade, screens everywhere flashing cartoon characters and brightly-lit graphics. Good was fighting Evil all over the arcade, but Smart Bomb had caught the punters' imagination. They'd had it in The Unity for a few months now. It was taking over. Whoever had the idea must be coining it, living a great life somewhere, straight down the travel agent's for a one-way flight to the Philippines, leaving the wife and kids to fend for themselves as the genius inventor prepared to enjoy the spoils of war.

Harry saw Nicky, her small frame popping up again, sitting on the edge of her bed with a cup of coffee and the photo album, running through the pictures one more time. He saw Nicky working in the Philippines with the not-so-good Catholic girls left behind by the Spanish, working the Manila go-go bars. Harry was pleased, though, because that was Christian Manila and Nicky was from Buddhist Thailand, and Smart Bomb wasn't bothered with Asian trading zones. The people were hard workers and had the right attitude. They grafted and wanted to get ahead, so accepted low wages and saved hard. No, Smart Bomb Parade was focused on the East but somewhere a little nearer home, pinpointing the wicked General Mahmet, leader of a deviant oil-stealing regime, concentrating on another kind of warfare. It was an exciting game, matching moral justification with high kill ratios and negligible personal risk.

Harry left the Germans to their war games and stopped at a pizza shop. He bought a big slice of ham and cheese from a skinny punk and went over to a bench, sitting in the sunshine feeding his gut and working on yesterday's hangover, wondering where to go next. He wasn't far from the Hotel Kasbah, and he smiled thinking of last night and this morning, the owner a fucking nutter doing everything he could to make the English invasion force feel at home. Berlin was a lot different to Amsterdam. It seemed more controlled in a lot of ways, but then you came across someone like Abdul at the reception desk, a reminder that Berlin was supposed to be a mad city. A big chunk of the Nazi party came from southern Germany and considered Berlin a centre of Mahmet-style deviance, so maybe he'd scout out something similar, but where did you start? He wasn't looking for whores, because he'd had enough of that for right now. He was happy and didn't want any hassle.

– Alright? Billy Bright said, coming and sitting next to Harry. What are you doing?

Harry had to think about that one. What the fuck was he doing? He was in Berlin and he'd read something about the place before leaving, about the music and clubs, investment pouring into a city busy building for a brighter future. It sounded good. But he wasn't doing much except thinking.

– Just having something to eat, Harry answered. What about you?

– I'm going to see the bunker where Hitler committed suicide.

Harry nodded and took a big bite of pizza. The cheese was thick and stringy, and a big blob dropped on his jeans.

– Fucking hell.

Billy sat down and Harry offered him a bite. Billy shook his head.

– The bunker's not marked because they don't want people finding out where it is in case it becomes a shrine. They're shit scared because they know there's still interest, specially among the East Germans who were pissed on for years by the reds. They had to deal with the Stasi their whole lives so swung to the right. They wanted to have some pride so they looked around. All they found was the neo-Nazis. That's why you get things like Rostock. People struggling to get by don't want millions of Turks turning up and nicking their jobs. They want to get on with life and have some pride.

– That Turk at the hotel's alright, Harry said.

– It's not the Turks I'm talking about, Billy said. It's people wanting to have some pride in their country and fighting back.

Harry nodded again because he knew Berlin could be an extreme place. He didn't want to get into a discussion about poverty-stricken, harshly-treated locals. He hadn't been here long, but Amsterdam was more his sort of place. He was probably one of the exceptions, because the others would like the energy extremes brought. Now he was here, he wanted to get into the future instead of the past. Berlin was the future of a united Europe. There was no point fighting the inevitable. Harry was going to enjoy his holiday no matter what.

Everywhere had its own atmosphere. He believed in these things, because when he looked at someone nine times out of ten he sussed them right off. He could tell a lot about people by how they looked. If someone had mean eyes they generally turned out to be a cunt, and if someone was friendly they were usually generous and honest. Harry went with the feeling. People were prejudiced, but that was because they stuck with what they were told to see. You had to work things out for yourself. He thought about Nicky and knew it could be hard getting through the wrapper.

– Eva Braun stood by Adolf right to the end. Imagine being stuck in the bunker with your woman and dog, with the Red Army getting closer and closer. They did the right thing and were dead before the scum arrived.

Berlin wasn't going to be easy. Harry understood that now, sitting on the bench with the smell of kebabs and the exploding rockets of the amusement arcade, and with Billy Bright doing a Nuremburg on him. No, Berlin was different, another planet to Amsterdam. The people had to deal with the same problems but Amsterdam was a melting pot, where the ideas blended together. Berlin, he didn't really know, but could guess. The buildings seemed so clean, yet under the roof behind him there was dirt and grease. England was halfway between the two countries, trying to con itself everything was running efficiently, the same as in Germany, while those in charge were fucking useless.

He saw Billy Bright sitting there like he was expecting something. Harry wondered what he wanted. The bloke was alright in his way, but went on a bit. Everyone had their views, but Billy's weren't the same as Harry's. He didn't give a toss about all that nonsense, just wanted an easy life, finishing the pizza and throwing the paper plate at a bin, missing and leaving it in the gutter. What the fuck was the bloke waiting for?

Billy was a Barnardo's boy and had never really got over the fact that his mum and dad had given him away. Harry had heard the story second-hand and never asked him what it was all about, because it wasn't the sort of thing you brought up over a pint. Even if he'd been a close mate he would've found it hard dealing with something so personal.

He saw Billy sitting there with his short hair and frowning face and thought of Nicky's kid and how the little boy must feel stuck in an orphanage, with his mum on the other side of the world, on the game. He wouldn't know about all that sex stuff, and so it wouldn't matter, but he must miss his mum. Maybe he saw other kids and they had mums and dads and he wondered what made him special. In the picture the kid had light brown skin and Oriental features. He didn't really stand out from the crowd and that was a good thing. It was better to blend in, keep your head down and not make too many waves.

The monks didn't look dodgy like some of the vicars you got in England, and the boy had a smile on his face. At least the kid was better off in a tropical paradise than a grey European city where it rained for months on end and the cold got right inside your bones. In Europe he'd go to a hard city school with none of the sun and calm he had in Thailand. Harry convinced himself the boy was happy and Harry felt good about that. Maybe one day Nicky would send for him and he'd go and live in Holland, the kid's old girl sitting pretty in a smart apartment, or maybe she'd get a one-way ticket to Bangkok and take the train south, settle on one of the islands and live happy ever after.

Harry thought about Balti and how he said he'd like to live in a tropical paradise one day, usually after a curry. Harry had dreamt about the tropics and wondered if it meant something, but it would be hard to give up everything because England was a difficult place to leave, with all the history and tradition nobody really knew about in any specific detail still strong enough to keep you tied down. Even though he moaned, England was home and the best country in the world, and that didn't stop him wanting the best Europe had to offer as well. Harry stopped himself because soon he'd be standing in the square singing God Save The Queen with Billy Bright.

According to the story he'd heard, Billy had spent the first ten years of his life in care before an elderly couple took him in. They were good people, but were old and the husband died when Billy was fifteen. He still lived near his foster mum and they were close. He'd been lucky, Harry supposed, because he could've gone through life without ever getting a chance. When the old girl got mugged one day coming back with her pension Billy went off his head. The attackers were black and the old bill never found them. She was knocked over and kicked in the face, and from that day on Billy was different. Harry didn't hate blacks but there was nothing he could say to Billy. He didn't necessarily want to change his mind, because he didn't care one way or the other, but because a couple of blokes were scum didn't mean everyone else was the same.

When Harry thought about it, the Nazis wouldn't have been too impressed with Billy. They wanted the same perfection as the modern corporations, and loved the sick experiments just like today's scientists. Look at the experiments and it was going on right now. It was round the back door. But Billy didn't give a toss about genetic engineering and artificial insemination, or whether the valves of a pig's heart would mould with human flesh. Harry saw Billy celebrating victory against the evil forces of international Jewry and communism, having helped clean the scum from the pond, standing in front of the Leader who was focusing on a new element, taking another step towards perfection with the erasing of physical deformities. Billy would expect better.

– Do you want to go and see the bunker? Billy asked.

– What bunker?

– The bunker where Hitler killed himself. We could get a taxi there if you want.

– I thought you said it was buried away so nobody could see it, so it won't become a shrine.

– It's just hidden, Billy said, thinking. I asked some of the others but none of them were interested. Said they'd rather have a drink. We're going to East Berlin tonight and meeting up with these blokes from Leipzig. See if we can have a row with some anarchists or reds, anyone who's up for it really.

Harry shook his head and said he wasn't interested either. He was going walkabout and tonight he was going to get a decent fräulein to suck his knob. Billy was obviously disappointed, then said what about Bang, they could all go there, take a big firm along and have a good night out. Harry had forgotten about the bar and the card that trendy bird gave him on the ferry. It was worth thinking about. She was well tasty and the boyfriend looked like a cunt. One of those sincere wankers who gave it the big one all the time but when it came down to everyday politeness was a slag. That's the way Harry preferred to see things. It meant he might have a chance. She was a cracker no matter what anyone said, and he had to be honest that Nicky had been cropping up a bit too often. It wasn't healthy and not something you read in the Carter training manual. Deliver your load and turn for home. It was the only way, but sometimes you had to be honest, and if Harry was totally honest what he needed was a good shag here in Berlin to burn away the memory of that Thai slag.

Billy was going on about Adolf and Eva again, and how it must've been hard to shoot the dog, and Harry agreed but said he had to get back to the hotel. He didn't have anything against the bloke, but he wanted to have a walk around on his own and go to that bar later, early evening maybe, after he'd seen some of Berlin. He was on a roll and didn't have time for all that political shit.

Three o'clock in the afternoon and the bars are packed. I'm fucked before we've even moved. It's kick-off time and I'm feeling the ten bottles of lager. That poof cunt of a waiter has stopped coming outside because there's hundreds of English on the pavement singing RULE BRITANNIA. Maybe his shift's finished and the timing's right. Let off the hook with some of his customers calling him a fucking German queer. We have to go inside for our drink, but at least there's more staff behind the counter now. The owner's smiling, everyone on the piss and enjoying themselves.

I'm in the bar starting another bottle and spot this familiar ginger head. I blink and make sure. Standing there a few feet away. Haven't seen the bloke for years. It's this nutter from Derby I met years back watching England. I start to move towards him but suddenly remember an incident between Chelsea and Derby. It worked out alright and I'm pissed, so I tap him on the shoulder and after a couple of seconds he smiles. We shake hands laughing, running through what we've been doing and all the usual bollocks. The years vanish. He's a good bloke. Running through Derby's end-of-season rows while I think of the incident. It was at night and he slashed Facelift. Right across the arse. I should've said something but kept quiet. It worked out okay with the old bill coming along at the right time. Didn't feel good about it and I'm glad Facelift's not here. I almost start laughing, thinking of him with his arse slashed, stabbed in the gut. Mark and Harris are nearby and they don't know Derby from Adam. It's fucking mental and doing my head in.

We have a couple of drinks together, but I'm fucked. Tell him I'll find him later on. Down the same bar. I go back to the hotel for the speed Harris has brought along from Amsterdam. That's what he says – skunk in Holland and whizz in Germany. Must be the train journey or sitting in the sun for hours doing me in. The streets are baking and it just means you drink more. I follow Harris, Mark and Carter to the Kasbah.

Harry was having a break in a bar, somewhere in East Berlin, because his feet were aching and he'd hoped for a repeat of that Amsterdam effort, where the girls were friendly and passed the dutchie, and where their Angel boyfriends were polite and bought you a bottle of lager. He'd struck lucky there, but this place was well quiet. He got himself a drink and sat by the window. His shirt was soaked from the walking. He must've done miles, and it had to be at least eighty degrees outside.

He'd been for a wander around Zoo station, and then caught the train from West to East. It passed over a stretch of land where he guessed the Berlin Wall had been. There was a big tent on some wasteland, a circus or rave venue maybe, everything moving on with new freaks and new sounds. One minute the Wall was there and the next it was gone in a puff of dust and the thud of pickaxes, East and West united. The English press said there was a new German superstate in the making and some hinted that the old Prussian spirit was stirring, except it hadn't really worked out like that, because instead of the goose-stepping they got love parades and techno drilling through the brick torture chambers, skinheads and punks eyeballing each other for the leftovers. He enjoyed the ride, getting off when his stop arrived.

The first thing Harry saw as he came out of the station was a sex shop and some dodgy cunt selling burgers, a few rancid boilers pushing snotty-nosed kids in pushchairs. There were a couple of cartoon drug dealers leaning against a fence doing their best to look like drug dealers, with dark shades and greased-back hair. He was in the shade of the station, with dirt ground into the stone and the ticket hall dark and dingy, smelling of piss. The sex shop was small and seedier than normal, the sort of business that only ever survived showing the hardest porn, something you'd be hard pressed to find in Soho. A man came out in the regulation mac, looked up and down the street and shot off, examining the pavement. It was June and the temperature was in the eighties and this wanker was going round like he didn't know the school holidays had started. Maybe they hadn't, but if the England boys found out they'd probably do him like they did that cunt in Amsterdam. The English had standards to maintain. Even Harry knew that.

The burgers were greasy and smelt like shit, and he didn't need that on a nice day like today. They were worse than the dog food you found outside football grounds. They reeked and even Carter wouldn't have touched them. The slags pushing the pushchairs had stopped to argue with the drug dealers and the snotty-nosed kids were looking on bored because they'd seen it all before. There was an argument and some bloke rolled over the street. A big fucker with tattoos up his arms and a long scar from cheek to chin, pissed and jabbering, having his say, and then suddenly they all strolled off in three separate directions as though nothing had happened.

Harry moved out of the shadows and into the sun, crossing a bridge and passing several small, busy cafés. There were decent Germans here sipping small glasses of spirit and watching the world. Harry kept going along wide roads lined by run-down, empty buildings. The cars were spewing out fumes and he was sweating, but finally found the street he was looking for. There were a lot of bars and a quieter atmosphere, but he didn't stop, taking notice of the bars as he'd be back. At the other end of the street he turned and found some grand buildings, a big church and the oversized communist architecture of Alexanderplatz. He looked at the church or cathedral or whatever the fuck it was for a couple of minutes, but he was fed up with religion and headed for Alexanderplatz itself.

Harry stood in the square and looked around. The buildings were major. There was a row of flats and the kind of building he'd only ever seen on the telly, big and grey and communist, most of all impressive. It reminded him of the photos of Hitler's buildings. These dictators knew how to build big and he supposed that when you could do whatever the fuck you wanted you tended to think big. He doubted whether Stalin or Hitler had to answer to an accountant when they went on a spree. He sat down on a bench and looked around. Alexanderplatz wasn't bad and it felt different from West Berlin, less commercial. When the Wall was still standing it would've been different again, one side free and packed with adverts, the other confined and advert-free, but despite the misery there had to be a strong belief in what they were doing. Maybe not, he didn't know. It was better to have everyone in together.

Harry drank his lager and watched the people pass outside. Alexanderplatz was something he'd never seen before and he preferred it to West Berlin. He was getting into the feel of the place now, having a cold drink in this small corner of the city wondering what time things livened up. He looked at his watch and it was almost six. A couple of women wandered in and sat at the bar, and the barman put some hip-hop or trip-hop or whatever on, but at least he kept the volume down. Harry tapped his foot and sipped his lager, relaxed and calm, Nicky in her right place and at peace with the world, getting into the European state of mind, loving every minute of his time on the Continent without any kind of media propaganda, doing his own thing, loving everything he saw. The tang of cold German lager tickling the back of his throat as he took things nice and slow.

* * *

Must be Millwall going into NO-ONE LIKES US substituting English lions for the lions of New Cross, the sound drifting down the street, and I'm walking back from the Kasbah after a shower and then some whizz with the rest of the boys, and we get back to the bar where there's more English than before and a couple of police vans parked across the road now that the evening's coming and the English are pissed up singing TWO WORLD WARS AND ONE WORLD CUP pointing at the old bill, trying to wind them up, and then moving straight into ONE BOMBER HARRIS and I wonder if the old bill know that we're taking the piss trying to wind them up about Dresden, Bomber doing Stalin a favour there, wonder if the cunts can understand English humour, but we're peaceful enough and this speed is good blowing my head off and I'm feeling fucking brilliant now looking at the lights, slowly clocking the street and for a few seconds I imagine we're in Hong Kong or somewhere, before the Chinese took the place back, typical English honesty that, keeping to agreements but suppose it had more to do with the Chinese army and a million men in uniform, but who cares about a chinky outpost because it's only money and the lights go on as the sun starts sinking and the cheers go up as a bird across the road blushes with hundreds of Englishmen singing DO YOU TAKE IT, DO YOU TAKE IT . . . a thin girl in her twenties with a short skirt and nicely tanned legs . . . DO YOU TAKE IT UP THE ARSE? and she understands what's being said and her face is red through the bronze skin but she waves and shakes her head, so the England boys give her a big cheer and she waves back, and everything's funny again because it's an old football favourite, and I'm thinking of the Charity Shield when David Beckham came down to the end where 30 or 40,000 Chelsea were sitting and started warming up and suddenly this mass of supposedly New Football Fans – the megastore, club-shirted, middle-class family support – suddenly 30,000 people (mostly working-class men – thirty-year-old men – men with short hair – those men – men like us – men like me), 30,000 geezers are taking the piss out of the bloke singing SHE'S A WHORE because lucky David's going out with a Spice Girl, and he holds his hand to his ear and

805

asks for something better seeing if the Chelsea boys are still up to scratch and within seconds there's 30 or 40,000 Chelsea singing DOES SHE TAKE IT UP THE ARSE? again and again until the stewards come over and off Beckham goes. It makes you laugh. Makes you grin. Makes you want to go over to that fräulein and give her one. Even the bird four rows down was singing at Wembley, my head racing ahead to the next game at Coventry and at half-time they bring on this troupe of thirteen- or fourteen-year-old girls in skirts and pom poms, get them doing the cheer-leader routine, a few harmless movements dancing about playing at baby pop stars, the way the media does, lowering the age of consent all the time, spreading fashion further down the scale just making a living, but the PA is turned up full crank and one or two blokes remember the David Beckham incident and try to get something going but nobody joins in because these kids are too young, knowing the boundaries, and then they come over and line up in front of 4,000 Chelsea, who are mainly half-cut blokes in their thirties sweating in the sun, and the girls do their routine and Chelsea give them a chorus of IF SHE DON'T COME I'LL TICKLE HER BUM WITH A LUMP OF CELERY, and I'm standing in Berlin and this comes in with the rush seeing that bird across the street, having another drink with the boys and there's a mob who were following England in the early eighties, someone says the Salonika 7 are there, and they start something the others pick up on, a golden oldie, singing OLD TED CROKER SAID, WHAT IS HAPPENING, WHAT IS HAPPENING, WHAT IS HAPPENING, OLD TED CROKER SAID, WHAT IS HAPPENING, AND THIS IS WHAT WE SAID, OH, THE ENGLAND BOYS ARE ON THE PISS AGAIN, ON THE PISS AGAIN, ON THE PISS AGAIN, THE ENGLAND BOYS ARE ON THE PISS AGAIN, THIS IS WHAT WE SAID, and I hold my bottle and half drain the lager and I suppose we've been making life hard for the FA for decades now, wherever they go the England mob are already there, shagging the local women and giving the local hooligans a slap, ready and waiting, spoiling the FA's foreign travel, and I'm feeling fucking great, feeling fucking brilliant, and I know it's going to be a good night as a few of us walk away following Harris, leaving the main mob of English behind – they're behaving themselves and not looking for trouble, minding their Ps and Qs, acting like gentlemen with none of those bad German swear words, ambassadors for Tony Blair and the suits at home, the G&T fossils in the British Embassy – walking away and turning down a side street to a taxi office.

We order two cabs driven by Nigerians – big old boys who've escaped their government and the oil industry – eight of us off to meet the Germans – do something for international relations – Billy says neo-Nazis from the East – distant tower blocks covered in football graffiti – no jobs and too much time – fed on hatred for their old controllers – bitter memories – and I sit by the window with the sun down – can't believe the time's gone – maybe the clocks are wrong – whizzing by the window – head on glass speeding through the present day – driver piling along – playing some classical stuff on the radio – friendly enough geezer – doesn't know who he's got on board – travelling with a Billy Boy Gruff – how serious does he take the right-wing stuff? – grown-up and bad tempered – the driver saying how his mum and dad and brothers died and he came to Europe to earn a crust – talking loud about tribal wars and how bad these things are – booming voice fills my ears – then the sound dips down – watching the cars and buses and people strolling along – suddenly look up and see the Reichstag – fucking hell, it's the Reichstag and Brandenburg Gate – seeing the sights but keeping it to myself – flashes of colour – drank too much and did the speed – gone a bit overboard if I'm honest – an Anglo-Saxon who likes his lager – but bollocks – it feels good and I fancy some more – dead silence inside the car – the music's gone and I wonder what's happened – the cab's stopped and I don't want to look – I mean, Brighty says he hates niggers and Harris likes cutting people – not enough to kill a man – not enough for Harris to lean over from the back seat and pull the driver's head back – hold it firm – the Nigerian trying to struggle and get loose – doesn't want to die like the rest of the family – doesn't want to die like the German kids in their villages – just wants the angels to come and spare his life – wants to live to fight another day – Harris holding him firm so Reich-Bright can do his Aryan Brotherhood routine – pull out a razor and laugh in the face of the black man – lean over and cut the pulsing throat – lean in close with his face distorted – watching the blood pump in a slaughterhouse massacre – tribesmen shagging blue monkeys – greasing the primate's arse and slipping in – buried to the hilt – only girl monkeys because there's nothing the tribes hate more than queers – and I suppose the old monkey doesn't have much choice – caught in a trap and brought into the village for some slap and tickle – slapping its face and tickling its bum – with celery – Reich-Bright leaning in close so the black man can smell the lager on his breath and the powder on his gums – leaning in close but saying fuck all – this deathly silence that does my fucking head in – knowing this is shit – fucking shit – just something Bright says for a laugh and I don't want to see anyone die – tiredness and the sun and drink and speed taking advantage – burning everything as it races forward – brain bulging – the blood pumping from a severed jugular and hitting the roof of this beat-up car – thought the Germans built quality cars and empires to last a thousand years – rust on the doors and the smell of petrol – stink of blood hitting the roof and hitting my face – eyes buried on the dark tarmac outside – hard jungle red – the tinkle of green as I raise my right hand to wipe away the blood – get rid of the sweat – red turning to green so the car starts moving again and I hear the band strike up with DJ Bright the man at the controls . . . the Expeditionary Force moving ahead – the driver laughing and saying he likes the music – where did you get the tape? – and Brighty must be fucked as well because he starts asking this bloke all these questions like where did your family die and how old were you and it's hard being an orphan and you better stop round the corner because the place we're going might not be too friendly – says good luck mate as we shut the door and I stumble on the pavement – the second cab stopping behind – eight of us crossing the road and heading for a bar near some place Harris calls Alexanderplatz.

I stand in the shadows, tapping Harris for a top-up, and he's ready enough. Hasn't been drinking like me because he's the leader of our team. Has to keep his head straight. Standing in the shadows knowing my head's fucked. Left myself wide open. Don't give a toss, because I make the effort and get the concentration pointing in the right direction here in some dark corner of East Berlin following the leader into this bar with the tinted windows, carved German words in the glass, walking in on a mini Nuremburg and a bar stuffed with fifty or so blokes, most of them in black combat jackets and DMs, feel like I've gone back a few years here though it's a German style they've picked up along the way and changed from the original just like the style English skinheads picked up from Jamaica and changed, shedding some skin and some weight, marching straight in, and a few of the Germans turn their heads at these eight England boys strolling in without a care in the world and I'm glad to see Harris spot the blokes he knows. We're soon sitting at the bar and the Germans are lining up the lager with a big selection of white noise sounding out, all Screwdriver and Skullhead and Blood & Honour tunes brought along by their own resident gruppen-DJ, keeping the reich-sounds going, settling in and taking a look at the bar, sipping lager with the whizz shifting my head forward a gear and cruising, because once you sit down and look at things more clearly they pan out, clocking the big reich-geezers, obviously the hardcore, and a mix of other blokes who look like they're along for the night out, Harris introducing us to several of these Germans whose names I don't understand, expecting them to launch into one and start going on about the Turks and asylum-seekers and the coming new world order, but they're very formal asking us what we think of Berlin, and one bloke who you'd never guess was an animal-lover asks Mark if he's been to the zoo. Mark obviously thinks it's a trick question and pauses, that the zoo's some inner-city ghetto full of Pakis, but the bloke's straight up because there's a panda on loan that they're trying to mate with this other panda who's also on loan as well but neither seems interested in sex, preferring the bamboo. We're sitting in Nuremburg with Ian Stuart belting out a song and we're in a conversation about pandas with this modern-day storm-trooper. Maybe the bloke's speeding as well, maybe there's a glut of the stuff and they're giving it away with the frankfurters in the train station. Another zoo. Laughing now with these fucking nutters talking about how the pandas can't be bothered having a shag because it's too much effort and they'd rather sit in the bar and have a few beers and then piss off for a bamboo special with water chestnuts, and we say we know a lot of geezers like that back home in London, like old Harry Roberts who's a good bloke but a pisshead who can't be bothered half the time, him and a hundred other blokes just the same, and this German is almost pissing himself, almost crying with laughter because he says he knows these people, he knows these men dedicated to another kind of life, the bierkeller and burger men. There's enough of them in Leipzig and every other German city. I say they're everywhere because they just can't be bothered with all that sex stuff when they can sit in front of the telly and have a wank over some skin flick of a bird getting serviced on their behalf. The old medical condition, Blow Job By Proxy, but then I go and spoil it all by saying that's the fucking chinks for you, been smoking too much opium.

– Yes, this bloke says, it is a problem in Germany. The immigrants are taking over with their drug dealers and pimps. There are four million Turks in Germany and millions of Germans unemployed.

I nod and have another drink and let Brighty and Harris lead the conversation, looking round at the men drinking and laughing, and there's quite a few with their hair grown out and a couple with flat-tops, and there's this little geezer, a real wide boy with a jack-in-the-box manner, explaining to Mark how the Europeans look at the English hooligans, that whatever they say and do to us, deep down they respect England for the trouble we've caused through the years. Whatever happens, England is the role model for football hooligans. They can't get over these mobs of barbarians who come over and raid their cities, pillaging but not raping, smashing up their shopping centres and causing havoc against the odds. Doesn't matter whether they come from London, Birmingham, Leeds, New-castle, whatever, they're on a different scale that frightens the shit out of the Continentals. He says the English are rebels. Not in their politics but in their young men, the working class who drink and riot, it's part of the Saxon nature to get pissed and have a laugh, and if anyone starts on them give them a kicking.

Have to admit this bloke knows what he's on about and he's not saying this like he's trying to lick anyone's arse. Has a feel about him that tells you he's dangerous. He knows we're Chelsea and says Chelsea have a cult support, a rebel following, and that the fans have made the club famous through the years. That the Europeans always talk about Chelsea with respect, whether it's Scandinavia, Germany, Croatia. He doesn't know about the Italians and Spanish because they're another set of people, fucking subhumans, and he starts going on about how Western Europe is split between the Saxons and the Latins, that the Germans and English share the same blood and that it was a tragedy how we fought each other during the war. With the English fighting next to the Germans, the Russians would have been annihilated, the Slavs working as slaves for their masters in the West. France wants to be Latin, but they can't pull it off, though there's no way you can connect the French and English or the French and Germans. Everyone does the French.

I think of that game in Paris and the French riot police were firing tear gas as the English gave a mob of French skinheads the run-around. I laugh out loud remembering Rod trying to piss on the eternal flame and wipe out their memories before he was nicked. Mark and the nutter look at me and another German leans in and says his grandfather died fighting the English. I don't know if he wants to have a go or what, but then he says it's stupid this was allowed to happen – friends fighting among themselves when there are better enemies to join forces against. We all nod because there's logic in that, what's the point of killing each other, and I'm off thinking of Vince Matthews and the stories he told us once about the World Cup in 1982 and how the Spanish riot police were always after the English, the police and local fascists both thinking along similar lines, cornering small groups of English when they had the numbers, and how the English were always up for it. The Spanish went for the race connection because we'd given the Argies a good kicking in the Falklands, and when England played Argentina in

Mexico a few years later, when Maradona punched the ball over Shilton, the England boys mobbed up outside waiting for the Argies who bottled out, but even so, I don't know about the English and Germans joining up because I hate the idea of European union. We have to keep ourselves separate, have a drink but go our own ways. I want to tell Hans or whatever the bloke's called that the English don't kill women and kids in concentration camps, no fucking way. It's an essential difference. I know it's not a good idea right now but I can feel the words forming, wondering if I should mention the bombing of London and the plans the Nazis had at the end of the war to execute English prisoners of war, and if that had happened I doubt we'd be sitting here now. But I know it's not the time or place and I have to fight back against laughing, so I look over and concentrate on these birds in the corner, focus on their tits and forget about the heavy stuff. There's three of them and they're fucking beautiful with the speed getting me in that mean-sex frame of mind so I want to go over and drag them in the bogs and fuck the arse off them one by one, humming under my breath THE GERMANS COME IN ONE BY ONE, AND ONE BY ONE THEY ALL GOT DONE to the tune of When Johnny Comes Marching Home, adapting an old Chelsea song from West Ham to Germany, looking at the man next to me and fighting the urge to nut the cunt, what's he fucking looking at, shifting back to the women.

I keep an eye on what they're up to and concentrate on the one with peroxide hair who looks more punk than skin, but it's not the hair I'm bothered about, concentrating on her tits. I'm not that bad yet that I don't show a bit of modesty and slowly look away when she turns her head. Keep her guessing. No need to stir up a bar full of krauts. I can imagine her in the old jackboots. Nothing else except a mouthful of English. I try to push this out of my head and get back in the conversation but the bar suddenly seems hot and stuffy and the white noise fuzzy, everything harder than before. I want to move and get some air and it seems the rest of the bar feels the same way, because we're up and moving, banging through the doors and out into the street, Harris saying how he met these blokes a few years back when he was on holiday in Majorca – imagine that, taking the kids away for a holiday and one night he gets talking with these Germans at the bar and there you go – and Billy met them when they were over in London for the weekend one time. He says they give it the big right-wing thing but most of them are normal aggro merchants. They're not the real thing, whatever they like to think, and I remember that old woman earlier today and how the Nazis stitched her up, how the Allies followed through and fucked her as well but paid for the privilege, and she was just a kid at the time and sees one thing, and there were the Russians getting shafted by the Germans and I suppose the bad blood goes back and forward with the tide. I think about the bombed-out English cities and all the English people the Germans killed. By rights we should be steaming this little lot instead of drinking with them. Fair enough, if it was neutral territory then we could have a laugh, but this seems wrong somehow. Our job is to come into Berlin and do the cunts. I don't know. It's all getting confused.

We walk for a while and come to a street with bars at fairly regular intervals. A lot of them are trendy, and looking through the windows of one or two they're full of wankers. The music's shit and the people look a bit too pleased with themselves and not too happy to see this mob turning up. When a bottle breaks a window our hosts pile in. They wreck the place and give some of the wankers inside a slap. It's no real battle. This one gruppen-geezer, suppose he's the main boy, says this is the easy place, now we're going to do some real communists. People with real politics who'll stand up and fight back and we'd better be ready, because they're more anarchists than reds, and I can almost feel some hidden respect in with the hate. The mob goes along the street sieg-heiling with me and Mark tagging along at the side, Harris and the others a bit further ahead. It's fucking mental because in my head there's films of rallies and I'm thinking how it was all ordered and controlled and now there's these blokes flowing along with the power as the people in the bars try to hide, a few bottles breaking glass, unreal somehow.

I look through a window that doesn't get the treatment and see this face looking back, watching the show, and I tell Mark to look as well because there's the man himself, Fat Harry, with a bottle in his hand and a smile on his face, some tasty-looking bird on his arm.

I slow down and the bar looks good enough, and it seems like it's stacked with crumpet. I'm thinking about peeling off when I hear the sirens. That does it for me and I pull Mark back because my head's fucked and I'm not into all this because we're England and it's all distorted. I call to the others but they're turning down a side street and we take our chance . . . dipping into the bar and giving Harry the surprise of his life . . . fucking hell Harry, you kept her quiet . . . speeding up and slowing down, taking things easy now . . . and Harry looked at Tom and Mark and knew they were pissed and speeding – he'd been enjoying the show outside and suddenly these two had appeared from nowhere. The German crew had disappeared off the main street, but even with the music going Harry could hear the smash of glass. But now he had to think about Tom and Mark and he could see problems ahead, his night ending in tears, because they were stumbling through to the bar and Ingrid was looking at them and asking who they were, and she laughed when he told her they were mates of his from London and said they seemed very happy to see him.

Harry was feeling good about life in general and this bird in particular. He'd been in the bar for a couple of hours when Ingrid turned up. It was down to chance whether she came in or not, but he didn't mind being on his own, and maybe she wouldn't even remember him, or if she did, then think he was a stalker. He was just the bloke by the window sitting alone, and it didn't matter if you were somewhere foreign because it was a different set of circumstances. It wasn't like back home, where if you sat in some club-type bar on your own you looked like a right old wanker, a sad case without any mates left to sniff bar stools.

Everything was a bit new in Bang, but the people coming in were nothing special. There was a theme to the bar, something from a tropical island. The people were laid back and friendly enough, but there wasn't the same warmth as Amsterdam, and it

814

wasn't Harry's sort of place. Here he was in East Berlin and this line of bars and clubs wasn't what he'd expected. The other streets were how he'd imagined this part of the city to look, run down and with a harder edge. He could imagine the secret police giving you grief and border guards shooting runaways making a break for the West, but this bar could've been anywhere. He didn't mind, especially when Ingrid walked in.

– Hello, she said, spotting him straight off.

She didn't seem surprised and this made Harry feel better.

– So you found the bar, she said, sitting right next to him.

Harry didn't want to look but couldn't help it. She had another mini-skirt on shorter than the one she'd been wearing on the ferry. It hitched even further up her legs when she sat down and he knew he had to get a look at the white pants peeping out. She was a fucking raver and much too good for a fat cunt like him, but you never knew, stranger things happened in life, but those legs were doing his head in. He started imagining her peeling off her panties and lying back on the bed, and it was the bed in Nicky's flat for some reason with a closed photo album and open-eyed statue; no, he shifted the scene somewhere else. It didn't matter where the fucking bed was because Ingrid was doing a strip, but Harry put himself in a Sunday dinner-time boozer with a plump old slapper on stage doing her routine, except Ingrid was a hundred times better-looking and stripping for fun. Then she was on Nicky's bed again and Harry was just about to get stuck in when he pulled back and went to buy her a drink.

– It is not my bar, Ingrid said, when he returned. I work here, but today I have the day off. I still come for a drink because the music is good. It is a nice place.

Harry was trying to think of something to say but was getting sidetracked. Whenever Ingrid moved on her stool the mini-skirt rode further up her arse. It wasn't fair, because she was doing his head in and didn't seem to realise. A lot of birds were like that, not knowing the power they had over a bloke's cock and acting like sex didn't exist, wandering around half-dressed flashing their tits and fanny, Ingrid sitting there on the stool with her panties on show, and all he could think about was pulling them off and knobbing her. It had to be the heat because he couldn't get his mind off her legs, and when she shifted a bit she even brushed against his knee, very faintly but still a touch, and he tried to ignore it because he didn't want to end up with a hard-on in the middle of the fucking bar. Funny thing was, Nicky was a cracker as well, but even though she was on the game and shagging ten blokes a night, with the smell of rubber between her legs and spunk in her mouth, this German bird was more dirty somehow. It didn't make much sense because Nicky was a professional, but she was different. He reckoned this Ingrid was a nympho, she had to be dressed like that, he bet she fucking loved it, the dirty cow. But even if she was a sex maniac he had to speak because she'd think he was dumb or thick. With a big effort he looked at her face.

– It's alright here, Harry said. A lot different to the bars in Amsterdam, but I suppose that's because the place is new. There's a lot of pictures on the wall. Where's it supposed to be?

– Hat Rin in Thailand, Ingrid said. It is a place a lot of travellers go, people who want to sit around and take drugs and go raving. I have been there a couple of times. It is not really Thailand, but it is somewhere you can live for a long time on not very much money.

Harry thought of Nicky again and wondered if she'd been to Hat Rin. He didn't think so, because the places she'd talked about were for men content to listen to disco covers and drink imported lager, and from what he could make out they didn't seem short of a few bob. He saw Nicky as a kid sent down from the north to service men two or three times her age and knew it was a different scene. Funny thing was, she told him a few stories about her time there in a matter-of-fact kind of way, and they didn't do anything for him. Watching wank videos he liked birds getting done at both ends or a couple of birds doing a bloke, or best of all two birds doing each other, but when she told him about exactly the same things in real life his cock didn't even flicker. Knowing her took something away and it was a mistake Carter wouldn't make, and thinking of Carter he realised he was on his own and out of the sex machine's shadow. Harry was doing very well for himself, without any help from the professional.

This cheered Harry up because maybe the shag man was losing his touch. There was no more total football from the flash cunt, just Sunday league leftovers, watching some tart trying to get her sagging tits to spin tassels, cheering with the rest of the lads. Harry had to laugh, the pictures on the wall a different world to the go-go bars and blow-job parlours of Nicky's life.

– The first time was best, Ingrid said. The second time I saw it differently, all these bums wandering around who weren't really bums at all. They weren't poor, and certainly not poor like the Thais, and the people who make the money from the businesses are often outsiders. They are from Bangkok. I won't go back to Hat Rin because there is a lack of respect for the local people.

Harry waited for her to light a fag. In Holland it would be dope, but here the drugs were designer rather than natural.

– A lot of the people who go to these places, Hat Rin and Goa and similar areas, don't care about the people who live there. They take but give nothing. The Thais are very traditional people, whatever the West says about them. They don't like to see Westerners naked on the beach and taking drugs. Why should they be pushed aside so the businessmen can build cabins and the travellers fill their beaches with bottles?

Ingrid smiled and shifted again, but Harry kept looking straight ahead, resisting the temptation.

– No, I will not go there again, but I think the bar is okay because it has the original spirit of places like Hat Rin. There is a world culture now of theme bars, techno, ecstasy, world music. All the cultures are blending together so soon there will be no more individual identities.

Harry nodded, but didn't believe all the cultures would disappear, whatever happened, though he wasn't going to argue. He wasn't going to rock the boat and tell her he didn't mind having the extended drinking and relaxed laws on drugs, but knew that his mates weren't going to suddenly start wearing berets and switching from lager to red wine, preferring Bernard's Bistro to Balti Heaven. They finished their drinks at the same time and Ingrid went to the bar and stayed there talking to the bloke serving, while he watched the night get going and more people come in. Ingrid returned and sat down, and Harry was both relieved and disappointed to see her pull her skirt towards her knees. He moved up her body and snuck a look at a nice pair of tits pushing through a thin shirt, nipples visible, moving up to her head. Very nice.

– I don't want to keep you here if you've got somewhere to go, he said, playing the gentleman, kind and considerate.

– I just came in for one drink, but now I have had two. It is not a problem. Do you remember on the boat from England, when you were sick on the heads of those English schoolgirls?

She smiled.

– They were very upset and you laughed. That was very funny. For me at least it was funny, but not for you or the girls.

Harry hoped he wasn't going red because it wasn't the kind of thing you wanted a woman to have in her head when you were looking to get your leg over. He remembered that time when Chelsea played Sheffield Wednesday. They'd gone to Northampton after for a night out and he'd pulled this bird in a club, and though she was nothing special she was game enough. He'd gone back with her and one thing led to another, and there he was pissed out of his fucking skull if he was honest, and this old tart was gagging for it and he wasn't going to disappoint her, but a couple of seconds after he'd got in and started giving it the big one he was sick on her face. He was so pissed he couldn't help himself. He didn't like to think about it too much because she'd gone off her trolley. At first she didn't get what had happened and he was willing himself to come before she found out, but then she worked out what the mess on her face was and she pushed him off and started hitting him. She'd punched him a couple of times then ran off to the bog to wash. He sat down in a chair and pulled his shirt on, but he was pissed and not thinking, giving her time to get clean, and then the fucking door opened and the light went on and she was standing there with a baseball bat. She'd gone for him big time and he had to leg it. Thinking back it was funny because it must've looked like something from Benny Hill, Harry getting

chased by this bird who was screaming her head off, and Balti
was servicing some sort next door and Carter was downstairs on
the couch with another one of her mates. This bird bashed
Harry on the head and chased him onto the landing. He was
pissed but couldn't hit her, couldn't do anything, and he legged
it down the stairs and into the living room where Carter was
standing behind this other bird giving her one, and the old sex
machine kept going while this psycho chased Harry around the
room and out through the back door. He'd done a runner and
looked back towards the room where Carter was carrying on
regardless, imagining the scene inside, the happy couple half-lit
by street lights.

Harry had hid in bushes across the road and waited. At about
six he went back to the house and tapped on the window. He
only had his shirt on and his balls were frozen, a bad hangover
made worse by the baseball bat. He had a lump on the side of
his head and one of his eyes was half shut. She'd done him good
and proper, but luckily Carter was sleeping on the couch and he
passed Harry's clothes out, smiled, then went back to his pillow
and blanket. Harry walked to the train station and waited on the
platform feeling like shit, carrying Carter's smug grin in his
head, the sex machine well pleased. Harry couldn't blame the
woman he supposed, but she was a fucking old slag all the same
going spastic like that just because he'd puked in her face. He
didn't see the others till he got back to London, and his balls
were aching so much from the interrupted sex he'd had to go in
and have a wank in the train bogs. That was the worst life could
get – attacked by a bird and left to wank in a smelly BR bog
early on Sunday morning. What a life. Still, you moved on and
things were definitely looking better now.

– I didn't mean to get sick, he said, weakly. It's the sea that
does it. I've always been like that. Wasn't the best introduction,
was it?

– I don't know, Ingrid said, for the first time showing this
might be more than a friendly chat about nothing in particular.
Sometimes it is not what people do but how they react. I liked
the way you laughed because it showed you did not care.
German men are too serious. Even the ones who hate being

German and want to escape the mentality can't because it is inside them. They want to relax and laugh, but they can't.

– The Germans have always seemed friendly enough to me.

– But you didn't care. You didn't care what the other people saw. Maybe they saw this man with short hair doing something disgusting, but you didn't care if they thought you were an idiot.

Harry thought she should go easy there. He wasn't an idiot and he never thought anyone else thought so, the fucking tart. Just because she had a nice pair of legs that went right up the crack of her arse, and probably had a perfect cunt to go with them, didn't mean she could take the piss.

– They might think you are an idiot because you were sick but you aren't, and you didn't care. Do you understand?

Harry wasn't sure. He nodded all the same because he didn't see why she'd want to make fun of him. It must be the language barrier.

– Anyway, I thought you were attractive so it was a good excuse to talk to you.

Harry felt his knob flutter, because that's what he wanted to hear. The green light was beaming and boyfriend or not he was in. Maybe she was kinky or something, getting turned on by the bulldog emptying his guts over young girls, but as long as she didn't expect a repeat performance he was happy enough, because he was the lover boy on tour and didn't need to splash out on prostitutes tonight. She was a fucking nympho this one, he could feel it in his bones and he could feel it in his bollocks. She was moving around on the stool and he could see the skirt shifting up her legs again, and this time he was less careful whether she noticed him having a peep. She did notice and smiled, and told him to look out of the window, and when Harry did as he was told he saw a strange sight. Two prostitutes in stockings and suspenders were walking down the street with a Turkish-looking bloke who must've been the pimp. They were well-built girls but not ugly. It was like something off a stage and he couldn't believe they were patrolling this street with its line of new bars. It was like in France where the girls waited for truck drivers by the side of the motorways dressed up to the nines in full view of everyone. It was a lot different to England where they were driven down side streets and kept away from the light, operating in shadows, and it was another European tradition he wouldn't mind England absorbing into everyday life.

– They walk up and down every night, Ingrid said. Do you think they are attractive?

Harry said they were okay, but nothing special. He watched them pass and turn the corner. He didn't care about prostitutes because he had something better and cheaper lined up. The windows in Amsterdam were strange, but seeing a couple of girls walking down the road in stockings was mental. You wouldn't get that round his way and it was a shame, it added a lot of spice. He knew The Unity would be packed to the ceiling twenty-four hours a day with crumpet like that marching past.

– Look at this, Ingrid said, pointing outside.

Harry followed her finger and saw this mob coming down the street, heading their way but stopping and steaming into another place. He could hear the glass going and when he leant forward he could've sworn Harris was in there somewhere, but knew they were Germans by the way they dressed. Fuck, there was another bloke who looked like Billy Bright, and it just went to show how international the English look had become, because now they were copying the fucking faces. Either that or Ingrid had been putting something in his drink.

The mob started moving again and passed the bar, and they were making a lot of noise, but Harry couldn't work out what they were doing down here when most of the English were over in West Berlin. Maybe it was too early and they were having a warm-up before they tried to take on England. He watched them go and was thinking he'd have to tell the rest of the lads about this and, fucking hell, he was seeing things because right there on the other side of the glass was Tom pointing his way. Mark came over and they were moving away from the others and heading for the bar. Maybe it was an English firm, but he didn't think so, didn't understand what was going on, realising it was too late to duck his head and avoid unwanted company.

– Shall we go somewhere else? Ingrid asked. There's a good club down the road if you would like to see some other places.

Harry thought it was a good idea but they were too late, Tom and Mark coming in and introducing themselves, then pissing off to the bar. They couldn't just walk out now and, anyway, Ingrid was looking at them and asking who they were, and she laughed when he said they were mates of his from London, and she said they seemed very happy to see him.

This was all he fucking needed and it was typical, because here he was out on the pull and doing well when these two turn up out of nowhere. They were either pissed or on something the way they were acting, the way they looked, and it was like he would never be able to escape his mates and their influence. Looking away from Ingrid he saw Billy Bright and Harris coming into the bar. Maybe someone was selling tickets. He wondered where Carter was.

– I thought I recognised the name, Brighty said.

– Hello darling, Harris said, leaning over and introducing himself to Ingrid.

Billy was standing next to Ingrid and staring at her legs.

– Very nice, he said, swaying.

When they went over to the bar Harry asked Ingrid if she wanted to go somewhere else. The others wouldn't mind and there was enough of them not to miss him.

– No, she said, your friends seem very nice. We can all have fun together.

Harry groaned. He didn't need this and knew the kind of fun the rest of the boys would enjoy. He looked over and saw Mark hanging over the bar saying something to the barman, who shrugged his shoulders.

– Why's this place called Bang? Billy asked, back from the bar. It sounds like a fucking queer place, but I can't see any poofs. A lot of wankers, but no obvious shirt-lifters.

– It is just a sound, Ingrid said. I don't know why they chose it.

– Do you want a drink? Billy asked. That's what I've come back for. We had to jump in here because the old bill have started nicking Nazis, suppressing free speech. Some blokes Harris knows. I'll tell you later.

Harry watched Billy push through to Harris and noticed the others chatting up some girls. This was his big chance to get out before he was lumbered. They were pissed and he could see trouble brewing. Fuck knows what they were doing with those Germans. Maybe he was getting things confused but he thought it was a football match coming up and that the English were the enemy. He'd got hold of something worthwhile here and wasn't going to let the rest of the lads fuck it up, because the same thing had happened enough times in the past. He could see the rest of the night and how it would develop with Ingrid either storming off or, worse than that, pulling one of the others. They were in better shape, but there again he was a sick bastard and Ingrid liked her men sick.

– Why don't you want to stay with your friends? She asked as they walked down the road. I don't mind if you want to talk with them.

– Just fancy going to that club you mentioned, Harry said, wondering where the fuck they were going to end up.

To be honest, Bang had started getting on his nerves. He'd come to Germany to see something German and instead he was in a fucking theme bar. It was like the rich cunts buying into certain areas of London who couldn't make do with the local boozers and had to have them ripped apart and rebuilt, killing the character. You could be anywhere. No, he fancied a few beers in a German bar, but Ingrid had other ideas.

She stopped a cab and he was sitting in the back while Ingrid did the honours, telling the driver where to go. They were driving along and then they were snogging in the back and Harry started to think that the driver was probably watching them in the mirror, the dirty cunt, but he didn't want to let the girl down. She broke off and said something else to the driver and he swore and did a big U-turn, making sure he burnt lots of rubber, the fucking slag. Harry didn't ask what she'd said and sat back watching the streets flash past. He was playing things easy now because he was in and didn't have any more work to do. He felt bad about walking out like that, but none of the others would notice or care. He knew tonight could well end in tears, and there were going to be murders tomorrow, the day of the game.

They were going on a long drive and Harry sat in silence listening to the radio. He got into the sound of the woman speaking and thought how German was a nice language. He knew people said it was hard and ugly, but Harry liked it. Then the woman stopped speaking and classical music filled the car. There was something grand about Berlin at night, with the street lights and music, a feeling Amsterdam didn't have. It probably depended on your mood, but driving through Berlin with this soundtrack was perfect. He leant back in the seat wondering if he'd fuck things up trying to get Ingrid to give him a blow job in the taxi, dismissing the idea and concentrating on the passing city. This was something he'd always remember.

They drove by the Reichstag and Harry thought long and hard, remembering the building from old war footage. He could also see images of Russian soldiers raising the red flag over a burning Berlin, and wondered if it was the same place. Where were the English when this was happening? He started recognising streets and eventually saw these West Berlin bars packed with drinking and singing Englishmen. There were police vans nearby but no German mob in sight. He didn't know if there'd been any trouble yet, imagining that most of the English would either be here or wandering around nearby, enjoying the nightlife. Tomorrow was D–Day. There must've been at least a thousand English milling around, with more tucked down side streets, mobbing the bars. Harris reckoned there'd be seven or eight thousand English attending the game, but you never could tell exactly.

The cab had to slow down and looking out of the window Harry tried to spot Carter, but there were too many people. They were cheering something or other and the old bill were looking nervous, and there were a lot of coppers as well. Someone had hung a big SCARBOROUGH Union Jack over a bar window and there was a couple of Crosses of St George with CHARLTON and CARLISLE on either side. The bars were jammed and everyone was having a laugh. Part of Harry wanted to jump out and go and join in the fun, leave this bird alone and get pissed, but there was time enough for that tomorrow and he couldn't let Ingrid down. He had to do his duty for England and keep the girl happy, because she said her flat was only five minutes away and did he mind listening to some music there instead of in a noisy club, because then they could be alone?

– That's alright with me.

– There's a lot of England supporters here, Ingrid said. They look very dangerous, don't they? I wouldn't like to be a German hooligan fighting with the English, but the police are very strict here and will stop anything that happens.

The England boys were singing GOD SAVE THE QUEEN as they passed and Harry couldn't help feeling proud that he was English and proud of the country's hooligan element. It was the feeling of power you could only get from everyone mobbing together. Sex gave you something, but the threat and use of violence was something else. It let you play God for a while, like you could do whatever the fuck you wanted and nothing could touch you and make you pay a price. He put his hand on Ingrid's leg and agreed that the police would know what to do with the hooligans.

It's one of those miracles that come round a couple of times in your life. Because I'm lying here thinking of last night. It's a bit after ten and I'm a lazy cunt, stuck in bed. Pulling the different strands apart. Fuck knows what time we got in but Abdul was awake and drinking coffee. Listening to the night-time sounds with a hotel full of pissed English sleeping off the drink. Last thing I remember is walking back from that street with the bars. Looked down this alley and there's two tarts in stockings. The alley's pitch black with an open door letting out a beam of light. They're standing around having a fag. On their tea break maybe. Real old grinders. I couldn't handle it and thought it was some kind of bad trip. Fat old girls with beer guts. Fuck that. I didn't tell the others and we kept on walking. Next thing we're by this bunker.

Couldn't believe it was right there beside us, that those things were still standing. You'd think the communists would've bulldozed the bunkers right away. It still had bullet and rocket dents in the brickwork and the entrance was made from this carved wood. Same as the porch of a Norman church in an English village. The others had disappeared round the corner and me and Mark were left standing there looking at this thing.

We were down a small street and the place was deserted. Mark goes up to the door and tries to open it, but it was locked with a padlock and thick chains. The links were old but strong. We backed off and just stood there for five minutes looking at this square block with tiny windows. I was slowing down. Finding this relic was clearing my head. Thinking of what the torturers got up to inside those walls. You wouldn't have a chance if the Gestapo got you in there. I'm standing in the middle of this fucking street lost in Berlin thinking about torture chambers and medical instruments. Mad cunts in white coats stripping the skin from men's legs while some nonce in a black leather coat asks where it's going off tomorrow. Where the England boys are mobbing up. Eventually we left the bunker because we had a long journey home and I didn't have a clue where we were going. We were looking for the Nigerians, but they were long gone, so we waved down a passing cab and the driver brought us back here.

The miracle is I don't have a hangover. Maybe it's the excitement of the game coming through and washing away the drink and chemicals, because the build-up starts here. There's this wave that comes from somewhere. I know it's going to be a great day out. I'm a kid in a way, even though I'm into my thirties now, because this is how I felt when I was a boy just thinking about going to see Chelsea play football. Now there's the other side. The chance to go on the rampage. See what the Germans can do. It's all bottled and ready to go and most of the England boys will be feeling the same way. All the preliminaries are over. Everyone will get in tight and target the enemy. Give it another ten minutes and I'll get up, because last night was mental and that part-time Nazi effort was a dream really, mixing drink and drugs and fucking up the newspaper headlines.

Today will be different. Time to be on our guard. Thinking

of that meeting makes me laugh. Fuck knows what it was all about. There's going to be some bigger boys over here with better connections. First the Nazis, then the bar and those birds we were chatting up. Then the trek back here after they blew us out. Must've been something we said. Or Billy grabbing that bird's arse. Right up the crack. I think we even saw Harry in a bar with some decent bird. But that's got to be another dream, because one minute he's there and the next he's gone. The bird I thought I saw him with was too good for a fat cunt like that.

– What time is it? Mark asks.

His voice sounds rough as fuck. I tell him ten.

– That's alright. It's still early.

There's silence. I stretch.

– Do you remember that bunker? he asks. We tried to get inside.

Mark tried to break the chain but it was a heavy duty effort. No chance. I tell him we were lucky the sound didn't wake the dead. Worse than that the living. They wouldn't have liked us breaking into the vaults because most Germans want to forget the past. Don't want to hear us singing about two World Wars and one World Cup.

– You think what it would've been like in there, Mark says. The Russians must've gone through the place and closed it, left everything how it was. It's funny they never got around to knocking it down.

– Probably left it as a reminder. Or maybe they didn't have the time or money for the bulldozers. You look round this area here and there's not a lot to remind you of the Third Reich, is there?

– That's because we bombed fuck out of the cunts. No-one's ever going to forget with that fucking bunker right there. It was built to last. There were other buildings I saw in East Berlin that had bullet holes in them. All those years and they've still got the scars.

He stops talking and is quiet for a while. Then the cunt's out of bed and opening the curtains, telling me to get up, and don't I feel like shit? He starts going on about how I was mouthing off with those birds and that's why they fucked off, but I say it was

Bright Spark squeezing that bird's arse and cunt, and Mark nods. Do I remember walking in and seeing Fat Harry with the Page 3 girl? We wonder what happened to them, but you have to fear the worst. The bloke's been sniffing around ever since we got to Europe and all the time I thought Carter was supposed to be the sex machine. Maybe it's to do with his mate getting topped. Sometimes blokes take that kind of thing out on women. Not hurting them, but getting in there and shagging them silly. It's like in a war, where all that death makes you want to make babies. Maybe he's gone soft in his old age, because by rights he should be hanging about with the rest of the boys a bit more.

It's another half-hour before we're across the road having some breakfast. Carter's sitting there with a cooked meal and an English paper he's dug up from somewhere. There's scare stories about the trouble that's coming to Berlin. Comments from various upright establishment figures. Rent-a-quote, do-nothing cunts trotting out the same old bollocks their mums and dads were using twenty years ago.

– You missed a good night, Carter said. We were out till gone two when the old bill started closing the bars. It was all going alright, just good clean fun and that, but they have to come along and start winding everyone up. They soon realised the English were up for it and backed off.

He cuts into a chunky-looking sausage and suddenly I'm starving hungry. This is better than the shit we were getting in Holland. More like English cooking. Something that'll give you energy. Good old-fashioned grease and gristle. Kevin's sitting at the next table with Crewe and they give us a nod. Ask where we got to last night. Laugh when Mark mentions the bunker.

– Have you seen Harry? Carter asks. He didn't come home last night.

– He was in this bar in East Berlin, Mark says, sitting down and pulling a couple of pages out from the middle of the paper. We saw him with some bird. She was fucking beautiful as well. I don't think you need to worry about him, because they seemed happy enough. She had this fucking mini-skirt on and the smallest pair of knickers you've ever seen.

Carter stops eating. Doesn't look too impressed.

– I don't know what's happened to the bloke, he says, with some moral distaste in his voice. How the fuck did he end up over there? One minute he's here, the next he's on the other side of the city. That's not Harry's style. Normally he's at the bar the whole time getting pissed.

From what I've seen and heard about Carter in the past he's the one who's usually sniffing, so I don't know what he's wound up about.

– At home he never bothers. I don't know what he's up to. He should get his priorities sorted out. His mates should come first.

We order some food and have a feed. Other England start coming over. Harris and Brighty roll in with a load of Chelsea and a mix of strays. I look twice and Facelift is standing there with High Street and Biggs. They shake our hands and I can see Facelift is buzzing. Says they got a flight over and beat the system. That they weren't going to miss today for anything. Everyone's steaming. Excited as kids, knowing there's going to be a major row in a few hours' time.

After our breakfast we walk ten minutes to this bar tucked down a side street, away from the main bars. We line up the lager and kick back, killing time. We're trying to be relaxed about things but there's this feeling in the air. It's always like this when it's going to go off against some tasty opposition. Everyone's trying to act calm, but inside they're boiling away. The excitement is there because it's what you live for. It's international level this, another step along. I can feel the buzz sitting with Dave Harris and this Chelsea crew tucked out of the way in Berlin while the rest of the English gather on the main street. I can feel the pride come through and it's starting to replace everything else. It's like Chelsea, but with a bonus track. Today is all about England, and our place in the pecking order is obvious. The patriotism comes through and it's a case of keeping everything under control. Maintaining discipline. All the other bollocks goes out the window and you stop thinking about all the ifs and buts. We strip it all down. That's what patriotism is really, stripping the machine down and getting rid of the accessories. This is the stripped-down England coming through, putting all the soft options on hold. We're England, united, we'll never be defeated.

We kill time in the bar swapping stories and rumours, then move back to the bigger bars filling with English. Fuck knows how many are down here now. Seems like thousands. It's going to be a big one. A rerun of the war. Tapping into the spirit of the Blitz. Firming up as the spirit takes over. Some of the England boys are knocking back the drink, others staying sober, most blokes somewhere in the middle. Depends who you are and what your angle is.

There's this bloke with a telephoto camera across the road and he snaps off a couple of shots. The England boys start cheering. He thinks this is the go-ahead and comes nearer inviting some sieg-heils. Bottles fly his way and one hits him on the head. There isn't any blood but it does the job. He staggers back rubbing his skull. Looks dazed. Two men leg it across the road and get hold of the wanker's camera. He tries to struggle so one of them smacks him. Down the photographer goes. Flat out on the pavement. The other bloke holds the camera in the air and exposes the film. Smashes the camera on the pavement. Everyone cheers louder than before, and as the photographer starts to haul himself up the same man kicks him in the face. Tells him he's a slimy paparazzi slag, that this one's for Diana. Everyone hates the press, and everyone cheers again.

— I didn't tell you, Carter says. There were these two journalists hanging about last night trying to be friendly. We got talking and that and they invited us for a drink round the corner. Wanted to know what was going on. Me, Gary and some others. We went to this bar for half an hour and the main one, David Morgan he said his name was, gave us five hundred marks, so Gary fed them this line about the leader of the English being this geezer Cromwell from Chelsea. Said there was a paramilitary mob called the New Model Army and that Cromwell had his boys tooled-up and was going to do the Germans on the steps of the Reichstag. He said Cromwell has links with the Loyalists. Then he says there's another firm called

The Dam Busters, who were going to steam in first, to soften the Germans up.

We're all pissing ourselves thinking of the journalists feeding the names through to London, because usually they get all that stuff wrong, but a name like Cromwell is going to stick in even the smallest brain. I try to imagine Gary Davison's face as he tells the cunts what they want to hear, Carter and the others trying not to laugh in their faces.

– Should've seen the cunts lapping it up, Gary says, sitting down. Almost as good as that story about Emu and the Kamikaze Kids. Talk about a wind up. I'm surprised they didn't work it out, but when you think about it Cromwell's a good name for a general. It's in the paper this morning, all over the front page, three extra pages inside.

Facelift passes the paper round and it's hard to believe those cunts are so dopey. It's a classic moment. One to remember.

– There was another journalist trying to get English skinheads to do sieg-heils and there was this trendy wanker from a radio station who asked us to make some threats in his microphone, Gary continues. You know, playground stuff. They're a bunch of wankers desperate for a story. They've got no souls. They weren't offering to pay either. I'd have done a sieg-heil for twenty quid, if the cunt had asked nicely. Would've sung the Red Flag for forty.

– Kevin poured his lager down the microphone, Carter says. The radio wanker was almost crying.

– It was nothing to do with me, Kev insists. It was Cromwell.

Everyone's cracking up. We start singing CROMWELL WHERE ARE YOU? and enough of the English already know the story and join in. The press will be over in big mobs for this game. Enjoying the expenses and pissing it up the wall. Shagging the bell boys and turning in some primary school essays. The blokes last night and that one today are the cunts who bother to come out of their four-star hotels. Usually they make it up, while there's always enough slags at home ready to claim some column inches. Makes you laugh. Gary says it's a shame more of them don't get out and about because it's easy money, good publicity and a chance to take the piss. They're a bunch of hypocrites and everyone here knows the score.

Funny thing is, when we're at home we're thinking about the surveillance cameras the whole time. The way the old bill have got things now you have to be smart. The tougher the police get the further underground it goes. Here in Europe we just don't give a fuck. We know the European old bill aren't going to bother tracking us down. Unless you do something major they'll just move the problem on. If you get nicked you'll probably get deported. So people like Gary Davison don't care if they're in the papers back home posing for the cameras. He's younger and coming through the ranks. None of us give a toss. It's all a laugh and this kind of publicity is a joke. A lot of the blokes love the attention and the media wankers get some action in their dull little lives. It's another collection of holiday snapshots. We're living without laws. We can do what we want. We haven't had respect for foreigners drilled into us. The way football is at home, Europe gives us more freedom, especially for those blokes who face long sentences if they get done again back in England.

The time's passing quickly and there's still no old bill around. Probably tucked down a street somewhere keeping out of sight so as not to stir things up. Small mobs of England are walking around having a look, but everything's sweet. The old bill will have their plan and the paper reckons all police leave has been cancelled. There's flags draped along the bars and enough noise, so they're not going to have any trouble finding us. It's not as hot as yesterday, but nice and sunny. A good proportion of the Expeditionary Force are having a drink, people like Harris making do with fizzy water. The army did the same thing. Gave the boys a drink before they went over the top. Poor cunts wiped out by the officer class then executed if the nerve gas and shell-shock got too much. Fucking wankers, and there's no officer core here, just a few blokes who earn respect and people follow, but overall we're bad-tempered Englishmen who do our own thing most of the time then come together when the occasion demands. Doesn't matter now if we're from London or Liverpool or anywhere else in between, because there's a common enemy and England's bigger than all the local rivalries.

It's moving on from family. You start with family and that's the core. Family is blood and you stick together. Nobody takes liberties with family. The closer the better. Your mum and dad and brothers and sisters, then cousins and aunts and uncles and all that. Your mates are next up. Close mates leading down to acquaintances. Then I suppose it's the area you grow up in with football fitting in somehow, and then the city and the country and so on. Probably gets into race or the bigger tribe, whatever you want to call it. That's what was wrong about last night. It was too far down the road. For a start me and Mark didn't have much interest, but bigger than that it felt wrong because today the Germans are going to get a kicking. Nice people who you can have a drink with any other time, but today it's different.

The singing dips and we drink up. Start moving. Chelsea and the London mobs start strolling. So do the Northerners and Midlanders and everyone else. It happens without much talk. The time's come and we cross the road and take a smaller side street. We move comfortably and silently. There's no old bill to be seen, which is suspicious. We take a few turns following the leaders, a mile or so from our meet with the Germans. We turn another corner and keep going. A missile cruising towards its target. Silent and controlled. Going back to silent films. Wanting to move faster but keeping ourselves together.

We turn a corner and it looks like the old bill are holding a fucking rally. They're waiting for us in full riot gear with a line of vans behind the ranks. It had to be expected somewhere because no way can this many blokes move without being seen. We stall with the surprise and several of the English start throwing bottles. Doesn't seem like a good move because the Germans don't hang about like the Dutch, and here they come with the batons and shields and every riot accessory money can buy. There's a split second when I wonder if this volunteer army is going to stand and fight, because this is the old bill. Should have more confidence. The English don't move and the police are getting pelted with bottles and bricks from a small building site and have to stop. There's one bloke down on the floor. With so many England here I reckon they've misjudged things. Played their cards early. It's not chance they're here, but maybe they didn't expect the numbers. Thought it was an invitation-only private party. Fifty a side or something. Dozy cunts. Because the shock wears off and this is a new battle. Adding to the day out.

The older blokes in their late thirties and forties are to one side, trying to get the English organised, and because there's so many different clubs and crews involved it's that bit harder, but there's some well-known faces here and we turn down another street. Skirting the authorities. Taking advantage of natural obstacles, concrete blocks. Piece of piss. We're trotting around the old bill and we're together and sussed and moving well. The old bill have fucked it up and the blokes at the front have been doing this sort of thing for donkey's years. England are in control, making sure we keep the appointment. Two decades of causing chaos across the Continent – France, Italy, Hungary, Norway, France, Luxembourg, Germany, Sweden, Switzerland, Denmark, Spain, Greece, Finland. Everywhere we go, people want to know, who we are, shall we tell them? We're England, putting the Europeans in their place.

We keep going, knowing the Germans will be waiting. Fucking hope so. We slow down. The old bill will be tracking us, but right now we've left them behind. Can't believe they were out-manoeuvred so easy. Shows why we won the war. A classic mix of bollocks and tactics. Slowing right down now, because the Germans should be here. No coppers to hide behind, the fucking slags. We're near a square with flats to one side. Things look quiet. Where the fuck are they? There's a shopping precinct to the left and I can't see it lasting if the cunts don't show. You don't expect the Germans to bottle out. Harris is shouting and going red in the face, where the fuck are they? Fucking German wankers. England fanning out and moving across the square.

After getting back to the Kasbah, Harry had a shower, changed his shirt and hurried to the bars where the English had been drinking since arriving in Berlin, but only found a hundred or so still there. The soldiers were on the move. He swore and kicked a wall. The sex had got in the way of the aggro and he was well fucked off, because apart from spending time seeing the sights he wanted to be there when it went off with the krauts. He couldn't fucking believe it and knew he was never going to live this down. He was a fucking mug, thinking with his knob instead of his brain. He didn't want the others thinking he'd bottled out, because it didn't look good, though they knew him well enough. More important, he wanted to be involved. You didn't want to miss the big dates. No fucking way.

He didn't know what to do next. He went in the bar where Carter and the rest of the boys had been drinking and looked around, but couldn't see anyone he recognised. The familiar faces had vanished and he didn't have a clue where they'd gone. He asked around, but these blokes weren't interested. He swore again and bought himself a bottle of lager and some schnapps, stood outside hoping someone would turn up. The England mob were out on the prowl and he was standing there like a fucking tart. He'd passed the same bar last night with that nutter Ingrid and he should've got out there and then, made sure of today. He really was a cunt sometimes. A right fucking donut. Fucking hell.

Harry's head was still wired from last night, and it just went to show you never knew what was waiting inside the wrapping, with Ingrid dripping by the time they got back to her place, and nothing was a bigger turn-on than knowing a bird wanted the business, and better than that, wanted it off you. Ingrid was a nice girl with white pants, but once indoors she turned into a nympho. She was a fucking raver and Harry made the most of the chance, lifting Ingrid onto a glass coffee table and banging her right there, pumping away till he dumped his load and slipped forward, crashing down through the table and smashing the glass. He looked at Ingrid and her eyes were glazed, and for a second he thought she was dead, skewered by a broken shard of glass, like a fucking vampire.

– Don't stop, she said. Don't finish yet. Come on you pig.

But Harry was over and done and the first thing he wanted after a bit of sex like that, after a bellyful of drink, was to crash out for a while. He pulled back and said sorry about the table, and Ingrid stood up with this dark look on her face, all psycho-like. She said she hadn't climaxed yet and what was the matter with men? Look what he'd done to the table. She stormed into the kitchen, but then came back with a couple of bottles and sat next to him on the couch. Harry took the drink. Who was she calling a pig, the fucking slag.

– Never mind, Ingrid said, fiddling with his cock. We can try again in a few minutes. We have got all night to get it right. My boyfriend won't be back for a couple of days.

Harry wished she'd keep her hands to herself.

– Where's he gone then? Harry asked, wondering about the all-night bit. He was knackered.

– He is visiting his family, Ingrid said. We went to England to sort out some problems we had. He was having sex with my sister and I caught them together. I walked in and they were on the sofa, right where we are sitting now. They did not expect me to come home. It is a hard thing to forget. I want him to know what it feels like.

Ingrid drank half her bottle in one go, and Harry couldn't say he minded filling in for that dozy German cunt, though he reckoned it was a bit iffy being used like some rent-a-dildo party filler, but still, it was decent fanny and he wasn't going to turn Ingrid down. If the girl wanted a portion then Harry was the man for the job, but he didn't want any grief. That was the English for you, get in, do the business, then piss off before the post-mortem starts. He should get going really, but he was fucked.

– Sorry, I shouldn't have said that. I like you Harry. You don't care about anything and you have no manners.

He almost choked on his lager, the stroppy fucking cunt. They sat in silence drinking, Harry narked, and then Ingrid stood up and said she had something that would make him happier.

The night picked up speed, with Ingrid going like a train. After the glass table, they moved to the bed, her mouth, and finally she was greasing her arse and Harry was being forced to run a bombing raid up the Rhine. By this time she'd fed him a

Gulf Boy, and once the chemicals took effect he was doing what he was told, right open to suggestion, obeying orders with Ingrid taking on the role of controller. His head was on fire and he had the vague idea he should be using a rubber, but didn't connect. He was doing what he was told and the Gulf pill made him invincible.

Harry was dead by five in the morning and drifted off to sleep, the next thing he felt a sharp pain under his gut. He sat up and found Ingrid chewing his cock, not sucking but digging her teeth in. It was fucking agony and he tried to get her off, pulling away, but the vampire was hanging on, razor teeth behind his helmet. It was murder and the bed was a war zone, Harry trying to coax the girl off, but she was out of her head and the Gulf Boy had turned their session into a blockbuster video where a soldier forcing a peasant woman to suck him off had his cock bit off and bled to death. It was the perfect revenge but Harry hadn't done anything wrong. The film and the reality merged and Harry was shitting it. He punched Ingrid in the head to get her off, and she went straight to sleep, running on automatic. Harry laid there for a while knowing he should get out, but he couldn't move.

Harry didn't wake up till after two and Ingrid had already gone to work, leaving a note telling him to come and see her later. He left the flat and took a taxi back to the Kasbah, going straight to the shower and washing the blood, shit and spunk from his cock, gritting his teeth as the soap stung cut skin. He stayed under the water a long time and cleaned well, scrubbing away the memory, looking forward to a fresh start.

Now Harry was sipping his lager, more concerned with missing the others than almost losing his knob. The Expedition-ary Force was out on patrol and he'd been left behind. He finished his drink and left the bar, went for a wander. His brain was running through old videos chopping at a dead image, thinking of Balti, surprisingly okay knowing the man who was more than a brother was dead and gone, his face blown away by a sad old cunt who'd lost his grandson to leukaemia, and now old McDonald was doing twenty years in another sort of farm, banged up sending his shit through the bars. It was bad news, but what could you do? Nothing at all. You were powerless.

What could you do but walk into the flashing amusement arcade and stand in front of the first machine that took your fancy, in among the pale boys and girls and old prowling perverts who didn't take any notice of the new arrival, Harry wondering if he was faceless, just like Balti, the poor cunt, both of them fucked. But they'd had some good times and that was all you could hope for in life, pulling out the change he needed to play the game, looking for the slot but turning his head when two teenage girls came up next to him and started yelling at a flashing red-orange-blue screen, teenage girls sucked into the chase, blonde runaways in a nicked Porsche accelerating away from the old bill cutting through East German side streets looking for the alley that was just wide enough to squeeze through, escaping through a gap in the wall, because speed was everything on the autobahns, no limit to expansion, they all needed living space, racing all the way to West Berlin.

Everything was easy these days and the English could march right in, when Europe was at peace, it was all so fucking easy, because if you had the cash you could do whatever the fuck you wanted, like that cunt in the corner eyeing the boys and girls and licking his lips. Harry could feel the anger rising because the Gulf Boy had sharpened his senses and the bloke was a fucking nonce, the scum of Europe, the boys had been talking about it in Amsterdam, pulling everyone together with the Cross of St George in the window, all the London geezers and Liverpool scallies and Pompey, Mancs and stray dogs from right across the country, and Harry was trying to pull his thoughts back, telling himself the bloke was probably alright, just wanted to play a game and get away from Berlin and its history, the fucking Berlin Wall and Cold War. Like Harry he wanted to sit pretty and take everything out on someone else, pay an easy target back for all the other bollocks coming his way in life. It was the safe option, picking a soft target and unloading your hatred.

Harry pulled himself straight and looked at the message on the screen, fluorescent green words on a black background, Harry sharp now, feeling his confidence return as he started reading, having trouble, brain ticking, looking sideways at the blondes, not bad really, but young, legal but young, fucking right, too young for a fat cunt like him, looking now at the screen and banging his fist on the control panel because it was ALL IN FUCKING GERMAN.

Fucking cunts. How was he supposed to read that? He breathed in deep and felt his confidence return, because he'd played this game in The Unity back home in London. It was Smart Bomb Parade, flavour of the month, year, decade. It was a piece of piss and he knew the rules, his coin going in the slot, Harry off on a run as the bells chimed and a soft robot voice told him to climb into the cockpit, and he did as he was told looking through the eyes of a fighter bomber pilot, a hero figure, Smart Bomb the biggest seller in Europe, looking through the eyes of Big Bob West the Gulf War veteran from the pub, the original Gulf Boy, but they said he was fucked up on chemicals, illegal substances rotting his brain and breaking down his defences. Harry laughed out loud and the girls looked at him nervously.

It was Flash Harry inside the cockpit preparing for take-off, part of the New Economic Order assault force, Christian idealists ready to take on the might of the wicked General Mahmet in the East, the mighty Mahmet and his conscript farmhands in their vintage killing machines, an evil empire far away over the horizon in a world of medieval cruelty, feudalist perversion, beyond the Slav slave-states, far away on the wisp of a cloud, with a Stone Island bull's-eye in front of his face chiselled into Harry's helmet because he'd paid his euros, feeling the button under his finger and hearing the girls next door, the sound of music and rockets all around the amusement arcade, Harry on a roll forgetting about the football. He was fighting for the NEO, for extended drinking, legalised drugs and cheaper sex. He was ready for take-off, knob red raw, mind wired into the circuits of the European machine.

—I'm scared suddenly in this dead village. I've walked in on Mangler and a crying woman. I ask him what he's doing. He tells me to fuck off and I back out of the room confused and bitter. Bullets explode against the concrete above me so I crouch down behind a broken wall. There's a child's body nearby and I brush maggots from her blonde hair. A small girl, I think, killed by Allied bombers. It's a necessary evil in the struggle for peace. All this evil is necessary if good is to prevail. I have to get the job finished and go home. I try not to think of Mangler and the woman because it is a mistake, my mind turned rotten by the constant destruction. There's a thud on the bricks in front of me, a sniper hidden further along the street. I hear one of the lads firing a mortar and shouting that the fucking flame-thrower isn't working right. I can hear a man shouting something in German. They won't surrender these Germans. They're fighting to the death. We start running forward but I'm not sure where we're going. I'm caught in the panic as a hand grenade blows a hole in the street. I peel away and charge along a small path, catching my head on some wire and ducking down. There's blood coming from my ear but nothing worth worrying about. I turn through the arch of a door and there's a boy in a grey uniform facing me. There's no time to think as I fire into his guts and see the tunic turn black. He stumbles and there's a second of silence as he tries to fight the shock and pain. My heart is pumping and I don't care about this German bastard because all I see is the gun in his hand. I fire again. I don't know how many bullets I drill into his body and I don't hear him scream or even cry. I fire into his head and it explodes. There's blood and brain everywhere and he twitches a lot, struggling in the mud. I stand over him and my mind is frozen. I don't know if it's hate, fear, confusion. His scared expression, shock and then pain are frozen inside me. I know I'll never escape the image, a horror film sitting in the cupboard. I roll him over and there's not much left of his face. I've killed this conscript forced to fight the mad English tommy with the bulging eyes and bloodstained boots. I hear more shouting and firing and run across what was once someone's front room looking for cover. I glance back at the corpse briefly and move forward with the rest of the unit.

We're strolling now. Waiting for the Germans to make their move. The krauts are coming down from a shopping area. It's a bit mixed up in the road, and one or two of the boys must be thinking about the Germans last night, how they had a good laugh. I'm wondering whether it's going to tone things down, and the right-wing lot are going to have their own thing lined up, whether it's political or not, but if it's football then this mob here is ready to go, because the thing is, despite what you read, most of us are just normal everyday patriots out for a punch-up, and while we love the Queen and support the Loyalists in Northern Ireland, we're not political. We just have our views. Because politics is shit. Lines of manky old cunts shouting at each other while they're on the box then it's straight down the bar for a cosy drink. We're English and that's it. And the German crew mobbing up by the railings are starting to look a bit tasty. England are moving and I look at Facelift and almost next to him is Derby and there's no recognition from either of them. Bright is fired up and Harris is straining like a mad man, Mark and Carter, all the boys. Kevin, Crewe and Bolton, Millwall on the left and Pompey on the right next to West Ham, Leeds in the middle, Chelsea everywhere. Strolling towards the Germans. Silent and picking up momentum.

Because it's two World Wars and one World Cup, and the first bottle comes over thrown by someone hiding at the back of their firm, and there's a right old mixture of Germans with smart skinheads and shabby old soulboy-meets-boot-boys with those silly short-at-the-side/long-at-the-back Deutschland hair-cuts, dodgy tashes and naff trainers. There's even a few scarves, the daft cunts, and I look and see Harris and Bright moving across the street and the rest of the boys follow, a small crew of scousers and a mixture of Midlanders behind, Yorkshiremen through the middle with some Geordies, all moving in together because now it's tightening up and the Germans are pushing forward as they chuck more bottles, the English moving aside to let them land on the ground, glass shattering in among the Deutschland chants, and I catch Facelift's face and the bloke's got a flare gun, the fucking Hayes sniper, moving on from glassing his brother-in-law to firing rockets at Germans.

We're off now fancying ourselves as a fucking commando unit, regiments from every corner of England, steaming straight into the heart of Germany, the English-design Hamburg and Berlin skins coming to meet us and I see the flare flash and that scatters the cunts, better than a fucking fire bomb, this is the fucking war right here with Harris piling in like he's old Bomber himself burning Dresden to a cinder teaching the German scum not to fuck about with the English, and there's waves of English steaming into small mobs of Germans, don't need any orders for this one, and I go full into some bloke and punch him in the head and kick him in the balls and kick him in the head as he goes down with Mark and Carter kicking him again, moving to the next German coming through and hitting him in the head and pulling the cunt forward by his shirt, head down, bringing my knee up and Harris slicing his back, and I get a fist in the face and bounce back, swinging at the German, a massive bloke this one, and it takes five or six English to push him back, head-to-head in the middle of the street with a mass of arms and legs, Facelift's flare sending red-white-and-blue smoke spewing through the air. There's no music now, no soundtrack playing or bands beating up a rhythm for the rows of men getting gunned down, because we're smarter than that, leaving the music behind with DJ Bright lashing out and some of the Germans have started running and we're after them quick as a flash. They've broken into different mobs and there must be a hundred of us going to this wasteland where a German takes out a knife and stabs an Englishman in the face. We circle round and try and do the cunt, his eyes mental flashing murder, knows he's gone further now and if we get him he's dead, but suddenly this little firm think better of it and close round the knife merchant and you can smell the shit as they leg it, moving faster than Schumacher. The bloke with the cut face keeps going and we move back to where there's the main mob of Germans, and they're lobbing bottles and singing this shit song about something or other none of us understands, and the English get together and go into them again.

My head is fucking roaring like a machine tapping into the size of the English mob that's turned out and the fact that we're so far from home in the heart of the fatherland and this is a big one and we're doing the business. Mark's with me, and Carter,

Harris, Facelift, Brighty, Biggs, Ken and Davison's mob and all the other blokes we've been travelling through Europe with, and it hits me that the Germans have their own club differences but that doesn't matter because there's West Ham further along doing some Germans and there's no sign of the old bill. We're fighting smaller mobs of Germans and the English keep together and move in some sort of casual order. The Germans have lost it and we start following their main crew to another square where there's bigger numbers determined to make a stand and I reckon they've been trying to suck us in here, looking to the right and there's a big skinhead mob who are obviously the top boys, some cunt in one of a hundred or so black combat jackets lobbing tear gas, so we back off and let it burn out, milling around as the rest of the English catch up, a nice little breather, chance for a cup of tea maybe. There's a bit of a lull with everyone buzzing, fucking speeding better than that shit last night, better than designer narcotics, a pure fucking natural high this one, an England special.

These skins are the ones we're really going to have to sort out and all of them look the business. They start coming down this grass slope and we fan out still watching the other mob of Germans, all these blokes from both sides of the Channel going to war again and this is a fucking serious row with some of the Germans carrying baseball bats, but you have to keep going and the further in you get the darker it gets and we know there's going to be murders because this is the SS contingent, but the mob to the side have already been run once so we know we can do them easy enough, and when the skinheads come through it goes off with English getting kicked and Germans getting kicked and Mark getting a baseball bat across his arm, sounds like bone cracking, and I see Harris stab the German who did it deep and hard and I fucking hope his heart's not there, more like his gut with his shirt soaked looking shocked dropping the baseball bat, watching the German stagger away glad to see he's alive but hurt and when you lose your concentration you get a slap and that's what happens to me, a fist in the side of the head, except it doesn't hurt much and I do the cunt with the help of a couple of others, but the Germans aren't bottling out, the fighting continuing with both sides standing firm.

A gap appears and this has been going on for a while now without a result and the other Germans have got behind the skins making it more or less equal numbers which is something in itself because fucking hell, lads, this is Germany, fucking Berlin, and we're on their manor and we pile in again like the old boys did in the war going fucking mental tearing up and this time they don't fancy it so much and some start running, the younger element shitting it as the Chelsea and West Ham and Leeds and Millwall and Stoke and Pompey and all the big Northern geezers who are the fucking business when it really comes down to serious street-fighting, the sort of no-nonsense heavy-duty industry nutters who usually hate Southerners but when it's England are united and hard as fucking nails, everyone piles in and thumps the Germans – on their own fucking manor – getting the result – winning the war – living up to reputations – doing our dads and granddads proud – following their example – and it's not over yet because different mobs filter different ways and there's smaller battles now as we go through a row of shops, windows breaking.

The Germans have moved further off so the English start doing cars and buildings, glass made for smashing. The ordinary people are hiding in packs and nobody bothers with them apart from some shouted insults about the war and Hitler and how they killed our women and kids, but it's a coach and these shops that really take a battering, the cars get their roofs dented and the coach its window wrecked, no-one bothering to turn the VWs over and burn them because the colours won't look so good in the light and we've got better things to do. A bit of looting fills in the time and the discipline has gone now. The younger lads are into the vandalism, the spoils of war or whatever you want to call it, and these blokes move forward through the ranks when things get easier and when I look at Mark and the others travelling with me none of us are really bothered about the shops, though it adds to the spectacle and it's something that's going to happen one way or the other, another way of grinding your foot into the Germans because this is part of what they're defending, I suppose, their property and territory.

It's up to the vandals to do what they want. Personally, it's the German mob that counts, but I watch the windows cave in one after the other, racks of vegetables turned over, café chairs and tables broken, moving aside from this old dear who must be eighty if she's a day, a granny who doesn't know any better coming after the hooligans wrecking her cornershop. She's tooled-up with this gnarled walking stick and she catches this scrawny little bloke on the back of the head. He yells and runs away and everyone's laughing because Granny's no bottle merchant, clearing a gap through the English as she marches along lashing out, smacking Harris on the arm hard so he moves out of the way sharpish, grinning with embarrassment as he's put in his place, Granny hobbling after us shouting in German, but the windows have all gone now and she keeps going, chasing a big Northerner who's trying to calm her down and he jogs off giving up saying she's a nutter, and Granny doesn't care, doesn't give a fuck, because she's got the scent and we move away from the shops and onto another big street, milling around on the corner trying to work out where we are.

We look back and Granny's standing there screaming at us saying we're nothing but hooligans, nothing but English hooligans, and she's got a point, and there's some cheering and we're looking round trying to work out which way to go, spotting the Germans up ahead, throwing bricks, Harris saying we're on the right way to the ground where we can have a drink because there's still a few hours till kick-off and there'll be more Germans there, more English as well, but first we're going to have to fight these krauts some more because it looks like they're coming back to have another go, making the most of their big day out, been building up to it ever since the fixture was suggested by the politicians as a show of unity between the two nations and their banking institutions, a sporting event to help promote the new economic order, laying firm foundations for a united Europe.

There's the sound of sirens and a column of flashing lights ahead, so we hang back to see what's going to happen next, enjoying the show. The lights are behind the German mob and there's the slamming of doors and the barking of dogs, a minute of silence as the English stragglers catch up, a few blokes with trays of jewellery shifting towards some flats looking to hide their haul. We wait and see what the old bill are going to do and suddenly they just steam straight into the German mob with their truncheons and that's something you wouldn't get in Spain or Italy, coppers attacking their own kind, and the Germans come running towards us and then realise they're getting chased into another kicking. They shift off to the side moving into the flats and we see the riot police coming at us again and this time they look like they mean business because there's tear gas popping off and it does your fucking eyes in like nothing else. We move back and this gives the old bill the advantage and when I look through the smoke the German mob have seen their chance and are following the coppers through like they're getting a Panzer escort. We've seen it before, where the local hooligans and old bill almost work together because they're all racist against the English, but usually it's the Latins, because Latins and Anglo-Saxons don't mix. They all want to do us and the only difference is the uniform and the fact that the police are legally tooled-up. This lot are just grabbing their chance, though, because the German old bill are like the English old bill and don't play the Latin game. A lot of English get battered by the riot police, but again we don't run and they can't fucking handle this because they don't spend years training in crowd control tactics just to get fronted by a load of hooligans and sheer weight of numbers forces them back along the road.

It's one of those no-win situations and there's enough clever English around to lead the way down another side street, mirroring the Germans who are looking to do the same thing, and when I think about this it's fucking mental, because it's not ending, usually it would fizzle out or the old bill would end things or someone would get done right off, but I suppose the Germans are like us because they're going to keep coming back for more and aren't prepared to give up, specially at home, while the old bill have to deal with all these nutters from across the Channel who don't care about their German laws and aren't too scared about getting nicked. They can't fucking win and we've put ourselves in a situation where sticking together and fighting back means we survive.

No drug does it the same as we run towards the Germans again down another street and the two sides are smaller, people getting lost along the way, filtering off. That's the way they do you, picking off small mobs not paying attention, or people who get unlucky left on their own, and it flares up again with the more dedicated on both sides going for it and there's a couple of English getting done and then it goes back and forward, and with Mark and the rest of the Chelsea boys and another big mix of clubs we run another load of Germans down another fucking street, slowing down not knowing where the fuck we are now, maybe two hundred of us waiting for the rest of the English to catch up, walking now causing havoc, moving through the building blocks, my brain speeding.

Harry was feeling the effects. This was no ordinary war. No ordinary Saturday night punch-up outside The Hide. No midnight runner from the Taj Mahal. No rowing with the bouncers at Blues. No nutting Sunderland coppers. No, this was special. Personal. Because Harry was riding with the soul of Big Bob West, a war hero from The Unity who'd fought in the Gulf and seen so much on his video screen that when he got home his life was fucked, just like the old boys who sat in the corner early evening with their bitter, grey hair and weary limbs, the old soldiers who ran onto the beaches and through the German guns, fighting for England and the English way of life, fighting the Nazis and ready to steam into the Soviets. Old soldiers with fuck all in their pension and a series of governments who stitched them up every step of the way. Businessmen who hid at home telling the squaddies to forget the horror and move on, bow down, do what you're told. There was no gratitude and they were forced to hobble through mean streets to sit in front of prim-and-proper young men and women who hated age and the spirit of former days. Harry had seen the films of Spitfire pilots and commando missions but had also drunk with Bob West, a regular who didn't like the dream.

847

Harry felt the power in his fingertips, hovering over the buttons. There was a chemical rush through his spine. Tips of his toes to the top of his head. This was the crunch, fighting for the cause from the safety of a seat in the amusement arcade. Jurgen the German giving out change. The boom of engines as Harry soared above the city, high above Berlin, because he was part of the great game now, one more soldier ant fighting for the NEO, a benevolent money-motivated Euro-dictatorship where decisions were made behind closed doors by unelected bureaucrats.

Big Bob burnt women and kids so the Brits and Yanks could march into Iraq, and though these colours don't run it was the politicians who told them to stop before they got carried away and took Baghdad. West said the politicians wouldn't let them finish the job and get rid of Saddam, because he was just a mate who'd gone a bit over the top; and that was all in the past because now the English were in Berlin and the rest of the lads would be near the ground and it would be going off all over the shop, and in among the exhaust fumes of Harry's head he could see the irony, how they were allowed to march straight in and turn the place over while the soldiers obeyed orders and were told to sit tight over the horizon.

Harry was absorbed by the graphics and colour, sucked into a world of heroism where you didn't bruise your knuckles. He was moving into the future at a thousand miles per hour because, like his old mate Mango said, you had to go with the flow, accepting his place in the new super-state and doing his part in securing the borders, House of Commons politicians sneering at the right- and left-wing sceptics, Harry pushing the image of Ted Heath aside because it was changing shape and he saw Balti in the street with his fucking head blown off, all that blood and gore that made him feel sick, refusing to stay with the memory. It was real life and he didn't want real life, because real life was shit.

Smart Bomb Parade was harmless fun and Harry was accepting things for what they were, going forward rather than back, looking down on a futuristic Berlin with its American skyscrapers and American burger chains, the biggest amusement park in Europe built on the site of the Führer's bunker, the laughter of cartoon characters replacing the screams of men and women strapped down to dissection tables and gang-raped by nonces, Harry shaking with rage as he thought of Nicky running for safety, feeling his lungs contract as he gasped for fresh air, wishing those German slags would put out the fag. Harry came through the rocks with a supersonic boom and a biblical city of sodomy and drug addiction was right there, white blocks of stone decorated with marble minarets and tiny ants running for cover going this way and that, circling in on themselves as Harry prepared to teach them a lesson they would never forget.

—I suppose we never learn. It's all in our genes and the images flashed at us through the screen. It seems like another life now and I suppose it was. The Second World War will be forgotten soon and I'll be another rack of bones in a cemetery overflowing with dead, but empty of mourners. My time has passed, but I lived. I was a tearaway when I was young, and maybe I'd have hanged if it hadn't been for the war. Who knows what would have happened in different circumstances. They were hard times to live through but there could never be anything to compare. The war was terrible, but there was a comradeship that has never existed in England since. The working class was given respect by the authorities while there was a war to win and then we went back to normal. I hate war and violence, but the worst thing is that it was exciting. I killed and at times maybe I enjoyed the chaos. Some men like killing and hurting people. A lot of men enjoy destroying buildings and property. The battles were spectacles. The colours and noise of the bombardments were incredible. Hand-to-hand it was hard, seeing the faces of the men you killed but not really taking them in. I've come back from The Unity and everyone's sad because last night they found Bob West hanging in his flat. He committed suicide and didn't bother to leave a note. There were no last words. Denise was crying and says she doesn't understand. He had nothing to say. He never saw the people he killed, just the beauty of the flames and the sunsets. He saw the spectacle and missed the horror. Later he realised what his role had been, but there was no answer and nobody to help. Maybe he killed a hundred people, perhaps a thousand. I saw the charred corpses of men, women and children killed by bombers and I saw the insanity of a concentration camp. I found my wife there, right at the bottom, raped and starved almost to death. She was a brilliant woman. We were happy and I was a figure in the park digging the soil and planting flowers, enjoying the air and work. Nobody knew what I'd seen and it didn't matter. It made me stronger than all of them. You accept your place in the world and the rich take what they want. It's always been this way. The best you can do is stay honest. There was a short time after my wife passed away that I went mad, but I'm okay now and since then I have been content to plod along. You get by. Counting the cost of the heating and going cold at my age isn't right, but there's nothing that can be done. I killed for England. I did it in a uniform and they gave me medals. But I sit with my cup of tea and watch the news and a story of rioting in Berlin. The man on the screen is talking from a London studio. He is very excited. I've heard it before, in a hundred different situations. When he gets tired there are other stories of death and destruction. They can't leave it be. Do the young men I pass in the street learn anything? Or the politicians and media? But old men get bitter and that's not for me. I'll see Eddie and the boys in a few months. I'm going to see the world and go to Australia. That's my decision and I'm sticking to it, because that's all you can really do. I've made my choices and won't complain. Maybe it's better to die with your mates overseas than at home all alone. But there's no point dying young. No point at all.

The youth's taking a hammering from a couple of Englishmen. He's wriggling on the concrete and covering himself. His hair is short and his shirt specked with blood. It's bright red, not black. The thuds are muffled and his fingers cracked from the kicks. The two men take their time and pick their spots. I think of that kicking I got at Millwall a few years back. Then I think of Derby and the time I stood aside and did nothing when Facelift had a go at him. Fitted in and behaved myself. Stood in the shadows. With Millwall I thought I was going to die. Maybe end up in a wheelchair. Or brain damaged. Kicked to death over a game of football. Murdered in some Peckham slum. Chelsea did the business but I was unlucky. It's the luck of the draw. Another kind of lottery. Because a fight's a fight. There's no rules these days. No Queen's regulations. Doubt there ever was. Nothing's different except the wrapping gets more high-tech. They add some colour. It's a load of bollocks. It's all down to what's inside and you make your choices. Have to live with them for the rest of your life. It's personal responsibility.

We're a democratic people. This German decided to have a go at the famous English football hooligans and he's lost out. The mob we've been rowing with has scattered and the rest of the England boys are chasing them for fun. The German on the floor is having a bad time of things from these two. He's pushed himself to get out on the streets with his mates and this is the comeback. It's time for the cunt to pay the bill. Taking the piss having a go at the English. Fitting in with his mates and playing his part. All that mutual respect is shit. Face in the gutter getting the shit kicked out of him by a couple of men ten years older. The bigger of the two hovers around him, stamping on the youth's head. He's deliberate in what he's doing. He wants to hurt this boy. He's trying to crack the skull. Damage that fucking kraut brain. That fucking German cunt responsible for bombing London and Coventry and Plymouth. Fucking slags the lot of them. Kill the boy and walk away with no second thoughts. Leave the body face down in the mud for his mum and dad to identify days later in some regimental morgue. Send the body home in a box. A few miles out of Berlin to some grubby German village. Do the cunt and let his old man sit by the grave crying in front of the wife. Looking soft. Bringing the back of his trainer down on the side of the boy's face.

I walk towards them and hit the one stamping on the German's head. I punch him in the face and I punch him hard. It's a good punch. There's no panic or excitement, but I want to break his nose. I screw my fist in and try to hurt him. He stumbles back holding his head, half from surprise and half from pain. He's the same size and a bit younger than me, but he's a wanker. It's the cowards and the psychos who stand there for hours kicking a dead man. Kicking a dead man to death. I hate that, going on and on when you've done the job and proved your point. These cunts have been hanging back waiting to pick up the leftovers. You never see these slags at the front when it goes off, and they're the first ones on their toes when things go bad. They're a couple of wankers. The kind who in a war torture prisoners and rape women. Scum basically. There's rotten apples everywhere. You have to have standards.

The second man turns round and says they're English. Thinks I've got them mixed up with the krauts. I tell him to fuck off and kick him in the balls. He moves sideways and it only half hurts. He chokes and leans forward, then snaps back as I kick him in the mouth. He's a tart and does as he's told. Not fit to call himself English. He pulls his mate away and they hurry off. I watch them go, then look down at the German. He's moving and trying to crawl away. I turn him over with my foot but he doesn't have a face, just blood from his nose smeared with grit. I think of what Harry was saying in London a couple of weeks ago, when we were getting stoned on some of Rod's dope. Up to your fucking eyeballs on Arab camel dung and Fat Boy's running off at the mouth, going into one. You'd think he'd slow down but he was so fucking chuffed about the coming trip two hours on the herb didn't knock him out. My old mate, new mate Harry going on about how he imagined the face of Balti after he'd been shot. Wanted to know whether you could see the features or just the skull. I didn't want to start thinking about all that because fuck knows with the camel shit. Didn't want the paranoia, but the image stuck. Now I connect everything looking at a face that could belong to anyone.

I lean down and grab the boy round the neck. Hold onto the collar of his shirt and pull him to his feet. He's unsteady at first. His legs are weak for a few seconds but then the messages start coming through as the computer reconnects. He leans into me. Realises I'm not going to hurt him. Probably thinks I'm a local. His weight's on my shoulder as I half-walk, half-carry him to a brick wall. He leans back and shakes his head. Takes a hanky from his pocket and wipes the blood off. Gets his thoughts together. Looks at me again and seems confused. Nods his head up and down. He seems a bit spastic as the current starts firing and I watch the pulse in his temple. I kill time looking down the street to where I can hear shouting and the sound of breaking glass. England are moving along another row of shops and wrecking the place. I can see men running after other men. England are on the rampage but everything has broken up and got confused. I want to get back with the others and enjoy the fun. Make every second count.

I stay for a minute or so. The noise drifts further away and there's nobody but the two of us in the street. It's a fucking ghost town suddenly. Everyone's hurried to keep up with the fighting and left us behind. I look at the youth again and he's got his hands on his knees and his head down. I think he's going to be sick, but nothing happens. There's the blood but it's just his nose. Nothing serious. Fuck knows if they've done his bones or something internal. He stands up, looking better. Starts to say something, but I shake my head, frown and turn away. I jog down the road to catch up with Mark, Carter and the rest of the boys.

—And when you're in that situation in a time of war, as I was, with the world going mad around you, with millions dead all over the globe, you have to make decisions. I saw the German youth crawling and his gun was in his hand. Maybe he was trying to turn, maybe not. I'd killed before and I could have kicked the gun away, but I couldn't be bothered. I'd seen men with their brains blown out and boys with their intestines torn from their guts crying for their mums. I'd seen men with their balls in the mud and exposed hearts filling with rain water. Men castrated by shrapnel and bleeding to death. A lot of them weren't men. I was only a kid myself and I'd seen too much, and when the boy moved I didn't try to think. My brain was heavy and maybe I was insane. I shot him in the head and blew his head open. I shattered his skull with the crack of my bullets. I don't know how many shots I fired but I didn't need them all. I stuck my bayonet into him as well, but by then he had to be dead. I dug it in ten or more times. I killed a boy younger than myself and he stayed in the mud as I moved forward. I doubt he was ever given a funeral. He was probably a brave boy who deserved better from his rulers. I left his corpse to rot. I was mad and angry and would have killed anyone. I lived and thought about everything that happened. I married a survivor from a concentration camp and hated the men who raped her, the men and women responsible for the rapes, murders, tortures and experiments. After the war I thought things through but never really came to a conclusion. I saw Mangler but what could I do? Nobody wanted to know. It was a war and bad things happen. It's not an excuse and I've always wondered about the boy and I still wonder today. There's rubbish everywhere. I did my duty, and things could've been different. I'll never be sure and that's the hardest part. When I see war veterans on the television meeting old enemies and shaking hands I wonder what it would be like to meet that boy all grown up with a wife and children and grandchildren of his own. What would it be like to have a drink with him in a German beer garden? I would be embarrassed and turn my head away when he thanked me for his life.

I pick up my suitcase when the bell rings and open the front door. My daughter is taking me to the airport. I'm excited now and my head is clear. We make our choices, and as a young man you think things will get better, but they don't. It's what we are. We fight and kill and breed to rebuild. It's the English way, but more than that it's the way of the world. When you get older you slow down and realise it's daft, but you can't really explain it in words, and anyway, nobody's listening. People get embarrassed and the likes of me don't count. Life moves on and there's no telling people.

No telling the General in his marble bunker, deep inside stone corridors where nobody hears the prostitutes scream. Nobody heard Balti die in the street, the only witness a woman with the shits who saw everything through glass, and Harry wanted revenge, because life was unfair and the screens all around him were pointing the way ahead. He was powerless, but if he played the game he could have it all. The machine offered a perfect world, where nobody asked questions and an all-powerful state was prepared to crush those animals over the horizon. Harry had to pay his dues and channel his anger in a new direction.

Smart Bomb was a great game and Harry was running up a decent score, watching his missiles hit home, the Gulf Boy mixing his thoughts as he remembered that story from the First World War, when the two sides called a truce for Christmas Day and the English and Germans left their trenches and stood in no-man's land together, had a drink and a game of football. It was a famous story, because after that the two sides stopped shooting at each other. The soldiers had to be replaced and the next year there was no fraternising with the enemy. Harry pumped the button and destroyed a gunship, amazed that the officers were that stupid, because if you saw the face of your enemy and knew him as a person, you weren't going to try and kill him. They were more sussed today, making things easy with smart rockets, conquering the world with consumer goods, and Harry understood this because he could see exactly where Nicky fitted in.

He would go and see her in Amsterdam. He smiled as he pictured Nicky opening the door of her flat and throwing her thin arms around his neck. His knob was aching, but he could trust her. Everyone wanted to return home a hero, Harry aiming at a cartoon tank and shattering its armour, knowing it was just a game – it had to be – the bright red blood of the tank crew seeping through crinkled silver metal.

There's blood on my feet and I'm back with the main mob of English. We're running the old bill. Chasing twenty of the cunts through their own streets. The fighting seems like it's been going on for ever, and there's not so many of us now. We have to watch ourselves because we're on foreign soil, surrounded by people who hate us, but we're doing England proud. Putting on a show the locals won't forget. We're here in Berlin, rioting in the centre of Europe. Maintaining a reputation we've built up through the centuries. Kicking the shit out of anyone who takes the piss. Slowing down now and letting the old bill escape.

We stop at a crossroads and try to work out where we are. Harris has a look at his map, and points the way to the ground. There's some Germans further down the street. As we get nearer they move forward and we pile in, punching and kicking the ones at the front. My fist connects with some bloke's chin and my knuckles jolt. I feel it right along my arm. They don't really fancy it and do a runner. We slow down again, covering the road and walking tall. Going from street to street doing whatever we want, flushing out resistance. Battering the fuck out of anyone who wants to have a go. We're proud to be English and proud of our culture. We're doing the stroppy cunts once and for all.